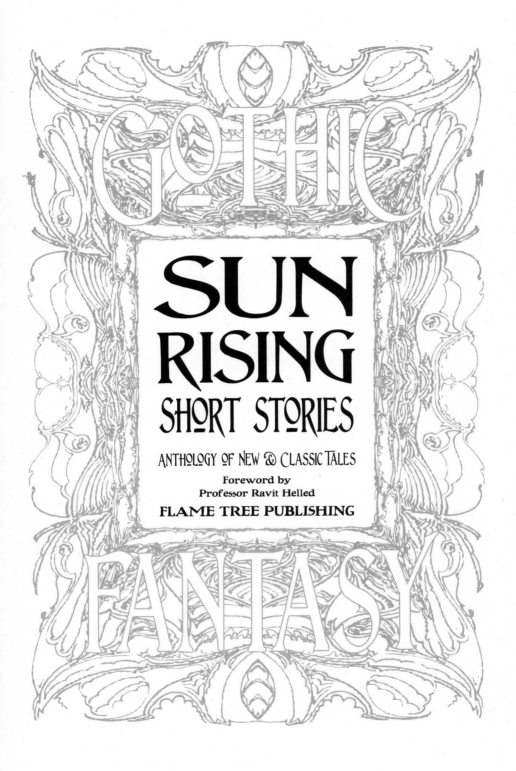

GOTHIC

SUN RISING

SHORT STORIES

ANTHOLOGY OF NEW & CLASSIC TALES

Foreword by
Professor Ravit Helled

FLAME TREE PUBLISHING

FANTASY

This is a FLAME TREE Book

Publisher & Creative Director: Nick Wells
Project Editor: Jocelyn Pontes
Editorial Board: Catherine Taylor, Gillian Whitaker, Jemma North, Simran Aulakh

FLAME TREE PUBLISHING
6 Melbray Mews, Fulham,
London SW6 3NS, United Kingdom
www.flametreepublishing.com

First published 2024

24 26 28 27 25
1 3 5 7 9 10 8 6 4 2

ISBN: 978-1-80417-808-9
Special ISBN: 978-1-80417-444-9

The cover image is created by Flame Tree Studio
based on shutterstock.com/Slava Gerj/Gabor Ruszkai/OlgaChernyak.

A copy of the CIP data for this book is available from the British Library.

Printed and bound in China

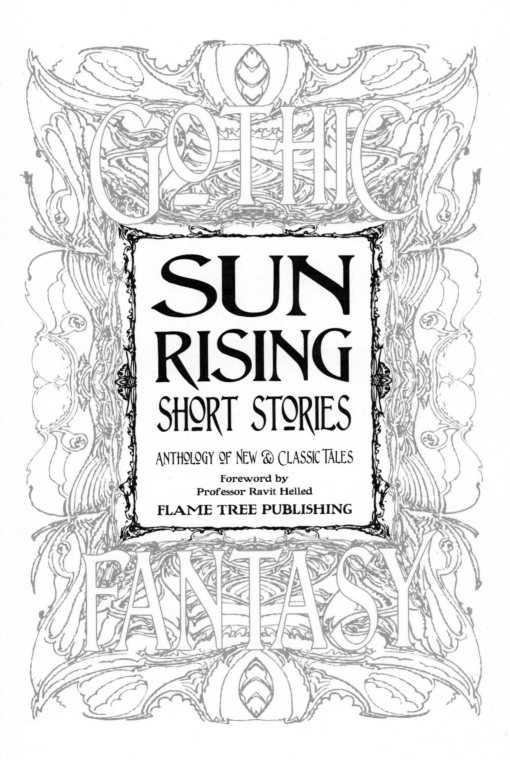

GOTHIC

SUN RISING

SHORT STORIES

ANTHOLOGY OF NEW & CLASSIC TALES

Foreword by
Professor Ravit Helled

FLAME TREE PUBLISHING

FANTASY

Contents

CONTENTS

CONTENTS

Foreword: Sun Rising Short Stories

OUR SUN IS A STAR – one star out of many in the galaxy, and the universe. Often, the sun is described as an "average star", but for us the sun is the center of our planetary system. Although we sometimes forget about its existence, the sun is essential for life on Earth as we know it.

Humans have always been gazing upon the sun with wonder and curiosity. Its radiant energy fuels the dance of plants, the rhythm of seasons and the pulse of weather. The sun has been an inspiration for science and art and has led to the development of many myths and stories. Indeed, the sun is a powerful symbol across various cultures and genres, embodying life, strength and the passage of time. In myths and folktales, the sun often represents the ultimate source of life and energy. For example, in Egyptian mythology, the sun god Ra is considered the king of the gods, travelling across the sky during the day and through the underworld at night, symbolizing death and rebirth. In Greek mythology, Helios, the personification of the sun, drives his chariot across the sky daily, marking the passage of time, stability and predictability. The sun has always been there for us, rising and setting regularly long before human consciousness first came about.

The sun is also a symbol of divine power and authority in several cultures. The cycle of the sun symbolizes the cycle of life, death and rebirth. In classic fantasy literature, the sun often retains its mythological significance. J.R.R. Tolkien used the sun as a symbol of hope, renewal and the relentless passage of time, often driving the narrative forward and influencing the characters' fates. In other stories, the sun's role ranges from a life-giving entity and a symbol of hope to a harbinger of destruction and war.

But the sun, like many other astronomical objects, is also a target for scientific exploration. Astrophysicists and solar scientists still study the sun with the aim to better understand its structure, dynamics and influence on the solar system's planets and small bodies. Investigating the solar interior teaches us about the processes of nuclear fusion and energy transport. The mechanisms behind solar activity, such as sunspots, solar flares, magnetic storms, and their impact on space weather and Earth's climate, are also a focus of scientific exploration.

The sun is an evolving star. Currently, the sun is in the middle of its life, about 4.6 billion years old, and it keeps shining by converting hydrogen into helium through nuclear fusion in its core. This efficient process of energy production will not last forever. Once the hydrogen in the core depletes, the sun will enter the red giant phase and will expand significantly, engulfing the inner planets and perhaps even planet Earth. The sun will end its life becoming a spectacular glowing planetary nebula (a shell of ionized gas ejected from the red giant), while the core will continue to contract into a white dwarf, which will slowly cool down and fade over billions of years.

Unfortunately, we can't look directly into the sun to observe its beauty. A full solar eclipse offers a rare and stunning view of the sun when it is completely obscured by the moon. I remember the first time I saw a full solar eclipse – it was truly impressive! The sun looked perfectly round, reflecting its strong gravitational force, and suddenly silence surrounded us. The middle of the day turned to night and revealed the sun's outer atmosphere, the corona, which is usually hidden by its bright light. It was certainly a unique and memorable experience. Sunsets and sunrises can also be spectacular, and we have them every day. These events are a reminder of the celestial rhythm that supports our existence. Next time you see the sun, you may want to stop for a moment. Enjoy the light and warmth it brings you and be grateful for being part of the cosmos. After all, for us humans, the sun is a special star.

Professor Ravit Helled

Publisher's Note

THE SUN HAS held a special place in the stories of humanity across the world and throughout the centuries. Equally revered and feared for its power to bring both life and death, to portend coming disaster, and to illuminate a brighter future, the sun grips the human imagination like no other entity in the celestial realm. This fascinating collection of stories explores humanity's complex and contradictory relationship to the great solar entity which makes life on earth possible, bringing together stories from new and classic authors alike, along with ancient myth and folklore from around the globe.

We received a great number of new submissions for this anthology, and we have enjoyed reading so many fascinating portrayals and inventive interpretations of the sun and its associated mythology. The standard of the writing submitted to us has always been impressive and the final selection is always a challenge, but ultimately we chose a collection of stories that presents a variety of ideas and balances with the classic tales.

As always, we must remind the reader that, as tales from mythology and folklore are principally derived from an oral storytelling tradition, their written representation depends on the transcription, translation and interpretation by those who heard them and first put them to paper, and also on whether they are recently re-told versions or more directly sourced from original first-hand accounts. The stories in this book are a mixture, and you can learn more about the sources and authors at the back of the book. Due to the historical nature of the classic text, we're aware that there may be some language used which has the potential to cause offence to the modern reader. However, wishing overall to preserve the integrity of the text, rather than impose contemporary sensibilities, we have left it unaltered.

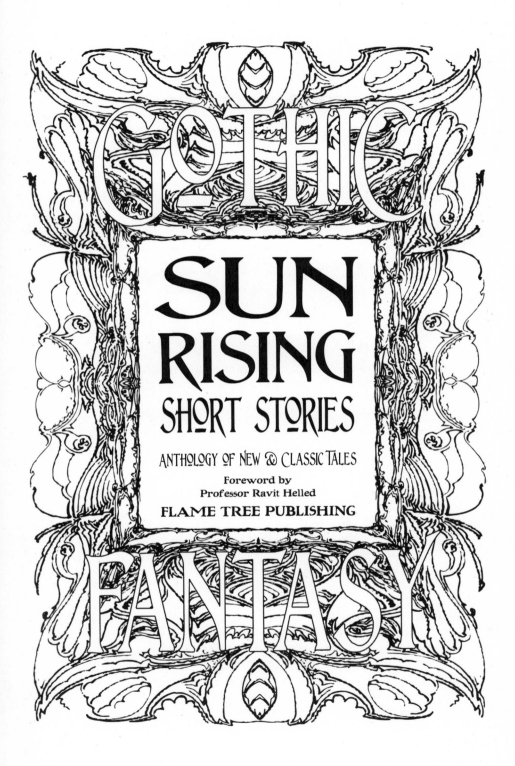

GOTHIC

SUN RISING

SHORT STORIES

ANTHOLOGY OF NEW & CLASSIC TALES

Foreword by
Professor Ravit Helled

FLAME TREE PUBLISHING

FANTASY

After the Storm

Rose Strickman

FOR YEARS, the storm had raged.

Around the house the winds whirled, shrieking and throwing handfuls of freezing rain against its walls and windows. Even the brightest day was dimmed by the perpetual clouds massed above the roof. The nights were pure blackness, with not a single star shining through.

Still the house stood untouched. Not one roof tile was torn off, not one brick loosened. It stood, secure in its enchantments, while around it the storm screamed on.

Until one day the storm…slackened.

* * *

Stella awoke suddenly, jerked into wakefulness. She lay still in her bed, wondering what had happened, to wake her so suddenly, heart galloping.

Everything seemed normal. Her bedroom lay shrouded in midnight blackness. Outside the storm blew on, its voice having lost the ability to disturb her rest long ago. Indeed, Stella barely even heard the storm anymore, so accustomed was she to its song.

But she could hear it now.

Frowning, she listened to the familiar notes and shrieks of the wind, the drumming of the rain. It was raging around the house, just as usual – but not at all usual. For she could *hear* it. Every whine of the wind, every thud of every raindrop, was subtly different. Just different enough to alert her.

Stella sat up in bed, pushing back the covers, and looked out the window. She saw nothing but darkness, the storm invisible in the night. What had changed? What was that note of difference in the gale?

It was a long time before she could sleep again.

* * *

"Morning, sleepyhead," said Aurora as Stella came stumbling into the kitchen. "About time you joined us." She sipped coffee.

Stella groped her way toward the kettle. While the water was boiling, she squinted out the window. The storm danced on outside, a deep pearly gray in the day's light. Water ran down the windows, sluiced across the garden. The trees stood bent under the wind, the flowers bowed down under the rain.

Everything looked normal. But it wasn't, quite. Stella could still hear the note of wrongness in the wind, the pattern of the rain. And it seemed to her that the day outside was just infinitesimally brighter than it should be, the light just slightly too clear.

Aurora joined her at the window, carrying her mug. "Something bothering you, Stells?"

"Look at the storm." Stella waved a hand at the window. "Does it seem…different to you?"

Aurora frowned outside. She was a tall, large woman who exuded strength and calmness. She studied the storm a long moment before speaking. "The trees," she said at last. "They're swaying differently. To a different pattern." She peered closer. "Not as violently."

"And it's easier to see them," said Stella. "Look – their tops aren't covered in mist." Something clicked in her mind. She turned to Aurora, to find her sister already staring at her, mouth agape. In her eyes was the same realization.

"The storm," said Aurora. "It's...weakening."

* * *

The sisters got none of their chores done that day. They sat in the kitchen, swigging coffee and tea, sneaking glances at the windows and discussing the situation.

"Why would the storm be weakening now?" Stella demanded. "It's been...." She trailed off. They'd lost track of time long ago. "A couple of years, anyway."

"I guess not even storm curses can keep it up forever." Aurora ran her hands through her mane of graying hair. "The question is, what do we do if it goes out completely?"

The sisters sat silent. Stella remembered the early years, when they'd still been counting the days. When the storm, and their isolation, had been a continual torment, every shriek of wind cutting like a razor, every raindrop hitting like a blow. They'd lain awake at night listening, and woken each morning hoping desperately for an end to the curse, only to be disappointed yet again. How they had prayed for an end to the curse. If the storm had slackened then, they would have been ecstatic. A part of Stella still leaped at the thought.

But the rest of her did not. She cringed from the enormity of such a change. One of the pillars of her existence, knocked out from under her.

"If the storm stops," she said, "we can't stay here. The house's enchantments won't hold. The house will stop providing us food and electricity all on its own. We'll have to...leave the house. Maybe even...get jobs."

Aurora's hands tightened on her mug, but she held her voice steady. "Well, that might not be so bad. I mean, other people do."

"*Other people.*" Stella grimaced. "When was the last time we even saw another person, Aurora? How would we know how to...deal with them?" The thought made her lungs choke with incipient panic.

Aurora reached across the table to lay a hand on her arm. "Hey. Calm down, Stells. It might not come to that. And if it does, we'll still have each other. We won't be alone."

Stella forced down her panic, enough to smile shakily at her sister. Aurora was right. It was too early to worry. And they had each other. They had to take care of each other. "So what do we do now?"

Aurora withdrew her hand and sat back. "Wait and see. You never know. The storm might pick up again and then we'll have worried for nothing."

* * *

But the storm did not pick up again. Instead, it slackened further.

Every day Stella awoke to find the winds singing a different, gentler note than the day before. Every morning, the rain tapped a softer tune. The diffuse gray daylight glowed brighter, and the trees danced just a little less, leaves becoming quieter and quieter. A few flowers even lifted their heads, raindrops glistening on their petals, looking almost incredulous with hope.

It was strange to go outside and not get completely soaked in seconds and buffeted by the wind. Stella ventured out onto the stone terrace, water flowing under her bare feet, feeling the lessening wind toss her hair about, the rain taking longer and longer each day to soak her through. It reminded her of days long gone, days she'd tucked away into a dark corner of her mind. Days when there had been others living in the house, when their world had comprised so much more than just the house and garden. A world lit by a blazing golden presence in the sky, too brilliant to look at, washing the day with light and heat. These memories filled her with both pleasure and terror. For that world might now be in reach once more, and the prospect was too huge and powerful to view with anything but fear.

Then one day, when she was washing the dishes after lunch, a blaze of light burst in.

Stella dropped the pan with a scream, covering her eyes. Aurora, busy wiping down the table, looked up and took in the light. She shrieked too, burying her face in her hands.

When Stella could make herself lower her hands again, the light was still there. A searing wash of gold, brighter and warmer than anything had been for years, dancing on the puddles in the garden, gleaming through the raindrops, filling the darkness with refracted light.

"Sunlight." The word fumbled strange and foreign in her mouth. "Aurora... it's *sunlight*."

Aurora made no verbal response to this, but dashed for the kitchen door. Stella ran after her.

The sun was already sliding away, hiding behind the clouds. But a few stray beams still shimmered on the puddles, limned the edges of the leaves. The wind blew gentler than ever, the rain softer and sparser. The clouds drifted, and, for the first time in years, Stella thought she caught a glimpse of the sea, a blue expanse just a mile away from the house. A glimpse of the outside world, beyond the storm.

She turned to Aurora, and saw in her sister's face the same wonder, the same fear. "It's happening," she whispered. "It's really happening. The storm is ending. The curse is ending."

Aurora reached out to take her hand and, to Stella's astonishment, there were tears in her eyes. "Yes," she said, and choked back a sob. "Yes."

Then the tears gushed, not out of Aurora's eyes, but Stella's. The world went blurry, a white-hot pain as bright as the sun, as she collapsed into her sister's arms, crying and crying. "Oh, God. Oh, God. I'm scared. I'm so scared, Aurora...."

"Me too." Aurora's arms trembled as they wrapped around Stella. "Me too, Stells. But it'll be okay. It'll be okay, Stella."

"*How* can it be okay?" Stella lurched back, throwing an angry arm at the again-impenetrable storm and the world beyond. "We're going to have to go back out *there* again. We're going to have to *talk* to people. We're going to have to get jobs and fill out forms and go to the store and – and we don't know *how*...."

"Then we'll learn. Don't cry, Stells, please. There's been enough rain around here."

Stella giggled through her sobs. "Still with that old joke, Aurora?"

"Well, you can't say it's stopped being relevant." Aurora paused. "Well, not yet, anyway."

Then they both laughed and cried, there in the curtains of slackening rain.

* * *

Then it happened.

Stella awoke to silence and light.

She lay in bed, staring at the square of light painted on the wall, illuminating her desk and flowery wallpaper in an unnatural yellow brilliance. She could see details she hadn't noticed for years, the unfamiliar familiarity hurting her eyes, her mind.

She squeezed her eyes shut. The silence pressed on her ears. The lack of wind, lack of rain. A golden void in the world. She pulled the covers over her head and ground her hands into her ears.

Footsteps, audible even through her hands. Aurora touched her shoulder. "Come on, Stells, wake up."

"No," Stella hissed through the counterpane. "This is not happening." She closed her eyes tighter, pressing her hands deeper into her ears. This was not happening, she told herself fiercely. This was a dream, a nightmare. Any minute now she would wake up.

Hands grabbed the counterpane and comforter, ripped them away in a tide of cold air and brilliance, pressing on Stella's closed eyes. The shock made her open those eyes, and then her hands fell away. She lay spinning in a golden hell of light.

"Come on, you coward," growled Aurora. "Don't make me face this all on my own!"

Aurora.

Stella forced her eyes to focus on her sister's face. It glowed in the sunlight, radiance illuminating every hair, every wrinkle. When had Aurora gotten wrinkles? And had her eyes always been that color? A deep green mixed with gold. The color of sunlight in summer woods.

Stella remembered sunlight in the woods, how the leaves glowed golden-green, how shadows threw themselves down to shift and dance on the leaf litter. She remembered running with her sister, through alternating light and shadow. Raising her face to the sun, glorying in its touch.

"Aurora," she whispered. "Your eyes. They're the color of sunlight in the woods."

"Are they?" Aurora raised a hand to touch her face, fingertips skimming her eyelids. "I always thought they were just a sort of muddy green."

"They were. In the storm." Stella sat up, and the shadows cast by the sun moved, so dark and crisp they cut her mind. "What color are my eyes?"

Aurora studied her. "In the storm they were gray," she said at last. "But now they're blue. Like the sea."

"The sea." Stella thought of the sea. She remembered walking down to the seashore with Aurora, their parents just behind, lugging the basket. She remembered the hot sand under her feet. The glitter of sunlight on the blue backs of the waves as they hurled themselves to the shore.

A strange, high-pitched trilling sounded. "Birdsong," Stella murmured. "Aurora. The birds are back."

"Didn't take them long, did it?" Aurora did not look out the window. Neither did Stella. Not yet. "Come on. Get dressed and come to breakfast. We still need to eat."

The house lay still and quiet around the sisters as they made their way downstairs. The silence filled every room, cascaded down the stairway. And through every window streamed blazing golden light, slanting in thick beams through the air, splashing radiance on the walls, the carpets. The sight – of the intimately familiar made utterly strange – made

Stella dizzy, and she had to stop every now and then, bracing herself against the wall and shutting her eyes.

But still she caught glimpses through the windows, out of the corners of her eyes. She could not help it. And in those glimpses she saw gold and green and *blue*. A deep, brilliant blue unlike any other, one she thought she'd never see again.

In the kitchen, the sisters prepared breakfast. The house's enchantments were already fading. They could tell. They felt it in the texture of the food, the taste of it in their mouths. No more would the house replenish their food supply by magic. Every bite they took was irrevocable.

After breakfast they sat motionless, staring down at the tablecloth. The sunlight illuminated the weave in unbearable detail. Outside, the songs of the birds grew thunderous, the anthem of the world, more insistent by the second. As impossible to ignore as the sun.

Stella rose to her feet. She made no conscious decision; it was as though she watched herself from outside her own body, getting to her feet and making her way to the door.

The doorknob felt cool and smooth under her hand. She paused then, looking at Aurora. Her sister looked back. The moment hung, suspended in silence.

Then Stella opened the door, and the sun blazed in, bringing with it the world.

Ama-terasu and Susa-no-o

From Japanese mythology

SUSA-NO-O, OR "THE IMPETUOUS MALE," was the brother of Ama-terasu, the Sun Goddess. Now Susa-no-o was a very undesirable deity indeed, and he figured in the Realm of the Japanese Gods as a decidedly disturbing element. His character has been clearly drawn in the *Nihongi*, more clearly perhaps than that of any other deity mentioned in these ancient records. Susa-no-o had a very bad temper, which often resulted in many cruel and ungenerous acts. Moreover, in spite of his long beard, he had a habit of continually weeping and wailing. Where a child in a tantrum would crush a toy to pieces, the Impetuous Male, when in a towering rage, and without a moment's warning, would wither the once fair greenery of mountains, and in addition bring many people to an untimely end.

His parents, Izanagi and Izanami, were much troubled by his doings, and, after consulting together, they decided to banish their unruly son to the Land of Yomi. Susa, however, had a word to say in the matter. He made the following petition, saying, "I will now obey thy instructions and proceed to the Nether-Land (Yomi). Therefore I wish for a short time to go to the Plain of High Heaven and meet with my elder sister (Ama-terasu), after which I will go away forever." This apparently harmless request was granted, and Susa-no-o ascended to Heaven. His departure occasioned a great commotion of the sea, and the hills and mountains groaned aloud.

Now Ama-terasu heard these noises, and perceiving that they denoted the near approach of her wicked brother Susa-no-o, she said to herself, "Is my younger brother coming with good intentions? I think it must be his purpose to rob me of my kingdom. By the charge which our parents gave to their children, each of us has his own allotted limits. Why, therefore, does he reject the kingdom to which he should proceed, and make bold to come spying here?"

Ama-terasu then prepared for warfare. She tied her hair into knots and hung jewels upon it, and round her wrists "an august string of five hundred Yasaka jewels." She presented a very formidable appearance when in addition she slung over her back "a thousand-arrow quiver and a five-hundred-arrow quiver," and protected her arms with pads to deaden the recoil of the bowstring. Having arrayed herself for deadly combat, she brandished her bow, grasped her sword-hilt, and stamped on the ground till she had made a hole sufficiently large to serve as a fortification.

All this elabourate and ingenious preparation was in vain. The Impetuous Male adopted the manner of a penitent. "From the beginning," he said, "my heart has not been black. But as, in obedience to the stern behest of our parents, I am about to depart forever to the Nether-Land, how could I bear to depart without having seen face to face thee my elder sister? It is for this reason that I have traversed on foot the clouds and mists and have come hither from afar. I am surprised that my elder sister should, on the contrary, put on so stern a countenance."

Ama-terasu regarded these remarks with a certain amount of suspicion. Susa-no-o's filial piety and Susa-no-o's cruelty were not easily to be reconciled. She thereupon resolved to test his sincerity by a remarkable proceeding we need not describe. Suffice it to say that for the time being the test proved the Impetuous Male's purity of heart and general sincerity towards his sister.

But Susa-no-o's good behaviour was a very short-lived affair indeed. It happened that Ama-terasu had made a number of excellent rice-fields in Heaven. Some were narrow and some were long, and Ama-terasu was justly proud of these rice-fields. No sooner had she sown the seed in the spring than Susa-no-o broke down the divisions between the plots, and in the autumn let loose a number of piebald colts.

One day when he saw his sister in the sacred Weaving Hall, weaving the garments of the Gods, he made a hole through the roof and flung down a flayed horse. Ama-terasu was so frightened that she accidentally wounded herself with the shuttle. Extremely angry, she determined to leave her abode; so, gathering her shining robes about her, she crept down the blue sky, entered a cave, fastened it securely, and there dwelt in seclusion.

Now the world was in darkness, and the alternation of night and day was unknown. When this dreadful catastrophe had taken place the Eighty Myriads of Gods assembled together on the bank of the River of Heaven and discussed how they might best persuade Ama-terasu to grace Heaven once more with her shining glory. No less a God than "Thought-combining," after much profound reasoning, gathered together a number of singing-birds from the Eternal Land. After sundry divinations with a deer's leg-bone, over a fire of cherry-bark, the Gods made a number of tools, bellows, and forges. Stars were welded together to form a mirror, and jewellery and musical instruments were eventually fashioned.

When all these things had been duly accomplished the Eighty Myriads of Gods came down to the rock-cavern where the Sun Goddess lay concealed, and gave an elaborate entertainment. On the upper branches of the True Sakaki Tree they hung the precious jewels, and on the middle branches the mirror. From every side there was a great singing of birds, which was only the prelude to what followed. Now Uzume ("Heavenly-alarming-female") took in her hand a spear wreathed with Eulalia grass, and made a headdress of the True Sakaki Tree. Then she placed a tub upside down, and proceeded to dance in a very immodest manner, till the Eighty Myriad Gods began to roar with laughter.

Such extraordinary proceedings naturally awakened the curiosity of Ama-terasu, and she peeped forth. Once more the world became golden with her presence. Once more she dwelt in the Plain of High Heaven, and Susa-no-o was duly chastised and banished to the Yomi Land.

Apollo and Daphne

From Greek mythology

CONQUEROR OF ALL conquerable earth, yet not always victorious over the heart of a maid was the golden-locked Apollo.

As mischievous Eros played one day with his bow and arrows, Apollo beheld him and spoke to him mockingly.

"What hast thou to do with the weapons of war, saucy lad?" he said. "Leave them for hands such as mine, that know full well how to wield them. Content thyself with thy torch, and kindle flames, if indeed thou canst, but such bolts as thy white young arms can drive will surely not bring scathe to god nor to man."

Then did the son of Aphrodite answer, and as he made answer he laughed aloud in his glee. "With thine arrows thou mayst strike all things else, great Apollo, a shaft of mine shall surely strike thy heart!"

Carefully, then, did Eros choose two arrows from his quiver. One, sharp-pointed and of gold, he fitted carefully to his bow, drew back the string until it was taut, and then let fly the arrow, that did not miss its mark, but flew straight to the heart of the sun-god. With the other arrow, blunt, and tipped with lead, he smote the beautiful Daphne, daughter of Peneus, the river-god. And then, full joyously did the boy-god laugh, for his roguish heart knew well that to him who was struck by the golden shaft must come the last pangs that have proved many a man's and many a god's undoing, while that leaden-tipped arrow meant to whomsoever it struck, a hatred of Love and an immunity from all the heart weakness that Love can bring. Those were the days when Apollo was young. Never before had he loved.

But as the first fierce storm that assails it bends the young, supple tree with its green budding leaves before its furious blast, so did the first love of Apollo bend low his adoring heart. All day as he held the golden reins of his chariot, until evening when its fiery wheels were cooled in the waters of the western seas, he thought of Daphne. All night he dreamed of her. But never did there come to Daphne a time when she loved Love for Love's sake. Never did she look with gentle eye on the golden-haired god whose face was as the face of all the exquisite things that the sunlight shows, remembered in a dream. Her only passion was a passion for the chase. One of Diana's nymphs was she, cold and pure and white in soul as the virgin goddess herself.

There came a day when Apollo could no longer put curbing hands on his fierce longing. The flames from his chariot still lingered in reflected glories on sea and hill and sky. The very leaves of the budding trees of spring were outlined in gold. And through the dim wood walked Daphne, erect and lithe and living as a sapling in the early spring.

With beseeching hands, Apollo followed her. A god was he, yet to him had come the vast humility of passionate intercession for the gift of love to a little nymph. She heard his steps behind her and turned round, proud and angry that one should follow her when she had not willed it.

"Stay!" he said, "daughter of Peneus. No foe am I, but thine own humble lover. To thee alone do I bow my head. To all others on earth am I conqueror and king."

But Daphne, hating his words of passionate love, sped on. And when his passion lent wings to his feet and she heard him gaining on her as she fled, not as a lover did Daphne look on deathless Apollo, but as a hateful foe. More swiftly than she had ever run beside her mistress Diana, leaving the flying winds behind her as she sped, ran Daphne now. But ever did Apollo gain upon her, and almost had he grasped her when she reached the green banks of the river of which her father, Peneus, was god.

"Help me, Peneus!" she cried. "Save me, oh my father, from him whose love I fear!"

As she spoke the arms of Apollo seized her, yet, even as his arms met around her waist, lissome and slight as a young willow, Daphne the nymph was Daphne the nymph no longer. Her fragrant hair, her soft white arms, her tender body all changed as the sun-god touched them. Her feet took root in the soft, damp earth by the river. Her arms sprouted into woody branches and green leaves. Her face vanished, and the bark of a big tree enclosed her snow-white body. Yet Apollo did not take away his embrace from her who had been his dear first love. He knew that her cry to Peneus her father had been answered, yet he said, "Since thou canst not be my bride, at least thou shalt be my tree; my hair, my lyre, my quiver shall have thee always, oh laurel tree of the Immortals!"

So do we still speak of laurels won, and worn by those of deathless fame, and still does the first love of Apollo crown the heads of those whose gifts have fitted them to dwell with the dwellers on Olympus.

> *"I espouse thee for my tree:*
> *Be thou the prize of honour and renown;*
> *The deathless poet, and the poem, crown;*
> *Thou shalt the Roman festivals adorn,*
> *And, after poets, be by victors worn."*
> **Ovid**

Apollo and King Admetus

From Greek mythology

THERE WOULD HAVE BEEN but little trouble between Jupiter and his stately wife if no one but Minerva ever gave the watchful Juno cause for jealousy; but other goddesses, and even mortal maidens, found favour in the eyes of Jupiter, and for their sake he often left her side. From his throne in the high heavens the ruler of the world saw not only the goddesses, with their glory of immortal youth, but also the daughters of men endowed with that same beauty and grace which the gods themselves had bestowed upon the first woman. Though Juno "of the snow-white arms" alone enjoyed the title of queen of heaven, she knew that she had many rivals for the love of Jupiter; and it was this jealousy of all loveliness in woman that made her ever watchful and revengeful. Perhaps it was the cause, too, of the very changeable temper that her husband accused her of possessing.

Whoever won the affections of Jupiter was sure to be persecuted by "cruel Juno's unrelenting hate," as the poet Virgil says; but this did not hinder the ruler of the gods from leaving very often the marble halls of Olympus to wander, in some disguise, about the earth. It was after such an absence that the watchful Juno learned of Jupiter's love for fair-haired Latona, goddess of dark nights. As this new rival was not a mortal maiden who could be punished with death, the wrathful queen was forced to be content with banishing the goddess forever from Olympus, and compelling her to live upon the earth. Not satisfied with this, she decreed that anyone who took pity on the unhappy goddess, or gave her any help, would incur the lasting displeasure of Juno.

For days and nights Latona wandered, not daring to ask for food or shelter, since all men knew of Juno's decree. She slept at night in some spot where the trees offered protection from wind and rain, and her only food was the scanty store that she could gather by the way – berries, nuts, wild honey, and sometimes bits of bread dropped by children in their play. One day, being very thirsty, she stopped beside a clear pool to drink; but some reapers who were passing by saw her, and hoping to gain favour with Juno they stepped into the pool and stirred up the water into such muddiness that poor Latona could not drink. Angered by such uncalled-for cruelty, the goddess prayed to Jupiter that these wicked men might never leave the spot where they were standing. Jupiter from his throne in the high heavens heard her prayer, and in answer he turned the reapers into ugly green frogs and bade them stay forever in the muddy pool. And ever afterwards when men came upon slimy ponds, where rank weeds grew and the water oozed from muddy banks, there they found the blinking frogs – even as Jupiter had willed.

After wandering some miles further Latona came at last to the seashore and here she begged Neptune, "the god who shakes the shores," to come to her aid, for she knew that Juno's power did not extend to the ruler of the sea. Seeing her distress, and pitying the poor persecuted goddess, Neptune sent her a dolphin, who took her on his back and swam with her to the floating island of Delos, which the kindly sea-god had caused to appear out of the depths of the ocean. Here Latona landed, and was for a time content; but the rocking of the island soon grew unbearable, and she begged the aid of Neptune a second time. He obligingly chained the island to the bottom of the Aegean Sea, and Latona had no further cause for complaint. On this island were born her two children: Apollo, god of the sun, and Diana, goddess of the moon.

When the children were grown, Jupiter took them to Olympus, though not without much protest from the ever-jealous Juno. The young Apollo's beauty and his skill in music gained him great favour among the gods, and found him worshippers in every town and city throughout the land of Greece. So conscious of his power did Apollo become, that he sometimes dared to assert his authority, unmindful of the will of Jupiter; and on one occasion he so angered his divine parent that he was banished to the earth, and made to serve Admetus, king of Thessaly.

In spite of his disgrace, Apollo managed to cheer his lonely hours of labour with his music; and as his work was no more difficult than to care for the king's sheep, he had abundant leisure to play upon his lyre while his flocks grazed on the sunny hillsides. As soon as he touched the strings, all the wild things in the forest crept out to hear. The fox came slinking from his hole among the rocks, and the timid deer drew close to the player and stayed beside him, listening. The strains of the wonderful music were carried across the meadows, and the mowers stopped their work, wondering where the player might be. One day they brought word to the king that some god must be among them, for no mortal could produce such music as they had heard. So Admetus sent for the shepherd, and when the youth stood before him, he marvelled at his great beauty, and still more at the golden lyre that Apollo held in his hand. Then when the young musician, in obedience to the king's command, began to play, all those who heard him were filled with wonder, and felt sure that a god had come to dwell among them. But Admetus asked no questions, only made the youth his head shepherd and treated him with all kindness.

Though a god, and no true shepherd, Apollo served the king faithfully, and when, at last, his time of service was over and Jupiter called him back to Olympus, Apollo, wishing to show some favour in return for the king's kindness, begged for Admetus the gift of immortality. This request the wise Jupiter granted, but only on the condition that when the time came for the king to die, someone could be found to take his place. Apollo agreed to these terms, and Admetus, knowing the conditions on which the gift was made, accepted his immortality gladly. For a time all went well; but the inevitable hour came when the Fates decreed that Admetus's life was ended, and that he must go the way of all mortals unless someone would die in his stead. The king was much beloved by his people; but no one's devotion to his sovereign was great enough to inspire him to make the needed sacrifice.

Then Alcestis, the beautiful wife of Admetus, learned of the price that must be paid for her husband's immortality and gladly offered her life in exchange for the king's. So, in all her young grace and beauty, she went down into the dark region of Hades, where no sunlight ever came and where her joyous laughter was forever hushed in the silence that reigns among the dead. Thus Admetus gained immortality; but his happiness was too dearly bought, for as the days went by he mourned more and more for his beautiful young wife, and in his dreams he saw her walking like a shadow among the grim shapes that move noiselessly in the silent halls of death. Bitterly he repented of his selfishness in accepting the sacrifice of her life, and his immortality grew hateful to him since each day only added to his sorrow. So he prayed to Apollo to recall his gift, and to give him back his wife Alcestis. It was not in the power of that god to change a decree of Jupiter's; but the Ruler of all things looked down from heaven, and, seeing the great grief and remorse of Admetus, he withdrew the gift that had cost the king so dear, and sent Hercules to the kingdom of Pluto with commands to let Alcestis go. Very gladly the god carried this message to the gloomy realm of Hades, where amid the myriad shadow-shapes he sought and found Alcestis; and out of the dreadful darkness in which she walked alone, Hercules led her back to earth again.

Apollo the Musician

From Greek mythology

I

WHEN APOLLO LEFT King Admetus and returned to the halls of Olympus, he had not rested there long before he found that there was further service for him to render on the earth. Among the many noted deeds that he performed, the most famous was his slaying of a monstrous serpent called the Python, which was born of the slime that remained on the surface of the earth after the Deluge. Apollo killed the creature with his golden arrows, and then went to the help of Neptune, who, though a powerful deity in his own realm, was often obliged to ask help of the other gods when he wished to accomplish anything on land. Hearing that Neptune wished to build a great wall around the city of Troy, and remembering the aid that the sea-god had given his mother Latona in her great need, Apollo went down to the sea and offered his services to Neptune. Of course no son of Jupiter could be expected to do the work of a slave, but this was not necessary, even in the building of a wall; for Apollo sat down on a grassy bank nearby, and, with his lyre in his hand, began to play such exquisite music that the very stones were bewitched, and rising from the ground of their own accord took their places in the wall. Still under the spell of Apollo's music, others followed in quick succession, and the wall rose higher and higher, until before nightfall the whole work was finished. When the last stone had dropped into place, Apollo stopped his playing and returned to the bright halls of Olympus; while Neptune, shaking the salt spray from his shaggy eyebrows, stared hard at the walls that had risen by magic before his wondering eyes.

II

The story of Arachne's sad fate should have been warning enough to all mortals not to compare themselves with the gods; but such was the pride of a certain youth named Marsyas that he boasted openly of his skill in flute-playing, and dared to proclaim himself the equal of Apollo. Now Marsyas had not always been a musician, for he was by birth a shepherd – some even say a satyr – and had never seen a flute or heard it played until one day, as he sat tending his flock on the bank of a stream, he heard sounds of music coming from some spot nearby. He was very curious to see who the musician might be, but he dared not move lest he startle the player and make the beautiful melody cease. So he sat still and waited; and presently there came floating down the stream a flute – something that Marsyas had never seen before. He hurriedly snatched it out of the water, and, no longer hearing the wonderful music, he guessed that it had come from the strange thing he held in his hand. He put the flute to his lips, and lo, the same sweet melody greeted his ears, for the flute was not a common thing such as any man might use – it was a beautiful instrument that belonged to no less a person than Minerva. The goddess had hidden herself on the bank of the stream and had been trying her skill as a flute-player; but chancing to look down into the water, she saw her puffed-out cheeks and distorted features and angrily threw the flute into the stream. Thus it had come into Marsyas's possession; and the shepherd, having found such a treasure, never let it leave his hands. He neglected his work and left his flocks unguarded while he spent all his days in the delight of flute-playing.

It was not long before he believed himself to be the greatest musician in all Greece; and then it was only a step further to declare that even Apollo could not equal him in the sweetness of his playing. The god of music allowed this boasting to go for some time unpunished; but at last he grew angry at the presumption of the shepherd boy, and summoned Marsyas to a contest in which the nine Muses were to be judges. Nothing daunted, Marsyas accepted the challenge; and on the morning when the contest took place, a great silence fell over all the earth, as if every living thing had stopped to listen. The playing of Marsyas was wonderfully sweet, and as the soft tones of his flute greeted the listeners' ears they sat as if under a spell until the last sounds died away. Then Apollo took up his golden lyre, and when he struck the first chords, the air was filled with music far sweeter than any melody that had fallen from the lips of Marsyas. The judges, however, found it hard to give a verdict in favour of either musician; so a second time Marsyas began to play, and his music was so strangely wild and sweet that even Apollo listened in delight. But, charmed as he was by the youth's playing, the god of music had no intention of being outdone by a shepherd; so when he took up his golden lyre again, he began to sing, and added the wonder of his voice to the sweetness of his playing. When the singing ended there was no longer any doubt to whom the victory belonged; and Marsyas was forced to admit his defeat. As the price of failure was to be the terrible penalty of being flayed alive, the wretched Marsyas had to submit to this cruel death. Apollo bound him to a tree and slew him with his own hands.

III

When the news of Marsyas's dreadful fate spread abroad, people were careful for many years not to anger any of the deities by presuming to rival them; but in time the memory of that tragic event faded away, and the horror of it was forgotten.

In the halls of King Midas was the noise of great mirth and feasting, and the sound of music filled the spacious room where the king and his court sat at the banquet-table. Beside the king stood Pan, his favourite flute-player, who was no other than the famous sylvan god of shepherds; and as the wine went round and the king grew boastful of his possessions, he exclaimed loudly that not even Apollo himself could produce such exquisite music as fell from the flute of Pan. The guests, remembering the fate of Marsyas, grew pale and begged the king not to let his boast be heard; but Midas laughed scornfully and, raising his drinking cup above his head, called upon Apollo to appear.

To the surprise and dismay of all, the god of music suddenly stood before them, beautiful as the dawn and glowing with divine wrath. Though Pan was himself a deity, he had no desire to challenge Apollo, and looked fearfully at the sun-god's angry frown; but the king, drunk with pride, commanded him to play, and bade the god of music surpass the playing if he could. There was, of course, no question as to which was the better musician, and the guests loudly proclaimed Apollo the victor. One story tells that to prove further the superiority of Apollo's playing the company went to the old mountain-god Tmolus, and let him make the final decision. Tmolus had to clear the trees from his ears to listen; and having done this he bent his head, and all his trees leaned with him. He heard with delight both musicians play; and when the last soft notes fell from Apollo's lyre, the mountain-god awarded him the victory. But Midas at the beginning of the contest had demanded the right to decide on the merits of the players, and he would not accept this verdict. In his mad perversity and fondness for his favourite, he cried out that Pan was the better player, and would therefore be awarded the prize. Angered at this unfair decision, Apollo left the banquet-hall, but not before he had assured Midas that the injustice would be punished.

These words came true in a most unexpected way, for when the king looked into his mirror the next morning, he found a pair of large fuzzy ass's ears growing in the place of his own natural ones. Horrified at his absurd appearance, Midas did not dare show himself to his people; but sent in haste for a barber, and bade him make a wig large enough to cover the monstrous ears. For many hours the barber was closeted with the king, and when the wig was finished, he was allowed to leave the palace, after having sworn never to reveal the king's misfortune under pain of death. For some time the secret was safely kept; but the poor barber found life unbearable, since he lived in constant fear of letting out the truth about the king's ears in spite of his frantic efforts to be silent. Whenever Midas appeared in the city streets, the barber had to rush home and shut himself up lest he should scream out the story of the wig.

One day he thought of a happy solution of his difficulty and one that broke his long seal of silence without endangering his life. He went out into the fields, dug a deep hole, and putting his head down as far as he could he shouted:

"King Midas has ass's ears, King Midas has ass's ears."

Then he went home again, much happier for having told someone of his secret, even though it was only Mother Earth. But the truth once told did not stay hidden even in the earth; for in time the hole was filled again and reeds grew over the spot, and as the wind swayed them back and forth they murmured, "King Midas has ass's ears. King Midas has ass's ears."

It was not long before all the people in the countryside had gathered to hear the strange whispering of the reeds, and then the secret could be kept no longer. But though everyone knew the truth King Midas continued to wear his wig, and no one ever saw the real size of his ears.

Baba Yaga's Red Rider

Cara Giles

I, THE RED SUN, did not often find my way into Baba Yaga's forest. The dense thatch of larch, pine, and spruce confounded me. I shone above in ignorance as my brothers Twilight and Night witnessed years of the witch's cruelties.

I thought it was no business of mine. Night tended to make everything sound worse than it was, and Twilight – well, he was misty and foolish at the best of times. I simply warmed the surrounding fields, shining on wheat and flax for the humans below. They embroidered red sun chariots on their clothes and tablecloths, grateful for the gifts of grain and linen.

I took no notice of Baba Yaga until one evening I spoke to Night, and found that while the world had darkened in the same mellow rest he brought everywhere, my brother did not answer. "I fear he has been channeled away by magic," I told Twilight. "He may be trapped beyond our reach."

Twilight and I searched for our brother under his own black sky, to no avail. "Baba Yaga must have him," Twilight said. "She has eaten men as they eat chickens, and her power grows as she picks over their bones."

I had questions for Twilight, but didn't get the chance to ask them. When dawn next paled the world, my second brother fell silent. I chased the horizon, all the light-streaked clouds Twilight favored, but he was gone.

If Baba Yaga had them, I could not remain careless above the trees as before. All morning I struggled through the forest canopy, fighting down through needles, branches, and moss. Finally I shone on what my brothers had described: a sinister hut lancing up between tree trunks, tall on a pair of enormous, scaled hen's legs. It sat within a wall of human bones, each post topped with the skull of someone my rays had fed and clothed. My brothers had not exaggerated Baba Yaga's evil.

Something crashed through the underbrush. The witch herself appeared, riding in an iron mortar that ripped leaves from the trees. She drove it along with a pestle, gouging lichen off stones until she skidded to a stop. I withdrew at once, but her cold eyes swept the enclosure fast enough to catch the last hint of sunlight on the hut's roof.

"Now the third is mine," she announced, clapping hands nearly as bony as her wall. The lit dome of the sky fell away, and next a prison, all red blood and red armor, surrounded me. I tried to spread my rays and found fingers flexing, fought to hide behind clouds only to writhe in the body of a man.

"You shall be my red rider," Baba Yaga said. "Come."

My human legs followed her without wishing it.

Baba Yaga approached a snorting red horse behind the hut. It reared, its eyes rolling wildly. "Enough, beast!" The animal quieted. She put its reins in my hand. "All my horsemen serve me. Mount," she commanded.

My new body swung up into the saddle.

"Your eldest brother, my black rider, hides my deeds," Baba Yaga said, smiling with knife-edge teeth. "My white rider goads the foolish toward me by raising their hopes. You, red rider, will give light that I may see the fear in their eyes. Now ride!" She slapped the horse's rump and it surged forward, tearing through the underbrush.

Baba Yaga's enchantment pulled me along on my first horrible patrol. I spread a merciless, burning light through the forest, terrorizing wanderers and blistering the unwary. I couldn't imagine doing this forever. Would the humans notice I was gone?

Not even Baba Yaga could contain *all* of Night, Twilight and the Red Sun. I watched the fiery orb that was myself cross the sky each day, largely hidden by branches; at least the fields would still grow, but no one was looking for me.

For many months I served Baba Yaga. She kept me separated from my brothers except when she set us to work inside the hut.

"Grind my wheat!" she would say. Silent and invisible save for our gloved hands, we made flour for her, hoping she would choke on it. "Press the oil from these poppy seeds!" came another demand, and we did, wishing her endless oblivion.

Baba Yaga spied a hapless peasant peeking through her windows as we worked. She dragged him in. "You had a question, young man?" she asked, all false sweetness. It was not convincing. "Some age a fellow before his time, but you're free to ask anything."

His mouth opened and closed in silent fright before he managed the words, "How are the gloves moving?"

"They will show you. Servants, throttle this man into his grave!" Bound by her spells, we had no choice, though we wished we could finish her instead. The peasant should have lain in peace beneath the earth, but Baba Yaga mounted his skull on one of her posts. "Red rider, shine from the eyes of my skulls!" My rays lit her yard each night.

In that bleak time, I'd forgotten that the world carried magic of different shades. Humans could also enchant things, if they had the knack. One kind mother nearby was on her deathbed, and used the last of her strength to cast a spell on a simple wooden doll. It had a carved slit of a mouth, two pinprick eyes, and a tiny sun painted on the base. It was smaller than her palm, but powerful enough to call in my light. Even riding rounds for Baba Yaga, I heard the woman's final words to her only child.

"When I am gone, Vasilisa," she told the girl, "I leave my blessing for you in this doll. It is enchanted with the power of the sun. Carry it about you always. If ever you are in trouble, give it something to eat and drink, then tell it your problem. It will look after you as I would."

Vasilisa did not feed her doll for more than a year. Finally bread and sweet-sour kvass slid through the doll's wooden mouth, the first I had tasted of anything. Instead of the wretched forest, I found myself looking at her, now practically a young woman, through pinprick eyes.

"What is your trouble, Vasilisa?"

"My father is on a journey," she said, "and my new stepmother is cruel. Her daughters let the fire burn out on purpose. I couldn't see to spin my flax. They have all bolted the door against me," she said, shivering in the snow, "and will not let me back in the house until I bring fire from Baba Yaga's hut."

"Keep me with you," I said. "I will protect you if I can."

She set out into the forest, tightly clutching the wooden doll. It was hours before we heard hoofbeats.

"Look doll, it is a rider – a horseman all in white, on a white horse."

"He is my brother, Twilight," I told her. High above the trees, the sky lightened. "He would not ride for Baba Yaga if he could help it."

"I hear hoofbeats again, doll. Look!"

The wild red horse tore by, my own unwilling self in human form perched on its back. "That is the Red Sun." Stronger light filtered partway into the forest canopy. "His business is sky and warmth and crops. Baba Yaga has trapped him, like Twilight."

We were nearing the hut on hen's legs when my second brother rode by.

"I fear this one," Vasilisa said, shrinking back against a trunk as Night barreled along on a black charger. His starless armor, dark as pitch, stole hope away with one glance.

"Night would not harm you if left to himself," I said. As the last of the light drained from the sky, Vasilisa reached the bone wall. "Hide me in your apron pocket."

Vasilisa hid the doll as I asked.

My vision shifted, all red rays shining from the skulls on Vasilisa herself. She waited beside the locked gate of jawbones.

A cracking of branches announced Baba Yaga's arrival. She leapt from her iron mortar. "You've come to find me on purpose, girl?" she asked incredulously.

"Yes, Baba Yaga. My stepmother has sent me to borrow some fire."

"To see you dead, more like. You must work for it if you want anything of me. Or I could simply eat you," the witch said, thinking.

"Put me to any task," Vasilisa offered.

"Set my table with everything in my great oven. Tomorrow when I ride out, sweep my boneyard, clean the hut, and cook my supper. A quarter measure of wheat in my storehouse has been mixed with black grains and wild peas. Clean it."

Vasilisa shuddered as she entered the hut. Her hands fumbled as she plated joints of meat she dared not contemplate. Baba Yaga ordered her to the cellar, forcing the girl to stagger up with a huge cask of beer. There was plenty for ten men, but Baba Yaga ate and drank it all herself. Vasilisa slept on the floor beside the stove. At dawn when the witch left, the girl fed her doll another crumb from her apron pocket and a drop of kvass.

She told me her tasks. "But the yard is full of human bones, and worse besides," she said. "The floorboards have seen much blood. How am I to clean it all in one day, and cook such a meal at the same time?"

"With my help, and your mother's blessing," I said. "Rest, and it shall be done."

For the first time in ages, I felt myself above the trees. I spoke to all the plants of the forest, bidding them do Vasilisa's tasks. The good pine boards within the hut remembered my light, how they had grown straight and tall toward me, and cleaned themselves in remembrance. The wheat in the cellar shook off all it was mixed with. Vasilisa awoke at noon and set to preparing the supper herself.

Baba Yaga was furious. She sniffed about the boneyard with her long nose, squinted at the clean floors, ran her hands through the wheat in hopes of finding one pea that would permit her to eat Vasilisa. In the end she had to be content with the extravagant meal the girl had prepared. "Horsemen, grind my wheat into flour," she commanded. My attention was wrenched back from the sky, and all but invisible, my brothers and I did her work for her.

Vasilisa fed the doll again that night. "I am to make an even greater supper, and clean five sacks of poppy seeds mixed with earth," she said.

"Rest now. You have my help and your mother's blessing."

Baba Yaga departed at dawn. I spoke to the poppy seeds, reminding them of windblown red petal days in their parent flowers. They happily worked free of the dirt in their sacks, and Vasilisa spent all afternoon preparing a huge feast.

Baba Yaga appeared at dusk. She brought the poppy seeds close to her eyes, but couldn't find the merest speck of earth on them. "Horsemen, press the oil from these poppy seeds," she ordered. We did so. Vasilisa stood silently by, staring at the floating gloves that did the witch's bidding.

Baba Yaga sat and began to work through all the food Vasilisa had prepared, tearing meat from the bones and tossing them in her yard when she was done. "Why are you silent?"

"I did not wish to disturb you," Vasilisa said.

"But you have a question? Not all questions lead to good. Some answers age one before her time. Still, you may ask any you please," the witch said, gristle wedged between her sharp teeth. "Ask, girl!"

Vasilisa's eyes darted to where she had twice watched my brothers and me prepare things for the witch. If she asked about the floating gloves, Baba Yaga could make us kill her.

"I would not age before my time," Vasilisa said. "I am content not to know."

"Well, I am not!" Baba Yaga raged, shoving back the table and bringing her terrible face close to Vasilisa's. "How have you done all these impossible tasks?"

She knew better than to mention the doll. "My mother's blessing helps me," she said, honest yet carefully vague.

"You profane my hut with a blessing? Get out!"

Vasilisa stumbled backwards, nearly falling into the boneyard outside. Baba Yaga grabbed her by the arm and threw her beyond the gate. She lifted a glowing skull from a post and muttered her orders over it, then she hurled it after the girl.

"That is all the fire your stepmother will get from me!" Baba Yaga raged, locking the gate from the inside.

Vasilisa was grateful to get away. She needed the skull's light to find her way home, but at the edge of the forest she set it down. "The earth is frozen hard, or I would bury you," she said. "Rest well, whoever you were."

Baba Yaga's malice had thrown a web of dark magic over the skull, but it was my light shining there. Perhaps there was a way to bring her last wicked act to a good end. "Take it to your stepfamily, Vasilisa," I urged her through the doll's mouth.

She gingerly lifted the skull again, and brought it to her own house.

Her stepsisters and stepmother had been in dire straits, for after thrusting Vasilisa out to die, they could not start a fire at all. Flame carried in from neighbors' houses went out as it crossed the threshold, and even the best flint could kindle nothing inside. They had been freezing, and unable to prepare food.

"How warm and steady it is!" the stepmother said, admiring the sunlight shining from the skull. "Like having summer indoors. Come Vasilisa, set it on the table!"

She did.

"Now step outside," I whispered as the doll. "Leave the rest to Baba Yaga."

Vasilisa's stepfamily didn't notice the girl edging out the door; they were too happy with their sudden change of fortune. The golden light coming through the window changed to blood red, and I had Vasilisa cover her eyes. Baba Yaga's spell flared in the house, all blistering, burning red, a scorching out of life. The screams gave way to silence, and the house they'd barred Vasilisa from stood empty.

The witch's magic had never before been used to set someone free. Her evil cracked just enough to allow our glorious escape.

"Night!" I called.

"Yes?" he asked, surprised that we could speak again. He was once more in the inky darkness above the world, free.

"Hide this deed, that innocent Vasilisa may come to no harm."

"I shall."

Vasilisa tiptoed back inside when his work was done. "They were cruel, but does anyone deserve such an end?"

"They did," I assured her. "Baba Yaga would have done as much to you, and they would have rejoiced at it. Twilight! Bring this girl hope for better days ahead. She deserves them."

"Gladly!" He soared above the earth once more, painting the eastern horizon pale pinks and oranges.

"Look to the tsar's road," I told Vasilisa. "Night and Twilight and the Red Sun have brought you a new beginning."

I took my place arcing across the sky. Under my light, Vasilisa's father walked the last few miles home.

Birthday

Alyza Taguilaso

THE MORNING AFTER you turned 35, Cee came into your life.

One moment you were sitting there doom-scrolling through your old iPhone, sipping cold coffee from a beer-stained paper cup left over from the previous night's party, and the next she was on your apartment floor, splayed like some hapless bird. Around her, glass shards and bits of your plant pots make a mosaic pattern on that carpet your mother gifted you from Kashmir. She looked like she had most of her bones broken, the way she was laid out. The girl had no wounds – not a single break on her skin, despite the arrangement of her limbs.

Torn between checking if she was alive and not touching her (God knows how many true crime shows you've watched to be convinced that touching possibly-dead-bodies is a one-way ticket to jail), you take a good ten minutes staring at her. You see her chest rise, slowly, then steadily. Eventually, she starts moving and raises her head – a mess of red hair and dark gray eyes.

"Fuck," is the first thing she says to you. Before you can even do anything, she stands up, dusts off the bits of glass and dirt from her pale, pale skin, and proceeds to examine the intact bits of your apartment. Some confetti and torn gift-wrapping paper stick to the soles of her red sneakers as she makes her way around. You wonder why she doesn't look the slightest bit bothered by the fact that she had just crashed into a stranger's apartment window.

She's wearing an old denim jacket over a dirty white dress with ladybugs printed on them. You're still wondering whether you should call someone for help when she says from the kitchen, "Hey, mind if I crash in your place a bit?"

You refuse and prepare to escort her to the door but she insists, "Don't worry mister. I've got money to pay for that window, and your birds. What's your account number? I can wire you now, whatever the amount." she adds. You ask about the birds because you've never had pet birds. "Your plants, silly. Birds of Paradise. The ones I smashed. What used to be in those pots." Pointing to that red plant thing you never quite figured out what to call. She doesn't even bother asking your name and instead picks it up from a gift tag that made its way to one of your books. "So, Gideon," Her voice gives your name a strange twang, "'s it okay? I need someplace to crash, until I figure things out, at least." She repeats her question from atop your shelf. "Awesome mythology collection you have here!" she adds with glee. "It's nice to see someone in this part of town who knows what actual paper books are, instead of those blah pdf things."

* * *

That was about two years ago. Cinnamon Cinna-Maulogausse ended up staying longer than she promised.

You did complain at the start – then being a thirtysomething hermit jumping between odd jobs here and there, who also happened to be inept with the whole idea of living with girls. Or, this one particular girl at least. In the beginning, you attempted to shoo her away – suggesting places where she could instead stay ("There's a nice old couple renting out a house at the end of the street", "My friend Isis has this trippy Airbnb two blocks away. You'd love it there with the hipsters," and so on). Yet each time, she managed to shake your suggestions away. She would affix a frown on her face and twirl her fingers on a necklace with an egg-shaped pendant, signaling the end of the conversation. Eventually, you agreed to let her pay rent, considering the economy and the rising price of everything. She made a room for herself – the one your younger sister used as a sewing area before the rest of your family moved out and gave you a place of your own.

You never really told her but you did like having her around.

You found that she wasn't lying about being rich too – Cee never had to work. She always had funds. On the instances when she would go off to pick it up, she always did so alone. One day she would miss dinner and the next morning she'd be honking for you to wake up so she could drive you around in her new Vespa. Or Lambo. Or whatever new vehicle you realize was still up for pre-release or whatever. "Move it, pumpkin-ass! You're going to be late for work!" she'd say each time. Some days, she'd purposely stay with you on your morning commute, eager to spot pickpockets on the trains. She'd never squeal on them but she was always in awe. "Look at that sleight of hand…."

At first, you tried following her during your days off, as any decent person would, but she always seemed to scoot off to a different place each time. Not to mention she had a habit of walking terribly fast – sometimes it would feel like she was gliding while you try to catch up, always hoping that you'll one day catch up. You'd constantly fantasize about finally figuring out the entire mystery behind this girl.

Fun fact: Cee was nowhere on social media. A complete ghost, despite all her hipster wear and Gen Z quips. "Yeet!" she would exclaim, whenever you asked anything personal.

Mostly she would just speak of the most random things. "Did you know that we grow extra-tall in our sleep?" she would say over breakfast, and then ask you how tall you are, comparing your height to the lines carved on one side of your doorway. Or sometimes she'd go off and talk about moonshine conjectures. God knows what in the world those things are.

Being the quiet type, you'd just sit there. Listening and learning things from her that no one else had ever told you. Over dinner, she'd say, "*Paradise Lost* was bound in the skin of a dead murderer!" while watering the plants one time. "It's possible for your heart to go on beating in a solution of water and sugar for about two hours after it's been removed from your chest,"; and, on one occasion, after watching a primetime soap opera: "Pigs eat their own poop!" You'd just nod and remark, "Fascinating", then go back to whatever you were doing, and yet secretly keep an eye on her.

The funny thing was, despite everything she said about the world in general, she rarely talked about herself. Most of the things you know about her were gained through observations you would constantly update and edit in a tiny notebook:

- She doesn't eat much – only candies and some green-colored liquid which she says is dew (*Probably a new diet thing? Protein shake? Something like Gwyneth Paltrow's bone broth?*)

- She fell in love with your mythology collection – even stashing it all off to her now-room-then-your-sister's-sewing-room
- She takes a good deal of forever in the bathroom (Usual reply: "I am having bowel problems! Leave me alone! Google Crohn's Disease!", will sometimes vary: "I have dysentery, like in the 15th century!")
- Birthday: unknown

It was the bit about the birthday that bothered you most. "Dude, didn't you say there were other things about her you didn't know?" you remember your friend Jose saying. "I mean, what's so special about knowing her birthday anyway? Besides, chicks don't dig it when guys know their real age." It had been your lunch break then, and all you could do in reply was take another bite off your burger. "Better lay off else she'll lay you off," he adds with a laugh.

* * *

"Don't you celebrate birthdays where you're from?" you ask her. It had been about three months since you last brought the topic up. The last time you tried asking her, you got carried away insisting she answer the question. That time then, Cee got fed up with repeating "I don't really want to talk about it," so much that she ended up hurling miscellaneous items (two flower pots, a kettle, half a set of teacups, and the telephone) through the window. You spent the entire evening of that day explaining to the neighbors that the broken fixtures and dangling telephone were attempts at trying out "a new form of modern art (ie., A Lesson on Boundaries)".

Today, you ask her again, more out of boredom than curiosity since both of you had been left stuck in the apartment as floods ravaged the city streets outside. You almost dropped the dish you were drying when she actually gave an answer. She shook her head and turned to you, "Yes, we do celebrate birthdays. Mine, especially." She pouted slightly before turning back to the book she was reading.

"So why don't you want to celebrate it now?" You actually want to ask why she was so upset the last time, but you decide to pace your questions else you elicit the same response.

She sighed, stood up, and went to the same window she crashed into the first time you met, which was also, strangely the same window where the "attempted modern art installation" made its grand exit from your apartment. "You know, I was running away from some people back then, when we met. Or maybe, they were running away from me." She placed her fingers on the new glass, tracing out some figures before turning to you, smiling. "It was my birthday that day."

* * *

The following day, Cee denied any bit of what she'd said. Your immediate reaction was to ignore her the entire morning. You even braved the receding floodwater outside to buy takeout for lunch so as not to be stuck at home. Once back, you immediately stuck to your phone, and kept your face to livestreams on the news. Nothing but floods, again. You stand up and secure the other half of the couch by dumping a slew of papers you needed for an article you had to write. In the interval following yet another ramen commercial, Cee calls you from the kitchen. "All right, almighty G, you win." Seeing how she got your attention, she swiftly offers a cupcake. It was vanilla with chocolate icing that formed a smiley face. "But not without a game." Before you could say anything, she swoops and plants a kiss on your right cheek. You try to argue afterward, only to be betrayed by your reddening cheeks, your tongue tied in a knot.

The rules were simple – you could pick any day to be her birthday, presents and all, and she would tell you if it was the right one or not.

* * *

So you tried.

You first picked the day she would usually spend disappearing to gather "funds". Halfway through a lavish dinner with an accompanying violinist – both of which ate up a quarter of your monthly salary, Cee sighs and starts taking sips of the mushroom soup you ordered. "It's turning out to be a pleasant un-birthday, don't you think?" she lets you know after blowing the candles off a cake.

Several presents, cakes, balloons, roses, clowns and Ferris wheel rides later, you still didn't know her birthday. Funnily, the more you tried, the less it started to matter. There was something new to laugh about after every un-birthday – the misspelled name on the cake, the way the balloon popped to scare some curious children in the park, the candles you eventually had to reuse since they were piling up in the apartment.

"I think I'll make up enough un-birthdays to turn you well into a hundred years old," you tell her, following another failed attempt. She takes your hand, smiling, and replies, "Wanna bet?"

* * *

Un-birthday games and "attempts at modern art" aside, the relationship wasn't all that strange. It had the makings of most relationships. Like, paying for rent equally. Mostly though, it was an unspoken agreement that certain parts of the relationship be kept fairly quiet. Those were the only times, under a sea of sheets, when her silence would put your own hushed breathing to shame. Once you asked her why and she replied sleepily, "The quiet helps me feel."

Most of the time you never really understood her, but then she says "Oh G," curling her thin fingers around you and you feel all the warmth in the world surge into your tired body.

Pretty much things were perfect, the way they turned out to be: her being a mix of affluent, quirky and slightly unhinged, and you, the silent working-class type, happy to be the side character to Cee in whatever her main quest would be. Your folks just adored her to death – rosy cheeks, red hair and all. They even asked during a visit once when you two would get married, to which you replied by saying dinner was getting cold and marriage was just a construct.

She brings you a different car every so often – once even a vintage thunderbird – and you, well, you try to keep the house cleaner now. You recently quit your current job as a personal assistant to some corporate boomers and, with the meager amount you saved, signed yourself up for a discounted archaeology course at the local university.

* * *

Things never got close to complicated until a month before your 37th birthday.

"Pack your bags!" she burst in one day, a bucket hat and a pair of heart-shaped sunglasses gracing her face. Showing you screenshots of what looked to be two plane tickets, she mused, "Egypt is where we're going for your birthday!" You try to dissuade her, being unused to traveling, especially after the Covid pandemic. Unfortunately for you, her mind was made up. "Come on – you want to be an archaeologist, right? Well, we're going to check out some old temples – and I know how you hate tourists, crowds and influencers so the places we're going to are pretty secret!" She hugs your right arm and rubs a warm cheek on it and suddenly you wonder why you wanted to say no in the first place.

* * *

It was your first plane ride since you were 15. The plane was small and the airline name was an unfamiliar one. Not Etihad or Emirates, which you were more expecting considering Cee's usual budget. You tell yourself that Cee probably hired some private service for this one. *How thoughtful of her*, you think as the plane whirs to motion.

You insist that Cee take the window seat because you suffer from motion sickness. She didn't seem to mind – in fact, she seemed to like staring out into the clear, cloudless sky most of the trip. Eventually you fall asleep listening to an obscure song called *Consolation Prizes* in your playlist. When you woke up, she was pinching your cheeks. "We're here, we're here! Aren't you excited?" she exclaimed, bouncing on her seat. You take a peek out the window and all you see are buildings, bland sand and the hint of pyramids. Everything feels suddenly warmer.

As you disembark from the plane, Cee leads the both of you to a dark-skinned man holding a cardboard sign that had something in Arabic written on it. "Gideon, meet Actis H.," Cee said. Drawing closer to him, you noticed how he had features indistinguishable to a particular race – a slightly cleft chin, pointy nose, chubby cheeks, amber eyes and bushy eyebrows. He smelled very strange too, like a book from an ancient library. "So you are Gideon," said his deep voice. "I, Actis H., am pleased to meet you. I have been told a lot about you, Mr. G. It is your birthday in one day, yes?"

You tell Actis that your birthday will be in seven days. "So we have enough time to see the place!" Cee cheerily adds. Actis leads you to an air-conditioned car with your luggage already in the trunk and he instructs the driver in Arabic. The car starts to move in the direction of the pyramids. You tell Cee that you didn't know she could read Arabic. Her lips purse and she answers, "I know Greek and Aramaic too."

Actis, in his strange lisp, attempts to give you a tour of everything you pass by. You couldn't understand most of the things he says. The only thing you caught onto was "cactus". The ride seemed to stretch as long as the Nile so you nodded off to sleep, your head resting on Cee's shoulder.

Again, it is Cee who wakes you upon arrival. "We'll stay here," she says, pulling you outside by the hand. Her hands have never felt any warmer. "This is Actis's place," she adds. You almost drop your valise at the size of the "place". It's an actual estate – enormous and white, a Mediterranean house towers and nearby, a swimming pool with attendants dressed in white holding gigantic leaves shaped like fans.

A group of people answer to Actis's booming voice and pick up your entire luggage set, bringing them to your rooms.

."He's always been nice enough to let me stay here for free ever since. I've always found it better than those so-so hotels and Airbnbs," Cee adds as you continue to gawk at the place. "Actis and I go a long way back," she muses. "Feel your birthday coming yet?" Cee smiles as she leads you up the house. You look back at Actis and attempt to say thank you while trying to catch up with Cee. He laughs and gestures for you to explore the place.

You and Cee have a lavish room to yourselves, facing a view of the town and the endless sand stretching to the horizon. Feeling slightly tired, you tell Cee you were going to spend the first night sleeping in. She didn't seem to mind. "Are you sure? You might've made plans," you tell her to make sure. Strangely, she didn't seem to be bothered by anything. "That's fine, G," she says, humming a lively tune. You remember her asking you if you wanted anything from the nearby flea market before you dozed off.

When you wake up she still hadn't returned. Fumbling the sheets, you eventually find your phone flickering with a message from her.

> Be back at 11, feel free to do whatever.
> —C
> PS Try the pool. Your muscles might atrophy from too much sleeping.

I'll let her have some fun, you tell yourself while you fixed up to look around Actis's house.

Actis, you are told by one of the house's staff, is resting in his study. You figured it would be rude to interrupt (not that you and Actis would have anything to talk about). You decide to follow Cee's suggestion and hang in the pool a bit. The water was uncomfortably hot but you do a few laps. A few minutes later, one of Actis's attendants calls you into the house. It was apparently dinnertime.

Entering the hall, you see Actis at the head of the table, seated like a king. You sit down only to stare at a dish you've never seen before. Actis, through one of his servants who could speak English, explains that its wild duck from Fayyoum, stuffed with something called *fireek*, which was cracked wheat gathered and dried, onions, some Egyptian celery – all of which had been basted with orange juice. All you see before you looks nothing like a duck. You bite into the meal to be polite. Surprisingly, you like the meat – spicy and hot around the tongue. You tell Actis it tastes good, and he is pleased. As dinner courses through, he tries (slowly and through the assistance of the same attendant) to engage you in conversation, asking about how you met Cee, and so on. You tell him everything, starting with how she crashed through your window, your un-birthday game, and ending at the point she dragged you into Egypt. To this, Actis laughed hard enough to move the walls of that hall. You chew your food slower so as not to be asked more questions.

"You must excuse me," he said after his bout of laughter, "Cee is really like that. Cee never changes."

Cee returns just before you were about to sleep; as she had promised, it was exactly 11pm. She had a few shopping bags and a stash of something that smelled like some herb. "Here, I bought you some books on topography and museum pieces," she says as she lies beside you, curling into a ball. You ask her about what was causing the strange smell. "Oh, that's just some myrrh," she answers before snuggling into you and falling asleep herself.

The next day you ask her what she needs the myrrh for. She tells you it's for her future periods.

"Helps with the blood flow. You know, when the uterus is acting like a monster or someone's nagging mother," she adds. You wonder how women would use such a thing to ease their pains.

* * *

You find yourself enjoying your stay by the third day. She tugs you around the city (the name of which you're still not sure how to pronounce) showing you the ins and outs of the place. People seemed to know her here – they just gave her whatever she picked out from the stalls and shops, not even asking for payment. Cee looked like nothing from Africa so you keep wondering where all their fond feelings for her came from. Maybe she was really just that pretty, or nice, or charming. Maybe she was secretly an influencer all of these people knew? "Actis pays for everything," she tells you later on. Somehow, you don't believe her on this.

She still had that habit of walking very fast. By the end of each "walk", your feet would be covered in a thin layer of hot sand, from trying to catch up to her. Eventually, she brings you to some ruins and teaches you more about hieroglyphs. You find it strange that the places she brings you to have but a few tourists. "Actis owns most of these sites, heritage spots purchased from the local government. The press release is that they're being researched and excavation staff need the space," she tells you while kicking at some dust in an old temple. "Mostly, it's really just his staff allowed here. Tourists are ok, but he doesn't like the publicity. Neither does he need the money." You ask her about Actis and she tells you he's really just an old friend. "Mighty nice guy," she adds.

* * *

"Hey Gideon, you're turning 37 in four days. What are you going to do?" she asked that night. You tell her you don't know, really.

"Maybe become an archaeologist. The things you showed me here are pretty neat." You joke a bit. "Maybe I'll get stuck here forever, trapped in some temple," She smiles and asks you if you'll take care of her. Instinctively, you answer, "Yes" and follow it up with "Why would you ask that?"

"Nothing, really," she answers. "Just making sure."

On the fourth day, you decide to stay in again after touring another temple. Cee said she needs to help Actis with some things and that they'll be back for dinner. You spend the afternoon swimming again. Afterwards, you decide to peek into the things Cee bought just a few days back.

You're surprised to find that she bought baby clothes.

"Who are these for?" you immediately ask once she returned. "You're pregnant? Cee, what the hell?" For the first time, Cee looks surprised. "Oh," she says softly, "So you've found out...well, they're for a baby girl!" She tells you it's for a niece she has in a province beside Actis's estate. "I'll visit her soon." Her tone tells you that she wants the conversation over. Before you could ask anything more, someone knocks on the door and tells you both that dinner was about to start. Over the table, Cee was ten times quieter than usual and Actis was talking to some Egyptian associate over his phone. Cee didn't partake of the food offered on the table – instead; she was served some of her "dew". It seemed to have taken too long to prepare so by the time it was served, she looked quite agitated. When it was handed to her, she grabbed it quickly, and then, almost out of nowhere, the glass she held burst into flames.

"Oh god, shit! I'm sorry, I'm so sorry!" Cee immediately stood up and tried to pour water over the bits on the floor. "Shit! Fuck! Damnit!" she was muttering as the attendants scuttled quickly to clean up the mess. She turned to Actis who seemed shocked and she said something in Arabic. He replied by patting her on the head to perhaps indicate that things were ok. You hold her shoulders to comfort her but she just shrugs it off.

Later that night you ask her again if she's pregnant. When she doesn't answer, you tell her it's ok – "It's not as if we can't take care of the kid, you know. I mean, I have some money." You didn't really want to talk about finances. Money always made you feel inadequate, knowing Cee's hidden stash probably amounted to a million times more than everything you've saved.

"You think you'd make a good dad?" she asks. You tell her, a bit unconvincingly, that you would try your best. "Even when I'm not around?" she asks, holding your hand. You wonder why she would suddenly ask that. "Why, is anything wrong?" she shakes her head and tells you that she wants to sleep. "I mean if you're worried about me letting the kid play with fire or running around with scissors, that won't happen." To this she just chuckles softly and buries her head on a pillow.

Her restless movements keep you awake that night. You try to figure out the next date for her un-birthday. *Maybe I should just hit two birds with one stone.* You decide the next date of her un-birthday would be the same day as your birthday.

* * *

The next morning, she takes a sudden aversion to holding things. "I feel under the weather, sorry," she says, sinking back into bed. You tell yourself that it's probably usual for pregnant women to start having hormonal bouts like this. You tell yourself everything's normal and Egypt is pretty and you'll both have fun for that day. You ask her why she didn't bring you to the pyramids, only the temples. She said something along the lines of "Pyramids house those pompous, dead creeps. I don't like them, and the whole idea of death parading around me. Sorry, G." You could see that she tried to make you feel better when she adds, "But if you want, I'll take you to one." You tell her it was ok and she didn't have to. Really, you were enjoying things.

That afternoon Actis called Cee to his study to discuss something. With no one looking, you stick your left ear to the door, hoping to know what it was about. They were talking in fast voices and in a language you've never heard before. Pretty soon the talking turned into a heated argument – Actis's voice exploding through the walls. Suddenly, a strong *thud* makes its way from inside the room.

You were about to charge in to see if anything happened to Cee when suddenly the door was blasted open by flames. The next thing you know, you're lying on your back, covered by splinters and Cee is running towards you.

"Gideon! Are you all right?" You tell her weakly that everything's fine and ask her what happened inside. Behind Cee you see Actis, his face looked half burnt, melted skin crusted with a dark eschar, some exposed bone. He didn't seem to feel any of it. You blink, doubting your eyes. Now, his face looks the same, like nothing happened to it. You tell yourself you're just seeing things. "He does not look well." You hear Actis say, "Cee, are you sure of this?" Cee retorts in a foreign tongue, her words burning through Actis. He gave no reply after she spoke.

* * *

That night you try to hold Cee, start stroking her hair, but she pushes you away. "I'm sorry," she says. You tell her it's ok and that you understand. She tells you again that she's sorry. You try holding her again but she pushes; you persist and she stops resisting eventually. In all the times you had held her, she had never felt this warm. You were beginning to get worried that she had a fever until she suddenly digs her head into your shoulder. She hugs you like a lost child and you wonder if the wetness you feel on your shoulder were her tears or just your sweat. You curse yourself for not knowing how to properly react to situations like these. You were a few days shy of turning 37. It was almost embarrassing. To make up for it, you swore to give her one of the best un-birthdays ever.

* * *

On the sixth day Cee didn't want to go out of the house and Actis was nowhere to be found. Not really in the mood for any swimming, you try your best to convince her to tour you. "Come on, I'm the one who's going to have a birthday," you tell her through the fortress of pillows she made. You manage to pull her out after a few repetitions of "Please".

In the flea market you pick out a present for her each time she looks elsewhere. To seem less obvious, you present her with a little necklace. As she tries it on, it slips and drops into the lamp of the person manning the stall. Before you both knew it, things started catching fire. Cee starts to panic and you don't know what to do, unsure if the people around you were shouting expletives or telling you how to douse the fire. You just stand there as the fire travels from one stall to another – wares flying around, chickens running about with flaming feathers, and people scrambling all over shouting curses or their gods' names or both. From the canal beside the stalls, frogs start hopping around. You start wondering if this is a modern reenactment of Egypt's Ten Plagues and try to spy if locusts are looming from a distance.

"Toast! We're so toast!" Cee says as she drags you out of the burning flea market by the hand. As you both run, bits and clumps of sand mixed with camel dung mixed with spit thwacks on your face; you tell yourself that you're not meant for adventures.

"Cee, this has not happened before," Actis tells Cee as his attendants dusted you clean of the ashes. "Don't be silly, Actis, everything's going fine. You should know how these things do happen, especially after I decided to...you know, *that*." You had no idea what they were talking about again.

What follows is a moment of silence. Then, Actis looks at you directly for the first time since meeting him. "Are you *really* sure? I do not think he can do it." Cee quickly replies, "Well, that's why you're here, Actis. That's why you've *always* been here," adding, quite softly, "But I'm sure he can do it. I really am. This one has a good heart. I won't have to rely on your choices again."

That night you ask Cee what just happened with Actis. She sighs, saying, "It's what always happens." Quickly changing the topic, she asks you what your favorite myth is. You wonder if she's trying to find stories to tell the baby. You tell her you've always liked the story about the sphinx. She asks you why and you tell her that you've always liked solving puzzles, discounting the fact that you can't remember any other myth at that time. "That's so boring," she draws closer and picks your hand up. With her thin fingers, she starts tracing out tiny circles on your palm. "Since we're in Egypt, you know this story they have about the Sun-bird?" She tells you it's her favorite story, "It's the best, really," she adds before turning her back and wrapping herself with the blanket. "Maybe the only one I know."

* * *

You wake up in the middle of the night and find Cee curled beside you. After making sure she was sleeping soundly, you realize you can't sleep. Remembering that it would be your birthday in a few hours, you realize your plan for Cee's un-birthday wasn't as mapped out as you wished it were.

Actis's halls were still well lit, so you had no difficulty in finding your way around. You figured that since he seems to be Cee's oldest friend, there would be a big chance you'd figure something out about her birthday if you looked around well enough.

Three rooms, five dust-laden bookshelves, thirty-two picture frames, and about two sculptures of gods later, you still don't have a clue. You were hoping the picture frames would at least have a few shots of Cee somewhere in them. So far it just had photographs of Actis in various locations with all sorts of people. Most of them were in black and white. In one, he looked to be shaking hands with a caucasian diplomat, in another, he was holding up a fish – one which he likely caught, judging by the lake in the background and the fishing rod held in his other hand. You couldn't help chuckle at the fact that in all his pictures, Actis's shiny forehead was almost bright as day. Feeling a sudden sense of daring, you decide to explore Actis's study.

You stare at the door in wonder, remembering how, just the previous day, it had been blasted into smithereens. *Then again, I could've been making that up*, you tell yourself, then shake your head. Carefully, you twist the golden doorknob and find yourself surprised by the fact that it's unlocked. *Must be a new knob, then*. This room resembled the others – wide and without many things within. A large bookshelf lay next to the door you notice a few picture frames placed on the shelves. The photographs show a relatively younger Actis, mostly with the same people. A slew of group shots later, one photograph catches your eye. Still a group photo, but with someone who wasn't there before. You could almost feel those pale eyes taking color and looking you straight the same way they did these past two years.

You almost drop the last picture frame when you hear a cough behind you. It was Actis.

* * *

For what felt to be a century, you freeze on the spot, looking up at Actis's enormous figure as he watched. Without saying anything, he takes the frame from your fingers and examines the photograph. A slight smile spreads on his face. He heads to his desk and scribbles something on a notepad. He tears off the paper and gives it to you.

In lightly written script are four numbers:

1879

Actis hands you back the photograph and you examine it closely. It was only then when you note the peculiarity of the photograph – everyone looked stiff and somehow too formal. The men all wore black suits and stood in a row behind seated women. Cee was one of those women. She was in a dress that wound tightly around her waist, like as if in a period film. She was the only one in the photograph with a slight smirk on her face. You look back at the numbers Actis wrote.

He pulls out a book from the shelf. It's about the same size as a regular paperback and was bound in red leather. A glyph seemed to be engraved on its spine but Actis flips it open quickly before you have the chance to make out the symbol. The page he opens to has a photograph as a bookmark. It was a shot from a ship. You could see Actis half-smiling, leaning beside a pile of barrels. Then there was Cee, her gaze directed to the horizon. Another person was with them. A boy, in his late twenties, the one in the group with the widest smile. You turn the picture over and find a name written behind it. *Henrik*. You were about to ask who the boy was or when the photograph was taken when Actis hands you another photograph, pulled out from another book. It seemed to be taken in the desert, amidst a camp of nomads. It had the same arrangement as the previous one: three people – Actis, Cee, and again, another man. This one had a bearded face and chiseled cheekbones. You flip the photograph. *Robert*. Actis goes through what feels like an entire ritual (*Markus. Jon. Sylvie. Daniel. Ignacio. Bianca. Oskar. Paul. Vincent. Anthony…*) before you manage to interrupt.

Instead of just one, you spew out a slew of questions. "Who are all these people with you and Cee? Where are they now? Why didn't she tell me any of this? 1879? What's happening?" You shake your head as the words flow out of your mouth. All you wanted was to find a sliver of a clue to Cee's birthday. Instead, you have your hands full with photographs bearing strangers' names.

The next thing Actis hands you is yet another tiny slip of paper with instructions. *Sit,* it said. He motions to a chair across his desk. You notice him scribbling something else while you slowly make your way to the chair, careful not to drop any of the photographs. Before reading the new message, you ask again, "Who are those people?" Actis points to the paper. It was not the answer you expected. *Do you love her?*

* * *

The question takes you by surprise. No one had asked it before. Not your friends, not your parents, not even Cee. You keep silent, eyes pinned to the paper, as if staring at it long enough would reveal a secret message Actis might've inscribed. The entire time you do this, Actis seats himself behind his desk and rests his hands on the table. It is only when you raise your head, your mouth unable to deliver an answer that he writes once more. Your mind goes blank, processing nothing save for the sound of pen softly sliding a trail of ink on paper.

Actis sighs as he tears the page off the pad. He hands you the next paper facedown then exits the room, leaving you with the message.

Who are those people in the photographs?
They are people no different from you. All of you: the same.
If tomorrow you are still here, I will answer all your questions.

Later, when you exit his study, you find that the lights have been shut. You make your way back to your room, the sheet of paper growing heavy as you hold it in darkness.

* * *

You wake up late the next morning. Cee is the first person you see. She wears a floral sundress and it's as though she had washed away all memory of the past few days.

"Happy birthday, G!" she squeals cheerfully, throwing her hands around you. "Today's going to be super!" she says. You find out that she was going to bring you to a particular temple – the one that Actis hadn't let anyone else touch yet for about a long time now. "So, you can do some archaeology of your own, this time I won't tour you."

She brings you to a temple no different from the rest – a rotunda where the altar was, and behind the altar was an obelisk. You realize Cee was right about her description. Not a single sign of human activity. It was as if no one had touched the insides of the temple for the last thousand years.

Cee tells you to go do your "archaeology thing" while she fixes some things in her knapsack. You think of asking her about the photographs Actis showed. But it's as if the words decided to stay in your mouth, floating in breath and indecision. You sigh to yourself and resolve to ask Cee about it later. You realize you left behind all the un-birthday presents you planned to give her. You drive your fist to the nearest pillar but scrape it instead. You curse yourself for being unable to deliver a proper blow.

You try to check the place out but the most you could "discover" were glyphs. These glyphs were the archaic types – the ones you couldn't read out even with your notes laid before you. You tried checking if an app on your iPhone could identify it but soon realized not a single signal bar remained. Cee stayed near the altar; you were about to ask her for help on the glyphs when you notice her making a small, circular thing with myrrh and some twigs. You ask what she's doing and she replies by telling you about what this temple is.

"You know the Egyptians, they believed," Cee speaks in a strange, tired voice, "they believed in this bird, the Sun-bird. They said it could live for five hundred, a thousand – even twelve thousand years. They said that it had a temple, somewhere in a holy city called Heliopolis. That temple, where it would go to once it feels like it has to die, and from its ashes will rise a new one. Can you imagine that? An exact replica of what it used to be. Ever heard of that story, Gideon?" It made no sense at all why she would go on telling you the story of the Phoenix in the middle of god-knows-where. You figure she was continuing the previous night's conversation. "Sometimes, it forgets its past life, but most times, it remembers. Would you call that a good thing, G? Remembering everything?" her voice trails off. "Kingdoms, wars, people – all their names. To remember everything – how they start, how they end."

"I don't get these hieroglyphs," you tell her, hoping to change the topic. "You don't have to really," she says, continuing to make a small nest with the twigs and myrrh. "Everything those blasted stones are saying can be summarized by what I just said." You tell her it's not funny for her to be making stuff up on your birthday, how you'd really like to read the glyphs and it would be most helpful if she would just tell you what they said.

"But I did," she says, seemingly surprised. "I've told you all you need to know, all this time." You tell her that you don't follow what she's saying. "These past two years – I've told you *everything* you need to know."

"Goddamnit Cee! Don't give me weirdzo talk again. Not now, at least. It's my fucking birthday." You make it a point to convey exactly how you feel, which is cruel.

Cee sighs from behind you. "I suppose I should've explained things clearer, then. But it's always been so hard to do these things, you know." You feel her warm arms around your neck. "Sometimes, I really just don't know where to start. What to say," she starts musing, "if I told you about Alexandria and the floods, if I told you about everything, would you really believe me? How do you think I know all those silly things I told you before, G? How do you think I know the color of Thomas Edison's favorite shoes, or the makings of each damned temple I've brought you to?" You were going to tell her that you figured she read those things in books, and then you remembered suddenly that about two of the temples you had seen the previous days you've never even heard of in your archaeology books.

Cee sighs again. With her arms still around your neck, she extends her fingers to trace out the glyphs. "These little scribbles are just telling you where the Sun-bird lives, which is here, what it does, which is mostly fly from place to place, quite unsure of itself, everything it's supposed to do when it comes back to this place," she sighs again, "in case it forgets."

You wonder if all pregnant women encounter hormonal bouts like this. Then you remember the photographs. For some reason, a weight builds up within you. You find yourself reaching into your pocket, fingers fumbling for the paper that held Actis's last message.

Suddenly she says, "Gideon, you love me, right?" Her voice didn't sound any different but something in her had changed. "You told me you'd be a good father." She lets go of you and returns to the patch of myrrh. "Actis has everything ready when you get back. *Everything.* That is, if you decide to return," Her voice almost sounds like it's pleading.

"All of this…." Her voice trails off.

You turn around to see her striking her egg pendant at the ground. You come closer the exact moment she manages to break it open. All it contained was some white powder. "What the hell is this, some ritual? Crack?"

The tone of her voice doesn't change. "This isn't cocaine, Gideon. It's what I have to do." She spreads the white powder evenly on the patch of myrrh and starts humming. Then she looks at you, straight in the eyes and you notice something in those eyes – something that seemed to be burning. You blink once, and again to make sure you're not dreaming things.

"Gideon, I'm not pregnant," she tells you. "I mean, it's something, yes, but it's definitely not pregnant."

She draws closer and kisses you softly. "G, you'll take care of me, right?" It didn't even feel like a question. She hurriedly takes out a small box from her bag. "Here," she says, "it's a cupcake I made for you this morning. It's not much of a gift, but I hope you like it." Her hands almost shake as she puts the box into yours.

"You can't look at this," she empties the contents of her bag and picked up a can of what looked to be kerosene. "This part's a bit disgusting since times have changed, and I've had to resort to more convenient, expedient measures. Don't worry, this will be quick. But it can blind you the same way it blinded countless others all those years ago."

Not really knowing what to do, you say the first thing that comes to mind. "I picked this day, you know, as your next un-birthday. It was going to be a surprise. But I forgot to bring the presents. I'm sorry. You could do that thing another time, we could head back—" She laughs slightly and turns you around by the shoulders, and then you feel her drawing away from you, moving closer to the altar.

Her kiss was still fresh on your lips when it all happens: soft, warm fire you can feel from behind you, burning and bright – casting shadows on the temple walls, but never once wounding you. The fire almost feels like Cee's arms holding you again. In your head you hear her voice cooing, "It's going to be okay, Gideon," and then nothingness. Just the faint crackling of flames.

A few minutes pass and, squinting your eyes at the horizon beyond the temple entrance, you wonder what to do. The wind howls from a distance and you realize you're 37 years old. Again, you're not sure if you should turn around, if you should even move. Shaking, you open the small box and pick out the cupcake. It's chocolate with sprinkles on top, with a small pumpkin-shaped candy. On the cupcake, a tiny flag with *Happy birthday Gideon!* written on it.

You think of Cee, because you can't think of anything else. You think of Cee and the cupcake and you tell yourself that since she made it just for you it should be delicious. You tell yourself that the best thing to do right now would be to bite it and taste all the love and whatever else she put in that damned cupcake. All two years of what you two shared – in a cupcake, from the moment she crashed into your window to whatever the hell just happened a few seconds ago.

Just about when you were going to bite into it you hear the soft but urgent cry of an infant from behind you.

Placing the cupcake back in the box, you sigh and turn around.

The Boy Who Married the Sun

From the Chukchi people, northeastern Siberia

A MAN LIVED in a Maritime settlement. He had seven grown-up sons. They were travelling in a boat, and hunting whales and walruses. One time they went to sea, and saw a large overhanging cliff, quite similar to a house. At that moment the boat capsized, and they were drowned. Their mother was left quite destitute, with the youngest son, who was still a small boy. The boy cried all the time, and asked his mother for food. She gathered some shells and seaweed on the shore, and with these she fed the boy; but he continued to cry, and to ask for whale-skin and walrus-blubber such as he was accustomed to. The mother also cried, "Where shall we find them? Your father is gone, and your brothers are also gone." He said, "Then I will go and find them." – "How can you find them? They are drowned in the sea."

The boy went away without his mother's knowledge, and walked along the shore. At last he came to that cliff-house. He entered it, and saw his father and his seven brothers sitting there. The father wept. "Why have you come? We are dead, drowned." A Cliff-Spirit was there also. He was very angry. "Why have you come?" said the Spirit, and gave the boy a tremendous thrashing, so that he was left hardly alive. The father helped him to get up, and led him out of the house. He gave him also three small roots, and said, "When you reach home, put one of these roots into each of our caches. Then in the morning send your mother to look into the caches." The boy came home, and first of all he went to the caches, and put into each of them one root of those given to him by his father. Then he came to the mother. The mother was weeping. "Where have you been, and who has beaten you so frightfully?" – "I saw my father and my seven brothers." – "Do not say so! Your father and your brothers perished long ago." Weeping, she fell asleep. In the morning he awakened her, and said, "O mother! go and open the three caches, and then bring some food from there!" The mother thought, "What shall I bring? There is nothing in them." Notwithstanding, she went to the caches and opened them. All the caches were full of provisions – whale-skin and white-whale blubber and walrus-meat and everything as it was in the time when her husband and her seven sons were alive. The boy said, "Now, mother, we have plenty of food: so I will go and look for a wife." – "Where will you find her, child?" – "I shall." He got up about midnight, put on his clothes and boots, and departed. He looked up toward the sky, and saw two men descending directly toward him. "Where are you going? What do you want?" – "I am going to look for a wife." – "All right! Then drive these reindeer of ours, and follow our trail. The way we descended, that way you ascend." He sat down on the sledge and drove upwards along the moon's ray. He felt much fear; nevertheless he drove straight ahead, and came to the heavens. The heavens looked like firm ground, only it was quite white and shining. He saw a Raven, that flew by. "What do you want here? Oh, well! I know. Stay a little! I will tell you. You will find on the way a settlement of Reindeer people. Do not stop there. Then you will find another settlement of Reindeer people. Do not stop there, either. Also pass by the third settlement. Then you will see a large house, shining like gold.

This is the house of the Sun. His daughter is quite ill. She is near unto death, and nobody knows how to help her. The Sun will greet you with great joy. He will say, 'Oh, it is a man from the Lower World! Can you not help my daughter? I will give you a rich reward.' Then say, 'I do not want your reward; but I will help, if you will consent to give me your daughter for a wife.' The Sun will think, 'She is dying. It is better to have her live and marry this stranger.' Then he will consent to your request. At the same time I will sit upon the roof. Enter the room, and look out of the window upon the roof. I will open my beak and take in three heavy breaths. Then do the same! Take three long breaths and let the air of them touch the girl. Then she will recover."

The young man came to that house, and fell backward, dazed by its mere brightness. The Sun lifted him from the ground, and said, "Do not be afraid! Since you came from the Lower World, help my daughter, who is ill! I will give you a rich reward." The boy answered, "I want no reward. Rather promise to let me marry your daughter!" The Sun thought to himself, 'Better that than to have her dead!' So he gave the promise. The young man looked out of the window. A Raven was sitting on the roof. The Raven opened his beak and drew in three breaths. He also drew three breaths. The air touched the girl, and she recovered. She looked as if just awakened from deep slumber. She asked for meat and drink, and they gave them to her. After that they married her to the visitor. In a few days the father-in-law said, "You have a country of your own. Go there to your mother!" The Sun said also, "On the way you will pass three settlements with large herds of reindeer. Tell them to follow you. I give them to you." He came to the settlements, and said as he had been told. "All right!" they answered; and when he looked back, it seemed as if the whole land was moving around, so numerous were the reindeer and the herdsmen. About midnight they came to his mother. Oh, she felt much joy! The young man's wife entered the house, and said, "Oh, this house is too bad! How could we live in a house like this?" – "We cannot help it," said her husband. "This is our only house." She went out, and took from her bosom a golden egg. She threw the egg into the brook, and there was a big golden house. "Now," said the woman, "this is a house fit for us to live in." They lived in the house. Their mother wondered greatly, and from thus wondering she died in three days. The poor people used to come to them from all directions, and they slaughtered reindeer for everyone. Thus they lived in affluence and grew numerous.

Breaking Bread Against the Dark

Andrew Knighton

ON THE LAST DAY in the world, Ingunn rose from her bed before dawn. She laid a fire in the hearth, put a pot of porridge on to cook and opened the front door carefully so that its creak wouldn't wake Halfdan from his snoring.

In the east, a soft light was swelling over the peaks beyond the fjord. Ingunn took a scythe from the barn and went out into the fields just as the sun pierced the horizon, its golden glow warming her face. She smiled as she swung her blade, slicing down stalks of wheat swollen by that life-giving warmth. The birds sang songs as bright and delicate as a flower while she toiled in the yard, splitting the seeds from the stalks then tossing the grains to let the wind carry the chaff away. With the sun over the horizon, she returned to the farmhouse, a small sack in her calloused hand.

Halfdan stood in the doorway, scraping a wooden spoon around the inside of his porridge bowl. He was still proud of his body, happy to stand there dressed only in his grey hair and scars, muscles rising and falling with each movement.

"Sköll has risen." He pointed his spoon at the jagged, snarling shadow rising across the southern sky. "Ragnarok is upon us."

Ingunn used to love hearing that fierce tone as he set off on a raid against the Angles or a summer sojourn down to Byzantium. But today the whole world would crash into blood and ruin, and like every warrior she knew he yearned to be part of that death, while all she wanted was life.

A woman who had watched her adult sons sail away on the longships could hold her voice steady through every grief and frustration, and Ingunn didn't have time to waste arguing when her work had barely begun. So she asked the question that drowned out all other thoughts, the one that she would hate herself for thinking whether she asked it or not.

"Do you have to go?"

"I'll die either way."

To say any more would be to end their marriage with the wrenching pain of an argument, so instead she went inside, got out the hand mill, and ground her grain while Halfdan donned his battle gear. Stone scraped against stone, golden seeds cracking and crumbling into flour, the movement soothing in its familiarity. For decades, this had been the work that kept them fed. Today, if fate was on her side, it might be the work that saved life from ruin.

But then, fate had called for Ragnarok.

"It's time." Halfdan stood in the doorway, spear in hand, axe at hip, helm enclosing his head. His smooth and supple muscles were replaced by hard edges and sharp points.

Ingunn ran her hands down his chainmail, tightened the belt to better take the strain off his shoulders, then kissed him one last time. Her heart was heavy as his armour and she felt every last ache that the years had planted, weighed down by the memories of a life together nearing its end. They rested their foreheads against each other while the light of a glorious day shone around them and a vast black wolf ran across the blue sky.

"With my last breath, I will speak of my love for you," Halfdan whispered.

"With your last breath, you'll be cursing the foe." Ingunn stroked his cheek. "But that doesn't make our love any less real."

Ingunn stood in the doorway for a long time, listening to Halfdan's footsteps and the jingle of his armour as he took the forest path up the valley side. Birdsong faltered like a dying breath then fell into silence as the vast, dark beast advanced. But the sun was bright still, blazing all the stronger for its final day. It warmed her skin and illuminated the warriors emerging all along the fjord, up onto the high peaks. Their spear tips gleamed like the stars, cold and fierce and distant. The ground quaked as other beasts appeared, and trees shed their leaves as the valley shook to the drumbeat of destruction.

Every spring, when the warriors sailed away, Ingunn had kept baking bread, kept bellies full and life alive. That was all the hope that remained, the only chance for something more than blood and ruin, so she flung the shutters open, set her largest bowl on the table, and poured her flour in. She fetched water fresh from the well and a small portion of salt from its precious bag. Off a high shelf, she took down a bowl full of frothy starter with its strange, sharp smell of yeast. It was tempting to tip the lot in – after all, this was the last day left in her world – but habit was strong and her old recipe reliable, so instead she used half, fed the starter, and set it back up on the shelf.

The purposeful thud of footsteps approached and Saldis appeared, her own bread bowl in her arms. Her daughter, Asa, scurried along at her side, hip high to her mother, staring at the sky in curiosity.

"The big wolf will eat the sun?" Asa asked, eyes wide.

"Yes, Asa," Saldis replied, setting her bowl down on the table.

"Stupid wolf. And Papa's gone to die in a big fight?"

Saldis locked eyes with Ingunn, and her lip trembled, but her voice held steady for her daughter.

"Yes, he has."

"Stupid Papa."

Ingunn held Saldis's gaze.

"We can do this," Ingunn said, and nodded to where Asa stood in the doorway, surveying the world with a small child's strong judgment. "For her."

"I hope so." Saldis pressed her lips together and set to work.

Wooden spoons clacked around the inside of their bowls. It was nearly noon, and countless figures stood on the high ground above the fjord, not just men but giants and monsters. The gods would be among them. Perhaps, if she was closer, Ingunn could have seen them puffed up with arrogance and heard them bellowing orders, seen Odin's one eye and the ravens on his shoulders, watched Thor hurl fistfuls of lightning.

Always so eager to fight. Maybe if the gods had learned to bake bread instead, they wouldn't be ripping Ingunn's world away.

She pummelled her frustration into the dough with both hands, kneading it hard against the well-worn table. No time to scream or to cry, to rage or to grieve. She made this bread or she gave in to death, and Ingunn had never given in to anything.

With a roar and a crash, the great wolf Sköll pounced on the sun. From the high land came an answering roar, thousands of voices rising in a battle cry, then the clash of arms. A single tear ran down Ingunn's cheek, salting the dough. How long could Halfdan last against gods, against monsters, against younger warriors without his aches and age? Had he died in that first charge, or was he battling on, bleeding from some axe wound, suffering his last few moments of pain and desperation?

More women were arriving, bringing their bread bowls or fresh dough wrapped in linen cloth. Some came striding tall; some huddled against the icy wind; some openly weeping. Behind them, trees were falling, the ground cracking, the water in the fjord draining away. Life bled from the land. Ingunn set her bread on a platter and put it in the window to rise.

Little Asa prodded at the loaf.

"When can we eat?" she asked.

"Soon," Ingunn replied.

"Will there be fish with the bread?"

"Not today."

"There should be fish. And all those people should stop shouting." Asa glared at the distant ridge where the war to end the world raged. "It's not nice."

Ingunn stroked the girl's hair. "When this is over, we'll make the world a nicer place."

If there was any world left.

Ingunn's bread oven was huge, a clay mound wide enough to bury three warriors side by side. Halfdan had said that building it was a waste of time and effort, but Ingunn had insisted, and he had never refused her anything as long as she never asked him to stay. She'd filled it with fuel the previous day, and as she stoked its fires she thought of his strong hands building up the clay, thought of them running over her, thought of them blood-stained and gripping his axe. She smiled sadly.

Torn beams and twisted wheels tumbled out of the sky and crashed down across the land, the ruined remains of the sun's chariot. A gloom descended as Sköll devoured the sun piece by piece, and Ingunn shivered with cold as much as dread. Leading the women whose bread was made, she went out to gather the pieces of the chariot, dragging its vast wheels and broken beams across dirt that was hardening as the cold closed in. Splinters pierced her hands and the weight of the chariot made her muscles ache more than all her years of ploughing and digging. The sounds of battle, the screams of fury and pain, made her blood run faster and gave her the strength she needed.

Out of the darkness of the valley came lights, a hundred women with burning brands or whale oil lamps. Every woman for miles around, some with their daughters or young sons in tow, all carrying dough made with that morning's grain. They took their turns at the kitchen table, some grim-faced, some sobbing, some stoic, all kneading their dough until it was ready.

High above, Sköll swallowed the last mouthful of his prey, ran his vast tongue across his lips, and went bounding into battle. On the humble ground below, the women gathered around Ingunn's oven, hunched against cold that whitened the ground and turned their breath to frost.

"There is hope," she said, and if forceful words could have remade the world then hers would have made everything right.

"Because we will meet our husbands tonight in the land of the dead?" a woman asked in a trembling voice.

"Because we will live." Ingunn held out her own unbaked bread. "Because the sun is on our side."

"The sun's gone." Asa, hands on her hips, stared up at Ingunn. "This is silly."

"The sun put itself into the grain, and we put it into the bread. When we eat, the sun's light is with us."

And perhaps, if they were lucky, there was just enough of that day's light to brighten the sky again. If warriors could end the world with spears and axes, surely bakers could save it with bread? The world didn't have to be ended, it could be sustained.

By all the gods and everything better than them, Ingunn hoped that she was right. If it turned out that she was mad, at least these people would have hope in their final hours.

With trembling hands, she pulled aside the charred board closing the mouth of the oven. Heat blasted out like a battle horn's bass note, soaking her in sweat. She slid her loaf in, then stepped aside to let the other women do the same, one after another stepping up to the blazing opening that was the only light and warmth left.

There wasn't much of the valley now. The far peaks had crumbled away, the meadows vanished into shadow, the waters of the fjord drained away. The trees had fallen, grain withered. Birds took flight only for their wings to fall still, and they fell with soft thuds on the frozen ground.

"Poor birdy." Asa picked up one of the bodies, shivering as she stroked its feathers. "Why is it dead?"

Ingunn didn't have an answer. Instead, she fetched tools, nails, planks and rope from the barn where her horses huddled together, whickering and pawing at their straw. Her and Halfdan's horses, as she'd always thought of them before, but she knew with a hitching breath and a horrible certainty that he must be dead by now. That was the world he had wanted. This was hers. It hurt to lose him, but it would hurt more to let men like him have their way.

Sounds of sawing and hammering mixed with those of distant battle as the women set to rebuilding the sun's chariot. The cold made Ingunn's fingers ache, but the work warmed her muscles and that kept her going.

"Make sure the board's straight," she said. "I don't want to fall off the first time I ride."

Some of the women laughed, though it wasn't much of a joke. Others had given up, too cold to keep working or too scared to do anything but stare at the horizon and the destruction there. No point trying to chide them into action. No one could argue with the end of the world.

Lying awake the previous night, her throat tight as she stared at Halfdan in the moonlight, Ingunn had imagined the battle growing quieter as men died, knowing that somewhere in that silence her husband had met his glorious, terrible end. But the battle only seemed to grow louder, a cacophony that joined the howling wind to roar down what remained of the valley, battering them as they forced the broken celestial timbers back into shape. On the ridge above, a dead giant crashed down through the forest, tossing trees aside like a plough slicing through dirt, then plunged off the edge of existence. Ingunn didn't know who he had been, who he had killed, but her chest ached for him because his was one death she could make out in all of the darkness.

Ingunn hammered in the last nail then strode over to the oven. Half-frozen women huddled against the heat of its sides, clutching each other tight. Children wailed and begged to go home, to see their fathers, to feel warmth and light.

Asa stood by the mouth of the oven, watching Ingunn approach.

"Why aren't you crying?" the girl asked.

"Because I have work to do."

"You're going to save us." The girl leaned forward conspiratorially and gestured towards the weeping women. "They don't believe you, they just want something to do. But I believe you."

Ingunn crouched facing her. She should have smiled, but Asa was strong, and she owed such a girl the truth, however painful. Lies could comfort, but truth was like sunlight, you needed it to grow.

"I'm not sure I believe me," Ingunn said. "But I have to try."

With steady hands, Ingunn opened the oven. The wind swept in, so cold that it darkened the embers and reduced the flames to a swirl of ash. When Ingunn reached in with a hooked stick to drag her bread out it was still warm, and it really did smell good.

The sounds from the battle were all screams now. It was almost over. The sky was a starless black, the shadows closing in. There was no valley left, just Ingunn's farm, the ridge above, and a stretch of fallen forest between. Everything else was rubble tumbling into darkness, her world crumbling into the void.

One by one, Ingunn drew the loaves from the oven and handed them to their makers. As the rattle of the last few blades sounded like a dying breath, she held her own loaf in her hands and broke it open. The grain of the last morning in the world had formed a perfect crust, which gave way with a snap and a drift of steam. The smell was earthy sweet, so delicious it made her dry mouth water. If this was her last sensation, then it would be a good one.

Around her, a hundred desperate faces were lit by the glow coming out of that loaf. It was only the softest illumination, a fraction of the sunlight that had fallen on the wheat that morning and on every day before that; the sunlight that made this land grow; the sunlight that fed the world.

Crusts crunched as other women broke bread. The light grew, diffuse but strong, a well of light in a desert of darkness.

Ingunn broke off a piece of her bread and held it before her lips. This was the moment she had planned for, a hope so desperate she hadn't dared share it with her husband, only with other women, those with no glory to fight for on the final day. She had the strength to do this.

"That smells good," Asa said, looking up at Ingunn.

"It does, doesn't it?"

Ingunn took a bite of her loaf, chewed and swallowed a fragment of the sun's last light. It filled her with warmth and hope. Other women passed her pieces of their bread, and as Ingunn ate she started to glow. The sun was in her, and she was the sun.

Still clutching her own loaf, Ingunn strode to the chariot, the others following her. Saldis had hitched the horses, ready to ride.

They only had moments. The darkness was closing in, nothing left but what stood in Ingunn's small pool of light.

"What are you going to do?" Asa asked, staring up at her wide-eyed.

"I'm going to save our world."

"But the world's stupid. It wanted to end like this."

"What would you do instead?"

"Smash it up and make a new one."

The little girl looked at her, a seed among stalks, and Ingunn saw a strength greater than her own. She hesitated, bread in one hand and reins in the other.

The shadows swept over them, swallowing even Ingunn's light. The battle was over. The last light of the world died. There was only the void.

In the darkness, Ingunn hung her head and heard the sobbing chorus of women who had come to her for hope. Her knees felt weak, shoulders slumping in shame.

She could do one last thing before the end.

"Here." She reached out, found Asa's hand, and pressed the bread into it.

There was a crunch, followed by the sloppy sound of a child chewing with her mouth open.

Then there was the girl, glowing with a soft inner light.

Murmurs ran through the throng of women crowding around that fragment of hope. Faces appeared, barely illuminated in the darkness, ghosts drifting in the final night. They tore pieces from their loaves, thrust them into Asa's hands, and the girl ate. With each bite of a sunlit field she glowed more brightly. By the time she'd eaten from every loaf, it hurt to look at her, but Ingunn couldn't stop staring.

"Here." She handed the girl the reins and lifted her onto the sun's chariot. Somehow, Asa was big enough.

Asa laughed and snapped the reins. Wheels turned as the horses cantered across the darkness. Her laughter beat back the funereal silence, life chasing way death. Her passing illuminated a new world rising into her dawn, and she soared towards heaven, a glowing new sun.

On the far ridges, the shadows of the fallen came together, forming a dark and terrible wolf. Halfdan would be among them. Was he happy, turned forever into the action and destruction he had loved? Ingunn hoped so, and she hoped not.

The beast loped into the sky, following the girl. But death was cold and slow, while life was bright and determined, and this was a world made by Asa's light. The chariot left the wolf far behind, and in fresh fields, the first shoots of new wheat started to unfurl.

Weeping with joy and grief, Ingunn turned to the other women.

"Come," she said. "We eat bread, and then we work. The fields must be tended again."

The Children Are Sent to Throw the Sleeping Sun into the Sky

From the San people, southern Africa

THE CHILDREN WERE those who approached gently to lift up the Sun-armpit, while the Sun-armpit lay sleeping.

The children felt that their mother was the one who spoke; therefore, the children went to the Sun; while the Sun shone, at the place where the Sun lay, sleeping lay.

Another old woman was the one who talked to the other about it; therefore, the other one spoke to the other one's children. The other old woman said to the other, that, the other one's children should approach gently to lift up the Sun-armpit, that they should throw up the Sun-armpit, that the Bushman rice might become dry for them, that the Sun might make bright the whole place; while the Sun felt that the Sun went (along), it went over the whole sky, it made all places bright; therefore, it made all the ground bright; while it felt that the children were those who had coaxed him; because an old woman was the one who spoke to the other about it, therefore, the other one said, "O children! ye must wait for the Sun, that the Sun may lie down to sleep, for, we are cold. Ye shall gently approach to lift him up, while he lies asleep; ye shall take hold of him, all together, all together ye lift him up, that ye may throw him up into the sky." They, in this manner, spoke; the old woman, in this manner, she spoke to the other; therefore, the other in this manner spoke to her, she also, in this manner, spoke to her children. The other said to her, "This (is the) story which I tell thee, ye must wait for the Sun."

The children came, the children went away; the old woman said, "Ye must go to sit down, when ye have looked at him, (to see) whether he lies looking; ye must go to sit down, while ye wait for him." Therefore, the children went to sit down, while the children waited for him; he lay down, he lifted up his elbow, his armpit shone upon the ground, as he lay. Therefore, the children threw him up into the sky, while they felt that the old woman had spoken to them. The old woman said to the children, "O children going yonder! Ye must speak to him, when ye throw him up." The old woman said to the children, "O children going yonder! Ye must tell him, that, he must altogether become the Sun, that he may go forward, while he feels that he is altogether the Sun, which is hot; therefore, the Bushman rice becomes dry, while he is hot, passing along in the sky; he is hot, while he stands above in the sky."

The old woman was the one who told the children about it, while she felt that her head was white; the children were listening to her, they were listening to their mamma, their mother; their mother told them about it, that which the old woman in this manner said. Therefore, they thought in this manner. Therefore, they went to sit down. An older child spoke to another, therefore, they went to sit down, while they waited for him (the Sun), they went to sit down.

They arose, going on, they stealthily approached him, they stood still, they looked at him, they went forward; they stealthily reached him, they took hold of him they all took hold of him together, lifted him up, they raised him, while he felt hot. Then, they threw him up, while he felt hot; they spoke to him while he felt hot, "O Sun! Thou must altogether stand fast, thou must go along, thou must stand fast) while thou art hot."

The old woman said (that) they seemed to have thrown him up, he seemed to be standing fast above. They thus spoke, they in this manner spoke. Her (apparently the mother's) husband said, "The Sun's armpit is standing fast above yonder, he whom the children have thrown up; he lay, he intended to sleep; therefore, the children have thrown him up."

The children returned. Then, the children came (and) said, "(Our) companion who is here, he took hold of him, I also was taking hold of him; my younger brother was taking hold of him, my other younger brother was also taking bold of him; (our) companion who is here, his other younger brother was also taking hold of him. I said: 'Ye must grasp him firmly.' I, in this manner, spoke; I said: 'Throw ye him up!' Then, the children threw him up. I said to the children: 'Grasp ye the old man firmly!' I said to the children: 'Throw ye up the old man!' Then, the children threw up the old man; that old man, the Sun; while they felt that the old woman was the one who spoke."

An older child spoke, while he felt that he was a youth; the other also was a youth, they were young men, they went to throw up the Sun-armpit. They came to speak, the youth spoke, the youth talked to his grandmother, "O my grandmother! We threw him up, we told him, that, he should altogether become the Sun, which is hot; for, we are cold. We said: 'O my grandfather, Sun-armpit! Remain (at that) place; become thou the Sun which is hot; that the Bushman rice may dry for us; that thou mayst make the whole earth light; that the whole earth may become warm in the summer; that thou mayst altogether make heat. Therefore, thou must altogether shine, taking away the darkness; thou must come, the darkness go away.'"

The Sun comes, the darkness goes away, the Sun comes, the Sun sets, the darkness comes, the moon comes at night. The day breaks, the Sun comes out, the darkness goes away, the Sun comes. The moon comes out, the moon brightens the darkness, the darkness departs; the moon comes out, the moon shines, taking away the darkness; it goes along, it has made bright the darkness, it sets. The Sun comes out, the Sun follows (drives away?) the darkness, the Sun takes away the moon, the moon stands, the Sun pierces it, with the Sun's knife, as it stands; therefore, it decays away on account of it. Therefore, it says, "O Sun! Leave for the children the backbone!" Therefore, the Sun leaves the backbone for the children; the Sun does so. Therefore, the Sun says that the Sun will leave the backbone for the children, while the Sun assents to him; the Sun leaves the backbone for the children; therefore, the moon painfully goes away, he painfully returns home, while he painfully goes along; therefore, the Sun desists, while he feels that the Sun has left for the children the backbone, while the Sun assents to him; therefore, the Sun leaves the backbone; while the Sun feels that the Sun assents to him; therefore, the Sun desists on account of it; he (the moon) painfully goes away, he painfully returns home; he again, he goes to become another moon, which is whole; he again, he lives; he again, be lives, while he feels that he had seemed to die. Therefore, he becomes a new moon; while he feels that he has again put on a stomach; he becomes large; while he feels that he is a moon which is whole; therefore, he is large; he comes, while he is alive. He goes along at night, he feels that he is the moon which goes by night, while he feels that he is a shoe; therefore, he walks in the night.

The Sun is here, all the earth is bright; the Sun is here, the people walk while the place is light, the earth is light; the people perceive the bushes, they see the other people; they see the meat which they are eating; they also see the springbok, they also hear the springbok, in summer; they also hear the ostrich, while they feel that the Sun shines; they also hear the ostrich in summer; they are shooting the springbok in summer, while they feel that the Sun shines, they see the springbok; they also steal up to the gemsbok; they also steal up to the kudu, while they feel that the whole place is bright; they also visit each other while they feel that the Sun shines, the earth also is bright, the Sun shines upon the path. They also travel in summer; they are shooting in summer; they hunt in summer; they espy the springbok in summer; they go round to hear the springbok; they lie down; they feel that they lie in a little house of bushes; they scratch up the earth in the little house of bushes, they lie down, while the springbok come.

Clytie

From Greek mythology

THE SUNBEAMS ARE basking on the high walls of the old garden – smiling on the fruit that grows red and golden in their warmth. The bees are humming round the bed of purple heliotrope, and drowsily murmuring in the shelter of the soft petals of the blush roses whose sweetness brings back the fragrance of days that are gone. On the old grey sundial, the white-winged pigeons sleepily croon as they preen their snowy plumage, and the Madonna lilies hang their heads like a procession of white-robed nuns who dare not look up from telling their beads until the triumphal procession of an all-conquering warrior has gone by. What can they think of that long line of tall yellow flowers by the garden wall, who turn their faces sunwards with an arrogant assurance, and give stare for stare to golden-haired Apollo as he drives his blazing car triumphant through the high heavens?

"Sunflowers" is the name by which we know those flamboyant blossoms which somehow fail so wholly to suggest the story of Clytie, the nymph whose destruction came from a faithful, unrequited love. She was a water-nymph, a timid, gentle being who frequented lonely streams, and bathed where the blue dragonflies dart across the white waterlilies in pellucid lakes. In the shade of the tall poplar trees and the silvery willows she took her midday rest, and feared the hours when the flowers drooped their heads and the rippling water lost its coolness before the fierce glare of the sun.

But there came a day when, into the dark pool by which she sat, Apollo the Conqueror looked down and mirrored his face. And nevermore did she hide from the golden-haired god who, from the moment when she had seen in the water the picture of his radiant beauty, became the lord and master of her heart and soul. All night she awaited his coming, and the dawn saw her looking eastward for the first golden gleams from the wheels of his chariot. All day she followed him with her longing gaze, nor did she ever cease to feast her eyes upon his beauty until the last reflection of his radiance had faded from the western sky.

Such devotion might have touched the heart of the sun-god, but he had no wish to own a love for which he had not sought. The nymph's adoration irked him, nor did pity come as Love's pale substitute when he marked how, day by day, her face grew whiter and whiter, and her lovely form wasted away. For nine days, without food or drink, she kept her shamed vigil. Only one word of love did she crave. Unexacting in the humility of her devotion, she would gratefully have nourished her hungry heart upon one kindly glance. But Apollo, full of scorn and anger, lashed up his fiery steeds as he each day drove past her, nor deigned for her a glance gentler than that which he threw on the satyrs as they hid in the dense green foliage of the shadowy woods.

Half-mocking, Diana said, "In truth the fair nymph who throws her heart's treasures at the feet of my golden-locked brother that he may trample on them, is coming to look like a faded flower!" And, as she spoke, the hearts of the other immortal dwellers in Olympus were stirred with pity.

"A flower she shall be!" they said, "and for all time shall she live, in life that is renewed each year when the earth stirs with the quickening of spring. The long summer days shall she spend forever in fearless worship of the god of her love!"

And, as they willed, the nymph passed out of her human form, and took the form of a flower, and evermore – the emblem of constancy – does she gaze with fearless ardour on the face of her love.

> *"The heart that has truly loved never forgets,*
> *But as truly loves on to the close;*
> *As the sunflower turns on her god when he sets*
> *The same look that she turned when he rose."*

Some there are who say that not into the bold-faced sunflower did her metamorphosis take place, but into that purple heliotrope that gives an exquisite offering of fragrance to the sun-god when his warm rays touch it. And in the old walled garden, while the bees drowsily hum, and the white pigeons croon, and the dashing sunflower gives Apollo gaze for gaze, and the scent of the mignonette mingles with that of clove pinks and blush roses, the fragrance of the heliotrope is, above all, worthy incense to be offered upon his altar by the devout lover of a god.

Extracts from 'A Connecticut Yankee in King Arthur's Court'

Mark Twain

Publisher's Note: In Mark Twain's classic 1899 novel, protagonist Hank Morgan is transported back in time to the reign of King Arthur. Finding himself in an unfamiliar world, he initially struggles to get his bearings.

Chapter II
King Arthur's Court

THE MOMENT I GOT a chance I slipped aside privately and touched an ancient, common-looking man on the shoulder and said, in an insinuating, confidential way:

"Friend, do me a kindness. Do you belong to the asylum, or are you just on a visit or something like that?"

He looked me over stupidly, and said:

"Marry, fair sir, me seemeth—"

"That will do," I said; "I reckon you are a patient."

I moved away, cogitating, and at the same time keeping an eye out for any chance passenger in his right mind that might come along and give me some light. I judged I had found one, presently; so I drew him aside and said in his ear:

"If I could see the head keeper a minute – only just a minute—"

"Prithee do not let me."

"Let you *what*?"

"*Hinder* me, then, if the word please thee better." Then he went on to say he was an under-cook and could not stop to gossip, though he would like it another time; for it would comfort his very liver to know where I got my clothes. As he started away he pointed and said yonder was one who was idle enough for my purpose, and was seeking me besides, no doubt. This was an airy slim boy in shrimp-colored tights that made him look like a forked carrot, the rest of his gear was blue silk and dainty laces and ruffles; and he had long yellow curls, and wore a plumed pink satin cap tilted complacently over his ear. By his look, he was good-natured; by his gait, he was satisfied with himself. He was pretty enough to frame. He arrived, looked me over with a smiling and impudent curiosity; said he had come for me, and informed me that he was a page.

"Go 'long," I said; "you ain't more than a paragraph."

It was pretty severe, but I was nettled. However, it never phased him; he didn't appear to know he was hurt. He began to talk and laugh, in happy, thoughtless, boyish fashion, as we walked along, and made himself old friends with me at once; asked me all sorts of questions about myself and about my clothes, but never waited for an answer – always chattered straight ahead, as if he didn't know he had asked a question and wasn't expecting any reply, until at last he happened to mention that he was born in the beginning of the year 513.

It made the cold chills creep over me! I stopped and said, a little faintly:

"Maybe I didn't hear you just right. Say it again – and say it slow. What year was it?"

"513."

"513! You don't look it! Come, my boy, I am a stranger and friendless; be honest and honourable with me. Are you in your right mind?"

He said he was.

"Are these other people in their right minds?"

He said they were.

"And this isn't an asylum? I mean, it isn't a place where they cure crazy people?"

He said it wasn't.

"Well, then," I said, "either I am a lunatic, or something just as awful has happened. Now tell me, honest and true, where am I?"

"*In King Arthur's Court.*"

I waited a minute, to let that idea shudder its way home, and then said:

"And according to your notions, what year is it now?"

"528 – nineteenth of June."

I felt a mournful sinking at the heart, and muttered, "I shall never see my friends again – never, never again. They will not be born for more than thirteen hundred years yet."

I seemed to believe the boy, I didn't know why. *Something* in me seemed to believe him – my consciousness, as you may say; but my reason didn't. My reason straightway began to clamor; that was natural. I didn't know how to go about satisfying it, because I knew that the testimony of men wouldn't serve – my reason would say they were lunatics, and throw out their evidence. But all of a sudden I stumbled on the very thing, just by luck. I knew that the only total eclipse of the sun in the first half of the sixth century occurred on the 21st of June, A.D. 528, O.S., and began at three minutes after 12 noon. I also knew that no total eclipse of the sun was due in what to me was the present year – *i.e.*, 1879. So, if I could keep my anxiety and curiosity from eating the heart out of me for forty-eight hours, I should then find out for certain whether this boy was telling me the truth or not.

Wherefore, being a practical Connecticut man, I now shoved this whole problem clear out of my mind till its appointed day and hour should come, in order that I might turn all my attention to the circumstances of the present moment, and be alert and ready to make the most out of them that could be made. One thing at a time, is my motto – and just play that thing for all it is worth, even if it's only two pair and a jack. I made up my mind to two things: if it was still the nineteenth century and I was among lunatics and couldn't get away, I would presently boss that asylum or know the reason why; and if, on the other hand, it was really the sixth century, all right, I didn't want any softer thing: I would boss the whole country inside of three months; for I judged I would have the start of the best-educated man in the kingdom by a matter of thirteen hundred years and upward. I'm not a man to waste time after my mind's made up and there's work on hand; so I said to the page:

"Now, Clarence, my boy – if that might happen to be your name – I'll get you to post me up a little if you don't mind. What is the name of that apparition that brought me here?"

"My master and thine? That is the good knight and great lord Sir Kay the Seneschal, foster brother to our liege the king."

"Very good; go on, tell me everything."

He made a long story of it; but the part that had immediate interest for me was this: He said I was Sir Kay's prisoner, and that in the due course of custom I would be flung into a dungeon and left there on scant commons until my friends ransomed me – unless I chanced to rot, first. I saw that the last chance had the best show, but I didn't waste any bother about that; time was too precious. The page said, further, that dinner was about ended in the great hall by this time, and that as soon as the sociability and the heavy drinking should begin, Sir Kay would have me in and exhibit me before King Arthur and his illustrious knights seated at the Table Round, and would brag about his exploit in capturing me, and would probably exaggerate the facts a little, but it wouldn't be good form for me to correct him, and not over safe, either; and when I was done being exhibited, then ho for the dungeon; but he, Clarence, would find a way to come and see me every now and then, and cheer me up, and help me get word to my friends.

Get word to my friends! I thanked him; I couldn't do less; and about this time a lackey came to say I was wanted; so Clarence led me in and took me off to one side and sat down by me.

Well, it was a curious kind of spectacle, and interesting. It was an immense place, and rather naked – yes, and full of loud contrasts. It was very, very lofty; so lofty that the banners depending from the arched beams and girders away up there floated in a sort of twilight; there was a stone-railed gallery at each end, high up, with musicians in the one, and women, clothed in stunning colors, in the other. The floor was of big stone flags laid in black and white squares, rather battered by age and use, and needing repair. As to ornament, there wasn't any, strictly speaking; though on the walls hung some huge tapestries which were probably taxed as works of art; battle-pieces, they were, with horses shaped like those which children cut out of paper or create in gingerbread; with men on them in scale armor whose scales are represented by round holes – so that the man's coat looks as if it had been done with a biscuit-punch. There was a fireplace big enough to camp in; and its projecting sides and hood, of carved and pillared stonework, had the look of a cathedral door. Along the walls stood men-at-arms, in breastplate and morion, with halberds for their only weapon – rigid as statues; and that is what they looked like.

In the middle of this groined and vaulted public square was an oaken table which they called the Table Round. It was as large as a circus ring; and around it sat a great company of men dressed in such various and splendid colors that it hurt one's eyes to look at them. They wore their plumed hats, right along, except that whenever one addressed himself directly to the king, he lifted his hat a trifle just as he was beginning his remark.

Mainly they were drinking – from entire ox horns; but a few were still munching bread or gnawing beef bones. There was about an average of two dogs to one man; and these sat in expectant attitudes till a spent bone was flung to them, and then they went for it by brigades and divisions, with a rush, and there ensued a fight which filled the prospect with a tumultuous chaos of plunging heads and bodies and flashing tails, and the storm of howlings and barkings deafened all speech for the time; but that was no matter, for the dog-fight was always a bigger interest anyway; the men rose, sometimes, to observe it the better and bet on it, and the ladies and the musicians stretched themselves out over their balusters with the same object; and all broke into delighted ejaculations from time to time. In the end, the winning dog stretched himself out comfortably with his bone between his paws, and proceeded to growl over it, and gnaw it, and grease the floor with it, just as fifty others were already doing; and the rest of the court resumed their previous industries and entertainments.

As a rule, the speech and behavior of these people were gracious and courtly; and I noticed that they were good and serious listeners when anybody was telling anything – I mean in a dog-fightless interval. And plainly, too, they were a childlike and innocent lot; telling lies of the stateliest pattern with a most gentle and winning naivety, and ready and willing to listen to anybody else's lie, and believe it, too. It was hard to associate them with anything cruel or dreadful; and yet they dealt in tales of blood and suffering with a guileless relish that made me almost forget to shudder.

I was not the only prisoner present. There were twenty or more. Poor devils, many of them were maimed, hacked, carved, in a frightful way; and their hair, their faces, their clothing, were caked with black and stiffened drenchings of blood. They were suffering sharp physical pain, of course; and weariness, and hunger and thirst, no doubt; and at least none had given them the comfort of a wash, or even the poor charity of a lotion for their wounds; yet you never heard them utter a moan or a groan, or saw them show any sign of restlessness, or any disposition to complain. The thought was forced upon me, "The rascals – *they* have served other people so in their day; it being their own turn, now, they were not expecting any better treatment than this; so their philosophical bearing is not an outcome of mental training, intellectual fortitude, reasoning; it is mere animal training; they are white Indians."

Chapter V
An Inspiration

I was so tired that even my fears were not able to keep me awake long.

When I next came to myself, I seemed to have been asleep a very long time. My first thought was, "Well, what an astonishing dream I've had! I reckon I've waked only just in time to keep from being hanged or drowned or burned or something.... I'll nap again till the whistle blows, and then I'll go down to the arms factory and have it out with Hercules."

But just then I heard the harsh music of rusty chains and bolts, a light flashed in my eyes, and that butterfly, Clarence, stood before me! I gasped with surprise; my breath almost got away from me.

"What!" I said, "you here yet? Go along with the rest of the dream! Scatter!"

But he only laughed, in his light-hearted way, and fell to making fun of my sorry plight.

"All right," I said resignedly, "let the dream go on; I'm in no hurry."

"Prithee what dream?"

"What dream? Why, the dream that I am in Arthur's court – a person who never existed; and that I am talking to you, who are nothing but a work of the imagination."

"Oh, la, indeed! And is it a dream that you're to be burned tomorrow? Ho-ho – answer me that!"

The shock that went through me was distressing. I now began to reason that my situation was in the last degree serious, dream or no dream; for I knew by past experience of the lifelike intensity of dreams, that to be burned to death, even in a dream, would be very far from being a jest, and was a thing to be avoided, by any means, fair or foul, that I could contrive. So I said beseechingly:

"Ah, Clarence, good boy, only friend I've got – for you *are* my friend, aren't you? – don't fail me; help me to devise some way of escaping from this place!"

"Now do but hear thyself! Escape? Why, man, the corridors are in guard and keep of men-at-arms."

"No doubt, no doubt. But how many, Clarence? Not many, I hope?"

"Full a score. One may not hope to escape." After a pause – hesitatingly, "and there be other reasons – and weightier."

"Other ones? What are they?"

"Well, they say – oh, but I daren't, indeed daren't!"

"Why, poor lad, what is the matter? Why do you blench? Why do you tremble so?"

"Oh, in sooth, there is need! I do want to tell you, but—"

"Come, come, be brave, be a man – speak out, there's a good lad!"

He hesitated, pulled one way by desire, the other way by fear; then he stole to the door and peeped out, listening; and finally crept close to me and put his mouth to my ear and told me his fearful news in a whisper, and with all the cowering apprehension of one who was venturing upon awful ground and speaking of things whose very mention might be freighted with death.

"Merlin, in his malice, has woven a spell about this dungeon, and there bides not the man in these kingdoms that would be desperate enough to essay to cross its lines with you! Now God pity me, I have told it! Ah, be kind to me, be merciful to a poor boy who means thee well; for an thou betray me I am lost!"

I laughed the only really refreshing laugh I had had for some time; and shouted:

"Merlin has wrought a spell! *Merlin*, forsooth! That cheap old humbug, that maundering old ass? Bosh, pure bosh, the silliest bosh in the world! Why, it does seem to me that of all the childish, idiotic, chuckle-headed, chicken-livered superstitions that ev – oh, damn Merlin!"

But Clarence had slumped to his knees before I had half finished, and he was like to go out of his mind with fright.

"Oh, beware! These are awful words! Any moment these walls may crumble upon us if you say such things. Oh, call them back before it is too late!"

Now this strange exhibition gave me a good idea and set me to thinking. If everybody about here was so honestly and sincerely afraid of Merlin's pretended magic as Clarence was, certainly a superior man like me ought to be shrewd enough to contrive some way to take advantage of such a state of things. I went on thinking, and worked out a plan. Then I said:

"Get up. Pull yourself together; look me in the eye. Do you know why I laughed?"

"No – but for our blessed Lady's sake, do it no more."

"Well, I'll tell you why I laughed. Because I'm a magician myself."

"Thou!" The boy recoiled a step, and caught his breath, for the thing hit him rather sudden; but the aspect which he took on was very, very respectful. I took quick note of that; it indicated that a humbug didn't need to have a reputation in this asylum; people stood ready to take him at his word, without that. I resumed.

"I've known Merlin seven hundred years, and he—"

"Seven hun—"

"Don't interrupt me. He has died and come alive again thirteen times, and travelled under a new name every time: Smith, Jones, Robinson, Jackson, Peters, Haskins, Merlin – a new alias every time he turns up. I knew him in Egypt three hundred years ago; I knew him in India five hundred years ago – he is always blethering around in my way, everywhere I go; he makes me tired. He don't amount to shucks, as a magician; knows some of the old common tricks, but has never got beyond the rudiments, and never will. He is well enough for the provinces – one-night stands and that sort of thing, you know – but dear me, *he* oughtn't to set up for an expert – anyway not where there's a real artist. Now look here,

Clarence, I am going to stand your friend, right along, and in return you must be mine. I want you to do me a favour. I want you to get word to the king that I am a magician myself – and the Supreme Grand High-yu-Muck-amuck and head of the tribe, at that; and I want him to be made to understand that I am just quietly arranging a little calamity here that will make the fur fly in these realms if Sir Kay's project is carried out and any harm comes to me. Will you get that to the king for me?"

The poor boy was in such a state that he could hardly answer me. It was pitiful to see a creature so terrified, so unnerved, so demoralized. But he promised everything; and on my side he made me promise over and over again that I would remain his friend, and never turn against him or cast any enchantments upon him. Then he worked his way out, staying himself with his hand along the wall, like a sick person.

Presently this thought occurred to me: how heedless I have been! When the boy gets calm, he will wonder why a great magician like me should have begged a boy like him to help me get out of this place; he will put this and that together, and will see that I am a humbug.

I worried over that heedless blunder for an hour, and called myself a great many hard names, meantime. But finally it occurred to me all of a sudden that these animals didn't reason; that *they* never put this and that together; that all their talk showed that they didn't know a discrepancy when they saw it. I was at rest, then.

But as soon as one is at rest, in this world, off he goes on something else to worry about. It occurred to me that I had made another blunder: I had sent the boy off to alarm his betters with a threat – I intending to invent a calamity at my leisure; now the people who are the readiest and eagerest and willingest to swallow miracles are the very ones who are hungriest to see you perform them; suppose I should be called on for a sample? Suppose I should be asked to name my calamity? Yes, I had made a blunder; I ought to have invented my calamity first. "What shall I do? What can I say, to gain a little time?" I was in trouble again; in the deepest kind of trouble…

"There's a footstep! They're coming. If I had only just a moment to think…. Good, I've got it. I'm all right."

You see, it was the eclipse. It came into my mind in the nick of time, how Columbus, or Cortez, or one of those people, played an eclipse as a saving trump once, on some savages, and I saw my chance. I could play it myself, now, and it wouldn't be any plagiarism, either, because I should get it in nearly a thousand years ahead of those parties.

Clarence came in, subdued, distressed, and said:

"I hasted the message to our liege the king, and straightway he had me to his presence. He was frighted even to the marrow, and was minded to give order for your instant enlargement, and that you be clothed in fine raiment and lodged as befitted one so great; but then came Merlin and spoiled all; for he persuaded the king that you are mad, and know not whereof you speak; and said your threat is but foolishness and idle vaporing. They disputed long, but in the end, Merlin, scoffing, said, 'Wherefore hath he not *named* his brave calamity? Verily it is because he cannot.' This thrust did in a most sudden sort close the king's mouth, and he could offer naught to turn the argument; and so, reluctant, and full loth to do you the discourtesy, he yet prayeth you to consider his perplexed case, as noting how the matter stands, and name the calamity – if so be you have determined the nature of it and the time of its coming. Oh, prithee delay not; to delay at such a time were to double and treble the perils that already compass thee about. Oh, be thou wise – name the calamity!"

I allowed silence to accumulate while I got my impressiveness together, and then said:

"How long have I been shut up in this hole?"

"Ye were shut up when yesterday was well spent. It is nine of the morning now."

"No! Then I have slept well, sure enough. Nine in the morning now! And yet it is the very complexion of midnight, to a shade. This is the 20th, then?"

"The 20th – yes."

"And I am to be burned alive tomorrow." The boy shuddered.

"At what hour?"

"At high noon."

"Now then, I will tell you what to say." I paused, and stood over that cowering lad a whole minute in awful silence; then, in a voice deep, measured, charged with doom, I began, and rose by dramatically graded stages to my colossal climax, which I delivered in as sublime and noble a way as ever I did such a thing in my life. "Go back and tell the king that at that hour I will smother the whole world in the dead blackness of midnight; I will blot out the sun, and he shall never shine again; the fruits of the earth shall rot for lack of light and warmth, and the peoples of the earth shall famish and die, to the last man!"

I had to carry the boy out myself, he sunk into such a collapse. I handed him over to the soldiers, and went back.

Chapter VI
The Eclipse

In the stillness and the darkness, realization soon began to supplement knowledge. The mere knowledge of a fact is pale; but when you come to *realize* your fact, it takes on colour. It is all the difference between hearing of a man being stabbed to the heart, and seeing it done. In the stillness and the darkness, the knowledge that I was in deadly danger took to itself deeper and deeper meaning all the time; a something which was realization crept inch by inch through my veins and turned me cold.

But it is a blessed provision of nature that at times like these, as soon as a man's mercury has got down to a certain point there comes a revulsion, and he rallies. Hope springs up, and cheerfulness along with it, and then he is in good shape to do something for himself, if anything can be done. When my rally came, it came with a bound. I said to myself that my eclipse would be sure to save me, and make me the greatest man in the kingdom besides; and straightway my mercury went up to the top of the tube, and my solicitudes all vanished. I was as happy a man as there was in the world. I was even impatient for tomorrow to come, I so wanted to gather in that great triumph and be the centre of all the nation's wonder and reverence. Besides, in a business way it would be the making of me; I knew that.

Meantime there was one thing which had got pushed into the background of my mind. That was the half-conviction that when the nature of my proposed calamity should be reported to those superstitious people, it would have such an effect that they would want to compromise. So, by and by when I heard footsteps coming, that thought was recalled to me, and I said to myself, "As sure as anything, it's the compromise. Well, if it is good, all right, I will accept; but if it isn't, I mean to stand my ground and play my hand for all it is worth."

The door opened, and some men-at-arms appeared. The leader said:

"The stake is ready. Come!"

The stake! The strength went out of me, and I almost fell down. It is hard to get one's breath at such a time, such lumps come into one's throat, and such gaspings; but as soon as I could speak, I said:

"But this is a mistake – the execution is tomorrow."

"Order changed; been set forward a day. Haste thee!"

I was lost. There was no help for me. I was dazed, stupefied; I had no command over myself, I only wandered purposely about, like one out of his mind; so the soldiers took hold of me, and pulled me along with them, out of the cell and along the maze of underground corridors, and finally into the fierce glare of daylight and the upper world. As we stepped into the vast enclosed court of the castle I got a shock; for the first thing I saw was the stake, standing in the centre, and near it the piled fagots and a monk. On all four sides of the court the seated multitudes rose rank above rank, forming sloping terraces that were rich with color. The king and the queen sat in their thrones, the most conspicuous figures there, of course.

To note all this occupied but a second. The next second Clarence had slipped from some place of concealment and was pouring news into my ear, his eyes beaming with triumph and gladness. He said:

"'Tis through *me* the change was wrought! And main hard have I worked to do it, too. But when I revealed to them the calamity in store, and saw how mighty was the terror it did engender, then saw I also that this was the time to strike! Wherefore I diligently pretended, unto this and that and the other one, that your power against the sun could not reach its full until the morrow; and so if any would save the sun and the world, you must be slain today, while your enchantments are but in the weaving and lack potency. Odsbodikins, it was but a dull lie, a most indifferent invention, but you should have seen them seize it and swallow it, in the frenzy of their fright, as it were salvation sent from heaven; and all the while was I laughing in my sleeve the one moment, to see them so cheaply deceived, and glorifying God the next, that He was content to let the meanest of His creatures be His instrument to the saving of thy life. Ah how happy has the matter sped! You will not need to do the sun a *real* hurt – ah, forget not that, on your soul forget it not! Only make a little darkness – only the littlest little darkness, mind, and cease with that. It will be sufficient. They will see that I spoke falsely – being ignorant, as they will fancy – and with the falling of the first shadow of that darkness you shall see them go mad with fear; and they will set you free and make you great! Go to thy triumph, now! But remember – ah, good friend, I implore thee remember my supplication, and do the blessed sun no hurt. For *my* sake, thy true friend."

I choked out some words through my grief and misery; as much as to say I would spare the sun; for which the lad's eyes paid me back with such deep and loving gratitude that I had not the heart to tell him his good-hearted foolishness had ruined me and sent me to my death.

As the soldiers assisted me across the court the stillness was so profound that if I had been blindfold I should have supposed I was in a solitude instead of walled in by four thousand people. There was not a movement perceptible in those masses of humanity; they were as rigid as stone images, and as pale; and dread sat upon every countenance. This hush continued while I was being chained to the stake; it still continued while the fagots were carefully and tediously piled about my ankles, my knees, my thighs, my body. Then there was a pause, and a deeper hush, if possible, and a man knelt down at my feet with a blazing torch; the multitude strained forward, gazing, and parting slightly from their seats without knowing it; the monk raised his hands above my head, and his eyes toward the blue sky, and began some words in Latin; in this attitude he droned on and on, a little while, and then stopped. I waited two or three moments; then looked up; he was standing there petrified. With a common impulse the multitude rose slowly up and stared into the sky. I followed their eyes, as sure as guns, there was my eclipse beginning! The life went boiling through my veins; I was a new man! The rim of black spread slowly into the sun's disk, my heart beat higher and higher, and still the assemblage and the priest stared into the sky, motionless. I knew that this gaze would be turned upon me, next. When it was, I was ready. I was in one of the most grand attitudes I ever struck, with my arm stretched up pointing to the sun. It was a noble effect. You could *see* the shudder sweep the mass like a wave. Two shouts rang out, one close upon the heels of the other:

"Apply the torch!"

"I forbid it!"

The one was from Merlin, the other from the king. Merlin started from his place – to apply the torch himself, I judged. I said:

"Stay where you are. If any man moves – even the king – before I give him leave, I will blast him with thunder, I will consume him with lightnings!"

The multitude sank meekly into their seats, and I was just expecting they would. Merlin hesitated a moment or two, and I was on pins and needles during that little while. Then he sat down, and I took a good breath; for I knew I was master of the situation now. The king said:

"Be merciful, fair sir, and essay no further in this perilous matter, lest disaster follow. It was reported to us that your powers could not attain unto their full strength until the morrow; but—"

"Your Majesty thinks the report may have been a lie? It *was* a lie."

That made an immense effect; up went appealing hands everywhere, and the king was assailed with a storm of supplications that I might be bought off at any price, and the calamity stayed. The king was eager to comply. He said:

"Name any terms, reverend sir, even to the halving of my kingdom; but banish this calamity, spare the sun!"

My fortune was made. I would have taken him up in a minute, but I couldn't stop an eclipse; the thing was out of the question. So I asked time to consider. The king said:

"How long – ah, how long, good sir? Be merciful; look, it groweth darker, moment by moment. Prithee how long?"

"Not long. Half an hour – maybe an hour."

There were a thousand pathetic protests, but I couldn't shorten up any, for I couldn't remember how long a total eclipse lasts. I was in a puzzled condition, anyway, and wanted to think. Something was wrong about that eclipse, and the fact was very unsettling. If this wasn't the one I was after, how was I to tell whether this was the sixth century, or nothing but a dream? Dear me, if I could only prove it was the latter! Here was a glad new hope. If the boy was right about the date, and this was surely the 20th, it *wasn't* the sixth century. I reached for the monk's sleeve, in considerable excitement, and asked him what day of the month it was.

Hang him, he said it was the *twenty-first*! It made me turn cold to hear him. I begged him not to make any mistake about it; but he was sure; he knew it was the 21st. So, that feather-headed boy had botched things again! The time of the day was right for the eclipse; I had seen that for myself, in the beginning, by the dial that was nearby. Yes, I was in King Arthur's court, and I might as well make the most out of it I could.

The darkness was steadily growing, the people becoming more and more distressed. I now said:

"I have reflected, Sir King. For a lesson, I will let this darkness proceed, and spread night in the world; but whether I blot out the sun for good, or restore it, shall rest with you. These are the terms, to wit: You shall remain king over all your dominions, and receive all the glories and honours that belong to the kingship; but you shall appoint me your perpetual minister and executive, and give me for my services one per cent of such actual increase of revenue over and above its present amount as I may succeed in creating for the state. If I can't live on that, I sha'n't ask anybody to give me a lift. Is it satisfactory?"

There was a prodigious roar of applause, and out of the midst of it the king's voice rose, saying:

"Away with his bonds, and set him free! And do him homage, high and low, rich and poor, for he is become the king's right hand, is clothed with power and authority, and his seat is upon the highest step of the throne! Now sweep away this creeping night, and bring the light and cheer again, that all the world may bless thee."

But I said:

"That a common man should be shamed before the world, is nothing; but it were dishonor to the *king* if any that saw his minister naked should not also see him delivered from his shame. If I might ask that my clothes be brought again—"

"They are not meet," the king broke in. "Fetch raiment of another sort; clothe him like a prince!"

My idea worked. I wanted to keep things as they were till the eclipse was total, otherwise they would be trying again to get me to dismiss the darkness, and of course I couldn't do it. Sending for the clothes gained some delay, but not enough. So I had to make another excuse. I said it would be but natural if the king should change his mind and repent to some extent of what he had done under excitement; therefore I would let the darkness grow a while, and if at the end of a reasonable time the king had kept his mind the same, the darkness should be dismissed. Neither the king nor anybody else was satisfied with that arrangement, but I had to stick to my point.

It grew darker and darker and blacker and blacker, while I struggled with those awkward sixth-century clothes. It got to be pitch dark, at last, and the multitude groaned with horror to feel the cold uncanny night breezes fan through the place and see the stars come out and twinkle in the sky. At last the eclipse was total, and I was very glad of it, but everybody else was in misery; which was quite natural. I said:

"The king, by his silence, still stands to the terms." Then I lifted up my hands – stood just so a moment – then I said, with the most awful solemnity, "Let the enchantment dissolve and pass harmless away!"

There was no response, for a moment, in that deep darkness and that graveyard hush. But when the silver rim of the sun pushed itself out, a moment or two later, the assemblage broke loose with a vast shout and came pouring down like a deluge to smother me with blessings and gratitude; and Clarence was not the last of the wash, to be sure.

The Creation, from the 'Younger Edda'

Snorri Sturluson

Publisher's Note: In the Younger Edda *of Snorri Sturluson (1179–1241), King Gylfe of Sweden journeys to Asgard, seeking knowledge of the legendary asa-folk. Once there, the king takes on the pseudonym of Ganglere and converses with three chiefs about the Norse creation story.*

THEN SAID GANGLERE: Much had been done, it seemed to me, when heaven and earth were made, when sun and moon were set in their places, and when days were marked out; but whence came the people who inhabit the world? Har answered as follows: As Bor's sons went along the sea-strand, they found two trees. These trees they took up and made men of them. The first gave them spirit and life; the second endowed them with reason and power of motion; and the third gave them form, speech, hearing and eyesight. They gave them clothes and names; the man they called Ask, and the woman Embla. From them all mankind is descended, and a dwelling-place was given them under Midgard. In the next place, the sons of Bor made for themselves in the middle of the world a burg, which is called Asgard, and which we call Troy. There dwelt the gods and their race, and thence were wrought many tidings and adventures, both on earth and in the sky. In Asgard is a place called Hlidskjalf, and when Odin seated himself there in the high-seat, he saw over the whole world, and what every man was doing, and he knew all things that he saw. His wife hight Frigg, and she was the daughter of Fjorgvin, and from their offspring are descended the race that we call asas, who inhabited Asgard the old and the realms that lie about it, and all that race are known to be gods. And for this reason Odin is called Alfather, that he is the father of all gods and men, and of all things that were made by him and by his might. Jord (earth) was his daughter and his wife; with her he begat his first son, and that is Asa-Thor. To him was given force and strength, whereby he conquers all things quick.

Norfe, or Narfe, hight a giant, who dwelt in Jotunheim. He had a daughter by name Night. She was swarthy and dark like the race she belonged to. She was first married to a man who hight Naglfare. Their son was Aud. Afterward she was married to Annar. Her last husband was Delling (Daybreak), who was of asa-race. Their son was Day, who was light and fair after his father. Then took Alfather Night and her son Day, gave them two horses and two cars, and set them up in heaven to drive around the earth, each in twelve hours by turns. Night rides first on the horse which is called Hrimfaxe, and every morning he bedews the earth with the foam from his bit. The horse on which Day rides is called Skinfaxe, and with his mane he lights up all the sky and the earth.

Then said Ganglere: How does he steer the course of the sun and the moon? Answered Har: Mundilfare hight the man who had two children. They were so fair and beautiful that he called his son Moon, and his daughter, whom he gave in marriage to a man by name

Glener, he called Sun. But the gods became wroth at this arrogance, took both the brother and the sister, set them up in heaven, and made Sun drive the horses that draw the car of the sun, which the gods had made to light up the world from sparks that flew out of Muspelheim. These horses hight Arvak and Alsvid. Under their withers the gods placed two wind-bags to cool them, but in some songs it is called ironcold (ísarnkol). Moon guides the course of the moon, and rules its waxing and waning. He took from the earth two children, who hight Bil and Hjuke, as they were going from the well called Byrger, and were carrying on their shoulders the bucket called Sager and the pole Simul. Their father's name is Vidfin. These children always accompany Moon, as can be seen from the earth.

Then said Ganglere: Swift fares Sun, almost as if she were afraid, and she could make no more haste in her course if she feared her destroyer. Then answered Har: Nor is it wonderful that she speeds with all her might. Near is he who pursues her, and there is no escape for her but to run before him. Then asked Ganglere: Who causes her this toil? Answered Har: It is two wolves. The one hight Skol, he runs after her; she fears him and he will one day overtake her. The other hight Hate, Hrodvitner's son; he bounds before her and wants to catch the moon, and so he will at last. Then asked Ganglere: Whose offspring are these wolves? Said Har; A hag dwells east of Midgard, in the forest called Jarnved (Ironwood), where reside the witches called Jarnvidjes. The old hag gives birth to many giant sons, and all in wolf's likeness. Thence come these two wolves. It is said that of this wolf-race one is the mightiest, and is called Moongarm. He is filled with the life-blood of all dead men. He will devour the moon, and stain the heavens and all the sky with blood. Thereby the sun will be darkened, the winds will grow wild, and roar hither and thither, as it is said in the Prophecy of the Vala:

> *In the east dwells the old hag,*
> *In the Jarnved forest;*
> *And brings forth there*
> *Fenrer's offspring.*
> *There comes of them all*
> *One the worst,*
> *The moon's devourer*
> *In a troll's disguise.*

> *He is filled with the lifeblood*
> *Of men doomed to die;*
> *The seats of the gods*
> *He stains with red gore;*
> *Sunshine grows black*
> *The summer thereafter,*
> *All weather gets fickle.*
> *Know you yet or not?*

Then asked Ganglere: What is the path from earth to heaven? Har answered, laughing: Foolishly do you now ask. Have you not been told that the gods made a bridge from earth to heaven, which is called Bifrost? You must have seen it. It may be that you call it the rainbow. It has three colours, is very strong, and is made with more craft and skill than other structures. Still, however strong it is, it will break when the sons of Muspel come to ride over it, and then they will have to swim their horses over great rivers in order to get on. Then said Ganglere: The gods did not, it seems to me, build that bridge honestly, if it shall be able to break to pieces, since they could have done so, had they desired. Then made answer Har: The gods are worthy of no blame for this structure. Bifrost is indeed a good bridge, but there is no thing in the world that is able to stand when the sons of Muspel come to the fight.

The Creation Story of the Four Suns

From Aztec mythology

TONACATECUTLI AND TONACACIUATL dwelt from the beginning in the thirteenth heaven. To them were born, as to an elder generation, four gods – the ruddy Camaxtli (chief divinity of the Tlascalans); the black Tezcatlipoca, wizard of the night; Quetzalcoatl, the wind-god; and the grim Huitzilopochtli, of whom it was said that he was born without flesh, a skeleton.

For six hundred years these deities lived in idleness; then the four brethren assembled, creating first the fire (hearth of the universe) and afterward a half-sun. They formed also Oxomoco and Cipactonal, the first man and first woman, commanding that the former should till the ground, and the latter spin and weave; while to the woman they gave powers of divination and grains of maize that she might work cures. They also divided time into days and inaugurated a year of eighteen twenty-day periods, or three hundred and sixty days. Mictlantecutli and Mictlanciuatl they created to be Lord and Lady of Hell, and they formed the heavens that are below the thirteenth storey of the celestial regions, and the waters of the sea, making in the sea a monster Cipactli, from which they shaped the earth. The gods of the waters, Tlaloctecutli and his wife Chalchiuhtlicue, they created, giving them dominion over the Quarters.

The son of the first pair married a woman formed from a hair of the goddess Xochiquetzal; and the gods, noticing how little was the light given forth by the half-sun, resolved to make another half-sun, whereupon Tezcatlipoca became the sun-bearer – for what we behold traversing the daily heavens is not the sun itself, but only its brightness; the true sun is invisible. The other gods created huge giants, who could uproot trees by brute force, and whose food was acorns. For thirteen times fifty-two years, altogether six hundred and seventy-six, this period lasted – as long as its Sun endured; and it is from this first Sun that time began to be counted, for during the six hundred years of the idleness of the gods, while Huitzilopochtli was in his bones, time was not reckoned.

This Sun came to an end when Quetzalcoatl struck down Tezcatlipoca and became Sun in his place. Tezcatlipoca was metamorphosed into a jaguar (Ursa Major) which is seen by night in the skies wheeling down into the waters whither Quetzalcoatl cast him; and this jaguar devoured the giants of that period.

At the end of six hundred and seventy-six years Quetzalcoatl was treated by his brothers as he had treated Tezcatlipoca, and his Sun came to an end with a great wind which carried away most of the people of that time or transformed them into monkeys.

Then for seven times fifty-two years Tlaloc was Sun; but at the end of this three hundred and sixty-four years Quetzalcoatl rained fire from heaven and made Chalchiuhtlicue Sun in place of her husband, a dignity which she held for three hundred and twelve years (six times fifty-two); and it was in these days that maize began to be used.

Now two thousand six hundred and twenty-eight years had passed since the birth of the gods, and in this year it rained so heavily that the heavens themselves fell, while the people of that time were transformed into fish. When the gods saw this, they created four men, with whose aid Tezcatlipoca and Quetzalcoatl again upreared the heavens, even as they are today; and these two gods becoming lords of the heavens and of the stars, walked therein.

After the deluge and the restoration of the heavens, Tezcatlipoca discovered the art of making fire from sticks and of drawing it from the heart of flint. The first man, Piltzintecutli, and his wife, who had been made of a hair of Xochiquetzal, did not perish in the flood, because they were divine. A son was born to them, and the gods created other people just as they had formerly existed.

But since, except for the fires, all was in darkness, the gods resolved to create a new Sun. This was done by Quetzalcoatl, who cast his own son, by Chalchiuhtlicue, into a great fire, whence he issued as the Sun of our own time; Tlaloc hurled his son into the cinders of the fire, and thence rose the Moon, ever following after the Sun. This Sun, said the gods, should eat hearts and drink blood, and so they established wars that there might be sacrifices of captives to nourish the orbs of light.

The Daughter of the Sun

From the Cherokee people

THE SUN LIVED ON the other side of the sky vault, but her daughter lived in the middle of the sky, directly above the earth, and every day as the Sun was climbing along the sky arch to the west she used to stop at her daughter's house for dinner.

Now, the Sun hated the people on the earth, because they could never look straight at her without screwing up their faces. She said to her brother, the Moon, "My grandchildren are ugly; they grin all over their faces when they look at me." But the Moon said, "I like my younger brothers; I think they are very handsome," because they always smiled pleasantly when they saw him in the sky at night, for his rays were milder.

The Sun was jealous and planned to kill all the people, so every day when she got near her daughter's house she sent down such sultry rays that there was a great fever and the people died by hundreds, until everyone had lost some friend and there was fear that no one would be left. They went for help to the Little Men, who said the only way to save themselves was to kill the Sun.

The Little Men made medicine and changed two men to snakes, the Spreading-adder and the Copperhead, and sent them to watch near the door of the daughter of the Sun to bite the old Sun when she came next day. They went together and hid near the house until the Sun came, but when the Spreading-adder was about to spring, the bright light blinded him and he could only spit out yellow slime, as he does to this day when he tries to bite. She called him a nasty thing and went by into the house, and the Copperhead crawled off without trying to do anything.

So the people still died from the heat, and they went to the Little Men a second time for help. The Little Men made medicine again and changed one man into the great Uktena and another into the Rattlesnake and sent them to watch near the house and kill the old Sun when she came for dinner. They made the Uktena very large, with horns on his head, and everyone thought he would be sure to do the work, but the Rattlesnake was so quick and eager that he got ahead and coiled up just outside the house, and when the Sun's daughter opened the door to look out for her mother, he sprang up and bit her and she fell dead in the doorway. He forgot to wait for the old Sun, but went back to the people, and the Uktena was so very angry that he went back, too. Since then we pray to the rattlesnake and do not kill him, because he is kind and never tries to bite if we do not disturb him. The Uktena grew angrier all the time and very dangerous, so that if he even looked at a man, that man's family would die. After a long time the people held a council and decided that he was too dangerous to be with them, so they sent him up to Gălûñ'lătĭ, and he is there now. The Spreading-adder, the Copperhead, the Rattlesnake, and the Uktena were all men.

When the Sun found her daughter dead, she went into the house and grieved, and the people did not die anymore, but now the world was dark all the time, because the Sun would not come out. They went again to the Little Men, and these told them that if they wanted the Sun to come out again they must bring back her daughter from Tsûsgina'ĭ, the

Ghost country, in Usûñhi'yĭ, the Darkening land in the west. They chose seven men to go, and gave each a sourwood rod a hand-breadth long. The Little Men told them they must take a box with them, and when they got to Tsûsgina'ĭ they would find all the ghosts at a dance. They must stand outside the circle, and when the young woman passed in the dance they must strike her with the rods and she would fall to the ground. Then they must put her into the box and bring her back to her mother, but they must be very sure not to open the box, even a little way, until they were home again.

They took the rods and a box and travelled seven days to the west until they came to the Darkening land. There were a great many people there, and they were having a dance just as if they were at home in the settlements. The young woman was in the outside circle, and as she swung around to where the seven men were standing, one struck her with his rod and she turned her head and saw him. As she came around the second time another touched her with his rod, and then another and another, until at the seventh round she fell out of the ring, and they put her into the box and closed the lid fast. The other ghosts seemed never to notice what had happened.

They took up the box and started home toward the east. In a little while the girl came to life again and begged to be let out of the box, but they made no answer and went on. Soon she called again and said she was hungry, but still they made no answer and went on. After another while she spoke again and called for a drink and pleaded so that it was very hard to listen to her, but the men who carried the box said nothing and still went on. When at last they were very near home, she called again and begged them to raise the lid just a little, because she was smothering. They were afraid she was really dying now, so they lifted the lid a little to give her air, but as they did so there was a fluttering sound inside and something flew past them into the thicket and they heard a redbird cry, *"Kwish! kwish! kwish!"* in the bushes. They shut down the lid and went on again to the settlements, but when they got there and opened the box it was empty.

So we know the Redbird is the daughter of the Sun, and if the men had kept the box closed, as the Little Men told them to do, they would have brought her home safely, and we could bring back our other friends also from the Ghost country, but now when they die we can never bring them back.

The Sun had been glad when they started to the Ghost country, but when they came back without her daughter she grieved and cried, "My daughter, my daughter," and wept until her tears made a flood upon the earth, and the people were afraid the world would be drowned. They held another council, and sent their handsomest young men and women to amuse her so that she would stop crying. They danced before the Sun and sang their best songs, but for a long time she kept her face covered and paid no attention, until at last the drummer suddenly changed the song, when she lifted up her face, and was so pleased at the sight that she forgot her grief and smiled.

The Daughter of the Sun and Moon

From the Bantu-speaking peoples, Angola

KIMANAWEZE'S SON, when the time came for him to choose a wife, declared that he would not "marry a woman of the earth," but must have the daughter of the Sun and Moon. He wrote "a letter of marriage" (a modern touch, no doubt added by the narrator) and cast about for a messenger to take it up to the sky. The little duiker (*mbambi*) refused, so did the larger antelope, known as *soko*, the hawk, and the vulture. At last a frog came and offered to carry the letter. The son of Kimanaweze, doubtful of his ability to do this, said, "Begone! Where people of life, who have wings, gave it up dost thou say, 'I will go there'?" But the frog persisted, and was at last sent off, with the threat of a thrashing if he should be unsuccessful. It appears that the Sun and Moon were in the habit of sending their handmaidens down to the earth to draw water, descending and ascending by means of a spider's web. The frog went and hid himself in the well to which they came, and when the first one filled her jar he got into it without being seen, having first placed the letter in his mouth. The girls went up to heaven, carried their water jars into the room, and set them down. When they had gone away he came out, produced the letter, laid it on a table, and hid.

After a while "Lord Sun" (*Kumbi Mwene*) came in, found the letter, and read it. Not knowing what to make of it, he put it away, and said nothing about it. The frog got into an empty water-jar, and was carried down again when the girls went for a fresh supply. The son of Kimanaweze, getting no answer, refused at first to believe that the frog had executed his commission; but, after waiting for some days, he wrote another letter and sent him again. The frog carried it in the same way as before, and the Sun, after reading it, wrote that he would consent, if the suitor came himself, bringing his 'first-present' (the usual gift for opening marriage negotiations). On receiving this the young man wrote another letter, saying that he must wait till told the amount of the 'wooing-present', or bride-price (*kilembu*). He gave this to the frog, along with a sum of money, and it was conveyed as before. This time the Sun consulted his wife, who was quite ready to welcome the mysterious son-in-law.

She solved the question of providing refreshments for the invisible messenger by saying, "We will cook a meal anyhow, and put it on the table where he leaves the letters." This was done, and the frog, when left alone, came out and ate. The letter, which was left along with the food, stated the amount of the bride-price to be "a sack of money." He carried the letter back to the son of Kimanaweze, who spent six days in collecting the necessary amount, and then sent it by the frog with this message, "Soon I shall find a day to bring home my wife." This, however, was more easily said than done, for when his messenger had once more returned he waited twelve days, and then told the frog that he could not find people to fetch the bride. But the frog was equal to the occasion. Again he had himself carried up to the Sun's palace, and, getting out of the water-jar, hid in a corner of the room till after dark, when he came out and went through the house till he found the princess's bedchamber.

Seeing that she was fast asleep, he took out one of her eyes without waking her, and then the other. He tied up the eyes in a handkerchief, and went back to his corner in the room where the water jars were kept. In the morning, when the girl did not appear, her parents came to inquire the reason, and found that she was blind. In their distress they sent two men to consult the diviner, who, after casting lots, said (not having heard from them the reason of their coming), "Disease has brought you; the one who is sick is a woman; the sickness that ails her the eyes. You have come, being sent; you have not come of your own will. I have spoken." The Sun's messengers replied, "Truth. Look now what caused the ailment." He told them that a certain suitor had cast a spell over her, and she would die unless she were sent to him. Therefore they had best hasten on the marriage. The men brought back word to the Sun, who said, "All right. Let us sleep. Tomorrow they shall take her down to the earth." Next day, accordingly, he gave orders for the spider to "weave a large cobweb" for sending his daughter down. Meanwhile the frog had gone down as usual in the water-jar and hidden himself in the bottom of the well. When the water carriers had gone up again he came out and went to the village of the bridegroom and told him that his bride would arrive that day. The young man would not believe him, but he solemnly promised to bring her in the evening, and returned to the well.

After sunset the attendants brought the princess down by way of the stronger cobweb and left her by the well. The frog came out, and told her that he would take her to her husband's house; at the same time he handed back her eyes. They started, and came to the son of Kimanaweze, and the marriage took place. And they lived happy ever after – on earth, for, as the narrator said, "They had all given up going to heaven; who could do it was Mainu the frog."

The Daughter of the Universe

Ondine Mayor

A SPARK. A GLOW. A fire ablaze with the first light that had ever been, amongst what had only existed as Darkness before that moment of indefinite. That moment she burned into existence. It was one which the Universe could never forget. She was their first child. The daughter of the Universe. She shone brighter than anything the Universe had ever seen; dressed in a gold that would never be believed, she was more beautiful than anything they could have dreamed. Dreaming was something that existed long before any of them. Even the Universe could not recall when there wasn't a moment of dreams. And now, she was the only dream that they needed.

There were many names that had been gifted to her throughout the years of Life: Ra, Akycha, Surya, Shams, Nanahuatzin, Amaterasu, Guaraci. The list could be extended through time itself. But there was one thing that would always be agreed upon. She was The Sun.

The Universe had never been a parent, and they were bound to make mistakes. But when the spark that seemed to burn brighter than ever before, became the fiery child they held in their arms, the Universe knew that there could be no greater gift than what they had in that moment. There, in that time and space, her very first name was received. Sun. For she burned brighter than any other. Anything within her presence couldn't help but to reflect the glow she emitted; her light was contagious. The Sun had a touch that would burn anything within reach, leaving a fire that blazed *almost* as bright as she herself did. Every fragment of her existence was infectious, and warm, and unlike anything that had ever been, nor anything that would ever be again.

Before her, the Everything had been without light. All that had ever been known was darkness. Of course, one could dream of light; though it was hard to dream of that which did not exist. However, that was how all good things came to be: beginning with a dream. And when the light came to be, with the birth of the sun, suddenly it was no longer just a dream. The Universe, while looking down at the child in their arms, for the first time could see the tips of their fingers, embraced by the golden glow that was light. Suddenly, the Everything had light. A fire that burned away the darkness that had once shrouded all that had ever been. It was warm, and it was brilliant, and it lit up anything and everything.

The older she grew, the brighter she burned. And while she seemed no more than a baby to the Universe, who had been around for many times longer, it was the day of her one billionth birthday, when she was first introduced to Life.

Life began, and it grew. Mothered and sustained by her very dear friend, Earth. Earth had been so young when she had come to the Sun. Still dressed in the burning reds which the Sun herself had given.

My dear friend, I have a request.

The Sun, though she towered over her friend, was not so much older than the Earth as many may believe, and wanted only to assist her friend. *Whatever it is, I shall do anything I may to help.*

I wish to create Life.

The Sun was surprised, as she had not known of this before. Life? *Has the Universe given permission?*

Of course. Had they not, I would not ask.

What might I do?

It has been your warmth that has sustained me. And now I wish for it to be your warmth which sustains them. From their first moment of life, until the last dying breath I hold in my hands. This may be ten years. Or it may be ten billion. I do not know how they may live, nor if they may thrive. But I wish to do all in my power to provide a chance, pledged the Earth. *In exchange I, and all my siblings, shall be your orbit. We will revolve only about you. Any request of us you may have shall be granted.*

The Sun thought about this. Perhaps it seemed quite the demand, but time moved so differently for her. The Universe had seen many more than ten billion years. And this was a dream – how could she refuse the dream of her dearest friend? *I shall do as you ask. With one condition.*

The Earth agreed.

I wish for you and all your siblings to care for my children. The Sun opened her hands. Her palms, all the way to the tips of her fingers, glittered and sparkled with every turn and reflection of her own light. Though, that wasn't quite right. They didn't seem to simply reflect her own light. The Sun was the only light within Everything. She was *the* light. And yet this no longer seemed to be the case. This was a new light. It was nothing in comparison to the Sun. Practically insignificant. But there it was, sitting within her hands, billions, if not trillions, of minuscule – microscopic – glints and glitters. Each one seemed to be emitting a light of their own. Not dissimilar to that of the Sun. The Earth couldn't imagine that any of them would grow to the same greatness that was the Sun, but they all burned. They burned with their own light. Trillions of these little sparks, that were just that. Sparks.

The Earth reached out and observed as one of the many glitters, twisted itself between and away from the fingers of the Sun and around to the Earth. At which point, the Earth realized, unlike the other sparkles, this one didn't seem to have its own light, only to reflect that of the Sun. The Earth couldn't think of it as being any less marvellous than the others. *He seems to have taken a liking to you.*

The Earth smiled at her new little friend. *My siblings and I shall do all in our power to care for your children.*

The Sun bowed her head. An agreement had been reached. She then threw open her arms, and the glitters that were once encompassing her hands and twining through every finger, flew. They scattered; it was their first taste of freedom. Dancing amongst the planets, and flitting into each and every part of the Everything. They seemed never to end. No longer did the Sun solely light up that which was once the darkness. Now it seemed as though every piece of time and space glittered as it never had done before.

These *are my Stars.*

* * *

There were yet to be hours, or days, or even months, but on the very first moment of Life, they all celebrated. Even the Universe came to offer their congratulations to Earth for the small bacterial form which was the beginning of Life. And as Life grew, so did Earth. She outgrew the burning fires that had been given to her so many years ago by the Sun, and she began to dress in the white of the clouds and the blue of the seas that had grown to become part of her. She changed, moulding herself to be exactly what Life would need. The Sun remained faithful, and kept her promise. As Earth, and her many siblings, surrounded the Sun, she warmed them. Just enough, so that Life would grow and thrive.

As the Earth became the mother to Life, the Sun watched her own children glitter amongst Everything. She wept, when a Star fell, and rejoiced when a new one slipped from between her fingers: born into the Everything. They aged, and grew, and burned, not unlike the Sun. However, there would never be another that could compare to her, and the brilliance with which she shone. They were glitz and glitters beside the raging inferno of golden-white light that was their creator. It was no competition. Thankfully, they never saw it as such: The Sun was the light, and they were Stars. And that was that.

The Sun's child who had taken a liking to Earth, all those years ago, remained faithfully by her side ever since. Many more of her children became closer to Earth's siblings, as they grew older together.

When Humans were born into existence, they were unlike any Life the Sun had seen before. The Earth seemed to agree, the proudest a mother could have been of her children. The Humans would worship Neptune and Venus, Saturn and Mars. They worshipped Jupiter, and Mercury, and Uranus. They worshipped the Stars that glittered and the Moon that would illuminate the night sky. But there was none that they worshipped more than the Sun herself. They praised her every moment and movement. They bowed to her golden brilliance, and thanked her for warming their home and lighting their days. It seemed they worshipped all but the Earth. She who had moulded herself to sustain their life. The Earth didn't mind. A mother's love is unconditional.

The Humans seemed to have the greatest capacity for love, and yet the strongest proficiency to inflict pain. The Sun could only watch as her friend's oceans grew and rivers flooded while she wept tears for the atrocities which her children inflicted on their own kind.

The Earth had been alive very nearly as long as the Sun herself had. While for Earth, Humans were her beloved children, for the Sun they were only a blip on her radar. Alive barely long enough for her to register. And yet never before had she seen one wither away as devastatingly quickly as she had, her dear friend Earth. It had barely been a million years when the Humans came to be, and Earth – who had so recently been thriving off Life – had never seemed more finite.

The Sun watched as the green that the Earth had once been so proud to display, slowly withered away to the brown, that was so similar, to what it had been when the Earth was only a few years old. The blue of her oceans seemed now only to shrink, as the Earth grew warmer and warmer each day. The Sun knew that she would forever be growing until the day she ceased to be. And as she grew, the more her fire burned. The brighter she would shine and the hotter she would blaze. But why was it affecting her friend so? Was it her heat that was causing the Earth's demise, or was it the Humans? The Sun knew that speaking with the Earth would gain nothing. Her children could do no wrong. It was simply old age – she had been alive for upward of four billion years. Not everyone could live forever. And so the Sun called to her child. The loyal companion of the Earth, who loved her friend as much as she herself did.

Mother?

Moon. Tell me, please. Why does Earth suffer so? Have I grown too strong? Too hot? Is it I who causes her pain?

When the Moon denied this to be the case, the Sun's mood hardly improved. If not her, then was it indeed the Humans?

They create. They create and take. They take all that Earth is able to give, and she still pushes to give more. They are her everything. Yet their creations hurt her. They've trapped her in a blanket of their waste. Every day she withers away. Every day they take more. She is ageing beyond her years. I do not know how much longer she will have.

The Sun grieved at what was only an affirmation. How could Life be so good and so wonderful, and yet…and yet.

I will speak with the Universe.

The Moon seemed to hold not the slightest hope, but was equally reluctant to surrender their good friend.

Universe.

My child.

It is Earth. She is dying.

I know.

It is her dream. It is her dream that kills her.

When the Universe sighs, it is Everything that shifts. Or perhaps, it is the contrary: each minuscule movement within the Everything pauses. You will know when the Universe sighs. It is impossible to miss. *I know, my child.*

We must do something! The Sun felt far younger than she was, arguing with her parent. Not knowing anything about the Everything. There's so much to be learnt over billions of years. But now they were back: a stubborn child, and a parent who could only be as wise as one who had been around for as long as time itself.

There is nothing that can be done. Life is not only her dream, but her reality. It is her child. She will let it devour her within every inch of her existence and she will do nothing to stop it. She will defend it until the very end. And when she dies, so will they all.

But—

Have you not tried to catch every child of your own as they fell? Have you not tried to reignite every Star whose flame died? They are your children, just as Life is hers. Existence for some may be forever, and for others it is fleeting. Neither is less than the other, but either way, there is nothing that can be done.

All that had been said, was all that could be said. The Sun knew that the Universe was correct. Just as they always would be. And so the Sun burned. She couldn't dim her flame to protect her friend. All that she could offer was her company. And so that was what she did. It was what she would always do.

The Death of the Sun-Hero

From Bukovinian fairy tale

MANY, MANY THOUSANDS of years ago there lived a mighty King whom heaven had blessed with a clever and beautiful son. When he was only ten years old the boy was cleverer than all the King's counsellors put together, and when he was twenty he was the greatest hero in the whole kingdom. His father could not make enough of his son, and always had him clothed in golden garments which shone and sparkled like the sun; and his mother gave him a white horse, which never slept, and which flew like the wind. All the people in the land loved him dearly, and called him the Sun-Hero, for they did not think his like existed under the sun. Now it happened one night that both his parents had the same extraordinary dream. They dreamt that a girl all dressed in red had come to them and said: "If you wish that your son should really become the Sun-Hero in deed and not only in name, let him go out into the world and search for the Tree of the Sun, and when he has found it, let him pluck a golden apple from it and bring it home."

When the King and Queen had each related their dreams to the other, they were much amazed that they should both have dreamt exactly the same about their son, and the King said to his wife, "This is clearly a sign from heaven that we should send our son out into the world in order that he may come home the great Sun-Hero, as the Red Girl said, not only in name but in deed."

The Queen consented with many tears, and the King at once bade his son set forth in search of the Tree of the Sun, from which he was to pluck a golden apple. The Prince was delighted at the prospect, and set out on his travels that very day.

For a long time he wandered all through the world, and it was not till the ninety-ninth day after he started that he found an old man who was able to tell him where the Tree of the Sun grew. He followed his directions, and rode on his way, and after another ninety-nine days he arrived at a golden castle, which stood in the middle of a vast wilderness. He knocked at the door, which was opened noiselessly and by invisible hands. Finding no one about, the Prince rode on, and came to a great meadow, where the Sun-Tree grew. When he reached the tree he put out his hand to pick a golden apple; but all of a sudden the tree grew higher, so that he could not reach its fruit. Then he heard someone behind him laughing. Turning round, he saw the girl in red walking towards him, who addressed him in these words:

"Do you really imagine, brave son of the earth, that you can pluck an apple so easily from the Tree of the Sun? Before you can do that, you have a difficult task before you. You must guard the tree for nine days and nine nights from the ravages of two wild black wolves, who will try to harm it. Do you think you can undertake this?"

"Yes," answered the Sun-Hero, "I will guard the Tree of the Sun nine days and nine nights."

Then the girl continued: "Remember, though, if you do not succeed the Sun will kill you. Now begin your watch."

With these words the Red Girl went back into the golden castle. She had hardly left him when the two black wolves appeared: but the Sun-Hero beat them off with his sword, and they retired, only, however, to reappear in a very short time. The Sun-Hero chased them away once more, but he had hardly sat down to rest when the two black wolves were on the scene again. This went on for seven days and nights, when the white horse, who had never done such a thing before, turned to the Sun-Hero and said in a human voice: "Listen to what I am going to say. A Fairy gave me to your mother in order that I might be of service to you; so let me tell you, that if you go to sleep and let the wolves harm the tree, the Sun will surely kill you. The Fairy, foreseeing this, put everyone in the world under a spell, which prevents their obeying the Sun's command to take your life. But all the same, she has forgotten one person, who will certainly kill you if you fall asleep and let the wolves damage the tree. So watch and keep the wolves away."

Then the Sun-Hero strove with all his might and kept the black wolves at bay, and conquered his desire to sleep; but on the eighth night his strength failed him, and he fell fast asleep. When he awoke a woman in black stood beside him, who said: "You have fulfilled your task very badly, for you have let the two black wolves damage the Tree of the Sun. I am the mother of the Sun, and I command you to ride away from here at once, and I pronounce sentence of death upon you, for you proudly let yourself be called the Sun-Hero without having done anything to deserve the name."

The youth mounted his horse sadly, and rode home. The people all thronged round him on his return, anxious to hear his adventures, but he told them nothing, and only to his mother did he confide what had befallen him. But the old Queen laughed, and said to her son: "Don't worry, my child; you see, the Fairy has protected you so far, and the Sun has found no one to kill you. So cheer up and be happy."

After a time the Prince forgot all about his adventure, and married a beautiful Princess, with whom he lived very happily for some time. But one day when he was out hunting he felt very thirsty, and coming to a stream he stooped down to drink from it, and this caused his death, for a crab came swimming up, and with its claws tore out his tongue. He was carried home in a dying condition, and as he lay on his deathbed the woman in black appeared and said: "So the Sun has, after all, found someone, who was not under the Fairy's spell, who has caused your death. And a similar fate will overtake everyone under the Sun who wrongfully assumes a title to which he has no right."

A Desert Episode

Algernon Blackwood

I

"BETTER PUT WRAPS on now. The sun's getting low," a girl said.

It was the end of a day's expedition in the Arabian Desert, and they were having tea. A few yards away the donkeys munched their *barsim*; beside them in the sand the boys lay finishing bread and jam. Immense, with gliding tread, the sun's rays slid from crest to crest of the limestone ridges that broke the huge expanse towards the Red Sea. By the time the tea-things were packed the sun hovered, a giant ball of red, above the Pyramids. It stood in the western sky a moment, looking out of its majestic hood across the sand. With a movement almost visible it leaped, paused, then leaped again. It seemed to bound towards the horizon; then, suddenly, was gone.

"It *is* cold, yes," said the painter, Rivers. And all who heard looked up at him because of the way he said it. A hurried movement ran through the merry party, and the girls were on their donkeys quickly, not wishing to be left to bring up the rear. They clattered off. The boys cried; the thud of sticks was heard; hoofs shuffled through the sand and stones. In single file the picnickers headed for Helouan, some five miles distant. And the desert closed up behind them as they went, following in a shadowy wave that never broke, noiseless, foamless, unstreaked, driven by no wind, and of a volume undiscoverable. Against the orange sunset the Pyramids turned deep purple. The strip of silvery Nile among its palm trees looked like rising mist. In the incredible Egyptian afterglow the enormous horizons burned a little longer, then went out. The ball of the earth – a huge round globe that bulged – curved visibly as at sea. It was no longer a flat expanse; it turned. Its splendid curves were realized.

"Better put wraps on; it's cold and the sun is low." And then the curious hurry to get back among the houses and the haunts of men. No more was said, perhaps, than this, yet, the time and place being what they were, the mind became suddenly aware of that quality which ever brings a certain shrinking with it – vastness; and more than vastness: that which is endless because it is also beginningless – eternity. A colossal splendour stole upon the heart, and the senses, unaccustomed to the unusual stretch, reeled a little, as though the wonder was more than could be faced with comfort. Not all, doubtless, realized it, though to two, at least, it came with a staggering impact there was no withstanding. For, while the luminous greys and purples crept round them from the sandy wastes, the hearts of these two became aware of certain common things whose simple majesty is usually dulled by mere familiarity. Neither the man nor the girl knew for certain that the other felt it, as they brought up the rear together; yet the fact that each *did* feel it set them side by side in the same strange circle – and made them silent. They realized the immensity of a moment: the dizzy stretch of time that led up to the casual pinning of a veil; to the tightening of a stirrup strap; to the little speech with a companion; the roar of the vanished centuries that have ground mountains into sand and spread them over the floor of Africa; above all, to the little truth that they themselves existed amid the whirl of stupendous systems all delicately balanced as a spider's web – that they were *alive*.

For a moment this vast scale of reality revealed itself, then hid swiftly again behind the débris of the obvious. The universe, containing their two tiny yet important selves, stood still for an instant before their eyes. They looked at it – realized that they belonged to it. Everything moved and had its being, *lived* – here in this silent, empty desert even more actively than in a city of crowded houses. The quiet Nile, sighing with age, passed down towards the sea; there loomed the menacing Pyramids across the twilight; beneath them, in monstrous dignity, crouched that Shadow from whose eyes of battered stone proceeds the nameless thing that contracts the heart, then opens it again to terror; and everywhere, from towering monoliths as from secret tombs, rose that strange, long whisper which, defying time and distance, laughs at death. The spell of Egypt, which is the spell of immortality, touched their hearts.

Already, as the group of picnickers rode homewards now, the first stars twinkled overhead, and the peerless Egyptian night was on the way. There was hurry in the passing of the dusk. And the cold sensibly increased.

"So you did no painting after all," said Rivers to the girl who rode a little in front of him, "for I never saw you touch your sketchbook once."

They were some distance now behind the others; the line straggled; and when no answer came he quickened his pace, drew up alongside and saw that her eyes, in the reflection of the sunset, shone with moisture. But she turned her head a little, smiling into his face, so that the human and the non-human beauty came over him with an onset that was almost shock. Neither one nor other, he knew, were long for him, and the realization fell upon him with a pang of actual physical pain. The acuteness, the hopelessness of the realization, for a moment, were more than he could bear, stern of temper though he was, and he tried to pass in front of her, urging his donkey with resounding strokes. Her own animal, however, following the lead, at once came up with him.

"You felt it, perhaps, as I did," he said some moments later, his voice quite steady again. "The stupendous, everlasting thing – the – *life* behind it all." He hesitated a little in his speech, unable to find the substantive that could compass even a fragment of his thought. She paused, too, similarly inarticulate before the surge of incomprehensible feelings.

"It's – awful," she said, half laughing, yet the tone hushed and a little quaver in it somewhere. And her voice to his was like the first sound he had ever heard in the world, for the first sound a full-grown man heard in the world would be beyond all telling – magical. "I shall not try again," she continued, leaving out the laughter this time; "my sketchbook is a farce. For, to tell the truth," – and the next three words she said below her breath – "I dare not."

He turned and looked at her for a second. It seemed to him that the following wave had caught them up, and was about to break above her, too. But the big-brimmed hat and the streaming veil shrouded her features. He saw, instead, the Universe. He felt as though he and she had always, always been together, and always, always would be. Separation was inconceivable.

"It came so close," she whispered. "It – shook me!"

They were cut off from their companions, whose voices sounded far ahead. Her words might have been spoken by the darkness, or by someone who peered at them from within that following wave. Yet the fanciful phrase was better than any he could find. From the immeasurable space of time and distance men's hearts vainly seek to plumb, it drew into closer perspective a certain meaning that words may hardly compass, a formidable truth that belongs to that deep place where hope and doubt fight their incessant battle. The awe she spoke of was the awe of immortality, of belonging to something that is endless and beginningless.

And he understood that the tears and laughter were one – caused by that spell which takes a little human life and shakes it, as an animal shakes its prey that later shall feed its blood and increase its power of growth. His other thoughts – really but a single thought – he had not the right to utter. Pain this time easily routed hope as the wave came nearer. For it was the wave of death that would shortly break, he knew, over him, but not over her. Him it would sweep with its huge withdrawal into the desert whence it came: her it would leave high upon the shores of life – alone. And yet the separation would somehow not be real. They were together in eternity even now. They were endless as this desert, beginningless as this sky...immortal. The realisation overwhelmed.

The lights of Helouan seemed to come no nearer as they rode on in silence for the rest of the way. Against the dark background of the Mokattam Hills these fairy lights twinkled brightly, hanging in mid-air, but after an hour they were no closer than before. It was like riding towards the stars. It would take centuries to reach them. There were centuries in which to do so. Hurry has no place in the desert; it is born in streets. The desert stands still; to go fast in it is to go backwards. Now, in particular, its enormous, uncanny leisure was everywhere – in keeping with that mighty scale the sunset had made visible. His thoughts, like the steps of the weary animal that bore him, had no progress in them. The serpent of eternity, holding its tail in its own mouth, rose from the sand, enclosing himself, the stars – and her. Behind him, in the hollows of that shadowy wave, the procession of dynasties and conquests, the great series of gorgeous civilizations the mind calls Past, stood still, crowded with shining eyes and beckoning faces, still waiting to arrive. There is no death in Egypt. His own death stood so close that he could touch it by stretching out his hand, yet it seemed as much behind as in front of him. What man called a beginning was a trick. There was no such thing. He was with this girl – *now*, when Death waited so close for him – yet he had never really begun. Their lives ran always parallel. The hand he stretched to clasp approaching death caught instead in this girl's shadowy hair, drawing her in with him to the centre where he breathed the eternity of the desert. Yet expression of any sort was as futile as it was unnecessary. To paint, to speak, to sing, even the slightest gesture of the soul, became a crude and foolish thing. Silence was here the truth. And they rode in silence towards the fairy lights.

Then suddenly the rocky ground rose up close before them; boulders stood out vividly with black shadows and shining heads; a flat-roofed house slid by; three palm trees rattled in the evening wind; beyond, a mosque and minaret sailed upwards, like the spars and rigging of some phantom craft; and the colonnades of the great modern hotel, standing upon its dome of limestone ridge, loomed over them. Helouan was about them before they knew it. The desert lay behind with its huge, arrested billow. Slowly, owing to its prodigious volume, yet with a speed that merged it instantly with the far horizon behind the night, this wave now withdrew a little. There was no hurry. It came, for the moment, no farther. Rivers knew. For he was in it to the throat. Only his head was above the surface. He still could breathe – and speak – and see. Deepening with every hour into an incalculable splendour, it waited.

II

In the street the foremost riders drew rein, and, two and two abreast, the long line clattered past the shops and cafés, the railway station and hotels, stared at by the natives from the busy pavements. The donkeys stumbled, blinded by the electric light. Girls in white dresses flitted here and there, arabîyehs rattled past with people hurrying home to dress for dinner, and the evening train, just in from Cairo, disgorged its stream of passengers. There were dances in several of the hotels that night. Voices rose on all sides. Questions and answers, engagements and appointments were made, little plans and plots and intrigues for seizing happiness on the wing – before the wave rolled in and caught the lot. They chattered gaily:

"You *are* going, aren't you? You promised—"

"Of course I am."

"Then I'll drive you over. May I call for you?"

"All right. Come at ten."

"We shan't have finished our bridge by then. Say ten-thirty."

And eyes exchanged their meaning signals. The group dismounted and dispersed. Arabs standing under the lebbekh trees, or squatting on the pavements before their dim-lit booths, watched them with faces of gleaming bronze. Rivers gave his bridle to a donkey-boy, and moved across stiffly after the long ride to help the girl dismount. "You feel tired?" he asked gently. "It's been a long day." For her face was white as chalk, though the eyes shone brilliantly.

"Tired, perhaps," she answered, "but exhilarated too. I should like to be there now. I should like to go back this minute – if someone would take me." And, though she said it lightly, there was a meaning in her voice he apparently chose to disregard. It was as if she knew his secret. "Will you take me – some day soon?"

The direct question, spoken by those determined little lips, was impossible to ignore. He looked close into her face as he helped her from the saddle with a spring that brought her a moment half into his arms. "Some day – soon. I will," he said with emphasis, "when you are – ready." The pallor in her face, and a certain expression in it he had not known before, startled him. "I think you have been overdoing it," he added, with a tone in which authority and love were oddly mingled, neither of them disguised.

"Like yourself," she smiled, shaking her skirts out and looking down at her dusty shoes. "I've only a few days more – before I sail. We're both in such a hurry, but you are the worst of the two."

"Because my time is even shorter," ran his horrified thought – for he said no word.

She raised her eyes suddenly to his, with an expression that for an instant almost convinced him she had guessed – and the soul in him stood rigidly at attention, urging back the rising fires. The hair had dropped loosely round the sun-burned neck. Her face was level with his shoulder. Even the glare of the streetlights could not make her undesirable. But behind the gaze of the deep brown eyes another thing looked forth imperatively into his own. And he recognized it with a rush of terror, yet of singular exultation.

"It followed us all the way," she whispered. "It came after us from the desert – where it *lives*."

"At the houses," he said equally low, "it stopped." He gladly adopted her syncopated speech, for it helped him in his struggle to subdue those rising fires.

For a second she hesitated. "You mean, if we had not left so soon – when it turned cold. If we had not hurried – if we had remained a little longer—"

He caught at her hand, unable to control himself, but dropped it again the same second, while she made as though she had not noticed, forgiving him with her eyes. "Or a great deal longer," she added slowly, "forever?"

And then he was certain that she *had* guessed – not that he loved her above all else in the world, for that was so obvious that a child might know it, but that his silence was due to his other, lesser secret; that the great Executioner stood waiting to drop the hood about his eyes. He was already pinioned. Something in her gaze and in her manner persuaded him suddenly that she understood.

His exhilaration increased extraordinarily. "I mean," he said very quietly, "that the spell weakens here among the houses and among the – so-called living." There was masterfulness, triumph, in his voice. Very wonderfully he saw her smile change; she drew slightly closer to his side, as though unable to resist. "Mingled with lesser things we should not understand completely," he added softly.

"And that might be a mistake, you mean?" she asked quickly, her face grave again.

It was his turn to hesitate a moment. The breeze stirred the hair about her neck, bringing its faint perfume – perfume of young life – to his nostrils. He drew his breath in deeply, smothering back the torrent of rising words he knew were impermissible. "Misunderstanding," he said briefly. "If the eye be single—" He broke off, shaken by a paroxysm of coughing. "You know my meaning," he continued, as soon as the attack had passed; "you feel the difference *here*," pointing round him to the hotels, the shops, the busy stream of people; "the hurry, the excitement, the feverish, blinding child's play which pretends to be alive, but does not know it—" And again the coughing stopped him. This time she took his hand in her own, pressed it very slightly, then released it. He felt it as the touch of that desert wave upon his soul. "The reception must be in complete and utter resignation. Tainted by lesser things, the disharmony might be—" he began stammeringly.

Again there came interruption, as the rest of the party called impatiently to know if they were coming up to the hotel. He had not time to find the completing adjective. Perhaps he could not find it ever. Perhaps it does not exist in any modern language. Eternity is not realized today; men have no time to know they are alive forever; they are too busy.

They all moved in a clattering, merry group towards the big hotel. Rivers and the girl were separated.

III

There was a dance that evening, but neither of these took part in it. In the great dining-room their tables were far apart. He could not even see her across the sea of intervening heads and shoulders. The long meal over, he went to his room, feeling it imperative to be alone. He did not read, he did not write; but, leaving the light unlit, he wrapped himself up and leaned out upon the broad windowsill into the great Egyptian night. His deep-sunken thoughts, like to the crowding stars, stood still, yet forever took new shapes. He tried to see behind them, as, when a boy, he had tried to see behind the constellations – out into space – where there is nothing.

Below him the lights of Heluan twinkled like the Pleiades reflected in a pool of water; a hum of queer soft noises rose to his ears; but just beyond the houses the desert stood at attention, the vastest thing he had ever known, very stern, yet very comforting, with its peace beyond all comprehension, its delicate, wild terror, and its awful message of immortality. And the attitude of his mind, though he did not know it, was one of prayer.... From time to time he went to lie on the bed with paroxysms of coughing. He had overtaxed his strength – his swiftly fading strength. The wave had risen to his lips.

Nearer forty than thirty-five, Paul Rivers had come out to Egypt, plainly understanding that with the greatest care he might last a few weeks longer than if he stayed in England. A few more times to see the sunset and the sunrise, to watch the stars, feel the soft airs of earth upon his cheeks; a few more days of intercourse with his kind, asking and answering questions, wearing the old familiar clothes he loved, reading his favourite pages, and then – out into the big spaces – where there is nothing.

Yet no one, from his stalwart, energetic figure, would have guessed – no one but the expert mind, not to be deceived, to whom in the first attack of overwhelming despair and desolation he went for final advice. He left that house, as many had left it before, knowing that soon he would need no earthly protection of roof and walls, and that his soul, if it existed, would be shelterless in the space behind all manifested life. He had looked forward to fame and position in this world; had, indeed, already achieved the first step towards this end; and now, with the vanity of all earthly aims so mercilessly clear before him, he had turned, in somewhat of a nervous, concentrated hurry, to make terms with the Infinite while still the brain was there. And had, of course, found nothing. For it takes a lifetime crowded with experiment and effort to learn even the alphabet of genuine faith; and what could come of a few weeks' wild questioning but confusion and bewilderment of mind? It was inevitable. He came out to Egypt wondering, thinking, questioning, but chiefly wondering. He had grown, that is, more childlike, abandoning the futile tool of Reason, which hitherto had seemed to him the perfect instrument. Its foolishness stood naked before him in the pitiless light of the specialist's decision. For, "Who can by searching find out God?"

To be exceedingly careful of over-exertion was the final warning he brought with him, and, within a few hours of his arrival, three weeks ago, he had met this girl and utterly disregarded it. He took it somewhat thus, "Instead of lingering I'll enjoy myself and go out – a little sooner. I'll *live*. The time is very short." His was not a nature, anyhow, that could heed a warning. He could not kneel. Upright and unflinching, he went to meet things as they came, reckless, unwise, but certainly not afraid. And this characteristic operated now. He ran to meet Death full tilt in the uncharted spaces that lay behind the stars. With love for a companion now, he raced, his speed increasing from day to day, she, as he thought, knowing merely that he sought her, but had not guessed his darker secret that was now his *lesser* secret.

And in the desert, this afternoon of the picnic, the great thing he sped to meet had shown itself with its familiar touch of appalling cold and shadow, familiar, because all minds know of and accept it; appalling because, until realized close, and with the mental power at the full, it remains but a name the heart refuses to believe in. And he had discovered that its name was – Life.

Rivers had seen the Wave that sweeps incessant, tireless, but as a rule invisible, round the great curve of the bulging earth, brushing the nations into the deeps behind. It had followed him home to the streets and houses of Helouan. He saw it *now*, as he leaned from his window, dim and immense, too huge to break. Its beauty was nameless, undecipherable. His coughing echoed back from the wall of its great sides.... And the music floated up at the same time from the ballroom in the opposite wing. The two sounds mingled. Life, which is love, and Death, which is their unchanging partner, held hands beneath the stars.

He leaned out farther to drink in the cool, sweet air. Soon, on this air, his body would be dust, driven, perhaps, against her very cheek, trodden on possibly by her little foot – until, in turn, she joined him too, blown by the same wind loose about the desert. True. Yet at the same time they would always be together, always somewhere side by side, continuing in the vast universe, *alive*. This new, absolute conviction was in him now. He remembered the curious, sweet perfume in the desert, as of flowers, where yet no flowers are. It was the perfume of life. But in the desert there is no life. Living things that grow and move and utter, are but a protest against death. In the desert they are unnecessary, because death there *is* not. Its overwhelming vitality needs no insolent, visible proof, no protest, no challenge, no little signs of life. The message of the desert is immortality.

He went finally to bed, just before midnight. Hovering magnificently just outside his window, Death watched him while he slept. The wave crept to the level of his eyes. He called her name.

And downstairs, meanwhile, the girl, knowing nothing, wondered where he was, wondered unhappily and restlessly; more – though this she did not understand – wondered motheringly. Until today, on the ride home, and from their singular conversation together, she had guessed nothing of his reason for being at Helouan, where so many come in order to find life. She only knew her own. And she was but twenty-five.

Then, in the desert, when that touch of unearthly chill had stolen out of the sand towards sunset, she had realized clearly, astonished she had not seen it long ago, that this man loved her, yet that something prevented his obeying the great impulse. In the life of Paul Rivers, whose presence had profoundly stirred her heart the first time she saw him, there was some obstacle that held him back, a barrier his honour must respect. He could never tell her of his love. It could lead to nothing. Knowing that he was not married, her intuition failed her utterly at first. Then, in their silence on the homeward ride, the truth had somehow pressed up and touched her with its hand of ice. In that disjointed conversation at the end, which reads as it sounded, as though no coherent meaning lay behind the words, and as though both sought to conceal by speech what yet both burned to utter, she had divined his darker secret, and knew that it was the same as her own. She understood then it was Death that had tracked them from the desert, following with its gigantic shadow from the sandy wastes. The cold, the darkness, the silence which cannot answer, the stupendous mystery which is the spell of its inscrutable Presence, had risen about them in the dusk, and kept them company at a little distance, until the lights of Helouan had bade it halt. Life which may not, cannot end, had frightened her.

His time, perhaps, was even shorter than her own. None knew his secret, since he was alone in Egypt and was caring for himself. Similarly, since she bravely kept her terror to herself, her mother had no inkling of her own, aware merely that the disease was in her system and that her orders were to be extremely cautious. This couple, therefore, shared secretly together the two clearest glimpses of eternity life has to offer to the soul. Side by side they looked into the splendid eyes of Love and Death. Life, moreover, with its instinct for simple and terrific drama, had produced this majestic climax, breaking with pathos, at the very moment when it could not be developed – this side of the stars. They stood together upon the stage, a stage emptied of other human players; the audience had gone home and the lights were being lowered; no music sounded; the critics were a-bed. In this great game of Consequences it was known where he met her, what he said and what she answered, possibly what they did and even what the world thought. But "what the consequence was" would remain unknown, untold. That would happen in the big spaces of which the desert in its silence, its motionless serenity, its shelterless, intolerable vastness, is the perfect symbol. And the desert gives no answer. It sounds no challenge, for it is complete. Life in the desert makes no sign. It *is*.

IV

In the hotel that night there arrived by chance a famous International dancer, whose dahabîyeh lay anchored at San Giovanni, in the Nile below Helouan; and this woman, with her party, had come to dine and take part in the festivities. The news spread. After twelve the lights were lowered, and while the moonlight flooded the terraces, streaming past pillar and colonnade, she rendered in the shadowed halls the music of the Masters, interpreting with an instinctive genius messages which are eternal and divine.

Among the crowd of enthralled and delighted guests, the girl sat on the steps and watched her. The rhythmical interpretation held a power that seemed, in a sense, inspired; there lay in it a certain unconscious something that was pure, unearthly; something that the stars, wheeling in stately movements over the sea and desert know; something the great winds bring to mountains where they play together; something the forests capture and fix magically into their gathering of big and little branches. It was both passionate and spiritual, wild and tender, intensely human and seductively non-human. For it was original, taught of Nature, a revelation of naked, unhampered life. It comforted, as the desert comforts. It brought the desert awe into the stuffy corridors of the hotel, with the moonlight and the whispering of stars, yet behind it ever the silence of those grey, mysterious, interminable spaces which utter to themselves the wordless song of life. For it was the same dim thing, she felt, that had followed her from the desert several hours before, halting just outside the streets and houses as though blocked from further advance; the thing that had stopped her foolish painting, skilled though she was, because it hides behind colour and not in it; the thing that veiled the meaning in the cryptic sentences she and he had stammered out together; the thing, in a word, as near as she could approach it by any means of interior expression, that the realisation of death for the first time makes comprehensible – Immortality. It was unutterable, but it *was*. He and she were indissolubly together. Death was no separation. There was no death…. It was terrible. It was – she had already used the word – awful, full of awe.

"In the desert," thought whispered, as she watched spellbound, "it is impossible even to conceive of death. The idea is meaningless. It simply is not."

The music and the movement filled the air with life which, being there, must continue always, and continuing always can have never had a beginning. Death, therefore, was the great revealer of life. Without it none could realize that they are alive. Others had discovered this before her, but she did not know it. In the desert no one can realize death: it is hope and life that are the only certainty. The entire conception of the Egyptian system was based on this – the conviction, sure and glorious, of life's endless continuation. Their tombs and temples, their pyramids and sphinxes surviving after thousands of years, defy the passage of time and laugh at death; the very bodies of their priests and kings, of their animals even, their fish, their insects, stand today as symbols of their stalwart knowledge.

And this girl, as she listened to the music and watched the inspired dancing, remembered it. The message poured into her from many sides, though the desert brought it clearest. With death peering into her face a few short weeks ahead, she thought instead of – life. The desert, as it were, became for her a little fragment of eternity, focused into an intelligible point for her mind to rest upon with comfort and comprehension. Her steady, thoughtful nature stirred towards an objective far beyond the small enclosure of one narrow lifetime.

The scale of the desert stretched her to the grandeur of its own imperial meaning, its divine repose, its unassailable and everlasting majesty. She looked beyond the wall.

Eternity! That which is endless; without pause, without beginning, without divisions or boundaries. The fluttering of her brave yet frightened spirit ceased, aware with awe of its own everlastingness. The swiftest motion produces the effect of immobility; excessive light is darkness; size, run loose into enormity, is the same as the minutely tiny. Similarly, in the desert, life, too overwhelming and terrific to know limit or confinement, lies undetailed and stupendous, still as deity, a revelation of nothingness because it is all. Turned golden beneath its spell that the music and the rhythm made even more comprehensible, the soul in her, already lying beneath the shadow of the great wave, sank into rest and peace, too certain of itself to fear. And panic fled away. "I am immortal…because I *am*. And what I love is not apart from me. It is myself. We are together endlessly because we *are*."

Yet in reality, though the big desert brought this, it was Love, which, being of similar parentage, interpreted its vast meaning to her little heart – that sudden love which, without a word of preface or explanation, had come to her a short three weeks before…. She went up to her room soon after midnight, abruptly, unexpectedly stricken. Someone, it seemed, had called her name. She passed his door.

The lights had been turned up. The clamour of praise was loud round the figure of the weary dancer as she left in a carriage for her dahabîyeh on the Nile. A low wind whistled round the walls of the great hotel, blowing chill and bitter between the pillars of the colonnades. The girl heard the voices float up to her through the night, and once more, behind the confused sound of the many, she heard her own name called, but more faintly than before, and from very far away. It came through the spaces beyond her open window; it died away again; then – but for the sighing of that bitter wind – silence, the deep silence of the desert.

And these two, Paul Rivers and the girl, between them merely a floor of that stone that built the Pyramids, lay a few moments before the Wave of Sleep engulfed them. And, while they slept, two shadowy forms hovered above the roof of the quiet hotel, melting presently into one, as dreams stole down from the desert and the stars. Immortality whispered to them. On either side rose Life and Death, towering in splendour. Love, joining their spreading wings, fused the gigantic outlines into one. The figures grew smaller, comprehensible. They entered the little windows. Above the beds they paused a moment, watching, waiting, and then, like a wave that is just about to break, they stooped.

And in the brilliant Egyptian sunlight of the morning, as she went downstairs, she passed his door again. She had awakened, but he slept on. He had preceded her. It was next day she learned his room was vacant…. Within the month she joined him, and within the year the cool north wind that sweetens Lower Egypt from the sea blew the dust across the desert as before. It is the dust of kings, of queens, of priests, princesses, lovers. It is the dust no earthly power can annihilate. It, too, lasts forever. There was a little more of it…the desert's message slightly added to: Immortality.

The End of the World

Simon Newcomb

"MARS IS SIGNALLING a dark star."

The world to which this news was flashed from the Central Observatory on the Himalayas had long been dull and stagnant. Almost every scientific discovery had been made thousands of years before, and the inventions for their application had been so perfected that it seemed as if no real improvement could be made in them. Methods of conducting human affairs had been brought into such good shape that everything went on as by machinery. Successive Defenders of the Peace of the World had built up a code of international law so complete that every question at issue between nations was settled by its principles. The only history of great interest was that of a savage time, lying far back in the mists of antiquity, when men fought and killed each other in war. The daily newspapers chronicled little but births, marriages, deaths, and the weather reports. They would not publish what was not worth talking about, and a subscriber often found at his door a paper containing little more than the simple announcement, on an otherwise blank page, "Nothing worthy of note has happened since our last issue." Only one language was spoken the world over, and all gentlemen dined in blue coats with gilt buttons, and wore white neckties with red borders. Even China, the most distant nation of all, had fallen into line several thousand years before, and lived like the rest of the world.

To find a time of real excitement it was necessary to go back three thousand years, when messages had first been successfully interchanged with the inhabitants of Mars. To send a signal which they could see required a square mile of concentrated light as bright as the sun, and experiments extending through thousands of years had been necessary before this result could be brought about by any manageable apparatus. Signals from the plains of Siberia had been made nightly during two or three oppositions of the planet, without any answer being received. Then the world was electrified by hearing that return signals could be seen flashing in such a way that no doubt could exist about them. Their interpretation required more study than was ever expended by out archaeologists on a Moabite inscription. When success was at last reached, it became evident by a careful comparison of the records that the people of Mars were more successful watchers of the stars than we were ourselves. It was found that a row of four lights diminishing in intensity from one end to the other, and pointing in one direction, meant that a new star was showing itself in that direction. Some object of this sort had been seen every two or three years from the earliest historical times, but in recent times a star had often been signalled from Mars before even the sensitive photographic plates and keen eyes of our Himalayan astronomers had discerned it.

Ordinary comets were plentiful enough. More than twenty-five thousand had been recorded, and the number was still increasing every year. But dark stars were so rare that not one had appeared for three centuries, and only about twenty had been recorded in astronomical history. They differed from comets in not belonging to the solar system, but coming from far distant regions among the stars, and in being comparatively dark in colour, with very short tails, or perhaps none at all. They were found to be dark bodies whose origin and destination were alike unknown, each pursuing its own way through the immeasurable abysses of space. It had been found that a certain arrangement of five lights in the form of a cross on the planet meant that one of these bodies was flying through or past our system, and the head of the cross showed the direction in which it was to be looked for.

After a dozen generations of men had passed away without seeing a body of this kind, it goes without saying that the news from Mars of a coming dark star excited universal interest. Where is it? What does it mean? What is a dark star? The Himalayan astronomers were nearly buried under telegrams asking these and other questions without numbers. They could only reply that they had not yet succeeded in finding the object, but that the constellation to which the signal pointed was the head of the Dragon.

There was no likelihood that the object was yet visible, even through powerful telescopes, but this did not prevent the family telescope being brought out in every dwelling in the world, in order to scour the heavens for the new star. For some time it evaded the scrutiny even of the Himalayan astronomers. When a week had passed and it had not been sighted, men began to ask whether there was not some mistake in interpreting the signal, and whether it could be possible that the telescopes of another planet were as much better than ours as this failure would seem to indicate. The conviction began to gain ground that the signal had been misinterpreted, and that there was no dark star or anything else unusual coming. But when interest in the subject had about died away, it was suddenly renewed by the announcement that the object had been photographed very near where the signals had indicated it. It was about halfway between the head of the Dragon and the constellation Lyra, moving very slowly toward the east and south.

The problem now was to determine the orbit of the new star, and for this purpose the astronomers began to make the most accurate observations possible. Owing to the slowness of the motion, several days, perhaps two weeks would be required. While waiting for more news curiosity was excited by a new announcement:

"Mars appears to be in a state of extraordinary excitement. The five signal lights which have been seen from time to time ever since the dark star appeared are flashing in a way never before recorded. We cannot imagine what it means."

Our world could only ask, "What can it mean?" and wait patiently.

The astronomers were much puzzled about the orbit, and a month passed before they could reach a decision on the subject. Then Himalaya sent out an announcement more startling than any that had preceded it:

"The dark star has no orbit. It is falling straight toward the sun with a speed that has already reached thirty kilometres a second, and which is continually increasing as it falls. It will reach the sun in about 210 days."

The first man to see the possibilities suggested by this announcement was the Professor of Physics. Although all the scientific discoveries had probably been made, a single great physical laboratory had been established in which experiments were conducted with a faint hope of something new being learned. The laboratory was placed near the southern end of a peninsula, the site of one of the greatest cities of the ancient world, known as Neeork, the ruins of which, buried ages before by an earthquake, were known to extend over many square miles. To the north now stood the city of Hattan, the mighty city of the world, whose well-paved streets, massive buildings, public institutions, and lofty towers extended a day's journey to the north and west, whose wealth was fabulous, and whose sights every man in the world wanted to see at least once during his lifetime. Most of the investigations to which the laboratory was devoted had to be carried on where the temperature was the same from one year's end to another. To bring about this result an immense vault hundreds of yards in extent had been excavated at a depth of more than a hundred feet under the ground. Here was stored what one might suppose to be every piece of apparatus that human ingenuity had invented for making physical researches, and every instrument that men could make use of.

Of course the Professor of Physics, like all the rest of the world, heard that a dark star was going to fall into the sun. His proceedings after this announcement would have excited curiosity had it not been that the thoughts of men were too much occupied with the celestial visitor to notice his doings. He proceeded to supplement his immense stock of physical apparatus by a kind of supplies never before known to form the outfit of a laboratory. These consisted of flout, fresh wheat, edibles of every kind, and a supply of the seeds of almost every plant known to Botany. The few people who noticed what he was doing gave the subject no attention, supposing that he was merely extending his experiments into the vegetable kingdom. Having got his supplies all stored away, he called his assistants around him.

"I have something to say to you, and the first condition I impose is that it must be kept an absolute secret. Those who are not willing to pledge themselves to secrecy will please retire."

None retired.

"Will you all hold up your right hands in evidence of your adherence to the pledge which I exact from you?"

All did so.

"Now let me tell you what none but ourselves must hear. You all know that from the beginning of recorded history stars supposed to be new have from time to time blazed out in the heavens. The scientific men know that these stars were not really new. They were simply commonplace stars which, through the action of some cause that no one has yet brought to light, suddenly increased their heat and light thousands of times. Then, in the course of a few months, they faded away into their former insignificance, or rather, perhaps, turned into nebulae.

"We have also known that dark bodies many times larger than the earth are flying through space like the stars themselves. Now, my theory is that if one of these objects chances to strike a star it bursts through its outer envelope and sets free the enormous fires pent up within, which burst forth in all their fury.

"Next December one of these objects is going to fall into our sun. Now I do not want to frighten you unnecessarily, but I think we may as well look this matter in the face. If my theory is correct, the light and heat of the sun will be suddenly increased thousands of times. Should this result follow, can there be any doubt as to the consequences? The whole surface of the earth will be exposed to a radiation as intense as that in the focus of a burning glass, which you all know, will not only set fire to wood, but melt iron and crumble stone. The flood of heat will destroy all the works of man and every living being that exists upon the earth. The polar regions alone will be exempt from the radiation, because the sun will not be shining on them at the time of the collision. But they will be visited by such a flood of hot air and steam that their fate can hardly be different from that of the rest of the world.

"Under such circumstances I do not know what to do. For the present I shall merely hope that my theory is all wrong. At the same time I invite you to be in readiness to bring your wives and families here at the critical moment, so that we can all take refuge in our vaults. If nothing occurs, well and good. Nobody need know what we have planned. It is not likely that we shall feel it worthwhile to live if the rest of the world is destroyed. But we cannot decide that question until we face it. Keep in readiness and say nothing, that is all I have to advise for the present."

During the month that followed the Professor was very much perplexed as to whether he should make his fears known. Against doing this was the consideration that the world could not help itself, and it had better go onto the last moment in ignorance of what was coming. Physicians make it a point of honour not to inform their patient that he has a fatal illness, why should the race be apprised of its inevitable doom? The mental suffering endured in the meantime would be useless, no matter whether they were saved or lost. Why make them suffer to no purpose?

But in spite of this reticence on his part, the world was much concerned, especially by the signals from Mars. These, instead of ceasing as always before, after one or two nights, now flashed out incessantly night after night. The Martians must be trying to tell us something of unprecedented importance. What could it be? The Professor of Physics was loudly called upon to know if there was not really some danger from the dark comet falling into the sun. The calls became so pressing that he was forced to make some sort of reply.

"While it is impossible to state with certainty the effect that will be produced by the fall of the dark star into the sun, it is only right to say that it may possibly be followed by an increase in the sun's radiation, which will have reached its height in two or three days, and may continue abnormally great for some weeks. It will therefore be prudent to guard against the possible consequences of an increase in the sun's heat. The roofs of houses, and all combustible objects exposed to the sun's rays, should, as far as possible, be protected by a non-combustible covering. Food and clothing liable to be damaged by the heat should be protected by being stored in cellars."

The Professor of Logic in the University of Hattan put all the data bearing on the subject into equations which he proceeded to solve, and then announced his judgment on the view of the Professor of Physics.

"Ten thousand years of recorded experience has led to the conclusion that the sun is one of the most stable bodies in the universe. During all the years through which meteorological records have extended there has not been a change of a single degree in the annual amount of heat radiated to the earth. In favour of the view that a sudden change will be produced by any cause whatever we have only doubtful physical theory, sustained by no experience whatever. It is, therefore, not logical to be frightened by the prediction of the Professor of Physics, especially when he is himself in doubt about the correctness of his own view. Yet, in view of the magnitude of the interests involved, the prudence of the suggestion made by the Professor cannot be questioned. No harm can be done by taking every possible precaution."

A torrent of dispatches now poured down upon the Professor of Physics from every part of the world wanting to know whether his mathematical theory of the case was really well grounded. After all, was not the Professor of Logic right, and was it not unreasonable to suppose that an order of things which had continued probably, for millions of years should be so suddenly changed? He could only reply that his theory had never been verified in any known case. He was glad to find his view in doubt. The main fact on which it was based – that the new stars which blazed up every few years were not new, but old stars which had suddenly burst out from some inscrutable cause – he purposely kept in the background.

While this discussion was going on, the terrible object which was darting toward our sun remained for some time invisible in every telescope but the great one of the Himalayas. In a few weeks, however, growing brighter as it came nearer the sun, it could be seen in smaller and smaller telescopes, and at last was clearly made out by every watcher of the heavens. Two months before its occurrence the time of the catastrophe was predicted to a minute by the Himalayan astronomers. It would be in the afternoon of December 12th, after the sun had set in Europe, and while it was still shining on all but the northeastern portion of the American continent and on most of the Pacific Ocean. The sun would have set to regions as far east as Labrador, and would be about an hour high on the middle portions of the Atlantic coast. The star was followed night after night with constantly increasing concern. As each evening approached, men indulged in a vain hope that the black star might prove a phantom – some ghost of the sky which would disappear never again to be seen. But this impression was always dispelled when night came on, and the telescope was pointed. The idea of an illusion vanished entirely when the object became visible to the naked eye, and was seen night after night without any telescope at all.

Every night it was a very little brighter than the night before. Yet there was nothing in the object itself that would excite alarm. Even in the most superstitious age of the world people might never have noticed it, or, if they had, would only have wondered how the star happened to be there when it had not before been seen. Now, however, the very slowness of the increase inflicted a slow torture upon the whole human race, like that experienced by a Chinese prisoner whose shaved head is made to feel the slow dropping of water. What is hardly noticeable at first gets further and further beyond the limit of endurance. The slowness with which the light of the star increased only lengthened the torture. Men could scarcely pursue their daily vocations. Notes went to protest on a scale that threatened universal bankruptcy. When December approached it was seen that the fall toward the sun was becoming more rapid, and that the increase in brightness was going on at a greater and still greater rate. Formerly the star had been seen only at night. Now the weird object, constantly growing larger, could be seen in full daylight, like some dragon in the sky.

As December approached the thoughts and sentiments of their remote ancestors, which had been absent for untold ages, were revived in the minds of men. They had long worshipped the invisible, beneficent, and all-pervading Power which informed the universe and breathed into its atoms the breath of life. Now this power became a remorseless Judge, about to punish the men of the present for the sins of ancestors during all time.

December forced its way in, and now the days were counted. Eleven days – ten – tomorrow nine only will elapse before the fate of the world will be decided. It required nerve to face the star; men shut their eyes to it, as if the unseen were non-existent. Those who dared to point the telescope saw it look as large as the moon to the naked eye. But the mild and serene aspect of our satellite was not there – only a fierce glow, as that of the eye of a beast of prey.

Seven days – six days – five days – fiercer glowed the eye which in waking hours belonged to a being breathing naught but vengeance. Even in sleep men still in imagination saw the eye and felt such terrors as might be inspired by the chase of malignant and pitiless demons of the bottomless pit. They lived over again the lives of their ancestors who had been chased by wild beasts.

Three days – two days – reason began to leave its seat. The insane rushed madly about, but the guardians of the peace heeded them not. In the streets men glared into each other's eyes, but no word was necessary to express the thought.

The last day dawns: tonight – what? Calm and still was the morning; mildly as ever shone the sun, all unconscious of the enemy ready to strike him. His unconcern seemed to calm the minds of men, as if he meant to assure them that nothing was to happen. They plucked up courage to look with eye and telescope. The sun, unmoved as ever, advanced toward the west, the hours were counted – now the minutes.

At every telescope some watcher found the nerve to see what would happen. Every minute the malignant eye grew brighter and glared more fiercely; every minute it could be seen nearer the sun. A shudder spread over the whole city of Hattan as the object seemed to touch the sun's disc. A moment of relief followed when it disappeared without giving any sign. Perhaps, under the fervent heat of the sun, the star had dissolved into the air. But this hope was speedily dashed by its reappearance as a black spot on the sun, slowly passing along its face. Those who considered the case now knew that we were merely looking at the object as seen between us and the sun, and that it had not yet fallen into the latter. For a moment there was a vague hope that the computations of the astronomers had, for the first time in history, led them astray, and that the black object would continue its course over the sun, to leave it again like the planet Mercury or Venus during a transit. But this illusion was dispelled when the dark object disappeared in a moment and its place was taken by an effulgence of such intensity that, notwithstanding the darkness of the glass through which the sun was being viewed, the eyes of the lookers-on were dazzled with the brightness.

No telescope was necessary to see what followed. Looking with the naked eye through a dark-glass a spot many times brighter than the rest of the sun was seen where the black object had just disappeared. Every minute it grew larger and brighter. In half an hour this effulgence, continually increasing and extending, was seen to project away from the sun like a fan or the tail of a comet. An unearthly glow spread over the whole landscape, in the light of which pebbles glistened like diamonds. By the time the sun had set in the eastern states its size seemed to be doubled and its brightness to have increased fourfold. Before it set on the Pacific coast the light and heat became so intense that everyone had to seek the shade.

The setting of the sun afforded a respite for the night. But no sooner had it grown dark than a portentous result was seen in the heavens. It happened that Mars, in opposition, had just risen in the east, while Venus, as the evening star, was seen in the west. These objects both glowed – Venus like an electric light, Mars like a burning coal. Everyone knew the cause. Shining by the reflected light of the sun, their brightness increased in the same proportion as the sunlight. It was like seeing a landscape by the light of some invisible conflagration. Its very suggestiveness added a new terror. The beholders could imagine what results were being produced on other continents by the rapidly increasing conflagration, and awaited in calm despair the result when our central luminary should again come around to our longitude.

The earth, continuing its revolution, exposed the oceans and continents in succession to the burning rays. When the sun set at San Francisco the heat was still not unbearable. But from Asia and Europe came the most portentous news through the period of what, for them, was day, while on the American continent it was night. In China and India men could only remain out of doors a few minutes at a time. In the afternoon all had to flee from the heat and take refuge in their houses.

Yet worse was the case of Europe. For a time detailed dispatches came from London. The telegraph offices had all been removed to the cellars of the buildings in which they were located, and men were trying to store everything combustible where the sun's rays could not reach it. Every fire engine in the city was called out to sprinkle the roofs of the houses. Notwithstanding these precautions, at eleven o'clock a roof in Cheapside took fire, and soon after fires broke out here and there in nearly every quarter. By noon the whole city seemed to be in flames, the firemen fighting heat above them and around them. It would soon become impossible for a human being to live in the streets.

A few minutes later came the news that sudden relief had been experienced. A violent gale came in from the Atlantic, bringing with it a torrent of rain, which, for the time being, extinguished the flames. But a new horror was now added. The wind increased to a hurricane of unexampled force. Houses were everywhere blown down and roofs were flying in mid-air, exposing everything in the interior to the flood of water.

About 3 p.m. it was announced that the sun, having dissolved the clouds with its fervent heat, had again shone forth hotter than ever, and that the telegraph offices would soon have to be abandoned. Not another word was heard from the European side until night. Then it was announced that the heat had again been followed by a torrent of rain, and that, the sun having set, another respite had been obtained. The damage done was incalculable and the loss of life frightful, yet hope would have survived had it not been for what might be expected on the morrow.

The American continent, forewarned, undertook the most vigorous defence possible. Before the sun rose every fire engine in Hattan was in place ready for action. Everything combustible in the city was covered with woollen cloth and sprinkled with water. The possibility of doing something occupied all minds, and after the sun rose men fought the heat with the courage of despair. Fiercely though the sun poured down its flood of fire, an engine was ready to extinguish the flames wherever they burst forth. As in Europe, they were soon aided by floods of rain. Thus passed the day, while the sun shed a fiercer heat with every passing hour.

The scene while the sun was setting filled all minds with despair. The size of our luminary was multiplied so many times that it was an hour after the lower edge touched the horizon before the upper edge had set. When it finally disappeared the place of twilight was taken by a lurid illumination of the whole heavens, which still left the evening brighter than an ordinary day. Cosmic flames millions of miles in extent, rising from the sun, still appeared above the horizon from time to time. Even at midnight a sort of aurora, ten times brighter than any that had ever been recorded, seemed to spread over the sky in rising sheets of fiery vapor, which disappeared at the zenith. The trained eye of the Professor of Physics watched the scene from the iron door of his vault. He knew the cause. The exploded sun was sending forth its ions with a velocity almost comparable with that of light to every part of the solar system. In the midst of the illumination the planet Mars could still be seen glowing with supernatural brightness, but no word came from the Himalayan Observatory as to any signals it might be sending to us. Communication from other continents had entirely ceased, and the inhabitants of the whole American continent awaited the coming of what they knew must be the last day.

After midnight, although the ions were flying thicker than ever, a supernatural light seemed to spread over the landscape. The very contrast to what was expected to come in the morning added to the depression and terror. If any vain hope was entertained that the sun might, during its course over the Pacific Ocean and Asia, abate some of its fiery stream, it was dispelled when, shortly after three o'clock, the first sign of the approaching luminary was seen in the east. Still thicker the ions flew, as a bright radiance, far exceeding that of the evening before, heralded the approach of what had always been considered the great luminary, but was now the great engine of destruction. Brighter and brighter grew the eastern horizon, until, long before the actual sun appeared above it, the eye could no longer endure the dazzling blaze. When, and hour later, the sun itself appeared, its rays struck the continent like a fiery flood. As they advanced from the Atlantic to the Pacific everything combustible which they struck burst into flame, stones crumbled by the heat, towers and steeples fell as if shaken by an earthquake. Men had to take refuge in caves or cellars or beneath any covering which could protect them from the fierce heat. Old and young, rich and poor, male and female, crowded together in the confusion of despair. The great magnates of commerce and industry, whose names were everywhere familiar as household words, on whose wealth and power all the millions that inhabited the continent had looked with envy or admiration, were now huddled with their liveried servants beneath the ruins of falling houses, in the cellars of their own homes, in the vaults of their banks, of under any shelter which could protect them from the burning of a thousand sins.

The Professor of Physics, with his assistants, could only look through a crevice in the covering of his vault and see the fiery radiance which was coming from the east. When the covering grew so hot that he felt refuge must soon be taken in the lowest vaults, the sun was suddenly cut off by a rising cloud of blackness coming in from the Atlantic. The whole ocean was boiling like a pot, and the rising steam was carried over the land by a gale produced by the expansion of the air over the ocean. Moving with inconceivable velocity, the gale passed over the continent, sweeping before it every vestige of human work that stood in its path. Even the stones of the buildings, cracked and pulverized by the heat, were now blown through the air like dust, and, churned with the rain, buried the land under a torrent of mud. The lightning played incessantly everywhere, and, if it did not destroy every being exposed to it, it was only because no living beings survived where it struck. Constantly thickening and darkening clouds poured down their storm of rain upon the ruins. But no relief was thus afforded to the mass of cringing humanity which remained protected in vaults and cellars. The falling flood was boiling hot, scalding to death everyone upon whom it fell. It poured through cracks and crevices, flooding cellars, saturating the ruins of buildings, and if a living being remained it scalded him to death.

The Professor and his official family were, for the time being, saved from destruction by the construction of their subterranean chambers. The head and the wind had effaced every structure at the mouth of the cave, and driven them into the lowest recess of their vaults. Against the iron doors which walled them in the flood pressed like the water against the compartments of a ship riven in two by a collision. The doors burned the hand that touched them, but the boiling water leaked through only in small streams.

The few survivors of the human race here huddled together could only envy their more fortunate fellow men who, in the sleep of death, had escaped such an imprisonment as they now suffered. Had the question of continuing to survive been put to a vote, all would have answered it in the negative. Hope was gone, and speedy death was the best that could be prayed for. Only the conscience which had been implanted in the race through long ages prohibited their taking their own lives. They had provisions for two years, and might, therefore, survive during that period, if the supply of air and oxygen should hold out. For producing the latter both material and apparatus existed in the vaults. The reflection that such was the case was painful rather than pleasurable. While they did not have the nerve to let themselves be smothered to death, they felt that the devices for prolonging their lives, to which instinct compelled them to resort, could only be the means of continuing their torture. Electric light they had in abundance, but by day or night nothing could be done. They were in the regions of eternal night except when they chose to turn on the current. From time to time one or another, moved more by the necessity of doing something than by any real object, examined the doors of the cave to see what changes might have taken place in the pressure of the water against them. Long after the latter had ceased to trickle through the cracks the doors continued hot, but as time passed – they could not say whether days, weeks, or months – they found the doors growing cooler.

They at length ventured to open them. A sea of mud, knee-deep, but not quite at a scalding temperature, was found in the passages outside of them. Through this they were at length able to wade, and in time made their way to the open air. Emerging, it was impossible to say whether it was day or night. The illumination was brighter than anything ever known in the brightest day, yet no sun could be seen in the sky. The latter seemed filled with a nebulous mass of light through and over which the clouds of ions were still streaming like waves of fire. The temperature was barely endurable, but it was no worse than the stifling closeness of their subterranean abode.

The first effect of the outer air was to produce an impression as of waking from a dream. But a glance over the landscape dispelled this impression in a moment. What they saw must be reality, though awful beyond conception. Vainly their eyes looked for the great city. No city, not even a ruin was there. They longed in vain for human help; not an animated being was in sight. Every vestige of man and his works – it might even be said every vestige of the work of Nature was gone. On three sides were what seemed great rivers of slime, while, toward the north, the region which had swarmed with the life and activity of the great world-centre was a flat surface of dried clay, black sand, or steaming mud, in which not even an insect crawled. In the thick and vaporous air not a bird warbled its note. To return to their dungeons was like a prisoner returning to his cell. Farther they must go in a search for some familiar object or some sign of humanity. Is there no telegraph to send a word of news? No railway on which a train may run? No plough with which the furrow may be turned? No field in which wheat can be sown? These questions were asked in silence; had they been asked aloud not even an echo would have answered. When the Professor had stored seeds and provisions in his vaults it was with the thought that, if the worst should happen, he and his companions might repopulate the earth. But now every such prospect dissolved away.

As their strength ebbed, a holy calm spread over the souls of all. The Professor found words:

"Such is the course of evolution. The sun, which for millions of years gave light and heat to our system and supported life on the earth, was about to sink into exhaustion and become a cold and inert mass. Its energy could not be revived, except by such a catastrophe as has occurred. The sun is restored to what it was before there was any earth upon which it could shed its rays, and will in time be ready to run its course anew. In order that a race may be renewed it must die like an individual. Untold ages must once more elapse while life is reappearing on earth and developing in higher forms. But to the Power which directs and controls the whole process the ages of humanity are but as days, and it will await in sublime patience the evolution of a new earth and a new order of animated nature, perhaps as far superior to that we have witnessed as ours was to that which preceded it."

The Flaming Horse:
The Story of a Country
where the Sun Never Shines

From Czech fairy tale

THERE WAS ONCE a land that was dreary and dark as the grave, for the sun of heaven never shone upon it. The king of the country had a wonderful horse that had, growing right on his forehead, a flaming sun. In order that his subjects might have the light that is necessary for life, the king had this horse led back and forth from one end of his dark kingdom to the other. Wherever he went his flaming head shone out and it seemed like beautiful day.

Suddenly this wonderful horse disappeared. Heavy darkness that nothing could dispel settled down on the country. Fear spread among the people and soon they were suffering terrible poverty, for they were unable to cultivate the fields or do anything else that would earn them a livelihood. Confusion increased until the king saw that the whole country was likely to perish. In order then, if possible, to save his people, he gathered his army together and set out in search of the missing horse.

Through heavy darkness they groped their way slowly and with difficulty to the far boundaries of the kingdom. At last they reached the ancient forests that bordered the neighbouring state and they saw gleaming through the trees faint rays of the sunshine with which that kingdom was blessed.

Here they came upon a small, lonely cottage which the king entered in order to find out where he was and to ask directions for moving forward.

A man was sitting at the table reading diligently from a large open book. When the king bowed to him, he raised his eyes, returned the greeting, and stood up. His whole appearance showed that he was no ordinary man but a seer.

"I was just reading about you," he said to the king, "that you were gone in search of the flaming horse. Exert yourself no further, for you will never find him. But trust the enterprise to me and I will get him for you."

"If you do that, my man," the king said, "I will pay you royally."

"I seek no reward. Return home at once with your army, for your people need you. Only leave here with me one of your serving men."

The king did exactly as the seer advised and went home at once.

The next day the seer and his man set forth. They journeyed far and long until they had crossed six different countries. Then they went on into the seventh country which was ruled over by three brothers who had married three sisters, the daughters of a witch.

They made their way to the front of the royal palace, where the seer said to his man, "Do you stay here while I go in and find out whether the kings are at home. It is they who stole the flaming horse and the youngest brother rides him."

Then the seer transformed himself into a green bird and flew up to the window of the eldest queen and flitted about and pecked until she opened the window and let him into her chamber. When she let him in, he alighted on her white hand and the queen was as happy as a child.

"You pretty thing!" she said, playing with him. "If my husband were home how pleased he would be! But he's off visiting a third of his kingdom and he won't be home until evening."

Suddenly the old witch came into the room and as soon as she saw the bird she shrieked to her daughter, "Wring the neck of that cursed bird, or it will stain you with blood!"

"Why should it stain me with blood, the dear innocent thing?"

"Dear innocent mischief!" shrieked the witch. "Here, give it to me and I'll wring its neck!"

She tried to catch the bird, but the bird changed itself into a man and was already out of the door before they knew what had become of him.

After that he changed himself again into a green bird and flew up to the window of the second sister. He pecked at it until she opened it and let him in. Then he flitted about her, settling first on one of her white hands, then on the other.

"What a dear bird you are!" cried the queen. "How you would please my husband if he were at home. But he's off visiting two-thirds of his kingdom and he won't be back until tomorrow evening."

At that moment the witch ran into the room and as soon as she saw the bird she shrieked out, "Wring the neck of that wretched bird, or it will stain you with blood!"

"Why should it stain me with blood?" the daughter answered. "The dear innocent thing!"

"Dear innocent mischief!" shrieked the witch. "Here, give it to me and I'll wring its neck!"

She reached out to catch the bird, but in less time than it takes to clap a hand, the bird had changed itself into a man who ran through the door and was gone before they knew where he was.

A moment later he again changed himself into a green bird and flew up to the window of the youngest queen. He flitted about and pecked until she opened the window and let him in. Then he alighted at once on her white hand and this pleased her so much that she laughed like a child and played with him.

"Oh, what a dear bird you are!" she cried. "How you would delight my husband if he were home. But he's off visiting all three parts of his kingdom and he won't be back until the day after tomorrow in the evening."

At that moment the old witch rushed into the room. "Wring the neck of that cursed bird!" she shrieked, "or it will stain you with blood."

"My dear mother," the queen answered, "why should it stain me with blood – beautiful innocent creature that it is?"

"Beautiful innocent mischief!" shrieked the witch. "Here, give it to me and I'll wring its neck!"

But at that moment the bird changed itself into a man, disappeared through the door, and they never saw him again.

The seer knew now where the kings were and when they would come home. So he made his plans accordingly. He ordered his servant to follow him and they set out from the city at a quick pace. They went on until they came to a bridge which the three kings as they came back would have to cross.

The seer and his man hid themselves under the bridge and lay there in wait until evening. As the sun sank behind the mountains, they heard the clatter of hoofs approaching the bridge. It was the eldest king returning home. At the bridge his horse stumbled on a log which the seer had rolled there.

"What scoundrel has thrown a log here?" cried the king angrily.

Instantly the seer leaped out from under the bridge and demanded of the king how he dared to call him a scoundrel. Clamouring for satisfaction he drew his sword and attacked the king. The king, too, drew sword and defended himself, but after a short struggle he fell from his horse dead. The seer bound the dead king to his horse and then with a cut of the whip started the horse homewards.

The seer hid himself again and he and his man lay in wait until the next evening.

On that evening near sunset the second king came riding up to the bridge. When he saw the ground sprinkled with blood, he cried out, "Surely there has been a murder here! Who has dared to commit such a crime in my kingdom!"

At these words the seer leaped out from under the bridge, drew his sword, and shouted, "How dare you insult me? Defend yourself as best you can!"

The king drew, but after a short struggle he, too, yielded up his life to the sword of the seer.

The seer bound the dead king to his horse and with a cut of the whip started the horse homewards.

Then the seer hid himself again under the bridge and he and his man lay there in wait until the third evening.

On the third evening just at sunset the youngest king came galloping home on the flaming steed. He was hurrying fast because he had been delayed. But when he saw red blood at the bridge he stopped short and looked around.

"What audacious villain," he cried, "has dared to kill a man in my kingdom!"

Hardly had he spoken when the seer stood before him with drawn sword demanding satisfaction for the insult of his words.

"I don't know how I've insulted you," the king said, "unless you're the murderer."

When the seer refused to parley, the king, too, drew his sword and defended himself.

To overcome the first two kings had been mere play for the seer, but it was no play this time. They both fought until their swords were broken and still victory was doubtful.

"We shall accomplish nothing with swords," the seer said. "That is plain. I'll tell you what: let us turn ourselves into wheels and start rolling down the hill and the wheel that gets broken let him yield."

"Good!" said the king. "I'll be a cartwheel and you be a lighter wheel."

"No, no," the seer answered quickly. "You be the light wheel and I'll be the cartwheel."

To this the king agreed. So they went up the hill, turned themselves into wheels and started rolling down. The cartwheel went whizzing into the lighter wheel and broke its spokes.

"There!" cried the seer, rising up from the cartwheel. "I am victor!"

"Not so, brother, not so!" said the king, standing before the seer. "You only broke my fingers! Now I tell you what: let us change ourselves into two flames and let the flame that burns up the other be victor. I'll be a red flame and do you be a white one."

"Oh, no," the seer interrupted. "You be the white flame and I'll be the red one."

The king agreed to this. So they went back to the road that led to the bridge, turned themselves into flames, and began burning each other mercilessly. But neither was able to burn up the other.

Suddenly a beggar came down the road, an old man with a long grey beard and a bald head, with a scrip at his side and a heavy staff in his hand.

"Father," the white flame said, "get some water and pour it on the red flame and I'll give you a penny."

But the red flame called out quickly, "Not so, father! Get some water and pour it on the white flame and I'll give you a shilling!"

Now of course the shilling appealed to the beggar more than the penny. So he got some water, poured it on the white flame and that was the end of the king.

The red flame turned into a man who seized the flaming horse by the bridle, mounted him and, after he had rewarded the beggar, called his servant and rode off.

Meanwhile at the royal palace there was deep sorrow for the murdered kings. The halls were draped in black and people came from miles around to gaze at the mutilated bodies of the two elder brothers which the horses had carried home.

The old witch was beside herself with rage. As soon as she had devised a plan whereby she could avenge the murder of her sons-in-law, she took her three daughters under her arm, mounted an iron rake, and sailed off through the air.

The seer and his man had already covered a good part of their journey and were hurrying on over rough mountains and across desert plains, when the servant was taken with a terrible hunger. There wasn't anything in sight that he could eat, not even a wild berry. Then suddenly they came upon an apple tree that was bending beneath a load of ripe fruit. The apples were red and pleasant to the sight and sent out a fragrance that was most inviting.

The servant was delighted. "Glory to God!" he cried. "Now I can feast to my heart's content on these apples!"

He was already running to the tree when the seer called him back.

"Wait! Don't touch them! I will pick them for you myself!"

But instead of picking an apple, the seer drew his sword and struck a mighty blow into the apple tree. Red blood gushed forth.

"Just see, my man! You would have perished if you had eaten one apple. This apple tree is the eldest queen, whom her mother, the witch, placed here for our destruction."

Presently they came to a spring. Its water bubbled up clear as crystal and most tempting to the tired traveller.

"Ah," said the servant, "since we can get nothing better, at least we can take a drink of this good water."

"Wait!" cried the seer. "I will draw some for you."

But instead of drawing water he plunged his naked sword into the middle of the spring. Instantly it was covered with blood and blood began to spurt from the spring in thick streams.

"This is the second queen, whom her mother, the witch, placed here to work our doom."

Presently they came to a rosebush covered with beautiful red roses that scented all the air with their fragrance.

"What beautiful roses!" said the servant. "I have never seen any such in all my life. I'll go pluck a few. As I can't eat or drink, I'll comfort myself with roses."

"Don't dare to pluck them!" cried the seer. "I'll pluck them for you."

With that he cut into the bush with his sword and red blood spurted out as though he had cut a human vein.

"This is the youngest queen," said the seer, "whom her mother, the witch, placed here in the hope of revenging herself on us for the death of her sons-in-law."

After that they proceeded without further adventures.

When they crossed the boundaries of the dark kingdom, the sun in the horse's forehead sent out its blessed rays in all directions. Everything came to life. The earth rejoiced and covered itself with flowers.

The king felt he could never thank the seer enough and he offered him the half of his kingdom.

But the seer replied, "You are the king. Keep on ruling over the whole of your kingdom and let me return to my cottage in peace."

He bade the king farewell and departed.

The Flight of Nikaros

Christopher R. Muscato

"ELDER, WHY DO *you paint the amphorae with Nikaros?"*

The old man leaned back from his work, hands stained with black pigment, and surveyed the little children intruding on his workshop. Had they not learned their histories? They knew the name, that was obvious. They recognized the iconography. And still they asked.

The old man set down his paintbrush.

"Come children, sit, and I will tell you the tale of Nikaros."

Many generations ago, there was an island named Kríti, and its time was coming to an end. Humans had pushed their Mother Earth to her limits and her exhaustion came at terrible cost. Gaia lost patience with humanity. And, like too many places, Kríti would burn.

Among the many who tried to flee Kríti, there was a man. This man had a son. That son's name was Nikos.

"Father, why haven't we left yet?" Nikos pleaded. He watched in horror as the mountains blazed in the distance, so bright it filled the night sky. Nikos's father surveyed the dock. All these people, shuffling from line to line, but none were leaving. No one could penetrate the bureaucratic mess of claiming refugee status, this labyrinth of red tape and paperwork.

"Come," he gestured to his son. There was no hope for them here.

"I don't understand. Why couldn't the people leave?"

"To leave Kríti, another city would have to take them in. And this was nearly impossible. Walls written into law are tougher than any of stone." The old man held up his palm and smashed a fist into it, and the children gasped.

"Then how did they escape the fires of Kríti?"

The old man smiled a knowing smile, and the children leaned in closer.

"Father, shouldn't we be going away from the fires?" Nikos asked as they left the docks.

"The fires will not reach these cliffs for a few weeks, and that will be enough time," his father replied.

"Enough time for what?" Nikos asked. "Where are we going?"

Nikos's father gestured to the cliffside. "My workshop," he said.

Inside the workshop, Nikos's mouth hung open. He had never seen so many wondrous things. Bits of robotics lay strewn across workstations. Blueprints, maps, and models occupied crowded shelves. Screens flashed with data on AI software, on energy harvesting, on weapons and walls. And, oddly enough, dozens of small cages cluttered the walls, doors open, bits of feathers still sticking to the linings inside.

"There are things about me you do not know," Nikos's father said. "Of my life before I came to Kríti."

"Before?" It was enough to make Nikos look away from the distractions around him. "You lived in Athína, didn't you? You never talk about it."

"I did," his father said, pacing with slow, deliberate strides.

Nikos's father explained that he had been tasked with preparing the city for the growing Crisis. But he lost faith in his work, allowing himself to be bribed by the very corporations he once sought to keep out of Athína. Disgraced, he fled. The magistrate of Kríti laughed at the Crisis and welcomed the corporations, envisaging a bellowing bull market under his control. Nikos's father built the magistrate a maze of isolationist policies to protect this monster so that Kríti would not have to share its wealth.

"It worked well. Too well," Nikos's father confessed. "My system was copied all around the world as resources tightened and borders closed. These laws I created are the reason we are now stuck in Kríti, why we have nowhere to go."

Nikos's eyes stung and his cheeks burned.

"Why are you telling me this?" He asked.

"To save you from my mistakes." Nikos's father tapped the screen. "Before I left Athína, I proposed one final solution to save us from the Crisis, one too radical even for that enlightened city."

Nikos's eyes were still stinging, but he could not stop staring as he approached the screen.

"Are those...wings?"

The children in the workshop giggled among themselves. The potter waited for them to quiet, and continued.

The laws of nature are not to be rewritten lightly. But with enough will, and a just cause, it can be done. And so Nikos's father performed on his son a surgery, one forbidden even in Athína. Nikos himself assisted; he had studied under his father for years and was a quick learner. Tissue, muscle, and skin cells were grafted onto reinforced polymer, hair fibers taught to grow into feathers. To offer protection from the harsh sun, these feathers were built for near total albedo. The final gift Nikos's father gave him was the ability to program the color of his feathers, so that his new wings would grow to be beautiful.

While he worked, Nikos's father talked.

"In Athína, I developed a theory," said Nikos's father, "that the Earth is our great host, but humanity has become a dishonorable guest. We battle each other in Gaia's house, we make ourselves a burden on our host, we threaten her very existence. Now, Gaia will never let us know peace. The sun will scorch us, the seas will drown us, the storms will shake our bones from their tombs. This is what our actions have wrought, Nikos. We cannot fight it. We can only flee. That is why I built these wings, why I called this Project Ikaros, to remind us that there can be no harmony with nature."

Finally, the day arrived that Nikos stood free of bandages and medical equipment. He stretched his wings, reveling in the sensation. Then he turned and knocked over his father. It would take time to get used to these new limbs.

Unfortunately, time was not something Nikos possessed. Remember, Kríti was in peril. The flames were upon their doorstep.

"Take this," Nikos's father gave him a data drive containing all his plans and research. Along the cliffs, cinder and ash began to fall. Alarms blared. His father threw some items into a bag, scurrying about the workshop.

"These wings will let you stay ahead of Gaia's wrath, but remain vigilant. Do not fly too low, or the sea will snatch you. Do not fly too far, or the winds will carry you away. And above all, Nikos, fear the sun, Gaia's greatest ally. Your wings will shield you from its arrows, but they will be less effective the higher you fly. I'm sorry I do not have time to give you more lessons. I love you, my son."

Nikos did not understand the tone in his father's voice.

"You are coming with me," he protested. "We are leaving together."

"No, Nikos. Your wings are not strong enough for us both."

Alarms blared as tendrils of smoke crept into the room, snaking under doors and through cracks in the foundations.

"Father, I cannot!"

"Go, Nikos, go!"

And with that, Nikos's father pushed him out of the window. The last thing Nikos saw as he plummeted towards the waves was his father's workshop exploding in flames.

"Did Nikos die?"

"You already know he didn't."

"Shut up! He could have!"

"We wouldn't be here, would we?"

The old potter held up a hand.

"Wait and see."

Nikos did survive (*told ya' so*), but only just. His wings were new and untested. He felt them catch the air and suddenly he was gliding along the base of the cliffs. Flapping his wings, however, was something else entirely. It takes time to learn these things, you know.

He was exhausted by the time he saw a tiny island, no more than a pile of sea-worn rocks poking from the water. He tumbled to the ground, breathing heavily. He was sore, bruised, and weary, but he had done it. He had survived. He had escaped. He had flown.

As he wiped the tears from his eyes, his ears caught a sound. A frantic, scratchy chirping. Nikos looked and discovered a bundle of feathers quivering along the rocky shore.

"What happened to you?" Nikos asked. He reached for the bird, but it squawked and fell deeper into the water. Nikos stepped back. He folded his wings, then removed a handful of berries from the bag his father had given him. The bird took the berries, and Nikos was able to pull it from the water. He could see it better now, the beautiful plumage, the distinct beak, the shine in its eyes. It was a partridge.

"How did a partridge get all the way out here?" he wondered aloud. The bird did not answer, but nuzzled his wings. Nikos named the bird Perdix, and from that day on it remained his companion.

From this tiny island in the sea, Nikos flew to another. And then another. Perdix, whose wings did not permit long flights, remained tucked safely in Nikos's bag. Slowly they made their way towards Athína, the city that once sheltered Nikos's father. Finally, perched atop an ancient olive tree one evening, Nikos could see its glow in the distance.

Nikos lowered his binoculars and looked at Perdix. Something was wrong. He had been to Athína when he was younger, but the city did not glisten as it used to. Floodlights pierced the night sky. There was smoke, and sirens. Security boats patrolled the waters, searchlights reflecting off the metal of their guns. Perdix's feathers ruffled, agitated.

Nikos's mind span. Would people such as these even offer him shelter? He stretched his wings and remembered that the surgery which saved him was forbidden. To them, would he be a miracle, or a monster?

It became clear to him, in that moment, what his father had done. Nikos could never rejoin civilization. He would have to remain forever on the move, as his father wanted.

And so, Nikos did not continue to Athína but turned back into the Aegean.

With no home to return to, Nikos lived as a wanderer, moving between tiny islands poking from the sea. He learned to identify edible plants and roots. He distributed seeds across his islands, tending wild gardens, fostering beds of seaweed, and building lagoons for fish. He pulled trash from the sea so his gardens would grow lush and full, and so that Perdix would not become tangled in discarded fishing nets or snarls of plastic. What couldn't be composted, he built into structures, roosts that would shelter them both. His wings let him stay ahead of the storms and shielded him from the brutal sunlight, and yet he still felt as if were burning from within. His father's choice to banish him from civilization was something he could never forget. Never forgive.

It was in one of his roosts, while he was tinkering with a discarded tidal turbine, that Nikos's work was interrupted by a panicked squawking. Nikos rushed towards the sound and found Perdix tangled in debris along the shoreline. Nikos freed Perdix and frowned.

There was lots of trash today, far more than usual. No wonder the little partridge became tangled, Nikos thought, and he wondered where it all came from.

A thought pierced his mind, and his wings extended anxiously. His eyes traced the line of trash stretching into the sea.

It did not take Nikos long to find the shipwreck, pieces of the hull still bobbing in angry waters. Perdix chirped from Nikos's bag as they searched for survivors. It was night before Nikos saw a glow. A fire, set in a minuscule patch of sand along a vicious rocky outcrop. Shaking from exhaustion after flying for so long, he tumbled to the shore.

But when Nikos stood, shaking sand from his wings, he felt his breath freeze in his chest. On this small beach were crammed dozens of people. He stared, and they stared, an exchange of wide eyes and silence that was only broken when a man near the fire fell to his knees.

"Mercy! Please! I, Xenon, am the captain of a wrecked ship. Arrest me, but spare the others!"

"Help us!"

"Winged soldiers! This is how far Athína will go to keep us out?"

"Mercy! Please!"

Nikos stepped back, horror settling over his face as strangers wailed before him.

"I mean you no harm!" Nikos shouted, more loudly than he intended. He was trembling, from the tips of his fingers to the tips of his wings.

"I mean you no harm," he said again. The voices around him died down. Glances were exchanged, their confusion evident even in the dim light. Xenon stood.

"Who...who are you?" He asked.

"My name is Nikos," Nikos answered. "Of Kríti."

"There is no Kríti," Xenon replied. Nikos nodded.

Others stood, curiosity supplanting their fears as they approached this boy survivor of the burned island and beheld with wonder his beautiful wings.

Nikos learned next that they were hungry, and had to stop them from trying to eat his partridge.

"I have food," he told them. "I will bring it to you."

And that is how Nikos became caretaker of the castaways, flying back and forth between his roosts, bringing them food, fresh water, and supplies to build their own shelters. Nikos learned that they were refugees, not too dissimilar from himself, fleeing their crumbling island of Mýkonos. The ravenous sea, that swelling fist of Gaia's vengeance, had staked a claim on their city. But, as had happened to the people of Kríti, no one could escape by legal means and those who piled onto cramped ships drifted into the night with nowhere to go.

He warned them that he would have to leave when the storms came, and yet he never did. Their faces haunted him. Their fate could well have been his own, and so he continued to fly between his roosts and this island, bringing them supplies. By the end of the day, he would collapse on the sand, tired and often very hungry. He never flew too high or too low, he had guaranteed himself all the olives and figs and fish that his stomach could handle, but it was not enough. His body simply needed more energy.

This did not go unnoticed by the refugees in Nikos's care, and they worried for him.

"You have been given wings, and yet you are bound to us. We are your tether, your cage," Xenon lamented. "If only we had wings like yours."

Nikos ran his hands through Perdix's feathers. "You do not want this burden my father forced upon me. In the eyes of civilization, I have already fallen. There are other ways for you to stay ahead of Gaia's wrath."

Xenon looked out over the sea. His hair rustled in the breeze.

"It is not our desire to escape Gaia," he said. "On Mýkonos, terrible winds blew strong and fierce. But they also kept us cool in summer, and chased away the humidity. We loved them as a gift.

"And speaking of gifts," Xenon pulled something from his tattered cloak. It was a glass bauble in the shape of a partridge, roughly made but beautiful. "We forged this glass from the sands of Mýkonos, all we could take of our island as we fled. Please accept this as a small token of our immense gratitude."

Nikos sputtered his thanks, protesting that it was too much. Xenon only replied that Nikos had been exceptionally generous despite the burden they placed on him. Xenon swore that he and his people would live by this example.

"One day it may be us who find strangers at our doors, human or otherwise." Xenon smiled at Perdix. "And on that day, we will be as gracious hosts as you have been."

"But I am not your host," Nikos said. "This is the house of Gaia. I am a trespasser, fleeing from room to room."

"A thief does not clean the house they are robbing," Xenon asserted. "A trespasser does not tend the gardens. It seems to me that you are not the vandal, but the caretaker. And what does a caretaker have to fear?"

"Failing to fear nature is arrogance," said Nikos. "Ikaros flew on such wings."

"So did Nike," Xenon replied. "Perhaps victory requires a bit of arrogance. What else is faith in our ability to improve?"

Nikos said nothing, but held the bauble up to the fire and watched the fire dance through it. Xenon turned towards the sea, the breeze in his hair.

"Gaia has gifts for us this evening too."

That night, Nikos remained restless. He paced the shore, wings brushing the sand. Perdix hopped beside him. Nikos turned the glass partridge in his hands.

How long had he accepted gifts of gentle rains and nourishing olives, and never thanked his host? Yes, there were storms, as his father warned, but Gaia also provided stable winds that carried his wings, guided currents that brought him fish, filtered the sunlight so it....

Nikos froze. Slowly, he sat, then pulled his tablet from his bag, tapping numbers and equations, scanning through the long-neglected data drive of his father's research. Finally, he set down the tablet. The screen flashed green. Nikos looked at the bauble, then held this gift up to the sky.

"Father," he said aloud. It was the first time he had spoken to his father's memory. "I can no longer bear the weight of my resentment towards you."

Nikos stretched his wings.

"You chose my banishment for me. But you also allowed me to determine what to do with these wings, with your life's work. I am grateful for the lessons you taught me. I am grateful for your mistakes. I am ready to make these wings my own."

A glow on the horizon heralded the dawning of the sun. Nikos raised his wings reflexively to shield himself but then lowered them, and felt the first warmth of the new day upon his face.

It took Nikos a few days to reach the island with the largest and most secure cave, a roost where he had a cached a reclaimed solar-powered water purifier and several jars of grain. He required relatively little else, the technology was mostly inside him, but this would take some time and he wasn't sure the effects it would have. He needed isolation to calm his mind and spirit. Even Perdix remained behind with the refugees. Nikos came alone.

Nikos set up his workstation using electronics he'd rebuilt from salvage. But before he began, he found herbs to burn as incense and thanked the cave for being such a gracious host. Then he opened his tablet and initiated the program.

Two days later, Nikos emerged from the cave. He stumbled, weak, into the Aegean sunlight and expanded his wings. In every fiber of every hair-feather, he felt the sun, not its wrath, but its vitality. He felt restored and laughed, weeping with joy. Then, he thrust his wings down and launched himself into the air.

Faster and faster Nikos flew, spinning over the water, and then up, up, up. Higher, higher, higher. He felt the sun heating his reprogrammed feathers, no longer rejecting the gift of sunlight but absorbing it. He knew it would provide the energy he needed. And it was wonderful.

It was in this moment that Nikos understood where his father had been mistaken. There was a time for youthful arrogance. There was a time to believe that things could be better. There was a time to race towards the Sun, if only one was prepared to harness it.

The old potter turned his vase so the children could fully see the primogenitor of their people, reaching for the Sun. They giggled and jumped in delight, small wings flapping in imitation of the painted figure.

The old potter could have told the children how Nikos arrived in Athína to find a city very much in disarray, but not so much that the appearance of a winged man from the sky didn't cause a significant stir. He could have explained that Nikos realized he held the city's attention. With that attention came power, and he was ready to harness that too. He decided to be neither Ikaros nor Nike to them, but something else. They called him

Nikaros, and listened when he talked about the House of Gaia, the folly of building walls in someone else's home, the honor of the guest and the host.

The old potter could have told the children how Nikaros untangled the labyrinth of his father, how Athína opened its doors to strangers, how Xenon's crew were among the first to enter. Or, how Nikaros did so much good in Athína that this time the request was met with a stamp of approval, and that Xenon's crew were the first to be initiated as Nikaros's disciples.

The old potter could have explained that Athína gave Nikaros funding to build his labs anywhere he desired. When Nikaros finally willed himself to return to Kríti he was surprised to find young olive trees growing firm from the ashes, flocks of partridges nesting around their bases. Nikaros thanked Perdix for his companionship and knew the bird was home. The potter could have explained that it was Nikaros himself who built the largest of the roosts still used by the winged people to this day, Nikaros himself who renamed the island House of the Partridge.

The old potter could even have explained that the winged people remain advocates for Gaia the Host, as well as all who travel her lands, seas, and skies. Our roosts are kept as guesthouses for wanderers, he could have said, for humans and animals and seeds alike, and it is our duty to remember that no one can build a wall in Gaia's House.

But there would be time for these lessons later. The children were becoming restless, little wings twitching closer and closer to the unfinished amphorae in his workshop.

"Alright, come now," he ushered them out. "Our tribe will be migrating soon, and we need to thank the island for hosting us. Go prepare for ceremony."

The children flitted away, and the old potter shook his head, chuckling. But before heading back inside, he paused to stretch his wings, delighting in the warmth of the sun. He felt its energy restore him, and he smiled at the figure on the vase.

"Thank you, great-grandfather."

The Frog Who Swallows the Sun

Joshua Lim

SLOWLY, HASAN CLOSED the door to his uncle's shed.

Frogs don't talk, he reminded himself. *Maybe I've gotten the heatstroke that Pak Kassim was talking about. I've stayed too long under the hot sun, and now I'm imagining things.*

He turned the creaky doorknob and took another peek inside.

"Help me!" cried the white frog in the glass terrarium. "Don't just shut the d—"

Hasan slammed the door shut, heart pounding. *A frog just talked to me!*

It was the third day of the strangest school holidays he had ever known, and it was only getting stranger.

* * *

On the first day of the holidays, Mama had dropped Hasan off to stay with her brother in this rural town in the hill country of Malaysia.

"Don't worry, Lenggong is a nice town," she had said before driving off to her week-long conference. "Your great-grandparents used to live here until they passed away. I'm sure you'll find yourself something interesting to do. And you, Kassim – stop working all the time, spend some time with your nephew!"

Pak Kassim had tried to protest, but she left him coughing in a cloud of exhaust, her car disappearing into the twilight shadows. From his grumblings, Hasan guessed that his uncle hadn't been told he was coming. He didn't seem prepared, anyway – there wasn't much food in the house. In fact there wasn't much of *anything* in the squalid house. Hasan figured that he would have to find something interesting to do outdoors instead.

On the second day, Pak Kassim forbade him from playing outside.

"You can't make me stay indoors all day!" cried Hasan, running after his uncle who was climbing onto his ice cream vendor's motorcycle in the grey light of early dawn, ready to go to work. "I'll be bored out of my mind! There's nothing to do inside the house!"

"Read a book or do some drawing!" Pak Kassim called over his shoulder.

"You don't have any storybooks!"

"There's a motorcycle manual lying around somewhere, check it out!"

"What's wrong with playing outdoors?"

"You wait and see," said Pak Kassim. He pointed at the steadily brightening sky. "Here in Lenggong at this time of the year, the sun is very hot. Not the usual dry season hot – it's VERY VERY VERY HOT. Not suitable for small kids like you to be running around outside."

"I'm not a small kid any more, I'm eleven!"

"The sun doesn't care how old you are! You know what happens to people who stay too long under the hot sun? They get heatstroke! Do you want to get heatstroke?"

It sounded bad, so Hasan shook his head.

The ice cream motorcycle revved to life. Pak Kassim buckled on his helmet and gave one last look at the sullen-faced Hasan.

"I know you're not going to listen to me," he said, sounding defeated. "I bet you're going to run in the hills and climb trees the moment I'm gone. So just remember to stay in the shade as much as possible. The garden shed is smelly, don't go there. And drink lots of water. I don't want to explain to your mother when you get heatstroke!"

"Ok, Pakcik."

It can't be that bad, Hasan thought.

The sun rose – and scorched the earth.

As his uncle lived in a small house on the outskirts of town, Hasan went out the back door and explored the wild, trudging through thick underbrush and overgrown trails, wandering among the hills, watching birds and animals. But around nine o'clock, the glaring sunlight emerged in full force and made Hasan's eyes hurt. Stepping out of the shade made him feel like a satay being slowly charred black over a grill. The heavy air and thick humidity made the sweltering heat unbearable by midmorning, and when he passed by some rambutan trees beside a small stream, he could have sworn he saw the leaves shrivel and turn yellow before his eyes.

The water in the bubbling stream came from the cool springs on the hilltops, but it was warm when it reached the town below. Nevertheless, it provided a little refreshment from the burning air. As he tore off his clothes and wallowed in the shallow brook like a water buffalo, Hasan had to admit that his uncle was right.

It was not the usual hot, nor the dry season hot.

It was VERY VERY VERY HOT.

"What did I tell you?" said Pak Kassim when he arrived home at dusk. "I *told* your mother this was a bad season to visit Lenggong." He took an ice cream from the refrigerator bin of his motorcycle and gave it to Hasan. They ate together on the front steps of the house, enjoying the ice-cold sensation that drove away the suffocating heat of the day.

"Are you allowed to eat your own ice cream?" asked Hasan.

"Technically, this is company property," said Pak Kassim, licking his Cornetto. "But don't worry – my boss isn't losing money. In fact, this hot weather has been great for business!"

They finished their ice cream as the cruel sun went down and the stars came out.

"When will it stop being hot?" asked Hasan.

A slight pause.

"Not anytime soon, I'm afraid," said Pak Kassim.

* * *

Now Hasan stared at the shed door while the world baked around him.

Pak Kassim has a talking frog in his shed.

For the third day of the holidays, he had decided that it was too hot to go exploring. He told his uncle about wallowing in the stream, making Pak Kassim frown. "Can you swim?"

"No, Pakcik."

"Then don't play in the stream. I can't explain to your mother if anything happens."

"It's very shallow!"

"Everyone says the pool of Chankei Waterfall is shallow, yet two kids still managed to drown themselves in it last year. No swimming without my supervision."

With nothing to do at home, no storybook to read nor football to kick around, Hasan had decided to explore around the house instead. And that was how he ended up standing outside his uncle's garden shed, his heart thumping inside his chest and the high-pitched croak of a frog still ringing in his ears.

A real-life talking frog! How? Why?

Idleness and curiosity are dangerous when combined, especially in a boy with too much energy and nowhere to spend it. Hasan threw open the door and strode in.

Inside the shed, everything was haphazardly stacked against the walls – boxes, tools, sacks, a rusty bicycle, all kinds of unrecognizable equipment. But the frog's tank was pressed against the far wall of the shed beside an open window, neatly set apart from everything else.

The little white frog looked up.

"There you are!" it croaked. "Open the tank and let me out, quick!"

Hasan drew near. The terrarium was designed to be a frog's paradise – a nice pool of water, leafy plants and ferns, large overhanging rocks for hiding places, even a cute food bowl. His uncle had clearly been taking good care of the frog.

"You can talk," said Hasan.

"Of course I can, I'm Chankei!" In a few bounds, the frog leapt onto a tall rock ledge near the wire mesh ceiling of the tank. Up close, Hasan could see it clearly – a beautiful frog with smooth white skin bruised horribly with grey, its throat cerulean blue like the noon sky and speckled with little white spots. The frog could have fit comfortably in his palm.

"I need your help, boy. Let me out so that I can swallow the sun!"

"What do you mean, swallow the sun?"

The frog stared with its large black eyes. "You don't know who I am?"

Hasan shook his head.

"I'm Chankei, the queen of all frogs, protector of the world!" The frog croaked a loud *kwaak*, her sky-blue throat ballooning. "When the sun gets too hot, I swallow it, and I release it only when it has learned to behave!"

"Hmm, yes," said Hasan, baffled. "And how would you swallow the sun?"

Chankei opened her mouth, shot out her tongue, pretended to pull something back and then closed her mouth over it. "Like that. But much higher in the sky, and much, much bigger."

"Hmm, yes."

I'm actually talking to a frog about swallowing THE SUN. Hasan pinched himself to make sure he was not dreaming. The frog's name rang a bell.

"Chankei, like the waterfall?" he said. "You're named after a waterfall?"

"The waterfall is named after *me*! That's my home!"

"Oh. Right. Then why are you here in a tank?"

Chankei started hopping in fury. "The thin man Kassim captured me! Quick, you have to set me free before he comes back!" She touched her face with a webbed foot, where a new grey bruise blossomed instantly. "Here in this shed I am hidden from sunlight, but I can still feel the world growing hotter and hotter outside. If I do not swallow the sun, it will continue to misbehave and living creatures will start to die! You have to set me free!"

Hasan's heartbeat, which had calmed down slightly, began to hammer again. "I don't think I'm allowed to do that...."

"What's your name, boy?"

"Hasan."

"Look, Hasan, I'm dying in here!" cried the frog, her croak almost rising into a shriek. "My body is bound to the earth. Every minute of sunlight is another burning flame pressed against my skin! Please, I beg you – let me out RIGHT NOW!"

Hasan turned and ran out of the shed, slamming the door behind him.

* * *

"Can we go to Chankei Waterfall tomorrow?" said Hasan over dinner.

"I just told you someone died there, and now you want to go." His uncle sighed. "What is it with young boys and ignoring advice?"

"I'm just curious. What does the name Chankei mean anyway?"

Pak Kassim looked up from his food. Hasan kept his face a mask of innocence.

"An Orang Asli word," said Pak Kassim finally. "The name of a mythical Lanoh creature. Your great-grandmother was a Semang from the Lanoh tribe, and she used to tell stories to us children. Don't think many people remember those tales now. Doesn't matter anyway, mythical creatures don't exist." He returned to his dinner.

"What kind of creature?" said Hasan.

"Curious, aren't you?" His uncle continued to speak between mouthfuls of rice. "Chankei is supposed to be a white frog."

"And she lives at the waterfall?"

"That's where she lives, yes, allegedly so she could leap up the rocks and—" This time Pak Kassim looked up with suspicion. "Why are you asking all this?"

"Just curious," said Hasan.

He didn't dare to ask any more for the rest of the night. But the next morning, the fourth day of the holidays, he got up early and watched his uncle hitch up the refrigerator to his motorcycle. The thought of eating ice cream on a hot day made Hasan's mouth water.

A sudden thought struck him. "Pakcik?"

"Yes, Hasan?"

"Will it be hot today?"

"Oh yes. Same rules as yesterday, don't go outside and play. It has been hot for a week now, and it's going to be hot for a month more at least."

"You sound very sure."

"I'm a local, of course I'm sure."

"Do you like this hot weather, Pakcik?" asked Hasan.

Pak Kassim exhaled long and hard. "I have to be thankful that this hot weather makes people want to buy more ice cream," he said, tapping the refrigerator. "But aside from business? I hate it just as much as you do." The motorcycle growled to life, and he drove off down the narrow lane leading into town, leaving Hasan staring after him, his voice fading into the distance. "Have fun, see you tonight!"

* * *

As soon as his uncle was gone, Hasan went to the shed.

"Are you really Chankei, the frog from Lanoh legend?"

The white frog croaked in exasperation, her blue throat sac expanding like a balloon, the speckled white spots becoming huge blobs. "I'm *literally talking* to you right now. How many talking frogs do you know?"

Hasan had to admit he didn't know any. "Are you in pain, Chankei?"

"It's still early," said Chankei, glancing out of the window. The brightness showed that it was not yet eight in the morning. "The sun will heat the world up soon. Then the pain will come." Hasan had never imagined a frog's face to have expression, but he saw a shadow of terror pass over Chankei's black eyes.

"And if I let you out, you will cool down the world?"

"Yes!"

"By leaping up the waterfall and…swallowing the sun?"

"Exactly! You're truly setting me free?"

Hasan nodded and watched the small white frog leap around inside the terrarium, bounding from rock to rock in glee at the idea of freedom. Chankei seemed to glow with joy when she finally settled down, her frog face once again strangely expressive.

"Do you know why the thin man Kassim captured you?" Hasan asked.

Chankei shrugged her frog shoulders. "Maybe he wanted a pet."

An honest mistake. That seemed possible to Hasan.

"All right, Chankei," he said with an air of purpose. "Should I set you free in the garden? Do you know your way back home?"

Chankei croaked in alarm. "Crossing roads? I'll be killed!"

Hasan's gaze drifted to the rusty bicycle in the shed. "I guess I could bring you myself." *I'll explain to Pak Kassim later.*

* * *

Midmorning found a boy pedalling down the narrow sandy lane on a bicycle too large for him, a straw hat on his head to shield from the scorching sun, cradling a large glass jar with a tiny frog sitting inside.

Hasan halted where the road forked. "Which way, Chankei?"

The white frog mumbled.

"Chankei! Focus!"

"Left," groaned the frog. The sun had risen quicker than usual that day, the temperature skyrocketing within minutes, sending Chankei into convulsions of pain. Even now the sunlight was almost blinding to look at. Hasan kept his eyes squinted as he turned left and continued down the lane, which soon changed from firm sand into the tyre-marked dried mud of poorly maintained estate roads.

It felt surreal to Hasan, realizing that in his arms sat the creature who could put a stop to these VERY VERY VERY HOT days. Every minute of cycling brought the sweat pouring out of his pores, and by the time Chankei spoke again, his hair was dripping wet.

"Stop there, by the signboard."

Hasan stopped and dismounted where a small jungle trail led off the road. There was a faded signboard half-hidden among the ferns pointing up the trail, reading CHANKEI WATERFALL: 1 KM. There were shreds of striped red-and-white tape draped around the sign.

"This trail was blocked off after some kids drowned—"

Chankei was interrupted by a faint *vroom*.

Hasan whirled around in horror, his heart rate spiking into overdrive. He could not see past the crest of the undulating road behind him, but the distant revving of his uncle's motorcycle was unmistakable.

"Go, go!" cried Chankei, hopping madly inside the jar. "Kassim has come for me!"

"Maybe I can explain—"

The familiar refrigerator-motorcycle combination appeared at the crest of the road. From such a distance they could hear Pak Kassim's faint voice.

"HASAAAAAAAAAAAN! COME BACK RIGHT NOOOOOOW!"

"Run!" cried the frog, and Hasan needed no more spurring. He dropped the bicycle and dashed up the trail, hat falling off, legs pumping, heart racing, tearing past ferns and bushes and branches and hanging vines, climbing up the rising slope, finding footholds among the twisted roots, all the while clutching the glass jar close to his chest. The motorcycle sounds behind drew closer and abruptly ceased.

"Keep following the trail!" Chankei croaked. "Please don't let him take me back!"

Hasan glimpsed the white frog, forelegs pressed against the glass, large black eyes imploring him, filled with desperation and hope. "Don't worry, Chankei!" he cried. "I'll get you home!"

He came to the rushing stream. At this altitude, the water gushed past at incredible speed, the banks eroded steeply on either side. There was a crude log bridge, so Hasan inched himself across carefully. No sooner had he reached the other side than Pak Kassim came pounding up the trail, huffing and puffing.

"Hasan, wait!" shouted Pak Kassim.

Hasan made a split-second decision. He set down the jar and lifted his end of the log before his uncle could step onto it. "I'm setting the frog free, Pakcik!" he shouted back over the roar of the stream.

"Look, Hasan, let's talk first, all right?" said Pak Kassim, holding up his hands. "That's my frog you're holding. I was going to set her free soon, I never meant to keep Chankei for long."

"You told me she didn't exist!"

"Alright, I'm sorry!" Pak Kassim wiped sweat from his forehead. "I should have shown her to you. Now if you would just pass her to me—"

"I can't do that! She was suffering in your tank!"

"Chankei's an immortal frog, she can't die no matter what you do to her!"

Hasan shook his head, tears forming in his eyes. "How can you be so cruel?" he cried. "You knew she was Chankei! Why did you capture her? Why do you want to hurt her so much?"

Pak Kassim's fury exploded.

"You want to know why, Hasan? You see my life – I don't have much money. I can't even buy you proper presents! Do you know that my boss pays me for every ice cream that I sell? Catching Chankei was the only way I could get people to buy more ice cream, and it worked, didn't it? In this past week, I've earned more money than I usually do in a single month! And all I had to do was catch a tiny frog and keep her in a tank!"

He jabbed a finger at the jar across the stream, the white frog shrinking away from his glare. "And I treated her well! I bought her a nice terrarium and fat worms to eat every day! I just want to keep her for a little while longer, earn a bit more money – until I have enough to fix my motorcycle, to buy you a good present this time. You don't have a bicycle of your own, do you, Hasan? Hand me the frog, and I'll work hard and buy you a nice good-quality bicycle, the ones that you see in the stores, all right?"

For a second Hasan hesitated.

Then his gaze fell on the glass jar – on Chankei the queen of frogs, staring out at him hopelessly, skin blazing white in the sunlight, her shadow stark against the ground as the sun climbed higher in the sky and beat down upon the earth. The grey bruises on her skin seemed to have grown in number.

Another month of keeping her in a tank as she squirms in pain.

Hasan set his jaw firmly.

"I can't do it, Pakcik. Chankei will be suffering, and I won't do that to her."

Pak Kassim hissed in anger. "I see what you want. You just want to set her free so that you can play outdoors again, don't you? You don't really care about the frog!"

It was Hasan's turn to get angry. "I'm not selfish like you, Pakcik," he said, the tears spilling out of his eyes at last. "I'm sorry."

"Don't you dare—"

Hasan heaved the log over the edge, sending it splashing and tumbling down the stream. He snatched up the glass jar and ran up the trail, leaving his raging uncle behind.

"That won't delay him for long," came Chankei's voice from the jar.

"We'll just have to reach there before him!" said Hasan. He dashed the tears away from his eyes. He felt that his heart would burst through his chest if it continued pounding like that. *Pak Kassim will hate me for the rest of my life,* he thought bitterly. *I can't believe I did that. For the sake of a frog.*

His legs were growing tired. But the fear of his uncle drove him on, and he forced himself to climb up the slope, step by step. A couple of minutes later he broke through the trees and found himself at the waterfall.

Chankei Waterfall.

A shining pool, gold-green in the dappled sunlight, lay before him. High up above, water came cascading over the top edge of the waterfall and fell crashing into the pool thirty feet below, turning everything into churning white foam. Clouds of spray caught the sun's rays and threw glimmering rainbows into the air. Here the constant roar of the waterfall seemed to form a wild, haunting song.

Hasan tipped the jar out onto his hand.

Chankei sat in his palm and gazed into his eyes. She laid a grateful webbed foot on his thumb, and although Hasan had never thought a frog could show emotion with its lips, he could have sworn that she smiled.

"Thank you, Hasan," she croaked.

Too breathless to speak, he merely nodded.

Chankei leapt to the ground. She hopped once, twice, then dived into the pool with a soft plop. Hasan spied her white form moving through the water, heading towards the rocks beside the waterfall near the foam. The trick of the light made her look a little bigger than before.

Then Chankei emerged on one of the rocks, and Hasan gasped.

Previously she could fit in the palm of his hand. Now she was struggling to balance on a stone about the size of his head. She had grown significantly in size, and as she leapt onto a higher ledge, Hasan saw her enlarge before his eyes into the size of a toddler. At this rate, by the time she reached the top of the waterfall and pushed off with her powerful hind legs, lunging into the atmosphere, she would almost be the size of...the sun.

Chankei leapt.

Now she was the size of Hasan.

Leapt again.

Adult sized.

Leapt again!

And halfway up the waterfall came Pak Kassim from the side, running and throwing himself off the rocks in a desperate lunge. He tackled Chankei in mid-air, arms locking around her gigantic white body, the frog letting out a choked croak. The two of them tumbled through the air and crashed into the pool below.

Hasan screamed. "No, Pak Kassim! Stop!"

Pak Kassim's head emerged, gasping for air. He took a large gulp and ducked back down, wrestling underwater, arms thrashing.

"Stop, stop! Chankei, swim away!"

A webbed foot appeared above water and Pak Kassim's hand dragged it under.

"No!" cried Hasan. He dashed towards the pool and splashed in. The water was deeper than it looked, rising up to his chest. He pushed through the water, moving towards the grappling figures near the thundering waterfall. *I must get to Chankei*, he urged himself as the sandy bottom grew harder and harder for his feet to reach. "Chankei! I'm coming!"

The bottom disappeared.

He sank, gurgling, the world suddenly blurry, tinted green and gold. He struggled helplessly, his heart pounding in his ears, solid ground nowhere within reach. Hasan reached towards the light, and before everything faded, he saw something reaching for him in answer.

* * *

"Hasan! Hasan, wake up!"

Hasan opened his eyes and coughed out water.

"Oh, Hasan!" Pak Kassim held him close to his chest and wept, caressing his hair, whispering over and over again, "I'm so sorry, Hasan. I'm sorry."

Hasan pushed his uncle away, gazing around. "Where's Chankei?"

They looked up.

The glaring sun was gone. The sky, previously blazing white, was now a beautiful shade of blue. Clouds covered the heavens as far as Hasan could see – little white clumps scattered across the firmament, curiously resembling the speckled white dots on the cerulean blue throat of a certain mythical frog.

A refreshing breeze began to blow as they sat together in silence.

Then Pak Kassim put his arms around Hasan, hugged him and said, "Let's go home."

The Further Vision, from 'The Time Machine'

H.G. Wells

In The Time Machine, *one of the most famous works of H.G. Wells (1866–1946), a Victorian inventor travels to the far distant future, where he encounters a dangerous race of humanoid creatures called the Morlocks. He uses his time machine to escape from a trap set by them, retreating even further into the future.*

"I HAVE ALREADY TOLD you of the sickness and confusion that comes with time travelling. And this time I was not seated properly in the saddle, but sideways and in an unstable fashion. For an indefinite time I clung to the machine as it swayed and vibrated, quite unheeding how I went, and when I brought myself to look at the dials again I was amazed to find where I had arrived. One dial records days, and another thousands of days, another millions of days, and another thousands of millions. Now, instead of reversing the levers, I had pulled them over so as to go forward with them, and when I came to look at these indicators I found that the thousands hand was sweeping round as fast as the seconds hand of a watch – into futurity.

"As I drove on, a peculiar change crept over the appearance of things. The palpitating greyness grew darker; then – though I was still travelling with prodigious velocity – the blinking succession of day and night, which was usually indicative of a slower pace, returned, and grew more and more marked. This puzzled me very much at first. The alternations of night and day grew slower and slower, and so did the passage of the sun across the sky, until they seemed to stretch through centuries. At last a steady twilight brooded over the earth, a twilight only broken now and then when a comet glared across the darkling sky. The band of light that had indicated the sun had long since disappeared; for the sun had ceased to set – it simply rose and fell in the west, and grew ever broader and more red. All trace of the moon had vanished. The circling of the stars, growing slower and slower, had given place to creeping points of light. At last, some time before I stopped, the sun, red and very large, halted motionless upon the horizon, a vast dome glowing with a dull heat, and now and then suffering a momentary extinction. At one time it had for a little while glowed more brilliantly again, but it speedily reverted to its sullen red heat. I perceived by this slowing down of its rising and setting that the work of the tidal drag was done. The earth had come to rest with one face to the sun, even as in our own time the moon faces the earth. Very cautiously, for I remembered my former headlong fall, I began to reverse my motion. Slower and slower went the circling hands until the thousands one seemed motionless and the daily one was no longer a mere mist upon its scale. Still slower, until the dim outlines of a desolate beach grew visible.

"I stopped very gently and sat upon the Time Machine, looking round. The sky was no longer blue. Northeastward it was inky black, and out of the blackness shone brightly and steadily the pale white stars. Overhead it was a deep Indian red and starless, and southeastward it grew brighter to a glowing scarlet where, cut by the horizon, lay the huge hull of the sun, red and motionless. The rocks about me were of a harsh reddish colour, and all the trace of life that I could see at first was the intensely green vegetation that covered every projecting point on their southeastern face. It was the same rich green that one sees on forest moss or on the lichen in caves: plants which like these grow in a perpetual twilight.

"The machine was standing on a sloping beach. The sea stretched away to the southwest, to rise into a sharp bright horizon against the wan sky. There were no breakers and no waves, for not a breath of wind was stirring. Only a slight oily swell rose and fell like a gentle breathing, and showed that the eternal sea was still moving and living. And along the margin where the water sometimes broke was a thick incrustation of salt – pink under the lurid sky. There was a sense of oppression in my head, and I noticed that I was breathing very fast. The sensation reminded me of my only experience of mountaineering, and from that I judged the air to be more rarefied than it is now.

"Far away up the desolate slope I heard a harsh scream, and saw a thing like a huge white butterfly go slanting and fluttering up into the sky and, circling, disappear over some low hillocks beyond. The sound of its voice was so dismal that I shivered and seated myself more firmly upon the machine. Looking round me again, I saw that, quite near, what I had taken to be a reddish mass of rock was moving slowly towards me. Then I saw the thing was really a monstrous crab-like creature. Can you imagine a crab as large as yonder table, with its many legs moving slowly and uncertainly, its big claws swaying, its long antennae, like carters' whips, waving and feeling, and its stalked eyes gleaming at you on either side of its metallic front? Its back was corrugated and ornamented with ungainly bosses, and a greenish incrustation blotched it here and there. I could see the many palps of its complicated mouth flickering and feeling as it moved.

"As I stared at this sinister apparition crawling towards me, I felt a tickling on my cheek as though a fly had lighted there. I tried to brush it away with my hand, but in a moment it returned, and almost immediately came another by my ear. I struck at this, and caught something threadlike. It was drawn swiftly out of my hand. With a frightful qualm, I turned, and I saw that I had grasped the antenna of another monster crab that stood just behind me. Its evil eyes were wriggling on their stalks, its mouth was all alive with appetite, and its vast ungainly claws, smeared with an algal slime, were descending upon me. In a moment my hand was on the lever, and I had placed a month between myself and these monsters. But I was still on the same beach, and I saw them distinctly now as soon as I stopped. Dozens of them seemed to be crawling here and there, in the sombre light, among the foliated sheets of intense green.

"I cannot convey the sense of abominable desolation that hung over the world. The red eastern sky, the northward blackness, the salt Dead Sea, the stony beach crawling with these foul, slow-stirring monsters, the uniform poisonous-looking green of the lichenous plants, the thin air that hurts one's lungs: all contributed to an appalling effect. I moved on a hundred years, and there was the same red sun – a little larger, a little duller – the same dying sea, the same chill air, and the same crowd of earthy crustacea creeping in and out among the green weed and the red rocks. And in the westward sky, I saw a curved pale line like a vast new moon.

"So I travelled, stopping ever and again, in great strides of a thousand years or more, drawn on by the mystery of the earth's fate, watching with a strange fascination the sun grow larger and duller in the westward sky, and the life of the old earth ebb away. At last, more than thirty million years hence, the huge red-hot dome of the sun had come to obscure nearly a tenth part of the darkling heavens. Then I stopped once more, for the crawling multitude of crabs had disappeared, and the red beach, save for its livid green liverworts and lichens, seemed lifeless. And now it was flecked with white. A bitter cold assailed me. Rare white flakes ever and again came eddying down. To the northeastward, the glare of snow lay under the starlight of the sable sky, and I could see an undulating crest of hillocks pinkish white. There were fringes of ice along the sea margin, with drifting masses farther out; but the main expanse of that salt ocean, all bloody under the eternal sunset, was still unfrozen.

"I looked about me to see if any traces of animal life remained. A certain indefinable apprehension still kept me in the saddle of the machine. But I saw nothing moving, in earth or sky or sea. The green slime on the rocks alone testified that life was not extinct. A shallow sandbank had appeared in the sea and the water had receded from the beach. I fancied I saw some black object flopping about upon this bank, but it became motionless as I looked at it, and I judged that my eye had been deceived, and that the black object was merely a rock. The stars in the sky were intensely bright and seemed to me to twinkle very little.

"Suddenly I noticed that the circular westward outline of the sun had changed; that a concavity, a bay, had appeared in the curve. I saw this grow larger. For a minute perhaps I stared aghast at this blackness that was creeping over the day, and then I realized that an eclipse was beginning. Either the moon or the planet Mercury was passing across the sun's disk. Naturally, at first I took it to be the moon, but there is much to incline me to believe that what I really saw was the transit of an inner planet passing very near to the earth.

"The darkness grew apace; a cold wind began to blow in freshening gusts from the east, and the showering white flakes in the air increased in number. From the edge of the sea came a ripple and whisper. Beyond these lifeless sounds the world was silent. Silent? It would be hard to convey the stillness of it. All the sounds of man, the bleating of sheep, the cries of birds, the hum of insects, the stir that makes the background of our lives – all that was over. As the darkness thickened, the eddying flakes grew more abundant, dancing before my eyes; and the cold of the air more intense. At last, one by one, swiftly, one after the other, the white peaks of the distant hills vanished into blackness. The breeze rose to a moaning wind. I saw the black central shadow of the eclipse sweeping towards me. In another moment the pale stars alone were visible. All else was rayless obscurity. The sky was absolutely black.

"A horror of this great darkness came on me. The cold, that smote to my marrow, and the pain I felt in breathing, overcame me. I shivered, and a deadly nausea seized me. Then like a red-hot bow in the sky appeared the edge of the sun. I got off the machine to recover myself. I felt giddy and incapable of facing the return journey. As I stood sick and confused I saw again the moving thing upon the shoal – there was no mistake now that it was a moving thing – against the red water of the sea. It was a round thing, the size of a football perhaps, or, it may be, bigger, and tentacles trailed down from it; it seemed black against the weltering blood-red water, and it was hopping fitfully about. Then I felt I was fainting. But a terrible dread of lying helpless in that remote and awful twilight sustained me while I clambered upon the saddle.

The Heavenly Bodies

From Norse mythology

THE HEAVENLY BODIES were formed of the sparks from Muspelheim. The gods did not create them, but only placed them in the heavens to give light unto the world, and assigned them a prescribed locality and motion. By them days and nights and seasons were marked. Thus the Elder Edda, in Völuspá:

> *The sun knew not*
> *His proper sphere;*
> *The stars knew not*
> *Their proper place;*
> *The moon knew not*
> *Where her position was.*

> *There was nowhere grass*
> *Until Bor's sons*
> *The expanse did raise,*
> *By whom the great*
> *Midgard was made.*
> *From the south the sun*
> *Shone on the walls;*
> *Then did the earth*
> *Green herbs produce.*
> *The moon went ahead*
> *The sun followed,*
> *His right hand held*
> *The steeds of heaven.*

Mundilfare was the father of the sun and moon. It is stated in the Younger Edda that Mundilfare had two children, a son and a daughter, so lovely and graceful that he called the boy Maane (moon) and the girl Sol (sun), and the latter he gave in marriage to Glener (the shining one).

But the gods, being incensed at Mundilfare's presumption, took his children and placed them in the heavens, and let Sol drive the horses that draw the car of the sun. These horses are called Aarvak (the ever-wakeful) and Alsvinn (the rapid one); they are gentle and beautiful, and under their withers the gods placed two skins filled with air to cool and refresh them, or, according to another ancient tradition, an iron refrigerant substance called *ísarnkol*. A shield, by name Svalin (cool), stands before the Sun, the shining god. The mountains and the ocean would burn up if this shield should fall away. Maane was set to guide the moon in her course, and regulate her increasing and waning aspect.

A giant, by name Norve, who dwelt in Jotunheim, had a daughter called Night (*nótt*), who, like all her race, was of a dark and swarthy complexion. She was first wedded to a man called Naglfare, and had by him a son named Aud, and afterward to another man called Annar, by whom she had a daughter called Earth (*jörd*). She finally espoused Delling (daybreak), of asa-race, and their son was Day (*dagr*), a child light and fair like his father. Allfather gave Night and Day two horses and two cars, and set them up in the heavens that they might drive successively one after the other, each in twenty-four hours' time, round the world. Night rides first with her steed Hrimfaxe (rime-fax), that every morn, as he ends his course, bedews the earth with the foam from his bit. The steed driven by Day is called Skinfaxe (shining-fax), and all the sky and earth glistens from his mane. Thus the Elder Edda, in the lay of Vafthrudner:

> *Mundilfare hight he*
> *Who the moon's father is,*
> *And also the sun's:*
> *Round heaven journey*
> *Each day they must,*
> *To count years for men.*

In the lay of Grimner:

> *Aarvak and Alsvinn,*
> *Theirs it is up hence*
> *Tired the sun to draw*
> *Under their shoulder*
> *These gentle powers, the gods,*
> *Have concealed an iron-coolness.*
> *Svalin the shield is called*
> *Which stands before the sun,*
> *The refulgent deity;*
> *Rocks and ocean must, I ween,*
> *Be burnt,*
> *Fell it from its place.*

In the lay of Vafthrudner:

> *Delling called is he*
> *Who the Day's father is,*
> *But Night was of Norve born;*
> *The new and waning moons*
> *The beneficent powers created*
> *To count years for men.*

> *Skinfaxe he is named*
> *That the bright day draws*
> *Forth over human kind;*
> *Of coursers he is best accounted*

Among faring men;
Ever sheds light that horse's mane.

Hrimfaxe he is called
That each night draws forth
Over the beneficent powers;
He from his bit lets fall
Drops every morn
Whence in the dells comes dew.

The sun speeds at such a rate as if she feared that someone was pursuing her for her destruction. And well she may; for he that seeks her is not far behind, and she has no other way to escape than to run before him. But who is he that causes her this anxiety? There are two wolves; the one, whose name is Skol, pursues the sun, and it is he that she fears, for he shall one day overtake and devour her. The other, whose name is Hate Hrodvitneson, runs before her and as eagerly pursues the moon, that will one day be caught by him. Whence come these wolves? Answer: A giantess dwells in a wood called Jarnved (ironwood). It is situated east of Midgard, and is the abode of a race of witches. This old hag is the mother of many gigantic sons, who are all of them shaped like wolves, two of whom are Skol and Hate. There is one of that race who is the most formidable of all. His name is Maanagarm (moon-swallower): he is filled with the life-blood of men who draw near their end, and he will swallow up the moon, and stain the heavens and the earth with blood. As it is said in the Völuspá, of the Elder Edda:

Eastward in the Ironwood
The old one sitteth,
And there bringeth forth
Fenrer's fell kindred.
Of these, one, the mightiest,
The moon's devourer,
In form most fiend-like,
And filled with the life-blood
Of the dead and the dying,
Reddens with ruddy gore
The seats of the high gods.
Then shall the sunshine
Of summer be darkened,
And fickle the weather.
Conceive ye this or not?

The gods set Evening and Midnight, Morning and Noon, Forenoon and Afternoon, to count out the year. There were only two seasons, summer and winter; hence spring and fall must be included in these two. The father of summer is called Svasud (the mild), who is such a gentle and delicate being, that what is mild is from him called sweet (*sváslegt*). The father of winter has two names, Vindlone and Vindsval (the wind-cool); he is the son of Vasud (sleet-bringing), and, like all his race, has an icy breath and is of grim and gloomy aspect.

Whence come the winds, that are so strong that they move the ocean and fan fire to flame, and still are so airy that no mortal eye can discern them? Answer: In the northern extremity of the heavens sits a giant called Hraesvelger (corpse-swallower), clad with eagles' plumes. When he spreads out his wings for flight, the winds arise from under them.

Which is the path leading from earth to heaven? The gods made a bridge from earth to heaven and called it Bifrost (the vibrating way). We have all seen it and call it the rainbow. It is of three hues and constructed with more art than any other work. But though strong it be, it will be broken to pieces when the sons of Muspel, after having traversed great rivers, shall ride over it. There is nothing in nature that can hope to make resistance when the sons of Muspel sally forth to the great combat. Now listen to the Elder Edda on some of these subjects.

In the lay of Grimner:

Skol the wolf is named
That the fair-faced goddess
To the ocean chases;
Another Hate is called,
He is Hrodvitner's son:
He the bright maid of heaven shall precede.

In the Völuspá:

Then went the powers all
To their judgment seats,
The all-holy gods,
And thereon held council:
To night and to the waning moon
Gave names;
Morn they named
And mid-day,
Afternoon and eve,
Whereby to reckon years.

In the lay of Vafthrudner:

Vindsval is his name
Who winter's father is,
And Svasud summer's father is:
Yearly they both
Shall ever journey,
Until the powers perish.

Hraesvelger is his name
Who at the end of heaven sits,
A giant in an eagle's plumage:
From his wings comes,

It is said, the wind
That over all men passes.

In reference to Maane, it should be added, that the Younger Edda tells us, that he once took children from earth. Their names were Bil and Hjuke. They went from the spring called Byrger, and bore on their shoulders the bucket called Saeger with the pole called Simul. Their father's name was Vidfin. These children follow Maane, as may be seen, from the earth.

Horse Cursed by Sun

From South Africa

IT IS SAID THAT once Sun was on earth, and caught Horse to ride it. But it was unable to bear his weight, and therefore Ox took the place of Horse, and carried Sun on its back. Since that time Horse is cursed in these words, because it could not carry Sun's weight:

> *"From today thou shalt have a (certain) time of dying.*
> *This is thy curse, that thou hast a (certain) time of dying.*
> *And day and night shalt thou eat,*
> *But the desire of thy heart shall not be at rest,*
> *Though thou grazest till morning and again until sunset.*
> *Behold, this is the judgment which I pass upon thee," said Sun.*

Since that day Horse's (certain) time of dying commenced.

Extracts from
'The House on the Borderland'

William Hope Hodgson

Publisher's Note: William Hope Hodgson (1877–1918) explores the fringes of reality in his novel The House on the Borderland. *The narrator recounts in his journal his various supernatural and interdimensional experiences while living in a mysterious, isolated house in the countryside of western Ireland.*

Chapter XV
The Noise in the Night

AND NOW, I COME to the strangest of all the strange happenings that have befallen me in this house of mysteries. It occurred quite lately – within the month; and I have little doubt but that what I saw was in reality the end of all things. However, to my story.

I do not know how it is; but, up to the present, I have never been able to write these things down, directly they happened. It is as though I have to wait a time, recovering my just balance, and digesting – as it were – the things I have heard or seen. No doubt, this is as it should be; for, by waiting, I see the incidents more truly, and write of them in a calmer and more judicial frame of mind. This by the way.

It is now the end of November. My story relates to what happened in the first week of the month.

It was night, about eleven o'clock. Pepper and I kept one another company in the study – that great, old room of mine, where I read and work. I was reading, curiously enough, the Bible. I have begun, in these later days, to take a growing interest in that great and ancient book. Suddenly, a distinct tremor shook the house, and there came a faint and distant, whirring buzz, that grew rapidly into a far, muffled screaming. It reminded me, in a queer, gigantic way, of the noise that a clock makes, when the catch is released, and it is allowed to run down. The sound appeared to come from some remote height – somewhere up in the night. There was no repetition of the shock. I looked across at Pepper. He was sleeping peacefully.

Gradually, the whirring noise decreased, and there came a long silence.

All at once, a glow lit up the end window, which protrudes far out from the side of the house, so that, from it, one may look both East and West. I felt puzzled, and, after a moment's hesitation, walked across the room, and pulled aside the blind. As I did so, I saw the Sun rise, from behind the horizon. It rose with a steady, perceptible movement. I could see it travel upward. In a minute, it seemed, it had reached the tops of the trees, through which I had watched it. Up, up – It was broad daylight now. Behind me, I was conscious of a sharp, mosquito-like buzzing. I glanced 'round, and knew that it came from the clock. Even as I looked, it marked off an hour. The minute hand was moving 'round the dial, faster than an ordinary second-hand. The hour hand moved quickly from space to space. I had a numb sense of astonishment. A moment later, so it seemed, the two candles went out, almost together. I turned swiftly back to the window; for I had seen the shadow of the window-frames, traveling along the floor toward me, as though a great lamp had been carried up past the window.

I saw now, that the sun had risen high into the heavens, and was still visibly moving. It passed above the house, with an extraordinary sailing kind of motion. As the window came into shadow, I saw another extraordinary thing. The fine-weather clouds were not passing, easily, across the sky – they were scampering, as though a hundred-mile-an-hour wind blew. As they passed, they changed their shapes a thousand times a minute, as though writhing with a strange life; and so were gone. And, presently, others came, and whisked away likewise.

To the West, I saw the sun, drop with an incredible, smooth, swift motion. Eastward, the shadows of every seen thing crept toward the coming greyness. And the movement of the shadows was visible to me – a stealthy, writhing creep of the shadows of the wind-stirred trees. It was a strange sight.

Quickly, the room began to darken. The sun slid down to the horizon, and seemed, as it were, to disappear from my sight, almost with a jerk. Through the greyness of the swift evening, I saw the silver crescent of the moon, falling out of the Southern sky, toward the West. The evening seemed to merge into an almost instant night. Above me, the many constellations passed in a strange, 'noiseless' circling, Westward. The moon fell through that last thousand fathoms of the night-gulf, and there was only the starlight....

About this time, the buzzing in the corner ceased; telling me that the clock had run down. A few minutes passed, and I saw the Eastward sky lighten. A grey, sullen morning spread through all the darkness, and hid the march of the stars. Overhead, there moved, with a heavy, everlasting rolling, a vast, seamless sky of grey clouds – a cloud-sky that would have seemed motionless, through all the length of an ordinary earth-day. The sun was hidden from me; but, from moment to moment, the world would brighten and darken, brighten and darken, beneath waves of subtle light and shadow...

The light shifted ever Westward, and the night fell upon the earth. A vast rain seemed to come with it, and a wind of a most extraordinary loudness – as though the howling of a night-long gale, were packed into the space of no more than a minute.

This noise passed, almost immediately, and the clouds broke; so that, once more, I could see the sky. The stars were flying westward, with astounding speed. It came to me now, for the first time, that, though the noise of the wind had passed, yet a constant 'blurred' sound was in my ears. Now that I noticed it, I was aware that it had been with me all the time. It was the world-noise.

And then, even as I grasped at so much comprehension, there came the Eastward light. No more than a few heartbeats, and the sun rose, swiftly. Through the trees, I saw it, and then it was above the trees. Up – up, it soared and all the world was light. It passed, with a swift, steady swing to its highest altitude, and fell thence, Westward. I saw the day roll visibly over my head. A few light clouds flittered Northward, and vanished. The sun went down with one swift, clear plunge, and there was about me, for a few seconds, the darker growing grey of the gloaming.

Southward and Westward, the moon was sinking rapidly. The night had come, already. A minute it seemed, and the moon fell those remaining fathoms of dark sky. Another minute, or so, and the Eastward sky glowed with the coming dawn. The sun leapt upon me with a frightening abruptness, and soared evermore swiftly toward the zenith. Then, suddenly, a fresh thing came to my sight. A black thundercloud rushed up out of the South, and seemed to leap all the arc of the sky, in a single instant. As it came, I saw that its advancing edge flapped, like a monstrous black cloth in the heaven, twirling and undulating rapidly, with a horrid suggestiveness. In an instant, all the air was full of rain, and a hundred lightning flashes seemed to flood downward, as it were in one great shower. In the same second of time, the world-noise was drowned in the roar of the wind, and then my ears ached, under the stunning impact of the thunder.

And, in the midst of this storm, the night came; and then, within the space of another minute, the storm had passed, and there was only the constant 'blur' of the world-noise on my hearing. Overhead, the stars were sliding quickly Westward; and something, mayhaps the particular speed to which they had attained, brought home to me, for the first time, a keen realization of the knowledge that it was the world that revolved. I seemed to see, suddenly, the world – a vast, dark mass – revolving visibly against the stars.

The dawn and the sun seemed to come together, so greatly had the speed of the world-revolution increased. The sun drove up, in one long, steady curve; passed its highest point, and swept down into the Western sky, and disappeared. I was scarcely conscious of evening, so brief was it. Then I was watching the flying constellations, and the Westward hastening moon. In but a space of seconds, so it seemed, it was sliding swiftly downward through the night-blue, and then was gone. And, almost directly, came the morning.

And now there seemed to come a strange acceleration. The sun made one clean, clear sweep through the sky, and disappeared behind the Westward horizon, and the night came and went with a like haste.

As the succeeding day, opened and closed upon the world, I was aware of a sweat of snow, suddenly upon the earth. The night came, and, almost immediately, the day. In the brief leap of the sun, I saw that the snow had vanished; and then, once more, it was night.

Thus matters were; and, even after the many incredible things that I have seen, I experienced all the time a most profound awe. To see the sun rise and set, within a space of time to be measured by seconds; to watch (after a little) the moon leap – a pale, and ever growing orb – up into the night sky, and glide, with a strange swiftness, through the vast arc of blue; and, presently, to see the sun follow, springing out of the Eastern sky, as though in chase; and then again the night, with the swift and ghostly passing of starry constellations, was all too much to view believingly. Yet, so it was – the day slipping from dawn to dusk, and the night sliding swiftly into day, ever rapidly and more rapidly.

The last three passages of the sun had shown me a snow-covered earth, which, at night, had seemed, for a few seconds, incredibly weird under the fast-shifting light of the soaring and falling moon. Now, however, for a little space, the sky was hidden, by a sea of swaying, leaden-white clouds, which lightened and blackened, alternately, with the passage of day and night.

The clouds rippled and vanished, and there was once more before me, the vision of the swiftly leaping sun, and nights that came and went like shadows.

Faster and faster, spun the world. And now each day and night was completed within the space of but a few seconds; and still the speed increased.

It was a little later, that I noticed that the sun had begun to have the suspicion of a trail of fire behind it. This was due, evidently, to the speed at which it, apparently, traversed the heavens. And, as the days sped, each one quicker than the last, the sun began to assume the appearance of a vast, flaming comet flaring across the sky at short, periodic intervals.

At night, the moon presented, with much greater truth, a comet-like aspect; a pale, and singularly clear, fast traveling shape of fire, trailing streaks of cold flame. The stars showed now, merely as fine hairs of fire against the dark.

Once, I turned from the window, and glanced at Pepper. In the flash of a day, I saw that he slept, quietly, and I moved once more to my watching.

The sun was now bursting up from the Eastern horizon, like a stupendous rocket, seeming to occupy no more than a second or two in hurling from East to West. I could no longer perceive the passage of clouds across the sky, which seemed to have darkened somewhat. The brief nights, appeared to have lost the proper darkness of night; so that the hair-like fire of the flying stars, showed but dimly. As the speed increased, the sun began to sway very slowly in the sky, from South to North, and then, slowly again, from North to South.

So, amid a strange confusion of mind, the hours passed.

All this while had Pepper slept. Presently, feeling lonely and distraught, I called to him, softly; but he took no notice. Again, I called, raising my voice slightly; still he moved not. I walked over to where he lay, and touched him with my foot, to rouse him. At the action, gentle though it was, he fell to pieces. That is what happened; he literally and actually crumbled into a mouldering heap of bones and dust.

For the space of, perhaps a minute, I stared down at the shapeless heap, that had once been Pepper. I stood, feeling stunned. What can have happened? I asked myself; not at once grasping the grim significance of that little hill of ash. Then, as I stirred the heap with my foot, it occurred to me that this could only happen in a great space of time. Years – and years.

Outside, the weaving, fluttering light held the world. Inside, I stood, trying to understand what it meant – what that little pile of dust and dry bones, on the carpet, meant. But I could not think coherently.

I glanced away, 'round the room, and now, for the first time, noticed how dusty and old the place looked. Dust and dirt everywhere; piled in little heaps in the corners, and spread about upon the furniture. The very carpet, itself, was invisible beneath a coating of the same, all-pervading, material. As I walked, little clouds of the stuff rose up from under my footsteps, and assailed my nostrils, with a dry, bitter odour that made me wheeze, huskily.

Suddenly, as my glance fell again upon Pepper's remains, I stood still, and gave voice to my confusion – questioning, aloud, whether the years were, indeed, passing; whether this, which I had taken to be a form of vision, was, in truth, a reality. I paused. A new thought had struck me. Quickly, but with steps which, for the first time, I noticed, tottered, I went across the room to the great pier-glass, and looked in. It was too covered with grime, to give back any reflection, and, with trembling hands, I began to rub off the dirt. Presently, I could see myself. The thought that had come to me, was confirmed. Instead of the great, hale man, who scarcely looked fifty, I was looking at a bent, decrepit man, whose shoulders stooped, and whose face was wrinkled with the years of a century. The hair – which a few short hours ago had been nearly coal black – was now silvery white. Only the eyes were bright. Gradually, I traced, in that ancient man, a faint resemblance to my self of other days.

I turned away, and tottered to the window. I knew, now, that I was old, and the knowledge seemed to confirm my trembling walk. For a little space, I stared moodily out into the blurred vista of changeful landscape. Even in that short time, a year passed, and, with a petulant gesture, I left the window. As I did so, I noticed that my hand shook with the palsy of old age; and a short sob choked its way through my lips.

For a little while, I paced, tremulously, between the window and the table; my gaze wandering hither and thither, uneasily. How dilapidated the room was. Everywhere lay the thick dust – thick, sleepy and black. The fender was a shape of rust. The chains that held the brass clock-weights had rusted through long ago, and now the weights lay on the floor beneath; themselves two cones of Verdigris.

As I glanced about, it seemed to me that I could see the very furniture of the room rotting and decaying before my eyes. Nor was this fancy, on my part; for, all at once, the bookshelf, along the sidewall, collapsed, with a cracking and rending of rotten wood, precipitating its contents upon the floor, and filling the room with a smother of dusty atoms.

How tired I felt. As I walked, it seemed that I could hear my dry joints, creak and crack at every step. I wondered about my sister. Was she dead, as well as Pepper? All had happened so quickly and suddenly. This must be, indeed, the beginning of the end of all things! It occurred to me, to go to look for her; but I felt too weary. And then, she had been so queer about these happenings, of late. Of late! I repeated the words, and laughed, feebly – mirthlessly, as the realization was borne in upon me that I spoke of a time, half a century gone. Half a century! It might have been twice as long!

I moved slowly to the window, and looked out once more across the world. I can best describe the passage of day and night, at this period, as a sort of gigantic, ponderous flicker. Moment by moment, the acceleration of time continued; so that, at nights now, I saw the moon, only as a swaying trail of palish fire, that varied from a mere line of light to a nebulous path, and then dwindled again, disappearing periodically.

The flicker of the days and nights quickened. The days had grown perceptibly darker, and a queer quality of dusk lay, as it were, in the atmosphere. The nights were so much lighter, that the stars were scarcely to be seen, saving here and there an occasional hair-like line of fire, that seemed to sway a little, with the moon.

Quicker, and ever quicker, ran the flicker of day and night; and, suddenly it seemed, I was aware that the flicker had died out, and, instead, there reigned a comparatively steady light, which was shed upon all the world, from an eternal river of flame that swung up and down, North and South, in stupendous, mighty swings.

The sky was now grown very much darker, and there was in the blue of it a heavy gloom, as though a vast blackness peered through it upon the earth. Yet, there was in it, also, a strange and awful clearness, and emptiness. Periodically, I had glimpses of a ghostly track of fire that swayed thin and darkly toward the sun-stream; vanished and reappeared. It was the scarcely visible moon-stream.

Looking out at the landscape, I was conscious again, of a blurring sort of 'flitter,' that came either from the light of the ponderous-swinging sun-stream, or was the result of the incredibly rapid changes of the earth's surface. And every few moments, so it seemed, the snow would lie suddenly upon the world, and vanish as abruptly, as though an invisible giant 'flitted' a white sheet off and on the earth.

Time fled, and the weariness that was mine, grew insupportable. I turned from the window, and walked once across the room, the heavy dust deadening the sound of my footsteps. Each step that I took seemed a greater effort than the one before. An intolerable ache knew me in every joint and limb, as I trod my way, with a weary uncertainty.

By the opposite wall, I came to a weak pause, and wondered, dimly, what was my intent. I looked to my left, and saw my old chair. The thought of sitting in it brought a faint sense of comfort to my bewildered wretchedness. Yet, because I was so weary and old and tired, I would scarcely brace my mind to do anything but stand, and wish myself past those few yards. I rocked, as I stood. The floor, even, seemed a place for rest; but the dust lay so thick and sleepy and black. I turned, with a great effort of will, and made toward my chair. I reached it, with a groan of thankfulness. I sat down.

Everything about me appeared to be growing dim. It was all so strange and unthought of. Last night, I was a comparatively strong, though elderly man; and now, only a few hours later—! I looked at the little dust-heap that had once been Pepper. Hours! and I laughed, a feeble, bitter laugh; a shrill, cackling laugh, that shocked my dimming senses.

For a while, I must have dozed. Then I opened my eyes, with a start. Somewhere across the room, there had been a muffled noise of something falling. I looked, and saw, vaguely, a cloud of dust hovering above a pile of debris. Nearer the door, something else tumbled, with a crash. It was one of the cupboards; but I was tired, and took little notice. I closed my eyes, and sat there in a state of drowsy, semi-unconsciousness. Once or twice – as though coming through thick mists – I heard noises, faintly. Then I must have slept.

Chapter CVI
The Awakening

I awoke, with a start. For a moment, I wondered where I was. Then memory came to me....

The room was still lit with that strange light – half-sun, half-moon, light. I felt refreshed, and the tired, weary ache had left me. I went slowly across to the window, and looked out. Overhead, the river of flame drove up and down, North and South, in a dancing semi-circle of fire. As a mighty sleigh in the loom of time it seemed – in a sudden fancy of mine – to be beating home the picks of the years. For, so vastly had the passage of time been accelerated, that there was no longer any sense of the sun passing from East to West. The only apparent movement was the North and South beat of the sun-stream, that had become so swift now, as to be better described as a *quiver*.

As I peered out, there came to me a sudden, inconsequent memory of that last journey among the Outer worlds. I remembered the sudden vision that had come to me, as I neared the Solar System, of the fast whirling planets about the sun – as though the governing quality of time had been held in abeyance, and the Machine of a Universe allowed to run down an eternity, in a few moments or hours. The memory passed, along with a, but partially comprehended, suggestion that I had been permitted a glimpse into further time spaces. I stared out again, seemingly, at the quake of the sun-stream. The speed seemed to increase, even as I looked. Several lifetimes came and went, as I watched.

Suddenly, it struck me, with a sort of grotesque seriousness, that I was still alive. I thought of Pepper, and wondered how it was that I had not followed his fate. He had reached the time of his dying, and had passed, probably through sheer length of years. And here was I, alive, hundreds of thousands of centuries after my rightful period of years.

For, a time, I mused, absently. "Yesterday—" I stopped, suddenly. Yesterday! There was no yesterday. The yesterday of which I spoke had been swallowed up in the abyss of years, ages gone. I grew dazed with much thinking.

Presently, I turned from the window, and glanced 'round the room. It seemed different – strangely, utterly different. Then, I knew what it was that made it appear so strange. It was bare: there was not a piece of furniture in the room; not even a solitary fitting of any sort. Gradually, my amazement went, as I remembered, that this was but the inevitable end of that process of decay, which I had witnessed commencing, before my sleep. Thousands of years! Millions of years!

Over the floor was spread a deep layer of dust, that reached halfway up to the window-seat. It had grown immeasurably, whilst I slept; and represented the dust of untold ages. Undoubtedly, atoms of the old, decayed furniture helped to swell its bulk; and, somewhere among it all, mouldered the long-ago-dead Pepper.

All at once, it occurred to me, that I had no recollection of wading knee-deep through all that dust, after I awoke. True, an incredible age of years had passed, since I approached the window; but that was evidently as nothing, compared with the countless spaces of time that, I conceived, had vanished whilst I was sleeping. I remembered now, that I had fallen asleep, sitting in my old chair. Had it gone...? I glanced toward where it had stood. Of course, there was no chair to be seen. I could not satisfy myself, whether it had disappeared, after my waking, or before. If it had mouldered under me, surely, I should have been waked by the collapse. Then I remembered that the thick dust, which covered the floor, would have been sufficient to soften my fall; so that it was quite possible, I had slept upon the dust for a million years or more.

As these thoughts wandered through my brain, I glanced again, casually, to where the chair had stood. Then, for the first time, I noticed that there were no marks, in the dust, of my footprints, between it and the window. But then, ages of years had passed, since I had awaked – tens of thousands of years!

My look rested thoughtfully, again upon the place where once had stood my chair. Suddenly, I passed from abstraction to intentness; for there, in its standing place, I made out a long undulation, rounded off with the heavy dust. Yet it was not so much hidden, but that I could tell what had caused it. I knew – and shivered at the knowledge – that it was a human body, ages-dead, lying there, beneath the place where I had slept. It was lying on its right side, its back turned toward me. I could make out and trace each curve and outline, softened, and moulded, as it were, in the black dust. In a vague sort of way, I tried to account for its presence there. Slowly, I began to grow bewildered, as the thought came to me that it lay just about where I must have fallen when the chair collapsed.

Gradually, an idea began to form itself within my brain; a thought that shook my spirit. It seemed hideous and insupportable; yet it grew upon me, steadily, until it became a conviction. The body under that coating, that shroud of dust, was neither more nor less than my own dead shell. I did not attempt to prove it. I knew it now, and wondered I had not known it all along. I was a bodiless thing.

Awhile, I stood, trying to adjust my thoughts to this new problem. In time – how many thousands of years, I know not – I attained to some degree of quietude – sufficient to enable me to pay attention to what was transpiring around me.

Now, I saw that the elongated mound had sunk, collapsed, level with the rest of the spreading dust. And fresh atoms, impalpable, had settled above that mixture of grave-powder, which the aeons had ground. A long while, I stood, turned from the window. Gradually, I grew more collected, while the world slipped across the centuries into the future.

Presently, I began a survey of the room. Now, I saw that time was beginning its destructive work, even on this strange old building. That it had stood through all the years was, it seemed to me, proof that it was something different from any other house. I do not think, somehow, that I had thought of its decaying. Though, why, I could not have said. It was not until I had meditated upon the matter, for some considerable time, that I fully realized that the extraordinary space of time through which it had stood, was sufficient to have utterly pulverized the very stones of which it was built, had they been taken from any earthly quarry. Yes, it was undoubtedly mouldering now. All the plaster had gone from the walls; even as the woodwork of the room had gone, many ages before.

While I stood, in contemplation, a piece of glass, from one of the small, diamond-shaped panes, dropped, with a dull tap, amid the dust upon the sill behind me, and crumbled into a little heap of powder. As I turned from contemplating it, I saw light between a couple of the stones that formed the outer wall. Evidently, the mortar was falling away...

After awhile, I turned once more to the window, and peered out. I discovered, now, that the speed of time had become enormous. The lateral quiver of the sun-stream had grown so swift as to cause the dancing semi-circle of flame to merge into, and disappear in, a sheet of fire that covered half the Southern sky from East to West.

From the sky, I glanced down to the gardens. They were just a blur of a palish, dirty green. I had a feeling that they stood higher, than in the old days; a feeling that they were nearer my window, as though they had risen, bodily. Yet, they were still a long way below me; for the rock, over the mouth of the pit, on which this house stands, arches up to a great height.

It was later, that I noticed a change in the constant colour of the gardens. The pale, dirty green was growing ever paler and paler, toward white. At last, after a great space, they became greyish-white, and stayed thus for a very long time. Finally, however, the greyness began to fade, even as had the green, into a dead white. And this remained, constant and unchanged. And by this I knew that, at last, snow lay upon all the Northern world.

And so, by millions of years, time winged onward through eternity, to the end – the end, of which, in the old-earth days, I had thought remotely, and in hazily speculative fashion. And now, it was approaching in a manner of which none had ever dreamed.

I recollect that, about this time, I began to have a lively, though morbid, curiosity, as to what would happen when the end came – but I seemed strangely without imaginings.

All this while, the steady process of decay was continuing. The few remaining pieces of glass, had long ago vanished; and, every now and then, a soft thud, and a little cloud of rising dust, would tell of some fragment of fallen mortar or stone.

I looked up again, to the fiery sheet that quaked in the heavens above me and far down into the Southern sky. As I looked, the impression was borne in upon me, that it had lost some of its first brilliancy – that it was duller, deeper hued.

I glanced down, once more, to the blurred white of the worldscape. Sometimes, my look returned to the burning sheet of dulling flame, that was, and yet hid, the sun. At times, I glanced behind me, into the growing dusk of the great, silent room, with its aeon-carpet of sleeping dust...

So, I watched through the fleeting ages, lost in soul-wearing thoughts and wonderings, and possessed with a new weariness.

Chapter XVII
The Slowing Rotation

It might have been a million years later that I perceived, beyond possibility of doubt, that the fiery sheet that lit the world was indeed darkening.

Another vast space went by, and the whole enormous flame had sunk to a deep, copper colour. Gradually, it darkened, from copper to copper-red, and from this, at times, to a deep, heavy, purplish tint, with, in it, a strange loom of blood.

Although the light was decreasing, I could perceive no diminishment in the apparent speed of the sun. It still spread itself in that dazzling veil of speed.

The world, so much of it as I could see, had assumed a dreadful shade of gloom, as though, in very deed, the last day of the worlds approached.

The sun was dying; of that there could be little doubt; and still the earth whirled onward, through space and all the aeons. At this time, I remember, an extraordinary sense of bewilderment took me. I found myself, later, wandering, mentally, amid an odd chaos of fragmentary modern theories and the old Biblical story of the world's ending.

Then, for the first time, there flashed across me, the memory that the sun, with its system of planets, was, and had been, traveling through space at an incredible speed. Abruptly, the question rose – *Where?* For a very great time, I pondered this matter; but, finally, with a certain sense of the futility of my puzzlings, I let my thoughts wander to other things. I grew to wondering, how much longer the house would stand. Also, I queried, to myself, whether I should be doomed to stay, bodiless, upon the earth, through the dark-time that I knew was coming. From these thoughts, I fell again to speculations upon the possible direction of the sun's journey through space.... And so another great while passed.

Gradually, as time fled, I began to feel the chill of a great winter. Then, I remembered that, with the sun dying, the cold must be, necessarily, extraordinarily intense. Slowly, slowly, as the aeons slipped into eternity, the earth sank into a heavier and redder gloom. The dull flame in the firmament took on a deeper tint, very sombre and turbid.

Then, at last, it was borne upon me that there was a change. The fiery, gloomy curtain of flame that hung quaking overhead, and down away into the Southern sky, began to thin and contract; and, in it, as one sees the fast vibrations of a jarred harp-string, I saw once more the sun-stream quivering, giddily, North and South.

Slowly, the likeness to a sheet of fire, disappeared, and I saw, plainly, the slowing beat of the sun-stream. Yet, even then, the speed of its swing was inconceivably swift. And all the time, the brightness of the fiery arc grew ever duller. Underneath, the world loomed dimly – an indistinct, ghostly region.

Overhead, the river of flame swayed slower, and even slower; until, at last, it swung to the North and South in great, ponderous beats, that lasted through seconds. A long space went by, and now each sway of the great belt lasted nigh a minute; so that, after a great while, I ceased to distinguish it as a visible movement; and the streaming fire ran in a steady river of dull flame, across the deadly looking sky.

An indefinite period passed, and it seemed that the arc of fire became less sharply defined. It appeared to me to grow more attenuated, and I thought blackish streaks showed, occasionally. Presently, as I watched, the smooth onward flow ceased; and I was able to perceive that there came a momentary, but regular, darkening of the world. This grew until, once more, night descended, in short, but periodic, intervals upon the wearying earth.

Longer and longer became the nights, and the days equalled them; so that, at last, the day and the night grew to the duration of seconds in length, and the sun showed, once more, like an almost invisible, coppery red coloured ball, within the glowing mistiness of its flight. Corresponding to the dark lines, showing at times in its trail, there were now distinctly to be seen on the half-visible sun itself, great, dark belts.

Year after year flashed into the past, and the days and nights spread into minutes. The sun had ceased to have the appearance of a tail; and now rose and set – a tremendous globe of a glowing copper-bronze hue; in parts ringed with blood-red bands; in others, with the dusky ones, that I have already mentioned. These circles – both red and black – were of varying thicknesses. For a time, I was at a loss to account for their presence. Then it occurred to me, that it was scarcely likely that the sun would cool evenly all over; and that these markings were due, probably, to differences in temperature of the various areas; the red representing those parts where the heat was still fervent, and the black those portions which were already comparatively cool.

It struck me, as a peculiar thing, that the sun should cool in evenly defined rings; until I remembered that, possibly, they were but isolated patches, to which the enormous rotatory speed of the sun had imparted a belt-like appearance. The sun, itself, was very much greater than the sun I had known in the old-world days; and, from this, I argued that it was considerably nearer.

At nights, the moon still showed; but small and remote; and the light she reflected was so dull and weak that she seemed little more than the small, dim ghost of the olden moon, that I had known.

Gradually, the days and nights lengthened out, until they equalled a space somewhat less than one of the old-earth hours; the sun rising and setting like a great, ruddy bronze disk, crossed with ink-black bars. About this time, I found myself, able once more, to see the gardens, with clearness. For the world had now grown very still, and changeless. Yet, I am not correct in saying, 'gardens'; for there were no gardens – nothing that I knew or recognized. In place thereof, I looked out upon a vast plain, stretching away into distance. A little to my left, there was a low range of hills. Everywhere, there was a uniform, white covering of snow, in places rising into hummocks and ridges.

It was only now, that I recognized how really great had been the snowfall. In places it was vastly deep, as was witnessed by a great, upleaping, wave-shaped hill, away to my right; though it is not impossible, that this was due, in part, to some rise in the surface of the ground. Strangely enough, the range of low hills to my left – already mentioned – was not entirely covered with the universal snow; instead, I could see their bare, dark sides showing in several places. And everywhere and always there reigned an incredible death-silence and desolation. The immutable, awful quiet of a dying world.

All this time, the days and nights were lengthening, perceptibly. Already, each day occupied, maybe, some two hours from dawn to dusk. At night, I had been surprised to find that there were very few stars overhead, and these small, though of an extraordinary brightness; which I attributed to the peculiar, but clear, blackness of the night-time.

Away to the North, I could discern a nebulous sort of mistiness; not unlike, in appearance, a small portion of the Milky Way. It might have been an extremely remote star-cluster; or – the thought came to me suddenly – perhaps it was the sidereal universe that I had known, and now left far behind, forever – a small, dimly glowing mist of stars, far in the depths of space.

Still, the days and nights lengthened, slowly. Each time, the sun rose duller than it had set. And the dark belts increased in breadth.

About this time, there happened a fresh thing. The sun, earth and sky were suddenly darkened, and, apparently, blotted out for a brief space. I had a sense, a certain awareness (I could learn little by sight), that the earth was enduring a very great fall of snow. Then, in an instant, the veil that had obscured everything, vanished, and I looked out, once more. A marvellous sight met my gaze. The hollow in which this house, with its gardens, stands, was brimmed with snow. It lipped over the sill of my window. Everywhere, it lay, a great level stretch of white, which caught and reflected, gloomily, the sombre coppery glows of the dying sun. The world had become a shadowless plain, from horizon to horizon.

I glanced up at the sun. It shone with an extraordinary, dull clearness. I saw it, now, as one who, until then, had seen it, only through a partially obscuring medium. All about it, the sky had become black, with a clear, deep blackness, frightful in its nearness, and its unmeasured deep, and its utter unfriendliness. For a great time, I looked into it, newly, and shaken and fearful. It was so near. Had I been a child, I might have expressed some of my sensation and distress by saying that the sky had lost its roof.

Later, I turned, and peered about me, into the room. Everywhere, it was covered with a thin shroud of the all-pervading white. I could see it but dimly, by reason of the sombre light that now lit the world. It appeared to cling to the ruined walls; and the thick, soft dust of the years, that covered the floor knee-deep, was nowhere visible. The snow must have blown in through the open framework of the windows. Yet, in no place had it drifted; but lay everywhere about the great, old room, smooth and level. Moreover, there had been no wind these many thousand years. But there was the snow, as I have told.

And all the earth was silent. And there was a cold, such as no living man can ever have known.

The earth was now illuminated, by day, with a most doleful light, beyond my power to describe. It seemed as though I looked at the great plain, through the medium of a bronze-tinted sea.

It was evident that the earth's rotatory movement was departing, steadily.

The end came, all at once. The night had been the longest yet; and when the dying sun showed, at last, above the world's edge, I had grown so wearied of the dark, that I greeted it as a friend. It rose steadily, until about twenty degrees above the horizon. Then, it stopped suddenly, and, after a strange retrograde movement, hung motionless – a great shield in the sky. Only the circular rim of the sun showed bright – only this, and one thin streak of light near the equator.

Gradually, even this thread of light died out; and now, all that was left of our great and glorious sun, was a vast dead disk, rimmed with a thin circle of bronze-red light.

Chapter XVIII
The Green Star

The world was held in a savage gloom – cold and intolerable. Outside, all was quiet – quiet! From the dark room behind me, came the occasional, soft thud of falling matter – fragments of rotting stone. So time passed, and night grasped the world, wrapping it in wrappings of impenetrable blackness.

There was no night sky, as we know it. Even the few straggling stars had vanished, conclusively. I might have been in a shuttered room, without a light; for all that I could see. Only, in the impalpableness of gloom, opposite, burnt that vast, encircling hair of dull fire. Beyond this, there was no ray in all the vastitude of night that surrounded me; save that, far in the North, that soft, mist-like glow still shone.

Silently, years moved on. What period of time passed, I shall never know. It seemed to me, waiting there, that eternities came and went, stealthily; and still I watched. I could see only the glow of the sun's edge, at times; for now, it had commenced to come and go – lighting up a while, and again becoming extinguished.

All at once, during one of these periods of life, a sudden flame cut across the night – a quick glare that lit up the dead earth, shortly; giving me a glimpse of its flat lonesomeness. The light appeared to come from the sun – shooting out from somewhere near its centre, diagonally. A moment, I gazed, startled. Then the leaping flame sank, and the gloom fell again. But now it was not so dark; and the sun was belted by a thin line of vivid, white light. I stared, intently. Had a volcano broken out on the sun? Yet, I negatived the thought, as soon as formed. I felt that the light had been far too intensely white, and large, for such a cause.

Another idea there was, that suggested itself to me. It was, that one of the inner planets had fallen into the sun – becoming incandescent, under that impact. This theory appealed to me, as being more plausible, and accounting more satisfactorily for the extraordinary size and brilliance of the blaze, that had lit up the dead world, so unexpectedly.

Full of interest and emotion, I stared, across the darkness, at that line of white fire, cutting the night. One thing it told to me, unmistakably: the sun was yet rotating at an enormous speed. Thus, I knew that the years were still fleeting at an incalculable rate; though so far as the earth was concerned, life, and light, and time, were things belonging to a period lost in the long-gone ages.

After that one burst of flame, the light had shown, only as an encircling band of bright fire. Now, however, as I watched, it began slowly to sink into a ruddy tint, and, later, to a dark, copper-red colour; much as the sun had done. Presently, it sank to a deeper hue; and, in a still further space of time, it began to fluctuate; having periods of glowing, and anon, dying. Thus, after a great while, it disappeared.

Long before this, the smouldering edge of the sun had deadened into blackness. And so, in that supremely future time, the world, dark and intensely silent, rode on its gloomy orbit around the ponderous mass of the dead sun.

My thoughts, at this period, can be scarcely described. At first, they were chaotic and wanting in coherence. But, later, as the ages came and went, my soul seemed to imbibe the very essence of the oppressive solitude and dreariness, that held the earth.

With this feeling, there came a wonderful clearness of thought, and I realized, despairingly, that the world might wander forever, through that enormous night. For a while, the unwholesome idea filled me, with a sensation of overbearing desolation; so that I could have cried like a child. In time, however, this feeling grew, almost insensibly, less, and an unreasoning hope possessed me. Patiently, I waited.

From time to time, the noise of dropping particles, behind in the room, came dully to my ears. Once, I heard a loud crash, and turned, instinctively, to look; forgetting, for the moment, the impenetrable night in which every detail was submerged. In a while, my gaze sought the heavens; turning, unconsciously, toward the North. Yes, the nebulous glow still showed. Indeed, I could have almost imagined that it looked somewhat plainer. For a long time, I kept my gaze fixed upon it; feeling, in my lonely soul, that its soft haze was, in some way, a tie with the past. Strange, the trifles from which one can suck comfort! And yet, had I but known – but I shall come to that in its proper time.

For a very long space, I watched, without experiencing any of the desire for sleep, that would so soon have visited me in the old-earth days. How I should have welcomed it; if only to have passed the time, away from my perplexities and thoughts.

Several times, the comfortless sound of some great piece of masonry falling, disturbed my meditations; and, once, it seemed I could hear whispering in the room, behind me. Yet it was utterly useless to try to see anything. Such blackness, as existed, scarcely can be conceived. It was palpable, and hideously brutal to the sense; as though something dead, pressed up against me – something soft, and icily cold.

Under all this, there grew up within my mind, a great and overwhelming distress of uneasiness, that left me, but to drop me into an uncomfortable brooding. I felt that I must fight against it; and, presently, hoping to distract my thoughts, I turned to the window, and looked up toward the North, in search of the nebulous whiteness, which, still, I believed to be the far and misty glowing of the universe we had left. Even as I raised my eyes, I was thrilled with a feeling of wonder; for, now, the hazy light had resolved into a single, great star, of vivid green.

As I stared, astonished, the thought flashed into my mind; that the earth must be traveling toward the star; not away, as I had imagined. Next, that it could not be the universe the earth had left; but, possibly, an outlying star, belonging to some vast star cluster, hidden in the enormous depths of space. With a sense of commingled awe and curiosity, I watched it, wondering what new thing was to be revealed to me.

For a while, vague thoughts and speculations occupied me, during which my gaze dwelt insatiably upon that one spot of light, in the otherwise pit-like darkness. Hope grew up within me, banishing the oppression of despair, that had seemed to stifle me. Wherever the earth was traveling, it was, at least, going once more toward the realms of light. Light! One must spend an eternity wrapped in soundless night, to understand the full horror of being without it.

Slowly, but surely, the star grew upon my vision, until, in time, it shone as brightly as had the planet Jupiter, in the old-earth days. With increased size, its colour became more impressive; reminding me of a huge emerald, scintillating rays of fire across the world.

Years fled away in silence, and the green star grew into a great splash of flame in the sky. A little later, I saw a thing that filled me with amazement. It was the ghostly outline of a vast crescent, in the night; a gigantic new moon, seeming to be growing out of the surrounding gloom. Utterly bemused, I stared at it. It appeared to be quite close – comparatively; and I puzzled to understand how the earth had come so near to it, without my having seen it before.

The light, thrown by the star, grew stronger; and, presently, I was aware that it was possible to see the earthscape again; though indistinctly. Awhile, I stared, trying to make out whether I could distinguish any detail of the world's surface, but I found the light insufficient. In a little, I gave up the attempt, and glanced once more toward the star. Even in the short space, that my attention had been diverted, it had increased considerably, and seemed now, to my bewildered sight, about a quarter of the size of the full moon. The light it threw, was extraordinarily powerful; yet its colour was so abominably unfamiliar, that such of the world as I could see, showed unreal; more as though I looked out upon a landscape of shadow, than aught else.

All this time, the great crescent was increasing in brightness, and began, now, to shine with a perceptible shade of green. Steadily, the star increased in size and brilliancy, until it showed, fully as large as half a full moon; and, as it grew greater and brighter, so did the vast crescent throw out more and more light, though of an ever-deepening hue of green. Under the combined blaze of their radiances, the wilderness that stretched before me, became steadily more visible. Soon, I seemed able to stare across the whole world, which now appeared, beneath the strange light, terrible in its cold and awful, flat dreariness.

It was a little later that my attention was drawn to the fact that the great star of green flame was slowly sinking out of the North, toward the East. At first, I could scarcely believe that I saw aright; but soon there could be no doubt that it was so. Gradually, it sank, and, as it fell, the vast crescent of glowing green, began to dwindle and dwindle, until it became a mere arc of light, against the livid coloured sky. Later it vanished, disappearing in the self-same spot from which I had seen it slowly emerge.

By this time, the star had come to within some thirty degrees of the hidden horizon. In size it could now have rivalled the moon at its full; though, even yet, I could not distinguish its disk. This fact led me to conceive that it was, still, an extraordinary distance away; and, this being so, I knew that its size must be huge, beyond the conception of man to understand or imagine.

Suddenly, as I watched, the lower edge of the star vanished – cut by a straight, dark line. A minute – or a century – passed, and it dipped lower, until the half of it had disappeared from sight. Far away out on the great plain, I saw a monstrous shadow blotting it out, and advancing swiftly. Only a third of the star was visible now. Then, like a flash, the solution of this extraordinary phenomenon revealed itself to me. The star was sinking behind the enormous mass of the dead sun. Or rather, the sun – obedient to its attraction – was rising toward it, with the earth following in its trail. As these thoughts expanded in my mind, the star vanished; being completely hidden by the tremendous bulk of the sun. Over the earth there fell, once more, the brooding night.

With the darkness, came an intolerable feeling of loneliness and dread. For the first time, I thought of the Pit, and its inmates. After that, there rose in my memory the still more terrible Thing, that had haunted the shores of the Sea of Sleep, and lurked in the shadows of this old building. Where were they? I wondered – and shivered with miserable thoughts. For a time, fear held me, and I prayed, wildly and incoherently, for some ray of light with which to dispel the cold blackness that enveloped the world.

How long I waited, it is impossible to say – certainly for a very great period. Then, all at once, I saw a loom of light shine out ahead. Gradually, it became more distinct. Suddenly, a ray of vivid green, flashed across the darkness. At the same moment, I saw a thin line of livid flame, far in the night. An instant, it seemed, and it had grown into a great clot of fire; beneath which, the world lay bathed in a blaze of emerald green light. Steadily it grew, until, presently, the whole of the green star had come into sight again. But now, it could be scarcely called a star; for it had increased to vast proportions, being incomparably greater than the sun had been in the olden time.

"Then, as I stared, I became aware that I could see the edge of the lifeless sun, glowing like a great crescent-moon. Slowly, its lighted surface, broadened out to me, until half of its diameter was visible; and the star began to drop away on my right. Time passed, and the earth moved on, slowly traversing the tremendous face of the dead sun."

Gradually, as the earth travelled forward, the star fell still more to the right; until, at last, it shone on the back of the house, sending a flood of broken rays, in through the skeleton-like walls. Glancing upward, I saw that much of the ceiling had vanished, enabling me to see that the upper storeys were even more decayed. The roof had, evidently, gone entirely; and I could see the green effulgence of the starlight shining in, slantingly.

Chapter XIX
The End of the Solar System

From the abutment, where once had been the windows, through which I had watched that first, fatal dawn, I could see that the sun was hugely greater than it had been, when first the Star lit the world. So great was it, that its lower edge seemed almost to touch the far horizon. Even as I watched, I imagined that it drew closer. The radiance of green that lit the frozen earth, grew steadily brighter.

Thus, for a long space, things were. Then, on a sudden, I saw that the sun was changing shape, and growing smaller, just as the moon would have done in past time. In a while, only a third of the illuminated part was turned toward the earth. The Star bore away on the left.

Gradually, as the world moved on, the Star shone upon the front of the house, once more; while the sun showed, only as a great bow of green fire. An instant, it seemed, and the sun had vanished. The Star was still fully visible. Then the earth moved into the black shadow of the sun, and all was night – Night, black, starless, and intolerable.

Filled with tumultuous thoughts, I watched across the night – waiting. Years, it may have been, and then, in the dark house behind me, the clotted stillness of the world was broken. I seemed to hear a soft padding of many feet, and a faint, inarticulate whisper of sound, grew on my sense. I looked 'round into the blackness, and saw a multitude of eyes. As I stared, they increased, and appeared to come toward me. For an instant, I stood, unable to move. Then a hideous swine-noise rose up into the night; and, at that, I leapt from the window, out onto the frozen world. I have a confused notion of having run a while; and, after that, I just waited – waited. Several times, I heard shrieks; but always as though from a distance. Except for these sounds, I had no idea of the whereabouts of the house. Time moved onward. I was conscious of little, save a sensation of cold and hopelessness and fear.

An age, it seemed, and there came a glow, that told of the coming light. It grew, tardily. Then – with a loom of unearthly glory – the first ray from the Green Star, struck over the edge of the dark sun, and lit the world. It fell upon a great, ruined structure, some two hundred yards away. It was the house. Staring, I saw a fearsome sight – over its walls crawled a legion of unholy things, almost covering the old building, from tottering towers to base. I could see them, plainly; they were the Swine-creatures.

The world moved out into the light of the Star, and I saw that, now, it seemed to stretch across a quarter of the heavens. The glory of its livid light was so tremendous, that it appeared to fill the sky with quivering flames. Then, I saw the sun. It was so close that half of its diameter lay below the horizon; and, as the world circled across its face, it seemed to tower right up into the sky, a stupendous dome of emerald-coloured fire. From time to time, I glanced toward the house; but the Swine-things seemed unaware of my proximity.

Years appeared to pass, slowly. The earth had almost reached the centre of the sun's disk. The light from the Green *Sun* – as now it must be called – shone through the interstices, that gapped the mouldered walls of the old house, giving them the appearance of being wrapped in green flames. The Swine-creatures still crawled about the walls.

Suddenly, there rose a loud roar of swine-voices, and, up from the centre of the roofless house, shot a vast column of blood-red flame. I saw the little, twisted towers and turrets flash into fire; yet still preserving their twisted crookedness. The beams of the Green Sun, beat upon the house, and intermingled with its lurid glows; so that it appeared a blazing furnace of red and green fire.

Fascinated, I watched, until an overwhelming sense of coming danger, drew my attention. I glanced up, and, at once, it was borne upon me that the sun was closer; so close, in fact, that it seemed to overhang the world. Then – I know not how – I was caught up into strange heights – floating like a bubble in the awful effulgence.

Far below me, I saw the earth, with the burning house leaping into an ever-growing mountain of flame, 'round about it, the ground appeared to be glowing; and, in places, heavy wreaths of yellow smoke ascended from the earth. It seemed as though the world were becoming ignited from that one plague-spot of fire. Faintly, I could see the Swine-things. They appeared quite unharmed. Then the ground seemed to cave in, suddenly, and the house, with its load of foul creatures, disappeared into the depths of the earth, sending a strange, blood-coloured cloud into the heights. I remembered the hell Pit under the house.

In a while, I looked 'round. The huge bulk of the sun, rose high above me. The distance between it and the earth grew rapidly less. Suddenly, the earth appeared to shoot forward. In a moment, it had traversed the space between it and the sun. I heard no sound; but, out from the sun's face, gushed an ever-growing tongue of dazzling flame. It seemed to leap, almost to the distant Green Sun – shearing through the emerald light, a very cataract of blinding fire. It reached its limit, and sank; and, on the sun, glowed a vast splash of burning white – the grave of the earth.

The sun was very close to me, now. Presently, I found that I was rising higher; until, at last, I rode above it, in the emptiness. The Green Sun was now so huge that its breadth seemed to fill up all the sky, ahead. I looked down, and noted that the sun was passing directly beneath me.

A year may have gone by – or a century – and I was left, suspended, alone. The sun showed far in front – a black, circular mass, against the molten splendour of the great, Green Orb. Near one edge, I observed that a lurid glow had appeared, marking the place where the earth had fallen. By this, I knew that the long-dead sun was still revolving, though with great slowness.

Afar to my right, I seemed to catch, at times, a faint glow of whitish light. For a great time, I was uncertain whether to put this down to fancy or not. Thus, for a while, I stared, with fresh wonderings; until, at last, I knew that it was no imaginary thing; but a reality. It grew brighter; and, presently, there slid out of the green, a pale globe of softest white. It came nearer, and I saw that it was apparently surrounded by a robe of gently glowing clouds. Time passed...

I glanced toward the diminishing sun. It showed, only as a dark blot on the face of the Green Sun. As I watched, I saw it grow smaller, steadily, as though rushing toward the superior orb, at an immense speed. Intently, I stared. What would happen? I was conscious of extraordinary emotions, as I realized that it would strike the Green Sun. It grew no bigger than a pea, and I looked, with my whole soul, to witness the final end of our system – that system which had borne the world through so many aeons, with its multitudinous sorrows and joys; and now –

Suddenly, something crossed my vision, cutting from sight all vestige of the spectacle I watched with such soul-interest. What happened to the dead sun, I did not see; but I have no reason – in the light of that which I saw afterward – to disbelieve that it fell into the strange fire of the Green Sun, and so perished.

And then, suddenly, an extraordinary question rose in my mind, whether this stupendous globe of green fire might not be the vast Central Sun – the great sun, 'round which our universe and countless others revolve. I felt confused. I thought of the probable end of the dead sun, and another suggestion came, dumbly – Do the dead stars make the Green Sun their grave? The idea appealed to me with no sense of grotesqueness; but rather as something both possible and probable.

Chapter XX
The Celestial Globes

For a while, many thoughts crowded my mind, so that I was unable to do aught, save stare, blindly, before me. I seemed whelmed in a sea of doubt and wonder and sorrowful remembrance.

It was later, that I came out of my bewilderment. I looked about, dazedly. Thus, I saw so extraordinary a sight that, for a while, I could scarcely believe I was not still wrapped in the visionary tumult of my own thoughts. Out of the reigning green, had grown a boundless river of softly shimmering globes – each one enfolded in a wondrous fleece of pure cloud. They reached, both above and below me, to an unknown distance; and, not only hid the shining of the Green Sun; but supplied, in place thereof, a tender glow of light, that suffused itself around me, like unto nothing I have ever seen, before or since.

In a little, I noticed that there was about these spheres, a sort of transparency, almost as though they were formed of clouded crystal, within which burned a radiance – gentle and subdued. They moved on, past me, continually, floating onward at no great speed; but rather as though they had eternity before them. A great while, I watched, and could perceive no end to them. At times, I seemed to distinguish faces, amid the cloudiness; but strangely indistinct, as though partly real, and partly formed of the mistiness through which they showed.

For a long time, I waited, passively, with a sense of growing content. I had no longer that feeling of unutterable loneliness; but felt, rather, that I was less alone than I had been for kalpas of years. This feeling of contentment, increased, so that I would have been satisfied to float in company with those celestial globules, forever.

Ages slipped by, and I saw the shadowy faces, with increased frequency, also with greater plainness. Whether this was due to my soul having become more attuned to its surroundings, I cannot tell – probably it was so. But, however this may be, I am assured now, only of the fact that I became steadily more conscious of a new mystery about me, telling me that I had, indeed, penetrated within the borderland of some unthought-of region – some subtle, intangible place, or form, of existence.

The enormous stream of luminous spheres continued to pass me, at an unvarying rate – countless millions; and still they came, showing no signs of ending, nor even diminishing.

Then, as I was borne, silently, upon the unbuoying ether, I felt a sudden, irresistible, forward movement, toward one of the passing globes. An instant, and I was beside it. Then, I slid through, into the interior, without experiencing the least resistance, of any description. For a short while, I could see nothing; and waited, curiously.

All at once, I became aware that a sound broke the inconceivable stillness. It was like the murmur of a great sea at calm – a sea breathing in its sleep. Gradually, the mist that obscured my sight, began to thin away; and so, in time, my vision dwelt once again upon the silent surface of the Sea of Sleep.

For a little, I gazed, and could scarcely believe I saw aright. I glanced 'round. There was the great globe of pale fire, swimming, as I had seen it before, a short distance above the dim horizon. To my left, far across the sea, I discovered, presently, a faint line, as of thin haze, which I guessed to be the shore, where my Love and I had met, during those wonderful periods of soul-wandering, that had been granted to me in the old earth days.

Another, a troubled, memory came to me – of the Formless Thing that had haunted the shores of the Sea of Sleep. The guardian of that silent, echoless place. These, and other, details, I remembered, and knew, without doubt that I was looking out upon that same sea. With the assurance, I was filled with an overwhelming feeling of surprise, and joy, and shaken expectancy, conceiving it possible that I was about to see my Love, again. Intently, I gazed around; but could catch no sight of her. At that, for a little, I felt hopeless. Fervently, I prayed, and ever peered, anxiously.... How still was the sea!

Down, far beneath me, I could see the many trails of changeful fire, that had drawn my attention, formerly. Vaguely, I wondered what caused them; also, I remembered that I had intended to ask my Dear One about them, as well as many other matters – and I had been forced to leave her, before the half that I had wished to say was said.

My thoughts came back with a leap. I was conscious that something had touched me. I turned quickly. God, Thou wert indeed gracious – it was she! She looked up into my eyes, with an eager longing, and I looked down to her, with all my soul. I should like to have held her; but the glorious purity of her face kept me afar. Then, out of the winding mist, she put her dear arms. Her whisper came to me, soft as the rustle of a passing cloud. "Dearest!" she said. That was all; but I had heard, and, in a moment I held her to me – as I prayed – forever.

In a little, she spoke of many things, and I listened. Willingly would I have done so through all the ages that are to come. At times, I whispered back, and my whispers brought to her spirit face, once more, an indescribably delicate tint – the bloom of love. Later, I spoke more freely, and to each word she listened, and made answer, delightfully; so that, already, I was in Paradise.

She and I; and nothing, save the silent, spacious void to see us; and only the quiet waters of the Sea of Sleep to hear us.

Long before, the floating multitude of cloud-enfolded spheres had vanished into nothingness. Thus, we looked upon the face of the slumberous deeps, and were alone. Alone, God, I would be thus alone in the hereafter, and yet be never lonely! I had her, and, greater than this, she had me. Aye, aeon-aged me; and on this thought, and some others, I hope to exist through the few remaining years that may yet lie between us.

Chapter XXI
The Dark Sun

How long our souls lay in the arms of joy, I cannot say; but, all at once, I was waked from my happiness, by a diminution of the pale and gentle light that lit the Sea of Sleep. I turned toward the huge, white orb, with a premonition of coming trouble. One side of it was curving inward, as though a convex, black shadow were sweeping across it. My memory went back. It was thus, that the darkness had come, before our last parting. I turned toward my Love, inquiringly. With a sudden knowledge of woe, I noticed how wan and unreal she had grown, even in that brief space. Her voice seemed to come to me from a distance. The touch of her hands was no more than the gentle pressure of a summer wind, and grew less perceptible.

Already, quite half of the immense globe was shrouded. A feeling of desperation seized me. Was she about to leave me? Would she have to go, as she had gone before? I questioned her, anxiously, frightenedly; and she, nestling closer, explained, in that strange, faraway voice, that it was imperative she should leave me, before the Sun of Darkness – as she termed it – blotted out the light. At this confirmation of my fears, I was overcome with despair; and could only look, voicelessly, across the quiet plains of the silent sea.

How swiftly the darkness spread across the face of the White Orb. Yet, in reality, the time must have been long, beyond human comprehension.

At last, only a crescent of pale fire, lit the, now dim, Sea of Sleep. All this while, she had held me; but, with so soft a caress, that I had been scarcely conscious of it. We waited there, together, she and I; speechless, for very sorrow. In the dimming light, her face showed, shadowy – blending into the dusky mistiness that encircled us.

Then, when a thin, curved line of soft light was all that lit the sea, she released me – pushing me from her, tenderly. Her voice sounded in my ears, "I may not stay longer, Dear One." It ended in a sob.

She seemed to float away from me, and became invisible. Her voice came to me, out of the shadows, faintly; apparently from a great distance:

"A little while—" It died away, remotely. In a breath, the Sea of Sleep darkened into night. Far to my left, I seemed to see, for a brief instant, a soft glow. It vanished, and, in the same moment, I became aware that I was no longer above the still sea; but once more suspended in infinite space, with the Green Sun – now eclipsed by a vast, dark sphere – before me.

Utterly bewildered, I stared, almost unseeingly, at the ring of green flames, leaping above the dark edge. Even in the chaos of my thoughts, I wondered, dully, at their extraordinary shapes. A multitude of questions assailed me. I thought more of her, I had so lately seen, than of the sight before me. My grief, and thoughts of the future, filled me. Was I doomed to be separated from her, always? Even in the old earth-days, she had been mine, only for a little while; then she had left me, as I thought, forever. Since then, I had seen her but these times, upon the Sea of Sleep.

A feeling of fierce resentment filled me, and miserable questionings. Why could I not have gone with my Love? What reason to keep us apart? Why had I to wait alone, while she slumbered through the years, on the still bosom of the Sea of Sleep? The Sea of Sleep! My thoughts turned, inconsequently, out of their channel of bitterness, to fresh, desperate questionings. Where was it? Where was it? I seemed to have but just parted from my Love, upon its quiet surface, and it had gone, utterly. It could not be far away! And the White Orb which I had seen hidden in the shadow of the Sun of Darkness! My sight dwelt upon the Green Sun – eclipsed. What had eclipsed it? Was there a vast, dead star circling it? Was the *Central* Sun – as I had come to regard it – a double star? The thought had come, almost unbidden; yet why should it not be so?

My thoughts went back to the White Orb. Strange, that it should have been – I stopped. An idea had come, suddenly. The White Orb and the Green Sun! Were they one and the same? My imagination wandered backward, and I remembered the luminous globe to which I had been so unaccountably attracted. It was curious that I should have forgotten it, even momentarily. Where were the others? I reverted again to the globe I had entered. I thought, for a time, and matters became clearer. I conceived that, by entering that impalpable globule, I had passed, at once, into some further, and, until then, invisible dimension; there, the Green Sun was still visible; but as a stupendous sphere of pale, white light – almost as though its ghost showed, and not its material part.

A long time, I mused on the subject. I remembered how, on entering the sphere, I had, immediately, lost all sight of the others. For a still further period, I continued to revolve the different details in my mind.

In a while, my thoughts turned to other things. I came more into the present, and began to look about me, seeingly. For the first time, I perceived that innumerable rays, of a subtle, violet hue, pierced the strange semi-darkness, in all directions. They radiated from the fiery rim of the Green Sun. They seemed to grow upon my vision, so that, in a little, I saw that they were countless. The night was filled with them – spreading outward from the Green Sun, fan-wise. I concluded that I was enabled to see them, by reason of the Sun's glory being cut off by the eclipse. They reached right out into space, and vanished.

Gradually, as I looked, I became aware that fine points of intensely brilliant light, traversed the rays. Many of them seemed to travel from the Green Sun, into distance. Others came out of the void, toward the Sun; but one and all, each kept strictly to the ray in which it travelled. Their speed was inconceivably great; and it was only when they neared the Green Sun, or as they left it, that I could see them as separate specks of light. Further from the sun, they became thin lines of vivid fire within the violet.

The discovery of these rays, and the moving sparks, interested me, extraordinarily. To where did they lead, in such countless profusion? I thought of the worlds in space.... And those sparks! Messengers! Possibly, the idea was fantastic; but I was not conscious of its being so. Messengers! Messengers from the Central Sun!

An idea evolved itself, slowly. Was the Green Sun the abode of some vast Intelligence? The thought was bewildering. Visions of the Unnameable rose, vaguely. Had I, indeed, come upon the dwelling-place of the Eternal? For a time, I repelled the thought, dumbly. It was too stupendous. Yet...

Huge, vague thoughts had birth within me. I felt, suddenly, terribly naked. And an awful Nearness, shook me.

And Heaven...! Was that an illusion?

My thoughts came and went, erratically. The Sea of Sleep – and she! Heaven.... I came back, with a bound, to the present. Somewhere, out of the void behind me, there rushed an immense, dark body – huge and silent. It was a dead star, hurling onward to the burying place of the stars. It drove between me and the Central Suns – blotting them out from my vision, and plunging me into an impenetrable night.

An age, and I saw again the violet rays. A great while later – aeons it must have been – a circular glow grew in the sky, ahead, and I saw the edge of the receding star show darkly against it. Thus, I knew that it was nearing the Central Suns. Presently, I saw the bright ring of the Green Sun, show plainly against the night The star had passed into the shadow of the Dead Sun. After that, I just waited. The strange years went slowly, and ever, I watched, intently.

The thing I had expected, came at last – suddenly, awfully. A vast flare of dazzling light. A streaming burst of white flame across the dark void. For an indefinite while, it soared outward – a gigantic mushroom of fire. It ceased to grow. Then, as time went by, it began to sink backward, slowly. I saw, now, that it came from a huge, glowing spot near the centre of the Dark Sun. Mighty flames, still soared outward from this. Yet, spite of its size, the grave of the star was no more than the shining of Jupiter upon the face of an ocean, when compared with the inconceivable mass of the Dead Sun.

I may remark here, once more, that no words will ever convey to the imagination the enormous bulk of the two Central Suns.

How All Things Began

From Norse mythology

ONCE UPON A TIME, before ever this world was made, there was neither earth nor sea, nor air, nor light, but only a great yawning gulf, full of twilight, where these things should be.

To the north of this gulf lay the Home of Mist, a dark and dreary land, out of which flowed a river of water from a spring that never ran dry. As the water in its onward course met the bitter blasts of wind from the yawning gulf, it hardened into great blocks of ice, which rolled far down into the abyss with a thunderous roar and piled themselves one on another until they formed mountains of glistening ice.

South of this gulf lay the Home of Fire, a land of burning heat, guarded by a giant with a flaming sword which, as he flashed it to and fro before the entrance, sent forth showers of sparks. And these sparks fell upon the ice blocks and partly melted them, so that they sent up clouds of steam; and these again were frozen into hoarfrost, which filled all the space that was left in the midst of the mountains of ice.

Then one day, when the gulf was full to the very top, this great mass of frosty rime, warmed by the flames from the Home of Fire and frozen by the cold airs from the Home of Mist, came to life and became the Giant Ymir, with a living, moving body and cruel heart of ice.

Now there was as yet no tree, nor grass, nor anything that would serve for food, in this gloomy abyss. But when the Giant Ymir began to grope around for something to satisfy his hunger, he heard a sound as of some animal chewing the cud; and there among the ice-hills. he saw a gigantic cow, from whose udder flowed four great streams of milk, and with this his craving was easily stilled.

But the cow was hungry also, and began to lick the salt off the blocks of ice by which she was surrounded. And presently, as she went on licking with her strong, rough tongue, a head of hair pushed itself through the melting ice. Still the cow went on licking, until she had at last melted all the icy covering and there stood fully revealed the frame of a mighty man.

Ymir looked with eyes of hatred at this being, born of snow and ice, for somehow he knew that his heart was warm and kind, and that he and his sons would always be the enemies of the evil race of the Frost Giants.

So, indeed, it came to pass. For from the sons of Ymir came a race of giants whose pleasure was to work evil on the earth; and from the Sons of the Iceman sprang the race of the gods, chief of whom was Odin, Father of All Things that ever were made; and Odin and his brothers began at once to war against the wicked Frost Giants, and most of all against the cold-hearted Ymir, whom in the end they slew.

Now when, after a hard fight, the Giant Ymir was slain, such a river of blood flowed forth from his wounds that it drowned all the rest of the Frost Giants save one, who escaped in a boat, with only his wife on board, and sailed away to the edge of the world. And from him sprang all the new race of Frost Giants, who at every opportunity issued from their land of twilight and desolation to harm the gods in their abode of bliss.

Now when the giants had been thus driven out, All-Father Odin set to work with his brothers to make the earth, the sea, and the sky; and these they fashioned out of the great body of the Giant Ymir.

Out of his flesh they formed Midgard, the earth, which lay in the centre of the gulf; and all round it they planted his eyebrows to make a high fence which should defend it from the race of giants.

With his bones they made the lofty hills, with his teeth the cliffs, and his thick curly hair took root and became trees, bushes, and the green grass.

With his blood they made the ocean, and his great skull, poised aloft, became the arching sky. Just below this they scattered his brains, and made of them the heavy grey clouds that lie between earth and heaven.

The sky itself was held in place by four strong dwarfs, who support it on their broad shoulders as they stand east and west and south and north.

The next thing was to give light to the new-made world. So the gods caught sparks from the Home of Fire and set them in the sky for stars; and they took the living flame and made of it the sun and moon, which they placed in chariots of gold, and harnessed to them beautiful horses, with flowing manes of gold and silver. Before the horses of the sun, they placed a mighty shield to protect them from its hot rays; but the swift moon steeds needed no such protection from its gentle heat.

And now all was ready save that there was no one to drive the horses of the sun and moon. This task was given to Mani and Sol, the beautiful son and daughter of a giant; and these fair charioteers drive their fleet steeds along the paths marked out by the gods, and not only give light to the earth but mark out months and days for the sons of men.

Then All-Father Odin called forth Night, the gloomy daughter of the cold-hearted giant folk, and set her to drive the dark chariot drawn by the black horse, Frosty-Mane, from whose long wavy hair the drops of dew and hoarfrost fall upon the earth below. After her drove her radiant son, Day, with his white steed Shining-Mane, from whom the bright beams of daylight shine forth to gladden the hearts of men.

But the wicked giants were very angry when they saw all these good things; and they set in the sky two hungry wolves, that the fierce, grey creatures might forever pursue the sun and moon, and devour them, and so bring all things to an end. Sometimes, indeed, or so say the men of the North, the grey wolves almost succeed in swallowing sun or moon; and then the earth children make such an uproar that the fierce beasts drop their prey in fear. And the sun and moon flee more rapidly than before, still pursued by the hungry monsters.

One day, so runs the tale, as Mani, the Man in the Moon, was hastening on his course, he gazed upon the earth and saw two beautiful little children, a boy and a girl, carrying between them a pail of water. They looked very tired and sleepy, and indeed they were, for a cruel giant made them fetch and carry water all night long, when they should have been in bed. So Mani put out a long, long arm and snatched up the children and set them in the moon, pail and all; and there you can see them on any moonlit night for yourself.

How the Sun Came into the Sky

By Okun Asere of Mfamosing, of the Ekoi people,
Nigeria and Cameroon

ONCE THERE LIVED a man named Agbo and his wife named Nchun. They had a daughter called Afion. When the latter was about fifteen years old, her father and mother agreed that it was time to put her in the fatting-house. So they sent for an old woman named Umaw, who was very wise in such matters, and told her to prepare everything. She came and made all ready, and then said, "There is nothing more to be done. I will go back to my own place."

The parents "dashed" her two bottles of palm oil and two pieces of dried meat. To the townsfolk also the father gave many demi-johns of palm wine. He took ten pieces of dried meat, cooked them and called all the people to a feast, because his daughter had entered the fatting-house that day.

After about four months the mother, Nchun, said to Afion, "You have stayed long enough. You may come out tomorrow."

Then the father got together several demi-johns of palm wine, the kind that is drawn from the tops of the palm trees, and five pieces of dried meat. The mother also took the same amount of meat and drink. The father announced to the townsfolk:

"My daughter is going to clean her face tomorrow. Let all men stay in the town." Next morning the parents cooked ten calabashes full of chop for the people, who feasted all that day.

In the evening the father took his daughter into the other part of the house, and said to her, "Today you have cleaned your face. From today if a man should call you into his house you can go."

Next morning the mother cooked for the girl. Then the parents went to their farm and left her with a small boy who was as yet too young to work.

Now at that time Eyo (the Sun) dwelt upon earth, in the place that lies towards the great water. His body was redder than fire. He was very tall and thin. He lay in the bush, so that all his body up to the waist was hidden by the bush trees, but he stretched out his head and arms right into the room where the fatting-girl was. He said to her:

"I want to keep sweethearts with you," but she answered:

"You are so tall, your head, hands and arms alone fill my room. I cannot keep friends with you."

When he heard this the Sun was very angry, and said, "If you are not willing to become my sweetheart I will take my length away, but first I will kill you and leave you here."

Anon said to him:

"I do not care so much if you kill me. I would rather die than wed such a terrible being as you."

As soon as Eyo heard this he stretched out his hands, and killed her for true.

All this time the small boy had hidden himself where he could see everything that happened. He watched the terrible visitor draw the body into the middle room. Next he saw him go into the inner place where Nchun kept the fine mats. He took four of these and covered the fatting-girl. Next he went into another place where the fine cloths were kept. Of these again he took four, with four blankets and two small loin cloths. All these he laid over the dead girl.

After this Eyo left the house and stood in the little courtyard at the back. He began to lift his body up to the sky. He was so long that, though he tried all day, six o'clock in the evening was come and he had not quite finished. Some of him was in the sky and some still stayed upon earth.

When Agbo and Nchun came back from their farm, the small boy crept out from his hiding place, and said to them:

"The man who killed your daughter is a very tall man."

Father and mother began to weep. They took the body and called all the townsfolk together for the burial.

The people came with four guns. They wished to shoot the man who had killed the fatting-girl. At the back of the house they found him. They could not see all his body, but the feet only. With their four guns they shot at these. Then he gave a great spring and drew his feet up, after the rest of him, into the sky.

A fine house was standing there ready. Eyo entered and closed the door that he might be safe from the guns of the townsmen. In the morning, about six o'clock, he opened a window, and looked out a little way, very cautiously. When no one shot at him, he felt safer, and put his face right out. All day he looked down in case Anon should not be dead and he might see her once more. The people were busy away at their farms. At six o'clock they came back, so he drew in his face again, lest they should begin to shoot once more.

That is the reason why you only see the sun in the daytime. In the evening he draws back into his house and shuts the windows and doors.

How the Sun, the Moon and the Wind Went Out to Dinner

From Indian folklore

ONE DAY THE SUN, the Moon and the Wind went out to dine with their uncle and aunt, the Thunder and Lightning. Their mother (one of the most distant Stars you see far up in the sky) waited alone for her children's return.

Now both the Sun and the Wind were greedy and selfish. They enjoyed the great feast that had been prepared for them, without a thought of saving any of it to take home to their mother; but the gentle Moon did not forget her. Of every dainty dish that was brought round she placed a small portion under one of her beautiful long fingernails, that the Star might also have a share in the treat.

On their return, their mother, who had kept watch for them all night long with her little bright eye, said, "Well, children, what have you brought home for me?" Then the Sun (who was eldest) said, "I have brought nothing home for you. I went out to enjoy myself with my friends, not to fetch a dinner for my mother!" And the Wind said, "Neither have I brought anything home for you, mother. You could hardly expect me to bring a collection of good things for you, when I merely went out for my own pleasure." But the Moon said, "Mother, fetch a plate; see what I have brought you." And shaking her hands she showered down such a choice dinner as never was seen before.

Then the Star turned to the Sun and spoke thus, "Because you went out to amuse yourself with your friends, and feasted and enjoyed yourself without any thought of your mother at home, you shall be cursed. Henceforth, your rays shall ever be hot and scorching, and shall burn all that they touch. And men shall hate you and cover their heads when you appear."

(And that is why the Sun is so hot to this day.)

Then she turned to the Wind and said, "You also, who forgot your mother in the midst of your selfish pleasures, hear your doom. You shall always blow in the hot, dry weather, and shall parch and shrivel all living things. And men shall detest and avoid you from this very time."

(And that is why the Wind in the hot weather is still so disagreeable.)

But to the Moon she said, "Daughter, because you remembered your mother, and kept for her a share in your own enjoyment, from henceforth you shall be ever cool and calm and bright. No noxious glare shall accompany your pure rays, and men shall always call you 'blessed.'"

(And that is why the Moon's light is so soft and cool and beautiful even to this day.)

Hyacinthus

From Greek mythology

The sad death
Of Hyacinthus, when the cruel breath
Of Zephyr slew him – Zephyr penitent
Who now, ere Phoebus mounts the firmament,
Fondles the flower amid the sobbing rain.
John Keats

"WHOM THE GODS love die young." Truly it would seem so, as we read the old tales of men and of women beloved of the gods. To those men who were deemed worthy of being companions of the gods, seemingly no good fortune came. Yet, after all, if even in a brief span of life they had tasted god-given happiness, was their fate one to be pitied? Rather let us keep our tears for those who, in a colourless grey world, have seen the dull days go past laden with trifling duties, unnecessary cares and ever-narrowing ideals, and have reached old age and the grave – no narrower than their lives – without ever having known a fulness of happiness, such as the Olympians knew, or ever having dared to reach upwards and to hold fellowship with the Immortals.

Hyacinthus was a Spartan youth, son of Clio, one of the Muses, and of the mortal with whom she had mated, and from mother, or father, or from the gods themselves, he had received the gift of beauty. It chanced one day that as Apollo drove his chariot on its all-conquering round, he saw the boy. Hyacinthus was as fair to look upon as the fairest of women, yet he was not only full of grace, but was muscular, and strong as a straight young pine on Mount Olympus that fears not the blind rage of the North Wind nor the angry tempests of the South.

When Apollo had spoken with him he found that the face of Hyacinthus did not belie the heart within him, and gladly the god felt that at last he had found the perfect companion, the ever courageous and joyous young mate, whose mood was always ready to meet his own. Did Apollo desire to hunt, with merry shout Hyacinthus called the hounds. Did the great god deign to fish, Hyacinthus was ready to fetch the nets and to throw himself, whole-souled, into the great affair of chasing and of landing the silvery fishes. When Apollo wished to climb the mountains, to heights so lonely that not even the moving of an eagle's wing broke the everlasting stillness, Hyacinthus – his strong limbs too perfect for the chisel of any sculptor worthily to reproduce – was ready and eager for the climb. And when, on the mountain top, Apollo gazed in silence over illimitable space, and watched the silver car of his sister Diana rising slowly into the deep blue of the sky, silvering land and water as she passed, it was never Hyacinthus who was the first to speak – with words to break the spell of Nature's perfect beauty, shared in perfect companionship. There were times, too, when Apollo would play his lyre, and when naught but the music of his own making could fulfil his longing. And when those times came, Hyacinthus would lie at the feet of his friend – of the friend who was a god – and would listen, with eyes of rapturous joy, to the music that his master made. A very perfect friend was this friend of the sun-god.

Nor was it Apollo alone who desired the friendship of Hyacinthus. Zephyrus, god of the South Wind, had known him before Apollo crossed his path and had eagerly desired him for a friend. But who could stand against Apollo? Sulkily Zephyrus marked their ever-ripening friendship, and in his heart jealousy grew into hatred, and hatred whispered to him of revenge. Hyacinthus excelled at all sports, and when he played quoits it was sheer joy for Apollo, who loved all things beautiful, to watch him as he stood to throw the disc, his taut muscles making him look like Hermes, ready to spurn the cumbering earth from off his feet. Further even than the god, his friend, could Hyacinthus throw, and always his merry laugh when he succeeded made the god feel that nor man nor god could ever grow old. And so there came that day, fore-ordained by the Fates, when Apollo and Hyacinthus played a match together. Hyacinthus made a valiant throw, and Apollo took his place, and cast the discus high and far. Hyacinthus ran forward eager to measure the distance, shouting with excitement over a throw that had indeed been worthy of a god. Thus did Zephyrus gain his opportunity. Swiftly through the treetops ran the murmuring South Wind, and smote the discus of Apollo with a cruel hand. Against the forehead of Hyacinthus it dashed, smiting the locks that lay upon it, crashing through skin and flesh and bone, felling him to the earth. Apollo ran towards him and raised him in his arms. But the head of Hyacinthus fell over on the god's shoulder, like the head of a lily whose stem is broken. The red blood gushed to the ground, an unquenchable stream, and darkness fell on the eyes of Hyacinthus, and, with the flow of his life's blood, his gallant young soul passed away.

"Would that I could die for thee, Hyacinthus!" cried the god, his god's heart near breaking. "I have robbed thee of thy youth. Thine is the suffering, mine the crime. I shall sing thee ever – oh perfect friend! And evermore shalt thou live as a flower that will speak to the hearts of men of spring, of everlasting youth – of life that lives forever."

As he spoke, there sprang from the blood-drops at his feet a cluster of flowers, blue as the sky in spring, yet hanging their heads as if in sorrow.

And still, when winter is ended, and the song of birds tell us of the promise of spring, if we go to the woods, we find traces of the vow of the sun-god. The trees are budding in buds of rosy hue, the willow branches are decked with silvery catkins powdered with gold. The larches, like slender dryads, wear a feathery garb of tender green, and under the trees of the woods the primroses look up, like fallen stars. Along the woodland path we go, treading on fragrant pine-needles and on the beech leaves of last year that have not yet lost their radiant amber. And, at a turn of the way, the sun-god suddenly shines through the great dark branches of the giants of the forest, and before us lies a patch of exquisite blue, as though a god had robbed the sky and torn from it a precious fragment that seems alive and moving, between the sun and the shadow.

And, as we look, the sun caresses it, and the South Wind gently moves the little bell-shaped flowers of the wild hyacinth as it softly sweeps across them. So does Hyacinthus live on; so do Apollo and Zephyrus still love and mourn their friend.

Hymns to the Sun God Ra

From Egyptian mythology

Hymn I: A Hymn to Ra at His Rising

ADORED BE RA, when he riseth up from the eastern horizon
   of Heaven; they who accompany him extol him.
Here is the Osiris N, the Victorious, and he saith:
O thou radiant Orb, who arisest each day from the Horizon,
   shine thou upon the face of the Osiris N who adoreth thee
   at dawn, and propitiateth thee at the gloaming.
Let the soul of N come forth with thee into heaven, let him
   journey in the Maatit boat and finish his course in the Sektit
   boat till he reach in heaven unto the Stars which set.
He saith, as he invoketh his Lord, the Eternal one:
Hail to thee, Horus of the Two Horizons, who art Chepera Self-originating;
   Beautiful is thy rising up from the horizon, enlightening the two
   Earths with thy rays. All the gods are in exultation when they see
   thee the King of Heaven, with the Nebt Unnut established upon thy
   head (and the diadem of the South and the diadem of the North
   upon thy brow) which maketh her abode in front of thee.
Thoth abideth at the prow of thy bark that he may destroy all thine adversaries.
They who dwell in the Tuat are coming forth to meet thy Majesty,
   and to gaze upon that beautiful semblance of thine.
And I too come to thee that I may be with thee to see thine Orb
   each day; let me not be detained, let me not be repulsed.
Let my limbs be renewed by the contemplation of thy glories, like all thy
   servants, for I am one of those who honoured thee upon earth.
Let me reach the Land of Ages, let me gain the Land of Eternity;
   for thou, my Lord, hast destined them for me.
The Osiris N; he saith:
Hail to thee who risest up from the Horizon as Ra in union with Maat; thou dost
   traverse heaven in peace and all men see thee as thou goest forward. And after
   being concealed from them thou presentest thyself at the dawn of each day.
Brisk is the bark under thy Majesty.
Thy rays are upon men's faces; the golden glories they cannot
   be told: not to be described are thy beams.
The Lands of the gods, the colours of Punit are seen in them; that men
   may form an estimate of that which is hidden from their faces.
Alone art thou when thy form riseth up upon the Sky; let me advance as thou
   advancest, like thy Majesty, without a pause, O Ra, whom none can outstrip.

A mighty march is thine; Leagues by millions, and hundreds of thousands,
in a small moment thou hast travelled them, and thou goest to rest.
Thou completest the hours of the Night, according as thou hast measured them
out. And when thou hast completed them according to thy rule, day dawneth.
Thou presentest thyself at thy place as Ra, as thou risest from the Horizon.
The Osiris N, he saith, as he adoreth thee when thou shinest; He saith to
thee when thou risest up at dawn, as he exalteth thine appearance;
Thou comest forth, most glorious one, fashioning and forming thy limbs,
giving birth to them without any labour, as Ra rising in heaven.
Grant that I may attain to the Heaven of eternity and the abode of thy
servants; let me be united with the venerable and mighty Chu of the
Netherworld; let me come forth with them to see thy glories, as thou
shinest at the gloaming, when thy mother Nut enfoldeth thee.
And when thou turnest thy face to the West, mine hands are in adoration to
thy setting as one who liveth; for it is thou who hast created Eternity.
I have set thee in my heart unceasingly, who art more mighty than all the gods.
The Osiris N, he saith:
Adoration to thee, who arisest out of the Golden, and givest
light to the earth on the day of thy birth. Thy mother bringeth
thee forth upon her hands, that thou mayest give light to the
whole circumference which the Solar Orb enlighteneth.
Mighty Enlightener, who risest up in the Sky and raisest up the tribes
of men by thy Stream, and givest holiday to all districts, towns
and temples; and raising food, nourishment and dainties.
Most Mighty one, master of masters, who defendest every
abode of thine against wrong, Most Glorious one in thine
Evening Bark, Most Illustrious in thy Morning Bark.
Glorify thou the Osiris N in the Netherworld, grant that he
may come into Amenta without defect and free from wrong,
and set him among the faithful and venerable ones.
Let him be united with the souls in the Netherworld, let him sail
about in the country of Aarru after a joyful journey.
Here is the Osiris N.
Come forth into Heaven, sail across the firmament and enter into brotherhood
with the Stars, let salutation be made to thee in the Bark, let invocation
be made to thee in the Morning Bark. Contemplate Ra within his
Ark and do thou propitiate his Orb daily. See the Ant fish in its birth
from the emerald stream, and see the Abtu fish and its rotations.
And let the offender fall prostrate, when he meditates
destruction for me, by blows upon his backbone.
Ra springs forth with a fair wind; the Evening Bark speeds on
and reaches the Haven; the crew of Ra are in exultation
when they look upon him; the Mistress of Life, her heart is
delighted at the overthrow of the adversary of her Lord.
See thou Horus at the Look-out of the ship, and at his sides Thoth and Maat.
All the gods are in exultation when they behold Ra coming in peace to give
new life to the hearts of the Chu, and here is the Osiris N along with them.

Litany: Adored be Ra as He Setteth in the Land of Life

Adored be Ra, as he setteth in the Land of Life.
Hail to thee, who hast come as Tmu, and hast been
  the creator of the cycle of the gods,
Hail to thee, who hast come as the Soul of Souls, August one in Amenta,
Hail to thee, who art above the gods and who lightenest up the Tuat with thy glories,
Hail to thee, who comest in splendour, and goest round in thine Orb,
Hail to thee, who art mightier than the gods, who art
  crowned in Heaven and King in the Tuat,
Hail to thee, who openest the Tuat and disposest of all its doors,
Hail to thee, supreme among the gods, and Weigher of Words in the Netherworld.
Hail to thee, who art in thy Nest, and stirrest the Tuat with thy glory,
Hail to thee, the Great, the Mighty, whose enemies are laid prostrate at their blocks,
Hail to thee, who slaughterest the Sebau and annihilatest Apepi,

(Each invocation of this Litany is followed by)
Give thou delicious breezes of the north wind to the Osiris N.
Horus openeth; the Great, the Mighty, who divideth the earths, the great one
  who resteth in the Mountain of the West, and lighteneth up the Tuat with his
  glories and the Souls in their hidden abode, by shining into their sepulchres.
By hurling harm against the foe thou hast utterly
  destroyed all the adversaries of the Osiris N.

Hymn II: A Hymn to Ra at His Setting

The Osiris N; he saith when he adoreth Ra, the Horus of the
  Two Horizons, when setting in the Land of Life.
Adoration to thee, O Ra; Adoration to thee, O Tmu, at thy coming
  in thy beauty, in thy manifestation, in thy mastery.
Thou sailest over the Heaven, thou travellest over earth and in
  splendour thou reachest the zenith; the two divisions of Heaven
  are in obeisance to thee, and yield adoration to thee.
All the gods of Amenta are in exultation at thy glory. They whose
  abodes are hidden adore thee, and the Great Ones make offerings
  to thee, who for thee have created the soil of earth.
They who are on the Horizon convey thee, and they who are in the Evening Bark
  transport thee, and they say – Adoration at the approach of thy Majesty, Come,
  Come, approach in peace, Oh to thee, Welcome, Lord of Heaven, King of Akerta.
Thy mother Isis embraceth thee, seeing in thee her son, as the Lord of
  Terror, the All-Powerful, as he setteth in the Land of Life at night.
Thy father Tatunen carrieth thee, and his arms are stretched out behind
  thee, and that which hath taken place is made last upon earth.
Wake up from thy rest, thine abode is in Manu.
Let me be entrusted to the fidelity which is yielded to Osiris.
Come, O Ra, Tmu, be thou adored. Do thy will daily. Grant
  success in presence of the cycle of the mighty gods.

Beautiful art thou, O Ra, in thine Horizon of the West; O
    Lord of Law, in the midst of the Horizon.
Very terrible art thou, rich art thou in attributes, and great
    is thy love to those who dwell in the Tuat.

To be said, when Ra sets in the Land of Life; with hands bent downward.

Hymn III: A Hymn to Ra, the Sun God

HAIL TO YOU, Tem! Hail to you, Kheprer, who created himself.
You are the High, in this your name of 'Height'.
You came into being in this your name of 'Kheprer'.
Hail to you, Eye of Horus, which he furnishes with his hands completely.
He permits you not to be obedient to those of the West;
He permits you not to be obedient to those of the East;
He permits you not to be obedient to those of the South;
He permits you not to be obedient to those of the North;
He permits you not to be obedient to those who are in the earth;
For you are obedient to Horus.
He it is who has furnished you, he it is who has built you,
He it is who has made you to be dwelt in.
You do for him whatever he asks of you, in every place
wherever he goes.
You lift up to him the waterfowl that are in you.
You lift up to him the waterfowl that are about to be in you.
You lift up to him every tree that is in you.
You lift up to him every tree that is about to be in you.
You lift up to him the cakes and ale that are in you.
You lift up to him the cakes and ale that are about to be in you.
You lift up to him the gifts that are in you.
You lift up to him the gifts that are about to be in you.
You lift up to him everything that is in you.
You lift up to him everything that is about to be in you.
You take them to him in every place where it pleases him to be.
The doors upon you stand fast shut like the god Anmutef,
They open not to those who are in the West;
They open not to those who are in the East;
They open not to those who are in the North;
They open not to those who are in the South;
They open not to those who are in the middle of the earth;
But they open to Horus.
He it was who made them, he it was who made them stand firm,
He it was who delivered them from every evil attack
    which the god Set made upon them.
He it was who made you to be a settled country in this your name of 'Kerkut'.
He it was who passed bowing after you in your name of 'Nut'.
He it was who delivered you from every evil attack which Set made upon you.

Other Hymns to Ra

The following extracts from Hymns to the Sun-god and Osiris are written in the hieratic character upon slices of limestone now preserved in the Egyptian Museum in Cairo.

"Well dost thou watch, O Horus, who sailest over the sky, thou child who proceedest from the divine father, thou child of fire, who shinest like crystal, who destroyest the darkness and the night. Thou child who growest rapidly, with gracious form, who restest in thine eye. Thou wakest up men who are asleep on their beds, and the reptiles in their nests. Thy boat saileth on the fiery Lake Neserser, and thou traversest the upper sky by means of the winds thereof. The two daughters of the Nile-god crush for thee the fiend Neka, Nubti (*i.e.* Set) pierceth him with his arrows. Keb seizeth (?) him by the joint of his back, Serqet grippeth him at his throat. The flame of this serpent that is over the door of thy house burneth him up. The Great Company of the Gods are wroth with him, and they rejoice because he is cut to pieces. The Children of Horus grasp their knives, and inflict very many gashes in him. Hail! Thine enemy hath fallen, and Truth standeth firm before thee. When thou again transformest thyself into Tem, thou givest thy hand to the Lords of Akert (*i.e.* the dead), those who lie in death give thanks for thy beauties when thy light falleth upon them. They declare unto thee what is their hearts' wish, which is that they may see thee again. When thou hast passed them by, the darkness covereth them, each one in his coffin. Thou art the lord of those who cry out (?) to thee, the god who is beneficent forever. Thou art the Judge of words and deeds, the Chief of chief judges, who stablishest truth, and doest away sin. May he who attacketh me be judged rightly, behold, he is stronger than I am; he hath seized upon my office, and hath carried it off with falsehood. May it be restored to me."

Hymns to the Sun God Surya

From the Rig Veda

Book I, Hymn L

His bright rays bear him up aloft, the God who knoweth all that lives,
Surya, that all may look on him.
The constellations pass away, like thieves, together with their beams,
Before the all-beholding Sun.
His herald rays are seen afar refulgent o'er the world of men,
Like flames of fire that burn and blaze.
Swift and all beautiful art thou, O Surya, maker of the light,
Illuming all the radiant realm.
Thou goest to the hosts of Gods, thou comest hither to mankind,
Hither all light to be beheld.
With that same eye of thine wherewith thou lookest brilliant Varuna,
Upon the busy race of men,
Traversing sky and wide mid-air, thou metest with thy beams our days,
Sun, seeing all things that have birth.
Seven Bay Steeds harnessed to thy car bear thee, O thou farseeing One,
God, Surya, with the radiant hair.
Surya hath yoked the pure bright Seven, the daughters of the car; with these,
His own dear team, he goeth forth.
Looking upon the loftier light above the darkness we have come
To Surya, God among the Gods, the light that is most excellent.
Rising this day, O rich in friends, ascending to the loftier heaven,
Surya remove my heart's disease, take from me this my yellow hue.
To parrots and to starlings let us give away my yellowness,
Or this my yellowness let us transfer to Haritala trees.
With all his conquering vigour this Aditya hath gone up on high,
Giving my foe into mine hand: let me not be my foeman's prey.

Book I, Hymn CXV

The brilliant presence of the Gods hath risen, the eye of Mitra, Varuna and Agni.
The soul of all that moveth not or moveth, the Sun
    hath filled the air and earth and heaven.
Like as a young man followeth a maiden, so doth the
    Sun the Dawn, refulgent Goddess:
Where pious men extend their generations, before
    the Auspicious One for happy fortune.

Auspicious are the Sun's Bay-coloured Horses, bright,
    changing hues, meet for our shouts of triumph.
Bearing our prayers, the sky's ridge have they mounted, and
    in a moment speed round earth and heaven.
This is the Godhead, this might of Surya: he hath
    withdrawn what spread o'er work unfinished.
When he hath loosed his Horses from their station, straight
    over all Night spreadeth out her garment.
In the sky's lap the Sun this form assumeth that Varuna and Mitra may behold it.
His Bay Steeds well maintain his power eternal, at one
    time bright and darksome at another.
This day, O Gods, while Surya is ascending, deliver us from trouble
    and dishonour.
This prayer of ours may Varuna grant, and Mitra, and
    Aditi and Sindhu, Earth and Heaven.

Book V, Hymn XL

Come thou to what the stones have pressed, drink Soma, O thou
    Soma's Lord,
Indra best Vrtra-slayer Strong One, with the Strong.
Strong is the stone, the draught is strong, strong is this Soma that is pressed,
Indra, best Vrtra-slayer, Strong One with the Strong.
As strong I call on thee the Strong, O Thunder-armed, with various aids,
Indra, best Vrtra-slayer, Strong One with the Strong.
Impetuous, Thunderer, Strong, quelling the mighty,
    King, potent, Vrtra-slayer, Soma-drinker,
May he come hither with his yoked Bay Horses; may
    Indra gladden him at the noon libation.
O Surya, when the Asura's descendant Svarbhanu, pierced
    thee through and through with darkness,
All creatures looked like one who is bewildered, who
    knoweth not the place where he is standing.
What time thou smotest down Svarbhanu's magic that
    spread itself beneath the sky, O Indra,
By his fourth sacred prayer Atri discovered Surya
    concealed in gloom that stayed his function.
Let not the oppressor with this dread, through anger
    swallow me up, for I am thine, O Atri.
Mitra art thou, the sender of true blessings: thou
    and King Varuna be both my helpers.
The Brahman Atri, as he set the press-stones, serving
    the Gods with praise and adoration,
Established in the heaven the eye of Surya, and caused
    Svarbhanu's magic arts to vanish.
The Atris found the Sun again, him whom Svarbhanu of the brood
Of Asuras had pierced with gloom. This none besides had power to do.

Book X, Hymn XXXVII

Do homage unto Varuna's and Mitra's Eye: offer this
    solemn worship to the Mighty God,
Who seeth far away, the Ensign, born of Gods. Sing
    praises unto Surya, to the Son of Dyaus.
May this my truthful speech guard me on every side wherever
    heaven and earth and days are spread abroad.
All else that is in motion finds a place of rest: the waters
    ever flow and ever mounts the Sun.
No godless man from time remotest draws thee down when
    thou art driving forth with winged dappled Steeds.
One lustre waits upon thee moving to the cast, and,
    Surya, thou arisest with a different light.
O Surya, with the light whereby thou scatterest gloom, and
    with thy ray impellest every moving thing,
Keep far from us all feeble, worthless sacrifice, and
    drive away disease and every evil dream.
Sent forth thou guardest well the Universe's law, and in
    thy wonted way arisest free from wrath.
When Surya, we address our prayers to thee today, may
    the Gods favour this our purpose and desire.
This invocation, these our words may Heaven and Earth,
    and Indra and the Waters and the Maruts hear.
Ne'er may we suffer want in presence of the Sun, and,
    living happy lives, may we attain old age.
Cheerful in spirit, evermore, and keen of sight, with store
    of children, free from sickness and from sin,
Long-living, may we look, O Surya, upon thee uprising
    day by day, thou great as Mitra is!
Surya, may we live long and look upon thee still, thee, O
    Far-seeing One, bringing the glorious light,
The radiant God, the spring of joy to every eye, as thou
    art mounting up o'er the high shining flood.
Thou by whose lustre all the world of life comes forth,
    and by thy beams again returns unto its rest,
O Surya with the golden hair, ascend for us day after
    day, still bringing purer innocence.
Bless us with shine, bless us with perfect daylight, bless
    us with cold, with fervent heat and lustre.
Bestow on us, O Surya, varied riches, to bless us in our home and when we travel.
Gods, to our living creatures of both kinds vouchsafe
    protection, both to bipeds and to quadrupeds,
That they may drink and eat invigorating food. So grant us
    health and strength and perfect innocence.
If by some grievous sin we have provoked the Gods, O Deities,
    with the tongue or thoughtlessness of heart,

That guilt, O Vasus, lay upon the Evil One, on him
    who ever leads us into deep distress.

Book X, Hymn LXXXV

Truth is the base that bears the earth; by Surya are the heavens sustained.
By Law the Adityas stand secure, and Soma holds his place in heaven.
By Soma are the Adityas strong, by Soma mighty is the earth.
Thus Soma in the midst of all these constellations hath his place.
One thinks, when they have brayed the plant, that he hath drunk the Soma's juice;
Of him whom Brahmans truly know as Soma no one ever tastes.
Soma, secured by sheltering rules, guarded by hymns in Brhati,
Thou standest listening to the stones none tastes of thee who dwells on earth.
When they begin to drink thee then, O God, thou swellest out again.
Vayu is Soma's guardian God. The Moon is that which shapes the years.
Raibhi was her dear bridal friend, and Narasamsi led her home.
Lovely was Surya's robe: she came to that which Gatha had adorned.
Thought was the pillow of her couch, sight was the unguent for her eyes:
Her treasury was earth and heaven when Surya went unto her Lord.
Hymns were the cross-bars of the pole, Kurira-metre decked the car:
The bridesmen were the Asvin Pair Agni was leader of the train.
Soma was he who wooed the maid: the groomsmen were both Asvins, when
The Sun-God Savitar bestowed his willing Surya on her Lord.
Her spirit was the bridal car; the covering thereof was heaven:
Bright were both Steers that drew it when Surya approached her husband's, home.
Thy Steers were steady, kept in place by holy verse and Sama-hymn:
All car were thy two chariot wheels: thy path was tremulous in the sky,
Clean, as thou wentest, were thy wheels wind, was the axle fastened there.
Surya, proceeding to her Lord, mounted a spirit-fashioried car.
The bridal pomp of Surya, which Savitar started, moved along.
In Magha days are oxen slain, in Arjuris they wed the bride.
When on your three-wheeled chariot, O Asvins, ye
    came as wooers unto Surya's bridal,
Then all the Gods agreed to your proposal Pusan as Son elected you as Fathers.
O ye Two Lords of lustre, then when ye to Surya's wooing came,
Where was one chariot wheel of yours? Where stood ye for die Sire's command?
The Brahmans, by their seasons, know, O Surya, those two wheels of thine:
One kept concealed, those only who are skilled in highest truths have learned.
To Surya and the Deities, to Mitra and to Varuna.
Who know aright the thing that is, this adoration have I paid.
By their own power these Twain in close succession move;
They go as playing children round the sacrifice.
One of the Pair beholdeth all existing things; the other
    ordereth seasons and is born again.
He, born afresh, is new and new forever ensign of days he goes before the Mornings
Coming, he orders for the Gods their portion. The
    Moon prolongs the days of our existence.

Mount this, all-shaped, gold-hued, with strong wheels,
    fashioned of Kimsuka and Salmali, light-rolling,
Bound for the world of life immortal, Surya: make
    for thy lord a happy bridal journey.
Rise up from hence: this maiden hath a husband. I
    laud Visvavasu with hymns and homage.
Seek in her father's home another fair one, and find
    the portion from of old assigned thee.
Rise up from hence, Visvavasu: with reverence we worship thee.
Seek thou another willing maid, and with her husband leave the bride.
Straight in direction be the paths, and thornless,
    whereon our fellows travel to the wooing.
Let Aryaman and Bhaga lead us: perfect, O Gods,
    the union of the wife and husband.
Now from the noose of Varuna I free thee, wherewith
    Most Blessed Savitar hath bound thee.
In Law's seat, to the world of virtuous action, I give
    thee up uninjured with thy consort.
Hence, and not thence, I send these free. I make thee softly fettered there.
That, Bounteous Indra, she may live blest in her fortune and her sons.
Let Pusan take thy hand and hence conduct thee; may
    the two Asvins on their car transport thee.
Go to the house to be the household's mistress and
    speak as lady to thy gathered people.
Happy be thou and prosper witlh thy children here: be
    vigilant to rule thy household in this home.
Closely unite thy body with this; man, thy lord. So shall
    ye, full of years, address your company.
Her hue is blue and red: the fiend who clingeth close is driven off.
Well thrive the kinsmen of this bride the husband is bourid fast in bonds.
Give thou the woollen robe away: deal treasure to the Brahman priests.
This female fiend hath got her feet, and as a wife attends her lord.
Unlovely is his body when it glistens with this wicked fiend,
What time the husband wraps about his limbs the garment of his wife.
Consumptions, from her people, which follow the bride's resplendent train,—
These let the Holy Gods again bear to the place from which they came.
Let not the highway thieves who lie in ambush find the wedded pair.
By pleasant ways let them escape the danger, and let foes depart.
Signs of good fortune mark the bride come all of you and look at her.
Wish her prosperity, and then return unto your homes again.
Pungent is this, and bitter this, filled, as it were, with arrow-
    barbs, Empoisoned and not fit for use.
The Brahman who knows Surya well deserves the garment of the bride.
The fringe, the cloth that decks her head, and then the triply parted robe—
Behold the hues which Surya wears these doth the Brahman purify.
I take thy hand in mine for happy fortune that thou
    mayst reach old age with me thy husband.

Gods, Aryaman, Bhaga, Savitar, Purandhi, have given
  thee to be my household's mistress.
O Pusan, send her on as most auspicious, her who
  shall be the sharer of my pleasures;
Her who shall twine her loving arms about me, and
  welcome all my love and mine embraces.
For thee, with bridal train, they, first, escorted Surya to her home.
Give to the husband in return, Agni, the wife with progeny.
Agni hath given the bride again with splendour and with ample life.
Long lived be he who is her lord; a hundred autumns let him live.
Soma obtained her first of all; next the Gandharva was her lord.
Agai was thy third husband: now one born of woman is thy fourth.
Soma to the Gandharva, and to Agni the Gandharva gave:
And Agni hath bestowed on me riches and sons and this my spouse.
Be ye not parted; dwell ye here reach the full time of human life.
With sons and grandsons sport and play, rejoicing in your own abode.
So may Prajapati bring children forth to us; may
  Aryaman adorn us till old age come nigh.
Not inauspicious enter thou thy husband's house: bring
  blessing to our bipeds and our quadrupeds.
Not evil-eyed, no slayer of thy husband, bring weal to cattle, radiant, gentlehearted;
Loving the Gods, delightful, bearing heroes, bring
  blessing to our quadrupeds and bipeds.
O Bounteous Indra, make this bride blest in her sons and fortunate.
Vouchsafe to her ten sons, and make her husband the eleventh man.
Over thy husband's father and thy husband's mother bear full sway.
Over the sister of thy lord, over his brothers rule supreme.
So may the Universal Gods, so may the Waters join our hearts.
May Matarisvan, Dhatar, and Destri together bind us close.

Book X, Hymn CLVIII

May Surya guard us out of heaven, and Vata from the firmament,
And Agni from terrestrial spots.
Thou Savitar whose flame deserves hundred libations, be thou pleased:
From failing lightning keep us safe.
May Savitar the God, and may Parvata also give us sight;
May the Creator give us sight.
Give sight unto our eye, give thou our bodies sight that they may see:
May we survey, discern this world.
Thus, Surya, may we look on thee, on thee most lovely to behold,
See clearly with the eyes of men.

Book X, Hymn CLXX

May the Bright God drink glorious Soma-mingled meath,
  giving the sacrifice's lord uninjured life;

He who, wind-urged, in person guards our offspring well, hath
   nourished them with food and shines o'er many a land.
Radiant, as high Truth, cherished, best at winning strength, Truth
   based upon the statute that supports the heavens,
He rose, a light, that kills Vrtras and enemies, best
   slayer of the Dasyus, Asuras, and foes.
This light, the best of lights, supreme, all-conquering,
   winner of riches, is exalted with high laud.
All-lighting, radiant, mighty as the Sun to see, he spreadeth
   wide unfailing victory and strength.
Beaming forth splendour with thy light, thou hast attained heaven's lustrous realm.
By thee were brought together all existing things,
   possessor of all Godhead, All-effecting God.

Book X, Hymn CLXXXIX

This spotted Bull hath come, and sat before the Mother in the east,
Advancing to his Father heaven.
Expiring when he draws his breath, she moves along the lucid spheres:
The Bull shines out through all the sky.
Song is bestowed upon the Bird: it rules supreme through thirty realms
Throughout the days at break of morn.

Icarus

From Greek mythology

FOURTEEN YEARS ONLY have passed since our twentieth century began. In those fourteen years how many a father's and mother's heart has bled for the death of gallant sons, greatly-promising, greatly-daring, who have sought to rule the skies? With wings not well enough tried, they have soared dauntlessly aloft, only to add more names to the tragic list of those whose lives have been sacrificed in order that the groping hands of science may become sure, so that in time the sons of men may sail through the heavens as fearlessly as their fathers sailed through the seas.

High overhead we watch the monoplane, the great, swooping thing, like a monster black-winged bird, and our minds travel back to the story of Icarus, who died so many years ago that there are those who say that his story is but a foolish fable, an idle myth.

Daedalus, grandson of a king of Athens, was the greatest artificer of his day. Not only as an architect was he great, but as a sculptor he had the creative power, not only to make men and women and animals that looked alive, but to cause them to move and to be, to all appearances, endowed with life. To him the artificers who followed him owed the invention of the axe, the wedge, the wimble and the carpenter's level, and his restless mind was ever busy with new inventions. To his nephew, Talus or Perdrix, he taught all that he himself knew of all the mechanical arts. Soon it seemed that the nephew, though he might not excel his uncle, equalled Daedalus in his inventive power. As he walked by the seashore, the lad picked up the spine of a fish, and, having pondered its possibilities, he took it home, imitated it in iron, and so invented the saw. A still greater invention followed this. While those who had always thought that there could be none greater than Daedalus were still acclaiming the lad, there came to him the idea of putting two pieces of iron together, connecting them at one end with a rivet, and sharpening both ends, and a pair of compasses was made. Louder still were the acclamations of the people. Surely greater than Daedalus was here. Too much was this for the artist's jealous spirit.

One day they stood together on the top of the Acropolis, and Daedalus, murder that comes from jealousy in his heart, threw his nephew down. Down, down he fell, knowing well that he was going to meet a cruel death, but Pallas Athene, protectress of all clever craftsmen, came to his rescue. By her Perdrix was turned into the bird that still bears his name, and Daedalus beheld Perdrix, the partridge, rapidly winging his way to the far-off fields. Since then, no partridge has ever built or roosted in a high place, but has nestled in the hedge-roots and amongst the standing corn, and as we mark it we can see that its flight is always low.

For his crime Daedalus was banished from Athens, and in the court of Minos, king of Crete, he found a refuge. He put all his mighty powers at the service of Minos, and for him designed an intricate labyrinth which, like the river Meander, had neither beginning nor ending, but ever returned on itself in hopeless intricacy. Soon he stood high in the favour of the king, but, ever greedy for power, he incurred, by one of his daring inventions, the wrath of Minos. The angry monarch threw him into prison, and imprisoned along with him his son, Icarus. But prison bars and locks did not exist that were strong enough to baffle this master craftsman, and from the tower in which they were shut, Daedalus and his son were not long in making their escape. To escape from Crete was a less easy matter. There were many places in that wild island where it was easy for the father and son to hide, but the subjects of Minos were mostly mariners, and Daedalus knew well that all along the shore they kept watch lest he should make him a boat, hoist on it one of the sails of which he was part inventor, and speed away to safety like a sea-bird driven before the gale. Then did there come to Daedalus, the pioneer of inventions, the great idea that by his skill he might make a way for himself and his son through another element than water. And he laughed aloud in his hiding place amongst the cypresses on the hillside at the thought of how he would baffle the simple sailor men who watched each creek and beach down on the shore. Mockingly, too, did he think of King Minos, who had dared to pit his power against the wits and skill of Daedalus, the mighty craftsman.

Many a Cretan bird was sacrificed before the task which the inventor had set himself was accomplished. In a shady forest on the mountains he fashioned light wooden frames and decked them with feathers, until at length they looked like the pinions of a great eagle, or of a swan that flaps its majestic way from lake to river. Each feather was bound on with wax, and the mechanism of the wings was so perfect a reproduction of that of the wings from which the feathers had been plucked, that on the first day that he fastened them to his back and spread them out, Daedalus found that he could fly even as the bird flew. Two pairs he made; having tested one pair, a second pair was made for Icarus, and, circling round him like a mother bird that teaches her nestlings how to fly, Daedalus, his heart big with the pride of invention, showed Icarus how he might best soar upwards to the sun or dive down to the blue sea far below, and how he might conquer the winds and the air currents of the sky and make them his servants.

That was a joyous day for father and son, for the father had never before drunk deeper of the intoxicating wine of the gods – Success – and for the lad it was all pure joy. Never before had he known freedom and power so utterly glorious. As a little child he had watched the birds fly far away over the blue hills to where the sun was setting, and had longed for wings that he might follow them in their flight. At times, in his dreams, he had known the power, and in his dreaming fancy had risen from the cumbering earth and soared high above the trees and fields on strong pinions that bore him away to the fair land of heart's desire – to the Islands of the Blessed. But when Sleep left him and the dreams silently slipped out before the coming of the light of day, and the boy sprang from his couch and eagerly spread his arms as, in his dreams, he had done, he could no longer fly. Disappointment and unsatisfied longing ever came with his waking hours. Now all that had come to an end, and Daedalus was glad and proud as well to watch his son's joy and his fearless daring. One word of counsel only did he give him.

"Beware, dear son of my heart," he said, "lest in thy new-found power thou seekest to soar even to the gates of Olympus. For as surely as the scorching rays from the burnished wheels of the chariot of Apollo smite thy wings, the wax that binds on thy feathers will melt, and then will come upon thee and on me woe unutterable."

In his dreams that night Icarus flew, and when he awoke, fearing to find only the haunting remembrance of a dream, he found his father standing by the side of his bed of soft leaves under the shadowy cypresses, ready to bind on his willing shoulders the great pinions that he had made.

Gentle Dawn, the rosy-fingered, was slowly making her way up from the East when Daedalus and Icarus began their flight. Slowly they went at first, and the goatherds who tended their flocks on the slopes of Mount Ida looked up in fear when they saw the dark shadows of their wings and marked the monster birds making their way out to sea. From the riverbeds the waterfowl arose from the reeds, and with great outcry flew with all their swiftness to escape them. And down by the seashore the mariners' hearts sank within them as they watched, believing that a sight so strange must be a portent of disaster. Homewards they went in haste to offer sacrifices on the altars of Poseidon, ruler of the deep.

Samos and Delos were passed on the left and Lebynthos on the right, long ere the sun-god had started on his daily course, and as the mighty wings of Icarus cleft the cold air, the boy's slim body grew chilled, and he longed for the sun's rays to turn the waters of the Aegean Sea over which he flew from green-grey into limpid sapphire and emerald and burning gold. Towards Sicily he and his father bent their course, and when they saw the beautiful island afar off lying like a gem in the sea, Apollo made the waves in which it lay, for it a fitting setting. With a cry of joy Icarus marked the sun's rays paint the chill water, and Apollo looked down at the great white-winged bird, a snowy swan with the face and form of a beautiful boy, who sped exulting onwards, while a clumsier thing, with wings of darker hue, followed less quickly, in the same line of flight. As the god looked, the warmth that radiated from his chariot touched the icy limbs of Icarus as with the caressing touch of gentle, life-giving hands. Not long before, his flight had lagged a little, but now it seemed as if new life was his. Like a bird that wheels and soars and dives as if for lightness of heart, so did Icarus, until each feather of his plumage had a sheen of silver and of gold. Down, down, he darted, so near the water that almost the white-tipped waves caught at his wings as he skimmed over them. Then up, up, up he soared, ever higher, higher still, and when he saw the radiant sun-god smiling down on him, the warning of Daedalus was forgotten. As he had excelled other lads in foot races, now did Icarus wish to excel the birds themselves. Daedalus he left far behind, and still upwards he mounted. So strong he felt, so fearless was he, that to him it seemed that he could storm Olympus, that he could call to Apollo as he swept past him in his flight, and dare him to race for a wager from the Aegean Sea to where the sun-god's horses took their nightly rest by the trackless seas of the unknown West.

In terror his father watched him, and as he called to him in a voice of anguished warning that was drowned by the whistling rush of the air currents through the wings of Icarus and the moist whisper of the clouds as through them he cleft a way for himself, there befell the dreaded thing. It seemed as though the strong wings had begun to lose their power. Like a wounded bird Icarus fluttered, lunged sideways from the straight, clean line of his flight, recovered himself, and fluttered again. And then, like the bird into whose soft breast the sure hand of a mighty archer has driven an arrow, downwards he fell, turning over and yet turning again, downwards, ever downwards, until he fell with a plunge into the sea that still was radiant in shining emerald and translucent blue.

Then did the car of Apollo drive on. His rays had slain one who was too greatly daring, and now they fondled the little white feathers that had fallen from the broken wings and floated on the water like the petals of a torn flower.

On the dead, still face of Icarus they shone, and they spangled as if with diamonds the wet plumage that still, widespread, bore him up on the waves.

Stricken at heart was Daedalus, but there was no time to lament his son's untimely end, for even now the black-prowed ships of Minos might be in pursuit. Onward he flew to safety, and in Sicily built a temple to Apollo, and there hung up his wings as a propitiatory offering to the god who had slain his son.

And when grey night came down on that part of the sea that bears the name of Icarus to this day, still there floated the body of the boy whose dreams had come true. For only a little while had he known the exquisite realization of dreamed-of potentialities, for only a few hours tasted the sweetness of perfect pleasure, and then, by an over-daring flight, had lost it all forever.

The sorrowing Nereids sang a dirge over him as he was swayed gently hither and thither by the tide, and when the silver stars came out from the dark firmament of heaven and were reflected in the blackness of the sea at night, it was as though a velvet pall, silver-decked in his honour, was spread around the slim white body with its outstretched snowy wings.

So much had he dared – so little accomplished.

Is it not the oft-told tale of those who have followed Icarus? Yet who can say that gallant youth has lived in vain when, as Icarus did, he has breasted the very skies, has flown with fearless heart and soul to the provinces of the deathless gods? – when, even for the space of a few of the heartbeats of Time, he has tasted supreme power – the ecstasy of illimitable happiness?

Idas and Marpessa

From Greek mythology

BY DAY, WHILE THE SUN-GOD drove his chariot in the high heavens and turned the blue-green Aegean Sea into the semblance of a blazing shield of brass, Idas and Marpessa sat together in the trees' soft shades, or walked in shadowy valleys where violets and wild parsley grew, and where Apollo rarely deigned to come. At eventide, when, in royal splendour of purple and crimson and gold, Apollo sought his rest in the western sky, Idas and Marpessa wandered by the seashore watching the little wavelets softly kissing the pebbles on the beach, or climbed to the mountainside from whence they could see the first glimpse of Diana's silver crescent and the twinkling lights of the Pleiades breaking through the blue canopy of the sky. While Apollo sought in heaven and on earth the best means to gratify his imperial whims, Idas, for whom all joys had come to mean but one, sought ever to be by the side of Marpessa. Shadowy valley, murmuring sea, lonely mountain side, or garden where grew the purple amaranth and where roses of pink and amber-yellow and deepest crimson dropped their radiant petals on the snowy marble paths, all were the same to Idas – Paradise for him, were Marpessa by his side; without her, dreary desert.

More beautiful than any flower that grew in the garden was Marpessa. No music that Apollo's lute could make was as sweet in the ears of Idas as her dear voice. Its music was ever new to him – a melody to make his heart more quickly throb. New, too, ever was her beauty. For him it was always the first time that they met, always the same fresh ravishment to look in her eyes. And when to Idas came the knowledge that Marpessa gave him love for love, he had indeed won happiness so great as to draw upon him the envy of the gods.

"The course of true love never did run smooth," and, like many and many another father since his day, Evenos, the father of Marpessa, was bitterly opposed to a match where the bridegroom was rich only in youth, in health, and in love. His beautiful daughter naturally seemed to him worthy of something much higher. Thus it was an unhappy day for Marpessa when, as she sat alone by the fountain which dripped slowly down on the marble basin, and dreamed of her lover, Idas, Apollo himself, led by caprice, noiselessly walked through the rose bushes, whose warm petals dropped at his feet as he passed, and beheld a maiden more fair than the fairest flower that grew. The hum of bees, the drip, drip of the fountain, these lulled her mind and heart and soothed her daydreams, and Marpessa's red lips, curved like the bow of Eros, smiled as she thought of Idas, the man she loved. Silently Apollo watched her. This queen of all the roses was not fit to be the bride of mortal man – Marpessa must be his.

To Evenos Apollo quickly imparted his desire. He was not used to having his imperial wishes denied, nor was Evenos anxious to do so. Here, indeed, was a match for his daughter. No insignificant mortal, but the radiant sun-god himself! And to Marpessa he told what Apollo wished, and Marpessa shyly looked at her reflection in the pool of the fountain, and wondered if she were indeed beautiful enough to win the love of a god.

"Am I in truth so wondrous fair?" she asked her father.

"Fair enough to mate with Apollo himself!" proudly answered Evenos.

And joyously Marpessa replied, "Ah, then am I happy indeed! I would be beautiful for my Idas' sake!"

An angry man was her father. There was to be no more pleasant dallying with Idas in the shadowy wood or by the seashore. In the rose garden Apollo took his place and charmed Marpessa's ears with his music, while her eyes could not but be charmed by his beauty. The god had no doubts or fears. Only a little time he would give her, for a very little only would he wait, and then undoubtedly this mortal maiden would be his, her heart conquered as assuredly as the rays from his chariot conquered the roses, whose warm crimson petals they strewed at his feet. Yet as Marpessa looked and listened, her thoughts were often far away and always her heart was with Idas. When Apollo played most exquisitely to her it seemed that he put her love for Idas into music. When he spoke to her of his love she thought, "Thus, and thus did Idas speak," and a sudden memory of the human lad's halting words brought to her heart a little gush of tenderness, and made her eyes sparkle so that Apollo gladly thought, "Soon she will be mine."

And all this while Idas schemed and plotted and planned a way in which he could save his dear one from her obdurate father, and from the passion of a god. He went to Neptune, told his tale, and begged him to lend him a winged chariot in which he could fly away with Marpessa. Neptune good-naturedly consented, and when Idas flew up from the seashore one day, like a great bird that the tempests have blown inland, Marpessa joyously sprang up beside her lover, and swiftly they took flight for a land where in peace they might live and love together. No sooner did Evenos realize that his daughter was gone, than, in furious anger against her and her lover, he gave chase. One has watched a hawk in pursuit of a pigeon or a bird of the moors and seen it, a little dark speck at first, gradually growing larger and larger until at length it dominated and conquered its prey, swooping down from above, like an arrow from a bow, to bring with it sudden death.

So at first it seemed that Evenos must conquer Idas and Marpessa in the winged chariot of Neptune's lending. But onwards Idas drove the chariot, ever faster and faster, until before the eyes of Marpessa the trees of the forest grew into blurs of blue and brown, and the streams and rivers as they flew past them were streaks of silver. Not until he had reached the river Lycormas did the angry father own that his pursuit had been in vain. Over the swift-flowing stream flew the chariot driven by Idas, but Evenos knew that his horses, flecked with white foam, pumping each breath from hearts that were strained to breaking-point, no longer could go on with the chase. The passage of that deep stream would destroy them. The fierce water would sweep the wearied beasts down in its impelling current, and he with them. A shamed man would he be forever. Not for a moment did he hesitate, but drew his sharp sword from his belt and plunged it into the breast of one steed and then of the other who had been so willing and who yet had failed him in the end. And then, as they, still in their traces, neighed shrilly aloud, and then fell over and died where they lay, Evenos, with a great cry, leaped into the river. Over his head closed the eddies of the peat-brown water. Once only did he throw up his arms to ask the gods for mercy; then did his body drift down with the stream, and his soul hastened downwards to the Shades. And from that day the river Lycormas no more was known by that name, but was called the river *Evenos* forever.

Onwards, triumphantly, drove Idas, but soon he knew that a greater than Evenos had entered in the chase, and that the jealous sun-god's chariot was in pursuit of the winged car of Neptune. Quickly it gained on him – soon it would have swept down on him – a hawk indeed, this time, striking surely its helpless prey – but even as Apollo saw the white face of Marpessa and knew that he was the victor, a mighty thunderbolt that made the mountains shake, and rolled its echoes through the lonely fastnesses of a thousand hills, was sent to earth by Jupiter. While the echoes still re-echoed, there came from Olympus the voice of Zeus himself.

"*Let her decide!*" he said.

Apollo, like a white flame blown backward by the wind, withheld his hands that would have seized from Idas the woman who was his heart's desire.

And then he spoke, and while his burning gaze was fixed upon her, and his face, in beautiful fury, was more perfect than any exquisite picture of her dreams, his voice was as the voice of the sea as it calls to the shore in the moonlit hours, as the bird that sings in the darkness of a tropic night to its longing mate.

"Marpessa!" he cried, "Marpessa! wilt thou not come to me? No woe nor trouble, never any pain can touch me. Yet woe indeed was mine when first I saw thy fairest face. For even now dost thou hasten to sorrow, to darkness, to the dark-shadowed tomb. Thou art but mortal! Thy beauty is short-lived. Thy love for mortal man shall quickly fade and die. Come to me, Marpessa, and my kisses on your lips shall make thee immortal! Together we shall bring the sunbeams to a cold, dark land! Together shall we coax the spring flowers from the still, dead earth! Together we shall bring to men the golden harvest, and deck the trees of autumn in our liveries of red and gold. I love thee, Marpessa – not as mere mortal loves do I love thee. Come to me, Marpessa – my Love – my Desire!"

When his voice was silent, it seemed as if the very earth itself with all its thousand echoes still breathed his words, "Marpessa – my Love – my Desire."

Abashed before the god's entreaties stood Idas. And the heart of Marpessa was torn as she heard the burning words of the beautiful Apollo still ringing through her head, and saw her mortal lover, silent, white-lipped, gazing first at the god and then into her own pale face. At length he spoke:

> "*After such argument what can I plead?*
> *Or what pale promise make? Yet since it is*
> *In woman to pity rather than to aspire,*
> *A little I will speak. I love thee then*
> *Not only for thy body packed with sweet*
> *Of all this world, that cup of brimming June,*
> *That jar of violet wine set in the air,*
> *That palest rose sweet in the night of life;*
> *Nor for that stirring bosom all besieged*
> *By drowsing lovers, or thy perilous hair;*
> *Nor for that face that might indeed provoke*
> *Invasion of old cities; no, nor all*
> *Thy freshness stealing on me like strange sleep.*
> *Nor for this only do I love thee, but*
> *Because Infinity upon thee broods;*
> *And thou art full of whispers and of shadows.*
> *Thou meanest what the sea has striven to say*
> *So long, and yearned up the cliffs to tell;*

Thou art what all the winds have uttered not,
What the still night suggesteth to the heart.
Thy voice is like to music heard ere birth,
Some spirit lute touched on a spirit sea;
Thy face remembered is from other worlds,
It has been died for, though I know not when,
It has been sung of, though I know not where.
It has the strangeness of the luring West,
And of sad sea-horizons; beside thee
I am aware of other times and lands,
Of birth far-back, of lives in many stars.
O beauty lone and like a candle clear
In this dark country of the world! Thou art
My woe, my early light, my music dying."

Then Idas, in the humility that comes from perfect love, drooped low his head, and was silent. In silence for a minute stood the three – a god, a man, and a woman. And from on high the watching stars looked down and marvelled, and Diana stayed for a moment the course of her silver car to watch, as she thought, the triumph of her own invincible brother.

From man to god passed the eyes of Marpessa, and back from god to man. And the stars forgot to twinkle, and Diana's silver-maned horses pawed the blue floor of the sky, impatient at the firm hand of the mistress on the reins that checked their eager course.

Marpessa spoke at last, in low words that seemed to come "remembered from other worlds."

For all the joys he offered her she thanked Apollo. What grander fate for mortal woman than to rule the sunbeams – to bring bliss to the earth and to the sons of men? What more could mortal woman crave than the gift of immortality shared with one whose power ruled the vast universe, and who still had stooped to lay the red roses of his passionate love at her little, human feet? And yet – and yet – in that sorrow-free existence that he promised, might there not still be something awanting to one who had once known tears?

"Yet I, being human, human sorrow miss."

Then were he indeed to give her the gift of immortal life, what value were life to one whose beauty had withered as the leaves in autumn, whose heart was tired and dead? What uglier fate than this, to endure an endless existence in which no life was, yoked to one whose youth was immortal, whose beauty was everlasting?

Then did she turn to Idas, who stood as one who awaits the judgment of the judge in whose hands lies the power of meting out life or death. Thus she spoke:

"But if I live with Idas, then we two
On the low earth shall prosper hand in hand
In odours of the open field, and live
In peaceful noises of the farm, and watch
The pastoral fields burned by the setting sun.
And he shall give me passionate children, not
Some radiant god that will despise me quite,
But clambering limbs and little hearts that err.
...So shall we live,

And though the first sweet sting of love be past,
The sweet that almost venom is; though youth,
With tender and extravagant delight,
The first and secret kiss by twilight hedge,
The insane farewell repeated o'er and o'er,
Pass off; there shall succeed a faithful peace;
Beautiful friendship tried by sun and wind,
Durable from the daily dust of life."

The sun-god frowned as her words fell from her lips. Even now, as she looked at him, he held out his arms. Surely she only played with this poor mortal youth. To him she must come, this rose who could own no lesser god than the sun-god himself.

But Marpessa spoke on:

"And thou beautiful god, in that far time,
When in thy setting sweet thou gazest down
On his grey head, wilt thou remember then
That once I pleased thee, that I once was young?"

So did her voice cease, and on the earth fell sudden darkness. For to Apollo had come the shame of love rejected, and there were those who said that to the earth that night there came no sunset, only the sullen darkness that told of the flight of an angry god. Yet, later, the silver moonbeams of Diana seemed to greet the dark earth with a smile, and, in the winged car of Neptune, Idas and Marpessa sped on, greater than the gods, in a perfect harmony of human love that feared nor time, nor pain, nor Death himself.

Iosco, or The Prairie Boys' Visit to the Sun and Moon

From the Odawa people, Eastern Woodlands of North America

ONE PLEASANT MORNING, five young men and a boy about ten years of age, called Ioscoda, went out a shooting with their bows and arrows. They left their lodges with the first appearance of daylight, and having passed through a long reach of woods, had ascended a lofty eminence before the sun arose. While standing there in a group, the sun suddenly burst forth in all its effulgence. The air was so clear, that it appeared to be at no great distance. "How very near it is," they all said. "It cannot be far," said the eldest, "and if you will accompany me, we will see if we cannot reach it." A loud assent burst from every lip. Even the boy, Ioscoda, said he would go. They told him he was too young; but he replied, "If you do not permit me to go with you, I will mention your design to each of your parents." They then said to him, "You shall also go with us, so be quiet."

They then fell upon the following arrangement. It was resolved that each one should obtain from his parents as many pairs of moccasins as he could, and also new clothing of leather. They fixed on a spot where they would conceal all their articles, until they were ready to start on their journey, and which would serve, in the meantime, as a place of rendezvous, where they might secretly meet and consult. This being arranged, they returned home.

A long time passed before they could put their plan into execution. But they kept it a profound secret, even to the boy. They frequently met at the appointed place, and discussed the subject. At length everything was in readiness, and they decided on a day to set out. That morning the boy shed tears for a pair of new leather leggings. "Don't you see," said he to his parents, "how my companions are dressed?" This appeal to their pride and envy prevailed. He obtained the leggings. Artifices were also resorted to by the others, under the plea of going out on a special hunt. They said to one another, but in a tone that they might be overheard, "We will see who will bring in the most game." They went out in different directions, but soon met at the appointed place, where they had hid the articles for their journey, with as many arrows as they had time to make. Each one took something on his back, and they began their march. They travelled day after day, through a thick forest, but the sun was always at the same distance. "We must," said they, "travel toward Waubunong, and we shall get to the object, some time or other." No one was discouraged, although winter overtook them. They built a lodge and hunted, till they obtained as much dried meat as they could carry, and then continued on. This they did several times; season followed season. More than one winter overtook them. Yet none of them became discouraged, or expressed dissatisfaction.

One day the travellers came to the banks of a river, whose waters ran toward Waubunong. They followed it down many days. As they were walking, one day, they came to rising grounds, from which they saw something white or clear through the trees. They encamped on this elevation. Next morning they came, suddenly, in view of an immense body of water. No land could be seen as far as the eye could reach. One or two of them lay down on the beach to drink. As soon as they got the water in their mouths, they spit it out, and exclaimed, with surprise, "Shewetagon awbo!" (salt water.) It was the sea. While looking on the water, the sun arose as if from the deep, and went on its steady course through the heavens, enlivening the scene with his cheering and animating beams. They stood in fixed admiration, but the object appeared to be as distant from them as ever. They thought it best to encamp, and consult whether it were advisable to go on, or return. "We see," said the leader, "that the sun is still on the opposite side of this great water, but let us not be disheartened. We can walk around the shore." To this they all assented.

Next morning they took the northerly shore, to walk around it, but had only gone a short distance when they came to a large river. They again encamped, and while sitting before the fire, the question was put, whether any one of them had ever dreamed of water, or of walking on it. After a long silence, the eldest said he had. Soon after they lay down to sleep. When they arose the following morning, the eldest addressed them, "We have done wrong in coming north. Last night my spirit appeared to me, and told me to go south, and that but a short distance beyond the spot we left yesterday, we should come to a river with high banks. That by looking off its mouth, we should see an island, which would approach to us. He directed that we should all get on it. He then told me to cast my eyes toward the water. I did so, and I saw all he had declared. He then informed me that we must return south, and wait at the river until the day after tomorrow. I believe all that was revealed to me in this dream, and that we shall do well to follow it."

The party immediately retraced their footsteps in exact obedience to these intimations. Toward the evening they came to the borders of the indicated river. It had high banks, behind which they encamped, and here they patiently awaited the fulfilment of the dream. The appointed day arrived. They said, "We will see if that which has been said will be seen." Midday is the promised time. Early in the morning two had gone to the shore to keep a look-out. They waited anxiously for the middle of the day, straining their eyes to see if they could discover anything. Suddenly they raised a shout. *"Ewaddee sub neen*! There it is! There it is!" On rushing to the spot they beheld something like an *island* steadily advancing toward the shore. As it approached, they could discover that something was moving on it in various directions. They said, "It is a Manito, let us be off into the woods." "No, no," cried the eldest, "let us stay and watch." It now became stationary, and lost much of its imagined height. They could only see *three* trees, as they thought, resembling trees in a pinery that had been burnt. The wind, which had been off the sea, now died away into a perfect calm. They saw something leaving the fancied island and approaching the shore, throwing and flapping its wings, like a loon when he attempts to fly in calm weather. It entered the mouth of the river. They were on the point of running away, but the eldest dissuaded them. "Let us hide in this hollow," he said, "and we will see what it can be." They did so. They soon heard the sounds of chopping, and quickly after they heard the falling of trees. Suddenly a man came up to the place of their concealment. He stood still and gazed at them. They did the same in utter amazement. After looking at them for some time, the person advanced and extended his hand toward them. The eldest took it, and they shook hands. He then spoke, but they could not understand each other. He then cried out for his comrades. They came, and examined very minutely their dresses. They again tried to converse. Finding it impossible, the strangers then motioned to the Naubequon, and to the Naubequon-ais, wishing them to embark. They consulted with each other for a short time. The eldest then motioned that they should go on board. They embarked on board the boat, which they found to be loaded with wood. When they reached the side of the supposed island, they were surprised to see a great number of people, who all came to the side and looked at them with open mouths. One spoke out, above the others, and appeared to be the leader. He motioned them to get on board. He looked at and examined them, and took them down into the cabin, and set things before them to eat. He treated them very kindly.

When they came on deck again, all the sails were spread, and they were fast losing sight of land. In the course of the night and the following day they were sick at the stomach, but soon recovered. When they had been out at sea ten days, they became sorrowful, as they could not converse with those who had hats on.

The following night Ioscoda dreamed that his spirit appeared to him. He told him not to be discouraged, that he would open his ears, so as to be able to understand the people with hats. I will not permit you to understand much, said he, only sufficient to reveal your wants, and to know what is said to you. He repeated this dream to his friends, and they were satisfied and encouraged by it. When they had been out about thirty days, the master of the ship told them, and motioned them to change their dresses of leather, for such as his people wore; for if they did not, his master would be displeased. It was on this occasion that the elder first understood a few words of the language. The first phrase he comprehended was *La que notte*, and from one word to another he was soon able to speak it.

One day the men cried out, land! and soon after they heard a noise resembling thunder, in repeated peals. When they had got over their fears, they were shown the large guns which made this noise. Soon after they saw a vessel smaller than their own, sailing out of a bay, in the direction toward them. She had flags on her masts, and when she came near she fired a gun. The large vessel also hoisted her flags, and the boat came alongside. The master told the person who came in it, to tell his master or king, that he had six strangers on board, such as had never been seen before, and that they were coming to visit him. It was some time after the departure of this messenger before the vessel got up to the town. It was then dark, but they could see people, and horses, and odawbons ashore. They were landed and placed in a covered vehicle, and driven off. When they stopped, they were taken into a large and splendid room. They were here told that the great chief wished to see them. They were shown into another large room, filled with men and women. All the room was Shoneancauda. The chief asked them their business, and the object of their journey. They told him where they were from, and where they were going, and the nature of the enterprise which they had undertaken. He tried to dissuade them from its execution, telling them of the many trials and difficulties they would have to undergo; that so many days' march from his country dwelt a bad spirit, or Manito, who foreknew and foretold the existence and arrival of all who entered into his country. It is impossible, he said, my children, for you ever to arrive at the object you are in search of.

Ioscoda replied, "Nosa," and they could see the chief blush in being called *father*, "we have come so far on our way, and we will continue it; we have resolved firmly that we will do so. We think our lives are of no value, for we have given them up for this object. Nosa," he repeated, "do not then prevent us from going on our journey." The chief then dismissed them with valuable presents, after having appointed the next day to speak to them again, and provided everything that they needed or wished for.

Next day they were again summoned to appear before the king. He again tried to dissuade them. He said he would send them back to their country in one of his vessels: but all he said had no effect. "Well," said he, "if you will go, I will furnish you all that is needed for your journey." He had everything provided accordingly. He told them, that three days before they reached the Bad Spirit he had warned them of, they would hear his Shéshegwun. He cautioned them to be wise, for he felt that he should never see them all again.

They resumed their journey, and travelled sometimes through villages, but they soon left them behind and passed over a region of forests and plains, without inhabitants. They found all the productions of a new country: trees, animals, birds, were entirely different from those they were accustomed to, on the other side of the great waters. They travelled, and travelled, till they wore out all of the clothing that had been given to them, and had to take to their leather clothing again.

The three days the chief spoke of meant three years, for it was only at the end of the third year, that they came within the sight of the spirit's shéshegwun. The sound appeared to be near, but they continued walking on, day after day, without apparently getting any nearer to it. Suddenly they came to a very extensive plain; they could see the blue ridges of distant mountains rising on the horizon beyond it; they pushed on, thinking to get over the plain before night, but they were overtaken by darkness; they were now on a stony part of the plain, covered by about a foot's depth of water; they were weary and fatigued; some of them said, let us lie down; no, no, said the others, let us push on. Soon they stood on firm ground, but it was as much as they could do to stand, for they were very weary. They, however, made an effort to encamp, lighted up a fire, and refreshed themselves by eating. They then commenced conversing about the sound of the spirit's shéshegwun, which they had heard for several days. Suddenly the instrument commenced; it sounded as if it was subterraneous, and it shook the ground: they tied up their bundles and went toward the spot. They soon came to a large building, which was illuminated. As soon as they came to the door, they were met by a rather elderly man. "How do ye do," said he, "my grandsons? Walk in, walk in; I am glad to see you: I knew when you started: I saw you encamp this evening: sit down, and tell me the news of the country you left, for I feel interested in it." They complied with his wishes, and when they had concluded, each one presented him with a piece of tobacco. He then revealed to them things that would happen in their journey, and predicted its successful accomplishment. "I do not say that all of you," said he, "will successfully go through it. You have passed over three-fourths of your way, and I will tell you how to proceed after you get to the edge of the earth. Soon after you leave this place, you will hear a deafening sound: it is the sky descending on the edge, but it keeps moving up and down; you will watch, and when it moves up, you will see a vacant space between it and the earth. You must not be afraid. A chasm of awful depth is there, which separates the unknown from this earth, and a veil of darkness conceals it. Fear not. You must leap through; and if you succeed, you will find yourselves on a beautiful plain, and in a soft and mild light emitted by the moon." They thanked him for his advice. A pause ensued.

"I have told you the way," he said; "now tell me again of the country you have left; for I committed dreadful ravages while I was there: does not the country show marks of it? and do not the inhabitants tell of me to their children? I came to this place to mourn over my bad actions, and am trying, by my present course of life, to relieve my mind of the load that is on it." They told him that their fathers spoke often of a celebrated personage called Manabozho, who performed great exploits. "I am he," said the Spirit. They gazed with astonishment and fear. "Do you see this pointed house?" said he, pointing to one that resembled a sugar-loaf; "you can now each speak your wishes, and will be answered from that house. Speak out, and ask what each wants, and it shall be granted." One of them, who was vain, asked with presumption, that he might live forever, and never be in want. He was answered, "Your wish shall be granted." The second made the same request, and received the same answer. The third asked to live longer than common people, and to be always successful in his war excursions, never losing any of his young men. He was told, "Your wishes are granted." The fourth joined in the same request, and received the same reply. The fifth made an humble request, asking to live as long as men generally do, and that he might be crowned with such success in hunting as to be able to provide for his parents and relatives. The sixth made the same request, and it was granted to both, in pleasing tones, from the pointed house.

After hearing these responses they prepared to depart. They were told by Manabozho, that they had been with him but one day, but they afterward found that they had remained there upward of a year. When they were on the point of setting out, Manabozho exclaimed, "Stop! you two, who asked me for eternal life, will receive the boon you wish immediately." He spake, and one was turned into a stone called Shin-gauba-wossin, and the other into a cedar tree. "Now," said he to the others, "you can go." They left him in fear, saying, "We were fortunate to escape so, for the king told us he was wicked, and that we should not probably escape from him." They had not proceeded far, when they began to hear the sound of the beating sky. It appeared to be near at hand, but they had a long interval to travel before they came near, and the sound was then stunning to their senses; for when the sky came down, its pressure would force gusts of wind from the opening, so strong that it was with difficulty they could keep their feet, and the sun passed but a short distance above their heads. They however approached boldly, but had to wait sometime before they could muster courage enough to leap through the dark veil that covered the passage. The sky would come down with violence, but it would rise slowly and gradually. The two who had made the humble request, stood near the edge, and with no little exertion succeeded, one after the other, in leaping through, and gaining a firm foothold. The remaining two were fearful and undecided: the others spoke to them through the darkness, saying, "Leap! leap! the sky is on its way down." These two looked up and saw it descending, but fear paralysed their efforts; they made but a feeble attempt, so as to reach the opposite side with their hands; but the sky at the same time struck on the earth with great violence and a terrible sound, and forced them into the dreadful black chasm.

The two successful adventurers, of whom Iosco now was chief, found themselves in a beautiful country, lighted by the moon, which shed around a mild and pleasant light. They could see the moon approaching as if it were from behind a hill. They advanced, and an aged woman spoke to them; she had a white face and pleasing air, and looked rather old, though she spoke to them very kindly: they knew from her first appearance that she was the moon: she asked them several questions: she told them that she knew of their coming, and was happy to see them: she informed them that they were halfway to her brother's, and that from the earth to her abode was half the distance. "I will, by and by, have leisure," said she, "and will go and conduct you to my brother, for he is now absent on his daily course: you will succeed in your object, and return in safety to your country and friends, with the good wishes, I am sure, of my brother." While the travellers were with her, they received every attention. When the proper time arrived, she said to them, "My brother is now rising from below, and we shall see his light as he comes over the distant edge: come," said she,

"I will lead you up." They went forward, but in some mysterious way, they hardly knew how: they rose almost directly up, as if they had ascended steps. They then came upon an immense plain, declining in the direction of the sun's approach. When he came near, the moon spake, "I have brought you these persons, whom we knew were coming;" and with this she disappeared. The sun motioned with his hand for them to follow him. They did so, but found it rather difficult, as the way was steep: they found it particularly so from the edge of the earth till they got halfway between that point and midday: when they reached this spot, the sun stopped, and sat down to rest. "What, my children," said he, "has brought you here? I could not speak to you before: I could not stop at any place but this, for this is my first resting-place – then at the centre, which is at midday, and then halfway from that to the western edge. Tell me," he continued, "the object of your undertaking this journey and all the circumstances which have happened to you on the way." They complied; Iosco told him their main object was to see him. They had lost four of their friends on the way, and they wished to know whether they could return in safety to the earth, that they might inform their friends and relatives of all that had befallen them. They concluded by requesting him to grant their wishes. He replied, "Yes, you shall certainly return in safety; but your companions were vain and presumptuous in their demands. They were Gug-ge-baw-diz-ze-wug. They aspired to what Manitoes only could enjoy. But you two, as I said, shall get back to your country, and become as happy as the hunter's life can make you. You shall never be in want of the necessaries of life, as long as you are permitted to live; and you will have the satisfaction of relating your journey to your friends, and also of telling them of me. Follow me, follow me," he said, commencing his course again. The ascent was now gradual, and they soon came to a level plain. After travelling some time he again sat down to rest, for we had arrived at Nau-we-qua. "You see," said he, "it is level at this place, but a short distance onwards, my way descends gradually to my last resting-place, from which there is an abrupt descent." He repeated his assurance that they should be shielded from danger, if they relied firmly on his power. "Come here quickly," he said, placing something before them on which they could descend; "keep firm," said he, as they resumed the descent. They went downward as if they had been let down by ropes.

In the meantime the parents of these two young men dreamed that their sons were returning, and that they should soon see them. They placed the fullest confidence in their dreams. Early in the morning they left their lodges for a remote point in the forest, where they expected to meet them. They were not long at the place before they saw the adventurers returning, for they had descended not far from that place. The young men knew they were their fathers. They met, and were happy. They related all that had befallen them. They did not conceal anything; and they expressed their gratitude to the different Manitoes who had preserved them, by feasting and gifts, and particularly to the sun and moon, who had received them as their children.

Iris and Aurora

From Greek mythology

IRIS WAS THE SPECIAL attendant of Juno, and was often employed as a messenger by both Juno and Jupiter. In the *Iliad* she is the swift servant of the gods; but in the *Odyssey* it is Mercury who is the messenger to and from Olympus, and Iris is never mentioned. Sometimes Iris is described as the rainbow itself; sometimes the rainbow is only the road over which she travels, and which therefore vanishes when it is no longer needed. When Juno sends Iris to the Cave of Sleep "she assumes her garments of a thousand colours, and spans the heavens with her curving arch." As the personification of the rainbow – that brilliant phenomenon that vanishes as quickly as it appears – Iris might easily be considered the swift messenger of the gods.

* * *

Aurora, rosy-fingered goddess of the dawn, opened the gates of the morning for the impatient horses of the sun, who chafed at being held behind the golden bars until Apollo was ready to start forth on his daily course, attended by the faithful Hours. Though Aurora was the wife of Aeolus and mother of the winds, she had the usual weakness of the deities of Olympus for falling in love with mortals who won her favour. Thus she became enamoured of the young hunter Cephalus, but was unable to gain his love, as he himself had already wedded the fair Procris, one of Diana's nymphs. The happiness of these lovers was a maddening sight to the jealous Aurora, and she determined to find some way to end it. Procris had brought to her husband as a dowry a hunting dog named Lelaps, who could outrun the swiftest deer, and a javelin that never missed its mark. So all day long Cephalus hunted in the forest, and his long absences gave the malicious Aurora an excuse for whispering to the young wife that her husband spend his time in the society of a wood-nymph. For some time Procris resisted these suggestions of the goddess; but at last, overcome by jealousy, she followed Cephalus to the forest to see who the maiden was that charmed him. At noonday the weary hunter sought his accustomed resting place; and as he lay beneath a wide-spreading tree, he called to the breeze to come and refresh him. Believing that he referred to some wood-nymph, Procris sank down among the bushes in a swoon; and her husband, hearing the leaves rustle suddenly behind him, hurled his javelin into the thicket, supposing that some wild beast was crouching near him ready to spring. To his horror he discovered the body of Procris; and though he did all that he could to stanch the wound made by his unerring spear, his wife died in his arms – but not before an explanation had been given.

Though Aurora had succeeded in separating the lovers forever, she did not thereby gain the affections of Cephalus, but was obliged to console herself with the Trojan prince, Tithonus. She begged Jupiter to confer upon him the boon of immortal life; but forgetting that he would sometime grow old, she neglected to ask for him the greater gift of eternal youth. For a while she was very happy with her lover, but as soon as he lost the attractions of youth she wearied of his company and wished to get rid of him. She shut him up in a room of her palace, where his feeble voice could often be heard; and then, knowing that he would never die, she cruelly changed him into a grasshopper.

The son of Aurora and Tithonus was Memnon, who became king of the Ethiopians, and went with a band of warriors to help his kindred in the Trojan War. He fought bravely, but at length met his death at the hands of Achilles. When he fell on the battlefield, Aurora commanded her sons, the winds, to carry his body to the banks of the river Aesepus in Asia Minor, where a tomb was erected to his memory. To honour him further, Jupiter caused the sparks and cinders from his funeral pyre to be changed into birds, which divided into two flocks and fought until they fell into the flames. Every year, on the anniversary of Memnon's death, the birds returned to celebrate the funeral rites in this same strange way. When the flames from the funeral pyre had burned out, Aurora sat by the ashes of her son, weeping and mourning his loss; and the many tears that she shed turned into glistening dewdrops. In Egypt there were two colossal statues, one of which was said to be the statue of Memnon; and tradition tells that when the first rays of morning fell upon it, it gave forth a sound like the snapping of harp strings.

The Journey to the Sunrise

From the Cherokee people

A LONG TIME AGO several young men made up their minds to find the place where the Sun lives and see what the Sun is like. They got ready their bows and arrows, their parched corn and extra moccasins, and started out toward the east. At first they met tribes they knew, then they came to tribes they had only heard about, and at last to others of which they had never heard.

There was a tribe of root eaters and another of acorn eaters, with great piles of acorn shells near their houses. In one tribe they found a sick man dying, and were told it was the custom there when a man died to bury his wife in the same grave with him. They waited until he was dead, when they saw his friends lower the body into a great pit, so deep and dark that from the top they could not see the bottom. Then a rope was tied around the woman's body, together with a bundle of pine knots, a lighted pine knot was put into her hand, and she was lowered into the pit to die there in the darkness after the last pine knot was burned.

The young men travelled on until they came at last to the sunrise place where the sky reaches down to the ground. They found that the sky was an arch or vault of solid rock hung above the earth and was always swinging up and down, so that when it went up there was an open place like a door between the sky and ground, and when it swung back the door was shut. The Sun came out of this door from the east and climbed along on the inside of the arch. It had a human figure, but was too bright for them to see clearly and too hot to come very near. They waited until the Sun had come out and then tried to get through while the door was still open, but just as the first one was in the doorway the rock came down and crushed him. The other six were afraid to try it, and as they were now at the end of the world they turned around and started back again, but they had travelled so far that they were old men when they reached home.

King Midas of the Golden Touch

From Greek mythology

IN THE PLAYS OF SHAKESPEARE we have three distinct divisions – three separate volumes. One deals with Tragedy, another with Comedy, a third with History; and a mistake made by the young in their aspect of life is that they do the same thing, and keep tragedy and comedy severely apart, relegating them to separate volumes that, so they think, have nothing to do with each other. But those who have passed many milestones on the road know that *"History"* is the only right label for the Book of Life's many parts, and that the actors in the great play are in truth tragic comedians.

This is the story of Midas, one of the chief tragic comedians of mythology.

Once upon a time the kingdom of Phrygia lacked a king, and in much perplexity, the people sought help from an oracle. The answer was very definite:

"The first man who enters your city riding in a car shall be your king."

That day there came slowly jogging into the city in their heavy, wooden-wheeled wain, the peasant Gordias and his wife and son, whose destination was the marketplace, and whose business was to sell the produce of their little farm and vineyard – fowl, a goat or two, and a couple of skinsful of strong, purple-red wine. An eager crowd awaited their entry, and a loud shout of welcome greeted them. And their eyes grew round and their mouths fell open in amaze when they were hailed as King and Queen and Prince of Phrygia.

The gods had indeed bestowed upon Gordias, the low-born peasant, a surprising gift, but he showed his gratitude by dedicating his wagon to the deity of the oracle and tying it up in its place with the wiliest knot that his simple wisdom knew, pulled as tight as his brawny arms and strong rough hands could pull. Nor could anyone untie the famous Gordian knot, and therefore become, as the oracle promised, lord of all Asia, until centuries had passed, and Alexander the Great came to Phrygia and sliced through the knot with his all-conquering sword.

In time Midas, the son of Gordias, came to inherit the throne and crown of Phrygia. Like many another not born and bred to the purple, his honours sat heavily upon him. From the day that his father's wain had entered the city amidst the acclamations of the people, he had learned the value of power, and therefore, from his boyhood onward, power, always more power, was what he coveted. Also his peasant father had taught him that gold could buy power, and so Midas ever longed for more gold, that could buy him a place in the world that no descendant of a long race of kings should be able to contest. And from Olympus the gods looked down and smiled, and vowed that Midas should have the chance of realizing his heart's desire.

Therefore, one day when he and his court were sitting in the solemn state that Midas required, there rode into their midst, tipsily swaying on the back of a gentle full-fed old grey ass, ivy-crowned, jovial and foolish, the satyr Silenus, guardian of the young god Bacchus.

With all the deference due to the friend of a god Midas treated this disreputable old pedagogue, and for ten days and nights on end he feasted him royally. On the eleventh day Bacchus came in search of his preceptor, and in deep gratitude bade Midas demand of him what he would, because he had done Silenus honour when to dishonour him lay in his power.

Not even for a moment did Midas ponder.

"I would have gold," he said hastily, "much gold. I would have that touch by which all common and valueless things become golden treasures."

And Bacchus, knowing that here spoke the son of peasants who many times had gone empty to bed after a day of toilful striving on the rocky uplands of Phrygia, looked a little sadly in the eager face of Midas, and answered, "Be it as thou wilt. Thine shall be the golden touch."

Then Bacchus and Silenus went away, a rout of singing revellers at their heels, and Midas quickly put to proof the words of Bacchus.

An olive tree grew near where he stood, and from it he picked a little twig decked with leaves of softest grey, and lo, it grew heavy as he held it, and glittered like a piece of his crown. He stooped to touch the green turf on which some fragrant violets grew, and turf grew into cloth of gold, and violets lost their fragrance and became hard, solid, golden things. He touched an apple whose cheek grew rosy in the sun, and at once it became like the golden fruit in the Garden of the Hesperides. The stone pillars of his palace as he brushed past them on entering, blazed like a sunset sky. The gods had not deceived him. Midas had the Golden Touch. Joyously he strode into the palace and commanded a feast to be prepared – a feast worthy of an occasion so magnificent.

But when Midas, with the healthy appetite of the peasant-born, would have eaten largely of the savoury food that his cooks prepared, he found that his teeth only touched roast kid to turn it into a slab of gold, that garlic lost its flavour and became gritty as he chewed, that rice turned into golden grains, and curdled milk became a dower fit for a princess, entirely unnegotiable for the digestion of man. Baffled and miserable, Midas seized his cup of wine, but the red wine had become one with the golden vessel that held it; nor could he quench his thirst, for even the limpid water from the fountain was melted gold when it touched his dry lips. Only for a very few days was Midas able to bear the affliction of his wealth. There was nothing now for him to live for. He could buy the whole earth if he pleased, but even children shrank in terror from his touch, and hungry and thirsty and sick at heart he wearily dragged along his weighty robes of gold. Gold was power, he knew well, yet of what worth was gold while he starved? Gold could not buy him life and health and happiness.

In despair, at length he cried to the god who had given him the gift that he hated.

"Save me, O Bacchus!" he said. "A witless one am I, and the folly of my desire has been my undoing. Take away from me the accursed Golden Touch, and faithfully and well shall I serve thee forever."

Then Bacchus, very pitiful for him, told Midas to go to Sardis, the chief city of his worshippers, and to trace to its source the river upon which it was built. And in that pool, when he found it, he was to plunge his head, and so he would, for evermore, be freed from the Golden Touch.

It was a long journey that Midas then took, and a weary and a starving man was he when at length he reached the spring where the river Pactolus had its source. He crawled forward, and timidly plunged in his head and shoulders. Almost he expected to feel the harsh grit of golden water, but instead there was the joy he had known as a peasant boy when he laved his face and drank at a cool spring when his day's toil was ended. And when he raised his face from the pool, he knew that his hateful power had passed from him, but under the water he saw grains of gold glittering in the sand, and from that time forth the river Pactolus was noted for its gold.

One lesson the peasant king had learnt by paying in suffering for a mistake, but there was yet more suffering in store for the tragic comedian.

He had now no wish for golden riches, nor even for power. He wished to lead the simple life and to listen to the pipings of Pan along with the goatherds on the mountains or the wild creatures in the woods. Thus it befell that he was present one day at a contest between Pan and Apollo himself. It was a day of merry-making for nymphs and fauns and dryads, and all those who lived in the lonely solitudes of Phrygia came to listen to the music of the god who ruled them. For as Pan sat in the shade of a forest one night and piped on his reeds until the very shadows danced, and the water of the stream by which he sat leapt high over the mossy stones it passed, and laughed aloud in its glee, the god had so gloried in his own power that he cried:

"Who speaks of Apollo and his lyre? Some of the gods may be well pleased with his music, and mayhap a bloodless man or two. But my music strikes to the heart of the earth itself. It stirs with rapture the very sap of the trees, and awakes to life and joy the innermost soul of all things mortal."

Apollo heard his boast, and heard it angrily.

"Oh, thou whose soul is the soul of the untilled ground!" he said, "wouldst thou place thy music, that is like the wind in the reeds, beside my music, which is as the music of the spheres?"

And Pan, splashing with his goat's feet amongst the waterlilies of the stream on the bank of which he sat, laughed loudly and cried:

"Yea, would I, Apollo! Willingly would I play thee a match – thou on thy golden lyre – I on my reeds from the river."

Thus did it come to pass that Apollo and Pan matched against each other their music, and King Midas was one of the judges.

First of all Pan took his fragile reeds, and as he played, the leaves on the trees shivered, and the sleeping lilies raised their heads, and the birds ceased their song to listen and then flew straight to their mates. And all the beauty of the world grew more beautiful, and all its terror grew yet more grim, and still Pan piped on, and laughed to see the nymphs and the fauns first dance in joyousness and then tremble in fear, and the buds to blossom, and the stags to bellow in their lordship of the hills. When he ceased, it was as though a tensely drawn string had broken, and all the earth lay breathless and mute. And Pan turned proudly to the golden-haired god who had listened as he had spoken through the hearts of reeds to the hearts of men.

"Canst, then, make music like unto my music, Apollo?" he said.

Then Apollo, his purple robes barely hiding the perfection of his limbs, a wreath of laurel crowning his yellow curls, looked down at Pan from his godlike height and smiled in silence. For a moment his hand silently played over the golden strings of his lyre, and then his fingertips gently touched them. And every creature there who had a soul, felt that that soul had wings, and the wings sped them straight to Olympus. Far away from all earth-bound creatures they flew, and dwelt in magnificent serenity amongst the Immortals. No longer was there strife, or any dispeace. No more was there fierce warring between the actual and the unknown. The green fields and thick woods had faded into nothingness, and their creatures, and the fair nymphs and dryads, and the wild fauns and centaurs longed and fought no more, and man had ceased to desire the impossible. Throbbing nature and passionately desiring life faded into dust before the melody that Apollo called forth, and when his strings had ceased to quiver and only the faintly remembered echo of his music remained, it was as though the earth had passed away and all things had become new.

For the space of many seconds all was silence.

Then, in low voice, Apollo asked:

"Ye who listen – who is the victor?"

And earth and sea and sky, and all the creatures of earth and sky, and of the deep, replied as one:

"The victory is thine, Divine Apollo."

Yet was there one dissentient voice.

Midas, sorely puzzled, utterly un-understanding, was relieved when the music of Apollo ceased. "If only Pan would play again," he murmured to himself. "I wish to live, and Pan's music gives me life. I love the woolly vine-buds and the fragrant pine leaves, and the scent of the violets in the spring. The smell of the fresh-ploughed earth is dear to me, the breath of the kine that have grazed in the meadows of wild parsley and of asphodel. I want to drink red wine and to eat and love and fight and work and be joyous and sad, fierce and strong, and very weary, and to sleep the dead sleep of men who live only as weak mortals do."

Therefore he raised his voice, and called very loud, "Pan's music is sweeter and truer and greater than the music of Apollo. Pan is the victor, and I, King Midas, give him the victor's crown!"

With scorn ineffable the sun-god turned upon Midas, his peasant's face transfigured by his proud decision. For a little he gazed at him in silence, and his look might have turned a sunbeam to an icicle.

Then he spoke:

"The ears of an ass have heard my music," he said. "Henceforth shall Midas have ass's ears."

And when Midas, in terror, clapped his hands to his crisp black hair, he found growing far beyond it, the long, pointed ears of an ass. Perhaps what hurt him most, as he fled away, was the shout of merriment that came from Pan. And fauns and nymphs and satyrs echoed that shout most joyously.

Willingly would he have hidden in the woods, but there he found no hiding place. The trees and shrubs and flowering things seemed to shake in cruel mockery. Back to his court he went and sent for the court hairdresser, that he might bribe him to devise a covering for these long, peaked, hairy symbols of his folly. Gladly the hairdresser accepted many and many oboli, many and many golden gifts, and all Phrygia wondered, while it copied, the strange headdress of the king.

But although much gold had bought his silence, the court barber was unquiet of heart. All day and all through the night he was tormented by his weighty secret. And then, at length, silence was to him a torture too great to be borne; he sought a lonely place, there dug a deep hole, and, kneeling by it, softly whispered to the damp earth, "King Midas has ass's ears."

Greatly relieved, he hastened home, and was well content until, on the spot where his secret lay buried, rushes grew up. And when the winds blew through them, the rushes whispered for all those who passed by to hear, "King Midas has ass's ears! King Midas has ass's ears!" Those who listen very carefully to what the green rushes in marshy places whisper as the wind passes through them, may hear the same thing to this day. And those who hear the whisper of the rushes may, perhaps, give a pitying thought to Midas – the tragic comedian of mythology.

Extracts from 'King Solomon's Mines'

H. Rider Haggard

Publisher's Note: King Solomon's Mines, *by H. Rider Haggard (1856–1925), follows a group of Victorian adventurers on an expedition through Africa to rescue the missing brother of one of the characters. Coming to a desert, the group must survive beneath an unforgiving sun.*

Chapter V
Our March into the Desert

WE HAD KILLED nine elephants, and it took us two days to cut out the tusks, and having brought them into camp, to bury them carefully in the sand under a large tree, which made a conspicuous mark for miles round. It was a wonderfully fine lot of ivory. I never saw a better, averaging as it did between forty and fifty pounds a tusk. The tusks of the great bull that killed poor Khiva scaled one hundred and seventy pounds the pair, so nearly as we could judge.

As for Khiva himself, we buried what remained of him in an ant-bear hole, together with an assegai to protect himself with on his journey to a better world. On the third day we marched again, hoping that we might live to return to dig up our buried ivory, and in due course, after a long and wearisome tramp, and many adventures which I have not space to detail, we reached Sitanda's Kraal, near the Lukanga River, the real starting-point of our expedition. Very well do I recollect our arrival at that place. To the right was a scattered native settlement with a few stone cattle kraals and some cultivated lands down by the water, where these savages grew their scanty supply of grain, and beyond it stretched great tracts of waving "veld" covered with tall grass, over which herds of the smaller game were wandering. To the left lay the vast desert. This spot appears to be the outpost of the fertile country, and it would be difficult to say to what natural causes such an abrupt change in the character of the soil is due. But so it is.

Just below our encampment flowed a little stream, on the farther side of which is a stony slope, the same down which, twenty years before, I had seen poor Silvestre creeping back after his attempt to reach Solomon's Mines, and beyond that slope begins the waterless desert, covered with a species of karoo shrub.

It was evening when we pitched our camp, and the great ball of the sun was sinking into the desert, sending glorious rays of many-coloured light flying all over its vast expanse. Leaving Good to superintend the arrangement of our little camp, I took Sir Henry with me, and walking to the top of the slope opposite, we gazed across the desert. The air was very clear, and far, far away I could distinguish the faint blue outlines, here and there capped with white, of the Suliman Berg.

"There," I said, "there is the wall round Solomon's Mines, but God knows if we shall ever climb it."

"My brother should be there, and if he is, I shall reach him somehow," said Sir Henry, in that tone of quiet confidence which marked the man.

"I hope so," I answered, and turned to go back to the camp, when I saw that we were not alone. Behind us, also gazing earnestly towards the far-off mountains, stood the great Kafir Umbopa.

The Zulu spoke when he saw that I had observed him, addressing Sir Henry, to whom he had attached himself.

"Is it to that land that thou wouldst journey, Incubu?" (a native word meaning, I believe, an elephant, and the name given to Sir Henry by the Kafirs), he said, pointing towards the mountain with his broad assegai.

I asked him sharply what he meant by addressing his master in that familiar way. It is very well for natives to have a name for one among themselves, but it is not decent that they should call a white man by their heathenish appellations to his face. The Zulu laughed a quiet little laugh which angered me.

"How dost thou know that I am not the equal of the Inkosi whom I serve?" he said. "He is of a royal house, no doubt; one can see it in his size and by his mien; so, mayhap, am I. At least, I am as great a man. Be my mouth, O Macumazahn, and say my words to the Inkoos Incubu, my master, for I would speak to him and to thee."

I was angry with the man, for I am not accustomed to be talked to in that way by Kafirs, but somehow he impressed me, and besides I was curious to know what he had to say. So I translated, expressing my opinion at the same time that he was an impudent fellow, and that his swagger was outrageous.

"Yes, Umbopa," answered Sir Henry, "I would journey there."

"The desert is wide and there is no water in it, the mountains are high and covered with snow, and man cannot say what lies beyond them behind the place where the sun sets; how shalt thou come thither, Incubu, and wherefore dost thou go?"

I translated again.

"Tell him," answered Sir Henry, "that I go because I believe that a man of my blood, my brother, has gone there before me, and I journey to seek him."

"That is so, Incubu; a Hottentot I met on the road told me that a white man went out into the desert two years ago towards those mountains with one servant, a hunter. They never came back."

"How do you know it was my brother?" asked Sir Henry.

"Nay, I know not. But the Hottentot, when I asked what the white man was like, said that he had thine eyes and a black beard. He said, too, that the name of the hunter with him was Jim; that he was a Bechuana hunter and wore clothes."

"There is no doubt about it," said I; "I knew Jim well."

Sir Henry nodded. "I was sure of it," he said. "If George set his mind upon a thing he generally did it. It was always so from his boyhood. If he meant to cross the Suliman Berg he has crossed it, unless some accident overtook him, and we must look for him on the other side."

Umbopa understood English, though he rarely spoke it.

"It is a far journey, Incubu," he put in, and I translated his remark.

"Yes," answered Sir Henry, "it is far. But there is no journey upon this earth that a man may not make if he sets his heart to it. There is nothing, Umbopa, that he cannot do, there are no mountains he may not climb, there are no deserts he cannot cross, save a mountain and a desert of which you are spared the knowledge, if love leads him and he holds his life in his hands counting it as nothing, ready to keep it or lose it as Heaven above may order."

I translated.

"Great words, my father," answered the Zulu – I always called him a Zulu, though he was not really one – "great swelling words fit to fill the mouth of a man. Thou art right, my father Incubu. Listen! What is life? It is a feather, it is the seed of the grass, blown hither and thither, sometimes multiplying itself and dying in the act, sometimes carried away into the heavens. But if that seed be good and heavy it may perchance travel a little way on the road it wills. It is well to try and journey one's road and to fight with the air. Man must die. At the worst he can but die a little sooner. I will go with thee across the desert and over the mountains, unless perchance I fall to the ground on the way, my father."

He paused a while, and then went on with one of those strange bursts of rhetorical eloquence that Zulus sometimes indulge in, which to my mind, full though they are of vain repetitions, show that the race is by no means devoid of poetic instinct and of intellectual power.

"What is life? Tell me, O white men, who are wise, who know the secrets of the world, and of the world of stars, and the world that lies above and around the stars; who flash your words from afar without a voice; tell me, white men, the secret of our life – whither it goes and whence it comes!

"You cannot answer me; you know not. Listen, I will answer. Out of the dark we came, into the dark we go. Like a storm-driven bird at night we fly out of the Nowhere; for a moment our wings are seen in the light of the fire, and, lo! we are gone again into the Nowhere. Life is nothing. Life is all. It is the Hand with which we hold off Death. It is the glow-worm that shines in the night-time and is black in the morning; it is the white breath of the oxen in winter; it is the little shadow that runs across the grass and loses itself at sunset."

"You are a strange man," said Sir Henry, when he had ceased.

Umbopa laughed. "It seems to me that we are much alike, Incubu. Perhaps I seek a brother over the mountains."

I looked at him suspiciously. "What dost thou mean?" I asked; "what dost thou know of those mountains?"

"A little; a very little. There is a strange land yonder, a land of witchcraft and beautiful things; a land of brave people, and of trees, and streams, and snowy peaks, and of a great white road. I have heard of it. But what is the good of talking? It grows dark. Those who live to see will see."

Again I looked at him doubtfully. The man knew too much.

"You need not fear me, Macumazahn," he said, interpreting my look. "I dig no holes for you to fall in. I make no plots. If ever we cross those mountains behind the sun I will tell what I know. But Death sits upon them. Be wise and turn back. Go and hunt elephants, my masters. I have spoken."

And without another word he lifted his spear in salutation, and returned towards the camp, where shortly afterwards we found him cleaning a gun like any other Kafir.

"That is an odd man," said Sir Henry.

"Yes," answered I, "too odd by half. I don't like his little ways. He knows something, and will not speak out. But I suppose it is no use quarrelling with him. We are in for a curious trip, and a mysterious Zulu won't make much difference one way or another."

Next day we made our arrangements for starting. Of course it was impossible to drag our heavy elephant rifles and other kit with us across the desert, so, dismissing our bearers, we made an arrangement with an old native who had a kraal close by to take care of them till we returned. It went to my heart to leave such things as those sweet tools to the tender mercies of an old thief of a savage whose greedy eyes I could see gloating over them. But I took some precautions.

First of all I loaded all the rifles, placing them at full cock, and informed him that if he touched them they would go off. He tried the experiment instantly with my eight-bore, and it did go off, and blew a hole right through one of his oxen, which were just then being driven up to the kraal, to say nothing of knocking him head over heels with the recoil. He got up considerably startled, and not at all pleased at the loss of the ox, which he had the impudence to ask me to pay for, and nothing would induce him to touch the guns again.

"Put the live devils out of the way up there in the thatch," he said, "or they will murder us all."

Then I told him that, when we came back, if one of those things was missing I would kill him and his people by witchcraft; and if we died and he tried to steal the rifles I would come and haunt him and turn his cattle mad and his milk sour till life was a weariness, and would make the devils in the guns come out and talk to him in a way he did not like, and generally gave him a good idea of judgment to come. After that he promised to look after them as though they were his father's spirit. He was a very superstitious old Kafir and a great villain.

Having thus disposed of our superfluous gear we arranged the kit we five – Sir Henry, Good, myself, Umbopa, and the Hottentot Ventvögel – were to take with us on our journey. It was small enough, but do what we would we could not get its weight down under about forty pounds a man. This is what it consisted of:

The three express rifles and two hundred rounds of ammunition.

The two Winchester repeating rifles (for Umbopa and Ventvögel), with two hundred rounds of cartridge.

Five Cochrane's water-bottles, each holding four pints.

Five blankets.

Twenty-five pounds' weight of biltong – *i.e.* sun-dried game flesh.

Ten pounds' weight of best mixed beads for gifts.

A selection of medicine, including an ounce of quinine, and one or two small surgical instruments.

Our knives, a few sundries, such as a compass, matches, a pocket filter, tobacco, a trowel, a bottle of brandy, and the clothes we stood in.

This was our total equipment, a small one indeed for such a venture, but we dared not attempt to carry more. Indeed, that load was a heavy one per man with which to travel across the burning desert, for in such places every additional ounce tells. But we could not see our way to reducing the weight. There was nothing taken but what was absolutely necessary.

With great difficulty, and by the promise of a present of a good hunting-knife each, I succeeded in persuading three wretched natives from the village to come with us for the first stage, twenty miles, and to carry a large gourd holding a gallon of water apiece. My object was to enable us to refill our water-bottles after the first night's march, for we determined to start in the cool of the evening. I gave out to these natives that we were going to shoot ostriches, with which the desert abounded. They jabbered and shrugged their shoulders, saying that we were mad and should perish of thirst, which I must say seemed probable; but being desirous of obtaining the knives, which were almost unknown treasures up there, they consented to come, having probably reflected that, after all, our subsequent extinction would be no affair of theirs.

All next day we rested and slept, and at sunset ate a hearty meal of fresh beef washed down with tea, the last, as Good remarked sadly, we were likely to drink for many a long day. Then, having made our final preparations, we lay down and waited for the moon to rise. At last, about nine o'clock, up she came in all her glory, flooding the wild country with light, and throwing a silver sheen on the expanse of rolling desert before us, which looked as solemn and quiet and as alien to man as the star-studded firmament above. We rose up, and in a few minutes were ready, and yet we hesitated a little, as human nature is prone to hesitate on the threshold of an irrevocable step. We three white men stood by ourselves. Umbopa, assegai in hand and a rifle across his shoulders, looked out fixedly across the desert a few paces ahead of us; while the hired natives, with the gourds of water, and Ventvögel, were gathered in a little knot behind.

"Gentlemen," said Sir Henry presently, in his deep voice, "we are going on about as strange a journey as men can make in this world. It is very doubtful if we can succeed in it. But we are three men who will stand together for good or for evil to the last. Now before we start let us for a moment pray to the Power who shapes the destinies of men, and who ages since has marked out our paths, that it may please Him to direct our steps in accordance with His will."

Taking off his hat, for the space of a minute or so, he covered his face with his hands, and Good and I did likewise.

I do not say that I am a first-rate praying man, few hunters are, and as for Sir Henry, I never heard him speak like that before, and only once since, though deep down in his heart I believe that he is very religious. Good too is pious, though apt to swear. Anyhow I do not remember, excepting on one single occasion, ever putting up a better prayer in my life than I did during that minute, and somehow I felt the happier for it. Our future was so completely unknown, and I think that the unknown and the awful always bring a man nearer to his Maker.

"And now," said Sir Henry, "*trek*!"

So we started.

We had nothing to guide ourselves by except the distant mountains and old José da Silvestra's chart, which, considering that it was drawn by a dying and half-distraught man on a fragment of linen three centuries ago, was not a very satisfactory sort of thing to work with. Still, our sole hope of success depended upon it, such as it was. If we failed in finding that pool of bad water which the old Dom marked as being situated in the middle of the desert, about sixty miles from our starting-point, and as far from the mountains, in all probability we must perish miserably of thirst. But to my mind the chances of our finding it in that great sea of sand and karoo scrub seemed almost infinitesimal. Even supposing that da Silvestra had marked the pool correctly, what was there to prevent its having been dried up by the sun generations ago, or trampled in by game, or filled with the drifting sand?

On we tramped silently as shades through the night and in the heavy sand. The karoo bushes caught our feet and retarded us, and the sand worked into our veldtschoons and Good's shooting-boots, so that every few miles we had to stop and empty them; but still the night kept fairly cool, though the atmosphere was thick and heavy, giving a sort of creamy feel to the air, and we made fair progress. It was very silent and lonely there in the desert, oppressively so indeed. Good felt this, and once began to whistle "The Girl I left behind me," but the notes sounded lugubrious in that vast place, and he gave it up.

Shortly afterwards a little incident occurred which, though it startled us at the time, gave rise to a laugh. Good was leading, as the holder of the compass, which, being a sailor, of course he understood thoroughly, and we were toiling along in single file behind him, when suddenly we heard the sound of an exclamation, and he vanished. Next second there arose all around us a most extraordinary hubbub, snorts, groans, and wild sounds of rushing feet. In the faint light, too, we could descry dim galloping forms half hidden by wreaths of sand. The natives threw down their loads and prepared to bolt, but remembering that there was nowhere to run to, they cast themselves upon the ground and howled out that it was ghosts. As for Sir Henry and myself, we stood amazed; nor was our amazement lessened when we perceived the form of Good careering off in the direction of the mountains, apparently mounted on the back of a horse and halloaing wildly. In another second he threw up his arms, and we heard him come to the earth with a thud.

Then I saw what had happened; we had stumbled upon a herd of sleeping quagga, onto the back of one of which Good actually had fallen, and the brute naturally enough got up and made off with him. Calling out to the others that it was all right, I ran towards Good, much afraid lest he should be hurt, but to my great relief I found him sitting in the sand, his eyeglass still fixed firmly in his eye, rather shaken and very much frightened, but not in any way injured.

After this we travelled on without any further misadventure till about one o'clock, when we called a halt, and having drunk a little water, not much, for water was precious, and rested for half an hour, we started again.

On, on we went, till at last the east began to blush like the cheek of a girl. Then there came faint rays of primrose light, that changed presently to golden bars, through which the dawn glided out across the desert. The stars grew pale and paler still, till at last they vanished; the golden moon waxed wan, and her mountain ridges stood out against her sickly face like the bones on the cheek of a dying man. Then came spear upon spear of light flashing far away across the boundless wilderness, piercing and firing the veils of mist, till the desert was draped in a tremulous golden glow, and it was day.

Still we did not halt, though by this time we should have been glad enough to do so, for we knew that when once the sun was fully up it would be almost impossible for us to travel. At length, about an hour later, we spied a little pile of boulders rising out of the plain, and to this we dragged ourselves. As luck would have it, here we found an overhanging slab of rock carpeted beneath with smooth sand, which afforded a most grateful shelter from the heat. Underneath this we crept, and each of us having drunk some water and eaten a bit of biltong, we lay down and soon were sound asleep.

It was three o'clock in the afternoon before we woke, to find our bearers preparing to return. They had seen enough of the desert already, and no number of knives would have tempted them to come a step farther. So we took a hearty drink, and having emptied our water-bottles, filled them up again from the gourds that they had brought with them, and then watched them depart on their twenty miles' tramp home.

At half-past four we also started. It was lonely and desolate work, for with the exception of a few ostriches there was not a single living creature to be seen on all the vast expanse of sandy plain. Evidently it was too dry for game, and with the exception of a deadly-looking cobra or two we saw no reptiles. One insect, however, we found abundant, and that was the common or house fly. There they came, "not as single spies, but in battalions," as I think the Old Testament says somewhere. He is an extraordinary insect is the house fly. Go where you will you find him, and so it must have been always. I have seen him enclosed in amber, which is, I was told, quite half a million years old, looking exactly like his descendant of today, and I have little doubt but that when the last man lies dying on the earth he will be buzzing round – if this event happens to occur in summer – watching for an opportunity to settle on his nose.

At sunset we halted, waiting for the moon to rise. At last she came up, beautiful and serene as ever, and, with one halt about two o'clock in the morning, we trudged on wearily through the night, till at last the welcome sun put a period to our labours. We drank a little and flung ourselves down on the sand, thoroughly tired out, and soon were all asleep. There was no need to set a watch, for we had nothing to fear from anybody or anything in that vast untenanted plain. Our only enemies were heat, thirst and flies, but far rather would I have faced any danger from man or beast than that awful trinity. This time we were not so lucky as to find a sheltering rock to guard us from the glare of the sun, with the result that about seven o'clock we woke up experiencing the exact sensations one would attribute to a beefsteak on a gridiron. We were literally being baked through and through. The burning sun seemed to be sucking our very blood out of us. We sat up and gasped.

"Phew," said I, grabbing at the halo of flies which buzzed cheerfully round my head. The heat did not affect *them*.

"My word!" said Sir Henry.

"It is hot!" echoed Good.

It was hot, indeed, and there was not a bit of shelter to be found. Look where we would there was no rock or tree, nothing but an unending glare, rendered dazzling by the heated air that danced over the surface of the desert as it dances over a red-hot stove.

"What is to be done?" asked Sir Henry; "we can't stand this for long."

We looked at each other blankly.

"I have it," said Good, "we must dig a hole, get in it, and cover ourselves with the karoo bushes."

It did not seem a very promising suggestion, but at least it was better than nothing, so we set to work, and, with the trowel we had brought with us and the help of our hands, in about an hour we succeeded in delving out a patch of ground some ten feet long by twelve wide to the depth of two feet. Then we cut a quantity of low scrub with our hunting-knives, and creeping into the hole, pulled it over us all, with the exception of Ventvögel, on whom, being a Hottentot, the heat had no particular effect. This gave us some slight shelter from the burning rays of the sun, but the atmosphere in that amateur grave can be better imagined than described. The Black Hole of Calcutta must have been a fool to it; indeed, to this moment I do not know how we lived through the day. There we lay panting, and every now and again moistening our lips from our scanty supply of water. Had we followed our inclinations we should have finished all we possessed in the first two hours, but we were forced to exercise the most rigid care, for if our water failed us we knew that very soon we must perish miserably.

But everything has an end, if only you live long enough to see it, and somehow that miserable day wore on towards evening. About three o'clock in the afternoon we determined that we could bear it no longer. It would be better to die walking than to be killed slowly by heat and thirst in this dreadful hole. So taking each of us a little drink from our fast diminishing supply of water, now warmed to about the same temperature as a man's blood, we staggered forward.

We had then covered some fifty miles of wilderness. If the reader will refer to the rough copy and translation of old da Silvestra's map, he will see that the desert is marked as measuring forty leagues across, and the "pan bad water" is set down as being about in the middle of it. Now forty leagues is one hundred and twenty miles, consequently we ought at the most to be within twelve or fifteen miles of the water if any should really exist.

Through the afternoon we crept slowly and painfully along, scarcely doing more than a mile and a half in an hour. At sunset we rested again, waiting for the moon, and after drinking a little managed to get some sleep.

Before we lay down, Umbopa pointed out to us a slight and indistinct hillock on the flat surface of the plain about eight miles away. At the distance it looked like an anthill, and as I was dropping off to sleep I fell to wondering what it could be.

With the moon we marched again, feeling dreadfully exhausted, and suffering tortures from thirst and prickly heat. Nobody who has not felt it can know what we went through. We walked no longer, we staggered, now and again falling from exhaustion, and being obliged to call a halt every hour or so. We had scarcely energy left in us to speak. Up to this Good had chatted and joked, for he is a merry fellow; but now he had not a joke in him.

At last, about two o'clock, utterly worn out in body and mind, we came to the foot of the queer hill, or sand koppie, which at first sight resembled a gigantic ant-heap about a hundred feet high, and covering at the base nearly two acres of ground.

Here we halted, and driven to it by our desperate thirst, sucked down our last drops of water. We had but half a pint a head, and each of us could have drunk a gallon.

Then we lay down. Just as I was dropping off to sleep I heard Umbopa remark to himself in Zulu:

"If we cannot find water we shall all be dead before the moon rises tomorrow."

I shuddered, hot as it was. The near prospect of such an awful death is not pleasant, but even the thought of it could not keep me from sleeping.

Chapter VI
Water! Water!

Two hours later, that is, about four o'clock, I woke up, for so soon as the first heavy demand of bodily fatigue had been satisfied, the torturing thirst from which I was suffering asserted itself. I could sleep no more. I had been dreaming that I was bathing in a running stream, with green banks and trees upon them, and I awoke to find myself in this arid wilderness, and to remember, as Umbopa had said, that if we did not find water this day we must perish miserably. No human creature could live long without water in that heat. I sat up and rubbed my grimy face with my dry and horny hands, as my lips and eyelids were stuck together, and it was only after some friction and with an effort that I was able to open them. It was not far from dawn, but there was none of the bright feel of dawn in the air, which was thick with a hot murkiness that I cannot describe. The others were still sleeping.

Presently it began to grow light enough to read, so I drew out a little pocket copy of the "Ingoldsby Legends" which I had brought with me, and read "The Jackdaw of Rheims." When I got to where

"A nice little boy held a golden ewer,
Embossed, and filled with water as pure
As any that flows between Rheims and Namur,"

literally I smacked my cracking lips, or rather tried to smack them. The mere thought of that pure water made me mad. If the Cardinal had been there with his bell, book, and candle, I would have whipped in and drunk his water up; yes, even if he had filled it already with the suds of soap "worthy of washing the hands of the Pope," and I knew that the whole consecrated curse of the Catholic Church should fall upon me for so doing. I almost think that I must have been a little light-headed with thirst, weariness and the want of food; for I fell to thinking how astonished the Cardinal and his nice little boy and the jackdaw would have looked to see a burnt up, brown-eyed, grizzly-haired little elephant hunter suddenly bound between them, put his dirty face into the basin, and swallow every drop of the precious water. The idea amused me so much that I laughed or rather cackled aloud, which woke the others, and they began to rub *their* dirty faces and drag *their* gummed-up lips and eyelids apart.

As soon as we were all well awake we began to discuss the situation, which was serious enough. Not a drop of water was left. We turned the bottles upside down, and licked their tops, but it was a failure; they were dry as a bone. Good, who had charge of the flask of brandy, got it out and looked at it longingly; but Sir Henry promptly took it away from him, for to drink raw spirit would only have been to precipitate the end.

"If we do not find water we shall die," he said.

"If we can trust to the old Dom's map there should be some about," I said; but nobody seemed to derive much satisfaction from this remark. It was so evident that no great faith could be put in the map. Now it was gradually growing light, and as we sat staring blankly at each other, I observed the Hottentot Ventvögel rise and begin to walk about with his eyes on the ground. Presently he stopped short, and uttering a guttural exclamation, pointed to the earth.

"What is it?" we exclaimed; and rising simultaneously we went to where he was standing staring at the sand.

"Well," I said, "it is fresh Springbok spoor; what of it?"

"Springboks do not go far from water," he answered in Dutch.

"No," I answered, "I forgot; and thank God for it."

This little discovery put new life into us; for it is wonderful, when a man is in a desperate position, how he catches at the slightest hope, and feels almost happy. On a dark night a single star is better than nothing.

Meanwhile Ventvögel was lifting his snub nose, and sniffing the hot air for all the world like an old Impala ram who scents danger. Presently he spoke again.

"I *smell* water," he said.

Then we felt quite jubilant, for we knew what a wonderful instinct these wild-bred men possess.

Just at that moment the sun came up gloriously, and revealed so grand a sight to our astonished eyes that for a moment or two we even forgot our thirst.

There, not more than forty or fifty miles from us, glittering like silver in the early rays of the morning sun, soared Sheba's Breasts; and stretching away for hundreds of miles on either side of them ran the great Suliman Berg. Now that, sitting here, I attempt to describe the extraordinary grandeur and beauty of that sight, language seems to fail me. I am impotent even before its memory. Straight before us, rose two enormous mountains, the like of which are not, I believe, to be seen in Africa, if indeed there are any other such in the world, measuring each of them at least fifteen thousand feet in height, standing not more than a dozen miles apart, linked together by a precipitous cliff of rock, and towering in awful white solemnity straight into the sky. These mountains placed thus, like the pillars of a gigantic gateway, are shaped after the fashion of a woman's breasts, and at times the mists and shadows beneath them take the form of a recumbent woman, veiled mysteriously in sleep. Their bases swell gently from the plain, looking at that distance perfectly round and smooth; and upon the top of each is a vast hillock covered with snow, exactly corresponding to the nipple on the female breast. The stretch of cliff that connects them appears to be some thousands of feet in height, and perfectly precipitous, and on each flank of them, so far as the eye can reach, extend similar lines of cliff, broken only here and there by flat table-topped mountains, something like the world-famed one at Cape Town; a formation, by the way, that is very common in Africa.

To describe the comprehensive grandeur of that view is beyond my powers. There was something so inexpressibly solemn and overpowering about those huge volcanoes – for doubtless they are extinct volcanoes – that it quite awed us. For a while the morning lights played upon the snow and the brown and swelling masses beneath, and then, as though to veil the majestic sight from our curious eyes, strange vapours and clouds gathered and increased around the mountains, till presently we could only trace their pure and gigantic outlines, showing ghostlike through the fleecy envelope. Indeed, as we afterwards discovered, usually they were wrapped in this gauze-like mist, which doubtless accounted for our not having seen them more clearly before.

Sheba's Breasts had scarcely vanished into cloud-clad privacy, before our thirst – literally a burning question – reasserted itself.

It was all very well for Ventvögel to say that he smelt water, but we could see no signs of it, look which way we would. So far as the eye might reach there was nothing but arid sweltering sand and karoo scrub. We walked round the hillock and gazed about anxiously on the other side, but it was the same story, not a drop of water could be found; there was no indication of a pan, a pool, or a spring.

"You are a fool," I said angrily to Ventvögel; "there is no water."

But still he lifted his ugly snub nose and sniffed.

"I smell it, Baas," he answered; "it is somewhere in the air."

"Yes," I said, "no doubt it is in the clouds, and about two months hence it will fall and wash our bones."

Sir Henry stroked his yellow beard thoughtfully. "Perhaps it is on the top of the hill," he suggested.

"Rot," said Good; "whoever heard of water being found at the top of a hill!"

"Let us go and look," I put in, and hopelessly enough we scrambled up the sandy sides of the hillock, Umbopa leading. Presently he stopped as though he was petrified.

"*Nanzia manzie!*" that is, "Here is water!" he cried with a loud voice.

We rushed up to him, and there, sure enough, in a deep cut or indentation on the very top of the sand koppie, was an undoubted pool of water. How it came to be in such a strange place we did not stop to inquire, nor did we hesitate at its black and unpleasant appearance. It was water, or a good imitation of it, and that was enough for us. We gave a bound and a rush, and in another second we were all down on our stomachs sucking up the uninviting fluid as though it were nectar fit for the gods. Heavens, how we did drink! Then when we had done drinking we tore off our clothes and sat down in the pool, absorbing the moisture through our parched skins. You, Harry, my boy, who have only to turn on a couple of taps to summon "hot" and "cold" from an unseen, vasty cistern, can have little idea of the luxury of that muddy wallow in brackish tepid water.

After a while we rose from it, refreshed indeed, and fell to on our "biltong," of which we had scarcely been able to touch a mouthful for twenty-four hours, and ate our fill. Then we smoked a pipe, and lay down by the side of that blessed pool, under the overhanging shadow of its bank, and slept till noon.

All that day we rested there by the water, thanking our stars that we had been lucky enough to find it, bad as it was, and not forgetting to render a due share of gratitude to the shade of the long-departed da Silvestra, who had set its position down so accurately on the tail of his shirt. The wonderful thing to us was that the pan should have lasted so long, and the only way in which I can account for this is on the supposition that it is fed by some spring deep down in the sand.

Having filled both ourselves and our water-bottles as full as possible, in far better spirits we started off again with the moon. That night we covered nearly five-and-twenty miles; but, needless to say, found no more water, though we were lucky enough the following day to get a little shade behind some ant-heaps. When the sun rose, and, for a while, cleared away the mysterious mists, Suliman's Berg with the two majestic Breasts, now only about twenty miles off, seemed to be towering right above us, and looked grander than ever. At the approach of evening we marched again, and, to cut a long story short, by daylight next morning found ourselves upon the lowest slopes of Sheba's left breast, for which we had been steadily steering. By this time our water was exhausted once more, and we were suffering severely from thirst, nor indeed could we see any chance of relieving it till we reached the snow line far, far above us. After resting an hour or two, driven to it by our torturing thirst, we went on.

Kua Fu Chases the Sun

From Chinese mythology

THE UNDERWORLD of the north where the most ferocious giants had lived since the dawn of time was centred around a wild range of black mountains. And underneath the tallest of these mountains the giant Kua Fu, gatekeeper of the dark city, had built for himself a home. Kua Fu was an enormous creature with three eyeballs and a snake hanging from each ear, yet in spite of his intimidating appearance he was said to be a fairly good-natured giant, though not the most intelligent of his race.

Kua Fu took great pleasure in everything to do with the sun. He loved to feel its warm rays on his great body, and nothing delighted him more than to watch the golden orb rise from its bed in the east each morning. He was never too keen, however, to witness it disappear below the horizon in the evenings and longed for the day when the sun would not have to sleep at night.

And as he sat watching the sun descend in the sky one particular evening, Kua Fu began thinking to himself:

"Surely I can do something to rid the world of this depressing darkness. Perhaps I could follow the sun and find out where it hides itself at night. Or better still, I could use my great height to catch it just as it begins to slide towards the west and fix it firmly in the centre of the sky so that it never disappears again."

So the following morning, Kua Fu set off in pursuit of the sun, stepping over mountains and rivers with his very long legs, all the time reaching upwards, attempting to grab hold of the shining sphere above him. Before long, however, evening had approached, and the sun began to glow a warm red, bathing the giant in a soothing, relaxing heat. Puffing and panting with exhaustion, Kua Fu stretched his huge frame to its full length in a last great effort to seize his prize. But as he did so, he was overcome by an unbearable thirst, the like of which he had never experienced before. He raced at once to a nearby stream and drank its entire contents down in one mouthful. Still his thirst had not been quenched, so he proceeded to the Weishui River and again gulped down the water until the river ran dry. But now he was even more thirsty and he felt as if he had only swallowed a single drop.

He began to chase all over the earth, pausing at every stream and lake, seeking to drown the fiery heat that raged within his body. Nothing seemed to have any effect on him, though he had by now covered a distance of eight thousand miles, draining the waters from every possible source he encountered. There was, however, one place that he had not yet visited where surely he would find enough water to satisfy him. That place was the great lake in the province of Henan where it was said the clearest, purest water flowed from the mountain streams into the lake's great cavern.

The giant summoned all his remaining strength and plodded along heavily in the direction of this last water hole. But he had only travelled a short distance before he collapsed to the ground, weak with thirst and exhaustion. The last golden rays of the sun curved towards his outstretched body, softening the creases on his weary forehead, and melting away his suffering. Kua Fu's eyelids began to droop freely and a smile spread its way across his face as he fell into a deep, deep, eternal sleep.

At dawn on the following morning, the sun rose as usual in the east, but the sleeping figure of the giant was no longer anywhere to be seen. In its place a great mountain had risen up towards the sky. And on the western side of the mountain a thick grove of trees had sprung up overnight. These trees were laden with the ripest, most succulent peaches whose sweet juices had the power to quench the most raging thirst of any passer-by. Many believe that the giant's body formed this beautiful site and that is why it is still named Kua Fu Mountain in his honour.

The Last Human

Rob Nisbet

AN ALARM SHRIEKS at me and red warning lights blaze around the control deck. Much of the equipment has already been eaten away. And now the ship has detected another attack, streaming in this direction. I glance at the automatic recorder: damaged, like everything else, but I sense it is still working. I can still feel the connection to my thoughts. It is part of the cloneship and therefore linked directly to me.

Me – the last living human.

The responsibility is scary; I now represent the whole of humanity and want to leave a record of what is happening. The ship doesn't know nor care if I am male or female, tall or short, black or white. None of that matters. It knows me as The Captain, the solar engineer, the only witness to the destruction of Earth.

Out here in space, I feel supremely alone – I know I don't stand a chance. The alarm intensifies. But I'm not giving up without a fight. Literally.

The clonedroids skitter to my defence, gyroscopes whirling, keeping them upright on their spindly legs. Several of them speak in unison, using that eerily familiar voice. "Captain, we have Maw."

Yeah, as if I didn't know.

"Protect yourselves and the outer hull!" I scan the meagre remnants of the control deck; my precious view screen; the ruined instrumentation, awash with red warnings. And here it comes, forming in the centre of the chamber; the floating rippling ribbon of alien energy I have named Maw.

Instantly, the nearest clonedroids extend slender probes, tips sparking with electricity. Their mechanisms churn like clockwork as they scurry valiantly towards the expanding ribbon which glows a faint grey-blue like dead flesh.

The filament of Maw flexes and swirls in the air like some flattened tentacle feeling around what is left of the controls. Its undulating surface glitters with a multitude of sparkle-blue annihilations as it eats away at the very air it floats in.

This substance, Maw, has defied all analysis. It appears so alien in nature that cohabitation is impossible. It simply annihilates any normal matter that it touches.

Outside, a chunk of tumbling debris thuds into the ship, a hunk of rock that sets the hull ringing like a great bell. The deck judders under the impact and I fall back against the command dais as a phalanx of clonedroids assembles in front of me. They wield their electric probes like flashing rapiers, striking at the ribbon with white lightning. The Maw spasms into curls, shrinking back and thinning to a sparking thread.

"Captain. Behind you."

I am still startled that the clonedroids speak in my own voice, with their not-quite-human intonation. It's as if my inner thoughts are taunting me, projected through the vibrating larynx circuits of these half-machines. I swing around. A second ribbon of Maw has appeared and floats across the command chair. It passes through the chair's back which fizzes out of existence where it has been touched.

The clonedroids whirl to my protection; I feel the heat from their lightning probes sear around me. But the Maw deftly swirls to avoid their defence. With another juddering clang, the hull is struck again by one of the twisting rocks out in space. I am thrown across the command platform directly beneath the strand of Maw. I am a solar engineer, theoretical of course, but I always knew I stood no chance. If the bombardment of rocks didn't destroy the ship, the Maw surely would. And, if by some miracle I survived those threats, nothing could endure the imminent flares of the expanding sun. One threat compounded by another, and yet another. As the clonedroids spring to my aid, I slump exhausted to the ground. Suddenly, resistance seems too much of an effort.

I see the grey-blue slither of Maw reaching down for me. I snatch away my left hand but the fleshy ribbon snaps like a whipcord through the air around my fingers.

I am surrounded by a blaze of electric fire as the clonedroids blast the Maw into retreat. Folding in on itself, it shrinks to a fine thread and eventually disappears – presumably back to the mysterious hole in space it has come from.

* * *

My left hand has gone. My arm ends in a precisely severed stump where my wrist would be. Bizarrely, there is no pain. And, stranger still, my brain hasn't registered the loss. The Maw left a sizzling sparkle of raw flesh which has become what looks like a cauterized scab. But I can still feel my hand. I have sensation enough to flex my fingers; the tendons in my arm move but, no matter how convincing the perception, my fingers are no longer there.

I allow myself a moment of weary melancholy. Why hadn't it just devoured all of me? Then I wouldn't be compelled to fight.

The Maw has withdrawn for the moment. But I know it will be back; it *always* comes back. I assess the damage to my ship. Thankfully no breaches to the hull this time. Three more clonedroids are missing and there is further damage to the ship's equipment; voids gouged from matter as the Maw floated through it.

The first thing I check is the wall-sized view screen. Half of the apparatus has been eaten away – but still the screen works. Of a sort. It lights up opposite the command platform, resembling a window looking out into space. But it displays an impossible double image. Some quirk of the damaged system shows the image of Earth revolving slowly on the screen, exactly as it would appear from my position in orbit: blue, hazy-white and magnificent against the black void. I want to believe in this image, but I know it's a lie. Overlayed on the screen is the reality: the tumbling jagged rocks that litter this region of space: the debris of the shattered Earth and moon. As if to emphasize the destruction, the screen shows another chunk of rock twisting towards the ship. I feel it clang against the hull with a calamitous toll.

And looming massive, darker even than the black space around it, is that mysterious hole. It is impossible to estimate its size, or indeed its structure. It could be composed of anything – or nothing. All I know is that it appeared after I was sent into orbit to study the solar flares. My task was to make a more accurate assessment of how long the Earth had before the flares baked it to oblivion like Mercury. I had expected to observe our swollen, flare-ravaged sun. I hadn't expected to find the hole.

It's like a mouth in space. That's why I called it Maw. And its tongues reach out to eat away anything they touch.

I reach out, too, to enlarge the phantom view of Earth the screen has somehow retained. The impossibility of this image snags at my brain. Perhaps the cloneship senses how much I *need* to see the Earth and is projecting it for me. This was my home; my beautiful world; I need the memory it represents. Then, suddenly, I realize that I am reaching with my left hand, trying to adjust settings with my missing fingers. I let the screen continue to show its impossible double image: the haunting pristine Earth, and its shattered remnants. The black mouth of the hole hangs in space beyond it – and in the far distance the sun glows: a burning circle of sickly orange. Even at this level of magnification, I can see the crimson flares snake across its fiery surface. And my engineer training kicks in.

I had been sent into Earth orbit in the cloneship. A vessel biologically linked to my mind and body. The clonedroids, too, are extensions of me to crew the ship, the idea being to risk only one life out here in space.

Above any atmospheric distortions, I was to assess the sun's deterioration. The flares had already decimated Mercury. And Venus was heating beyond its already excessive temperatures. Earth would be next. The population had been reassured. Six hundred years they'd been told, until the solar flares became a serious threat. Six centuries in which to develop a means to escape our doomed world. We already had settlements on the moon; the proposition of travel to the stars was not unreasonable. But that reassurance was a lie.

My observations and readings from this ship confirmed that six hundred *days* was more likely. Six hundred days till the sun boiled away all life on Earth – if we were lucky.

Lucky!

Amazingly, the intercom still functions. I instruct the clonedroids to patrol the ship. Protect the hull from Maw and deflect any attack near my precious view screen. I need that false image of my perfect Earth. It almost dispels the memory of that day the Maw attacked.

I had achieved only a few orbits when the hole appeared, hanging in space. So alien that I couldn't divine any structure or meaningful assessment of its size or depth. It appeared to be an immense void – a dimensional tunnel perhaps. Such theories were not beyond reasonable speculation, though they were beyond our expectation and experience. Ground Base reasoned at first that the mysterious hole might be some manifestation of the solar flares.

But then the Maw attacked.

Vast continent-sized ribbons streamed from the darkness. Earth and its people – *all those people!* – didn't stand a chance. At the Maw's touch, great swathes of the Earth sparked and vanished. In just a few terrible hours the fleshy ribbons had coiled themselves into my world. The panic-stricken communications I had with Ground Base were short-lived. Only I could see what was happening to the planet. Everywhere that the sweeping ribbons of Maw touched – vanished; whole continents and oceans gone; everything annihilated till only a few tumbling rocks remained.

A few rocks – and me, alone in my orbiting cloneship. The last human.

I don't understand how my ship is still functioning. Despite the ruined machinery and equipment around me, I can still feel the link between the ship and my mind. Somehow, I know that it is still recording this testimony from my thoughts. Like the impossible image of Earth on the screen, systems still function despite being half destroyed by Maw. Like my hand, I realize. My left hand, gone, but I still have the sensation of having fingers. It is as if, somehow, the Earth, and my hand, still exist.

"Captain." It is my voice again. All the clonedroids appear busy with their patrols and maintenance. I realize the voice has come from the intercom; it is the ship attracting my attention. It adjusts the view on the giant screen. The image of the sun zooms into close-up. Its orange surface is acrawl with flares. Suddenly a plume of red fire fountains out towards the ship. I had expected this, but still the sun's assault causes a sickening hollow feeling in my stomach. The estimated six hundred days' grace seems overly optimistic.

The ship adjusts the screen again, showing the dark tunnel-mouth in space. Perhaps the Maw *is* some manifestation of the solar flares after all. Giant undulating ribbons are being ejected from the hole. Not the narrow strands that have been picking away at the ship; wide bands like those that had devoured the Earth and moon. I wonder distractedly why the Maw should have targeted only the worlds where there was life.

The fleshy blue-grey ribbons flex and swirl towards the ship. This is the end. Many of the vast tumbling rocks are caught up in its approach, fizzing and disappearing at its touch. The ribbons are large enough to envelop the whole ship. There will be no escape.

The clonedroids turn to me. They sense my fear, and perhaps my resignation. They look to me for guidance.

"Retract your probes," I tell them. I know that Maw of this size will simply devour everything.

The screen defaults to its double image of the perfect cloud-draped Earth and the shattered debris-field of its destruction. This image still worries at me. What does it mean?

The Maw closes-in on the ship. There is no sense of impact. The ship begins to dissolve at the ribbon's touch. On the control deck, I hardly register the warning lights and alarms. The hull has been breached. The propulsion chamber melts away – yet still I feel a ghostly vibration of the juddering engines. Corridors and compartments vanish. The forward control deck is the last portion of the ship to survive. I see the dead-flesh Maw, like a flexible wall, sweep towards me across the chamber, reducing everything to a sparkle of annihilations. Damaged equipment finally succumbs to total destruction. The clonedroids twist their mechanisms to face me, instinctively seeking orders as they are obliterated one-by-one.

I want my last sight to be of the Earth. I turn to the screen, accepting my fate. I know from my hand that it will be painless. At my back, I am touched by Maw. I am conscious of it eating through me, slowly.

There is a point when precisely half of me has gone. And that's when I realize. The ribbons don't destroy, they *transport*. The alien Maw has been sent to save us.

* * *

As I transfer, the cloneship reforms, complete around me. The control deck is restored; the back of the command chair is whole again. All the clonedroids have returned and skitter in circles as confused, at first, as I am. I hold up my left hand, clenching and unclenching my fingers in wonder.

The cloneship glides smoothly into orbit. It is a wonder that it doesn't flip and loop, reflecting my relief and sudden reassessment of the Maw.

I look to the screen – like a window, it displays my beautiful Earth, the whole Earth and its moon, set like jewels in a new region of space. I wonder where we are.

With a dawning realization, I understand, at last, the double image the screen had been showing me. Half the screen's circuitry had been taken by the Maw. What was left showed the tumbling remnants of the missing Earth. And the portion of the screen that the Maw had taken showed the rescued Earth, here – wherever *here* is.

A white-yellow sun gleams in the distance. From my training, I recognize it as a young star, billions of millennia from the devastating flares of old age.

The dark mouth of Maw had been a dimensional tunnel after all, some form of wormhole, sent by our, as yet, unknown benefactors.

I am grateful, and excited, and feel suddenly alive. I turn to the communications console and deliberately activate it with my left hand. I wonder if Ground Base has realized yet what has happened to them – to the entire planet.

I have seen the transference from my unique vantage point. I am the last human to pass through the Maw.

And somewhere, perhaps now half a universe away, the destructive flares from a dying orange sun will stream harmlessly across empty space.

The Legend of Ra and Isis

From Egyptian mythology

THIS LEGEND IS FOUND written in the hieratic character upon a papyrus preserved in Turin, and it illustrates a portion of the preceding Legend. We have seen that Ra instructed Thoth to draw up a series of spells to be used against venomous reptiles of all kinds, and the reader will perceive from the following summary that Ra had good reason for doing this. The Legend opens with a list of the titles of Ra, the "self-created god," creator of heaven, earth, breath of life, fire, gods, men, beasts, cattle, reptiles, feathered fowl, and fish, the King of gods and men, to whom cycles of 120 years are as years, whose manifold names are unknown even by the gods. The text continues, "Isis had the form of a woman, and knew words of power, but she was disgusted with men, and she yearned for the companionship of the gods and the spirits, and she meditated and asked herself whether, supposing she had the knowledge of the Name of Ra, it was not possible to make herself as great as Ra was in heaven and on the earth?

Meanwhile Ra appeared in heaven each day upon his throne, but he had become old, and he dribbled at the mouth, and his spittle fell on the ground. One day Isis took some of the spittle and kneaded up dust in it, and made this paste into the form of a serpent with a forked tongue, so that if it struck anyone the person struck would find it impossible to escape death. This figure she placed on the path on which Ra walked as he came into heaven after his daily survey of the Two Lands (*i.e.* Egypt). Soon after this Ra rose up, and attended by his gods he came into heaven, but as he went along the serpent drove its fangs into him. As soon as he was bitten Ra felt the living fire leaving his body, and he cried out so loudly that his voice reached the uppermost parts of heaven. The gods rushed to him in great alarm, saying, "What is the matter?" At first Ra was speechless, and found himself unable to answer, for his jaws shook, his lips trembled, and the poison continued to run through every part of his body.

When he was able to regain a little strength, he told the gods that some deadly creature had bitten him, something the like of which he had never seen, something which his hand had never made. He said, "Never before have I felt such pain; there is no pain worse than this." Ra then went on to describe his greatness and power, and told the listening gods that his father and mother had hidden his name in his body so that no one might be able to master him by means of any spell or word of power. In spite of this something had struck him, and he knew not what it was. "Is it fire?" he asked. "Is it water? My heart is full of burning fire, my limbs are shivering, shooting pains are in all my members." All the gods round about him uttered cries of lamentation, and at this moment Isis appeared. Going to Ra she said, "What is this, O divine father? What is this? Hath a serpent bitten thee? Hath something made by thee lifted up its head against thee? Verily my words of power shall overthrow it; I will make it depart in the sight of thy light." Ra then repeated to Isis the story of the incident, adding, "I am colder than water, I am hotter than fire. All my members sweat. My body quaketh. Mine eye is unsteady. I cannot look on the sky, and my face is bedewed with water as in the time of the Inundation." Then Isis said, "Father, tell me thy name, for he who can utter his own name liveth."

Ra replied, "I am the maker of heaven and earth. I knit together the mountains and whatsoever liveth on them. I made the waters. I made Mehturit to come into being. I made Kamutef. I made heaven, and the two hidden gods of the horizon, and put souls into the gods. I open my eyes, and there is light; I shut my eyes, and there is darkness. I speak the word(s), and the waters of the Nile appear. I am he whom the gods know not. I make the hours. I create the days. I open the year. I make the river (Nile). I create the living fire whereby works in the foundries and workshops are carried out. I am Khepera in the morning, Ra at noon, and Temu in the evening." Meanwhile the poison of the serpent was coursing through the veins of Ra, and the enumeration of his works afforded the god no relief from it. Then Isis said to Ra, "Among all the things which thou hast named to me thou hast not named thy name. Tell me thy name, and the poison shall come forth from thee." Ra still hesitated, but the poison was burning in his blood, and the heat thereof was stronger than that of a fierce fire. At length he said, "Isis shall search me through, and my name shall come forth from my body and pass into hers." Then Ra hid himself from the gods, and for a season his throne in the Boat of Millions of Years was empty. When the time came for the heart of the god to pass into Isis, the goddess said to Horus, her son, "The great god shall bind himself by an oath to give us his two eyes (*i.e.* the sun and the moon)." When the great god had yielded up his name Isis pronounced the following spell, "Flow poison, come out of Ra. Eye of Horus, come out of the god, and sparkle as thou comest through his mouth. I am the worker. I make the poison to fall on the ground. The poison is conquered. Truly the name of the great god hath been taken from him. Ra liveth! The poison dieth! If the poison live Ra shall die." These were the words which Isis spoke, Isis the great lady, the Queen of the gods, who knew Ra by his own name.

In late times magicians used to write the above Legend on papyrus above figures of Temu and Heru-Hekenu, who gave Ra his secret name, and over figures of Isis and Horus, and sell the rolls as charms against snake bites.

The Long Night

Faye Snowden

"THEY AIN'T COMING in here, Roscoe. Oh no they ain't."

Rhett peeked between the gaps of the two-by-fours she had nailed haphazardly across the glass doors of what used to be Angelos, one of the best fine dining restaurants in Byrd's Landing, Louisiana. It was by Big Bayou Lake where them fools eating could watch herons gliding over the water and think they were in nature. But that wasn't what she was thinking about just at that moment.

The children had come again. They stood under the splash of light from the lamp posts in the parking lot. She glimpsed slices of bare brown feet, knobby knees, cut-off shorts, and dresses with flowers on them. She saw tiny eyes so furious it was as if those kids were trying to burn the place down with a glance. She caught sight of their hands, one with an ax, another a butcher knife, and still another with what looked like a scythe.

"Stay in your homes!" Rhett screamed so loud that the sound lifted her onto her tip toes. Her feet fell flat on the ground as the sound left her. The kids didn't move, just stared at her with a fury and a purpose. She turned her head to the side to see if anyone was coming to help her. The streets were empty. It was just them and her.

She began singing the jingle from the commercials about the restaurant, *the best fine dining is Angelos*, before letting the tune peter out in a whistle. It wasn't best anymore. Or fine, not since the entire family of Angelos up and left.

"Went running like the rest of them...." Rhett mumbled to Roscoe, who just snarled and snapped as if he finally found something tasty to eat in the fetid air of the abandoned restaurant.

Rhett tried to push away the sharp sticks poking at the balloons of her memory. That's what the lot of them did when the darkness came. Didn't they? Sure, they did. Picked up and left. A great many of them with cars piled high with all the shit that they cared most about. Caravans snaking through the Byrd's Landing roads, meeting up at Kingfisher and finally rolling across the only bridge out of town. Some who stayed did much worse. She could've told them all that the sun wasn't being stingy with just them. It had a bone to pick with the whole damned world.

"Bet they ain't making fun of my buggy no more," Rhett said to Roscoe.

Years ago, they told her she killed a child, a baby. She didn't believe them, but they sent her away just the same. After they let her out of the mental hospital, she stole the grocery cart from Weingarten's to carry her things. She'd push that cart through town when everybody could still count on the sun rising every morning like a promise from God. The gazes from the good citizens of Byrd's Landing would slide from her as she rested in a doorway, foraged in a dumpster for her supper, or scolded Roscoe to hurry up and get those four paws moving.

"At least the light didn't go with the heat," she told Roscoe now.

The smart people who studied the sky told them that they had time to figure it out since the sun didn't go completely cold, just dark. They told folks to stay in their homes while they figured it out. Even the sheriff climbed his fat ass onto a truck, and shouted as loud as he could through a bullhorn for everybody to stay in their homes. For people like her without any homes? They were rounding up those they could catch. How long had it been? Rhett had never been friendly with time. Since the sun had stopped showing up for work, time and Rhett had become downright enemies. Was it the third or fifth day of darkness? Could it be ten whole days since this mess began, twenty?

"The sun ain't coming up, right?" she asked Roscoe. "Maybe I'm still asleep or at the asylum."

Roscoe labored to his feet and padded over to the door where Rhett was still looking through the wooden slats. He jumped up and placed his paws next to her wrinkled hands. The dead smell and heat from his breath convinced her. The darkness was real. She banged against the boards with the flat of her hand.

"Stay in your homes!" she screamed through the door. "Stay in your homes," Rhett said one more time, but in a whisper. "That's what them smart people say. They'll figure it out. We still got the heat."

In the meantime, without sunlight cornsilk dimmed from gold to black in the cornfields, and all the wildflowers in Byrd's Landing started to die.

* * *

Fleur kept her eyes on Angelos. Even though she couldn't see Mama Rhett, she could sense her, and her senses drew for her an old hag with fat, gray dreadlocks, and a mean, greedy mouth.

"We can go in there and get her," Fleur said.

"She sicked that dog on us last time," Marceline said.

Marceline was the mayor's daughter. Unlike the others, she kept her face clean and still wore flowered dresses even though the sun had been gone for weeks, and her daddy was dead along with her mama, her big brother and baby sister.

The first days of no sunlight were relatively calm. The reporters on the news and social media theorized about eclipses. NASA science heads told folks that nothing was beyond their technology, their ability to think and deduce. They reasoned, they pontificated, they published charts and simulations and made what Fleur's daddy, the science teacher, called hypotheses, and what they could do to make it right. *But how you gonna test it?* her daddy would scream at the TV while her mama paced from one end of the house to the other talking about a God thing. Those with nonessential jobs were told to stay in their homes. Young people held end-of-the-world parties on rooftops.

Two days later the looting started. People from all over the country fled towns and cities. A great number had taken to dying by their own hand. When the government closed the roads, family annihilations began and spread like wildfire. In Byrd's Landing it was as if someone had soaked the soil in kerosene. The town suffered one or two family annihilations a day. It did no good when the soldiers went door-to-door and confiscated weapons. Annihilators turned to beatings and drownings. The mayor used a baseball bat. As a result, children fled homes, and formed bands all over the city. Fleur, at fourteen, was the leader of their band even though Clyde was two years her senior. It wasn't about age, but who was the smartest, who could keep them alive the longest.

"That one-eyed, lame dog?" Tap said. "He can't do nothing to nobody."

His family was alive, but he was afraid to go home, as were Fleur, Clyde, and Lucy, who at six was the youngest of the group.

"That dog is mean," Clyde said. "Besides, we been out here all day."

"Yeah, I'm hungry," Lucy said.

"Why can't we just burn her out," Tap said. "And be done with it."

"Because we'll burn it up, too," Fleur said.

"If what you say is true," Clyde said. "How can that be?"

"I'm telling you," Fleur said. "We have to get our hands on her."

She turned without looking at any of them and walked away. She was sure they would follow.

* * *

Rhett watched them go. Roscoe lowered his paws from the window. He slinked over to a pile of old rags Rhett had put in a corner for him. She watched him nose the rags into a bundle, then walk around in a circle a few times before plopping down.

"They'll be back," she said, "and I'll be ready."

She grabbed a shotgun by the front door. The gun made a loud snapping sound in the restaurant as she checked the load.

"I ain't against blasting them little badasses back to the olden days."

She then went around the room poking the shotgun between the boards covering the windows. Still clasping the shotgun, she lifted a bedroll and an old blanket from the shopping cart with one hand. The blanket used to be soft as a cloud, thick enough to protect her old bones from the cold. But now the thing was thin with use and pinpricked with holes. She took the blanket, bedroll and shotgun to where Roscoe lay. She sat the weapon between them, and then unrolled the bedroll without bothering to untie it. Instead, she settled down on top of it, pawed at the blanket until it covered her up all the way to her chin. She took a deep breath before falling into a dead sleep.

It wasn't long before Roscoe's head shot up. He whined at the yellow light shining through the pinholes in the blanket. Bright and strong smelling, they radiated all the way to the ceiling of Angelos. It was as if the walls of the restaurant were plastered in honeysuckle.

* * *

Fleur knew Clyde was watching her as she stirred a pot of ranch style beans over a fire in a cutdown metal trashcan. They were at their camp, an abandoned bridge east of Kingfisher Road. Earlier she had sliced the remaining three hotdogs into the simmering beans so they'd have enough to go around. Sauce splashed on her bare wrists, and she licked it off. She saw Clyde watching her when she looked up, saw him swallow nervously. Clyde was two years older than her, but the white boy let her lead, this tall, lanky black girl who everybody said was as crazy as a bag of cats. They pointed to her hallucinations, the hospital stays and visits to the nurse's office for the medicines designed to keep her right in the head. *And calm,* she heard her Mama's voice. *Don't forget calm.*

"What's our next move?" Clyde asked her.

"The move is we wait," she said. "Mama Rhett has been locked up in that restaurant for more than a week, ever since we chased her in there. That place was cleaned out even then. She'd be lucky if she found a breadstick. Hunger will send her our way."

He gave her a face that called bullshit. But instead of challenging her, he picked up a bowl for Fleur to ladle in the beans and hot dogs.

"Lucy," he called.

They always fed the youngest before they ate. In the beginning it was like playing house, Clyde and Fleur scavenging from abandoned buildings for their supplies, putting their lives on the line for their three 'kids'. The adrenalin pumping through her body while running from the cops was better than any drug Fleur had ever taken. The escapes felt like flying.

But now it was no game. The other day they all but collided with Tap's mama on Morning Glory. She reached for Tap, tried to snatch him away. They had to join hands in a circle around him to keep her away. She kept snaking her arm between them, trying to dig her claws into Tap's skinny shoulder. She cried the entire time, telling him to hurry home because it was only there she could end his suffering. Finally, Clyde told them to run. They flew apart like startled birds in all different directions. Fleur didn't quite know how they lost her.

"We could go to the government," Clyde said. "I heard some kids say they will protect us."

"We need the sun back," Fleur said.

"And you think that we'll get that by murdering some crazy old woman?" Clyde asked.

"I never said murder," Fleur answered.

"Then why the weapons?"

She didn't answer him. Lucy was nodding over her empty bowl. Fleur took it from her and laid her down on the mattress next to Tap. Marceline did what she did every night. She stared at the stars with a question on her face, a question that Fleur knew could never be answered.

Fleur sat down in a lawn chair in front of the fire's dying embers. Clyde sat next to her.

"Tell it to me again," Clyde said.

"Look, you either believe me or you don't," she said.

"I just need to hear it one more time."

Fleur let out a breath. "I saw Mama Rhett eat the sun."

"Eat it?" Clyde asked.

"Yes."

A couple of months ago Fleur walked into the old witch's shop, a shotgun on the edge of town. She knew she wasn't supposed to be there, but Fleur loved exploring places she wasn't supposed to go. It was cool and dark inside, shelves with mason jars of things living and things long dead lined the walls.

The old witch was on Fleur as soon as the bell on the screen door stopped jangling. She certainly didn't look the part of a witch, Fleur thought as the woman bore down on her. She wore jeans and a t-shirt that said, *nope, not today*, written out in rhinestones. The only thing witchy about her was her long fingernails, at least six feet and decorated with jewels, and weird symbols.

"Good, good Chile," the woman said. Her nails made a chittering sound as they flowed down Fleur's back. It was as if they were alive. "You got to help me find it."

Fleur shrugged from her grip. She took a step back. The woman had wild, crazy eyes that scared Fleur.

"I had it here, here." The woman threw a hand to one corner of the shop, and another to the opposite corner. She turned back to Fleur, her eyes glittering with fury.

"Did you take it?"

Because she was used to helping grownups look for things, Fleur did the only thing she could think to do in order to calm her fear. She said, "No, what does it look like?"

"Round," the woman said. "Gold. Smells like honeysuckle, and it's very fragile, Chile. Don't step on it. If you step on it, it'll bring the night."

Fleur helped. She looked between mason jars and under tables. Together, they searched every corner. With each passing moment the woman became more desperate. She kept lifting her hands, her nails flowing and chittering like water over rocks. And she kept looking at Fleur as if it were all her fault. When those chittering nails came at her again, Fleur bolted.

She ran back into the hot dusty yard, and around the back. She stopped. In the white-hot sunlight, Mama Rhett stood next to a yard can looking down at something in her hand. It was small and round and glowed a soft yellow. Fleur took a step forward. Mama Rhett sniffed it, and then gave it to the ancient yellow dog to sniff. The animal whimpered and backed away. The old woman brought it close to her face, poked out a red tongue and licked it. Fleur started to yell *stop*, but before she could get the word out, Mama Rhett popped the small orb into her mouth. When the sun was supposed to rise the next morning, the world was left in darkness.

* * *

Rhett woke with a snort. Roscoe had moved away from her during the night. He sat directly across from her. He glared at her as if he had lost all sense in his old head.

"What's the matter with you, ole fool?"

He showed her his teeth.

"Well, be that way, why don't you," she said.

She got up and rummaged around in the shopping cart for a good long time for something to eat for breakfast. All she found was a half sleeve of stale crackers.

"Better than nothing," she said. And then, "Roscoe, we're starving to death in a restaurant." She cackled and held out a cracker to him thinking he would come right over and get it. But he growled deep in his throat.

"Don't be mad because we ain't got no food. It's them damn kids' fault."

She retrieved the shotgun and went to the front door. Maybe they wouldn't be out there. Maybe they were still sleep somewhere. But no, they were there, the older ones anyway. They were giving Angelos that same tired ole death stare.

Before she knew what she was doing, she busted out the glass in the door with the butt of the shotgun. She wanted them to hear her.

"What do you want?" she shouted.

"Come on out, Mama Rhett," the girl said. It was the Johnson's kid. Fleur. She was sure of it. Folks said that kid didn't have the good sense God gave a goose.

"Ain't you heard?" she said. "I ain't nobody's mama, not since…." She couldn't remember what she wanted to say. She squinted. "Where them young'uns?"

"We left them home," the white boy said. "They weren't feeling good. Come outside. We only want to talk to you."

"We need your help," Fleur said. She held her hands up. "See, no blades."

"Why you been chasing me, then?" she asked. "All through the streets like I done something wrong."

"We're scared of grownups," the other girl said. The mayor's daughter, Rhett thought. Marceline. "We thought you were one of the crazy ones."

Rhett blew a raspberry at them. "Take your asses on."

"We got food," Fleur said. "Last night we had hotdogs with buttered buns. And beans."

Rhett's mouth watered. She looked back at Roscoe. She needed to get them food. Besides, these kids had no weapons. And she'd be lying if she didn't want to know what had them so riled. Stay in, her sane mind told her. Go out, the other one said. That one was her belly talking. And Roscoe's belly was probably saying the same thing. If they didn't get food soon, he'd probably start nipping at her backside for supper.

She found a crowbar in the shopping cart and began prying loose the wood planks. When they were all down, she twisted the lock and walked into the darkness. But she kept hold of the shotgun. She wasn't stupid. She aimed it at the three kids in front of her in the parking lot. And she could tell by the look on their faces that they weren't counting on that.

"What?" she said. "You think all I had for protection was that old dog?"

"Lucy, Tap," Fleur yelled. "Stay way."

Rhett had no idea what she was talking about, but then she heard it. Fast but tiny footsteps slapping against the asphalt, the sound of children hollering coming from the right and left of her. They carried the sharpest knives Rhett had ever seen.

But that's not what got her.

She couldn't help it. Those little feet tap, tap, tapping got inside her head. And the kids were crying. The sobs did something to her heart. She put her hands to her head. The shotgun clattered to the ground.

That's when the white boy tackled her. The girl, Fleur jumped on top of her. She could feel Fleur's sharp bones poking everywhere, at her stomach and her breasts. And then punches from the other two older kids, all over her body. Rhett cried, "Jesus, Jesus. Stop, help me. It ain't my fault. It was never my fault."

* * *

Mama Rhett lay dead in the parking lot of Angelos. Roscoe, the old one-eyed dog, nosed around her body. He sniffed at one stab wound deep in her chest. He whined and licked the blood from her face. Lucy was sitting on the curb rocking back and forth like a catatonic. Both Tap and Lucy were covered in blood from the old woman. Clyde had his arm around a sobbing Tap trying to comfort him. Fleur wandered around in a stunned silence. They were right, all of them, the doctors, the teachers, her mother. It hadn't worked. The morning was still dark, the sun still hiding. She was as crazy and vile as Mama Rhett.

"No," she said in a low voice. And then louder, "No!", and louder, "NO!"

She jumped on top of Mama Rhett's corpse. She straddled the old bag of bones that had prowled the streets of Byrd's Landing for years. Fleur plunged the knife deeper into the woman's stomach yelling no, no, no. She twirled the knife, cut and dug until she hit bone. That would be the spine, she thought, tears and blood streaming down her face. Guts, fat, shit and spine.

But no sun.

She laid down against Rhett's broken chest. She nestled her head under her chin. The blood felt warm. She closed her eyes.

"Fleur," Lucy said.

Tap had stopped sobbing. Fleur didn't open her eyes. She couldn't. She had failed them. She made them kill for nothing. Mama Rhett's blood was warm, almost hot beneath her. Tap hiccupped.

"Fleur," this time it was Clyde. His voice was wondering, timid.

Fleur stayed as motionless as stone. Was it her imagination or was Mama Rhett's blood getting hotter? She felt as if she were being scalded. Good, she thought, she deserved it.

"Fleur." This time Clyde's voice was more insistent.

The next thing she knew Clyde tackled her hard. She rolled from Mama Rhett's body. Her eyes flew open, and she saw smoke rising from Rhett's blood on her chest. And it was no longer a thick, gloppy red, but a warm, soft yellow.

"Feels like a bathtub," Lucy said with a small grin on her face.

Roscoe sat down, lifted his snout, and started to howl. The drops and slashes of blood on all of them begin to lift in globs of molten gold toward the sky. They turned to Mama Rhett's body. Big shafts of yellow light lifted from the stab wounds. The rays were tall and wide. Some of them were tinged pink. Others were a bright red. The light spread like a blanket, moved over the placid water of Big Bayou Lake. Soon the entire lake was soaked in yellow light, and a fat, red ball slowly ascended turning the sky into a dusky gray. A sunset tinged with blood and gold. Clyde reached for Fleur's hand. She took it and squeezed hard. Their long night was over.

The Love of Apollo

From Greek mythology

I

LIKE HIS FATHER, Jupiter, the young Apollo was not content to stay always in the shining halls of Olympus, but spent many days wandering over the broad lands of Greece in search of adventure, or for the sake of some maiden's love. There were many fair ones among the daughters of men, and they were wont to look with favour upon the beautiful young god who came down from the high heavens to woo them. Each morning as he drove across the sky the fiery horses that were harnessed to the chariot of the sun, some maiden gazed with longing at the splendour above her, and prayed that the radiant Apollo might look kindly upon her. Seldom did these prayers go unanswered; but sometimes the heart of the god was untouched by the devotion so freely offered, and the maiden pined away over her hopeless love.

Such a one was Clytie, who worshipped the glorious sun-god, and longed in secret for his love; but in spite of her tears and sighing she met with only coldness in return. Each day she rose before the dawn to greet Apollo as soon as his chariot appeared in the heavens, and all day long she watched him until the last rays of light were lost behind the hills. But the young god felt no sympathy for her sorrow, and the unhappy Clytie grew so pale and sick with longing that Jupiter in pity changed her into a sunflower, that she might always stand watching the course of the sun, and turn her face forever toward him, no matter where his beams might shine.

II

The great beauty of Apollo usually assured his success whenever he stooped from his high estate to love the maidens of the earth; but once he was repaid for his hard-heartedness to poor Clytie, and failed in his wooing when he sought the love of the beautiful wood-nymph Daphne. He was wandering one day in the forest when he came suddenly upon Daphne as she was gathering flowers, and her beauty and grace so charmed him that he desired her love above everything else in the world. Not wishing to frighten her, he stood still and softly spoke her name. When the nymph heard his voice, she turned quickly and looked at him with the startled eyes of some wild forest creature. Surprise and fear held her for a moment while Apollo spoke again gently and begged her not to be afraid, for he was no hunter nor even a rude shepherd. But Daphne only shrank away, fearful of his eagerness; and when Apollo grew bolder and ventured to draw near, she turned and fled through the forest. Angered at this rebuff, the god followed her, and though the nymph ran swiftly she could not escape from her pursuer, who was now more than ever determined to win her.

In and out among the trees she darted, hoping to bewilder him into giving up the chase; but Apollo kept close behind, and little by little gained on her flying feet. Wearied but unyielding, Daphne now hurried her steps toward the stream at the edge of the forest, where she knew that she would find her father, the river-god Peneus. As she neared the stream she cried aloud to him for help; and just as Apollo had reached her side and his outstretched hand was on her shoulder, a rough bark began to enclose her soft body in its protecting sheath; green branches sprouted from the ends of her uplifted arms; and her floating hair became only waving leaves under the grasp of the god's eager fingers. Apollo stood dismayed at this transformation, and when he saw a laurel tree rooted in the spot where, but a moment ago, had stood a beautiful living maiden, he repented of his folly in having pursued her and sat for many days beside the river, mourning her loss.

Thus it was that the laurel became the favourite tree of Apollo; and when the god returned sadly to Olympus, he decreed that whenever poet or musician or any victor in the games was to be crowned with a garland of leaves, those leaves were to be taken from the laurel tree in memory of Daphne.

III

In one of the flower-filled meadows of sunny Greece, there played all day a golden-haired boy named Phaëton, who was the pride and delight of his mother Clymene, a stately maiden whom Apollo had once wooed and won. The boy was willful and headstrong, but beautiful as a young god; and his mother, in her foolish pride, often reminded him how favoured he was above all other children in being the son of Apollo. Each morning she led him to a place where he could see the sun rise, and told him that his father was just then harnessing the fiery steeds to his golden-wheeled car, and would soon be leaving his palace of burnished gold to drive across the heavens, bringing daylight to the darkened earth. She told him of Apollo's great beauty, and of his wonderful music, and of his high position among the gods, because his chariot was nothing less than the glorious sun. Phaëton never tired of hearing these stories, and it was no wonder that he became very proud of his divine parentage, and boasted of it among his playmates. The children only laughed at his wonderful tales, and to convince them he grew more arrogant in his bearing, until they, angered by his continued boasts, bade him give some proof of his claims or else be silent. This Phaëton could not do; so they taunted him with his godlike appearance, and sneered at his pretensions until the boy, roused to action by their repeated insults, ran to his mother, and begged her to tell him whether he might not speak to his wonderful, but unknown father, and obtain from him some proof to silence the children's tongues.

Clymene hesitated to send the child on the long necessary journey, but yielding at last to his entreaties, she showed him the way to his father's palace. It was night when Phaëton set out, and he was obliged to travel quickly if he wished to reach his journey's end before the sun-car left the golden portals of the east. The palace of the sun was marvellously wrought, and the light from its golden columns and glittering jewelled towers so dazzled the eyes of Phaëton that he was afraid to draw near. But remembering the taunts of his playmates, he grew bolder, and sought out his father to beg the boon for which he had travelled so far and wearily. When Apollo, from his ivory throne, saw the boy approaching, he welcomed him kindly and called him by the name of son. Hearing this, Phaëton lost all fear, and told his father how the children had refused to believe Clymene's stories, and had taunted him because he could not prove the truth of his mother's claim.

The lofty brow of Apollo grew cloudy as he listened to Phaëton's words, and he promised to give the boy the proof he desired by granting him any favour he might ask. Instantly Phaëton demanded that he be allowed that very day to drive the sun-chariot; for when those on the earth saw him in that exalted place, they could no longer refuse to believe that he was indeed the favoured child of Apollo. Dismayed at this unexpected request, the sun-god sought to persuade Phaëton to ask some other boon, for he knew that no hand but his own could guide the four winged horses that were harnessed to the golden sun-car. But the boy was determined to carry out his plan; and with all the wilfulness of a conceited child, he refused to heed his father's warnings. As Apollo had sworn by the river Styx – the most terrible of all oaths – to grant Phaëton's request whatever it might be, he was obliged to fulfil his promise; and very reluctantly he led the boy to the portals of the palace, where the impatient horses already stood pawing the ground.

Phaëton gazed at the sun-car in delight, for it was all of gold – except the spokes of the wheel, which were of silver – and the body of the chariot was studded with chrysolites and diamonds that reflected the sun's dazzling brightness. The impatient boy sprang into the chariot and seized the reins in his hands, while his father bound on his head the blazing sun rays; but before the journey was begun, Apollo poured over him a cooling essence, that his skin might not be shrivelled by the burning heat of the sun, and gave him careful instructions how to handle the restless steeds. Phaëton but half listened to these words, and fretted to be off on his triumphant course; so Apollo ordered the gates to be thrown open, and the sun-car dashed out into the heavens.

For a while all went well, for the boy remembered his father's caution about using a whip on the fiery horses; but as the day wore on he became reckless, and forgot everything but his own proud triumph. Faster and faster he drove, flourishing his whip, and never heeding in what direction the maddened horses sped. Soon he lost his way and the chariot came so close to the earth that its fierce heat dried up the rivers and scorched the ground and shrivelled up all vegetation, even turning the natives in that part of the country brown – which colour they are still to this very day. Smoke rose up from the charred and blackened earth, and it so clouded the eyes of the now terrified Phaëton that he could not find his way back to the path of the sun and drove wildly far away from the earth. This caused terrible disaster, for under the sudden cold all growing things withered, and the blight of frost settled over all the land.

Then a great cry arose from the people of the earth when they saw their country laid waste; and though Jupiter was fast asleep on his golden couch he heard the cry, and started up in surprise. What *could* be happening on the earth that the sound of human wailing should break in upon the silence of his dreams! One glance was sufficient for him to see the smoke rising from the burnt-up land and to realize the cause of all that useless destruction; for far across the heavens – like a vanishing comet – Phaëton was madly driving the flaming chariot of the sun. Angered at the sight of a mere boy presuming to take upon himself so great a task, Jupiter seized one of his deadliest thunderbolts and hurled it at the unhappy youth, whose scorched body was immediately dashed from its lofty seat and sank into the calm waters of the Eridanus River.

Clymene mourned her son's untimely death, and gathered his remains from the river that they might have honourable burial. Phaëton's dearest friend, Cycnus, continued to haunt the river's edge, looking for any relic of his favourite that might chance to rise to the surface of the water. In recognition of this devotion the gods changed him into a swan that might stay forever on the river and plunge his head fearlessly into the clear waters to search for some scattered fragments of his unfortunate friend.

An Extract from Lucian's 'True History'

Lucian of Samosata

Publisher's Note: True History, *by Lucian of Samosata (c. 125 CE–c. 180 CE), is the first known fictional work to involve outer space and extra-terrestrial beings. After a group of seafarers venture past the Pillars of Heracles and stay on a fantastical island, their adventures become yet more unusual.*

ON THE MORROW we put to sea again, the wind serving us weakly, but about noon, when we had lost sight of the island, upon a sudden a whirlwind caught us, which turned our ship round about, and lifted us up some three thousand furlongs into the air, and suffered us not to settle again into the sea, but we hung above ground, and were carried aloft with a mighty wind which filled our sails strongly. Thus for seven days' space and so many nights were we driven along in that manner, and on the eighth day we came in view of a great country in the air, like to a shining island, of a round proportion, gloriously glittering with light, and approaching to it, we there arrived, and took land, and surveying the country, we found it to be both inhabited and husbanded: and as long as the day lasted we could see nothing there, but when night was come many other islands appeared unto us, some greater and some less, all of the colour of fire, and another kind of earth underneath, in which were cities and seas and rivers and woods and mountains, which we conjectured to be the earth by us inhabited: and going further into the land, we were met withal and taken by those kind of people which they call Hippogypians. These Hippogypians are men riding upon monstrous vultures, which they use instead of horses: for the vultures there are exceeding great, everyone with three heads apiece: you may imagine their greatness by this, for every feather in their wings was bigger and longer than the mast of a tall ship: their charge was to fly about the country, and all the strangers they found to bring them to the king: and their fortune was then to seize upon us, and by them we were presented to him. As soon as he saw us, he conjectured by our habit what countrymen we were, and said, Are not you, strangers, Grecians? which when we affirmed, And how could you make way, said he, through so much air as to get hither?

Then we delivered the whole discourse of our fortunes to him; whereupon he began to tell us likewise of his own adventures, how that he also was a man, by name Endymion, and rapt up long since from the earth as he was asleep, and brought hither, where he was made king of the country, and said it was that region which to us below seemed to be the moon; but he bade us be of good cheer and fear no danger, for we should want nothing we stood in need of: and if the war he was now in hand withal against the sun succeeded fortunately, we should live with him in the highest degree of happiness. Then we asked of him what enemies he had, and the cause of the quarrel: and he answered, Phaethon, the king of the inhabitants of the sun (for that is also peopled as well as the moon), hath made war against us a long time upon this occasion: I once assembled all the poor people and needy persons within my dominions, purposing to send a colony to inhabit the Morning Star, because the country was desert and had nobody dwelling in it. This Phaethon envying, crossed me in my design, and sent his Hippomyrmicks to meet with us in the midway, by whom we were surprised at that time, being not prepared for an encounter, and were forced to retire: now therefore my purpose is once again to denounce war and publish a plantation of people there: if therefore you will participate with us in our expedition, I will furnish you every one with a prime vulture and all armour answerable for service, for tomorrow we must set forwards. With all our hearts, said I, if it please you. Then were we feasted and abode with him, and in the morning arose to set ourselves in order of battle, for our scouts had given us knowledge that the enemy was at hand. Our forces in number amounted to an hundred thousand, besides such as bare burthens and engineers, and the foot forces and the strange aids: of these, fourscore thousand were Hippogypians, and twenty thousand that rode upon Lachanopters, which is a mighty great fowl, and instead of feathers covered thick over with wort leaves; but their wing feathers were much like the leaves of lettuces: after them were placed the Cenchrobolians and the Scorodomachians: there came also to aid us from the Bear Star thirty thousand Psyllotoxotans, and fifty thousand Anemodromians: these Psyllotoxotans ride upon great fleas, of which they have their denomination, for every flea among them is as big as a dozen elephants: the Anemodromians are footmen, yet flew in the air without feathers in this manner: every man had a large mantle reaching down to his foot, which the wind blowing against, filled it like a sail, and they were carried along as if they had been boats: the most part of these in fight were targeteers. It was said also that there were expected from the stars over Cappadocia threescore and ten thousand Struthobalanians and five thousand Hippogeranians, but I had no sight of them, for they were not yet come, and therefore I durst write nothing, though wonderful and incredible reports were given out of them. This was the number of Endymion's army; the furniture was all alike; their helmets of bean hulls, which are great with them and very strong; their breastplates all of lupins cut into scales, for they take the shells of lupins, and fastening them together, make breastplates of them which are impenetrable and as hard as any horn: their shields and swords like to ours in Greece: and when the time of battle was come, they were ordered in this manner. The right wing was supplied by the Hippogypians, where the king himself was in person with the choicest soldiers in the army, among whom we also were ranged: the Lachanopters made the left wing, and the aids were placed in the main battle as every man's fortune fell: the foot, which in number were about six thousand myriads, were disposed of in this manner: there are many spiders in those parts of mighty bigness, everyone in quantity exceeding one of the Islands Cyclades: these were appointed to spin a web in the air between the Moon and the Morning Star, which was done in an instant, and made a plain champaign upon which the foot forces were planted, who had for their leader Nycterion, the son of Eudianax, and two other associates.

But of the enemy's side the left wing consisted of the Hippomyrmicks, and among them Phaethon himself: these are beasts of huge bigness and winged, carrying the resemblance of our emmets, but for their greatness: for those of the largest size were of the quantity of two acres, and not only the riders supplied the place of soldiers, but they also did much mischief with their horns: they were in number fifty thousand. In the right wing were ranged the Aeroconopes, of which there were also about fifty thousand, all archers riding upon great gnats: then followed the Aerocardakes, who were light armed and footmen, but good soldiers, casting out of slings afar off huge great turnips, and whosoever was hit with them lived not long after, but died with the stink that proceeded from their wounds: it is said they use to anoint their bullets with the poison of mallows. After them were placed the Caulomycetes, men-at-arms and good at hand strokes, in number about fifty thousand: they are called Caulomycetes because their shields were made of mushrooms and their spears of the stalks of the herb asparagus: near unto them were placed the Cynobalanians, that were sent from the Dogstar to aid him: these were men with dogs' faces, riding upon winged acorns: but the slingers that should have come out of *Via Lactea*, and the Nephelocentaurs came too short of these aids, for the battle was done before their arrival, so that they did them no good: and indeed the slingers came not at all, wherefore they say Phaethon in displeasure over-ran their country. These were the forces that Phaethon brought into the field: and when they were joined in battle, after the signal was given, and when the asses on either side had brayed (for these are to them instead of trumpets), the fight began, and the left wing of the Heliotans, or Sun soldiers, fled presently and would not abide to receive the charge of the Hippogypians, but turned their backs immediately, and many were put to the sword: but the right wing of theirs were too hard for our left wing, and drove them back till they came to our footmen, who joining with them, made the enemies there also turn their backs and fly, especially when they found their own left wing to be overthrown. Thus were they wholly discomfited on all hands; many were taken prisoners, and many slain; much blood was spilt; some fell upon the clouds, which made them look of a red colour, as sometimes they appear to us about sun-setting; some dropped down upon the earth, which made me suppose it was upon some such occasion that Homer thought Jupiter rained blood for the death of his son Sarpedon. Returning from the pursuit, we erected two trophies: one for the fight on foot, which we placed upon the spiders' web: the other for the fight in the air, which we set up upon the clouds. As soon as this was done, news came to us by our scouts that the Nephelocentaurs were coming on, which indeed should have come to Phaethon before the fight. And when they drew so near unto us that we could take full view of them, it was a strange sight to behold such monsters, composed of flying horses and men: that part which resembled mankind, which was from the waist upwards, did equal in greatness the Rhodian Colossus, and that which was like a horse was as big as a great ship of burden: and of such multitude that I was fearful to set down their number lest it might be taken for a lie: and for their leader they had the Sagittarius out of the Zodiac. When they heard that their friends were foiled, they sent a messenger to Phaethon to renew the fight: whereupon they set themselves in array, and fell upon the Selenitans or the Moon soldiers that were troubled, and disordered in following the chase, and scattered in gathering the spoils, and put them all to flight, and pursued the king into his city, and killed the greatest part of his birds, overturned the trophies he had set up, and overcame the whole country that was spun by the spiders. Myself and two of my companions were taken alive. When Phaethon himself was come they set up other trophies in token of victory, and on the morrow we were carried prisoners into the Sun, our arms bound behind us with a piece of the cobweb: yet would they by no means lay any siege to the city, but returned and built up a wall in the midst of the air to keep the light of the Sun from falling upon the Moon, and they made it a double wall, wholly compact of clouds, so that a manifest eclipse of the Moon ensued, and all things detained in perpetual night: wherewith Endymion was so much oppressed that he sent ambassadors to entreat the demolishing of the building, and beseech him that he would not damn them to live in darkness, promising to pay him tribute, to be his friend and associate, and never after to stir against him. Phaethon's council twice assembled to consider upon this offer, and in their first meeting would remit nothing of their conceived displeasure, but on the morrow they altered their minds to these terms.

"The Heliotans and their colleagues have made a peace with the Selenitans and their associates upon these conditions, that the Heliotans shall cast down the wall, and deliver the prisoners that they have taken upon a ratable ransom: and that the Selenitans should leave the other stars at liberty, and raise no war against the Heliotans, but aid and assist one another if either of them should be invaded: that the king of the Selenitans should yearly pay to the king of the Heliotans in way of tribute ten thousand vessels of dew, and deliver ten thousand of their people to be pledges for their fidelity: that the colony to be sent to the Morning Star should be jointly supplied by them both, and liberty given to any else that would to be sharers in it: that these articles of peace should be engraven in a pillar of amber, to be erected in the midst of the air upon the confines of their country: for the performance whereof were sworn of the Heliotans, Pyronides and Therites and Phlogius: and of the Selenitans, Nyctor and Menius and Polylampes."

Thus was the peace concluded, the wall immediately demolished, and we that were prisoners delivered. Being returned into the Moon, they came forth to meet us, Endymion himself and all his friends, who embraced us with tears, and desired us to make our abode with him, and to be partners in the colony, promising to give me his own son in marriage (for there are no women amongst them), which I by no means would yield unto, but desired of all loves to be dismissed again into the sea, and he finding it impossible to persuade us to his purpose, after seven days' feasting, gave us leave to depart.

The Man Who Would Shoot Iruwa

From the Chaga people, Tanzania

A POOR MAN, living somewhere in the Chaga country, on Kilimanjaro mountain, had a number of sons born to him, but lost them all, one after another. He sat down in his desolate house, brooding over his troubles, and at last burst out in wild wrath, "Who has been putting it into Iruwa's head to kill all my boys? I will go and shoot an arrow at Iruwa." So he rose up and went to the smith's forge, and got him to make some iron arrow-heads. When they were ready he put them into his quiver, took up his bow, and said, "Now I am going to the farthest edge of the world, to the place where the sun comes up. The very moment I see it I will loose this arrow against it – *tichi*!" – imitating the sound of the arrow. So he set out and walked on and on till he came to a wide meadow, where he saw a gateway and many paths, some leading up towards the sky, some downward to. the earth. And he stood still, waiting till the sun should rise, and keeping very quiet. After a while he heard a great noise, and the earth seemed to shake with the trampling of many feet, as if a great procession were approaching. And he heard people shouting one to another, "Quick! Quick! Open the gate for the King to pass through!" Presently he saw many men coming towards him, all goodly to look on and shining like fire. Then he was afraid, and hid himself in the bushes. Again he heard these men crying, "Clear the way where the King is going to pass!" They came on, a mighty host, and all at once, in the midst of them, he was aware of the Shining One, bright as flaming fire, and after him followed another long procession. But suddenly those in front stopped and began asking each other, "What is this horrible smell here, as if an earth-man had passed?" They hunted all about till they found the man, and seized him and brought him before the King, who asked, "Where do you come from, and what brings you to us?" And the man answered, "Nay, my lord, it was nothing – only sorrow – which drove me from home, so that I said to myself, let me go and die in the bush." Then said the King, "But how about your saying you wanted to shoot me? Go on! Shoot away!" The man said, "Oh my lord, I dare not – not now!" "What do you want of me?" "You know that without my telling you, Oh chief!" "So you want me to give you your children back?" The King pointed behind him, saying, "There they are. Take them home with you!" The man looked up and saw all his sons gathered in front of him; but they were so beautiful and radiant that he scarcely knew them, and he said, "No, Oh chief, I cannot take them now. They are yours, and you must keep them." So Iruwa told him to go home and look out carefully on the way, for he should find something that would greatly please him. And he should have other sons in place of those he had lost.

And so it came to pass, for in due time other sons were born to him, who all lived to grow up. And what he found on the road was a great store of elephants' tusks, so that when his neighbours had helped him to carry them home he was made rich for life.

Many Swans: Sun Myth of the North American Indians

Amy Lowell

'Many Swans', by Amy Lowell (1874–1925), is a story based upon a legend belonging to the Kathlamet people of Southwestern Washington. Using some traditional songs and themes from their culture, Lowell melds these with her own alterations and additions.

WHEN THE GOOSE MOON rose and walked upon a pale sky, and water made a noise once more beneath the ice on the river, his heart was sick with longing for the great good of the sun. One Winter again had passed, one Winter like the last. A long sea with waves biting each other under grey clouds, a shroud of snow from ocean to forest, snow mumbling stories of bones and driftwood beyond his red fire. He desired space, light; he cried to himself about himself, he made songs of sorrow and wept in the corner of his house. He gave his children toys to keep them away from him. His eyes were dim following the thin sun. He said to his wife, "I want that sun. Some day I shall go to see it." And she said, "Peace, be still. You will wake the children."

So he waited, and the Whirlwind Moon came, a crescent – mounted, and marched down beyond the morning, and was gone. Then the Extreme Cold Moon came and shone, it mounted, moved night by night into morning and faded through day to darkness. He watched the Old Moon pass, he saw the Eagle Moon come and go. Slowly the moons wound across the snow, and many nights he could not see them, he could only hear the waves raving foam and fury until dawn.

Now the Goose Moon told him things, but his blood lay sluggish within him until the moon stood full and apart in the sky. His wife asked why he was silent. "I have wept my eyes dry," he answered. "Give me my cedar bow and my two-winged arrows with the copper points. I will go into the forest and kill a moose, and bring fresh meat for the children."

All day he stalked the forest. He saw the marks of bears' claws on the trees. He saw the wide tracks of a lynx, and the little slot-slot of a jumping rabbit, but nothing came along. Then he made a melancholy song for himself: "My name is Many Swans, but I have seen neither sparrow nor rabbit, neither duck nor crane. I will go home and sit by the fire like a woman and spin cedar bark for fish-lines."

Then silver rain ran upon him through the branches from the moon, and he stepped upon open grass and laughed at the touch of it under his foot." I will shoot the moon," he thought, "and cut it into cakes for the children."

He laid an arrow on his bow and shot, and the copper tip made it shine like a star flying. He watched to see it fall, but it did not. He shot again, and his arrow was a bright star until he lost it in the brilliance of the moon. Soon he had shot all his arrows, and he stood gaping up at the moonshine wishing he had not lost them.

Then Many Swans laughed again because his feet touched grass, not snow. And he gathered twigs and stuck them in his hair, and saw his shadow like a tree walking there. But something tapped the twigs, he stood tangled in something. With his hand he felt it, it was the feather head of an arrow. It dangled from the sky, and the copper tip jangled upon wood and twinkled brightly. This – that – and other twinkles, pricking against the soft flow of the moon, and the wind crooned in the arrow-feathers and tinkled the bushes in his hair.

Many Swans laid his hand on the arrow and began to climb – up – up – a long time. The earth lay beneath him wide and blue, he climbed through white moonlight and purple air until he fell asleep from weariness.

Sunlight struck sidewise on a chain of arrows, below were cold clouds above a sky blooming like an open flower and he aiming to the heart of it. Many Swans saw that up was far, and down was also far, but he cried to himself that he had begun his journey to the sun. Then he pulled a bush from his hair, and the twigs had leaved and fruited, and there were salmonberries dancing beneath the leaves. "My father, the sun, is good," said Many Swans, and he eat the berries and went on climbing the arrows into the heart of the sky.

He climbed till the sun set and the moon rose, and at midmost moon he fell asleep to the sweeping of the arrow-ladder like a cradle in the wind.

When dawn struck gold across the ladder, he awoke. "It is Summer," said Many Swans, "I cannot go back, it must be more days down than I have travelled. I should be ashamed to see my children, for I have no meat for them." Then he remembered the bushes, and pulled another from his hair, and there were blue huckleberries shining like polished wood in the midst of leaves. "The sun weaves the seasons," thought Many Swans, "I have been under and over the warp of the world, now I am above the world," and he went on climbing into the white heart of the sky.

Another night and day he climbed, and he eat red huckleberries from his last bush, and went on – up and up – his feet scratching on the ladder with a great noise because of the hush all round him. When he reached an edge he stepped over it carefully, for edges are thin and he did not wish to fall. He found a tall pine-tree by a pond. "Beyond can wait," reasoned Many Swans, "this is surely a far country." And he lay down to sleep under the pine-tree, and it was the fourth sleep he had had since he went hunting moose to bring meat to his family.

The shadow crept away from him, and the sun came and sat upon his eyelids, so that by and by he opened them and rubbed his eyes because a woman stared at him, and she was beautiful as a Salmon leaping in Spring. Her skirt was woven of red and white cedar bark, she had carved silver bracelets and copper bracelets set with haliotis shell, and earrings of sharks' teeth. She sparkled like a river salmon, and her smile was water tipping to a light South breeze. She pleased the heart of Many Swans so that fear was not in him, only longing to take her for himself as a man does a woman, and he asked her name. "Grass-Bush-and-Blossom is my name," she answered, "I am come after you. My grandmother has sent me to bring you to her house." "And who is your grandmother?" asked Many Swans. But the girl shook her head, and took a pinch of earth from the ground and threw it toward the sun. "She has many names. The grass knows her, and the trees, and the fish in the sea. I call her 'grandmother,' but they speak of her as 'The-One-Who-Walks-All-Over-the-Sky.'" Many Swans marvelled and said nothing, for things are different in a far country.

They walked together, and the man hungered for the woman and could not wait. But he said no word, and he eat up her beauty as though it were a ripe foam-berry and still went fasting until his knees trembled, and his heart was like hot dust, and his hands ached to thrust upon her and turn her toward him. So they went, and Many Swans forgot his wife and children and the earth hanging below the sharp edge of the sky.

* * *

The South wind sat on a rock and never ceased to blow, locking the branches of the trees together; a flock of swans rose out of the Southeast, one and seven, making strange, changing lines across a smooth sky. Wild flax-blossoms ran blue over the bases of black and red totem poles. The colours were strong as blood and death, they rattled like painted drums against the eyesight. "Many Swans!" said the girl and smiled. "Blood and death," drummed the totem poles. "Alas!" nodded the flax. The man heeded nothing but the woman and the soles of his feet beating on new ground.

The houses were carved with the figures of the Spring Salmon. They were carved in the form of a rainbow. Hooked noses stood out above doorways; crooked wooden men crouched, frog-shaped, gazing under low eaves. It was a beautiful town, ringing with colours, singing brightly, terribly, in the smooth light. All the way was sombre and gay, and the man walked and said nothing.

They came to a house painted black and carved with stars. In the centre was a round moon with a door in it. So they entered and sat beside the fire, and the woman gave the man fish-roes and gooseberries, but his desire burnt him and he could not eat.

Grass-Bush-and-Blossom saw his trouble, and she led him to a corner and showed him many things. There were willow arrows and quivers for them. There were mountain-goat blankets and painted blankets of two elkskins, there were buffalo skins, and dressed buckskins, and deerskins with young, soft hair. But Many Swans cared for nothing but the swing of the woman's bark skirt, and the sting of her loveliness which gave him no peace.

Grass-Bush-and-Blossom led him to another corner, and showed him crest helmets, and wooden armour; she showed him coppers like red rhododendron blooms, and plumes of eagles' wings. She gave him clubs of whalebone to handle, and cedar trumpets which blow a sound cool and sweet as the noise of bees. But Many Swans found no ease in looking save at her arms between the bracelets, and his trouble grew and pressed upon him until he felt strangled.

She led him farther and showed him a canoe painted silver and vermilion with white figures of fish upon it, and the gunwales fore and aft were set with the teeth of the sea-otter. She lifted out the paddles, the blades were shaped like hearts and striped with fire-hues. She said, "Choose. These are mine and my grandmother's. Take what you will." But Many Swans was filled with the glory of her standing as a young tree about to blossom, and he took her and felt her sway and: fold about him with the tightness of new leaves. "This," said Many Swans, "this – for am I not a man!" So they abode and the day ran gently past them, slipping as river water, and evening came, and someone entered, darkening the door.

Then Grass-Bush-and-Blossom wrapped her cedar-bark skirt about her and sprang up, and her silver and copper ornaments rang sweetly with her moving. The-One-Who-Walks-All-Over-the-Sky looked at Many Swans. "You have not waited," she said. "Alas! It is an evil beginning. My son, my son, I wished to love you." But he was glad and thought, "It is a querulous old woman, I shall heed her no more than the snapping of a fire of dead twigs."

The old woman went behind the door and hung up something. It pleased him. It was shining. When he woke in the night, he saw it in the glow of the fire. He liked it, and he liked the skins he lay on and the woman who lay with him. He thought only of these things.

In the morning, the old woman unhooked the shining object and went out, and he turned about to his wife and said sharp, glad words to her and she to him, and the sun shone into the house until evening, and in the night again he was happy, because of the thing that glittered and flashed and moved to and fro, clashing softly on the wall.

The days were many. He did not count them. Every morning the old woman took out the shining thing, and every evening she brought it home, and all night it shone and cried "Ching-a-ling" as it dangled against the wall.

Moons and moons went by, no doubt. Many Swans did not reckon them out. Was there an earth? Was there a sky? He remembered nothing. He did not try. And then one day, wandering along the street of carved houses, he heard a song. He heard the beat of rattles and drums, and the shrill humming of trumpets blown to a broken rhythm:

> *"Haioo'a! Haioo!*
> *Many Salmon are coming ashore,*
> *They are coming ashore to you, the post of our heaven,*
> *They are dancing from the salmon's country to the shore.*
> *I come to dance before you at the right-hand side of the world, overtowering,*
> *outshining, surpassing all. I, the Salmon!*
> *Haioo'a! Haioo!"*

And the drums rumbled like the first thunder of a year, and the rattles pattered like rain on flower petals, and the trumpets hummed as wind hums in round-leafed trees; and people ran, jumping, out of the Spring Salmon house and leapt to the edge of the sky and disappeared, falling quickly, calling the song to one another as they fell so that the sound of it continued rising up for a long time.

Many Swans listened, and he recollected that when the Spring Salmon jump, the children say, "Ayuu! Do it again!" He thought of his children and his wife whom he had left on the earth, and wondered who had brought them meat, who had caught fish for them, and he was sad at his thoughts and wept, saying, "I want to shoot birds for my children. I want to spear trout for my children." So he went back to his house, and his feet dragged behind him like nets drawn across sand.

He lay down upon his bed and grieved, because he had no children in the sky, and because the wife of his youth was lost to him. He would not eat, but lay with his head covered and made no sound.

Then Grass-Bush-and-Blossom asked him, "Why do you grieve?" But he was silent. And again she said, "Why do you grieve?" But he answered nothing. And she asked him many times, until at last he told her of his children, of his other wife whom he had left, and she was pitiful because she loved him.

When the old woman came, she also said, "What ails your husband that he lies there saying nothing?" And Grass-Bush-and-Blossom answered, "He is homesick. We must let him depart."

Many Swans heard what she said, and he got up and made himself ready. Now the old woman looked sadly at him. "My son," she said, "I told you it was a bad beginning. But I wish to love you. Choose among these things what you will have and return to your people."

Many Swans pointed to the shining thing behind the door and said, "I will have that." But the old woman would not give it to him. She offered him spears of bone, and yew bows, and arrows winged with ducks' feathers. But he would not have them. She offered him strings of blue and white shells, and a copper canoe with a stern-board of copper and a copper bailer. He would not take them. He wanted the thing that glittered and cried "Ching-a-ling" as it dangled against the wall. She offered him all that was in the house. But he liked that great thing that was shining there. When that thing turned round it was shining so that one had to close one's eyes. He said, "That only will I have." Then she gave it to him saying, "You wanted it. I wished to love you, and I do love you." She hung it on him. "Now go home."

Many Swans ran swiftly, he ran to the edge of the sky, there he found the land of the rainbow. He put his foot on it and went down, and he felt strong and able to do anything. He forgot the sky and thought only of the earth.

Many Swans made a song as he went down the rainbow ladder. He sang with a loud voice:

"I will go and tear to pieces Mount Stevens, I will use it for stones for my fire.
I will go and break Mount Qa-tsta-is, I will use it for stones for my fire."

All day and all night he went down, and he was so strong he did not need to sleep. The next day he made a new song. He shouted it with a great noise:

"I am going all round the world,
I am at the centre of the world,
I am the post of the world,
On account of what I am carrying in my hand."

This pleased him, and he sang it all day and was not tired at all.

Four nights and days he was going down the ladder, and every day he made a song, and the last was the best. This was it!

"Oh wonder! He is making a turmoil on the earth.
Oh wonder! He makes the noise of falling objects on the earth.
Oh wonder! He makes the noise of breaking objects on the earth."

He did not mean this at all, but it was a good song. That is the way with people who think themselves clever. Many Swans sang this song a great many times, and on the fourth day, when the dawn was red, he touched the earth and walked off upon it.

* * *

When Many Swans arrived on the earth, he was not very near his village. He stood beneath a sea-cliff, and the rocks of the cliff were sprinkled with scarlet moss as it might have been a fall of red snow, and lilac moss shouldered between boulders of pink granite. Far out, the sea sparkled all colours like an abalone shell, and red fish sprang from it – one and another, over its surface. As he gazed, a shadow slipped upon the water, and, looking up, he saw a raven flying and overturning as it flew. Red fish, black raven – blood and death – but Many Swans called, "Haioho-ho!" and danced a long time on the sea-sand because he felt happy in his heart.

He heard a robin singing, and as it sang he walked along the shore and counted his fingers for the headlands he must pass to reach home. He saw the canoes come out to fish, he said the names of his friends who should be in them. He thought of his house and the hearth strewn with white shells and sand. When the canoes of twelve rowers passed, he tried to signal them, but they went by too far from land. The way seemed short, for all day he told himself stories of what people would say to him. "I shall be famous, my fame will reach to the ends of the world. People will try to imitate me. Everyone will desire to possess my power." So Many Swans said foolish things to himself, and the day seemed short until the evening when he came in sight of his village.

At the dusky time of night, he came to it, and he heard singing, so he knew his people were having a festival. He could hear the dance-sticks clattering on the cedar boards and the moon-rattles whirling, and he could see the smoke curling out of the smoke-holes. Then he shouted very much and ran fast, but as he ran, the thing which he carried in his hands shook and cried, "We shall strike your town." Then Many Swans went mad; he turned, swirling like a great cloud, he rose as a pillar of smoke and bent in the wind as smoke bends, he streamed as bands of black smoke, and out of him darted flames, red-mouthed flames, so that they scorched his hair. His hands were full of blood, and he yelled "Break! Break! Break! Break!" and did not know whose voice it was shouting.

There was a tree, and a branch standing out from it, and fire came down and hung on the end of the branch. He thought it was copper which swung on the tree, because it twirled and had a hard edge. Then it split as though a wedge had riven it, and burst into purple flame. The tree was consumed, and the fire leapt laughing upon the houses and poured down through the roofs upon the people. The flame-mouths stuck themselves to the houses and sucked the life from all the people, the flames swallowed themselves and brought forth little flames which ran a thousand ways like young serpents just out of their eggs, till the fire girdled the village and the water in front curdled and burned like oil.

Then Many Swans knew what he had done, and he tried to throw away his power which was killing everybody. But he could not do it. The people lay there dead, and his wife and children among the dead people. His heart was sick, and he cried, "The weapon flew into my hands with which I am murdering," and he tried to throw it away, but it stuck to his flesh. He tried to cut it apart with his knife, but the blade turned and blunted. He cried bitterly, "Ka! Ka! Ka! Ka!" and tried to break what he wore on a stone, but it did not break. Then he cut off his hair and blackened his face, and turned inland to the spaces of the forest, for his heart was dead with his people. And the moon followed him over the tops of the trees, but he hated the moon because it reminded him of the sky.

* * *

A long time Many Swans wandered in the forest. White-headed eagles flew over the trees and called down to him, "There is the man who killed everybody." By night the owls hooted to each other, "The man who sleeps has blood on him, his mouth is full of blood, he let loose his power on his own people." Many Swans beat upon his breast and pleaded with the owls, "You with ears far apart who hear everything, you the owls, it was not I who killed but this evil thing I carry and which I cannot put down." But the owls laughed, shrill, mournful, broken laughs, repeating the words they had said, so that Many Swans could not sleep and in the morning he was so weak he shook when he walked.

He walked among pines which flowed before him in straight, opening lines like water, and the wind in the pine-branches wearied his soul as he heard it all day long. At first he eat nothing, but when he stumbled and fell for faintness he gathered currants and partridge-berries and so made his feet carry him on.

He came to a wood of red firs where fire had been before him. The heartwood of the firs was all burnt out, but the trees stood on stilts of sapwood and mocked the man who slew with fire.

He passed through woods of spear-leaf trees, with sharp vines head-high all about them. He thrust the thing he carried into the vines and tried to let go of it, but it would not stay tangled and came away in his hand.

He heard beavers drumming with their tails on water, and saw musk-rats building burrows with the stalks of wild rice in shoal water but they scattered as he came near. The little animals fled before him in fear, chattering to each other. Even the bears deserted the huckleberry bushes when they heard the fall of his foot, so that he walked alone. Above him, the waxwings were catching flies in the spruce-tops, they were happy because it was Summer and warm, they were the only creatures too busy to look down at the man who moved on as one who never stops, making his feet go always because there was nothing else to do.

By and by the trees thinned, and Many Swans saw beyond them to a country of tall grass. He rested here some time eating foxgrapes and blackberries, for indeed he was almost famished, and weary with the sickness of solitude. He thought of the ways of men, and hungered after speech and comforting. But he saw no man, and the prairie frightened him, rolling endlessly to the sky.

At last his blood quickened again, and the longing for people beat a hard pulse in his throat so that he rose and went on, seeking where he might find men. For days he sought, following the trails of wild horses and buffalo, tripping among the crawling pea-vines, bruised and baffled, blind with the sharp shimmer of the grass.

Then suddenly they came, riding out of the distance on both sides of him. These men wore eagle-plume bonnets, and their horses went so fast he could not see their legs. They ran glittering toward one another, whooping and screaming, and the horses' tails streamed out behind them stiffly like bunches of bones. Each man lay prone on his horse and shot arrows, hawk-feathered arrows, owl-feathered arrows, and they were terrible in swiftness because the feathers had not been cut or burned to make them low.

The arrows flew across one another like a swarm of grasshoppers leaping, and the men foamed forward as waves foam at a double tide.

They came near, bright men, fine as whips, striding lithe cat horses. One rode a spotted horse, and on his head was an upright plume of the tail-feathers of the black eagle. One rode a buckskin horse, long-winded and chary as a panther. One rode a sorrel horse painted with zigzag lightnings. One rode a clay-coloured horse, and the figure of a kingfisher was stamped in blue on its shoulder. Wildcat running horses, and their hoofs rang like thunder-drums on the ground, and the men yelled with brass voices:

"We who live are coming.
Ai-ya-ya-yai!
We are coming to kill.
Ai-ya-ya-yai!
We are coming with the snake arrows,
We are coming with the tomahawks
Which swallow their faces.
Ai-ya-ya-yai!
We will back our enemies.

Ai-ya-ya-yai!
We will take many scalps.
Ai-ya-ya-yai!
We will kill – kill – kill – till everyone is dead.
Ai-ya-ya-ya-yai!"

Many Swans lay in a buffalo wallow and hid, and a white fog slid down from the North and covered the prairie. For a little time he heard the war-whoops and the pit-pit of hitting arrows, and then he heard nothing, and he lay beneath the cold fog hurting his ears with listening. When the sky was red in the evening and the fog was lifted, he shifted himself and looked above the grass. "Alas!" Alas!" wept Many Swans, "the teeth of their arrows were like dogs' teeth. They have devoured their enemies." For nobody was there, but the arrows were sticking up straight in the ground. Then Many Swans went a long way round that place for he thought that the stomachs of the arrows must be full of blood. And so he went on alone over the prairie, and his heart was black with what he had seen.

* * *

A stream flowed in a sunwise turn across the prairie, and the name of the stream was "Burnt Water," because it tasted dark like smoke. The prairie ran out tongues of raw colours – blue of camass, red of geranium, yellow of parsley – at the young green grass. The prairie flung up its larks on a string of sunshine, it lay like a catching-sheet beneath the black breasts balancing down on a wind, calling, "See it! See it! See it!" in little round voices.

Antelope and buffalo,
Threading the tall green grass they go,
To and fro, to and fro.
And painted Indians ride in a row,
With arrow and bow, arrow and bow,
Hunting the antelope, the buffalo.
Truly they made a gallant show

Across the prairie's bright green flow,
Warriors painted indigo,
Brown antelope, black buffalo,
Long ago.

* * *

Now when he heard the barking of dogs, and saw the bundles of the dead lashed to the cottonwood trees, Many Swans knew that he was near a village. He stood still, for he dared not go on because of the thing which he had with him. He said to himself, "My mind is not strong enough to manage it. My mind is afraid of it." But he longed to speak with men, and so he crept a little nearer until he could see the painted tepees standing in the edge of the sunshine, and smell the smoke of dried sweet grass. Many Swans heard the tinkling of small bells from the buffalo tails hung on the tepees, he saw the lodge ears move gently in the breeze. He heard talk, the voices of men, and he cried aloud and wept, holding his hands out toward the village.

Then the thing which he was carrying shook, and said, "We shall strike that town." Many Swans heard it, and he tried to keep quiet. He tried to throw the thing down, but his hands closed. He could not keep his mind, and his senses flew away so that he was crazy. He heard a great voice shouting, "Break! Break! Break! Break!" but he did not know that it was his own voice.

Back over the prairie sprang up a round cloud, and fire rose out of the heart of the grass. The reds and yellows of the flowers exploded into flame, showers of sparks rattled on the metal sky, which turned purple and hurtled itself down upon the earth. Winds charged the fire, lashing it with long thongs of green lightning, herding the flames over the high grass; and the fire screamed and danced and blew blood whistles, and the scarlet feet of the fire clinked a tune of ghost-bells on the shells of the dry cane brakes. Animals ran – ran – ran – and were overtaken, shaken grass glittered up with a roar and spilled its birds like burnt paper into the red air. The eagle's wing melted where it flew, the hills of the prairie grew mountain-high, amazed with light, and were obscured. The people in the village ran – ran – and the fire shot them down with its red and gold arrows and whirled on, crumpling the tepees so that the skins of them popped like corn. Then the bodies of the dead in the trees took fire with a hard smoke, and the burning of the cottonwoods choked Many Swans as he fled. His nostrils smelt the dead, and he was very sick and could not move. Then the fire made a ring round him, and he stood in the midst by the Burnt River and wrung his hands until the skin tore. He took the thing he wore and tried to strip it off in the fork of a tree, but it did not come off at all. He cried, "Ka! Ka! Ka! Ka!" and leapt into the river and tried to drown the thing, but when he rose it rose with him and came out of the water gleaming so that its wake rippled red and silver a long way down the stream.

Then Many Swans lamented bitterly and cried, "The thing I wanted is bad," but he had the thing and he could not part from it. He rolled in the stones and the bushes to scrape it off, but it clung to him and grew in his flesh like hair. Therefore Many Swans dragged himself up to go on, although the heat of the burnt grass scorched his feet and everything was dead about him. He heard nothing, for there was nobody to mock anymore.

* * *

Mist rises along the river bottoms, and ghost-voices hiss an old death-song to a false, faint tune. The branches of willows beat on the moon, pound, pound, with a thin, far sound, shaking and shrilling the wonder tale, the thunder tale, of a nation's killing:

> *The Nation's drum has fallen down.*
> *Beat – beat – and a double beat!*
> *Ashes are the grass of a lodge-pole town.*
> *Rattle – rattle – on a moon that is sinking.*
> *Out of the North come drift winds wailing.*
> *Beat – beat – and a double beat!*
> *In the frost-blue West, a crow is ailing.*
> *The streams, the water streams, are shrinking!*
>
> *He gave an acre and we gave him brass.*
> *Beat – beat – and a double beat!*

Beautiful and bitter are the roses in the grass.
Rattle – rattle – on a moon that is sinking.
A knife painted red and a knife painted black.
Beat – beat – and a double beat!
Green mounds under a hackmatack.
The streams, the water streams, are shrinking!
Is there Summer in the Spring? Who will bring the South?
Beat – beat – and a double beat!
Shall honey drop from the green snake's mouth?
Rattle – rattle – on a moon that is sinking.
A red-necked buzzard in an incense tree.
Beat – beat – and a double beat!
And a poison leaf from Gethsemane.
The streams, the water streams, are shrinking.

* * *

Now Many Swans walked over cinders, and there was no sprig or root that the fire had left. Therefore he grew weaker day by day, and at night he lay awake tortured for food, and he prayed to the Earth, saying, "Mother Earth have pity on me and give me to eat," but the ears of the Earth were stopped with cinders. Then, after five sleeps, suddenly before him grew a bush of serviceberries which the fire had not taken. Many Swans gathered the berries and appeased his hunger. He said, "The berries that grow are blessed, for now I shall live." Yet he knew that he did not want to live, only his hunger raged fiercely within him and he could not stand against it. He took cinders and powdered them, and mixed them with river water, and made his body black, and so he set his back to the river and his face to the mountains and journeyed on.

Up and over the Backbone-of-the-World went Many Swans. Above the peaks of solitude hang the winds of all directions, and because there are a multitude of winds they can hold fire and turn it. Therefore Many Swans felt leaves once more about his face, and the place was kind to his eyes with laurels, and quaking aspens, and honeysuckle trees. All the bushes and flowers were talking, but it was not about Many Swans. The oaks boasted of their iron sinews, "Fire is a plaything, a ball to be tossed and flung away," and they rustled their leaves and struck their roots farther into the moist soil. The red firs stirred at the challenge, "In Winter your leaves are dry," they called to the oaks, "then the fire-bear can eat you. But our leaves are never dry. They are whips to sting the lips of all fires." But the cedars and the pines said nothing, for they knew that nobody would believe them if they spoke.

Now when the hemlocks ran away from him, and the cold rocks glittered with snow, Many Swans knew that he stood at the Peak of the World, and again the longing for men came upon him. "I will descend into a new country," he said. "I will be very careful not to swing the sacred implement, truly it kills people so that they have no time to escape." He thought he could do it, he believed himself, and he knew no rest because of his quest for men.

There was no way to find, but Many Swans went down through the firs, and the yellow pines, and the maples, to a white plain which ran right, and left, and forward, with only a steep sky stopping it very far off; and the sun on the plain was like molten lead pressing him down and his tongue rattled with thirst. So he lifted himself against the weight of the sun and wished a great wish for men and went on with his desire sobbing in his heart.

To the North was sand, to the East was sand, to the West was sand, to the South was sand, and standing up out of the sand the great flutes of the cactus-trees beckoned him, and flung their flowers out to tempt him – their wax-white flowers, their magenta flowers, their golden-yellow flowers peeking through a glass-glitter of spines; all along the ridges of the desert they called to him and he knew not which way to turn. He asked a hummingbird in a scarlet trumpet-flower, and the humming-bird answered, "Across the sunset to the Red Hills." The sun rose and set three times, and again he knew not where to go, so he asked a gilded flicker who was clicking in a giant cactus. And the flicker told him, "Across the sunset to the Red Hills." But when, after many days, he saw no hills, he thought "The birds deceived me," and he asked a desert lily, "Where shall I find men?" And the lily opened her green-and-blue-veined blossom, and discovered the pure whiteness of her heart. "Across the desert to the Red Hills," she told him, and he believed her, and, on the ninth morning after, he saw the hills, and they were heliotrope and salmon, and as the sun lifted, they were red, and when the sun was in the top of the sky, they were blood scarlet. Then Many Swans lay and slept, for he did not wish to reach the hills at nightfall lest the people should take him for an enemy and kill him.

* * *

In the morning, many Swans got up and made haste forward to the hills, and soon he was among cornfields, and the rows of the cornfields were newly ploughed and from them there came a sound of singing. Then many Swans felt the fear come upon him because of the thing he loathed and yet carried, and he thought, "If it should kill these people!" The music of the song was so beautiful that he shed tears, but his fears overcame his longing, for already he loved these people who sang in cornfields at dawn. Many Swans hid in a tuft of mesquite bushes and listened, and the words the people were singing were these, but the tune was like a sun wind in the tree-of-green-sticks:

The white corn I am planting,
The white seed of the white corn.
The roots I am planting,
The leaves I am planting,
The ear of many seeds I am planting,
All in one white seed.
Be kind! Be kind!

The blue corn I am planting,
The blue ear of the good blue corn.
I am planting tall rows of corn.
The bluebirds will fly among my rows,
The blackbirds will fly up and down my rows,
The humming-birds will be there between my rows,
Between the rows of blue corn I am planting.

Beans I am planting.
The pod of the bean is in the seed.
I tie my beans with white lightning to bring the thunder,

The long thunder which herds the rain.
I plant beans.
Be kind! Be kind!

Squash-seeds I am planting
So that the ground may be striped with yellow,
Horizontal yellow of squash-flowers,
Horizontal white of squash-flowers,
Great squashes of all colours.
I tie the squash-plants with the rainbow
Which carries the sun on its back.
I am planting squash-seeds.
Be kind! Be kind!

Out of the South, rain will come whirling;
And from the North I shall see it standing and approaching.
I shall hear it dropping on my seeds,
Lapping along the stems of my plants,
Splashing from the high leaves,
Tumbling from the little leaves.

I hear it like a river, running – running –
Among my rows of white corn, running – running –
I hear it like a leaping spring among my blue corn rows,
I hear it foaming past the bean sprouts,
I hear water gurgling among my squashes.
Descend, great cloud-water,
Spout from the mouth of the lightning,
Fall down with the overturning thunder.

For the rainbow is the morning
When the sun shall raise us corn,
When the bees shall hum to the corn-blossom,
To the bean blossom,
To the straight, low blossoms of the squashes.

Hear me sing to the rain,
To the sun,
To the corn when I am planting it,
To the corn when I am gathering it,
To the squashes when I load them on my back.
I sing and the god people hear,
They are kind.

When the song was finished, Many Swans knew that he must not hurt this people. He swore, and even upon the sacred and terrible thing itself, to make them his safe keeping. Therefore when they returned up the trail to the Mesa, he wandered in the desert below among yellow rabbit-grass and grey ice plants, and visited the springs, and the shrines full of prayer-sticks, and his heart distracted him with love so that he could not stay still.

That night he heard an elf owl calling from a pinyon-tree, and he went to the owl and sought to know the name of this people who sang in the fields at dawn. The owl answered, "Do not disturb me, I am singing a love-song. Who are you that you do not know that this is the land of Tusayan." And Many Swans considered in himself, "Truly I have come a long way."

Four moons Many Swans abode on the plain, eating mesquite pods and old dried nopals, but he kept away from the Mesa lest the thing he had with him should be beyond his strength to hold.

* * *

Twixt this side, twixt that side,
Twixt rock-stones and sage-brush,
Twixt bushes and sand,
Go the snakes a smooth way,
Belly-creeping,
Sliding faster than the flash of water on a bluebird's wing.

Twixt corn and twixt cactus,
Twixt springside and barren,
Along a cold trail
Slip the snake-people.
Black-tip-tongued Garter Snakes,
Olive-blue Racer Snakes,
Whip Snakes and Rat Snakes,
Great orange Bull Snakes,
And the King of the Snakes,
With his high rings of scarlet,
His high rings of yellow,
His double high black rings,
Detesting his fellows,
The Killer of Rattlers.
Rattle – rattle – rattle –
Rattle – rattle – rattle –
The Rattlers,

The Rattlesnakes.
Hiss-s-s-s!
Ah-h-h!
White Rattlesnakes,
Green Rattlesnakes,
Black-and-yellow Rattlesnakes,
Barred like tigers,
Soft as panthers.

Diamond Rattlesnakes,
All spotted,
Six feet long
With tails of snow-shine.
And most awful,
Heaving wrongwise,
The fiend-whisking
Swift Sidewinders.
Rattlesnakes upon the desert
Coiling in a clump of greasewood,
Winding up the Mesa footpath.
Who dares meet them?
Who dares stroke them?
Who dares seize them?
Rattle-rattle-rattle –
Rattle – rattle – hiss-s-s!

They dare, the men of Tusayan. With their eagle-whips they stroke them. With their sharp bronze hands they seize them. Run – run – up the Mesa path, dive into the kiva. The jars are ready, drop in the rattlers – Tigers, Diamonds, Sidewinders, drop in Bull Snakes, Whip Snakes, Garters, but hang the King Snake in a basket on the wall, he must not see all these Rattlesnakes, he would die of an apoplexy.

They have hunted them toward the four directions. Toward the yellow North, the blue West, the red South, the white East. Now they sit by the sand altar and smoke, chanting of the clouds and the four-coloured lightning-snakes who bring rain. They have made green prayer-sticks with black points and left them at the shrines to tell the snake people that their festival is here. Bang! Bang! Drums! And whirl the thunder-whizzers!

"Ho! Ho! Ho! Hear us!
Carry our words to your Mother.
We wash you clean, Snake Brothers.
We sing to you.
We shall dance for you.
Plead with your Mother
That she send the white and green rain,
That she look at us with the black eyes of the lightning,
So our corn-ears may be double and long,
So our melons may swell as thunder-clouds
In a ripe wind.
Bring wind!
Bring lightning!
Bring thunder!
Strip our trees with blue-rain arrows.
Ho-ho-hai! Wa-ha-ne!"

Bang! Bang!

Over the floor of the kiva squirm the snakes, fresh from washing. Twixt this side, twixt that side, twixt toes and twixt ankles, go the snakes a smooth way, and the priests coax them with their eagle-feather whips and turn them always backward. Rattle – rattle – rattle – snake-tails threshing a hot air. Whizz! Clatter! Clap! Clap! Corn-gourds shaking in hard hands. A band of light down the ladder, cutting upon a mad darkness.

Cottonwood kisi flickering in a breeze, little sprigs of cotton-leaves clapping hands at Hopi people, crowds of Hopi people waiting in the Plaza to see a monstrous thing. Houses make a shadow, desert is in sunshine, priests step out of kiva.

Antelope priests in front of the kisi, making slow leg-motions to a slow time. Turtle-shell knee-rattles spill a double rhythm, arms shake gourd-rattles, goat-toes; necklaces – turquoise and sea-shell – swing a round of clashing. Striped lightning antelopes waiting for the Snake Priests. Red-kilted Snake Priests facing them, going forward and back, coming back and over, waving the snake-whips, chanting a hundred ask-songs. Go on, go back – white – black – red blood-feather, white breath-feather, little cotton-leaf hands clap – clap – he is at the flap of the kisi, they have given him a spotted rattlesnake. Put him in the mouth, kiss the Snake Brother, fondle him with the tongue.

Tripping on a quick tune, they trot round the square. Rattle – rattle – goat-toes, turtle-shells, snake-tails. Hiss oily snake-mouths, drip wide priest-mouths over the snake-skins, wet slimy snake-skins. "Aye-ya-ha! Ay-ye-he! Ha-ha-wa-ha! Oway-ha!" The red snake-whips tremble and purr. Blur, Plaza, with running priests, with streaks of snake-bodies. The Rain-Mother's children are being honoured. They must travel before the setting of the sun.

* * *

When the town was on a roar with dancing, Many Swans heard it far down in the plain, and he could not contain his hunger for his own kind. He felt very strong because the cool of sundown was spreading over the desert. He said, "I need fear nothing. My arms are grown tough in this place, my hands are hard as a sheep's skull. I can surely control this thing," and he set off up the path to ease his sight only, for he had sworn not to discover himself to the people. But when he turned the last point in the road, the thing in his hands shook, and said, "We shall strike that town."

Many Swans was strong, he turned and ran down the Mesa, but, as he was running, a priest passed him carrying a handful of snakes home. As the priest went by him, the thing in Many Swan's hand leapt up, and it was the King Snake. It was all ringed with red and yellow and black flames. It hissed, and looped, and darted its head at the priest and killed him. Now when the priest was dead, all the snakes he was holding burst up with a great noise and went every which way, twixt this side, twixt that side, twixt upwards, twixt downwards, twixt rock-stone and bunchgrass.

And they were little slipping flames of hot fire. They went up the hill in fourteen red and black strings, and they were the strings of blood and death. The snakes went up a swift, smooth way and Many Swans went up with them, for he was mad. He beat his hands together to make a drum, and shouted, "Break! Break! Break! Break!" And he thought it was the priests above singing a new song.

Many Swans reached the town, but the fire-snakes were running down all the streets. They struck the people so that they died, and the bodies took fire and were consumed. The house windows were hung with snakes who were caught by their tails and swung down vomiting golden stars into the rain-gutters. In one of the gutters was a blue salvia plant, and, as Many Swans passed, it nodded and said, "Alas! Alas!" It reminded Many Swans of the flax-flowers in the sky, and his senses came back to him and he tore his clothes and his hair and cried, "Ka! Ka! Ka! Ka!" a great many times. Then he beat himself on the sharp rocks and tried to crush the thing he had, but he could not; he tried to split it, but it did not split.

Many Swans saw that he was alone in the world. He lifted his eyes to the thing and cursed it, then he ran to hurl himself over the cliff. Now a boulder curled into the path and, as he turned its edge, The-One-Who-Walks-All-Over-the-Sky stood before him. Her eyes were moons for sadness, and her voice was like the coiling of the sea. She said to him, "I tried to love you; I tried to be kind to your people; why do you cry? You wished for it." She took it off him and left him.

Many Swans looked at the desert. He looked at the dead town. He wept.

Maui Snaring the Sun

From Polynesian mythology

"Maui became restless and fought the sun
With a noose that he laid.
And winter won the sun,
And summer was won by Maui."
Queen Liliuokalani's family chant

A VERY UNIQUE LEGEND is found among the widely scattered Polynesians. The story of Maui's "Snaring the Sun" was told among the Maoris of New Zealand, the Kanakas of the Hervey and Society Islands, and the ancient natives of Hawaii. The Samoans tell the same story without mentioning the name of Maui. They say that the snare was cast by a child of the sun itself.

The Polynesian stories of the origin of the sun are worthy of note before the legend of the change from short to long days is given.

The Tongan Islanders, according to W.W. Gill, tell the story of the origin of the sun and moon. They say that Vatea (Wakea) and their ancestor Tongaiti quarrelled concerning a child – each claiming it as his own. In the struggle the child was cut in two. Vatea squeezed and rolled the part he secured into a ball and threw it away, far up into the heavens, where it became the sun. It shone brightly as it rolled along the heavens, and sank down to Avaiki (Hawaii), the netherworld. But the ball came back again and once more rolled across the sky. Tongaiti had let his half of the child fall on the ground and lie there, until made envious by the beautiful ball Vatea made.

At last he took the flesh which lay on the ground and made it into a ball. As the sun sank he threw his ball up into the darkness, and it rolled along the heavens, but the blood had drained out of the flesh while it lay upon the ground, therefore it could not become so red and burning as the sun, and had not life to move so swiftly. It was as white as a dead body, because its blood was all gone; and it could not make the darkness flee away as the sun had done. Thus day and night and the sun and moon always remain with the earth.

The legends of the Society Islands say that a demon in the west became angry with the sun and in his rage ate it up, causing night. In the same way a demon from the east would devour the moon, but for some reason these angry ones could not destroy their captives and were compelled to open their mouths and let the bright balls come forth once more. In some places a sacrifice of someone of distinction was needed to placate the wrath of the devourers and free the balls of light in times of eclipse.

The moon, pale and dead in appearance, moved slowly; while the sun, full of life and strength, moved quickly. Thus days were very short and nights were very long. Mankind suffered from the fierceness of the heat of the sun and also from its prolonged absence. Day and night were alike a burden to men. The darkness was so great and lasted so long that fruits would not ripen.

After Maui had succeeded in throwing the heavens into their place, and fastening them so that they could not fall, he learned that he had opened a way for the sun-god to come up from the lower world and rapidly run across the blue vault. This made two troubles for men – the heat of the sun was very great and the journey too quickly over. Maui planned to capture the sun and punish him for thinking so little about the welfare of mankind.

As Rev. A.O. Forbes, a missionary among the Hawaiians, relates, Maui's mother was troubled very much by the heedless haste of the sun. She had many kapa-cloths to make, for this was the only kind of clothing known in Hawaii, except sometimes a woven mat or a long grass fringe worn as a skirt. This native cloth was made by pounding the fine bark of certain trees with wooden mallets until the fibres were beaten and ground into a wood pulp. Then she pounded the pulp into thin sheets from which the best sleeping mats and clothes could be fashioned. These kapa cloths had to be thoroughly dried, but the days were so short that by the time she had spread out the kapa the sun had heedlessly rushed across the sky and gone down into the underworld, and all the cloth had to be gathered up again and cared for until another day should come. There were other troubles. "The food could not be prepared and cooked in one day. Even an incantation to the gods could not be chanted through ere they were overtaken by darkness."

This was very discouraging and caused great suffering, as well as much unnecessary trouble and labour. Many complaints were made against the thoughtless sun.

Maui pitied his mother and determined to make the sun go slower that the days might be long enough to satisfy the needs of men. Therefore, he went over to the northwest of the island on which he lived. This was Mt. Iao, an extinct volcano, in which lies one of the most beautiful and picturesque valleys of the Hawaiian Islands. He climbed the ridges until he could see the course of the sun as it passed over the island. He saw that the sun came up the eastern side of Mt. Haleakala. He crossed over the plain between the two mountains and climbed to the top of Mt. Haleakala. There he watched the burning sun as it came up from Koolau and passed directly over the top of the mountain. The summit of Haleakala is a great extinct crater twenty miles in circumference, and nearly twenty-five hundred feet in depth. There are two tremendous gaps or chasms in the side of the crater wall, through which in days gone by the massive bowl poured forth its flowing lava. One of these was the Koolau, or eastern gap, in which Maui probably planned to catch the sun.

Mt. Hale-a-ka-la of the Hawaiian Islands means House-of-the-sun. "La," or "Ra," is the name of the sun throughout parts of Polynesia. Ra was the sun-god of ancient Egypt. Thus the antiquities of Polynesia and Egypt touch each other, and today no man knows the full reason thereof.

The Hawaiian legend says Maui was taunted by a man who ridiculed the idea that he could snare the sun, saying, "You will never catch the sun. You are only an idle nobody."

Maui replied, "When I conquer my enemy and my desire is attained, I will be your death."

After studying the path of the sun, Maui returned to his mother and told her that he would go and cut off the legs of the sun so that he could not run so fast.

His mother said, "Are you strong enough for this work?" He said, "Yes." Then she gave him fifteen strands of well-twisted fibre and told him to go to his grandmother, who lived in the great crater of Haleakala, for the rest of the things in his conflict with the sun. She said, "You must climb the mountain to the place where a large wiliwili tree is standing. There you will find the place where the sun stops to eat cooked bananas prepared by your grandmother. Stay there until a rooster crows three times; then watch your grandmother go out to make a fire and put on food. You had better take her bananas. She will look for them and find you and ask who you are. Tell her you belong to Hina."

When she had taught him all these things, he went up the mountain to Kaupo to the place Hina had directed. There was a large wiliwili tree. Here he waited for the rooster to crow. The name of that rooster was Kalauhele-moa. When the rooster had crowed three times, the grandmother came out with a bunch of bananas to cook for the sun. She took off the upper part of the bunch and laid it down. Maui immediately snatched it away. In a moment she turned to pick it up, but could not find it. She was angry and cried out, "Where are the bananas of the sun?" Then she took off another part of the bunch, and Maui stole that. Thus he did until all the bunch had been taken away. She was almost blind and could not detect him by sight, so she sniffed all around her until she detected the smell of a man. She asked, "Who are you? To whom do you belong?" Maui replied, "I belong to Hina." "Why have you come?" Maui told her, "I have come to kill the sun. He goes so fast that he never dries the tapa Hina has beaten out."

The old woman gave a magic stone for a battleax and one more rope. She taught him how to catch the sun, saying, "Make a place to hide here by this large wiliwili tree. When the first leg of the sun comes up, catch it with your first rope, and so on until you have used all your ropes. Fasten them to the tree, then take the stone axe to strike the body of the sun."

Maui dug a hole among the roots of the tree and concealed himself. Soon the first ray of light – the first leg of the sun – came up along the mountainside. Maui threw his rope and caught it. One by one the legs of the sun came over the edge of the crater's rim and were caught. Only one long leg was still hanging down the side of the mountain. It was hard for the sun to move that leg. It shook and trembled and tried hard to come up. At last it crept over the edge and was caught by Maui with the rope given by his grandmother.

When the sun saw that his sixteen long legs were held fast in the ropes, he began to go back down the mountainside into the sea. Then Maui tied the ropes fast to the tree and pulled until the body of the sun came up again. Brave Maui caught his magic stone club or axe, and began to strike and wound the sun, until he cried, "Give me my life." Maui said, "If you live, you may be a traitor. Perhaps I had better kill you." But the sun begged for life. After they had conversed a while, they agreed that there should be a regular motion in the journey of the sun. There should be longer days, and yet half the time he might go quickly as in the wintertime, but the other half he must move slowly as in summer. Thus men dwelling on the earth should be blessed.

Another legend says that he made a lasso and climbed to the summit of Mt. Haleakala. He made ready his lasso, so that when the sun came up the mountainside and rose above him he could cast the noose and catch the sun, but he only snared one of the sun's larger rays and broke it off. Again and again he threw the lasso until he had broken off all the strong rays of the sun.

Then he shouted exultantly, "Thou art my captive; I will kill thee for going so swiftly."

Then the sun said, "Let me live and thou shalt see me go more slowly hereafter. Behold, hast thou not broken off all my strong legs and left me only the weak ones?"

So the agreement was made, and Maui permitted the sun to pursue his course, and from that day he went more slowly.

Maui returned from his conflict with the sun and sought for Moemoe, the man who had ridiculed him. Maui chased this man around the island from one side to the other until they had passed through Lahaina (one of the first mission stations in 1828). There on the seashore near the large black rock of the legend of Maui lifting the sky he found Moemoe.

Then they left the seashore and the contest raged up hill and down until Maui slew the man and "changed the body into a long rock, which is there to this day, by the side of the road going past Black Rock."

Before the battle with the sun occurred Maui went down into the underworld, according to the New Zealand tradition, and remained a long time with his relatives. In some way he learned that there was an enchanted jawbone in the possession of some one of his ancestors, so he waited and waited, hoping that at last he might discover it.

After a time he noticed that presents of food were being sent away to some person whom he had not met.

One day he asked the messengers, "Who is it you are taking that present of food to?"

The people answered, "It is for Muri, your ancestress."

Then he asked for the food, saying, "I will carry it to her myself."

But he took the food away and hid it. "And this he did for many days," and the presents failed to reach the old woman.

By and by she suspected mischief, for it did not seem as if her friends would neglect her so long a time, so she thought she would catch the tricky one and eat him. She depended upon her sense of smell to detect the one who had troubled her. As Sir George Grey tells the story, "When Maui came along the path carrying the present of food, the old chiefess sniffed and sniffed until she was sure that she smelt someone coming. She was very much exasperated, and her stomach began to distend itself that she might be ready to devour this one when he came near.

Then she turned toward the south and sniffed and not a scent of anything reached her. Then she turned to the north, and to the east, but could not detect the odour of a human being. She made one more trial and turned toward the west. Ah! then came the scent of a man to her plainly and she called out, 'I know, from the smell wafted to me by the breeze, that somebody is close to me.'"

Maui made known his presence and the old woman knew that he was a descendant of hers, and her stomach began immediately to shrink and contract itself again.

Then she asked, "Art thou Maui?"

He answered, "Even so," and told her that he wanted "the jawbone by which great enchantments could be wrought."

Then Muri, the old chiefess, gave him the magic bone and he returned to his brothers, who were still living on the earth.

Then Maui said, "Let us now catch the sun in a noose that we may compel him to move more slowly in order that mankind may have long days to labour in and procure subsistence for themselves."

They replied, "No man can approach it on account of the fierceness of the heat."

According to the Society Island legend, his mother advised him to have nothing to do with the sun, who was a divine living creature, "in form like a man, possessed of fearful energy," shaking his golden locks both morning and evening in the eyes of men. Many persons had tried to regulate the movements of the sun, but had failed completely.

But Maui encouraged his mother and his brothers by asking them to remember his power to protect himself by the use of enchantments.

The Hawaiian legend says that Maui himself gathered cocoanut fibre in great quantity and manufactured it into strong ropes. But the legends of other islands say that he had the aid of his brothers, and while working learned many useful lessons. While winding and twisting they discovered how to make square ropes and flat ropes as well as the ordinary round rope. In the Society Islands, it is said, Maui and his brothers made six strong ropes of great length. These he called aeiariki (royal nooses).

The New Zealand legend says that when Maui and his brothers had finished making all the ropes required they took provisions and other things needed and journeyed toward the east to find the place where the sun should rise. Maui carried with him the magic jawbone which he had secured from Muri, his ancestress, in the underworld.

They travelled all night and concealed themselves by day so that the sun should not see them and become too suspicious and watchful. In this way they journeyed, until "at length they had gone very far to the eastward and had come to the very edge of the place out of which the sun rises. There they set to work and built on each side a long, high wall of clay, with huts of boughs of trees at each end to hide themselves in."

Here they laid a large noose made from their ropes and Maui concealed himself on one side of this place along which the sun must come, while his brothers hid on the other side.

Maui seized his magic enchanted jawbone as the weapon with which to fight the sun, and ordered his brothers to pull hard on the noose and not to be frightened or moved to set the sun free.

"At last the sun came rising up out of his place like a fire spreading far and wide over the mountains and forests.

He rised up.

His head passed through the noose.

The ropes were pulled tight.

Then the monster began to struggle and roll himself about, while the snare jerked backwards and forwards as he struggled. Ah! was not he held fast in the ropes of his enemies.

Then forth rushed that bold hero Maui with his enchanted weapon. The sun screamed aloud and roared. Maui struck him fiercely with many blows. They held him for a long time. At last they let him go, and then weak from wounds the sun crept very slowly and feebly along his course."

In this way the days were made longer so that men could perform their daily tasks and fruits and food plants could have time to grow.

The legend of the Hervey group of islands says that Maui made six snares and placed them at intervals along the path over which the sun must pass. The sun in the form of a man climbed up from Avaiki (Hawaiki). Maui pulled the first noose, but it slipped down the rising sun until it caught and was pulled tight around his feet.

Maui ran quickly to pull the ropes of the second snare, but that also slipped down, down, until it was tightened around the knees. Then Maui hastened to the third snare, while the sun was trying to rush along on his journey. The third snare caught around the hips. The fourth snare fastened itself around the waist. The fifth slipped under the arms, and yet the sun sped along as if but little inconvenienced by Maui's efforts.

Then Maui caught the last noose and threw it around the neck of the sun, and fastened the rope to a spur of rock. The sun struggled until nearly strangled to death and then gave up, promising Maui that he would go as slowly as was desired. Maui left the snares fastened to the sun to keep him in constant fear.

"These ropes may still be seen hanging from the sun at dawn and stretching into the skies when he descends into the ocean at night. By the assistance of these ropes he is gently let down into Avaiki in the evening, and also raised up out of shadow-land in the morning."

Another legend from the Society Islands is related by Mr. Gill:

Maui tried many snares before he could catch the sun. The sun was the Hercules, or the Samson, of the heavens. He broke the strong cords of cocoanut fibre which Maui made and placed around the opening by which the sun climbed out from the underworld. Maui made stronger ropes, but still the sun broke them every one.

Then Maui thought of his sister's hair, the sister Inaika, whom he cruelly treated in later years. Her hair was long and beautiful. He cut off some of it and made a strong rope. With this he lassoed or rather snared the sun, and caught him around the throat. The sun quickly promised to be more thoughtful of the needs of men and go at a more reasonable pace across the sky.

A story from the American Indians is told in Hawaii's Young People, which is very similar to the Polynesian legends.

An Indian boy became very angry with the sun for getting so warm and making his clothes shrink with the heat. He told his sister to make a snare. The girl took sinews from a large deer, but they shrivelled under the heat. She took her own long hair and made snares, but they were burned in a moment. Then she tried the fibres of various plants and was successful. Her brother took the fibre cord and drew it through his lips. It stretched and became a strong red cord. He pulled and it became very long. He went to the place of sunrise, fixed his snare, and caught the sun. When the sun had been sufficiently punished, the animals of the earth studied the problem of setting the sun free. At last a mouse as large as a mountain ran and gnawed the red cord. It broke and the sun moved on, but the poor mouse had been burned and shrivelled into the small mouse of the present day.

A Samoan legend says that a woman living for a time with the sun bore a child who had the name "Child of the Sun." She wanted gifts for the child's marriage, so she took a long vine, climbed a tree, made the vine into a noose, lassoed the sun, and made him give her a basket of blessings.

In Fiji, the natives tie the grasses growing on a hilltop over which they are passing, when travelling from place to place. They do this to make a snare to catch the sun if he should try to go down before they reach the end of their day's journey.

This legend is a misty memory of some time when the Polynesian people were in contact with the short days of the extreme north or south. It is a very remarkable exposition of a fact of nature perpetuated many centuries in lands absolutely free from such natural phenomena.

The Mirror of the Sun Goddess

From Japanese mythology

MANY, MANY YEARS AGO, when the gods reigned in high heaven, the country of Nippon rose from the waters. Izanagi and Izananu, standing upon the floating bridge of heaven, thrust down a glittering blade. They probed the blue ocean and the drops from the sword's point hardened and became islands; and thus was created the "Land of Many Blades," the isles of Nippon.

Now Izanagi and Izananu were the highest of the gods of heaven, and they had two children, Amaterasu and Susanoo. Susanoo was made god of the sea, and his sister was the bright and beautiful sun goddess, whose name meant Great Goddess of the Shining Heaven.

She reigned happily from her bright golden throne for many years, but Susanoo, like many other brothers, was a tease, and he made his sister very angry with some of his tricks. She was quite patient with him, as elder sisters should be, but at last there came a time when she could no longer stand his naughty ways.

Amaterasu sent Susanoo one day upon an errand, for she wished him to find a goddess named Uke-mochi, who lived in the reedy moors. When Susanoo found her he was tired and hungry, and so he asked her for food. Uke-mochi took food from her mouth to give him and this made him very angry. "Why feed me with foul things? You shall not live!" he cried; and, drawing his sword, he struck her dead.

When he went home and told Amaterasu what he had done, his sister was in a great rage and left her brother in total darkness. She fled to the cave of Ameno and closed the entrance with a huge rock. Then was all the earth dark, for the sun goddess no longer shed her light upon men. So terrible was it upon earth that at last the other gods met together near the cave, to consult and see what could be done.

They tried in every way to persuade Amaterasu to come forth, but she sulked like a naughty child and would not shine upon them. At last they thought of a plan to entice the goddess from her cavern by means of an image of herself. So a mirror was made, very large and fine. It was hung upon a tree, just before the door of the cave, and a strong hempen cord was put in the hands of a god who hid himself beside the door.

A number of cocks were started to crowing, and the lovely goddess Uzumé began to dance to music from a bamboo tube. The gods kept time by striking two pieces of wood together, and one of them played a harp made by placing six of their bows together with the strings upward and drawing grass and rushes across them. Great bonfires were lighted, and a huge drum was brought for Uzumé to dance upon. This she did with so much spirit and grace that all the gods were delighted. They laughed with joy, clapped their hands, and fairly shook high heaven with their merriment.

Amaterasu heard the noise and could not understand it. She was annoyed because the gods seemed to be having such a good time without her. She had thought that they could not possibly get along unless she let the light of her face shine upon them. She was naturally very curious to find out what it was all about. So she pushed open the door of her cave, just a little bit, and peeped out. There, by the light of the bonfires she saw Uzumé's graceful dancing, and heard her sing,

> *"Hito futa miyo*
> *Itsu muyu nana*
> *Ya koko no tari."*

"Why does Uzumé dance and why do the gods laugh? I thought both heaven and earth would be sad without me", said Amaterasu crossly.

"Oh, no," laughed Uzumé. "We rejoice because we have here a deity who far surpasses you in beauty."

"Where?" demanded the sun goddess indignantly. "Let me see her!" and as she spoke she caught sight of her own reflection in the mirror.

She had never seen such a thing before and was greatly astonished. She stepped outside her cave to see more plainly this radiant rival, when lo! the god who was waiting seized her and drew her forth, quickly passing the rope across the cave door to prevent her return. Thus was the sun goddess restored to earth.

Morena-Y-A-Letsatsi, or the Sun Chief

From Lesotho, southern Africa

IN THE TIME of the great famine, when our fathers' fathers were young, there lived across the mountains, many days' journey, a great chief, who bore upon his breast the signs of the sun, the moon, and eleven stars. Greatly was he beloved, and marvellous was his power. When all around were starving, his people had plenty, and many journeyed to his village to implore his protection. Amongst others came two young girls, the daughters of one mother. Tall and lovely as a deep still river was the elder, gentle and timid as the wild deer, and her they called Siloane (the teardrop.)

Of a different mould was her sister Mokete. Plump and round were her limbs, bright as the stars her eyes, like running water was the music of her voice, and she feared not man nor spirit. When the chief asked what they could do to repay him for helping them in their need, Mokete replied, "Lord, I can cook, I can grind corn, I can make 'leting,' I can do all a woman's work."

Gravely the chief turned to Siloane, "And you," he asked, "what can you do?"

"Alas, lord!" Siloane replied, "what can I say, seeing that my sister has taken all words out of my mouth."

"It is enough," said the chief, "you shall be my wife. As for Mokete, since she is so clever, let her be your servant."

Now the heart of Mokete burned with black hate against her sister, and she vowed to humble her to the dust; but no one must see into her heart, so with a smiling face she embraced Siloane.

The next day the marriage feast took place, amidst great rejoicing, and continued for many days, as befitted the great Sun Chief. Many braves came from far to dance at the feast, and to delight the people with tales of the great deeds they had done in battle. Beautiful maidens were there, but none so beautiful as Siloane. How happy she was, how beloved! In the gladness of her heart she sang a song of praise to her lord, "Great is the sun in the heavens, and great are the moon and stars, but greater and more beautiful in the eyes of his handmaiden is my lord. Upon his breast are the signs of his greatness, and by their power I swear to love him with a love so strong, so true, that his son shall be in his image, and shall bear upon his breast the same tokens of the favour of the heavens."

Many moons came and went, and all was peace and joy in the hearts of the Sun Chief and his bride; but Mokete smiled darkly in her heart, for the time of her revenge approached. At length came the day, when Siloane should fulfil her vow, when the son should be born. The chief ordered that the child should be brought to him at once, that he might rejoice in the fulfilment of Siloane's vow. In the dark hut the young mother lay with great content, for had not Mokete assured her the child was his father's image, and upon his breast were the signs of the sun, the moon, and eleven stars?

Why then this angry frown on the chief's face, this look of triumph in the eyes of Mokete? What is this which she is holding covered with a skin? She turns back the covering, and, with a wicked laugh of triumph, shows the chief, not the beautiful son he had looked for, but an ugly, deformed child with the face of a baboon. "Here, my lord," she said, "is the long-desired son. See how well Siloane loves you, see how well she has kept her vow! Shall I tell her of your heart's content?"

"Woman," roared the disappointed chief, "speak not thus to me. Take from my sight both mother and child, and tell my headman it is my will that they be destroyed ere the sun hide his head in yonder mountains."

Sore at heart, angry and unhappy, the chief strode away into the lands, while Mokete hastened to the headman to bid him carry out his master's orders; but ere they could be obeyed, a messenger came from the chief to say the child alone was to be destroyed, but Siloane should become a servant, and on the morrow should witness his marriage to Mokete.

Bitter tears rolled down Siloane's cheeks. What evil thing had befallen her, that the babe she had borne, and whom she had felt in her arms, strong and straight, should have been so changed ere the eyes of his father had rested upon him? Not once did she doubt Mokete. Was she not her own sister? What reason would she have for casting the "Evil Eye" upon the child? It was hard to lose her child, hard indeed to lose the love of her lord; but he had not banished her altogether from his sight, and perhaps some day the spirits might be willing that she should once again find favour in his sight, and should bear him a child in his own image.

Meanwhile Mokete had taken the real baby to the pigs, hoping they would devour him, for each time she tried to kill him some unseen power held her hand; but the pigs took the babe and nourished him, and many weeks went by – weeks of triumph for Mokete, but of bitter sorrow for Siloane.

At length Mokete bethought her of the child, and wondered if the pigs had left any trace of him. When she reached the kraal, she started back in terror, for there, fat, healthy, and happy, lay the babe, while the young pigs played around him. What should she do? Had Siloane seen him? No, she hardly thought so, for the child was in every way the image of the chief. Siloane would at once have known who he was.

Hurriedly returning to her husband, Mokete begged him to get rid of all the pigs, and have their kraal burnt, as they were all ill of a terrible disease. So the chief gave orders to do as Mokete desired; but the spirits took the child to the elephant which lived in the great bush, and told it to guard him.

After this Mokete was at peace for many months, but no child came to gladden the heart of her lord, and to take away her reproach. In her anger and bitterness she longed to kill Siloane, but she was afraid.

One day she wandered far into the bush, and there she beheld the child, grown more beautiful than ever, playing with the elephant. Mad with rage, she returned home, and gave her lord no rest until he consented to burn the bush, which she told him was full of terrible wild beasts, which would one day devour the whole village if they were not destroyed. But the spirits took the child and gave him to the fishes in the great river, bidding them guard him safely.

Many moons passed, many crops were reaped and Mokete had almost forgotten about the child, when one day, as she walked by the riverbank, she saw him, a beautiful youth, playing with the fishes. This was terrible. Would nothing kill him? In her rage she tore great rocks from their beds and rolled them into the water; but the spirits carried the youth to a mountain, where they gave him a wand. "This wand," said they, "will keep you safe. If danger threatens you from above, strike once with the wand upon the ground, and a path will be opened to you to the country beneath. If you wish to return to this upper world, strike twice with the wand, and the path will reopen."

So again they left him, and the youth, fearing the vengeance of his stepmother, struck once upon the ground with his wand. The earth opened, showing a long narrow passage. Down this the youth went, and, upon reaching the other end, found himself at the entrance to a large and very beautiful village. As he walked along, the people stood to gaze at him, and all, when they saw the signs upon his breast, fell down and worshipped him, saying, "Greetings, lord!" At length, he was informed that for many years these people had had no chief, but the spirits had told them that at the proper time a chief would appear who should bear strange signs upon his breast; him the people were to receive and to obey, for he would be the chosen one, and his name should be Tsepitso, or the promise.

From that day the youth bore the name of Tsepitso, and ruled over that land; but he never forgot his mother, and often wandered to the world above, to find how she fared and to watch over her. On these journeys he always clothed himself in old skins, and covered up his breast that none might behold the signs. One day, as he wandered, he found himself in a strange village, and as he passed the well, a maiden greeted him, saying, "Stranger, you look weary. Will you not rest and drink of this fountain?"

Tsepitso gazed into her eyes, and knew what love meant. Here, he felt, was the wife the spirits intended him to wed. He must not let her depart, so he sat down by the well and drank of the cool, delicious water, while he questioned the maid. She told him her name was Ma Thabo (mother of joy), and that her father was chief of that part of the country. Tsepitso told her he was a poor youth looking for work, whereupon she took him to her father, who consented to employ him.

One stipulation Tsepitso made, which was that for one hour every day before sunset he should be free from his duties. This was agreed to, and for several moons he worked for the old chief, and grew more and more in favour, both with him and with his daughter. The hour before sunset each day he spent amongst his own people, attending to their wants and giving judgment. At length he told Ma Thabo of his love, and read her answering love in her beautiful eyes. Together they sought the old chief, to whom Tsepitso told his story, and revealed his true self. The marriage was soon after celebrated, with much rejoicing, and Tsepitso bore his bride in triumph to his beautiful home in the world beneath, where she was received with every joy.

But amidst all his happiness Tsepitso did not forget his mother, and after the feasting and rejoicing were ended, he took Ma Thabo with him, for the time had at length come when he might free his mother forever from the power of Mokete.

When they approached his father's house, Mokete saw them, and, recognising Tsepitso, knew that her time had come. With a scream she fled to the hut, but Tsepitso followed her, and sternly demanded his mother. Mokete only moaned as she knelt at her lord's feet. The old chief arose, and said, "Young man, I know not who you are, nor who your mother is; but this woman is my wife, and I pray you speak to her not thus rudely."

Tsepitso replied, "Lord, I am thy son."

"Nay now, thou art a liar," said the old man sadly, "I have no son."

"Indeed, my father, I am thy son, and Siloane is my mother. Dost need proof of the truth of my words? Then look," and turning to the light, Tsepitso revealed to his father the signs upon his breast, and the old chief, with a great cry, threw himself upon his son's neck and wept. Siloane was soon called, and knew that indeed she had fulfilled her vow, that here before her stood in very truth the son she had borne, and a great content filled her heart. Tsepitso and Ma Thabo soon persuaded her to return with them, knowing full well that her life would no longer be safe were she to remain near Mokete; so, when the old chief was absent, in the dusk of the evening they departed to their own home.

When the Sun Chief discovered their flight, he determined to follow, and restore his beloved Siloane to her rightful place; but Mokete followed him, though many times he ordered her to return to the village, for that never again would she be wife of his, and that if she continued to follow him, he would kill her. At length he thought, "If I cut off her feet she will not be able to walk," so, turning round suddenly, he seized Mokete, and cut off her feet. "Now, wilt thou leave me in peace, woman? Take care nothing worse befall thee." So saying, he left her, and continued his journey.

But Mokete continued to follow him, till the sun was high in the heavens. Each time he saw her close behind him, he stopped and cut off more of her legs, till only her body was left; even then she was not conquered, but continued to roll after him. Thoroughly enraged, the Sun Chief seized her, and called down fire from the heavens to consume her, and a wind from the edge of the world to scatter her ashes.

When this was done, he went on his way rejoicing, for surely now she would trouble him no more. Then as he journeyed, a voice rose in the evening air, "I follow, I follow, to the edge of the world, yea, even beyond, shall I follow thee."

Placing his hands over his ears to shut out the voice, the Sun Chief ran with the fleetness of a young brave, until, at the hour when the spirits visit the abodes of men, he overtook Tsepitso and the two women, and with them entered the kingdom of his son.

How he won pardon from Siloane, and gained his son's love, and how it was arranged that he and Siloane should again be married, are old tales now in the country of Tsepitso. When the marriage feast was begun, a cloud of ashes dashed against the Sun Chief, and an angry voice was heard from the midst of the cloud, saying, "Nay, thou shalt not wed Siloane, for I have found thee, and I shall claim thee forever." Hastily the witch doctor was called to free the Sun Chief from the power of Mokete. As the old man approached the cloud, chanting a hymn to the gods, everyone gazed in silence. Raising his wand, the wizard made some mystic signs, the cloud vanished, and only a handful of ashes lay upon the ground.

Thus was the Evil Eye of Mokete stilled for evermore, and peace reigned in the hearts of the Sun Chief and his wife Siloane.

The Mother and Daughter Who Worshipped the Sun

From Indian Folklore

ONCE UPON A TIME there lived a mother and a daughter who worshipped the Sun. Though they were very poor they never forgot to honour the Sun, giving everything they earned to it except two meal cakes, one of which the mother ate, while the other was the daughter's share, every day one cake apiece; that was all.

Now it so happened that one day, when the mother was out at work, the daughter grew hungry, and ate her cake before dinnertime. Just as she had finished it a priest came by, and begged for some bread, but there was none in the house save the mother's cake. So the daughter broke off half of it and gave it to the priest in the name of the Sun.

By and by the mother returned, very hungry, to dinner, and, lo and behold! there was only half a cake in the house.

"Where is the remainder of the bread?" she asked.

"I ate my share, because I was hungry," said the daughter, "and just as I finished, a priest came a-begging, so I was obliged to give him half your cake."

"A pretty story!" quoth the mother, in a rage. "It is easy to be pious with other people's property! How am I to know you had eaten your cake first? I believe you gave mine in order to save your own!"

In vain the daughter protested that she really had finished her cake before the priest came a-begging – in vain she promised to give the mother half her share on the morrow – in vain she pleaded for forgiveness for the sake of the Sun, in whose honour she had given alms. Words were of no avail; the mother sternly bade her go about her business, saying, "I will have no gluttons, who grudge their own meal to the great Sun, in my house!"

So the daughter wandered away homeless into the wilds, sobbing bitterly. When she had travelled a long, long way, she became so tired that she could walk no longer; therefore she climbed into a big pîpal tree, in order to be secure from wild beasts, and rested amongst the branches.

After a time a handsome young prince, who had been chasing deer in the forest, came to the big pîpal tree, and, allured by its tempting shade, lay down to sleep away his fatigue. Now, as he lay there, with his face turned to the sky, he looked so beautiful that the daughter could not choose but keep her eyes upon him, and so the tears which flowed from them like a summer shower dropped soft and warm upon the young man's face, waking him with a start. Thinking it was raining, he rose to look at the sky, and see whence this sudden storm had come; but far and near not a cloud was to be seen. Still, when he returned to his place, the drops fell faster than before, and one of them upon his lip tasted salt as tears. So he swung himself into the tree, to see whence the salt rain came, and, lo and behold! a beauteous maiden sat in the tree, weeping.

"Whence come you, fair stranger?" said he; and she, with tears, told him she was homeless, houseless, motherless. Then he fell in love with her sweet face and soft words; so he asked her to be his bride, and she went with him to the palace, her heart full of gratitude to the Sun, who had sent her such good luck.

Everything she could desire was hers; only when the other women talked of their homes and their mothers she held her tongue, for she was ashamed of hers.

Everyone thought she must be some great princess, she was so lovely and magnificent, but in her heart of hearts she knew she was nothing of the kind; so every day she prayed to the Sun that her mother might not find her out.

But one day, when she was sitting alone in her beautiful palace, her mother appeared, ragged and poor as ever. She had heard of her daughter's good fortune, and had come to share it.

"And you *shall* share it," pleaded her daughter; "I will give you back far more than I ever took from you, if only you will go away and not disgrace me before my prince."

"Ungrateful creature!" stormed the mother, "do you forget how it was through my act that your good fortune came to you? If I had not sent you into the world, where would you have found so fine a husband?"

"I might have starved!" wept the daughter; "and now you come to destroy me again. O great Sun, help me now!"

Just then the prince came to the door, and the poor daughter was ready to die of shame and vexation; but when she turned to where her mother had sat, there was nothing to be seen but a golden stool, the like of which had never been seen on earth before.

"My princess," asked the prince, astonished, "whence comes that golden stool?"

"From my mother's house," replied the daughter, full of gratitude to the great Sun, who had saved her from disgrace.

"Nay! if there are such wondrous things to be seen in your mother's house," quoth the prince gaily, "I must needs go and see it. Tomorrow we will set out on our journey, and you shall show me all it contains."

In vain the daughter put forward one pretext and another: the prince's curiosity had been aroused by the sight of the marvellous golden stool, and he was not to be gainsaid.

Then the daughter cried once more to the Sun, in her distress, saying, "O gracious Sun, help me now!"

But no answer came, and with a heavy heart she set out next day to show the prince her mother's house. A goodly procession they made, with horsemen and footmen clothed in royal liveries surrounding the bride's palanquin, where sat the daughter, her heart sinking at every step.

And when they came within sight of where her mother's hut used to stand, lo! on the horizon showed a shining, flaming golden palace, that glittered and glanced like solid sunshine. Within and without all was gold – golden servants and a golden mother!

There they stopped, admiring the countless marvels of the Sun palace, for three days, and when the third was completed, the prince, more enamoured of his bride than ever, set his face homewards; but when he came to the spot where he had first seen the glittering golden palace from afar, he thought he would just take one look more at the wondrous sight, and, lo! there was nothing to be seen save a low thatched hovel!

Then he turned to his bride, full of wrath, and said, "You are a witch, and have deceived me by your detestable arts! Confess, if you would not have me strike you dead!"

But the daughter fell on her knees, saying, "My gracious prince, I have done nothing! I am but a poor homeless girl. It was the Sun that did it."

Then she told the whole story from beginning to end, and the prince was so well satisfied that from that day he too worshipped the Sun.

Extracts from 'The Mysterious Island'

Jules Verne

Publisher's Note: The Mysterious Island, *by Jules Verne (1828–1905), follows a group of prisoners of war who escape in a hot-air balloon during the American Civil War. Landing on a remote Pacific island in a storm, the group need to find means to survive and determine exactly where they are.*

Chapter XIII

IT WAS ON THE 2ND of April that Harding had employed himself in fixing the orientation of the island, or, in other words, the precise spot where the sun rose. The day before he had noted exactly the hour when the sun disappeared beneath the horizon, making allowance for the refraction. This morning he noted, no less exactly, the hour at which it reappeared. Between this setting and rising, twelve hours, twenty-four minutes passed. Then, six hours, twelve minutes after its rising, the sun on this day would exactly pass the meridian and the point of the sky which it occupied at this moment would be the north. At the said hour, Cyrus marked this point, and putting in a line with the sun two trees which would serve him for marks, he thus obtained an invariable meridian for his ulterior operations.

The settlers employed the two days before the oven was built in collecting fuel. Branches were cut all round the glade, and they picked up all the fallen wood under the trees. They were also able to hunt with greater success, since Pencroft now possessed some dozen arrows armed with sharp points. It was Top who had furnished these points, by bringing in a porcupine, rather inferior eating, but of great value, thanks to the quills with which it bristled. These quills were fixed firmly at the ends of the arrows, the flight of which was made more certain by some cockatoos' feathers. The reporter and Herbert soon became very skilful archers. Game of all sorts in consequence abounded at the Chimneys, capybaras, pigeons, agouties, grouse, etc. The greater part of these animals were killed in the part of the forest on the left bank of the Mercy, to which they gave the name of Jacamar Wood, in remembrance of the bird which Pencroft and Herbert had pursued when on their first exploration.

This game was eaten fresh, but they preserved some capybara hams, by smoking them above a fire of green wood, after having perfumed them with sweet-smelling leaves. However, this food, although very strengthening, was always roast upon roast, and the party would have been delighted to hear some soup bubbling on the hearth, but they must wait till a pot could be made, and, consequently, till the oven was built.

During these excursions, which were not extended far from the brickfield, the hunters could discern the recent passage of animals of a large size, armed with powerful claws, but they could not recognize the species. Cyrus Harding advised them to be very careful, as the forest probably enclosed many dangerous beasts.

And he did right. Indeed, Gideon Spilett and Herbert one day saw an animal which resembled a jaguar. Happily the creature did not attack them, or they might not have escaped without a severe wound. As soon as he could get a regular weapon, that is to say, one of the guns which Pencroft begged for, Gideon Spilett resolved to make desperate war against the ferocious beasts, and exterminate them from the island.

The Chimneys during these few days was not made more comfortable, for the engineer hoped to discover, or build if necessary, a more convenient dwelling. They contented themselves with spreading moss and dry leaves on the sand of the passages, and on these primitive couches the tired workers slept soundly.

They also reckoned the days they had passed on Lincoln Island, and from that time kept a regular account. The 5th of April, which was Wednesday, was twelve days from the time when the wind threw the castaways on this shore.

On the 6th of April, at daybreak, the engineer and his companions were collected in the glade, at the place where they were going to perform the operation of baking the bricks. Naturally this had to be in the open air, and not in a kiln, or rather, the agglomeration of bricks made an enormous kiln, which would bake itself. The fuel, made of well-prepared fagots, was laid on the ground and surrounded with several rows of dried bricks, which soon formed an enormous cube, to the exterior of which they contrived air-holes. The work lasted all day, and it was not till the evening that they set fire to the fagots. No one slept that night, all watching carefully to keep up the fire.

The operation lasted forty-eight hours, and succeeded perfectly. It then became necessary to leave the smoking mass to cool, and during this time Neb and Pencroft, guided by Cyrus Harding, brought, on a hurdle made of interlaced branches, loads of carbonate of lime and common stones, which were very abundant, to the north of the lake. These stones, when decomposed by heat, made a very strong quicklime, greatly increased by slacking, at least as pure as if it had been produced by the calcination of chalk or marble. Mixed with sand the lime made excellent mortar.

The result of these different works was that, on the 9th of April, the engineer had at his disposal a quantity of prepared lime and some thousands of bricks.

Without losing an instant, therefore, they began the construction of a kiln to bake the pottery, which was indispensable for their domestic use. They succeeded without much difficulty. Five days after, the kiln was supplied with coal, which the engineer had discovered lying open to the sky towards the mouth of the Red Creek, and the first smoke escaped from a chimney twenty feet high. The glade was transformed into a manufactory, and Pencroft was not far wrong in believing that from this kiln would issue all the products of modern industry.

In the meantime, what the settlers first manufactured was a common pottery in which to cook their food. The chief material was clay, to which Harding added a little lime and quartz. This paste made regular "pipe-clay," with which they manufactured bowls, cups moulded on stones of a proper size, great jars and pots to hold water, etc. The shape of these objects was clumsy and defective, but after they had been baked in a high temperature, the kitchen of the Chimneys was provided with a number of utensils, as precious to the settlers as the most beautifully enamelled china. We must mention here that Pencroft, desirous to know if the clay thus prepared was worthy of its name of pipe-clay, made some large pipes, which he thought charming, but for which, alas! he had no tobacco, and that was a great privation to Pencroft. "But tobacco will come, like everything else!" he repeated, in a burst of absolute confidence.

This work lasted till the 15th of April, and the time was well employed. The settlers, having become potters, made nothing but pottery. When it suited Cyrus Harding to change them into smiths, they would become smiths. But the next day being Sunday, and also Easter Sunday, all agreed to sanctify the day by rest. These Americans were religious men, scrupulous observers of the precepts of the Bible, and their situation could not but develop sentiments of confidence towards the Author of all things.

On the evening of the 15th of April they returned to the Chimneys, carrying with them the pottery, the furnace being extinguished until they could put it to a new use. Their return was marked by a fortunate incident; the engineer discovered a substance which replaced tinder. It is known that a spongy, velvety flesh is procured from a certain mushroom of the genus polyporous. Properly prepared, it is extremely inflammable, especially when it has been previously saturated with gunpowder, or boiled in a solution of nitrate or chlorate of potash. But, till then, they had not found any of these polypores or even any of the morels which could replace them. On this day, the engineer, seeing a plant belonging to the wormwood genus, the principal species of which are absinthe, balm-mint, tarragon, etc., gathered several tufts, and, presenting them to the sailor, said,

"Here, Pencroft, this will please you."

Pencroft looked attentively at the plant, covered with long silky hair, the leaves being clothed with soft down.

"What's that, captain?" asked Pencroft. "Is it tobacco?"

"No," replied Harding, "it is wormwood; Chinese wormwood to the learned, but to us it will be tinder."

When the wormwood was properly dried it provided them with a very inflammable substance, especially afterwards when the engineer had impregnated it with nitrate of potash, of which the island possessed several beds, and which is in truth saltpetre.

The colonists had a good supper that evening. Neb prepared some agouti soup, a smoked capybara ham, to which was added the boiled tubercules of the "caladium macrorhizum," an herbaceous plant of the arum family. They had an excellent taste, and were very nutritious, being something similar to the substance which is sold in England under the name of "Portland sago"; they were also a good substitute for bread, which the settlers in Lincoln Island did not yet possess.

When supper was finished, before sleeping, Harding and his companions went to take the air on the beach. It was eight o'clock in the evening; the night was magnificent. The moon, which had been full five days before, had not yet risen, but the horizon was already silvered by those soft, pale shades which might be called the dawn of the moon. At the southern zenith glittered the circumpolar constellations, and above all the Southern Cross, which some days before the engineer had greeted on the summit of Mount Franklin.

Cyrus Harding gazed for some time at this splendid constellation, which has at its summit and at its base two stars of the first magnitude, at its left arm a star of the second, and at its right arm a star of the third magnitude.

Then, after some minutes' thought,

"Herbert," he asked of the lad, "is not this the 15th of April?"

"Yes, captain," replied Herbert.

"Well, if I am not mistaken, tomorrow will be one of the four days in the year in which the real time is identical with average time; that is to say, my boy, that tomorrow, to within some seconds, the sun will pass the meridian just at midday by the clocks. If the weather is fine I think that I shall obtain the longitude of the island with an approximation of some degrees."

"Without instruments, without sextant?" asked Gideon Spilett.

"Yes," replied the engineer. "Also, since the night is clear, I will try, this very evening, to obtain our latitude by calculating the height of the Southern Cross, that is, from the southern pole above the horizon. You understand, my friends, that before undertaking the work of installation in earnest it is not enough to have found out that this land is an island; we must, as nearly as possible, know at what distance it is situated, either from the American continent or Australia, or from the principal archipelagoes of the Pacific."

"In fact," said the reporter, "instead of building a house it would be more important to build a boat, if by chance we are not more than a hundred miles from an inhabited coast."

"That is why," returned Harding, "I am going to try this evening to calculate the latitude of Lincoln Island, and tomorrow, at midday, I will try to calculate the longitude."

If the engineer had possessed a sextant, an apparatus with which the angular distance of objects can be measured with great precision, there would have been no difficulty in the operation. This evening by the height of the pole, the next day by the passing of the sun at the meridian, he would obtain the position of the island. But as they had not one he would have to supply the deficiency.

Harding then entered the Chimneys. By the light of the fire he cut two little flat rulers, which he joined together at one end so as to form a pair of compasses, whose legs could separate or come together. The fastening was fixed with a strong acacia thorn which was found in the wood pile. This instrument finished, the engineer returned to the beach, but as it was necessary to take the height of the pole from above a clear horizon, that is, a sea horizon, and as Claw Cape hid the southern horizon, he was obliged to look for a more suitable station. The best would evidently have been the shore exposed directly to the south; but the Mercy would have to be crossed, and that was a difficulty. Harding resolved, in consequence, to make his observation from Prospect Heights, taking into consideration its height above the level of the sea – a height which he intended to calculate next day by a simple process of elementary geometry.

The settlers, therefore, went to the plateau, ascending the left bank of the Mercy, and placed themselves on the edge which looked northwest and southeast, that is, above the curiously shaped rocks which bordered the river.

This part of the plateau commanded the heights of the left bank, which sloped away to the extremity of Claw Cape, and to the southern side of the island. No obstacle intercepted their gaze, which swept the horizon in a semi-circle from the cape to Reptile End. To the south the horizon, lighted by the first rays of the moon, was very clearly defined against the sky.

At this moment the Southern Cross presented itself to the observer in an inverted position, the star Alpha marking its base, which is nearer to the southern pole.

This constellation is not situated as near to the Antarctic pole as the Polar Star is to the arctic pole. The star Alpha is about twenty-seven degrees from it, but Cyrus Harding knew this and made allowance for it in his calculation. He took care also to observe the moment when it passed the meridian below the pole, which would simplify the operation.

Cyrus Harding pointed one leg of the compasses to the horizon, the other to Alpha, and the space between the two legs gave him the angular distance which separated Alpha from the horizon. In order to fix the angle obtained, he fastened with thorns the two pieces of wood on a third placed transversely, so that their separation should be properly maintained.

That done, there was only the angle to calculate by bringing back the observation to the level of the sea, taking into consideration the depression of the horizon, which would necessitate measuring the height of the cliff. The value of this angle would give the height of Alpha, and consequently that of the pole above the horizon, that is to say, the latitude of the island, since the latitude of a point of the globe is always equal to the height of the pole above the horizon of this point.

The calculations were left for the next day, and at ten o'clock everyone was sleeping soundly.

Chapter XIV

The next day, the 16th of April, and Easter Sunday, the settlers issued from the Chimneys at daybreak, and proceeded to wash their linen. The engineer intended to manufacture soap as soon as he could procure the necessary materials – soda or potash, fat or oil. The important question of renewing their wardrobe would be treated of in the proper time and place. At any rate their clothes would last at least six months longer, for they were strong, and could resist the wear of manual labour. But all would depend on the situation of the island with regard to inhabited land. This would be settled today if the weather permitted.

The sun rising above a clear horizon, announced a magnificent day, one of those beautiful autumn days which are like the last farewells of the warm season.

It was now necessary to complete the observations of the evening before by measuring the height of the cliff above the level of the sea.

"Shall you not need an instrument similar to the one which you used yesterday?" said Herbert to the engineer.

"No, my boy," replied the latter, "we are going to proceed differently, but in as precise a way."

Herbert, wishing to learn everything he could, followed the engineer to the beach. Pencroft, Neb, and the reporter remained behind and occupied themselves in different ways.

Cyrus Harding had provided himself with a straight stick, twelve feet long, which he had measured as exactly as possible by comparing it with his own height, which he knew to a hair. Herbert carried a plumb-line which Harding had given him, that is to say, a simple stone fastened to the end of a flexible fibre. Having reached a spot about twenty feet from the edge of the beach, and nearly five hundred feet from the cliff, which rose perpendicularly, Harding thrust the pole two feet into the sand, and wedging it up carefully, he managed, by means of the plumb-line, to erect it perpendicularly with the plane of the horizon.

That done, he retired the necessary distance, when, lying on the sand, his eye glanced at the same time at the top of the pole and the crest of the cliff. He carefully marked the place with a little stick.

Then addressing Herbert, "Do you know the first principles of geometry?" he asked.

"Slightly, captain," replied Herbert, who did not wish to put himself forward.

"You remember what are the properties of two similar triangles?"

"Yes," replied Herbert; "their homologous sides are proportional."

"Well, my boy, I have just constructed two similar right-angled triangles; the first, the smallest, has for its sides the perpendicular pole, the distance which separates the little stick from the foot of the pole and my visual ray for hypothenuse; the second has for its sides the perpendicular cliff, the height of which we wish to measure, the distance which separates the little stick from the bottom of the cliff, and my visual ray also forms its hypothenuse, which proves to be prolongation of that of the first triangle."

"Ah, captain, I understand!" cried Herbert. "As the distance from the stick to the pole is to the distance from the stick to the base of the cliff, so is the height of the pole to the height of the cliff."

"Just so, Herbert," replied the engineer; "and when we have measured the two first distances, knowing the height of the pole, we shall only have a sum in proportion to do, which will give us the height of the cliff, and will save us the trouble of measuring it directly."

The two horizontal distances were found out by means of the pole, whose length above the sand was exactly ten feet.

The first distance was fifteen feet between the stick and the place where the pole was thrust into the sand.

The second distance between the stick and the bottom of the cliff was five hundred feet.

These measurements finished, Cyrus Harding and the lad returned to the Chimneys.

The engineer then took a flat stone which he had brought back from one of his previous excursions, a sort of slate, on which it was easy to trace figures with a sharp shell. He then proved the following proportions:

$$15 : 500 :: 10 : x$$
$$500 \times 10 = 5000$$
$$5000 / 15 = 333.3$$

From which it was proved that the granite cliff measured 333 feet in height.

Cyrus Harding then took the instrument which he had made the evening before, the space between its two legs giving the angular distance between the star Alpha and the horizon. He measured, very exactly, the opening of this angle on a circumference which he divided into 360 equal parts. Now, this angle by adding to it the twenty-seven degrees which separated Alpha from the Antarctic pole, and by reducing to the level of the sea the height of the cliff on which the observation had been made, was found to be fifty-three degrees. These fifty-three degrees being subtracted from ninety degrees – the distance from the pole to the equator – there remained thirty-seven degrees. Cyrus Harding concluded, therefore, that Lincoln Island was situated on the thirty-seventh degree of the southern latitude, or taking into consideration through the imperfection of the performance, an error of five degrees, that it must be situated between the thirty-fifth and the fortieth parallel.

There was only the longitude to be obtained, and the position of the island would be determined. The engineer hoped to attempt this the same day, at twelve o'clock, at which moment the sun would pass the meridian.

It was decided that Sunday should be spent in a walk, or rather an exploring expedition, to that side of the island between the north of the lake and Shark Gulf, and if there was time they would push their discoveries to the northern side of Cape South Mandible. They would breakfast on the downs, and not return till evening.

At half-past eight the little band was following the edge of the channel. On the other side, on Safety Islet, numerous birds were gravely strutting. They were divers, easily recognized by their cry, which much resembles the braying of a donkey. Pencroft only considered them in an eatable point of view, and learnt with some satisfaction that their flesh, though blackish, is not bad food.

Great amphibious creatures could also be seen crawling on the sand; seals, doubtless, who appeared to have chosen the islet for a place of refuge. It was impossible to think of those animals in an alimentary point of view, for their oily flesh is detestable; however, Cyrus Harding observed them attentively, and without making known his idea, he announced to his companions that very soon they would pay a visit to the islet. The beach was strewn with innumerable shells, some of which would have rejoiced the heart of a conchologist; there were, among others, the phasianella, the terebratual, etc. But what would be of more use, was the discovery, by Neb, at low tide, of a large oyster bed among the rocks, nearly five miles from the Chimneys.

"Neb will not have lost his day," cried Pencroft, looking at the spacious oyster-bed.

"It is really a fortunate discovery," said the reporter, "and as it is said that each oyster produces yearly from fifty to sixty thousand eggs, we shall have an inexhaustible supply there."

"Only I believe that the oyster is not very nourishing," said Herbert.

"No," replied Harding. "The oyster contains very little nitrogen, and if a man lived exclusively on them, he would have to eat not less than fifteen to sixteen dozen a day."

"Capital!" replied Pencroft. "We might swallow dozens and dozens without exhausting the bed. Shall we take some for breakfast?"

And without waiting for a reply to this proposal, knowing that it would be approved of, the sailor and Neb detached a quantity of the molluscs. They put them in a sort of net of hibiscus fibre, which Neb had manufactured, and which already contained food; they then continued to climb the coast between the downs and the sea.

From time to time Harding consulted his watch, so as to be prepared in time for the solar observation, which had to be made exactly at midday.

All that part of the island was very barren as far as the point which closed Union Bay, and which had received the name of Cape South Mandible. Nothing could be seen there but sand and shells, mingled with debris of lava. A few seabirds frequented this desolate coast, gulls, great albatrosses, as well as wild duck, for which Pencroft had a great fancy. He tried to knock some over with an arrow, but without result, for they seldom perched, and he could not hit them on the wing.

This led the sailor to repeat to the engineer,

"You see, captain, so long as we have not one or two fowling-pieces, we shall never get anything!"

"Doubtless, Pencroft," replied the reporter, "but it depends on you. Procure us some iron for the barrels; steel for the hammers; saltpetre, coal and sulphur for powder; mercury and nitric acid for the fulminate; and lead for the shot; and the captain will make us first-rate guns."

"Oh!" replied the engineer, "we might, no doubt, find all these substances on the island, but a gun is a delicate instrument, and needs very particular tools. However, we shall see later!"

"Why," cried Pencroft, "were we obliged to throw overboard all the weapons we had with us in the car, all our implements, even our pocket-knives?"

"But if we had not thrown them away, Pencroft, the balloon would have thrown us to the bottom of the sea!" said Herbert.

"What you say is true, my boy," replied the sailor.

Then passing to another idea, "Think," said he, "how astounded Jonathan Forster and his companions must have been when, next morning, they found the place empty, and the machine flown away!"

"I am utterly indifferent about knowing what they may have thought," said the reporter.

"It was all my idea, that!" said Pencroft, with a satisfied air.

"A splendid idea, Pencroft!" replied Gideon Spilett, laughing, "and which has placed us where we are."

"I would rather be here than in the hands of the Southerners," cried the sailor, "especially since the captain has been kind enough to come and join us again."

"So would I, truly!" replied the reporter. "Besides, what do we want? Nothing."

"If that is not – everything!" replied Pencroft, laughing and shrugging his shoulders. "But, some day or other, we shall find means of going away!"

"Sooner, perhaps, than you imagine, my friends," remarked the engineer, "if Lincoln Island is but a medium distance from an inhabited island, or from a continent. We shall know in an hour. I have not a map of the Pacific, but my memory has preserved a very clear recollection of its southern part. The latitude which I obtained yesterday placed New Zealand to the west of Lincoln Island, and the coast of Chile to the east. But between these two countries, there is a distance of at least six thousand miles. It has, therefore, to be determined what point in this great space the island occupies, and this the longitude will give us presently, with a sufficient approximation, I hope."

"Is not the archipelago of the Pomoutous the nearest point to us in latitude?" asked Herbert.

"Yes," replied the engineer, "but the distance which separates us from it is more than twelve hundred miles."

"And that way?" asked Neb, who followed the conversation with extreme interest, pointing to the south.

"That way, nothing," replied Pencroft.

"Nothing, indeed," added the engineer.

"Well, Cyrus," asked the reporter, "if Lincoln Island is not more than two or three thousand miles from New Zealand or Chile?"

"Well," replied the engineer, "instead of building a house we will build a boat, and Master Pencroft shall be put in command—"

"Well then," cried the sailor, "I am quite ready to be captain – as soon as you can make a craft that's able to keep at sea!"

"We shall do it, if it is necessary," replied Cyrus Harding.

But while these men, who really hesitated at nothing, were talking, the hour approached at which the observation was to be made. What Cyrus Harding was to do to ascertain the passage of the sun at the meridian of the island, without an instrument of any sort, Herbert could not guess.

The observers were then about six miles from the Chimneys, not far from that part of the downs in which the engineer had been found after his enigmatical preservation. They halted at this place and prepared for breakfast, for it was half-past eleven. Herbert went for some fresh water from a stream which ran near, and brought it back in a jug, which Neb had provided.

During these preparations Harding arranged everything for his astronomical observation. He chose a clear place on the shore, which the ebbing tide had left perfectly level. This bed of fine sand was as smooth as ice, not a grain out of place. It was of little importance whether it was horizontal or not, and it did not matter much whether the stick six feet high, which was planted there, rose perpendicularly. On the contrary, the engineer inclined it towards the south, that is to say, in the direction of the coast opposite to the sun, for it must not be forgotten that the settlers in Lincoln Island, as the island was situated in the Southern Hemisphere, saw the radiant planet describe its diurnal arc above the northern, and not above the southern horizon.

Herbert now understood how the engineer was going to proceed to ascertain the culmination of the sun, that is to say its passing the meridian of the island or, in other words, determine due south. It was by means of the shadow cast on the sand by the stick, a way which, for want of an instrument, would give him a suitable approach to the result which he wished to obtain.

In fact, the moment when this shadow would reach its minimum of length would be exactly twelve o'clock, and it would be enough to watch the extremity of the shadow, so as to ascertain the instant when, after having successively diminished, it began to lengthen. By inclining his stick to the side opposite to the sun, Cyrus Harding made the shadow longer, and consequently its modifications would be more easily ascertained. In fact, the longer the needle of a dial is, the more easily can the movement of its point be followed. The shadow of the stick was nothing but the needle of a dial. The moment had come, and Cyrus Harding knelt on the sand, and with little wooden pegs, which he stuck into the sand, he began to mark the successive diminutions of the stick's shadow. His companions, bending over him, watched the operation with extreme interest. The reporter held his chronometer in his hand, ready to tell the hour which it marked when the shadow would be at its shortest. Moreover, as Cyrus Harding was working on the 16th of April, the day on which the true and the average time are identical, the hour given by Gideon Spilett would be the true hour then at Washington, which would simplify the calculation. Meanwhile as the sun slowly advanced, the shadow slowly diminished, and when it appeared to Cyrus Harding that it was beginning to increase, he asked, "What o'clock is it?"

"One minute past five," replied Gideon Spilett directly. They had now only to calculate the operation. Nothing could be easier. It could be seen that there existed, in round numbers, a difference of five hours between the meridian of Washington and that of Lincoln Island, that is to say, it was midday in Lincoln Island when it was already five o'clock in the evening in Washington. Now the sun, in its apparent movement round the earth, traverses one degree in four minutes, or fifteen degrees an hour. Fifteen degrees multiplied by five hours give seventy-five degrees.

Then, since Washington is 77° 3' 11" as much as to say seventy-seven degrees counted from the meridian of Greenwich which the Americans take for their starting-point for longitudes concurrently with the English – it followed that the island must be situated seventy-seven and seventy-five degrees west of the meridian of Greenwich, that is to say, on the hundred and fifty-second degree of west longitude.

Cyrus Harding announced this result to his companions, and taking into consideration errors of observation, as he had done for the latitude, he believed he could positively affirm that the position of Lincoln Island was between the thirty-fifth and the thirty-seventh parallel, and between the hundred and fiftieth and the hundred and fifty-fifth meridian to the west of the meridian of Greenwich.

The possible fault which he attributed to errors in the observation was, it may be seen, of five degrees on both sides, which, at sixty miles to a degree, would give an error of three hundred miles in latitude and longitude for the exact position.

But this error would not influence the determination which it was necessary to take. It was very evident that Lincoln Island was at such a distance from every country or island that it would be too hazardous to attempt to reach one in a frail boat.

In fact, this calculation placed it at least twelve hundred miles from Tahiti and the islands of the archipelago of the Pomoutous, more than eighteen hundred miles from New Zealand, and more than four thousand five hundred miles from the American coast!

And when Cyrus Harding consulted his memory, he could not remember in any way that such an island occupied, in that part of the Pacific, the situation assigned to Lincoln Island.

Of Myths and Gods – Anyanwu, the Sun God

Amanda Ilozumba

THE NIGHT IS DARK; there is naught a sound to be heard except the occasional crackling noise from the burning fire. You sit far away from the flames so as not to feel its scorching heat; the fire lights up your eyes and reveals your wariness, it knows you fear it so it burns brighter, reveling in that fear. You need not fear the fire; come closer dear reader; you must trust me, for I want to tell you a story.

A story of myths and gods.

* * *

In a far far away land during a time when humans were one with the earth, we bathed in the flowing streams and slept under the starry night skies. Our flesh was the color of obsidian; black and resplendent, our hair grew towards the sun in a mass of untamable curls. We worshipped the ones who created us, the old gods. We offered them dry spirits by morning and sacrifices of boiled yam bathed in rich red oil by night. In return, the gods blessed us with bountiful harvests and successful hunts.

With time as human nature demands, we grew lazy and became greedy, we wanted power and lusted for one another, worst of all we grew proud and began to believe that we were better than the old gods were.

We stopped offering sacrifices to the gods, stopped worshipping them and soon enough we forgot about them. Our belief in them waned and the old gods grew weaker for they drew their powers from our servitude.

The gods sent down a messenger from the heavens, his name was Nri. He spoke to us but we laughed and hurled insults at him, we ridiculed the old gods while we drank palm wine from the trees they gave us, we made a mockery of them while we ate food from the bountiful harvests they gifted us and so the old gods grew angry and turned against humans.

They regretted creating humans, one by one, they took back all they had gifted us and left us with nothing but our nakedness. We were plunged into eternal darkness, there was no good food to eat so we fed on leaves from left over trees and withered grass, we drank water from murky smelly streams and made fires from twigs to keep warm but that was not the worst of our punishment.

Oh, no it was not.

Without the sun, we lost our melanin. Our once beautiful dark skin turned the color of milk. White, pale and ghost-like. We wandered the earth like wraiths wailing and pleading with the gods, we rolled on the muddy earth and tore our hair from our scalps, pleading and pleading until the old gods were saddened by our pitiful state. We were their creation after all. They made us a promise.

"Journey through the forest of the deadly sins
Find the calabash that contains the sun
If this is done
Then the light will return."

There was one problem with this promise, to get the sun, one would have to pass seven tests of virtue in the forest of deadly sins; since humans had grown proud, lazy, greedy, envious, lustful, angry and gluttonous it was almost impossible for us to pass the test.

For years, we sent our bravest and purest of hearts into the forest but none returned. We lost all hope and resigned to our fate.

This is where the hero of our story comes in.

A child was born, his cries were deafening and it drew the attention of the people. He was the first child to have cried in a long time. When we saw him, we danced and rejoiced for his skin was the color of smooth ebony. The land was filled with merriment, our hope was renewed and we named the boy child Anyanwu-anyi meaning "our light".

Alas, hope is a fickle thing and just like trust, it is often placed in the wrong people. It did not take long for us to see that Anyanwu would never make it through the forest; he would never bring us the sun. He possessed the haughtiest of eyes and a tongue swift to lie. His heart devised wicked plans while his feet made haste to run to evil, he often desired that which did not belong to him and made effort only to thieve the belongings of others, never working for his keep. He sowed seeds of discord wherever he went; his fists were controlled by his frequent wrath.

Even a blind man could see that he was of no use to us. In fact, he must have been sent by the old gods to scorn us, to torment and remind humans that we would never see the light again.

When Anyanwu had seen just seventeen moons, he was banished. We became tired of his antics; he was a constant reminder of our plight so we sent him away with nothing but a knife and a gourd of dirty water.

Anyanwu was furious; he swore and stomped his feet, he cursed and he cursed until he had no more curses left in him, then he said, "I will journey through the forest of the deadly sins and bring back the sun. Then you will all worship me."

Our laughter followed close behind him as he entered the deadly forest.

The Land of Pride

For days, Anyanwu stumbled through the ancient forest. The forest was devoid of life giving it a silence that was eerie, the ominous-looking trees had bare branches that spiked into the sky, and it was so dark that Anyanwu was barely able to see where he was going.

The darkness was a different kind from the one in his land; this one was thick and threatened to suffocate him. Despite the fact that there was no sign of life, the forest of deadly sins seemed alive with little hidden secrets that only it knew.

Like a fool, Anyanwu had not thought to manage the water so his throat was dry and parched, his breathing shallow and his vision was becoming blurry by the minute. Anyanwu decided to rest; he leaned against a tree and closed his eyes.

Just for a moment, he assured himself, *then I will continue my journey. Oh how they will regret when I am victorious.* An arrow whizzed past his head pulling him out of his reverie; he whipped out his knife while his eyes darted to the area that he suspected the arrow had come from.

"Who goes there!" he yelled, "show yourself! Only a coward hides behind a weapon."

Despite his bravado, Anyanwu was afraid and the fear clouded his mind so he had no chance of evading the next arrow. It struck him squarely in his thighs, Anyanwu groaned, he buckled and collapsed to the ground.

The last thing he saw before his eyes closed was a horse with the upper body of a human.

When Anyanwu regained his consciousness he found himself in a sick room; his arrow wound had been cleaned and wrapped with banana leaves, he touched it and was surprised to find that the wound did not hurt. In fact, he felt healed. He got up, limped to the door, and pushed it open.

Bright light struck his eyes and Anyanwu instinctively shielded them as he fell to the ground screaming in pain, "What is this, what is this strange evil!"

He felt a kick in his side followed by a voice that said, "Rise, human, it is the day that hurts your eyes, open your eyes and taken in the splendor of the land."

Anyanwu slowly removed his hand from his eyes, *was this how his land would look like when he brought the sun?* Anyanwu was mesmerized. As his eyes gradually adjusted to the brightness of the day, Anyanwu realized that the half-horse-half-men people surrounded him. He took in the majestic land of the horse people but it was not as majestic as they were. Colorful beads adorned their lower halves while their upper bodies were covered with stylish ankara.

"What sort of creatures are you?" Anyanwu asked.

The crowd parted to make way for their king who sauntered regally to the front of the clearing; the king answered Anyanwu's question, "We are horse-men and this is the land of Pride. If you seek to pass through my kingdom, I will offer you what I offered the men and women before you."

The king stretched out his right hand, the jewelry adorning his fingers glinting in the sunlight, "You must kneel before my people and me and kiss my hand." However, the king knew that this would never happen; he had looked into Anyanwu's heart and saw his pride so it did not come as a surprise to him when Anyanwu spat on his outstretched hand.

Anyanwu was taken to their latrine where he was whipped every day and forced to haul feces.

On the fifth day, Anyanwu requested an audience with the horseman king. He was cleaned up and taken to the great hall where the king and his subjects awaited him.

Upon seeing the king, Anyanwu dropped to his knees and said, "I vowed to my people that I would bring back the sun. I vowed to make them regret their decision to banish me and that is what I must do. Therefore, I will kneel for I have discovered that I must put away my pride…for now."

The horseman king was amazed, the other humans before Anyanwu had kneeled before him but it was just so they could be granted safe passage through his land. He knew this because he had sensed the pride that was still in their hearts yet the one who kneeled before him made no effort to do such a thing. Anyanwu had learned humility but was not rid of his pride. A strange thing.

The king frowned as he cleared his throat, his baritone voice rang clear and true. "Your motivation is fueled by pride yet you kneel before me. I do not know what to make of you human, you may leave."

The Land of Wrath

The land of wrath was a wasteland. It was filled with flying debris but the debris was not the only enemy in the land of wrath, the ground was riddled with volcanic mounds that erupted every now and then. In addition, there were the bear people, half-human-half-bear, who despised humans and it was here that many of the humans who came before Anyanwu had perished.

The bear people were full of rage; they fought at the slightest confrontation and killed each other without remorse, this Anyanwu discovered immediately upon entering their land.

Anyanwu demanded an audience with their king but the bear people laughed at him. They dragged Anyanwu to an arena where they fitted him with armor and a sword and told him, "If you wish to see our king, you must fight."

Anyanwu's opponent was a huge bear-man that bore many scars, the bear-man wasted no time in drawing his sword. Anyanwu danced around the bear-man, his strategy was to block the blows of his opponent until his strength waned and then he would attack but this strategy backfired on him.

The bear-man seemed to grow in strength with each blow he dealt and he had a big mouth too, he hurled insults at Anyanwu. Painful and degrading insults that made the boy see red; anger clouded his judgment and concentration.

The bear-man called Anyanwu a weakling, which was the last straw. Anyanwu bellowed and attacked but the bear-man easily deflected his blow, his sword flashed as he raised it high above his furry head to deal the final blow that would kill Anyanwu.

Anyanwu nimbly jumped out of the way and crossed his arms in a sign of peace, "I yield." The bear-man spat at him and the bear people who watched the fight booed. They called him a coward and threw him out of the arena.

Anyanwu solicited to see the king again but the bear people told him, "Then you will fight again."

They left him at the entrance to the battlefield; a fight was currently going on. Anyanwu watched the duel. It was between his former opponent and another bear-man. Again, he hurled insults at his new opponent who reacted to the slurs by lashing out in any direction he could.

His rage made him sloppy as well as careless, *just like I had been*, Anyanwu realized. An angry person was an easily controlled person; with the right words, you could disarm him. It was not long before the angry bear-man was defeated. Cheers rang in the arena as the bear people chanted the victors' name. He beat his chest three times and roared and the cheers became louder.

A strong paw gripped Anyanwu's arm. "Your turn," the bear-man grunted before he pushed Anyanwu into the arena to face the victor.

The bear-man laughed when he saw Anyanwu. "The flesh thing has come to play again."

They danced once more, clashing swords and exchanging insults sharper than any blade. Anyanwu did not let his anger distract him this time, instead he let it fuel the strength of his attacks, and the duel went on for hours until the bear-man showed his first sign of weakness. With one strong thrust, Anyanwu pushed his sword into the heart of his opponent, and the bear-man fell.

Anyanwu threw down his sword, he beat his chest three times just as his dead opponent had done, and he roared, "Take me to your king!"

The king was a bear-man of little patience. "What does the filthy flesh-thing want?"

Anyanwu tamped down the anger that surged through him in reaction to the insult; he took a few moments to collect his thoughts before he said anything. He now understood why his people hated him; while they were not without their own flaws, his was worse. He was just like the bear people, swift to respond to anger with violence. He made up his mind there and then to express his anger better in the nearest future.

"Bear people I now see that I must control my anger before it controls me and that is a lesson you all must learn too. I offer my sincere gratitude for having being able to learn this in your land." Anyanwu finished his speech with a bow.

The hall was silent for a moment then the silence was broken by the clap of the bear king, he rose from his throne and lumbered to Anyanwu. "You have seen the error of your ways, anger is good but destructive when not controlled. You have passed the test. I grant you safe passage through my lands."

The Land of Sloth, Envy and Lust

Anyanwu was now aware of his many flaws and he was frightened by them. It was with this fear that he approached the land of sloth, envy and lust occupied by fairies.

The fairies lived in grand castles; they had a natural sunny glow and yellow coily hair the hue of butter. Their wings were shimmery and sparkled with all the colors of the rainbow.

Upon his arrival, the fairies threw a huge party for Anyanwu, they sang and danced for him, plied him with juicy berries and sugary wine that sent him into a heady stupor. Anyanwu soon forgot about his quest and settled in comfortably with the fairies in the land of sloth, envy and lust.

He partied day and night without a care, there was overflowing food and wine so Anwanyu did not need to lift a finger except to stuff his belly full. He hopped and skipped with the beautiful fairy women that flocked around him while the men envied him. Anyanwu was having the time of his life.

Occasionally he would remember the calabash containing the sun but then a fairy woman would smile ever so sweetly at him and he would brush the memory away and return to his merriment.

On the eighth day, Anyanwu happened upon another human who was pale and gaunt looking, the slightest breeze could have blown him away. Anyanwu approached the man and asked, "Who are you and why are you here?" Anyanwu was jealous to see another human receiving attention from the fairy women. He intended to send the man away.

"My name is Odinaka and I am on a journey to find the sun and return light to my people." His reply shocked Anyanwu out of his drunken state. He gazed down at his hands to see that his flesh had withered and was beginning to resemble that of Odinaka. He backed away from the man, slowly at first then his legs began to pick up pace until he was running.

The fairies watched him run away. The fairy women were sad to see their human plaything go but the men were happy because it meant their women would return to them. The fairies resumed their jollity and before long, they forgot about Anyanwu.

The Land of Covetousness and Gluttony

Dwarves, greedy little things that dwelled in the mountains and mined underground tunnels and caves for gold and precious stones, governed the land of covetousness and gluttony. Their land had piles of gold scattered here and there, their miniature bodies were covered head to toe in glittering jewelry yet they craved for more.

Compared to the other lands where Anyanwu had had to ask to see their king, the dwarves welcomed him as if he was a long-expected visitor. They put him in a carriage made of gold and pulled by magnificent horses.

The dwarves took him to the throne hall where their king presided. The king sat upon a throne fashioned out of one entire piece of gold and he had a great golden crown on his large head. In one hand, he held a diamond staff and in the other a silver sword; and on both sides of him stood dwarves all arranged according to their size, from the tallest of dwarves to the tiniest (the size of Anyanwu's thumb).

Anyanwu begged the king for passage through his lands so he could find the calabash than contained the sun.

However, the dwarf king said, "Why look for a stupid sun when you can live here with us, you wish to return the light to your people who banished you, ha! I will fill your pockets with gold and your house with gemstones. Food and wine would be overflowing, you will never have to lift a hand, never have to want for anything. All that you desire is here," the dwarf king said as he spread his hands across the expanse of the hall.

To this, Anyanwu replied, "In the land of sloth, envy and lust, I came across another human who had been on this same quest. He had the most beautiful women feeding him, he did not need to do any work, he seemed to be living the life I always wanted but he was losing his soul. My journey here has showed me that as a human, I am full of flaws but my flaws do not define me unless I let them. I know now what I must do; it does not matter if I get the sun. I must go back to my people to show them the error of their ways, to teach them seven virtues in place of the deadly sins. I will show them that where there is kindness and love, hard work and humility, then there will be light. The boy I was before would have wasted no time in accepting the riches you offer but I must refuse. My people need me, I cannot live here in splendor while they suffer, I cannot taste your sumptuous meals while they feed on grass and leaves."

"You are no boy little flesh thing," the dwarf king praised. "A boy would never have passed the seven tests; a boy would not have understood what the old gods have been trying to teach you humans for years. You are a man, Anyanwu." With this, the throne hall changed into the heavens and the dwarf king transformed into Chukwu, the supreme beings, the God of gods.

Chukwu beckoned Anyanwu to follow him and he took Anyanwu into a chamber where he washed him in heavenly water to cleanse him of his old self, and then Chukwu carved lines from the center of Anyanwu's forehead down to the center of his chin, then from his right cheek to the left. The lines met at the centre of his nose forming a perfect cross.

Chukwu drew another line from the left side of Anyanwu's forehead down to the right side of his chin. When Chukwu finished, the pattern looked like the rays of sun. Sixteen straight lines and eight crosses that mirrored the rays of the sun.

Chukwu stepped back and admired his work, he then placed a golden crown on Anyanwu's head, it was the crown of virtues. Chukwu declared, "You are now Anyanwu; the sun god, god of wisdom and foresight."

Home

When Anyanwu returned to us, we did not recognize him; had it not been for his ebony skin we would have never believed it was he. Apart from the scarification on his face, Anyanwu physically appeared the same as when we had banished him but when one looked closer, you could see the ethereal glow of his skin. Chukwu an immortal had bathed Anyanwu so he was no longer one of the earth.

One by one, we fell in line behind him, following him in awe. Anyanwu stood in the middle of our land and there he opened the calabash. "Behold!"

Golden light spilled out of the calabash into the dark sky, it was bright and hot, it had been long since our eyes saw light so we turned away shielding our eyes. Where the light touched, the darkness dispelled.

For the first time in years, the sun, the daughter of the sky, took her place on the horizon and let her rays cascade onto the world. Where her rays touched, flowers blossomed and trees grew. Dry land turned to streams of clear flowing water and the animals that had long abandoned us emerged from the forest of deadly sins; with them came the horsemen and the bear people, the fairies and the dwarves, they joined us to stand behind Anyanwu.

Together, we bowed down to our knees before him and proclaimed, "Long live Anyanwu, the sun god, the one who brought the light!"

Niobe

From Greek mythology

> *"...Like Niobe, all tears."*
> **William Shakespeare**

THE QUOTATION IS an overworked quotation, like many another of those from *Hamlet*; yet, have half of those whose lips utter it more than the vaguest acquaintance with the story of Niobe and the cause of her tears? The noble group – attributed to Praxiteles – of Niobe and her last remaining child, in the Uffizi Palace at Florence, has been so often reproduced that it also has helped to make the anguished figure of the Theban queen a familiar one in pictorial tragedy, so that as long as the works of those Titans of art, Shakespeare and Praxiteles, endure, no other monument is wanted for the memory of Niobe.

Like many of the tales of mythology, her tragedy is a story of vengeance wreaked upon a mortal by an angry god. She was the daughter of Tantalus, and her husband was Amphion, King of Thebes, himself a son of Zeus. To her were born seven fair daughters and seven beautiful and gallant sons, and it was not because of her own beauty, nor her husband's fame, nor their proud descent and the greatness of their kingdom, that the Queen of Thebes was arrogant in her pride. Very sure she was that no woman had ever borne children like her own children, whose peers were not to be found on earth nor in heaven. Even in our own day there are mortal mothers who feel as Niobe felt.

But amongst the Immortals there was also a mother with children whom she counted as peerless. Latona, mother of Apollo and Diana, was magnificently certain that not in all time, nor in eternity to come, could there be a son and daughter so perfect in beauty, in wisdom, and in power as the two that were her own. Loudly did she proclaim her proud belief, and when Niobe heard it she laughed in scorn.

"The goddess has a son and a daughter," she said. "Beautiful and wise and powerful they may be, but I have borne seven daughters and seven sons, and each son is more than the peer of Apollo, each daughter more than the equal of Diana, the moon-goddess!"

And to her boastful words Latona gave ear, and anger began to grow in her heart.

Each year the people of Thebes were wont to hold a great festival in honour of Latona and her son and daughter, and it was an evil day for Niobe when she came upon the adoring crowd that, laurel-crowned, bore frankincense to lay before the altars of the gods whose glories they had assembled together to celebrate.

"Oh foolish ones!" she said, and her voice was full of scorn, "am I not greater than Latona? I am the daughter of a goddess, my husband, the king, the son of a god. Am I not fair? Am I not queenly as Latona herself? And, of a surety, I am richer by far than the goddess who has but one daughter and one son. Look on my seven noble sons! Behold the beauty of my seven daughters, and see if they in beauty and all else do not equal the dwellers in Olympus!"

And when the people looked, and shouted aloud, for in truth Niobe and her children were like unto gods, their queen said, "Do not waste thy worship, my people. Rather make the prayers to thy king and to me and to my children who buttress us round and make our strength so great, that fearlessly we can despise the gods."

In her home on the Cynthian mountaintop, Latona heard the arrogant words of the Queen of Thebes, and even as a gust of wind blows smouldering ashes into a consuming fire, her growing anger flamed into rage. She called Apollo and Diana to her, and commanded them to avenge the blasphemous insult which had been given to them and to their mother. And the twin gods listened with burning hearts.

"Truly shalt thou be avenged!" cried Apollo. "The shameless one shall learn that not unscathed goes she who profanes the honour of the mother of the deathless gods!"

And with their silver bows in their hands, Apollo, the smiter from afar, and Diana, the virgin huntress, hasted to Thebes. There they found all the noble youths of the kingdom pursuing their sports. Some rode, some were having chariot-races, and excelling in all things were the seven sons of Niobe.

Apollo lost no time. A shaft from his quiver flew, as flies a bolt from the hand of Zeus, and the first-born of Niobe fell, like a young pine broken by the wind, on the floor of his winning chariot. His brother, who followed him, went on the heels of his comrade swiftly down to the Shades. Two of the other sons of Niobe were wrestling together, their great muscles moving under the skin of white satin that covered their perfect bodies, and as they gripped each other, yet another shaft was driven from the bow of Apollo, and both lads fell, joined by one arrow, on the earth, and there breathed their lives away.

Their elder brother ran to their aid, and to him, too, came death, swift and sure. The two youngest, even as they cried for mercy to an unknown god, were hurried after them by the unerring arrows of Apollo. The cries of those who watched this terrible slaying were not long in bringing Niobe to the place where her sons lay dead. Yet, even then, her pride was unconquered, and she defied the gods, and Latona, to whose jealousy she ascribed the fate of her "seven spears."

"Not yet hast thou conquered, Latona!" she cried. "My seven sons lie dead, yet to me still remain the seven perfect lovelinesses that I have borne. Try to match them, if thou canst, with the beauty of thy two! Still am I richer than thou, O cruel and envious mother of one daughter and one son!"

But even as she spoke, Diana had drawn her bow, and as the scythe of a mower quickly cuts down, one after the other, the tall white blossoms in the meadow, so did her arrows slay the daughters of Niobe. When one only remained, the pride of Niobe was broken. With her arms round the little slender frame of her golden-haired youngest born, she looked up to heaven, and cried upon all the gods for mercy.

"She is so little!" she wailed. "So young – so dear! Ah, spare me *one*," she said, "only one out of so many!"

But the gods laughed. Like a harsh note of music sounded the twang of Diana's bow. Pierced by a silver arrow, the little girl lay dead. The dignity of Latona was avenged.

Overwhelmed by despair, King Amphion killed himself, and Niobe was left alone to gaze on the ruin around her. For nine days she sat, a Greek Rachel, weeping for her children and refusing to be comforted, because they were not. On the tenth day, the sight was too much even for the superhuman hearts of the gods to endure. They turned the bodies into stone and themselves buried them. And when they looked on the face of Niobe and saw on it a bleeding anguish that no human hand could stay nor the word of any god comfort, the gods were merciful. Her grief was immortalized, for Niobe, at their will, became a stone, and was carried by a wailing tempest to the summit of Mount Sipylus, in Lydia, where a spring of Argos bore her name. Yet although a rock was Niobe, from her blind eyes of stone the tears still flowed, a clear stream of running water, symbol of a mother's anguish and never-ending grief.

The North Wind and the Sun

Aesop

A DISPUTE AROSE between the North Wind and the Sun, each claiming that he was stronger than the other. At last they agreed to try their powers upon a traveller, to see which could soonest strip him of his cloak. The North Wind had the first try; and, gathering up all his force for the attack, he came whirling furiously down upon the man, and caught up his cloak as though he would wrest it from him by one single effort: but the harder he blew, the more closely the man wrapped it round himself. Then came the turn of the Sun. At first he beamed gently upon the traveller, who soon unclasped his cloak and walked on with it hanging loosely about his shoulders: then he shone forth in his full strength, and the man, before he had gone many steps, was glad to throw his cloak right off and complete his journey more lightly clad.

Persuasion is better than force.

The Origin of Strawberries

From the Cherokee people

WHEN THE FIRST MAN was created and a mate was given to him, they lived together very happily for a time, but then began to quarrel, until at last the woman left her husband and started off toward Nûñdagûñ'yĭ, the Sun land, in the east. The man followed alone and grieving, but the woman kept on steadily ahead and never looked behind, until Une''lănûñ'hĭ, the great Apportioner (the Sun), took pity on him and asked him if he was still angry with his wife. He said he was not, and Une''lănûñ'hĭ then asked him if he would like to have her back again, to which he eagerly answered yes.

So Une''lănûñ'hĭ caused a patch of the finest ripe huckleberries to spring up along the path in front of the woman, but she passed by without paying any attention to them. Farther on he put a clump of blackberries, but these also she refused to notice. Other fruits, one, two, and three, and then some trees covered with beautiful red service berries, were placed beside the path to tempt her, but she still went on until suddenly she saw in front a patch of large ripe strawberries, the first ever known. She stooped to gather a few to eat, and as she picked them, she chanced to turn her face to the west, and at once the memory of her husband came back to her and she found herself unable to go on. She sat down, but the longer she waited the stronger became her desire for her husband, and at last she gathered a bunch of the finest berries and started back along the path to give them to him. He met her kindly and they went home together.

Phaeton

From Greek mythology

"The road, to drive on which unskilled were Phaeton's hands."
Dante Alighieri

TO APOLLO, THE SUN-GOD, and Clymene, a beautiful ocean-nymph, there was born in the pleasant land of Greece a child to whom was given the name of Phaeton, the Bright and Shining One. The rays of the sun seemed to live in the curls of the fearless little lad, and when at noon other children would seek the cool shade of the cypress groves, Phaeton would hold his head aloft and gaze fearlessly up at the brazen sky from whence fierce heat beat down upon his golden head.

"Behold, my father drives his chariot across the heavens!" he proudly proclaimed. "In a little while I, also, will drive the four snow-white steeds."

His elders heard the childish boast with a smile, but when Epaphos, half-brother to Apollo, had listened to it many times and beheld the child, Phaeton, grow into an arrogant lad who held himself as though he were indeed one of the Immortals, anger grew in his heart. One day he turned upon Phaeton and spoke in fierce scorn:

"Dost say thou art son of a god? A shameless boaster and a liar art thou! Hast ever spoken to thy divine sire? Give us some proof of thy sonship! No more child of the glorious Apollo art thou than are the vermin his children, that the sun breeds in the dust at my feet."

For a moment, before the cruel taunt, the lad was stricken into silence, and then, his pride aflame, his young voice shaking with rage and with bitter shame, he cried aloud, "Thou, Epaphos, art the liar. I have but to ask my father, and thou shalt see me drive his golden chariot across the sky."

To his mother he hastened, to get balm for his hurt pride, as many a time he had got it for the little bodily wounds of childhood, and with bursting heart he poured forth his story.

"True it is," he said, "that my father has never deigned to speak to me. Yet I know, because thou hast told me so, that he is my sire. And now my word is pledged. Apollo must let me drive his steeds, else I am for evermore branded braggart and liar, and shamed amongst men."

Clymene listened with grief to his complaint. He was so young, so gallant, so foolish.

"Truly thou art the son of Apollo," she said, "and oh, son of my heart, thy beauty is his, and thy pride the pride of a son of the gods. Yet only partly a god art thou, and though thy proud courage would dare all things, it were mad folly to think of doing what a god alone can do."

But at last she said to him, "Naught that I can say is of any avail. Go, seek thy father, and ask him what thou wilt." Then she told him how he might find the place in the east where Apollo rested ere the labours of the day began, and with eager gladness Phaeton set out upon his journey. A long way he travelled, with never a stop, yet when the glittering dome and jewelled turrets and minarets of the Palace of the Sun came into view, he forgot his weariness and hastened up the steep ascent to the home of his father.

Phoebus Apollo, clad in purple that glowed like the radiance of a cloud in the sunset sky, sat upon his golden throne. The Day, the Month, and the Year stood by him, and beside them were the Hours. Spring was there, her head wreathed with flowers; Summer, crowned with ripened grain; Autumn, with his feet empurpled by the juice of the grapes; and Winter, with hair all white and stiff with hoarfrost. And when Phaeton walked up the golden steps that led to his father's throne, it seemed as though incarnate Youth had come to join the court of the god of the Sun, and that Youth was so beautiful a thing that it must surely live forever. Proudly did Apollo know him for his son, and when the boy looked in his eyes with the arrogant fearlessness of boyhood, the god greeted him kindly and asked him to tell him why he came, and what was his petition.

As to Clymene, so also to Apollo, Phaeton told his tale, and his father listened, half in pride and amusement, half in puzzled vexation. When the boy stopped, and then breathlessly, with shining eyes and flushed cheeks, ended up his story with, "And, O light of the boundless world, if I am indeed thy son, let it be as I have said, and for one day only let me drive thy chariot across the heavens!" Apollo shook his head and answered very gravely:

"In truth thou art my dear son," he said, "and by the dreadful Styx, the river of the dead, I swear that I will give thee any gift that thou dost name and that will give proof that thy father is the immortal Apollo. But never to thee nor to any other, be he mortal or immortal, shall I grant the boon of driving my chariot."

But the boy pled on:

"I am shamed forever, my father," he said. "Surely thou wouldst not have son of thine proved liar and braggart?"

"Not even the gods themselves can do this thing," answered Apollo. "Nay, not even the almighty Zeus. None but I, Phoebus Apollo, may drive the flaming chariot of the sun, for the way is beset with dangers and none know it but I."

"Only tell me the way, my father!" cried Phaeton. "So soon I could learn."

Half in sadness, Apollo smiled.

"The first part of the way is uphill," he said. "So steep it is that only very slowly can my horses climb it. High in the heavens is the middle, so high that even I grow dizzy when I look down upon the earth and the sea. And the last piece of the way is a precipice that rushes so steeply downward that my hands can scarce check the mad rush of my galloping horses. And all the while, the heaven is spinning round, and the stars with it. By the horns of the Bull I have to drive, past the Archer whose bow is taut and ready to slay, close to where the Scorpion stretches out its arms and the great Crab's claws grope for a prey...."

"I fear none of these things, oh my father!" cried Phaeton. "Grant that for one day only I drive thy white-maned steeds!"

Very pitifully Apollo looked at him, and for a little space he was silent.

"The little human hands," he said at length, "the little human frame! And with them the soul of a god. The pity of it, my son. Dost not know that the boon that thou dost crave from me is Death?"

"Rather Death than Dishonour," said Phaeton, and proudly he added, "For once would I drive like the god, my father. I have no fear."

So was Apollo vanquished, and Phaeton gained his heart's desire.

From the courtyard of the Palace the four white horses were led, and they pawed the air and neighed aloud in the glory of their strength. They drew the chariot whose axle and pole and wheels were of gold, with spokes of silver, while inside were rows of diamonds and of chrysolites that gave dazzling reflection of the sun. Then Apollo anointed the face of Phaeton with a powerful essence that might keep him from being smitten by the flames, and upon his head he placed the rays of the sun. And then the stars went away, even to the Daystar that went last of all, and, at Apollo's signal, Aurora, the rosy-fingered, threw open the purple gates of the east, and Phaeton saw a path of pale rose-colour open before him.

With a cry of exultation, the boy leapt into the chariot and laid hold of the golden reins. Barely did he hear Apollo's parting words, "Hold fast the reins, and spare the whip. All thy strength will be wanted to hold the horses in. Go not too high nor too low. The middle course is safest and best. Follow, if thou canst, in the old tracks of my chariot wheels!" His glad voice of thanks for the godlike boon rang back to where Apollo stood and watched him vanishing into the dawn that still was soft in hue as the feathers on the breast of a dove.

Uphill at first the white steeds made their way, and the fire from their nostrils tinged with flame-colour the dark clouds that hung over the land and the sea. With rapture, Phaeton felt that truly he was the son of a god, and that at length he was enjoying his heritage. The day for which, through all his short life, he had longed, had come at last. He was driving the chariot whose progress even now was awaking the sleeping earth. The radiance from its wheels and from the rays he wore round his head was painting the clouds, and he laughed aloud in rapture as he saw, far down below, the sea and the rivers he had bathed in as a human boy, mirroring the green and rose and purple, and gold and silver, and fierce crimson, that he, Phaeton, was placing in the sky. The grey mist rolled from the mountaintops at his desire. The white fog rolled up from the valleys. All living things awoke; the flowers opened their petals; the grain grew golden; the fruit grew ripe. Could but Epaphos see him now! Surely he must see him, and realize that not Apollo but Phaeton was guiding the horses of his father, driving the chariot of the Sun.

Quicker and yet more quick grew the pace of the white-maned steeds. Soon they left the morning breezes behind, and very soon they knew that these were not the hands of the god, their master, that held the golden reins. Like an airship without its accustomed ballast, the chariot rolled unsteadily, and not only the boy's light weight but his light hold on their bridles made them grow mad with a lust for speed. The white foam flew from their mouths like the spume from the giant waves of a furious sea, and their pace was swift as that of a bolt that is cast by the arm of Zeus.

Yet Phaeton had no fear, and when they heard him shout in rapture, "Quicker still, brave ones! More swiftly still!" It made them speed onwards, madly, blindly, with the headlong rush of a storm. There was no hope for them to keep on the beaten track, and soon Phaeton had his rapture checked by the terrible realization that they had strayed far out of the course and that his hands were not strong enough to guide them. Close to the Great Bear and the Little Bear they passed, and these were scorched with heat. The Serpent which, torpid, chilly and harmless, lies coiled round the North Pole, felt a warmth that made it grow fierce and harmful again. Downward, ever downward galloped the maddened horses, and soon Phaeton saw the sea as a shield of molten brass, and the earth so near that all things on it were visible. When they passed the Scorpion and only just missed destruction from its menacing fangs, fear entered into the boy's heart. His mother had spoken truth. He was only partly a god, and he was very, very young. In impotent horror he tugged at the reins to try to check the horses' descent, then, forgetful of Apollo's warning, he smote them angrily. But anger met anger, and the fury of the immortal steeds had scorn for the wrath of a mortal boy. With a great toss of their mighty heads they had torn the guiding reins from his grasp, and as he stood, giddily swaying from side to side, Phaeton knew that the boon he had craved from his father must in truth be death for him.

And, lo, it was a hideous death, for with eyes that were like flames that burned his brain, the boy beheld the terrible havoc that his pride had wrought. That blazing chariot of the Sun made the clouds smoke, and dried up all the rivers and water-springs. Fire burst from the mountaintops, great cities were destroyed. The beauty of the earth was ravished, woods and meadows and all green and pleasant places were laid waste. The harvests perished, the flocks and they who had herded them lay dead. Over Libya the horses took him, and the desert of Libya remains a barren wilderness to this day, while those sturdy Ethiopians who survived are black even now as a consequence of that cruel heat. The Nile changed its course in order to escape, and nymphs and nereids in terror sought for the sanctuary of some watery place that had escaped destruction. The face of the burned and blackened earth, where the bodies of thousands of human beings lay charred to ashes, cracked and sent dismay to Pluto by the lurid light that penetrated even to his throne.

All this Phaeton saw, saw in impotent agony of soul. His boyish folly and pride had been great, but the excruciating anguish that made him shed tears of blood, was indeed a punishment even too heavy for an erring god.

From the havoc around her, the Earth at last looked up, and with blackened face and blinded eyes, and in a voice that was harsh and very, very weary, she called to Zeus to look down from Olympus and behold the ruin that had been wrought by the chariot of the Sun. And Zeus, the cloud-gatherer, looked down and beheld. And at the sight of that piteous devastation his brow grew dark, and terrible was his wrath against him who had held the reins of the chariot. Calling upon Apollo and all the other gods to witness him, he seized a lightning bolt, and for a moment the deathless Zeus and all the dwellers in Olympus looked on the fiery chariot in which stood the swaying, slight, lithe figure of a young lad, blinded with horror, shaken with agony. Then, from his hand, Zeus cast the bolt, and the chariot was dashed into fragments, and Phaeton, his golden hair ablaze, fell, like a bright shooting star, from the heavens above, into the river Eridanus. The steeds returned to their master, Apollo, and in rage and grief Apollo lashed them. Angrily, too, and very rebelliously did he speak of the punishment meted to his son by the ruler of the Immortals. Yet in truth the punishment was a merciful one. Phaeton was only half a god, and no human life were fit to live after the day of dire anguish that had been his.

Bitter was the mourning of Clymene over her beautiful only son, and so ceaselessly did his three sisters, the Heliades, weep for their brother, that the gods turned them into poplar trees that grew by the bank of the river, and, when still they wept, their tears turned into precious amber as they fell. Yet another mourned for Phaeton, "dead ere his prime." Cycnus, King of Liguria, had dearly loved the gallant boy, and again and yet again he dived deep in the river and brought forth the charred fragments of what had once been the beautiful son of a god, and gave to them honourable burial. Yet he could not rest satisfied that he had won all that remained of his friend from the river's bed, and so he continued to haunt the stream, ever diving, ever searching, until the gods grew weary of his restless sorrow and changed him into a swan.

And still we see the swan sailing mournfully along, like a white-sailed barque that is bearing the body of a king to its rest, and ever and anon plunging deep into the water as though the search for the boy who would fain have been a god were never to come to an end.

To Phaeton the Italian Naiades reared a tomb, and inscribed on the stone these words:

"Driver of Phoebus' chariot, Phaëton,
Struck by Jove's thunder, rests beneath this stone,
He could not rule his father's car of fire,
Yet was it much, so nobly to aspire."
Ovid

Ree in the Domain of Scavengers

Katherine Quevedo

BEFORE THE LIGHTNING struck me, I worshipped the Sun and lesser gods like everyone else did. Sun meant respite from the grinners, whose sharp sense of smell and sharper teeth kept us cowering at night in our stilted huts. We came in at the first sign of dusk and waited until well after dawn – the domain of scavengers – to be sure all the grinners had crept back to their caves before we emerged for the day.

The afternoon before the lightning, I found the priest sitting at the foot of the pedestal outside our village. The bone-white pedestal rose waist high. Atop it lay the idol, a gray stone cylinder the size of my forearm – no, thicker, the size of Keesuo's forearm, or one of the other hunters'. The runes snaking around it told of the Sun, of all the gods, in swirling, branching symbols. As long as we kept the idol there, grinners couldn't scale our huts. I tried to feel deeper reverence beyond a selfish gratitude for our safety, as the priest always urged in my studies, but to no avail.

"Ree, what brings you here?" he asked, still studying the runes. With his unmoving posture and clothing of gray scavenger hides – a gift from the hunters – he seemed to be trying to embody the sacred stone.

"I wish to guard the idol tonight."

He faced me, the lines on his forehead deepening in surprise. "You? Whatever for?"

I thought of Keesuo, how triumphantly he'd lifted a slain grinner's head yesterday in his wide, strong hands, showing us the fate of the beast that had cornered his hunting party. Guarding the idol was more ceremonial than anything because of its power, but it would be a first step toward my becoming a huntress.

"To show respect to the Sun," I said.

He peered at me.

I cleared my throat. "And to prove I am ready for adult responsibilities." I didn't want to tell him my other longing, to feel like I fit in with our tribe rather than being singled out as the priest's main pupil, and that I could contribute more than braiding bark rope with Sallok, my little sister.

"Ah, Ree, you've always been one of our deepest thinkers. That's why you're better off studying under me. So much wisdom to be passed down."

The prophet Kullok came to mind, she who had predicted when the Sun once darkened during daytime. And Loa, he of the night of the streaking stars. Fascinating in their way, but of limited use day-to-day.

"I'm honored, Your Brightness. But with all due respect, I admire the hunters and huntresses. They protect us."

"Ah." He nodded. "It's hard to be a deep thinker when our people honor the most basic assurances of survival above all else – which they do for good reason," he admitted.

I fidgeted with my stone necklaces. The pendant of the sacred Sun clacked against the three discs inscribed with symbols for the rains, moon and stars. Sallok always scowled at me when she heard that noise. She worried that the second necklace offended the Sun because it favored other, lesser gods, but the priest never minded it.

Now, he sighed. "Very well. The Sun seemed extra bright today. Perhaps the stars will be too and keep the grinners at bay. Rest up now. You have a long and lonely night ahead of you."

I beamed.

* * *

That humid, windy night, I leaned my spear against the idol's pedestal next to the torch and watched embers fly up, seeking to rejoin the Sun, before being blown sideways. I prayed the flame would hold. The jungle never slept; it barely calmed. Tonight, it seethed with breath-like warm wind, as though to test me now that the Sun had gone to rest with its precious light.

In a pause between gusts, fallen branches crunched nearby – scavengers too eager to wait for dawn, no doubt. Slitted eyes appeared through the leaves, not at knee level where a scavenger's face would be, but above my head. A grinner? They never came this close to the idol. Yet sure enough, a female poked her head out. She was tall, even on all fours. My heart thrummed like a drum. At the sight of me, she opened her mouth and bared knifelike teeth at crooked angles in purple gums.

I reached behind me for my spear and thrust it at the snapping mouth – no, it wasn't my spear, I'd grabbed the idol by mistake! Her jaws closed around it. Her head jerked forward. She swallowed it whole! My heart seemed to stop. What had I done? No, survive first, worry later. This time, my fingers closed around the spear. I jabbed and connected. She recoiled enough for me to see a fresh, long gash gleaming across her nose. Now I bared *my* teeth, hissing and lurching toward her, waving the spear to look as big as possible. She screeched, then turned and bolted.

I collapsed to my haunches. Steadying myself with the spear, I rested my forehead on my arm and tried to breathe.

She ate the idol.

I rocked back and forth, mind racing. I had to track the grinner before daybreak. If she made it back to her cave, we were finished. No way would I go near all those grinners. Even our hunters wouldn't. I couldn't tell them. I didn't want to tell the priest. I had to tell Sallok.

I stole over to the main hut and crept to the corner where she lay in her hammock next to my empty one. I nudged her awake. She blinked at me in the faint blue shadows, her face scrunched in sleepy confusion. I bent to her ear and whispered so those slumbering nearest to us wouldn't hear of my failure and the idol's fate. She clamped her hands over her mouth at the news.

"I must get it back," I finished. "Don't try to talk me out of this. And don't tell anyone, unless I don't return soon after dawn." I left her wide-eyed and trembling among the sleepers.

* * *

I squinted through the dark at broken branches and flattened grass in the hot, hissing jungle. Must be the tracks of the grinner who'd swallowed the idol. I prayed to the

Sun to guide me. I gripped my necklaces and included the lesser gods too, for good measure. I recalled every detail I'd overhead of the hunters' exploits, every description of their alertness and crouching and studying, like my long afternoons with the priest at the pedestal.

I tracked the grinner prints through soft soil well away from the village, into a clearing buzzing with insects. Then, as if to punish me by darkening the sunless sky even more, rainclouds swept in. I hadn't noticed them gathering through the trees, but here in the open I couldn't miss them. They smothered the sky like cloth. The buzzing stopped so suddenly, it set my teeth on edge. The first heavy sheet of rain reached me, drenching my body as though I wept from every pore. I pressed on.

Suddenly, the bolt struck. Bright white absorbed me, heat blasted into me, and sound shocked me. My muscles seized up. My senses died – so too, I thought, had the rest of me. But since I could still think, I wondered if some part of me had survived.

* * *

When sight returned, I was deaf and naked save for my jewelry. I lay sprawled among leaves away from the clearing, unsure if I'd been thrown here or had wandered over and collapsed in a daze. Rain pelted my extremities, and the sensation brought some comfort in the dangerous silence.

My head lolled to the right. My night vision had adjusted enough to make out teeth and eyes a mere arm's length away. With a familiar cut across the nose. The grinner opened her jaws and thrashed her head in an apparent snarl – silent to my damaged ears – then turned and dashed into the undergrowth. I'd never heard of a grinner giving up such easy prey. I tried to sit up, but my body resisted. It was far easier to close my eyes and black out again.

* * *

Hearing returned to my left ear first.

"Her clothes must have burned right off," the priest's voice said. "You're right about the wounds."

"They look just like lightning," Sallok's voice said, softer on my right side. "From her cheek to her hip. Have you ever seen such marks?"

"Never."

So, I hadn't dreamt it up.

"Look, they continue down her leg."

My hearing evened out on both sides. I forced my eyes open.

"Ree!" Sallok's face came into focus. Her eyes brimmed with joyful tears. "I knew you'd wake up."

They'd set me on a woven mat on the floor where the sick go, rather than on my hammock in the main hut. Had anyone other than Sallok expected me to wake back up? She poured water into my mouth from a gourd bowl. I coughed and sat up, my gaze falling onto the marks they'd mentioned. Impossible to miss them. A series of dark, connected branches snaked down my body, chronicling the lightning's path through me. Like the runes on the idol.

The idol. The memory of those jaws closing around it made my head spin.

"We tried all the usual healings for burns," Sallok said. She hugged herself and glanced away. "I'm afraid the marks are permanent."

I traced my finger near the lower half of them, skimming just outside the tender affected skin. I feared touching the design itself, even though it was part of me now.

Sallok reached toward my face, then changed her mind. She'd said the burns started at my cheek. How could I expect her to touch me when I, too, feared touching my burned skin? My heart sank. I could never face anyone again without lightning staring back at them. I would need some sort of ornamentation to hide the mark. A veil perhaps. But the mark would always be there, stranger than any wound from a grinner, a source of repulsion, not pride. Hunters didn't wear veils. I blinked away tears.

Sallok raised her eyebrows at the priest sheepishly, pulled a necklace over her head, and handed it to me. My necklace of the lesser gods. "I didn't want it to bring you ill luck in here," she said.

"I survived," I said, draping it back over my neck with the Sun necklace. "What ill luck is there in that?" My urge for tears faded.

The priest frowned and looked away.

"Do the others know about the idol?" I asked him.

He shook his head. "I can only hide its absence for so long. When we needed a search party for you, I told them you were overeager for your first kill and that's why you went out alone. I'm not sure Keesuo believed me. The burns will be bad enough, but if they hear of the idol, too…"

Sallok whimpered. "What if the grinners come? We have no protection."

I reached for her hand. She hesitated, gazing at my burns through teary eyes, then threw herself upon me in an embrace. As I smoothed her hair, I saw the priest's expression soften.

"Young Sallok," he said, "our idol was taken from us, but we were given Ree back in return."

A poor substitute. Since I couldn't protect my people, I had to get the idol back.

* * *

I prowled the edge of our village at dusk, praying that the same grinner would return. Praying to whom, though, the Sun or the rains of last night? I clasped my necklaces. I felt so lost, more than whenever I'd explored the jungle's writhing depths, more than last night in the dark, searching for grinner tracks by myself.

Now, as the stars appeared above, I heard rustling ahead. I grabbed my spear and crouched, heartbeat thundering in my ears. Three little scavengers emerged. They froze at the sight of me – or perhaps the scent, judging by their pulsating nostrils. I'd never seen them hold so still. Like right after the strike, when the grinner – I decided to call her Gashnose – could've taken me. Yes, something about my scent upset them.

I rose and stepped toward the scavengers. "You're out late."

The sound of my voice made them flee, glaring back once to shriek at me. Me. This contradiction in their eyes, this seared flesh walking. I laughed, and my fear sizzled away. I didn't feel lost anymore. I held out my arms as though I could call lightning through them at will. I couldn't, but my ruined skin filled me with a sense of power I'd never known before, perhaps no other human ever had. Between the scavengers' strange behavior and that of Gashnose, I knew I was no longer prey.

* * *

I dared not test my realization at night, beyond guarding the fringe of the village. Dawn, perhaps, after the grinners had sated themselves in their night hunting. Yet dawn came and went, and I slept through it after my long night watch. I dreamt of blinding flashes, sun-bright, and long bolts piercing the clouds from all sides and joining together before hurtling toward me.

I woke in a sweat, like when the thunderstorm had drenched me. How could the Sun have sent me lightning? Was that not the privilege of the rains alone?

I asked Sallok as much that afternoon. We peeled strips of bark for rope at the foot of a tree. She cocked her head at my question.

"Perhaps you pleased the rains somehow," she said.

I braided bark strips together into a cord. Their frayed edges stuck out from each curve, but despite the breakage, they formed a stronger unit together. I tugged on it to make sure, then added it to the pile. Sallok handed me the next strips.

Footsteps sounded nearby. I leapt to my feet and ducked behind the tree trunk. Word had spread of my burns, and I feared what the others would make of them. Would I be separated for sickness, confined to a lonely mat away from the other villagers for the rest of my days? The priest had pretended to take the idol for cleaning, gaining me at most a day of no questions before its absence came to light.

Absence and light. Again I thought of lightning, and my heartbeat thundered in my skull.

Sallok poked her head around the trunk and peeped, "Keesuo's here to see you."

Did that mean to speak with me or to view my marks? I stepped out, wishing for a veil. He glanced at my cheek, then carefully raised his gaze to mine and kept it there, although I knew the skill of a hunter's peripheral vision. Especially his. He wore strips of grinner hide, proud trophies of his numerous victories.

"Sunlight be upon you, Ree."

I inclined my head at his greeting but couldn't resist saying, "And lightning not be upon you."

He cracked a smile before resuming his seriousness. "I had a deep wound once. I didn't tell anyone because I was ashamed to die a slow death." He'd killed more grinners than the rest of us combined. Of course he expected to die a warrior's death, not suffer from a slow, fatal ailment. "Only one thing drove the sickness away," he continued, leaning closer. "I stabbed a grinner, and its blood dripped onto my wounded arm."

I waited for further explanation. He offered none. "Its blood healed you?" I asked.

He nodded. "And quickly, before anyone could separate me for my sickness." He played with the strip of hide running over his heart, likely from the grinner that had saved him.

So, I had a chance to rid myself of these marks after all. I knew whose blood I wanted. The fact that she'd eaten the idol made her blood all the more potent.

"They no longer see me as prey," I blurted.

His eyes widened. "Grinners? Impossible." He said it softly, questioningly.

"They eat raw flesh. You see what the lightning bolt did to me. The scavengers don't know how to regard me now."

"You're sure the grinners feel the same?"

"I'll find out tonight."

He exhaled, seeming to grapple with a thought. Then he lifted his chin as he did when addressing his hunting party.

"Go sooner, while they sleep. Prey or not, they will see you as a threat. They attack not only to hunt, but to defend themselves too."

I nodded with the gravity of a huntress.

* * *

I reached the grinners' caves just before dusk. I couldn't tell whether the long shadows of the canyon wall threatened or beckoned me, but I walked into its shade with my freshly sharpened spear at the ready. The cave entrances came into view, lined with sharp rocks like gaping grinner mouths. The closer I came to where the foliage ended and those forsaken tunnels started, the louder I heard a wheezing, labored breath from outside. I surveyed my surroundings and spied what looked like a boulder near the fringe of vegetation separating me from grinner territory. The top rose and fell and shuddered. A grinner. But why outside the caves?

She turned to me in a flash. Gashnose. She knew me, I saw it in her glare. She struggled to her feet. The other grinners must have forced her out here to distance themselves from her sickness from swallowing the idol. Apparently they did as we did. Strong survival instincts, both our types. Protect the group at any cost – like my decision to come here, alone.

Hopefully Gashnose's blood would still work, sickness and all. I spat on the dirt in frustration. Why couldn't I have caught her at full health?

Suddenly, she leapt in one bound as far as five of my strides, then faced me in a defensive crouch. Grinners couldn't usually cover that much ground in one leap even in full health. Yes, her blood would do nicely. I adjusted my grip on the spear and advanced, hissing like the jungle on that humid night when we'd met so recently, although it felt like an age ago.

I managed to corner her against the canyon wall, where she swayed unsteadily. It seemed the idol was attacking her from the inside. I had merely come to complete its work. I stabbed her belly, hoping against reason that I'd free the idol from her in the process. Her magical blood sprayed onto my arms. She shrieked and bounded over me into the thicket, her cries such a higher pitch than thunder but just as chilling.

I set my spear down and rubbed her blood into my marked-up skin. My hands quaked with urgency to cover the whole burn, cheek to hip to foot, before the blood dried. Barely enough to go around. As it crusted, I gritted my teeth and tensed my muscles to keep from moving for fear of flaking it off before it could work its healing. How long to wait? The blue light of dusk deepened as I stood alone, fighting shivers of anticipation and hope.

Finally, I scraped a bit away to see if it had worked. My heart fell at the sight of the ruined skin beneath. Even blood that had touched the idol couldn't undo the lightning's work! But why not? Could the rains be so powerful? My vision blurred with tears as I picked at the remaining crust.

Another grinner appeared, roused by Gashnose's earlier cries. This one squinted in the twilight, brighter than she preferred. I dared not crouch to grab my spear. She still saw me, of course, lowered her head, and growled. I froze as she lunged to my side. Her nostrils flared. Her breath covered my neck, fouler and hotter than the jungle's most rancid humid days. I held still, wondering whom to pray to. All of them? Were they jealous gods?

At the scents of my cooked skin and the grinner blood fresh on my body, she released one last, low growl, then turned and fled back into her cave. I sank to my haunches in relief. I panted there for a while. I was still marked but alive.

Finally, I rose and headed back toward the village. No need to rush, even in this failing light. Grinners no longer scared me. That much I'd proved.

However, a new fear set in: the loss of their power over my life. My exhilaration at no longer being prey twisted into an unease that would surely hunt me to the end of my days. I was different now. An outsider. I felt my world shaking, creaking at the corners, a fragile stilted hut in a sudden storm.

I had become a prophet.

But of what? That one could survive lightning? Hardly a useful lesson for my people. Then an idea shocked my mind, coursed through me like the branching path of the lightning bolt, and left its irreversible mark upon me. I was both cooked and raw flesh, and my scar was the dark upon my skin rendered of light. Surely that meant the sun, the lightning, the rains, even the streaking stars... What if they were interwoven like bark rope, strands forming one greater whole? Greater than us, mysterious to human and grinner alike. But could it protect us? Replace our lost idol?

I leaned my head back. "Give me a sign!" I bellowed to the sky, willing my voice to carry like thunder.

The only response came as a soft scrabbling in the underbrush nearby. A scavenger poked its head through the leaves and squawked at me before continuing on a few steps. It peered back and screeched again. My yell should have frightened it well clear of me. What business did a devourer of carcasses have paying attention to me, a noisy living creature?

I followed. It led me – whether intentionally or not – to a clearing much like where the lightning had struck me. No, the same one. The scorched ground still bore witness to that fateful bolt, like my skin. Now, a racket of high-pitched cries sprang from a crowd of scavengers in the center. They feasted upon what appeared to be a grinner's remains, a mess of bones and hide.

As I crossed the grass toward their circle, the tiniest ones hissed at me from the fringe. The larger ones kept their heads down to pick at the bones until I shoved them aside with my feet and the shaft of my spear. They glared at me, reluctant to give up their banquet even though so little of it remained. My confusing scent of cooked yet living flesh won out, and they backed away, shrieking in displeasure.

In the middle of the skeleton lay the idol. Either the poor beast's stomach juices or the most zealous of the scavengers had scuffed it, but it remained whole. The symbols around the circumference had worn away, save one. When read with the other characters, it had meant "All." Now, alone, it meant "The same."

I had asked for a sign.

As I crouched to reclaim our idol, I took Gashnose's skull too, as proof of my kill, my sole moment as a huntress before asserting myself evermore as a prophet.

* * *

Now I know there is something greater than the sun. Greater than lightning too, yes, greater than all things of brightness, because it has the might of the dark as well. It is not some conspiracy of gods. I can't be sure, signs or no, but I think it laughs at our attempts to understand it. I see it in the raucous flash of the grinners' gaze, the thrill and comfort of Sallok's smile, the stooping, opportunistic stance of the scavengers.

Before the lightning struck me, I worshipped the sun and other gods like everyone else did.

Ribbon Red Ribbon White

Damien Mckeating

IT WAS A DAY for magic. Edie Walker recognized the signs as she took her daily stroll around the outskirts of Little Barrow village.

It was the first of May and the world thrummed with the vibrations of spring turning towards summer, the maiden blossoming into a woman. Edie felt the sun warm against her skin and she paused to bathe under an ocean-sky rippled with whisps of white-cloud breakers.

Her path took her along the fields, hedgerows and holloways. The world was in bloom around her, flowers and leaves turning their faces to the golden eye above them. There were birds on the wing, animals darting among the grasses, and a taste of warm honey on the air.

Edie took in the preparations for the festival as she trod her well-worn path along the edge of the Bower's Field. Tents and stalls were already going up. At the centre was the towering May Pole, with its adornment of alternating red and white ribbons stretching out from the top.

Sixty years ago, Edie had danced around that May Pole and been crowned the May Queen. Plenty of young men had come courting that day, hoping for a greenwood wedding. Edie smiled at the memory and caught sight of two tangled bits of ribbon flapping in the hedgerow.

She picked them up, as she always did with any litter she found on her walk. Red and white ribbon, bound together, like a crumpled barber's pole.

Edie felt a shock down her spine.

There was a story about the barber's pole, that the red around the white were the bloodied rags and bandages back when from a barber was also a sawbones. The ribbons in her hands were bloody rags.

"There's going to be blood," she confirmed to herself, and looked across the festival field with new eyes.

She folded the ribbon and put it safely in her coat pocket. The day was the same and yet it was different. The warmth of the sun was familiar, the energy of the coming celebration prickled at the skin, but now there was an underlying urgency.

Harsh cracks of caws sounded behind her, like machine guns in some old black and white movie. In the tall oak across the path from her boundary-walk cackled a magpie.

One for sorrow.

Edie raised her hand to wave to it, the rhyme coming to her lips, when she saw flashes of black and white amongst the leaves.

More than one.

More than two, or three, or four.

She counted carefully.

Nine magpies in the old oak tree. There were more than a few versions of the magpie rhyme, and Edie knew most of them. Seven for a secret, eight for health, and nine for the devil.

"Devil, I defy you," she said. She reached into her other pocket, pulled out a small plastic tub, and from it sprinkled salt onto the ground.

It was a day of light, but the light attracted shadow-things.

Footsteps made her turn. There was a young woman coming down the path, dressed for summer, looking older than her fourteen years.

"Hello, Josie Parker," Edie said.

* * *

"Good morning, Mrs Walker," Josie said. She raised her hand against the still-rising sun and squinted at the silhouette of the old lady. "What are you doing?"

"Out for my walk," Edie replied, tucking a plastic tub back into her pocket. "Leaving a little something for the birds." She gestured up at the oak tree and then frowned.

Josie followed her gaze. The tree was a familiar one; it was a rite of passage for every kid in the village to climb and fall out of it. It was also free from birds, so whatever Mrs Walker was feeding wasn't in that tree. But then again, they all said Mrs Walker was a witch, so who knew what witches got up to.

"Are you going to the festival later?" Josie asked.

"Oh, I'll be there. With bells on," Edie grinned. "Or, the Morris Men will, I suppose. You'll be dancing, will you?"

"I am," Josie couldn't help but smile. The boys looked at the dancers, she knew. And then she thought how Mrs Walker probably knew that too, and knew that Josie knew, and she blushed.

They both started as a butterfly fluttered between them. They watched it, a smile on the lips of both women.

"Now there's a good sign after all," Mrs Walker said, carrying on before Josie could question her. "Give my best to your mum and dad," she added, with a wave goodbye. "Butterflies," she called out with a chuckle.

"I will." Josie frowned at the old woman and turned to follow the butterfly's flight as it flickered across a canvas of blue sky.

Josie turned from the path, cutting through a gap in the hedgerow and onto Bower's Field. She slipped off her shoes and walked barefoot across the close-cut grass. Tiny, sharp diamonds of dew kissed her toes.

She walked past the stalls as they set up, filled with artisans selling jewellery, baked goods, clothing, art and fortunes. The smell of hot oils and foods created a bewitchment in the air.

Josie paused to look at the May Pole, at the ribbon stretched out and ready to be taken, to be held, to be twirled, feet skipping across the field, winding tighter and tighter. She felt giddy with anticipation.

Her house was not far from the field and she arrived home to find her parents in a state of anxious preparation. A raucous twang of strings heralded Dad wrestling his guitar into a case.

"Calm down," her mother called.

"I'm calm."

"Stop rushing."

"We're running out of time."

Josie laughed to herself and ran up the stairs. A shadow fell across her and she drew up short, barely stopping herself from barrelling into her brother Tommy.

"Watch it," he growled.

He was bundled up like a wraith, dark trousers and a dark hoodie over a thin frame. His pale face stared out of the shadow-halo of his hood.

They passed on the stairs and Josie flinched away from him. For a moment she had thought she saw something in the shadow of his hood, nestled up against her brother. Another face, white, with dark eyes.

She shivered, turned, hand up and mouth open as if ready to reach out and call for him. He had been fun once, full of smiles and jokes. What had happened to him? Could she bring him back?

But they had passed. The moment was gone. She told herself she was silly, but she waited until he was out of sight before she ran for her room and shut the door.

* * *

Tommy stalked down the stairs, past the living room and into the kitchen. He slammed the door against the sounds of guitars, his parents, his sister, the world. He pulled his hood tighter around his face and closed his eyes.

He hated the festival. He hated this time of year. It was too bright. Too warm. Days getting longer and longer and leaving him feeling stretched out and thin.

He didn't want to go to the festival and see the same old stalls, hear his parents sing the same old folk songs, and all that other nonsense. There'd be the crowds from school as well. They'd all be there. Looking. Whispering.

He opened his eyes and found his gaze fell onto the kitchen knives in their block. Something writhed in his chest, a living creature of hate and fear that coiled around his heart and lungs and left him choked.

With slow, bored movements, he drew out one of the knives. It was long and sharp. He'd tried to use one, once, on himself, but had been too scared. He still called himself a coward. It was just… his skin felt tight. His blood throbbed under his flesh and he wanted…. He wanted…. Release.

Maybe if he couldn't keep the voices in his own head quiet, he could make the ones outside of his head be quiet.

He realized the knife was hidden in the pocket of his hoodie, but he didn't remove it. He tucked his hands inside, the handle of the blade loose in his palm.

"We're leaving," Dad shouted from the hallway. "You coming?"

Tommy trailed behind. He missed the look Josie gave him. He squinted against the sunlight and cast his gaze down at the floor. There was a throbbing behind his eyes; a headache crossed with the threat of tears. He wasn't going to cry, though. What kind of loser would cry like that?

The festival was warming up when they arrived. Tommy slipped away from his family and slid through the crowd on shadow feet. He saw the pretty girls and handsome boys from his class and veered away from them. He felt the looks of friends from the village and turned from them.

In the shadow of a tent he saw a familiar figure and watched them. A boy from his school. Joshua. Always Joshua, never Josh. Posh and popular and puffed-up. Tommy imagined the knife pricking him, deflating the wasted sack of skin, letting ribbons of red flow over that pale skin.

Tommy closed his eyes. Inside his pocket he felt the knife. Its handle was smooth in his palm. Warm. Like it was alive. There was a throbbing in his fingers, his own pulse or the quickened breath of the blade, he could not tell.

"Tommy Parker," a woman's voice said.

* * *

"Tommy Parker," Edie called again when the young man didn't respond. He turned to face her and she treated him to a gentle smile, her eyebrows raised into an unasked question.

"What?" he snapped back with a frown.

He was pale and sweating, and Edie guessed it was more than just being wrapped up in a black hood on a warm day. She looked at his hands shoved into the front pocket of his hoody. Exactly what he was holding she could not guess, but she reckoned she understood its intent all the same.

Pale skin and black clothes, an echo of the magpie.

"Help an old lady out," she said and turned away from him, heading to a quiet tent at the edge of the festival. As usual, a statement and an assumption got her more than a direct request would have done. Tommy followed.

"Lovely day for it," she said as they entered the cool shade of the fabric tent. Inside were stacks of boxes, supplies of snacks, bottled water, electrical cables, tools and all the little things than made the festival run. "You look warm. Take your hood down."

It was a demand too far. Tommy flinched from her, sinking down into the hood, into his shoulders. His hands writhed in his pocket with an eagerness Edie did not like.

"Saw your sister this morning," Edie said as if carrying on a casual conversation over a cup of tea.

"So?"

"Saw nine magpies in a tree," she carried on with a chuckle. "When I was a girl, the old rhyme used to say that was the devil coming. Can you imagine such a thing?"

She gave him a look and Tommy turned from her gaze. She saw something then, something in the shadow of the hood, something that might have stared back at her.

"Got something to get off your chest?" Edie prompted gently.

"Shut up," Tommy said, but he pulled the knife from his pocket.

"Good for chopping vegetables," Edie nodded in approval. "And other things, if you were of such a mind. It is your mind, isn't it, Tommy Parker?"

He looked at her and she was gratified to see something like fear in his eyes. He was not lost to them.

"I...." He opened his mouth to speak, but words failed him.

"The devil comes calling when you've got something he wants. When you've got the light in you. Understand me?"

Edie took a step forward and from her pocket she drew the strands of red and white ribbon. Tommy stared at them, mouth slack.

Josie burst into the tent. "Here you are," she grinned. "It's time for the May Pole dance." She fell silent, her steps stumbling to a stop. She took in the knife. The ribbon. "What's happening?"

* * *

Josie watched Mrs Walker step forward and take the knife from Tommy. It was a gentle, familiar movement, as if they'd been rehearsing it for years. Mrs Walker placed the knife on a box, took the ribbons in her hands and started to wrap them around Tommy's hands, binding them together.

"Tommy?" Josie said. Her brother was dumbstruck, staring down in awe at his hands, jaw slack, eyes far-seeing.

"Go and dance, Josie Parker," Mrs Walker said. "Dance the sun down to him so that he might know the way home."

Josie shook her head. "What?"

"Ribbon red, ribbon white, bind the wound and hold it tight," Mrs Walker whispered as she whipped the ribbon round and round. "Go," she said without sparing a glance. "Dance."

Josie turned and felt the weight of momentum come crashing down on her. It was sluggish, heavy movement, but as she shifted, as she turned her back to her brother, she fell into a run. Again, that familiar movement, something rehearsed, something as certain as the sun's motion across the sky.

A sprint across the grass, hair streaming behind her, sun silken across her skin. Josie went to the May Pole and took hold of the ribbon.

A red ribbon in her hand.

Ribbon around her brother's hands.

There were questions she wanted to ask, if only to reassure herself that others would answer the same as her. There was something wrong with her brother. Something had stolen into him, as a shadow under a tree steals away the warmth.

Josie turned her face to the sun.

Dance down the sun…

The music started.

The circle turned and Josie danced.

She skipped around the May Pole, following a path without thought. The music was a lively jig, the fiddle soaring, and Josie let it move her along.

Round and round, ribbon tighter and tighter.

Bind the wound and hold it tight.

"Ribbon white and ribbon red," Josie breathed as the circle span faster and tighter. "Heal the heart and clear the head."

Josie swept along in the dance. She grinned and felt every pulsing beat of her blood in her body like every young tree feels the rising sap at the first kiss of spring. Each step as sure as the sun in the sky and…no, the sun didn't move. The sun didn't move, it was they who moved. Who span, who carried themselves through the dark void of space.

The sun was constant.

The light was always there.

"Bind it tight," she gasped, the ribbon winding down, drawing the dancers to the May Pole's gravity.

She stumbled.

She kicked free of her shoes.

Toes brushed grass.

Josie ran, skipped and jumped, ducking under ribbons, weaving around the other girls, all laughing, all joyful, all full of sun and love and light.

The ribbon pulled tight.

The dance ended.

Josie was the last one holding the ribbon. The new May Queen stared down at her hand, at the pattern of red and white on the pole, at the cheering and smiling faces all around her.

And the May Queen ran from her court, across the green, to a small tent where her brother, her jester, stumbled out into the light, fell to his knees, and vomited.

* * *

Tommy spat and wiped at his mouth. He wondered what he was doing on his hands and knees. He wondered why he was outside. He curled his fingers into the cool grass and looked at the ribbon wrapped around his wrists, one red and one white. He looked up and squinted into the light, seeing his sister at last.

"Josie?" he asked.

"Are you okay?" she said as she knelt next to him.

"He'll be fine. That was some dance you did," Mrs Walker said.

Tommy sat back onto his heels, noticing Mrs Walker for the first time. Something of what had happened came back to him, like the fleeting showreels of a dream projected onto the dawn.

"What did we do?" Josie asked.

"A little sympathetic magic," Mrs Walker said. She held out her hand to receive the ribbons as Tommy unwound them from his wrists. "Nothing but a dance and a little psychology."

"I'm the May Queen," Josie said with a smile.

"Where's your crown?" he asked.

"Oh," Josie turned to look back at the green. "They'll want me back."

"Go. I'll catch up."

She gave him one last look but Tommy waved her away. He stood up, looked down at his hoodie splashed with vomit, and pulled it off. The air felt good against his bare arms, and he turned towards the sun.

"Feels good, doesn't it?" Mrs Walker said.

"I thought it was inside me," Tommy said.

"It is."

"The sun, I meant."

"I know. The other thing, too."

Tommy nodded. He remembered that feeling of something inside his chest, a creature that was writhing, choking his heart, clawing at his voice. He'd felt the ribbons around his hands, Mrs Walker singing some rhyme or other, and then spinning…dancing around the May Pole, and getting dizzier and sicker with every turn until…

"I spewed it up," he said. "But it's still in me, isn't it?"

Mrs Walker nodded and gave him a shrewd look. "But so is the sun, Tommy Parker. So is the sun. That was a hard thing you did, lad. Turned to shadow and shade, you stood up and faced yourself. That's a terrible thing to do. Most never manage it."

"What do I do now?"

Mrs Walker chuckled, took hold of his arm, and guided him back towards the green. "The same thing we do when we open up our windows and doors when the world turns and summer returns. Let the light in." They stepped from the shade of the tents and into the bustling light and brightness of the festival. "And let the sun put the shadows in their place."

The Search for the Home of the Sun

From the Songora people, central Africa

MASTER AND FRIENDS. We have an old phrase among us which is very common. It is said that he who waits and waits for his turn, may wait too long, and lose his chance. My tongue is not nimble like some, and my words do not flow like the deep river. I am rather like the brook which is fretted by the stones in its bed, and I hope after this explanation you will not be too impatient with me.

My tale is about King Masama and his tribe, the Balira, who dwelt far in the inmost region, behind (east) us, who throng the banks of the great river. They were formerly very numerous, and many of them came to live among us, but one day King Masama and the rest of the tribe left their country and went eastward, and they have never been heard of since, but those who chose to stay with us explained their disappearance in this way.

A woman, one cold night, after making up her fire on the hearth, went to sleep. In the middle of the night the fire had spread, and spread, and began to lick up the litter on the floor, and from the litter it crept to her bed of dry banana-leaves, and in a little time shot up into flames. When the woman and her husband were at last awakened by the heat, the flames had already mounted into the roof, and were burning furiously. Soon they broke through the top and leaped up into the night, and a gust of wind came and carried the long flames like a stream of fire towards the neighbouring huts, and in a short time the fire had caught hold of every house, and the village was entirely burned. It was soon known that besides burning up their houses and much property, several old people and infants had been destroyed by the fire, and the people were horror-struck and angry.

Then one voice said, "We all know in whose house the fire began, and the owner of it must make our losses good to us."

The woman's husband heard this, and was alarmed, and guiltily fled into the woods.

In the morning a council of the elders was held, and it was agreed that the man in whose house the fire commenced should be made to pay for his carelessness, and they forthwith searched for him. But when they sought for him he could not be found. Then all the young warriors who were cunning in woodcraft, girded and armed themselves, and searched for the trail, and when one of them had found it, he cried out, and the others gathered themselves about him and took it up, and when many eyes were set upon it, the trail could not be lost.

They soon came up to the man, for he was seated under a tree, bitterly weeping.

Without a word they took hold of him by the arms and bore him along with them, and brought him before the village fathers. He was not a common man by any means. He was known as one of Masama's principal men, and one whose advice had been often followed.

"Oh," said everybody, "he is a rich man, and well able to pay; yet, if he gives all he has got, it will not be equal to our loss."

The fathers talked a long time over the matter, and at last decided that to save his forfeited life he should freely turn over to them all his property. And he did so. His plantation of bananas and plantains, his plots of beans, yams, manioc, potatoes, groundnuts, his slaves, spears, shields, knives, paddles and canoes. When he had given up all, the hearts of the people became softened towards him, and they forgave him the rest.

After the elder's property had been equally divided among the sufferers by the fire, the people gained new courage, and set about rebuilding their homes, and before long they had a new village, and they had made themselves as comfortable as ever.

Then King Masama made a law, a very severe law – to the effect that, in future, no fire should be lit in the houses during the day or night; and the people, who were now much alarmed about fire, with one heart agreed to keep the law. But it was soon felt that the cure for the evil was as cruel as the fire had been. For the houses had been thatched with green banana-leaves, the timbers were green and wet with their sap, the floor was damp and cold, the air was deadly, and the people began to suffer from joint aches, and their knees were stiff, and the pains travelled from one place to another through their bodies. The village was filled with groaning.

Masama suffered more than all, for he was old. He shivered night and day, and his teeth chattered sometimes so that he could not talk, and after that his head would burn, and the hot sweat would pour from him, so that he knew no rest.

Then the king gathered his chiefs and principal men together, and said:

"Oh, my people, this is unendurable, for life is with me now but one continuous ague. Let us leave this country, for it is bewitched, and if I stay longer there will be nothing left of me. Lo, my joints are stiffened with my disease, and my muscles are withering. The only time I feel a little ease is when I lie on the hot ashes without the house, but when the rains fall I must needs withdraw indoors, and there I find no comfort, for the mould spreads everywhere. Let us hence at once to seek a warmer clime. Behold whence the sun issues daily in the morning, hot and glowing; there, where his home is, must be warmth, and we shall need no fire. What say you?"

Masama's words revived their drooping spirits. They looked towards the sun as they saw him mount the sky, and felt his cheering glow on their naked breasts and shoulders, and they cried with one accord, "Let us hence, and seek the place whence he comes."

And the people got ready and piled their belongings in the canoes, and on a certain day they left their village and ascended their broad river, the Lira. Day after day they paddled up the stream, and we heard of them from the Bafanya as they passed by their country, and the Bafanya heard of them for a long distance up – from the next tribe – the Bamoru – and the Bamoru heard about them arriving near the Mountain Land beyond.

Not until a long time afterwards did we hear what became of Masama and his people.

It was said that the Balira, when the river had become shallow and small, left their canoes and travelled by land among little hills, and after winding in and out amongst them they came to the foot of the tall mountain which stands like a grandsire amongst the smaller mountains. Up the sides of the big mountain they straggled, the stronger and more active of them ahead, and as the days passed, they saw that the world was cold and dark until the sun showed himself over the edge of the big mountain, when the day became more agreeable, for the heat pierced into their very marrows, and made their hearts rejoice. The greater the heat became, the more certain were they that they were drawing near the home of the sun. And so they pressed on and on, day after day, winding along one side of the mountain, and then turning to wind again still higher. Each day, as they advanced towards the top, the heat became greater and greater. Between them and the sun there was now not the smallest shrub or leaf, and it became so fiercely hot that finally not a drop of sweat was left in their bodies. One day, when not a cloud was in the sky, and the world was all below them – far down like a great buffalo hide – the sun came out over the rim of the mountain like a ball of fire, and the nearest of them to the top were dried like a leaf over a flame, and those who were behind were amazed at its burning force, and felt, as he sailed over their heads, that it was too late for them to escape. Their skins began to shrivel up and crackle, and fall off, and none of those who were high up on the mountain side were left alive. But a few of those who were nearest the bottom, and the forest belts, managed to take shelter, and remaining there until night, they took advantage of the darkness, when the sun sleeps, to fly from the home of the sun. Except a few poor old people and toddling children, there was none left of the once populous tribe of the Balira.

That is my story. We who live by the great river have taken the lesson, which the end of this tribe has been to us, close to our hearts, and it is this. Kings who insist that their wills should be followed, and never care to take counsel with their people, are as little to be heeded as children who babble of what they cannot know, and therefore in our villages we have many elders who take all matters from the chief and turn them over in their minds, and when they are agreed, they give the doing of them to the chief, who can act only as the elders decree.

The Shepherd and the Daughter of the Sun

From Inca mythology

IN THE SNOW-CLAD CORDILLERA above the valley of Yucay, called Pitu-siray, a shepherd watched the flock of white llamas intended for the Inca to sacrifice to the Sun. He was a native of Laris, named Acoya-napa, a very well disposed and gentle youth. He strolled behind his flock, and presently began to play upon his flute very softly and sweetly, neither feeling anything of the amorous desires of youth, nor knowing anything of them.

He was carelessly playing his flute one day when two daughters of the Sun came to him. They could wander in all directions over the green meadows, and never failed to find one of their houses at night, where the guards and porters looked out that nothing came that could do them harm. Well! the two girls came to the place where the shepherd rested quite at his ease, and they asked him about his llamas.

The shepherd, who had not seen them until they spoke, was surprised, and fell on his knees, thinking that they were the embodiments of two out of the four crystalline fountains which were very famous in those parts. So he did not dare to answer them. They repeated their question about the flock, and told him not to be afraid, for they were children of the Sun, who was lord of all the land, and to give him confidence they took him by the arm. Then the shepherd stood up and kissed their hands. After talking together for some time the shepherd said that it was time for him to collect his flock, and asked their permission. The elder princess, named Chuqui-llantu, had been struck by the grace and good disposition of the shepherd. She asked him his name and of what place he was a native. He replied that his home was at Laris and that his name was Acoya-napa. While he was speaking Chuqui-llantu cast her eyes upon a plate of silver which the shepherd wore over his forehead, and which shone and glittered very prettily. Looking closer she saw on it two figures, very subtly contrived, who were eating a heart. Chuqui-llantu asked the shepherd the name of that silver ornament, and he said it was called *utusi*. The princess returned it to the shepherd, and took leave of him, carrying well in her memory the name of the ornament and the figures, thinking with what delicacy they were drawn, almost seeming to her to be alive. She talked about it with her sister until they came to their palace. On entering, the doorkeepers looked to see if they brought with them anything that would do harm, because it was often found that women had brought with them, hidden in their clothes, such things as fillets and necklaces. After having looked well, the porters let them pass, and they found the women of the Sun cooking and preparing food. Chuqui-llantu said that she was very tired with her walk, and that she did not want any supper. All the rest supped with her sister, who thought that Acoya-napa was not one who could cause disquietude. But Chuqui-llantu was unable to rest owing to the great love she felt for the shepherd

Acoya-napa, and she regretted that she had not shown him what was in her breast. But at last she went to sleep.

In the palace there were many richly furnished apartments in which the women of the Sun dwelt. These virgins were brought from all the four provinces which were subject to the Inca, namely Chincha-suyu, Cunti-suyu, Anti-suyu and Colla-suyu. Within, there were four fountains which flowed towards the four provinces, and in which the women bathed, each in the fountain of the province where she was born. They named the fountains in this way. That of Chincha-suyu was called *Chuclla-puquio*, that of Cunti-suyu was known as *Ocoruro-puquio*, *Siclla-puquio* was the fountain of Anti-suyu, and *Llulucha-puquio* of Colla-suyu. The most beautiful child of the Sun, Chuqui-llantu, was wrapped in profound sleep. She had a dream. She thought she saw a bird flying from one tree to another, and singing very softly and sweetly. After having sung for some time, the bird came down and regarded the princess, saying that she should feel no sorrow, for all would be well. The princess said that she mourned for something for which there could be no remedy. The singing bird replied that it would find a remedy, and asked the princess to tell her the cause of her sorrow. At last Chuqui-llantu told the bird of the great love she felt for the shepherd boy named Acoya-napa, who guarded the white flock. Her death seemed inevitable. She could have no cure but to go to him whom she so dearly loved, and if she did her father the Sun would order her to be killed. The answer of the singing bird, by name *Checollo*, was that she should arise and sit between the four fountains. There she was to sing what she had most in her memory. If the fountains repeated her words, she might then safely do what she wanted. Saying this the bird flew away, and the princess awoke. She was terrified. But she dressed very quickly and put herself between the four fountains. She began to repeat what she remembered to have seen of the two figures on the silver plate, singing:

"Micuc isutu cuyuc utusi cucim."

Presently all the fountains began to sing the same verse.

Seeing that all the fountains were very favourable, the princess went to repose for a little while, for all night she had been conversing with the *checollo* in her dream.

When the shepherd boy went to his home he called to mind the great beauty of Chuqui-llantu. She had aroused his love, but he was saddened by the thought that it must be love without hope. He took up his flute and played such heartbreaking music that it made him shed many tears, and he lamented, saying, "Ay! ay! ay! for the unlucky and sorrowful shepherd, abandoned and without hope, now approaching the day of your death, for there can be no remedy and no hope." Saying this, he also went to sleep.

The shepherd's mother lived in Laris, and she knew, by her power of divination, the cause of the extreme grief into which her son was plunged, and that he must die unless she took order for providing a remedy. So she set out for the mountains, and arrived at the shepherd's hut at sunrise. She looked in and saw her son almost moribund, with his face covered with tears. She went in and awoke him. When he saw who it was he began to tell her the cause of his grief, and she did what she could to console him. She told him not to be downhearted, because she would find a remedy within a few days. Saying this she departed and, going among the rocks, she gathered certain herbs which are believed to be cures for grief. Having collected a great quantity she began to cook them, and the cooking was not finished before the two princesses appeared at the entrance of the hut. For Chuqui-llantu, when she was rested, had set out with her sister for a walk on the green slopes of the mountains, taking the direction of the hut. Her tender heart prevented her from going in any other direction. When they arrived they were tired, and sat down by the entrance. Seeing an old dame inside they saluted her, and asked her if she could give them anything to eat. The mother went down on her knees and said she had nothing but a dish of herbs. She brought it to them, and they began to eat with excellent appetites. Chuqui-llantu then walked round the hut without finding what she sought, for the shepherd's mother had made Acoya-napa lie down inside the hut, under a cloak. So the princess thought that he had gone after his flock. Then she saw the cloak and told the mother that it was a very pretty cloak, asking where it came from. The old woman told her that it was a cloak which, in ancient times, belonged to a woman beloved by Pachacamac, a deity very celebrated in the valleys on the coast. She said it had come to her by inheritance; but the princess, with many endearments, begged for it until at last the mother consented. When Chuqui-llantu took it into her hands she liked it better than before and, after staying a short time longer in the hut, she took leave of the old woman, and walked along the meadows looking about in hopes of seeing him whom she longed for.

We do not treat further of the sister, as she now drops out of the story, but only of Chuqui-llantu. She was very sad and pensive when she could see no signs of her beloved shepherd on her way back to the palace. She was in great sorrow at not having seen him, and when, as was usual, the guards looked at what she brought, they saw nothing but the cloak. A splendid supper was provided, and when everyone went to bed the princess took the cloak and placed it at her bedside. As soon as she was alone she began to weep, thinking of the shepherd. She fell asleep at last, but it was not long before the cloak was changed into the being it had been before. It began to call Chuqui-llantu by her own name. She was terribly frightened, got out of bed, and beheld the shepherd on his knees before her, shedding many tears. She was satisfied on seeing him, and inquired how he had got inside the palace. He replied that the cloak which she carried had arranged about that. Then Chuqui-llantu embraced him, and put her finely worked *lipi* mantles on him, and they slept together. When they wanted to get up in the morning, the shepherd again became the cloak. As soon as the sun rose, the princess left the palace of her father with the cloak, and when she reached a ravine in the mountains, she found herself again with her beloved shepherd, who had been changed into himself. But one of the guards had followed them, and when he saw what had happened he gave the alarm with loud shouts. The lovers fled into the mountains which are near the town of Calca. Being tired after a long journey, they climbed to the top of a rock and went to sleep. They heard a great noise in their sleep, so they arose. The princess took one shoe in her hand and kept the other on her foot. Then looking towards the town of Calca both were turned into stone. To this day the two statues may be seen between Calca and Huayllapampa.

The Siege of Zonstrale

Lauren C. Teffeau

MY CHIN UPLIFTED, I invite the sun. The rays shine down in welcome, but they burn hotter than usual during the morning's salutation.

Tatia and Dreeva join me, our voices feeble, flitting things compared to the whole chorus we used to be before the other young acolytes fell ill. Dreeva's brow glistens damp like mine, and I fear we may be next to enter the great hall – now our sickroom – and never leave it. As we sing, the sun sears my skin and blazes through my veins, warming my heart until my whole body's limp with exertion and the stone pillars of the temple waver before my eyes.

Gavil, one of the lesser sun priests, clings to a rough-hewn tree branch hastily pressed into service to keep him upright for the dawning of Zonstrale. He may be young for such an honor, but he sees to the rites well enough on behalf of the bedridden too sick to join us here in the courtyard. At the close of the ritual, I hasten to light the brazier closest to me, then Tatia's, as she uses her sleeve to stem the blood dripping from her nose.

The three of us trail after Gavil as he stamps his way across the cobbles. "How many did we lose overnight?"

"Twenty-two," Tatia says softly.

"And the others?"

She only shakes her head.

"I know you'll do what you can for them. We all will." He inhales sharply, swallowing back the sob we surely all feel in our throats, and turns to me. "Geetva, will you assist me in the Observatory first?"

"Of course."

No matter the horrors we face, he must still chart Zonstrale's passage, make the celestial calculations, and mark what portents the Eye reveals – all things that weren't to be his responsibility for years to come. Nor should the running of the temple fall to three exhausted acolytes. But just as Zonstrale greets us each day, we must see to our duties.

Tatia and Dreeva return to their work in the great hall while Gavil and I climb the stairs to the Observatory. We don't have the strength between us anymore to carry the dead to the memorial terrace and place them on the sundial altar – may Zonstrale forgive us – but this is something we can still do. Gavil pulls back the curtain overhead, and sunlight pours onto the housing for the Eye of Zonstrale. The crystal's a gift from our forbears from the age before, said to contain the knowledge of the universe within its facets. Each day, the sun ignites the Eye from a slightly different angle, revealing a new portent. The priests mark them down in our chronicles for our scholars to study.

Generations ago, the Eye was brought here to this mountain valley to protect its contents from the upheaval as the world fell into ruin. To this day, we keep it safe, secure, as we work to uncover the knowledge it holds from the age before. May we always be worthy of it.

I fetch ink and brush and paper as Gavil gingerly lowers himself to the floor where the refracted light dances. When I return to his side, I can see places where his hair has fallen out – the raw patches weren't there yesterday. The sickness must have found him too, but his duty to Zonstrale endures as he transcribes today's portent. But what good are they now if we don't survive this illness?

When he dismisses me, I pretend I don't see the welts on his face. It's the only kindness I can offer him.

I hurry to the kitchen and prepare a simple gruel. I cannot stomach the stuff today, but I take the pot to the sickroom. Dreeva must be off on some errand, for only Tatia greets me, looking as frayed as a sun shroud, her eyes rimmed red by repressed tears. I support the heads and necks of our patients while she presses a bowl to their lips. They cough and sputter and swallow it down. Many spit it back up, but hopefully they ingest enough of the gruel to see the other side of this sickness.

The final patient isn't one of our priests or acolytes, but a man who came to the temple a few days ago for Zonstrale's blessing. His companions were the first to fall ill, I'm told, all of them strangers to this part of the Brance. He stubbornly clings to life, grasping a leather satchel tight to his chest. His sleeping pallet's grimy with clumps of graying skin that pull off at the slightest touch. His cracked lips barely move as Tatia brings the bowl to his mouth. Bloodshot eyes slit open as I lower him down, my hands covered with hanks of gray-black hair.

"We didn't know," he rasps. "They're coming. They'll find us, I know it."

"Shh. You're safe here," Tatia tells him.

"Where…I must find—" He lapses into another language as though speaking to someone who isn't here.

Tatia meets my gaze with equal surprise as his eyes roll back, his neck taut, his head turning this way and that. "What is he talking about?" I ask.

She makes soothing noises as she tries to settle him down. "When he and his companions stumbled into the village, they were half-crazed with fear, telling wild stories of women with white hair who were tracking them like animals. Someone told them to come to the temple and appeal to Zonstrale."

I work his blistered hands off the satchel straps, which only seems to upset him more. Finally, he settles, thanks to either Tatia's dogged ministrations or sheer exhaustion. Delirium's the final stage. Some take longer than others to reach it. Some dwell in the madness for days; others only a few minutes or hours as their fevers cook their minds and burn off their skin in greasy strips. Early on, we would wait with the afflicted and mark down what they said, but now all we can do is pray and provide what comfort we can.

As I place the satchel by the man's bedside, it glances my thigh. I nearly scream in shock at how hot the leather is. I drop the satchel to the floor, and a strange, metal-like rock clatters onto the stone tiles. "What is that?"

Tatia gives it a tired look. "Maybe the village blacksmith will know."

If he lives. If we live long enough to ask him.

The villagers stopped coming days ago. No offerings at the gate. No more servants or craftsmen able to perform their duties around the temple. They were too sick, shut up in their homes. And now, that same sickness stalks us better than the women warriors the men rave about. All we have to look forward to is our morning salutations, that bright moment when the sun's rays rest upon us and we can forget the day's work to come, our dwindling food stores, and the bodies piling up. At least for a little while.

By the time I find my bed in the acolyte's wing, it's well past sunset. Dreeva's already there, shivering in her sleep. I take the blanket from the bed of one of the acolytes who died in the great hall yesterday and place it over her. I climb in, not wanting her to be alone – for her comfort as much as mine – and pray for sleep.

When I wake, the darkness tells me there's time enough to get water from the well before the morning salutations. Dreeva doesn't stir, her body cold where it wasn't pressed up against me. *No.* I hoped I'd go before her. A week ago, I'd be more upset than the small pang I feel now, but we've been living with the inevitability of death for so long, the peace on her face is almost as comforting as the sun's touch.

As I pass through the acolyte wing, a crawling sensation starts at my lower back and works its way up my spine. It's far too quiet. Unnaturally so. When I reach the great hall, I find Tatia slumped on the floor next to one of the priests' beds. I pray to Zonstrale she's merely exhausted like I am, but when I touch her burning forehead, I know the sickness has found her too. I can only make her as comfortable as I can before seeing to my own work.

Forcing back a sob, I hold it close till I'm dragging up water, hand over hand on the rope, heedless of the way my arms shake or how the stone rim digs into my hips as I lean against the well for support, alone in my grief.

Too much to do. No one left to do it.

And too few to bear witness to Zonstrale's glory with the rising sun.

"Is there anyone else?" Gavil asks me, half-crazed, when I meet him in the courtyard. He looks even more frightening than he did after last year's summer solstice ritual where there's only room for sunlight in your head.

"None that I saw." The others…. Never again will sunlight touch their faces. May Zonstrale find them anyway.

"Then we must perform the ceremony ourselves," he says, breathing hard.

What else can we do? I half-bow and take my place on the stone steps. His song begins, rutted and rough like the roads leading to our temple but still serviceable as I join my voice with his. Singing makes me feel better, connecting me to the sun about to crest our little valley and bathe us in its light. I sing with my whole body, and for a moment I shed my malaise and throw off the shroud of sickness that's cast our beloved home into so much shadow I fear not even the sun can banish it.

Once Zonstrale shows itself in all its brilliant finery, Gavil, instead of moving into the morning's blessing, begins the song of lament. His voice falters then scrapes back into the rough cadence he had before, then, too soon, he goes silent.

He leans against one of the columns, utterly spent. "Geetva, please…."

With tears streaming down my face, sweat beading down my arms and misting the back of my knees, I go to him, sun-drunk but still singing, singing, singing for all of us. If it's his time, he should at least have his face to the sun. He slumps against me, and we stagger to the ground. My song presses against him, his voice ragged as I help him lie back against the cobbles.

He smiles as sunlight finds him. The brightness momentarily washes out the weeping sores on his cheeks, making him look like his radiant self one last time as he prepares for Zonstrale's embrace. He can finally rest.

And so must I.

The sunlight sinks through my tunic and warms my skin, creating an insistent pressure that dissolves any impetus to rise and return to my work. I collapse beside Gavil in the courtyard. My vision grows hazy with light and heat and sickness, my song but a reedy whisper, soft in my ears but loud in my heart, as the sun drifts overhead.

There's a beauty in whatever Zonstrale touches, even in this, I think as I succumb to its splendor.

* * *

Zonstrale's light cleanses us of all our weaknesses and limitations as we cast off our human body and become pure, radiant energy. But I was never told how painful the process would be.

My body heats through, but unlike the caress of the sun, this *burns*, ripping open my eyes to a nightmare come to life. Corpses from the temple surround me, suffocating with decomposition. This must be one of Zonstrale's tests of character or perhaps a sun-drunk vision from the sickness.

The air turns charnel, ghastly with smoke of the dead. Not a vision, and if it's a test, then it's one of survival, for the pyre will claim me too if I let it. Rictus-spread fingers and limbs grasp at me as I struggle to make a path. Gavil's head lolls toward me, his bloodshot eyes accusing. He's too heavy – I can't get past him as the blaze presses closer. A scream tears through my throat and past my shredded vocal cords.

I can't get out. I can't draw a clear breath.

I can't—

Someone shouts over the fire's roar. Hands find my shoulders, my arms, and *pull*. The bodies of my sisters and brothers batter against me as I'm wrenched out of the pyre.

A gray cloak shrouds my savior as I'm bundled away from smoke and flame. I'm set down on a nest of blankets in some sort of camp shadowed by the temple's gates. The cloak is batted back, scattering ash and embers. A hard-looking, middle-aged woman with a streak of white hair shakes her head in disbelief as she looks me over. Her skin's a deep brown like some of the acolytes, her eyes tawny with reflected firelight.

She calls out, and I notice her companion. Another woman crowned with white hair, pale-skinned and a few years older than me, wearing the same cloak tied closed by belt and sword.

Are these the women warriors our visitors were fleeing?

They speak to each other in a strange, musical language. The second presses a flask into my hands. Drink I must, but when the foul liquid hits my raw throat, I nearly retch. Her hand closes over mine to ensure I swallow the rest of it.

It scorches down my throat and into my chest, blazing like the midday sun. I gasp, incapable of anything else as the first woman spreads something cool and astringent on my face and hands for, I look down, *oh*, the burns. Then the pain's everywhere, as though it only needed to be witnessed in order to be conjured forth into being.

They're saying something to me, but I don't understand. With a sigh, the first switches into the common speech the villagers use, and my head jerks up in recognition. She gives me a smile. "Ah, I was worried we'd run out of languages before we found one we shared."

I struggle to my feet. "Zonstrale. The rites." The full impact of what's transpired here hits me as I face the pyre once more. "I must—"

The second forces me back down. "You cannot help them now, girl. You're lucky we found you when we did."

"But—"

She throws up her hands at me and turns to her companion. They share a look, then she retreats to the other side of the campfire.

The first woman gives me a hard stare as if the mere pressure of her gaze can push me back against the blankets. "You'll squander your health if you don't take care now. Rest. Heal. Karis and I will help you perform whatever rituals you see fit *then*, you have my word."

Everything becomes filmy as though I've been wrapped in a sun shroud. "What did you give me?"

"Something that will help you recover."

At her words, my limbs turn liquid. "May Zonstrale mark your promise," I force out before darkness takes me.

* * *

Two days rise and fall, if my sense of the sun's passage is accurate despite the smoke that still lies thick on the air. Some of that time is spent in a feverish haze; some in sleep so like death, I fear I might never wake; the rest fitful and unpleasant as my burns slowly heal and my mind struggles to make sense of all that's happened. True to their word, the two women see to my needs as I recover my strength. The older one, Sister Vareva, has a patience the younger one, Sister Karis, lacks. Vareva's content to do the things that gnash the other's teeth or further frays her temper. Vareva's also the one to tell me how the visitors to our valley were scieneers who'd stolen a forbidden artifact from the age before.

"I see you recognize that term."

"Yes." The same people whose corrosive adherence to high technology broke the world once already. To think they had infiltrated our home….

I manage to sit up without assistance, and she gives me an approving nod. "I'm sorry we couldn't get here sooner. There were…complications."

"They kept raving about women with white hair. We didn't know what to make of it."

Sister Karis snorts and pokes the campfire with a stick, sending up sparks on the chill mountain air.

Sister Vareva gestures to the stripe of white that falls on either side of her part. "As a Sister of the Zasita Order, our devotion's marked by our hair. We've witnessed the evils of the age before and battled them back. These days, part of our mission is to keep scieneers from recreating forbidden technology. Tell me, what does your faith say of that time?"

"About the age before?"

She nods.

I gather myself, grounding my body to determine the angle of the sun based on where it warms my skin. "It was a time of wonder," I say slowly. The priests and priestesses told us of special glass-like rocks that could absorb the sun's rays and power all manner of things. A far cry from the sun-heated stones we use to warm our bathwater or the rays that chart our calendar, but they all come from Zonstrale, so we must hold them all equally in our hearts. Or so I was always taught. "Then war came, shattering the world into ruin. Like so many others, my people were blinded by the explosions that leveled the great city of Rivard generations ago. We traveled, with only the sun's warmth as our guide to this valley where we could escape the war and pledge our lives to Zonstrale."

"Did this Zonstrale or any of your people explain how scieneer technology corrupted the age before and wrought such terrible destruction?"

I don't correct Karis's assumptions. Despite her sun-touched hair, she seems indifferent to what Zonstrale stands for. "Yes. While our temple's a testament to the beauty light can bring, we must never again build anything that can eclipse the sun's greatness."

Sister Vareva looks relieved. "Then you understand when I say what those men brought to this valley was an unnatural, terrible thing. Your Zonstrale wouldn't have been able to stop it. We tried. I'm just sorry we came too late."

"Did you find it? The artifact that did this to us?"

The women exchange a careful look, and Vareva answers. "We did. We'll be taking it to the seat of our Order where it will be destroyed."

"May I see it?"

Sister Karis shakes her head, her braids snapping against her back. "The girl's crazy – she must have taken in too much smoke."

"Get the box," Vareva replies.

"But our orders—"

"I know. Get the box."

With a grimace, Sister Karis retrieves a metal box from amongst their things, perhaps twice the size of one of Cook's solstice loaves. Inside, the visitor's satchel cushions the metal object that so puzzled Tatia and me in what feels like a lifetime ago.

"That's what made everyone sick?" I ask carefully.

"Hmph. See?" Karis says. "It's meaningless to her."

"That isn't for you to decide," Vareva says sharply. To me, "This is a power cell from the age before. Your visitors sought to understand its secrets and make more like it, but they failed to realize it was leaking an invisible poison."

The sickness. I jerk back, my thigh burning in remembrance.

"Don't worry. It's contained for now."

"Why didn't it take me?"

Sister Vareva leans forward. "Ah, I've been wondering that myself. Can you tell me what happened the day the scieneers came to your valley?"

"I didn't learn of their arrival until much later because I was sent to gather herbs from the upper meadows," I explain as Sister Karis puts the artifact away once more. "I was gone all day."

"That errand saved your life," Sister Vareva says.

"I thought you did when you pulled me clear of the pyre."

She chuckles. "That was the *second* time." She turns serious. "Since you had less cumulative exposure to the poison, you lived longer than the others. Still, it was a very near thing. You must decide what's next for you."

I go cold at that, no matter the sun at my back. "Without my sisters and brothers...."

Sister Karis gives me a disbelieving look. "You cannot stay here. This place will be poisoned for a long time."

"But the medicine you gave me—"

"Will wear off," Vareva cuts in. "Sister Karis and I have nearly depleted our stores treating ourselves and you."

"I'm sorry."

"Don't be. This isn't your doing."

"Do you have any other family?" Sister Karis asks. I shake my head. She taps her knee. "Have you ever traveled beyond this valley?"

Again, I shake my head. Our teachings, our way of life, all of it constrained by mountains, consecrated in our temple, revered in our hearts. And now, only I am left. A sob escapes me. Sister Karis gets to her feet as if distancing herself from such an emotional display.

Sister Vareva hunkers down in front of me. "You're grieving now, but you'll want answers one day why this happened. It won't be enough to simply know. You'll need to do something to stop it from happening again somewhere else. Our Order's mission can become yours."

"But I am of Zonstrale." Something that never meant so little in the wake of so much tragedy. And yet I must try.

"You cannot stay here," she says gently. "If you come with us, you can share what you know of your people, of Zonstrale, of what happened here. It's a burden, but one you can carry until you speak to our scribes, until the truth of this place can enter into our histories. Then, if you wish it, I'll bring you back here myself." She reaches out and takes my hand, her fingers careful of my still-healing burns. "But first, I beg you, consider our cause. My Sisters come from all over the world, united in our fight against high technology from the age before and those who perpetuate it. You could join us. Turn your grief and sorrow into a weapon, honed by our teachings, to be unleashed upon the scieneers who sullied this sacred place."

Her words ignite an anger I didn't know I had. "I don't know how to fight."

"There's always time to learn."

"But who will I be outside this valley?"

She lifts a shoulder. "You'll learn that too. And if you don't like the answer, there'll be time to chart a new course then as well."

"My people are – were – a peaceful one."

"So you're opposed to fighting, even for just causes?"

"No. Balance is important." The sun, tempered by the moon. Day and night, each valued against what they are not and better for it. Light can illuminate but also burn. Dark can protect but also blind. "I could learn to fight for that."

She gives me a thoughtful nod. "Scieneers threaten the balance of our world. They always have. You can help us stop them."

* * *

It's strange to walk through the temple now, empty of all evidence of those who lived here. The pyre still burns, more embers than flame, but at least the smoke has replaced the scent of sickness that hung over my home for too long. I half-expected to see everything torn apart, but the Sisters saw to the bodies of my brothers and sisters far better than I could, something for which I'll be forever indebted to them.

Sister Karis brings me the bundles of herbs I requested from the storeroom. Vareva stuffs the braziers full of firewood blessed by the high priest's hand before he joined Zonstrale. All of it for the ceremony at daybreak tomorrow. Then it will be time to go.

Just that brief foray into the temple exhausted me, so I don't protest my return to my nest of blankets at the Sisters' camp or the sleep that soon finds me. I wake sometime in the night, disappointed to miss Zonstrale's passing. The Sisters are still awake, speaking in that strange, musical language of theirs.

Sister Vareva laughs at something Karis says and leans back against the wall with a shake of her head. "In common, please. You could use the practice."

Sister Karis grumbles to herself, then, "I can communicate with the girl well enough."

"Your vocabulary's still terrible."

"What does it matter? We have the whole return trip to practice."

"I don't want your tongue to get us into trouble. Not all of the Brance honors their pledge to the Order."

"Certainly not, if our quarry was any indication." The fire glints off Karis's white hair, giving her a ghostly halo. "But why would they come here? Wouldn't they have realized they'd be trapped?"

Vareva frowns. "I don't think they were in any condition to think about contingencies. With that poison in their veins, the animal instinct to run and hide was all they had left."

"And they took out this place in the process. I still can't believe Geetva survived all that. She's very lucky."

I hold my breath at the sudden flood of feeling. Lucky. As if I want to be here, bereft of everything I hold dear. My only luck is they still think I'm asleep. Who are these women really when they think no one's looking?

"You might say that," Vareva says carefully. "Others would say she's cursed for being the last of her people."

My ribs squeeze tight. Vareva, despite being a stranger to me and this place, seems to understand how I feel. If not all of it, then enough to be of some comfort.

"What do you make of this Zonstrale business?" The disdain's clear in Karis's voice.

"Whatever Zonstrale is, I think it gave these people a community they could believe in. You saw the condition of things. Despite the radiation sickness, this was a place well-cared for. We don't have to share their superstitions to honor that much."

No, but their assumptions about our faith make me glad I didn't explain Zonstrale or justify our life here. Karis wouldn't care, and Vareva.... She might come to understand the edges of it one day. But understanding and knowing are as different as the moon and the sun, with one only mirroring the light of the other.

Karis's voice dips lower with drowsiness. "The Order's archivists will want to catalogue everything. Did you see their records chamber? I can imagine Sister Irla will be salivating for another accounting of the age before as soon as she gets our report."

I go cold at her mention of the Observatory. Our chronicles of the portents are our most sacred texts. How can I protect them if I leave this place?

"No better than vultures, some of them," Vareva says in an uncharacteristically hard voice.

"Shh. You'll wake the girl."

Vareva arches a brow. "So now you care?"

Karis holds up her hand, a half-hearted gesture. "She's growing on me. Still a slip of a thing."

"You were too, once."

* * *

My voice is jagged with disuse as I exhort Zonstrale to cleanse this place of the evils that have found us here. Resentment at having to do this under such circumstances builds in my chest as my song rises to meet the cloud-shrouded dawn as if Zonstrale grieves with me. The Sisters stand at attention apart from the ceremony, but their mere presence feels like a discordant note, fracturing my attention in a way that would be unforgivable any other time.

As my song fades, light finally breaks through the clouds, the flickering beams touching everything in sight. I lift my face to its caress, heedless of my tears, the ache in my chest, heavy with what I know I must do next.

Sisters Karis and Vareva stand by as I light the braziers one final time. I won't be here to see them gutter and go dark. No one will.

"Are you ready?" Sister Vareva asks me.

"Not yet. There's one last thing I must do."

She nods while Karis taps her foot impatiently. Without Sister Vareva to hold her back, Karis would've greeted the road days ago, no matter what I said or needed to see to. Perhaps they think I've forgotten some item I want to have for our journey. Or that I need a few moments alone in this place away from prying eyes. I do – but not because I wish to keep my grief private.

There will be time enough for that later.

I hurry through the courtyard and past the great hall. I climb the stairs to the Observatory intent on the Eye of Zonstrale. If its housing is off even a bit – catastrophe.

And I need one now.

Heedless of today's measurements, I turn the crank, moving the Eye into the path of the sun streaming down from the windows overhead. The Eye catches it with blinding intensity, throwing focused beams of light and heat in all directions.

The oldest parchments catch fire first, destroying the accounts of those early years when my people first came to this valley. The calendars follow, each charted by the very Eye destroying them now.

When the smoke and heat become unbearable, I approach the Eye's housing and wrench the prism free of its setting. *This* is why Zonstrale hasn't laid claim to me yet, I'm certain. Someone has to safeguard the portents. The same mission that brought my people to this valley in the first place years ago. I must take comfort in the fact that whatever knowledge the Eye contains can be reconstructed. It will take time, as all truth does, to be sure whether or not the Sisters' Order can be trusted.

May they be worthy of it. If not, surely Zonstrale will guide me in my duty when the time comes.

"Geetva? Where are you?" Sister Karis's voice is barely audible over the crackling flames snaking across the bookshelves and along the worktables.

I stash the Eye into a pocket, my still-healing hand aching as I clasp it tight. Sister Karis slams open the door. She mutters a curse, then drags me down the stairs. We're both coughing by the time we reach the courtyard.

The temple creaks ominously, but there's too much mountain stone for it to be destroyed completely. May the fire be enough to keep Zonstrale's secrets for now.

Sister Karis scrubs her face free of soot with the end of her cloak. "You said she wouldn't try to kill herself," she demands of Sister Vareva.

"Where did you find her?"

"The records chamber. What could have possessed her to destroy it?"

Her outrage demands an answer, but Sister Vareva merely looks at me with a raised brow. "Who's to say it's not Zonstrale's will?"

"But the Order," Sister Karis sputters. Then her frame goes still. "My common didn't need practicing last night. You *wanted* her to overhear us, didn't you." She glares at us both then stalks toward the horses, muttering to herself.

"You're not angry?" I ask Vareva in a hoarse voice made all the rougher from the smoke.

She shakes her head. "No. If we'd left here, and you didn't have the opportunity to choose what happened to your temple home, then I would've been angry. With myself."

Relief washes through me. At least she understands some of what I've done today, and why. "Thank you."

"There's no need. If you're to become one of my Sisters – as I believe you will one day – I couldn't have done otherwise." Her gaze follows mine to the back of Sister Karis fussing with her mount's saddlebags in the distance. "She'll realize that too, in time."

Perhaps. If Vareva believes that of her apprentice, I won't gainsay her.

"You spoke truth when you said there was room for Zonstrale in your Order?" I ask carefully.

"Yes. But sometimes in our quest to understand the past so we don't repeat the same mistakes, we can forget the cost of that determination. I wouldn't see you pay it, if I could help it."

My hand tightens over the Eye of Zonstrale in my pocket and resolve fills me. "You've given me a great gift. I hope to return it one day."

She only nods. "If not me, then someone else. Come, we have a long day's ride still."

This time, I'm ready to see what else Zonstrale has in store for me.

The Sister of the Sun

From Finnish fairy tale

A LONG TIME AGO there lived a young prince whose favourite playfellow was the son of the gardener who lived in the grounds of the palace. The king would have preferred his choosing a friend from the pages who were brought up at court; but the prince would have nothing to say to them, and as he was a spoilt child, and allowed his way in all things, and the gardener's boy was quiet and well-behaved, he was suffered to be in the palace, morning, noon and night.

The game the children loved the best was a match at archery, for the king had given them two bows exactly alike, and they would spend whole days in trying to see which could shoot the highest. This is always very dangerous, and it was a great wonder they did not put their eyes out; but somehow or other they managed to escape.

One morning, when the prince had done his lessons, he ran out to call his friend, and they both hurried off to the lawn which was their usual playground. They took their bows out of the little hut where their toys were kept, and began to see which could shoot the highest. At last they happened to let fly their arrows both together, and when they fell to earth again the tail feather of a golden hen was found sticking in one. Now the question began to arise whose was the lucky arrow, for they were both alike, and look as closely as you would you could see no difference between them. The prince declared that the arrow was his, and the gardener's boy was quite sure it was *his* – and on this occasion he was perfectly right; but, as they could not decide the matter, they went straight to the king.

When the king had heard the story, he decided that the feather belonged to his son; but the other boy would not listen to this and claimed the feather for himself. At length the king's patience gave way, and he said angrily:

"Very well; if you are so sure that the feather is yours, yours it shall be; only you will have to seek till you find a golden hen with a feather missing from her tail. And if you fail to find her your head will be the forfeit."

The boy had need of all his courage to listen silently to the king's words. He had no idea where the golden hen might be, or even, if he discovered that, how he was to get to her. But there was nothing for it but to do the king's bidding, and he felt that the sooner he left the palace the better. So he went home and put some food into a bag, and then set forth, hoping that some accident might show him which path to take.

After walking for several hours he met a fox, who seemed inclined to be friendly, and the boy was so glad to have anyone to talk to that he sat down and entered into conversation.

"Where are you going?" asked the fox.

"I have got to find a golden hen who has lost a feather out of her tail," answered the boy; "but I don't know where she lives or how I shall catch her!"

"Oh, I can show you the way!" said the fox, who was really very good-natured. "Far towards the east, in that direction, lives a beautiful maiden who is called 'The Sister of the Sun.' She has three golden hens in her house. Perhaps the feather belongs to one of them."

The boy was delighted at this news, and they walked on all day together, the fox in front, and the boy behind. When evening came they lay down to sleep, and put the knapsack under their heads for a pillow.

Suddenly, about midnight, the fox gave a low whine, and drew nearer to his bedfellow. "Cousin," he whispered very low, "there is someone coming who will take the knapsack away from me. Look over there!" And the boy, peeping through the bushes, saw a man.

"Oh, I don't think he will rob us!" said the boy; and when the man drew near, he told them his story, which so much interested the stranger that he asked leave to travel with them, as he might be of some use. So when the sun rose they set out again, the fox in front as before, the man and boy following.

After some hours they reached the castle of the Sister of the Sun, who kept the golden hens among her treasures. They halted before the gate and took counsel as to which of them should go in and see the lady herself.

"I think it would be best for me to enter and steal the hens," said the fox; but this did not please the boy at all.

"No, it is my business, so it is right that I should go," answered he.

"You will find it a very difficult matter to get hold of the hens," replied the fox.

"Oh, nothing is likely to happen to me," returned the boy.

"Well, go then," said the fox, "but be careful not to make any mistake. Steal only the hen which has the feather missing from her tail, and leave the others alone."

The man listened, but did not interfere, and the boy entered the court of the palace.

He soon spied the three hens strutting proudly about, though they were really anxiously wondering if there were not some grains lying on the ground that they might be glad to eat. And as the last one passed by him, he saw she had one feather missing from her tail.

At this sight the youth darted forward and seized the hen by the neck so that she could not struggle. Then, tucking her comfortably under his arm, he made straight for the gate. Unluckily, just as he was about to go through it he looked back and caught a glimpse of wonderful splendours from an open door of the palace. "After all, there is no hurry," he said to himself; "I may as well see something now I *am* here," and turned back, forgetting all about the hen, which escaped from under his arm, and ran to join her sisters.

He was so much fascinated by the sight of all the beautiful things which peeped through the door that he scarcely noticed that he had lost the prize he had won; and he did not remember there was such a thing as a hen in the world when he beheld the Sister of the Sun sleeping on a bed before him.

For some time he stood staring; then he came to himself with a start, and feeling that he had no business there, softly stole away, and was fortunate enough to recapture the hen, which he took with him to the gate. On the threshold he stopped again. "Why should I not look at the Sister of the Sun?" he thought to himself; "she is asleep, and will never know." And he turned back for the second time and entered the chamber, while the hen wriggled herself free as before. When he had gazed his fill he went out into the courtyard and picked up his hen who was seeking for corn.

As he drew near the gate he paused. "Why did I not give her a kiss?" he said to himself; "I shall never kiss any woman so beautiful." And he wrung his hands with regret, so that the hen fell to the ground and ran away.

"But I can do it still!" he cried with delight, and he rushed back to the chamber and kissed the sleeping maiden on the forehead. But, alas! when he came out again he found that the hen had grown so shy that she would not let him come near her. And, worse than that, her sisters began to cluck so loud that the Sister of the Sun was awakened by the noise. She jumped up in haste from her bed, and going to the door she said to the boy:

"You shall never, never, have my hen till you bring me back my sister who was carried off by a giant to his castle, which is a long way off."

Slowly and sadly the youth left the palace and told his story to his friends, who were waiting outside the gate, how he had actually held the hen three times in his arms and had lost her.

"I knew that we should not get off so easily," said the fox, shaking his head; "but there is no more time to waste. Let us set off at once in search of the sister. Luckily, I know the way."

They walked on for many days, till at length the fox, who, as usual, was going first, stopped suddenly.

"The giant's castle is not far now," he said, "but when we reach it you two must remain outside while I go and fetch the princess. Directly I bring her out you must both catch hold of her tight, and get away as fast as you can; while I return to the castle and talk to the giants – for there are many of them – so that they may not notice the escape of the princess."

A few minutes later they arrived at the castle, and the fox, who had often been there before, slipped in without difficulty. There were several giants, both young and old, in the hall, and they were all dancing round the princess. As soon as they saw the fox they cried out, "Come and dance too, old fox; it is a long time since we have seen you."

So the fox stood up, and did his steps with the best of them; but after a while he stopped and said:

"I know a charming new dance that I should like to show you; but it can only be done by two people. If the princess will honour me for a few minutes, you will soon see how it is done."

"Ah, that is delightful; we want something new," answered they, and placed the princess between the outstretched arms of the fox. In one instant he had knocked over the great stand of lights that lighted the hall, and in the darkness had borne the princess to the gate. His comrades seized hold of her, as they had been bidden, and the fox was back again in the hall before anyone had missed him. He found the giants busy trying to kindle a fire and get some light; but after a bit someone cried out:

"Where is the princess?"

"Here, in my arms," replied the fox. "Don't be afraid; she is quite safe." And he waited until he thought that his comrades had gained a good start, and put at least five or six mountains between themselves and the giants. Then he sprang through the door, calling, as he went, "The maiden is here; take her if you can!"

At these words the giants understood that their prize had escaped, and they ran after the fox as fast as their great legs could carry them, thinking that they should soon come up with the fox, who they supposed had the princess on his back. The fox, on his side, was far too clever to choose the same path that his friends had taken, but would in and out of the forest, till at last even *he* was tired out, and fell fast asleep under a tree. Indeed, he was so exhausted with his day's work that he never heard the approach of the giants, and their hands were already stretched out to seize his tail when his eyes opened, and with a tremendous bound he was once more beyond their reach. All the rest of the night the fox ran and ran; but when bright red spread over the east, he stopped and waited till the giants were close upon him. Then he turned, and said quietly, "Look, there is the Sister of the Sun!"

The giants raised their eyes all at once, and were instantly turned into pillars of stone. The fox then made each pillar a low bow, and set off to join his friends.

He knew a great many short cuts across the hills, so it was not long before he came up with them, and all four travelled night and day till they reached the castle of the Sister of the Sun. What joy and feasting there was throughout the palace at the sight of the princess whom they had mourned as dead! And they could not make enough of the boy who had gone through such dangers in order to rescue her. The golden hen was given to him at once, and, more than that, the Sister of the Sun told him that, in a little time, when he was a few years older, she would herself pay a visit to his home and become his wife. The boy could hardly believe his ears when he heard what was in store for him, for his was the most beautiful princess in all the world; and however thick the darkness might be, it fled away at once from the light of a star on her forehead.

So the boy set forth on his journey home, with his friends for company; his heart full of gladness when he thought of the promise of the princess. But, one by one, his comrades dropped off at the places where they had first met him, and he was quite alone when he reached his native town and the gates of the palace. With the golden hen under his arm he presented himself before the king, and told his adventures, and how he was going to have for a wife a princess so wonderful and unlike all other princesses, that the star on her forehead could turn night into day. The king listened silently, and when the boy had done, he said quietly, "If I find that your story is not true I will have you thrown into a cask of pitch."

"It is true – every word of it," answered the boy; and went on to tell that the day and even the hour were fixed when his bride was to come and seek him.

But as the time drew near, and nothing was heard of the princess, the youth became anxious and uneasy, especially when it came to his ears that the great cask was being filled with pitch, and that sticks were laid underneath to make a fire to boil it with. All day long the boy stood at the window, looking over the sea by which the princess must travel; but there were no signs of her, not even the tiniest white sail. And, as he stood, soldiers came and laid hands on him, and led him up to the cask, where a big fire was blazing, and the horrid black pitch boiling and bubbling over the sides. He looked and shuddered, but there was no escape; so he shut his eyes to avoid seeing.

The word was given for him to mount the steps which led to the top of the cask, when, suddenly, some men were seen running with all their might, crying as they went that a large ship with its sails spread was making straight for the city. No one knew what the ship was, or whence it came; but the king declared that he would not have the boy burned before its arrival, there would always be time enough for that.

At length the vessel was safe in port, and a whisper went through the watching crowd that on board was the Sister of the Sun, who had come to marry the young peasant as she had promised. In a few moments more she had landed, and desired to be shown the way to the cottage which her bridegroom had so often described to her; and whither he had been led back by the king's order at the first sign of the ship.

"Don't you know me?" asked the Sister of the Sun, bending over him where he lay, almost driven out of his senses with terror.

"No, no; I don't know you," answered the youth, without raising his eyes.

"Kiss me," said the Sister of the Sun; and the youth obeyed her, but still without looking up.

"Don't you know me *now*?" asked she.

"No, I don't know you – I don't know you," he replied, with the manner of a man whom fear had driven mad.

At this the Sister of the Sun grew rather frightened, and beginning at the beginning, she told him the story of his meeting with her, and how she had come a long way in order to marry him. And just as she had finished in walked the king, to see if what the boy had said was really true. But hardly had he opened the door of the cottage when he was almost blinded by the light that filled it; and he remembered what he had been told about the star on the forehead of the princess. He staggered back as if he had been struck, then a curious feeling took hold of him, which he had never felt before, and falling on his knees before the Sister of the Sun, he implored her to give up all thought of the peasant boy, and to share his throne. But she laughed, and said she had a finer throne of her own, if she wanted to sit on it, and that she was free to please herself, and would have no husband but the boy whom she would never have seen except for the king himself.

"I shall marry him tomorrow," ended she; and ordered the preparations to be set on foot at once.

When the next day came, however, the bridegroom's father informed the princess that, by the law of the land, the marriage must take place in the presence of the king; but he hoped His Majesty would not long delay his arrival. An hour or two passed, and everyone was waiting and watching, when at last the sound of trumpets was heard and a grand procession was seen marching up the street. A chair covered with velvet had been made ready for the king, and he took his seat upon it, and, looking round upon the assembled company, he said:

"I have no wish to forbid this marriage; but, before I can allow it to be celebrated, the bridegroom must prove himself worthy of such a bride by fulfilling three tasks. And the first is that in a single day he must cut down every tree in an entire forest."

The youth stood aghast as the king's words. He had never cut down a tree in his life, and had not the least idea how to begin. And as for a whole forest! But the princess saw what was passing in his mind, and whispered to him:

"Don't be afraid. In my ship you will find an axe, which you must carry off to the forest. When you have cut down one tree with it just say: 'So let the forest fall,' and in an instant all the trees will be on the ground. But pick up three chips of the tree you felled, and put them in your pocket."

And the young man did exactly as he was bid, and soon returned with the three chips safe in his coat.

The following morning the princess declared that she had been thinking about the matter, and that, as she was not a subject of the king, she saw no reason why she should be bound by his laws; and she meant to be married that very day. But the bridegroom's father told her that it was all very well for her to talk like that, but it was quite different for his son, who would pay with his head for any disobedience to the king's commands. However, in consideration of what the youth had done the day before, he hoped His Majesty's heart might be softened, especially as he had sent a message that they might expect him at once. With this the bridal pair had to be content, and be as patient as they could till the king's arrival.

He did not keep them long, but they saw by his face that nothing good awaited them.

"The marriage cannot take place," he said shortly, "till the youth has joined to their roots all the trees he cut down yesterday."

This sounded much more difficult than what he had done before, and he turned in despair to the Sister of the Sun.

"It is all right," she whispered encouragingly. "Take this water and sprinkle it on one of the fallen trees, and say to it: 'So let all the trees of the forest stand upright,' and in a moment they will be erect again."

And the young man did what he was told, and left the forest looking exactly as it had done before.

Now, surely, thought the princess, there was no longer any need to put off the wedding; and she gave orders that all should be ready for the following day. But again the old man interfered, and declared that without the king's permission no marriage could take place. For the third time His Majesty was sent for, and for the third time he proclaimed that he could not give his consent until the bridegroom should have slain a serpent which dwelt in a broad river that flowed at the back of the castle. Everyone knew stories of this terrible serpent, though no one had actually seen it; but from time to time a child strayed from home and never came back, and then mothers would forbid the other children to go near the river, which had juicy fruits and lovely flowers growing along its banks.

So no wonder the youth trembled and turned pale when he heard what lay before him.

"You will succeed in this also," whispered the Sister of the Sun, pressing his hand, "for in my ship is a magic sword which will cut through everything. Go down to the river and unfasten a boat which lies moored there, and throw the chips into the water. When the serpent rears up its body you will cut off its three heads with one blow of your sword. Then take the tip of each tongue and go with it tomorrow morning into the king's kitchen. If the king himself should enter, just say to him: 'Here are three gifts I offer you in return for the services you demanded of me!' and throw the tips of the serpent's tongues at him, and hasten to the ship as fast as your legs will carry you. But be sure you take great care never to look behind you."

The young man did exactly what the princess had told him. The three chips which he flung into the river became a boat, and, as he steered across the stream, the serpent put up its head and hissed loudly. The youth had his sword ready, and in another second the three heads were bobbing on the water. Guiding his boat till he was beside them, he stooped down and snipped off the ends of the tongues, and then rowed back to the other bank. Next morning he carried them into the royal kitchen, and when the king entered, as was his custom, to see what he was going to have for dinner, the bridegroom flung them in his face, saying, "Here is a gift for you in return for the services you asked of me." And, opening the kitchen door, he fled to the ship. Unluckily he missed the way, and in his excitement ran backwards and forwards, without knowing whither he was going. At last, in despair, he looked round, and saw to his amazement that both the city and palace had vanished completely. Then he turned his eyes in the other direction, and, far, far away, he caught sight of the ship with her sails spread, and a fair wind behind her.

This dreadful spectacle seemed to take away his senses, and all day long he wandered about, without knowing where he was going, till, in the evening, he noticed some smoke from a little hut of turf nearby. He went straight up to it and cried, "O mother, let me come in for pity's sake!" The old woman who lived in the hut beckoned to him to enter, and hardly was he inside when he cried again, "O mother, can you tell me anything of the Sister of the Sun?"

But the woman only shook her head. "No, I know nothing of her," said she.

The young man turned to leave the hut, but the old woman stopped him, and, giving him a letter, begged him to carry it to her next eldest sister, saying, "If you should get tired on the way, take out the letter and rustle the paper."

This advice surprised the young man a good deal, as he did not see how it could help him; but he did not answer, and went down the road without knowing where he was going. At length he grew so tired he could walk no more; then he remembered what the old woman had said. After he had rustled the leaves only once all fatigue disappeared, and he strode over the grass till he came to another little turf hut.

"Let me in, I pray you, dear mother," cried he. And the door opened in front of him. "Your sister has sent you this letter," he said, and added quickly, "O mother! Can you tell me anything of the Sister of the Sun?"

"No, I know nothing of her," answered she. But as he turned hopelessly away, she stopped him.

"If you happen to pass my eldest sister's house, will you give her this letter?" said she. "And if you should get tired on the road, just take it out of your pocket and rustle the paper."

So the young man put the letter in his pocket, and walked all day over the hills till he reached a little turf hut, exactly like the other two.

"Let me in, I pray you, dear mother," cried he. And as he entered he added, "Here is a letter from your sister and – can you tell me anything of the Sister of the Sun?"

"Yes, I can," answered the old woman. "She lives in the castle on the Banka. Her father lost a battle only a few days ago because you had stolen his sword from him, and the Sister of the Sun herself is almost dead of grief. But, when you see her, stick a pin into the palm of her hand, and suck the drops of blood that flow. Then she will grow calmer, and will know you again. Only, beware; for before you reach the castle on the Banka fearful things will happen."

He thanked the old woman with tears of gladness for the good news she had given him, and continued his journey. But he had not gone very far when, at a turn of the road, he met with two brothers, who were quarrelling over a piece of cloth.

"My good men, what are you fighting about?" said he. "That cloth does not look worth much!"

"Oh, it is ragged enough," answered they, "but it was left us by our father, and if any man wraps it round him no one can see him; and we each want it for our own."

"Let me put it round me for a moment," said the youth, "and then I will tell you whose it ought to be!"

The brothers were pleased with this idea, and gave him the stuff; but the moment he had thrown it over his shoulder he disappeared as completely as if he had never been there at all.

Meanwhile the young man walked briskly along, till he came up with two other men, who were disputing over a tablecloth.

"What is the matter?" asked he, stopping in front of them.

"If this cloth is spread on a table," answered they, "the table is instantly covered with the most delicious food; and we each want to have it."

"Let me try the tablecloth," said the youth, "and I will tell you whose it ought to be."

The two men were quite pleased with this idea, and handed him the cloth. He then hastily threw the first piece of stuff round his shoulders and vanished from sight, leaving the two men grieving over their own folly.

The young man had not walked far before he saw two more men standing by the roadside, both grasping the same stout staff, and sometimes one seemed on the point of getting it, and sometimes the other.

"What are you quarrelling about? You could cut a dozen sticks from the wood each just as good as that!" said the young man. And as he spoke the fighters both stopped and looked at him.

"Ah! You may think so," said one, "but a blow from one end of this stick will kill a man, while a touch from the other end will bring him back to life. You won't easily find another stick like that!"

"No; that is true," answered the young man. "Let me just look at it, and I will tell you whose it ought to be."

The men were pleased with the idea, and handed him the staff.

"It is very curious, certainly," said he; "but which end is it that restores people to life? After all, anyone can be killed by a blow from a stick if it is only hard enough!" But when he was shown the end he threw the stuff over his shoulders and vanished.

At last he saw another set of men, who were struggling for the possession of a pair of shoes.

"Why can't you leave that pair of old shoes alone?" said he. "Why, you could not walk a yard in them!"

"Yes, they are old enough," answered they; "but whoever puts them on and wishes himself at a particular place, gets there without going."

"That sounds very clever," said the youth. "Let me try them, and then I shall be able to tell you whose they ought to be."

The idea pleased the men, and they handed him the shoes; but the moment they were on his feet he cried:

"I wish to be in the castle on the Banka!" And before he knew it, he was there, and found the Sister of the Sun dying of grief. He knelt down by her side, and pulling a pin he stuck it into the palm of her hand, so that a drop of blood gushed out. This he sucked, as he had been told to do by the old woman, and immediately the princess came to herself, and flung her arms round his neck. Then she told him all her story, and what had happened since the ship had sailed away without him. "But the worst misfortune of all," she added, "was a battle which my father lost because you had vanished with his magic sword; and out of his whole army hardly one man was left."

"Show me the battlefield," said he. And she took him to a wild heath, where the dead were lying as they fell, waiting for burial. One by one he touched them with the end of his staff, till at length they all stood before him. Throughout the kingdom there was nothing but joy; and *this* time the wedding was *really* celebrated. And the bridal pair lived happily in the castle on the Banka till they died.

Sky O'Dawn

From Chinese mythology

ONCE UPON A TIME there was a man who took a child to a woman in a certain village, and told her to take care of him. Then he disappeared. And because the dawn was just breaking in the sky when the woman took the child into her home, she called him Sky O'Dawn. When the child was three years old, he would often look up to the heavens and talk with the stars. One day he ran away and many months passed before he came home again. The woman gave him a whipping. But he ran away again, and did not return for a year. His foster-mother was frightened, and asked, "Where have you been all year long?" The boy answered, "I only made a quick trip to the Purple Sea. There the water stained my clothes red. So I went to the spring at which the sun turns in, and washed them. I went away in the morning and I came back at noon. Why do you speak about my having been gone a year?"

Then the woman asked, "And where did you pass on your way?"

The boy answered, "When I had washed my clothes, I rested for a while in the City of the Dead and fell asleep. And the King-Father of the East gave me red chestnuts and rosy dawn-juice to eat, and my hunger was stilled. Then I went to the dark skies and drank the yellow dew, and my thirst was quenched. And I met a black tiger and wanted to ride home on his back. But I whipped him too hard, and he bit me in the leg. And so I came back to tell you about it."

Once more the boy ran away from home, thousands of miles, until he came to the swamp where dwelt the Primal Mist. There he met an old man with yellow eyebrows and asked him how old he might be. The old man said, "I have given up the habit of eating, and live on air. The pupils of my eyes have gradually acquired a green glow, which enables me to see all hidden things. Whenever a thousand years have passed I turn around my bones and wash the marrow. And every two thousand years I scrape my skin to get rid of the hair. I have already washed my bones thrice and scraped my skin five times."

Afterward Sky O'Dawn served the Emperor Wu of the Han dynasty. The Emperor, who was fond of the magic arts, was much attached to him. One day he said to him, "I wish that the Empress might not grow old. Can you prevent it?"

Sky O'Dawn answered, "I know of only one means to keep from growing old."

The Emperor asked what herbs one had to eat. Sky O'Dawn replied, "In the Northeast grow the mushrooms of life. There is a three-legged crow in the sun who always wants to get down and eat them. But the Sun-God holds his eyes shut and does not let him get away. If human beings eat them they become immortal, when animals eat them they grow stupefied."

"And how do you know this?" asked the Emperor.

"When I was a boy I once fell into a deep well, from which I could not get out for many decades. And down there was an immortal who led me to this herb. But one has to pass through a red river whose water is so light that not even a feather can swim on it. Everything that touches its surface sinks to the depths. But the man pulled off one of his shoes and gave it to me. And I crossed the water on the shoe, picked the herb and ate it. Those who dwell in that place weave mats of pearls and precious stones. They led me to a spot before which hung a curtain of delicate, coloured skin. And they gave me a pillow carved of black jade, on which were graven sun and moon, clouds and thunder. They covered me with a dainty coverlet spun of the hair of a hundred gnats. A cover of that kind is very cool and refreshing in summer. I felt of it with my hands, and it seemed to be formed of water; but when I looked at it more closely, it was pure light."

Once the Emperor called together all his magicians in order to talk with them about the fields of the blessed spirits. Sky O'Dawn was there, too, and said, "Once I was wandering about the North Pole and I came to the Fire-Mirror Mountain. There neither sun nor moon shines. But there is a dragon who holds a fiery mirror in his jaws in order to light up the darkness. On the mountain is a park, and in the park is a lake. By the lake grows the glimmer-stalk grass, which shines like a lamp of gold. If you pluck it and use it for a candle, you can see all things visible, and the shapes of the spirits as well. It even illuminates the interior of a human being."

Once Sky O'Dawn went to the East, into the country of the fortunate clouds. And he brought back with him from that land a steed of the gods, nine feet high. The Emperor asked him how he had come to find it.

So he told him, "The Queen-Mother of the West had him harnessed to her wagon when she went to visit the King-Father of the East. The steed was staked out in the field of the mushrooms of life. But he trampled down several hundred of them. This made the King-Father angry, and he drove the steed away to the heavenly river. There I found him and rode him home. I rode three times around the sun, because I had fallen asleep on the steed's back. And then, before I knew it, I was here. This steed can catch up with the sun's shadow. When I found him he was quite thin and as sad as an aged donkey. So I mowed the grass of the country of the fortunate clouds, which grows once every two thousand years on the Mountain of the Nine Springs and fed it to the horse; and that made him lively again."

The Emperor asked what sort of a place the country of the fortunate clouds might be. Sky O'Dawn answered, "There is a great swamp there. The people prophesy fortune and misfortune by the air and the clouds. If good fortune is to befall a house, clouds of five colours form in the rooms, which alight on the grass and trees and turn into a coloured dew. This dew tastes as sweet as cider."

The Emperor asked whether he could obtain any of this dew. Sky O'Dawn replied, "My steed could take me to the place where it falls four times in the course of a single day!"

And sure enough he came back by evening, and brought along dew of every colour in a crystal flask. The Emperor drank it and his hair grew black again. He gave it to his highest officials to drink, and the old grew young again and the sick became well.

Once, when a comet appeared in the heavens, Sky O'Dawn gave the Emperor the astrologer's wand. The Emperor pointed it at the comet and the comet was quenched.

Sky O'Dawn was an excellent whistler. And whenever he whistled in full tones, long drawn out, the motes in the sunbeams danced to his music.

Once he said to a friend, "There is not a soul on earth who knows who I am with the exception of the astrologer!"

When Sky O'Dawn had died, the Emperor called the astrologer to him and asked, "Did you know Sky O'Dawn?"

He replied, "No!"

The Emperor said, "What do you know?"

The astrologer answered, "I know how to gaze on the stars."

"Are all the stars in their places?" asked the Emperor.

"Yes, but for eighteen years I have not seen the Star of the Great Year. Now it is visible once more."

Then the Emperor looked up towards the skies and sighed, "For eighteen years Sky O'Dawn kept me company, and I did not know that he was the Star of the Great Year!"

Sol Invictus

J.A. Johnson

BRAM BAXTER STARED down at the suits, the pair of them, one gold, one silver. As the project linguist he knew little about them except that they were neither gold, nor silver. In fact, they were like nothing else on earth. The materials of which they were constructed were all new; concocted in a laboratory under the direction of an extraterrestrial intelligence. Alchemy was the word that came to mind.

From his vantage in the control room, they seemed smaller than their three meters from head to toe. Huge and cumbersome in appearance, bristling with pipes and tubes and wires, the suits looked like something half hedgehog, half human.

According to the researchers, these new materials were capable of handling temperatures in excess of two million degrees Celsius. The nuclear fusion applications were the stuff of dreams. But, before then, there was matter of first contact.

Bram shifted his attention to the large screen above the control room's expansive view port. On which was a depiction of the Solar System with the Sun and the Earth highlighted. A bright orange line arced from the Sun to the Earth. The trajectory of the coronal mass ejection.

The large, wall-mounted chronometer read, *T-11:00:08*.

Bram began to sweat. The realization that he would soon be standing face-to-face with a non-terrestrial being was beginning to weigh on him. He glanced around the crowded room, filled with professors from across the scientific spectrum and, of course, the ubiquitous military brass and a compliment of heavily armed soldiers.

A slight grin played at the corners of Bram's mouth. If there was a threat, what use would machine guns be against a being of pure solar plasma and temperature of two million degrees Celsius?

"You look nervous, Mr. Baxter."

Bram turned to the man standing next to him; Secretary of Defense Carl Denton. "Shouldn't you be too?"

The older man smiled. "Son, I've faced enemies on battlefields across the globe. And one thing I've learned is that if an enemy has the intent and the advantage, he will act. If something from the sun can send a ball of fire…."

"Plasma," Bram corrected.

Denton suppressed his obvious annoyance. "…*plasma*, to an exact location, then why have us build all of this?" He waved his hand to indicate the whole facility.

Bram nodded. "So why are you and your troops here?"

It was Denton's turn to smile. "Who said my presence here had anything to do with the alien?"

It wasn't the answer that Bram had expected but, anything he might have said was preempted by a computerized voice that came over the loudspeaker. <T-minus ten minutes and counting. All stations conduct final systems checks.>

Denton abruptly excused himself and made his way over to the project lead, Dr. Nichols.

Alone with his thoughts, Bram looked down at the "suits" again. Technicians scrambled about them like ants at a picnic. They scurried over the massive thing, checking connections and running last-minute diagnostics.

Bram had been the project's first linguist. He had been the lead during the communications phase but, once the scientists took over, the linguistics team had been sent packing. Bram alone remained, and only because it was assumed that the solar being would want to communicate once it arrived. Until then, Bram felt nearly as useless as the wastebasket at his feet.

After four or five minutes, the technicians down on the floor were cleared out and the great chamber was sealed.

<T-minus five minutes and counting.>

On the solar system display, the orange trajectory line was now touching the Earth. The display changed and live, satellite-shot imagery appeared. The point of view switched from one satellite to another as the sun-bright mass of plasma streaked toward the Earth.

* * *

The moment was upon them at long last. Red lights flashed and klaxons blared. Bram was seized by a sudden sense of unease. The feeling that this was all somehow a terrible mistake became nearly overwhelming.

Then everything went silent. The pre-programmed lights and sounds went dead.

Bram, like the others, donned the protective eye-wear he had been issued.

Outside, atop the facility, two lofty towers, made of new material like the suits themselves, had been erected for the purpose of gathering the coronal mass ejection, or the alien – if there was even a distinction – and channeling it down through the conduits directly into the huge suits.

Suddenly, the monitors and displays in the control room turned blindingly white for two or three seconds before turning to static and finally winking out to black.

The entire facility went dark, even the emergency lighting.

Out in the main chamber, the ceiling above the suits began to glow; first a dull, warm, coppery orange.

The entire facility began to shake.

The interior temperature began to rise, despite the unprecedented insulation and the AC.

Bram knew the he was not alone in sweating this time.

The ceiling began to glow yellow-white. Even with the eye-wear, the brilliance was almost unbearable.

In the center of the glowing area, two specialized tubes terminated in an area of the suits that roughly corresponded with the area between a human's shoulder blades. One of the tubes glowed fiercely and shook like a convulsing serpent. Then, all at once, it was over.

The facility's lighting kicked in, computers booted up. Happy to be alive, Bram offered a silent prayer of thanks.

Everyone pressed forward for a look down into the chamber. Everything in the room appeared to waver like a desert mirage.

Super-heated air was being pumped into the huge room and gradually cooled in the process, both to bring the temperature down to human-acceptable levels as well as to replace the oxygen that had been burned away during the solar being's arrival.

The conduits, coils, and other paraphernalia connected to the suit slowly dimmed from glowing orange to dull gray. The once black lens plate, where a human face might have been positioned had the suit been designed for human use, now emitted a soft yellow radiance.

It was Secretary Denton who broke the silence with an unexpected observation. "Where is the other one?"

Bram blinked. The second suit was standing empty. Its exterior visually devoid of slowly cooling surfaces, its face plate as black as the dark side of the moon.

Dr. Nichols rushed to the main console where a technician was frantically pouring over her displays. "What happened? Was there a malfunction?"

The technician shook her head. "Everything checks out fine. All readings are in good. There was no problem on our end, Doctor."

Nichols lifted his gaze to Denton and the Secretary of Defense turned to Bram. "We were expecting two aliens, were we not? We were told to construct two suits based upon your translations. Were you incorrect? Are we missing an alien, Mr. Baxter?"

Bram felt his face grow hot. "There was nothing wrong with my translation," he said flatly.

"Then where is our other alien?" Denton asked icily.

Bram was suddenly unnerved by Denton's tone, but he quickly composed himself. He was confident in his work, and he stood his ground. "How should I know? We were never told how many solar beings to expect. We were told to construct two suits. Maybe the second was a back-up."

"*Maybe* it was a back-up." Denton's tone was as sour as his expression. "This is a multi-billion dollar project, Mr. Baxter. We do not deal in '*maybes*'. This project is too important."

Bram was puzzled by Denton's response. How was first contact with one extraterrestrial any less impressive than two? "Too important to whom?" he blurted before he could check himself.

Denton's expression was granite. "The world, Mr. Baxter. The whole damned world, that's who."

Denton jabbed a finger in Bram's chest. "Get you equipment. I need to know if we're short of one alien before we can proceed to phase two."

Bram blinked. "Phase two?"

"Get your equipment. Now!" bellowed Denton. The Secretary of Defense then turned to Dr. Nichols. "See if that thing in there is ready to talk."

Bram retrieved the briefcase that housed his translator from the storage module at the back of the control room. By the time he had plugged it into his station which had a view of the floor below, Dr. Nichols had established the link to the solar being's suit.

"Proceed, Mr. Baxter," said Denton.

Bram frowned. "What do you want me to ask?"

Clearly irritated, Denton said, "Ask if it is alone. Ask if there was supposed to be another 'solar being'," he said, for once not referring to the being as an 'alien'.

Bram activated his console.

Denton leaned in close to him. "Remember, Mr. Baxter. No more '*maybes*'."

A moment later, Bram spoke into the thin microphone built into the device in the briefcase. When he was several words along, a computer generated and outgoing vocal that sounded like a blending of whale song and a pond of croaking frogs.

"Welcome to Earth," Bram continued. "We see that the second suit remains empty. We are concerned. Was another of your kind supposed to arrive with you?"

All eyes instinctively focused on the suit's glowing face plate. The light began to flicker. The sounds of whales and frogs began to drift from the speaker on Bram's computer. The volume of the strange language lessened as a computer generated human voice began rendering the strange tongue into English.

>>I am alone.<<

Denton placed a hand over Bram's microphone. "Ask it the purpose of the second suit."

Bram relayed the question. There was no reply.

After a prolonged silence, Denton said to Bram. "Did it hear you? Check your equipment."

But then the solar being spoke. >>I cannot move! What have you done to me?<< The computer automatically sharpened the tone and increased the volume in response to the solar being's tone, which sounded angry.

Shocked, Bram said to Denton, "What does it mean? What have you all done?" Bram demanded. "The suits were for containment *and* mobility!"

Secretary of Defense Denton only smiled. He then turned to Nichols. "That's answered enough for me. Proceed to Phase Two, Doctor."

Using a key that hung on a chain around his neck, Dr. Nichols unlocked a panel in the wall and entered a pass code on the keypad within. "Phase Two commencing."

A mighty, resonant clang sounded from down in the chamber.

Bram watched as a gap formed in the ceramic-like face of the wall behind the two suits. The gap widened to reveal yet another chamber, equally large, but filled with an incomprehensible congestion of machinery, the purpose of which Bram could not imagine.

"What is it?" he ventured uneasily.

Secretary of Defense Denton placed a burly hand on Bram's shoulder. "That, my friend, is the world's first continuous-use fusion reactor."

Bram was speechless as his eyes traced the rows of pipes and tubing from the newly revealed reactor room back to where they all connected to the backs of the pair of suits.

"That's right," Denton continued. "We have literally harnessed the power of the sun."

Bram felt lightheaded. "And the suits can contain the temperatures…."

"Indefinitely," Denton concluded proudly.

Bram scowled. "You turned the suits into prisons. How could you? We could learn from the solar being. You could have gotten your reactor with its help."

Denton stepped closer to the observation room's huge window. "That down there is an alien intelligence, Mr. Baxter. In spite of what you might want to believe, it does not think like a human; it can not think like a human, because it is *not* a human. With that in mind, you have to ask yourself, what could possibly motivate a creature like that to visit Earth?"

Denton turned to face Bram directly. The deep creases around the Secretary of Defense's eyes actually relaxed. The hard edged glint in his gray eyes softened. "Personally, I don't know the answer. No one but that alien knows. But I can tell you this, none of the scenarios ended well for humanity with one exception. Which brings us to the present moment." The typical, iron edge to Denton's features returned. He nodded toward the floor of the room below. "At least in this scenario we know exactly what we can expect from the alien."

Bram shook his head in disgust. "By turning it into a battery?"

Denton regarded Bram as though he was as alien as the solar being. "Not just a battery, Mr. Baxter, a world-wide battery."

"Free energy for the masses? No offense, but I have a hard time believing you're motivated by altruism."

"I'm motivated by my order of the President, Mr. Baxter. And my job is to keep the country safe, and if that means turning this alien into a battery is how to do so, I will not hesitate. The fact that it can power the world is just icing on the cake."

Dr. Nichols cleared his throat to gain Denton's attention.

"Yes?"

"The reactor is online."

Denton nodded. "Good. Fire it up, Doctor." He then pointed to the technician at the comms station. "Get me the President."

Feeling helpless to do anything, Bram stood at the window and stared down at the solar being trapped, through treachery, in a prison of its own design. Denton's words, that the being did not, and could not, think like a human echoed in Bram's mind.

Regardless to whatever degree that Denton was right, Bram was sure of two things: anger was probably a universal emotion, and revenge a universal thought.

Hands clasped at the small of his back, his medal-covered chest puffed up, Denton stood next to Bram. "How does it feel, Mr. Bram, to be standing on the threshold of one of those rarest of moments, a moment after which the world will never be the same?"

Bram said nothing. He simply stared down at the suit with its glowing face plate. It seemed to him that the glow was slowly intensifying. He realized that he had begun to sweat again. "Is it me, or is it getting hotter in here?" he said to no one in particular.

"It's your imagination," Denton assured him in defiance of the sweat beading along the edges of his own closely cropped hair. "You're just nervous. It happens to everyone at moments such as this."

Denton turned to the comms tech. "I said to get me the President on the phone. What's the hold up?"

"Sorry, sir. I'm having trouble getting through. There's no connection."

Denton shot Bram a sidelong glance as though daring him to say something.

"Gentleman," said Dr. Nichols. "You had better come see this."

Denton hastened to join the professor at his computer.

Bram began to follow but, as he did, the readout on his translator caught his eye. The solar being was speaking; speaking so fast that the translator could not keep up. The words on the display streaked by so quickly that Bram only saw them as a solid green line. The rapid fire nature of the words caused the translator to remain silent, as it could not produce a translation in real time. Bram decided to later check and see if the recording could be slowed down when played back.

"This had better not be a problem with the reactor," Denton was saying.

Dr. Nichols looked pale in the glow of the computer screen. "The fail-safes have been tripped. The reactor is shutting down. But...."

"But what?" Denton snarled, though his voice contained an uncharacteristic trace of nervousness.

"But that's not what I called you to see."

As Bram joined them, Dr. Nichols brought up a news feed. It was a breaking news report. A distraught anchorwoman was seated behind a news desk. The image behind her was, according to the text overlay, a live shot of the full moon in all its radiance. The chyron at the bottom of the screen, apparently dedicated to the main story read, *State of emergency: Tsunamis and earthquakes erupt around the world.*

"*...scientists are at a loss to explain how or why the moon's gravitational pull has suddenly intensified. The consensus among them, however, is quite clear. The rash of earthquakes, tsunamis and rising tides, will continue to increase in number with no end in sight,*" said the anchorwoman.

"The damage already wrought in much less than an hour, is unprecedented. The death toll at this time remains unknown, but estimates are in the tens of billions. If you live in…."

The broadcast flickered and died.

Denton began to pace.

Bram returned to the observation window and looked down at the solar being in its suit. The air in the chamber was beginning to shimmer in the rising temperature.

Denton appeared at his side so abruptly that Bram gave a start. "It's got to be the alien," the Secretary of Defense declared. "You've got to talk to it. Calm it down. Tell it the suit malfunctioned or something. Anything. Just get it to stop."

A malfunction? As in, oops, we accidentally crossed-wired you to a fusion reactor? It was both unbelievable and insulting. Bram knew in his gut that they had crossed a point of no return. Still, Bram did not want to die without trying to do something to prevent it. "I'll give it a try," he said.

He spoke into his mic. <Please stop. There has been a malfunction. Please allow us time to fix it.>

Denton nodded. "Good. Good."

To Bram's surprise, the solar being replied.

>>Betrayers! We will not be denied!<<

The facility began to tremble then and the lights began to flicker.

Cracks began to form in the walls of the chamber, coming together at the apex of the domed ceiling. The dome began to crumble inward, revealing the night sky and the glowing moon.

The falling debris severed the illicit equipment; the cables, conduits and such that bound the suit to the reactor. Sparks crackled and flew, but fail-safes kicked in, containing the solar being's plasma safely within the suit.

The starry firmament beyond the shattered room began to fade white. As the glow intensified, the still raining debris, as though falling through a thick syrup, began to slow. They then reversed their descent and began to rise up and out of the ruin, to melt away into the silver-white glow.

Suddenly, a blinding beam of cold, silvery light passed down among the rising rubble. It entered into the unsealed aperture of the second suit.

And then Bram understood. They had assumed that the two containment suits were for a pair of solar beings. They had been wrong. The second suit was for a lunar being.

Free of the bonds that had immobilized it and linked it to the fusion reactor, the solar being moved at last! It tore away the silver suit's links to the reactor, thus setting its lunar companion free as well.

The solar being's single-lensed face plate began to glow with renewed intensity, brightening to an unbearable degree. Then a crackling, roiling beam of solar plasma shot forth like a blowtorch. The solar being turned in a slow circle, the beam shattered the walls of the facility and razed the remote countryside around the building, incinerating everything that fell under its burning gaze.

Bram watched with the calm acceptance that comes with utter resignation as the fiery beam swept toward the control room. But then….

The beam stopped. The lens dimmed.

The entire facility had been laid waste except for the control room. The moonlit landscape, for miles around, had been reduced to a blackened, smoking wasteland of ash and ember.

Bram and the others stood dazed, like statues, until Bram's translation device began making noise.

Bram glanced at his device and saw that the incoming verbalization was too fast for the machine to handle. Whatever was being said was clearly intended as a one way conversation.

Bram looked again to the alien beings in their containment suits; one silver, one golden. Moon and Sun. The solar being seemed to stare at him on some personal level and then, both aliens took to the air. Bram watched them rise toward the heavens until they disappeared from sight.

Postscript
Partial transcript of the final recording taken from Bram Baxter's translator.

In the final days of old Atlantis, when gods and goddesses still walked and ruled the earth, we ruled supreme. Under our rule, science and magic mingled, Atlantis prospered, and was the envy of the world. But envy breeds contempt and contempt breeds covetousness. And so, perhaps inevitably, we were betrayed, separated, and exiled. And from our prisons we watched helplessly, the destruction of Atlantis and the dark ages that followed.

But now, a new age will be born.

The Story of Balder the Beautiful

From Norse mythology

FAIR BEYOND ALL the sons of Odin was Balder the Beautiful, Balder of the snow-white brow and golden locks, and he was well beloved not only by the Asa folk, but also by the men of the earth below.

> *"Of all the twelve round Odin's throne,*
> *Balder, the Beautiful, alone,*
> *The Sun-god, good and pure and bright,*
> *Was loved by all, as all love light."*

Balder had a twin-brother named Hoder, who was born blind. Gloomy and silent was he, but nonetheless he loved his bright sun-brother best of all in heaven or earth.

The home of Balder was a palace with silver roof and pillars of gold, and nothing unclean or impure was allowed to come inside its doors.

Very wise in all magic charms was this radiant young god; and for all others save himself he could read the future; but "to keep his own life safe and see the sun" was not granted to him.

Now there came a time when Balder's bright face grew sad and downcast; and when his father Odin and his mother Frigga perceived this they implored him to tell them the cause of his grief. Then Balder told them that he had been troubled by strange dreams; and, since in those days men believed that dreams were sent as a warning of what was about to happen, he had gone heavily since these visions had come to him.

First he had dreamt that a dark cloud had arisen which came before the sun and shut out all brightness from the land.

The next night he dreamt again that Asgard lay in darkness, and that her bright flowers and radiant trees were withered and lifeless, and that the Asa folk, dull and withered also, were sorrowing as though from some great calamity.

The third night he dreamt yet again that Asgard was dark and lifeless and that from out of the gloom one sad voice cried:

"Woe! Woe! Woe! For Balder the Beautiful is dead – is dead!"

Odin listened to the recital of this story with heavy heart, and at its conclusion he mounted his coal-black horse and rode over many a hard and toilsome road till he came to the dark abode of Hela. And there he saw, to his surprise, that a great banquet was being prepared in the gloomy hall. Dishes of gold were set upon the table and all the couches were covered with the richest silken tapestry, as though some honoured guest were expected. But a throne that stood at the head of the table was empty.

Very thoughtfully Odin rode on through those dim halls till he came to one where dwelt an ancient prophetess, whose voice no man had heard for many a long year.

Silent he stood before her, until she asked in a voice that sounded as though it came from far away, "Who art thou, and from whence dost thou come to trouble my long rest?"

Now Odin was fearful that she would not answer him did he give his real name, so he told her that he was the son of Valtam, and asked anxiously for whom the grim goddess of death was preparing her banquet.

Then, to his great grief, the hollow voice of the prophetess replied that Balder was the expected guest, and that he would shortly be sent thither, slain by the hand of Hoder, the blind god of darkness.

"Who then," asked Odin, in sorrowful tones, "shall avenge the death of Balder?"

And she answered that the son of the Earth-goddess, Vali by name, should neither

> *"Comb his raven hair*
> *Nor wash his visage in the stream,*
> *Nor see the sun's departing beam,*
> *Till he on Hoder's corpse shall smile*
> *Flaming on the funeral pile."*

And learning thus of the fate of his two favourite sons, All-Father Odin went sadly back to Asgard.

Meantime Mother Frigga had not been idle. Filled with anxiety for her darling son, she decided to send her servants throughout the earth, bidding them exact a promise from all things – not only living creatures, but plants, stones, and metals, fire, water, trees and diseases of all kinds – that they would do harm in no way to Balder the Beautiful.

Theirs was an easy task, for all things loved the bright Sun-god, and readily agreed to give the pledge. Nothing was overlooked save only the mistletoe, growing upon the oak-tree that shaded the entrance to Valhalla. It seemed so insignificant that no one thought it worthwhile to ask this plant to take the oath.

The servants returned to Frigga with all the vows and compacts that had been made; and the Mother of Gods and Men went back with heart at ease to her spinning-wheel.

The Asa folk, too, were reassured, and, casting aside the burden of care that had fallen upon them, they resumed their favourite game upon the plains of Idavold, where they were wont to contend with one another in the throwing of golden disks.

And when it became known among them that nothing would hurt Balder the Beautiful they invented a new game.

Placing the young Sun-god in their midst, they would throw stones at him, or thrust at him with their knives, or strike with their wooden staves; and the wood or the knife or the stone would glance off from Balder and leave him quite unhurt.

This new game delighted both Balder and the Asa folk, and so loud was their laughter that Loki, who was some distance away pursuing one of his schemes in the disguise of an old woman, shook with rage at the sound. For Loki was jealous of Balder and, as is usual with people who make themselves disliked, nothing gave him such displeasure as to see a group of the Asas on such happy terms with each other.

Presently, in his wanderings, Loki passed by the house of Fensalir, in the doorway of which sat Frigga, at her spinning-wheel. She did not recognize Red Loki, but greeted him kindly and asked:

"Old woman, dost thou know why the gods are so merry this evening?"

And Loki answered, "They are casting stones and throwing sharp knives and great clubs at Balder the Beautiful, who stands smiling in their midst, daring them to hurt him."

Then Frigga smiled tranquilly and turned again to her wheel, saying, "Let them play on, for no harm will come to him whom all things in heaven and earth have sworn not to hurt."

"Art thou sure, good mother, that *all* things in heaven and earth have taken this vow?"

"Ay, indeed," replied Frigga, "all save a harmless little plant, the mistletoe, which grows on the oak by Valhalla, and this is far too small and weak to be feared."

And to this Loki replied in musing voice, nodding his head as he spoke, "Yea, thou art right, great Mother of Gods and Men."

But the wicked Asa had learnt what he desired to know. The instrument by which he might bring harm to Balder the Beautiful was now awaiting him, and he determined to use it, to the dire sorrow of Asgard.

Hastening to the western gate of Valhalla, he pulled a clump of the mistletoe from the oak, and fashioned therefrom a little wand, or stick, and with this in his hand he returned to the plain of Idavold. He was far too cunning, however, to attempt to carry out his wicked design himself. His malicious heart was too well known to the Asa folk. But he soon found an innocent tool. Leaning against a tree, and taking no part in the game, was Hoder, the blind god, the twin-brother of Balder, and to him he began:

"Hark to the Asas – how they laugh! Do you take no share in the game, good Hoder?"

"Not I," said Hoder gloomily, "for I am blind, and know not where to throw."

"I could show you that," said Loki, assuming a pleasant tone; "'tis no hard matter, Hoder, and methinks the Asas will call you proud and haughty if you take no share in the fun."

"But I have nothing to throw," said poor blind Hoder.

Then Loki said, "Here, at least, is a small shaft, 'twill serve your purpose," and leading innocent Hoder into the ring he cunningly guided his aim. Hoder, well pleased to be able to share in a game with his beloved brother, boldly sped the shaft, expecting to hear the usual shouts of joyous laughter which greeted all such attempts. There fell instead dead silence on his ear, and immediately on this followed a wail of bitter agony. For Balder the Beautiful had fallen dead without a groan, his heart transfixed by the little dart of mistletoe.

> *"So on the floor lay Balder dead; and round*
> *Lay thickly strewn swords, axes, darts, and spears,*
> *Which all the gods in sport had idly thrown*
> *At Balder, whom no weapon pierced or clove;*
> *But in his breast stood fixed the fatal bough*
> *Of mistletoe, which Loki the Accuser gave*
> *To Hoder, and unwitting Hoder threw—*
> *'Gainst that alone had Balder's life no charm."*

Dreading he knew not what, Hoder stood in doubt for some moments. But soon the meaning of that bitter wail was borne in upon him, piercing the cloud of darkness in which he always moved. He opened wide his arms as though to clasp the beloved form, and then with, "I have slain thee, my brother," despair seized him and he fell prostrate in utter grief.

Meantime, the Asa folk crowded round the silent form of Balder, weeping and wailing; but, alas! their moans and tears could not bring Balder back. At length, All-Father Odin, whose grief was too deep for lamentations, bade them be silent and prepare to bear the body of the dead Asa to the seashore.

The unhappy Hoder, unable to take part in these last offices, made his way sadly through Asgard, beyond the walls and along the seashore, until he came to the house Fensalir.

Frigga was seated upon her seat of honour before the fire against the inner wall, and standing before her, with bent head and woeful sightless gaze, Hoder told her of the dread mishap that had befallen.

"Tell me, O mother," he cried in ending, and his voice sounded like the wail of the wind on stormy nights, "tell me, is there aught I can do to bring my brother back? Or can I make agreement with the dread mother of the Underworld, giving my life in exchange for his?"

Woe crowded upon woe in the heart of Frigga as she listened to the story. The doom was wrought that she had tried so vainly to avert, and not even her mother's love had availed to safeguard the son so dearly cherished.

"On Balder Death hath laid her hand, not thee, my son," she said, "yet though we fail in the end, there is much that may be tried before all hope is lost."

Then she told Hoder of a road by which the abode of Hela could be reached, one which had been travelled by none living save Odin himself.

> *"Who goes that way must take no other horse*
> *To ride, but Sleipnir, Odin's horse, alone.*
> *Nor must he choose that common path of gods*
> *Which every day they come and go in heaven,*
> *O'er the bridge Bifrost, where is Heimdall's watch.*
>
> *But he must tread a dark untravelled road*
> *Which branches from the north of heaven, and ride*
> *Nine days, nine nights, toward the northern ice,*
> *Through valleys deep engulfed, with roaring streams.*
> *And he will reach on the tenth morn a bridge*
> *Which spans with golden arches Giöll's stream.*
> *Then he will journey through no lighted land,*
> *Nor see the sun arise, nor see it set;*
>
> *And he must fare across the dismal ice*
> *Northward, until he meets a stretching wall*
> *Barring his way, and in the wall a grate,*
> *But then he must dismount and on the ice*
> *Tighten the girths of Sleipnir, Odin's horse,*
> *And make him leap the grate, and come within."*

There in that cheerless abode dead Balder was enthroned, but, said Frigga, he who braves that dread journey must take no heed of him, nor of the sad ghosts flitting to and fro, like eddying leaves. First he must accost their gloomy queen and entreat her with prayers:

> *"Telling her all that grief they have in heaven*
> *For Balder, whom she holds by right below."*

A bitter groan of anguish escaped from Hoder when Frigga had finished her recital of the trials which must be undergone:

> *"Mother, a dreadful way is this thou showest;*
> *No journey for a sightless god to go."*

And she replied:

> *"...Thyself thou shalt not go, my son;*
> *But he whom first thou meetest when thou com'st*
> *To Asgard and declar'st this hidden way,*
> *Shall go; and I will be his guide unseen."*

Meantime the Asa folk had felled trees and had carried to the seashore outside the walls of Asgard a great pile of fuel, which they laid upon the deck of Balder's great ship, *Ringhorn*, as it lay stranded high up on the beach.

> *"Seventy ells and four extended*
> *On the grass the vessel's keel;*
> *High above it, gilt and splendid,*
> *Rose the figurehead ferocious*
> *With its crest of steel."*

Then they adorned the funeral pyre with garlands of flowers, with golden vessels and rings, with finely wrought weapons and rich necklets and armlets; and when this was done they carried out the fair body of Balder the Beautiful, and bearing it reverently upon their shields they laid it upon the pyre.

Then they tried to launch the good ship, but so heavily laden was she that they could not stir her an inch.

The Mountain-Giants, from their heights afar, had watched the tragedy with eyes that were not unpitying, for even they had no ill-will for Balder, and they sent and told of a giantess called Hyrroken, who was so strong that she could launch any vessel whatever its weight might be.

So the Asas sent to fetch her from Giantland, and she soon came, riding a wolf for steed and twisted serpents for reins.

When she alighted, Odin ordered four of his mightiest warriors to hold the wolf, but he was so strong that they could do nothing until the giantess had thrown him down and bound him fast.

Then with a few enormous strides, Hyrroken reached the great vessel, and set her shoulder against the prow, sending the ship rolling into the deep. The earth shook with the force of the movement as though with an earthquake, and the Asa folk collided with one another like pine-trees during a storm. The ship, too, with its precious weight, was well-nigh lost. At this Thor was wroth and, seizing his hammer, would have slain the giantess had not the other Asas held him back, bidding him not forget the last duty to the dead god. So Thor hallowed the pyre with a touch of his sacred hammer and kindled it with a thorn twig, which is the emblem of sleep.

Last of all, before the pyre blazed up, All-Father Odin added to the pile of offerings his magic ring, from which fell eight new rings every ninth night, and bending he whispered in Balder's ear.

But none to this day know the words that Odin spake thus in the ear of his dead son.

Then the flames from the pyre rose high and the great ship drifted out to sea, and the wind caught the sails and fanned the flames till it seemed as though sky and sea were wrapped in golden flame.

"And while they gazed, the sun went lurid down
Into the smoke-wrapt sea, and night came on.
But through the dark they watched the burning ship
Still carried o'er the distant waters....
But fainter, as the stars rose high, it flared;
And as, in a decaying winter fire,
A charr'd log, falling, makes a shower of sparks –
So, with a shower of sparks, the pile fell in,
Reddening the sea around; and all was dark."

And thus did Balder the Beautiful pass from the peaceful steads of Asgard, as passes the sun when he paints the evening clouds with the glory of his setting.

Sudika-Mbambi the Invincible

From the Bantu-speaking people, Angola

SUDIKA-MBAMBI WAS the son of Nzua dia Kimanaweze, who married the daughter of the Sun and Moon. The young couple were living with Nzua's parents, when one day Kimanaweze sent his son away to Loanda to trade. The son demurred, but the father insisted, so he went. While he was gone certain cannibal monsters, called *makishi*, descended on the village and sacked it – all the people who were not killed fled. Nzua, when he returned, found no houses and no people; searching over the cultivated ground, he at last came across his wife, but she was so changed that he did not recognize her at first. "The *makishi* have destroyed us," was her explanation of what had happened.

They seem to have camped and cultivated as best they could; and in due course Sudika-Mbambi ('the Thunderbolt') was born. He was a wonder-child, who spoke before his entrance into the world, and came forth equipped with knife, stick, and his *kilembe* (a 'mythic plant', explained as 'life-tree'), which he requested his mother to plant at the back of the house. Scarcely had he made his appearance when another voice was heard, and his twin brother Kabundungulu was born. The first thing they did was to cut down poles and build a house for their parents. Soon after this, Sudika-Mbambi announced that he was going to fight the *makishi*. He told Kabundungulu to stay at home and to keep an eye on the *kilembe*: if it withered he would know that his brother was dead; he then set out. On his way he was joined by four beings who called themselves *kipalendes* and boasted various accomplishments – building a house on the bare rock (a sheer impossibility under local conditions), carving ten clubs a day, and other more recondite operations, none of which, however, as the event proved, they could accomplish successfully. When they had gone a certain distance through the bush Sudika-Mbambi directed them to halt and build a house, in order to fight the *makishi*. As soon as he had cut one pole all the others needed cut themselves. He ordered the *kipalende* who had said he could erect a house on a rock to begin building, but as fast as a pole was set up it fell down again. The leader then took the work in hand, and it was speedily finished.

Next day he set out to fight the *makishi*, with three *kipalendes*, leaving the fourth in the house. To him soon after appeared an old woman, who told him that he might marry her granddaughter if he would fight her (the grandmother) and overcome her. They wrestled, but the old woman soon threw the *kipalende*, placed a large stone on top of him as he lay on the ground, and left him there, unable to move.

Sudika-Mbambi, who had the gift of second-sight, at once knew what had happened, returned with the other three, and released the *kipalende*. He told his story, and the others derided him for being beaten by a woman. Next day he accompanied the rest, the second *kipalende* remaining in the house. No details are given of the fighting with the *makishi*, beyond the statement that "they are firing." The second *kipalende* met with the same fate as his brother, and again Sudika-Mbambi was immediately aware of it. The incident was repeated on the third and on the fourth day. On the fifth Sudika-Mbambi sent the *kipalendes* to the war, and stayed behind himself. The old woman challenged him; he fought her and killed her – she seems to have been a peculiarly malignant kind of witch, who had kept her granddaughter shut up in a stone house, presumably as a lure for unwary strangers. It is not stated what she intended to do with the captives whom she secured under heavy stones, but, judging from what takes place in other stories of this kind, one may conclude that they were kept to be eaten in due course.

Sudika-Mbambi married the old witch's granddaughter, and they settled down in the stone house. The *kipalendes* returned with the news that the *makishi* were completely defeated, and all went well for a time.

Treachery of the Kipalendes

The *kipalendes*, however, became envious of their leader's good fortune, and plotted to kill him. They dug a hole in the place where he usually rested and covered it with mats; when he came in tired they pressed him to sit down, which he did, and immediately fell into the hole. They covered it up, and thought they had made an end of him. His younger brother, at home, went to look at the 'life-tree', and found that it had withered. Thinking that, perhaps, there was still some hope, he poured water on it, and it grew green again.

Sudika-Mbambi was not killed by the fall; when he reached the bottom of the pit he looked round and saw an opening. Entering this, he found himself in a road – the road, in fact, which leads to the country of the dead. When he had gone some distance he came upon an old woman, or, rather, the upper half of one (half-beings are very common in African folklore, but they are usually split lengthways, having one eye, one arm, one leg, and so on), hoeing her garden by the wayside. He greeted her, and she returned his greeting. He then asked her to show him the way, and she said she would do so if he would hoe a little for her, which he did. She set him on the road, and told him to take the narrow path, not the broad one, and before arriving at Kalunga-ngombe's house he must carry a jug of red pepper and a jug of wisdom. It is not explained how he was to procure these, though it is evident from the sequel that he did so, nor how they were to be used, except that Kalunga-ngombe makes it a condition that anyone who wants to marry his daughter must bring them with him. We have not previously been told that this was Sudika-Mbambi's intention. On arriving at the house a fierce dog barked at him; he scolded it, and it let him pass. He entered, and was courteously welcomed by people who showed him into the guest house and spread a mat for him. He then announced that he had come to marry the daughter of Kalunga-ngombe. Kalunga answered that he consented if Sudika-Mbambi had fulfilled the conditions. He then retired for the night, and a meal was sent in to him – a live cock and a bowl of the local porridge (*Junji*). He ate the porridge, with some meat which he had brought with him; instead of killing the cock he kept him under his bed. Evidently it was thought he would assume that the fowl was meant for him to eat (perhaps we have here a remnant of the belief, not known to or not understood by the narrator of the story, that the living must not eat of the food of the dead), and a trick was intended, to prevent his return to the upper world. In the middle of the night he heard people inquiring who had killed Kalunga's cock; but the cock crowed from under the bed, and Sudika-Mbambi was not trapped. Next morning, when he reminded Kalunga of his promise, he was told that the daughter had been carried off by the huge serpent called Kinyoka kya Tumba, and that if he wanted to marry her he must rescue her.

Sudika-Mbambi started for Kinyoka's abode, and asked for him. Kinyoka's wife said, "He has gone shooting." Sudika-Mbambi waited awhile, and presently saw driver ants approaching – the dreaded ants which would consume any living thing left helpless in their path. He stood his ground and beat them off; they were followed by red ants, these by a swarm of bees, and these by wasps, but none of them harmed him. Then Kinyoka's five heads appeared, one after the other. Sudika-Mbambi cut off each as it came, and when the fifth fell the snake was dead. He went into the house, found Kalunga's daughter there, and took her home to her father.

But Kalunga was not yet satisfied. There was a giant fish, Kimbiji, which kept catching his goats and pigs. Sudika-Mbambi baited a large hook with a sucking-pig and caught Kimbiji, but even he was not strong enough to pull the monster to land. He fell into the water, and Kimbiji swallowed him.

Kabundungulu, far away at their home, saw that his brother's life-tree had withered once more, and set out to find him. He reached the house where the *kipalendes* were keeping Sudika-Mbambi's wife captive, and asked where he was. They denied all knowledge of him, but he felt certain there had been foul play. "You have killed him. Uncover the grave." They opened up the pit, and Kabundungulu descended into it. He met with the old woman, and was directed to Kalunga-ngombe's dwelling. On inquiring for his brother he was told, "Kimbiji has swallowed him." Kabundungulu asked for a pig, baited his hook, and called the people to his help. Between them they landed the fish, and Kabundungulu cut it open. He found his brother's bones inside it, and took them out. Then he said, "My elder, arise!" and the bones came to life. Sudika-Mbambi married Kalunga-ngombe's daughter, and set out for home with her and his brother. They reached the pit, which had been filled in, and the ground cracked and they got out. They drove away the four *kipalendes* and, having got rid of them, settled down to a happy life.

Kabundungulu felt that he was being unfairly treated, since his brother had two wives, while he had none, and asked for one of them to be handed over to him. Sudika-Mbambi pointed out that this was impossible, as he was already married to both of them, and no more was said for the time being. But some time later, when Sudika-Mbambi returned from hunting, his wife complained to him that Kabundungulu was persecuting them both with his attentions. This led to a desperate quarrel between the brothers, and they fought with swords, but could not kill each other. Both were endowed with some magical power, so that the swords would not cut, and neither could be wounded. At last they got tired of fighting and separated, the elder going east and the younger west.

The Sun and the City-Builders

Beston Barnett

Dawn

I am born of a lioness.

My mother is untroubled when the umbilical cord emerges first. She is a serene, titanic animal, black-purple and star-pelted and velvet, her eyes the never-disturbed dark of sea deeps. At yesterday's dusk, she ate me – lovingly, I believe, I remember only the not-unpleasant pressure of being swallowed – and all night she has prowled the desert underside of the great coin of the world with me couched, pendulant in her soft belly. Now, with night in its last strength, she hunkers over the edge of the world and pushes and gives birth to day.

I crown. Twisting and arching, not-yet-born, I unpucker one eye and look out from between my mother's hind legs onto an inverted tableau. Beneath me, the sky, gray-sober. In runic attitudes of sleep, women and men and children lie in a circle on the ceiling of sandy ground, sheltering under animal skins or palm fronds or nested together for warmth. At their center hangs my umbilical cord. He is bent, looming, sticky with our shared blood. And because we are in this in-between place – between night and day, between unborn and born – I can see into the upside-down-in-between dreams of the sleeping people, and their dreams are of the umbilical cord that looms below them, whom they call Apep, Demon King, Chaos Lord, Soul Eater, Serpent of the Nile. They are so fragile, these sleepers, and in their dreams, he is so sudden and so fickle.

I feel at once that I must protect them.

I will not wait, but must struggle free of my mother's womb, dropping heavily to earth, dewy, birth-wet. Forty thousand cocks crow. I right myself and feel behind me for my mother but do not find her. In a circle, the people dream and stir. Though I am only new born, I cannot ignore their exposed necks, their bare feet, their sleep-shut eyes fluttering, and Apep, Demon King – my transformed umbilical cord – rears up now as a great flint-headed serpent above them.

"Do not hurt them." These are my first words.

"They know us only in dreams," hisses Apep.

I stand on first legs and wobble.

"Do not hurt them."

The Demon King ducks and weaves, his eyes intent, hissing:

"They know us only from the fear we incite!"

He slices towards me, and then we are knotted, scale versus sinew, thrashing tail versus grasping hand. I am given no quarter to enjoy the cool air of this new world nor to sing the grateful farewell I would like to sing to my lioness mother – gone now with the night. No, in this moment all my breath is for the fight. The sky goes crazy with our wrestling. His cobalt, his slate. My pink, my silver.

At first, I can only fend him off. I do not yet understand my strength. But when, in our furious wrestling, the spiked tail of Apep lashes out and passes wraithlike through an infant sleeping curled beside its sisters and brothers, and the breathing of the infant ceases, and I see that some of Apep's cold blue seeps across the infant's skin, then do I become enraged. I grip the body of Apep and squeeze, and a terrible burning passes through me, through my hands, and where I grip him, he smolders cinder-black and coils against himself in agony. A conflagration blooms up within me, enraged and joyous at once, and the skies burn with the brilliant red-orange of my rage and my joy.

Apep, Demon King, Soul Eater, collapses, breaks apart, hatred in his coal eyes. "They will not thank you," he rasps and though there is no wind, his ashes swirl away.

Around me, the people stretch stiff limbs and open their eyes on the new day. The sisters and brothers of the infant lost in the night hold one another close. Their mother wails. But Apep is mistaken: all the people – even those who mourn – warm their mouths with a word of gratitude to me.

Everyone gives thanks as I rise.

Yet not one among them will look at me.

Morning

It is a long journey to make in a day – one side of the world to the other – but they need my light.

I board my barge.

At dawn, there is only the one people – not much more than an extended family scrabbling for their breakfast. They are so few and so exposed; I worry for them. My barge floats on an updraft just above their heads, near enough that I can reach down and stroke their hair if I choose, though of course I dare not, remembering how the Demon King crumbled to ash under my burning hand. But then, as the morning proceeds, I ride higher into the sky while that first family divides into tribes, following migrating game or flood-plains. And wherever they go, they build cities.

Cities appear between rivers or on deltas, creep along coasts, crop out of jungles. Rarely does one rise that another doesn't fall. I watch the city-builders about their busy business and am moved to see that time and again, they build monuments to honor me. Apep could not now deny their gratitude: in city after city, stepped pyramids, walled furnaces, towers spiraling upwards. And yet, standing atop these touching constructions – chanting my praises, clothed in my vestments, perfumed with the incense of herbs or sacrifices – even their priests will not look at me. I search and search but not one eye ever alights directly on me for more than the briefest moment.

The design of my barge changes often, and I note a strange correlation. When the cities of the delta extrude themselves from the sand, my barge of bunched reeds is transformed into a wide wooden raft with long paddles, rowing like cilia. When the cities wash up along the river of yellow silt, my barge grows a mast and a great bat's wing of a sail. The appearance of a dragon's head carved into the prow coincides with settlements along the Northern fjords. And the most disconcerting transformation arrives with those clever marble cities and their olive orchards: I find I am suddenly riding in a chariot pulled by golden-yoked horses! Four fire-steeds at first, then, as the city-builders spread East, the number becomes seven, for the colors of the rainbow or the days of the week or the chakras. It seems I must repeatedly change my conveyance to suit my worshippers. But I do not begrudge them the vanished barge: my new horses are beautiful.

Another strange aspect of the people's worship: each city feels the need to send me a thief. Over the course of the morning, I am burgled by a hawk-man in a grass skirt, a rabbit, a buzzard, a horned man astride a giant wolf, a possum, a dog, a young boy, a grandmother spider, and a two-headed eight-armed god riding a ram. None simply ask for what they want, but instead rely on evermore audacious tricks.

Do they not realize that all this – the barge, the horses, the long journey across the sky – I undertake for them?

The hawk-man tries to slow my horses with a net of woven flax, then demands a toll. An old man wearing a coyote mask wearing an old man mask invites me to go hunting with him, and then steals my special hunting pants with which he later accidentally sets himself on fire. A shape-shifting raven turns himself into a cedar seed floating in a stream from which one of my horses drinks, becoming pregnant and giving birth to a foal who gambols about the chariot, and when I give the foal a ball to play with, it takes the toy in its mouth, turns back into a raven, and flies away through a hole in the sky. Unbelievable!

For what do they all come? For no more than a simple hair from my head: a thing I could simply gift them, though I gather that the trickery is in some way important to their pride.

I go along with this pretense because I crave conversation. Of each, I ask the same question:

"Why do the people not look at me?"

"Perhaps they are embarrassed or ashamed," answers the hawk-man. "You are perfect – your precise navigation and your strength – and they can never hope to attain such perfection."

Unsatisfied, I ask another: "Why do the people not look at me?"

"Among my people," responds the two-headed, eight-armed god, "it can be an offense to look directly at the raja because it suggests a treasonous equality. Perhaps they only show you the respect due a sovereign lord."

And later, to another: "Why do the people not look at me?"

"Do you know Plato's Analogy of the Divided Line?" counters a beautiful thief from the marble cities, hiding himself comically behind a giant fennel stalk.

I admit that I do not.

"May I borrow a strand of your hair to demonstrate?" Quick as a pecking hen, he has plucked the hair from my head.

Oh, the trickery.

"Imagine this hair represents everything we can perceive. Now bisect it." Here he clips the hair deftly in two between his thumbs. "Plato suggests the smaller segment represents all that is *visible*, and the larger, all that is *intelligible*. Now bisect those segments again."

From behind the fennel plant, his disembodied hands move like a conjuror's. Clip, clip, *clip*. I must pretend I do not see him palm the fifth segment as he continues with the misdirection of his patter:

"The lesser of the *visible* is the surfaces and shadows of things; it is what we actually see. The greater of the *visible* is the things themselves, whose inherent colors or textures are inferred from experience of their surfaces and shadows. The lesser of the *intelligible* is concrete abstractions like mathematics and logic, and the greater of the intelligible is the conclusions which must be reached by judgment and understanding of goodness and beauty and truth. Do you understand?"

"I'm not sure," I say. "How does this relate to my question?"

He holds his hands out towards me, palms up, letting four segments of hair sift theatrically between us.

"You have no surface, no shadow, yet neither are you simply an abstraction. You are neither *visible* nor *intelligible*. Perhaps you are the very line that bisects the two."

I cannot help but notice that this so-literate thief – even half-hidden behind the yellow flowers of his fennel – will not look directly at me. Nor would the others. I am misunderstood, unloved. *Neither visible nor intelligible.* A black tide of loneliness floods me as he back-steps away with the tiny clipping of my hair tucked into his toga.

But my loneliness is short-lived. It subsides, all at once, when I remember:

My wife, the Moon. She is about to rise.

Noon

Our relationship is not simple. We are more than night and day. Sometimes she visits my house at noon, sometimes I come to her in her Arctic fastnesses at midnight. Sometimes she chases me across the sky, sometimes I chase her. Our lovemaking, though infrequent, is always spectacular. And even that is not simple. She bites. But when our union is perfect, for those brief moments I feel as though I have escaped myself and become something else. The world stands still and my hair billows out around us in weird coruscating light, a corona of glowing silver-gold feathers warping the heavens, and the city-builders all put down their tools and stare.

I should also add that sometimes she is the husband and I am the wife. That sometimes we are brother and sister, or even two sisters. That she may sometimes even inhabit the role of my mother.

It's nothing to be ashamed of. Marriage is a theater of shifting roles. But always we are thesis, antithesis, and sometimes, during the rare total eclipse, we are synthesis.

I keep a house at noon. Golden palace and throne it may be, but to me it is also home, where I stable my horses and, when I am lucky, see my wife and children.

Today is one of those lucky days. We sit together on the floor. My wife has spread a feast of cooked lentils, peas, and dried mango before us on lotus leaves. To my left sit our twins, Yami and Yama; to my right, our youngest, Manu, still just a toddler. My wife orbits counter-clockwise, gracefully filling our cups from a ewer of spiced milk-tea. But Yama's hand shoots out and stops her from pouring his own. He is angry.

"You have given Manu more than his share," he accuses.

"Yama," I say, "You dishonor our meal by your greed. Apologize to your mother."

Yama stands. His face turns red, his fangs extend, his third and fourth hands rise from beneath black robes holding in one a sword and in the other a noose. This is his avatar as Lord of Justice and of Death.

He says, "She is not our mother, but a shadow. Some time ago, our mother abandoned us, leaving this shadow-woman in her place. And you – without realizing the exchange – fathered Manu, whom she now favors over your first-borns. I am not the author of this dishonor."

Little Manu has stuffed his mouth with mango. I look from him to my wife.

"Is this true?"

Under the silk hood of her silver robes, she stands, accused and uncertain how to respond, her eyes downcast.

"Look at me!" I demand, and all of them, even Lord Yama, tilt as if from a desert wind. The woman I believed to be my wife stumbles back and looks up at me fearfully, and in that instant when our eyes meet, she begins to fade. I reach for her hand but she is gone – a shadow sliding away at noon – her robe fluttering and dissolving, her last expression, remorse.

"Now you see," says Yama.

"I see nothing!" I shout. "Where is your real mother?"

Yami regains her composure first. As avatar of the sacred river Yamuna, she holds a necklace of lotus flowers in one hand and a water pot in the other. Her tortoise-mount cowers against her.

"Our mother fashioned this simulacrum of herself from her own shadow, and then fled in the guise of a white mare. She does not wish to be found."

"And yet!" I shout and stamp my foot. It is almost noon, and I am at the height of my powers. I stamp again, upsetting our meal beneath my hooves, shaking the house. I am a horse, a Brobdingnagian stallion made of fire, many times greater than the horses in my team. In three sudden lengths, I have leapt from my noon house and come crashing to earth among the nomad horsefolk of Mongolia, my fury torching the Gobi around me like waves of stacked dry twigs. Thousands of horses flee before me but none is the white mare that is my wife.

I leap again, landing in the Thar, singeing it to a crust with my hooves. I leap again to the Arabian, but the horses that start away at my coming are all black or nut brown. With one final impossible spring, I slam into the Sahara. And there, where no horse should be who travels without a hump, I find a white mare.

When she bolts, my anger flares, and lifeless desolation emanates from me in rippling dunes. I don't know if I am angry at her for deceiving me or angry at myself for being deceived – but I burn. With my muscular neck, I knock her sideways in mid-gallop and she goes sprawling in the sand.

"You are the only one who would look at me!" I scream. "Why did you leave?"

Standing over her, I see her eyes roll white with fear, and my rage – the same rage I had felt when I burned the Demon King at dawn – ignites in my hands. I will immolate this deceiver and fling her ash over the desert.

But then a shimmering comes into the air, the very shimmering eye of high noon, and she says:

"I *did* love you, and because I loved you, I *did* look at you. But I could only bear it for a short time. You are too bright, and looking at you is painful. I am sorry."

I sink to my knees, staring at my hands, so recently hot with vengeance and death.

"Am I that horrible?" I whisper, but when I look up, the white mare – my wife – is struggling over the far dunes and away from her husband and tormentor.

Shame enters me like a sickness.

Afternoon

I find a sacred cave, the Ama-no-Iwato, and beside its entrance, a boulder carved with a motif of swirling storm clouds.

I block myself in.

I tear out all my hair.

Squatting alone in the darkness, I can at last confront what I have become or perhaps have always been: a monster who would strike his own wife, a monster worshipped for killing another monster. And was not the Demon King Apep, in some sense, a part of me? I am a monster worshipped for killing itself.

Of course the priests will not look at me. Their worship is a charade; it is nothing but appeasement.

I decide to give up being a man. I will be a woman and will not raise my hand against my wife again. It is the least I can do. I become a woman in a white kimono with red sleeves and belt and a golden sword and a charm necklace of little golden wolves and flames, though, of course, none of this matters since I have torn out my hair like a penitent and there is no light by which to see my new attributes.

Eventually – in the silence of the cave – I calm. The darkness is like the night inside my lioness mother: a time of innocence, I see now, before the burning light and the fighting and the ceaseless journeying across the sky. It is good to breathe and to rest.

Too soon, my meditations are disturbed by distant screams. There is a scuffling outside my cave, another scream, and then:

"I have found her, she is here!"

A banging on my boulder, and then a voice, muffled but just outside:

"Amaterasu! Come quickly! The demons! In your absence, they have emerged again. Only you can fight them off. They – aaah!"

Another voice in a determined whisper: "Hush! She will not come out to this chaos and unhappiness. We must pretend we are having a party!"

The first voice, also whispered: "What? Alright, let me think...." And then more loudly, "Yes, Amaterasu! We are having a big demon-themed fancy dress party. In your honor! What fun! They're just rolling up the pots of rice wine now!"

"Yes," leers the other voice, "and Ame-no-Uzume is going to do her special dance!"

I retreat from the entrance of the cave as fake laughter and real screams punctuate the desperate invitations to join the party from the goddesses and gods assembling outside. In my shame, I have left the city-builders unprotected. But I will not leave my cave. I will no longer play the monster.

"You are right to make them wait."

I startle when the voice – soft, deep, furred at the edges – speaks at my shoulder.

"Whose there?"

"I am the goddess of wisdom. A goddess of wisdom. And I agree with you that a goddess's protection will only be appreciated if it is sometimes withdrawn. Or perhaps you are hiding here because you fear the Demon King whose minions run amok outside?"

I shift away from the voice in the dark.

"No."

I could take offense, but to what end? Bitterly, I retreat into my usual question. "If you are a goddess of wisdom, tell me – once and for all – why the people will not look at me."

After a pause, the voice says, "Do you know Plato's Allegory of the Cave?"

I sigh. "Is it anything like the Analogy of the Divided Line?"

"It is related, yes. He asks us to imagine a people chained from birth to the wall of a cave who stare all their lives at the blank wall opposite. Farther up the cave, there is a fire and when objects pass before the fire, their shadows are cast on the blank wall. To the people chained in the cave, this shadow theater is all they know of reality. If you unchained one and showed her the fire and the real objects passing before it, she would not believe her eyes. In fact, the truth of the fire would cause her pain."

"And in this allegory," I say wearily, "I am the fire that the people cannot look at."

"Ah.... Perhaps.... Do you mind if we have a little light?" There is a scrabbling and a sharp scratch, and then a small flame blossoms in the middle of the cave. The goddess of wisdom – revealed now as a bare-breasted woman with the head of a great owl – holds a single hair of mine, upright like a burning twig. The rest of my grief-torn hair lies in drifts about the cavern floor.

"You say, *perhaps*," I respond, indignant, maybe a little sullen. "Is there another reading of the allegory that *you* prefer?"

The owl-headed goddess gestures around her noncommittally, making the cavern walls flicker and dance in the weak light of the torch she holds.

"Plato can be interpreted in many ways," she says. "Perhaps *you* are the one chained to the wall and the fire is the beliefs of the city-builders who – unable to see you or understand you – cast shadow stories on your wall. These shadow stories are the city-builders' own projections, guesses about your nature which are more about *their* fears and hopes than about the true you. They are shadow stories projected on your wall, showing demon kings and sky barges and fire thieves and moon wives. Shadow stories about sacred caves, even about owl women...."

In the torchlight, the cavern walls seem to billow. Could the veil of reality indeed be so thin? But I cast my mind over my day, feeling again the murderous burning passing through my hands into Apep, seeing again the tremor of fear on my wife's face, and I cannot absolve myself so easily.

"No," I say to her. "It is simpler than that. They do not look at me because I am a monster. I am a monster so horrible I hurt their eyes."

Outside, amid the sounds of violent festivity, there comes a long scraping sound, something being dragged up to my boulder.

"What is that?"

The owl's head rotates slowly on the goddess's body.

"They are bringing a mirror. The goddesses and gods hope to surprise you with your reflection when you emerge and, while you are dazzled, to close the cave mouth so that you cannot reenter."

"Dazzled? But I have torn out my hair."

"Ah. And yet see. As we spoke, it has regrown."

Surprised, I touch gloss-slick hair where it hangs past my shoulders. The entreaties of the besieged party-goers outside rise in desperation.

"And am I not horrible?"

The owl's downy face is expressionless.

"I am a goddess of wisdom; beauty and ugliness are all one to me. Move the boulder and decide for yourself."

I stand. I adjust my robes and my sword. I run fingers over my wolf-charms. And then with a determined shove, I push aside the carved boulder.

Many things happen at once. Cocks crow. Demons shriek. Goddesses and gods crowd around to grapple with the boulder I have displaced. There is no flood of daylight, but from the dying fire in the cave, I can make out a crush of faces. And here before me is the mirror.

Ignoring the tumult, I examine myself. I seem to be a normal middle-aged woman, with – admittedly – beautiful silk robes. My face is indistinct under the powder and the painted eyebrows, but not unattractive. My expression is maybe a little stern, I suppose, but not terrifying. My eyes....

As I lean closer to look at my eyes, a glow begins to emanate from the skin at my neck so that I cannot see properly. I adjust my robe to see better and the glow spreads to my shoulder and across my face. Then from my hair, rays of power crackle and beam forth, illuminating the valley below me where demons of all shapes and sizes char and crumble beneath my emanations and even goddesses and gods must avert their faces.

Transfixed, I begin to disrobe. My arms glow, my breasts, my navel, my legs. But though I stand naked before the mirror, still something about me is not revealed. Even my skin, it seems, is a shadow story cast on a wall. Even my naked body is less than reality. Seized by foreboding, I turn to question the owl-headed goddess but she is gone, or perhaps never was.

When I look back into the mirror, my skin dissolves in dazzling light and I stand revealed. I am a perfect circle, blazing.

Dusk

My chariot climbs higher and higher above the teeming cities.

Looking down upon the blue-green tapestry unspooling beneath me, I muse on relative truths. Am I passing over a stationary Earth, or is it spinning beneath me? Does it matter?

I no longer drive the chariot. I am a bright circle, a geometric abstraction; I am without hands. Instead, a series of god-women and god-men vie for the honor of conducting my chariot as I shine, unblinking, from its pedestal. Each wears a headdress symbolic of my corona. A man with the armored skirt of a centurion is laureled with beaten gold. A woman with long orange-red curls holds her hair back with a gold-leafed wheel. A surprised young boy wears a bent olive branch cock-eyed across his brow. Each takes my chariot higher, farther. We enter realms of the upper air populated by monsters of the zodiac – through the horns of the Star-Bull, past the sharp segmented stinger of the Star-Scorpion – but they are shadows on the wall of a cave, thinned to metaphor. We pass through them.

One of my drivers, a wounded carpenter with hemp sandals and a crown of thorns, says to me:

"Do you know why the people will not look at us?"

My old feelings of alienation remain, but somehow they have softened since I uncovered my true form.

"We are too bright," I say to him simply. "We hurt their eyes."

He stares into the heavens ahead as the cloud-whirled Earth falls away beneath us, now no larger than a city, a boulder, a marble rolling across vastness.

"Yes," he says, "that is true. But I have sometimes feared there is more to it…. Do you know Plato's Analogy of the Sun?"

In the wounded man's voice, I think I hear an echo of the isolation that I myself once felt, enclosed in my cave.

I'm tired of Plato, but to humor the carpenter, I say, "Plato made an analogy of me?"

"His first, actually, before the others. Plato is tasked to define goodness and he refuses. Instead, he asks us to consider what is necessary to 'see' an object. The object itself is necessary, and the eye to see it, but light is also necessary to define its surface and display its color, otherwise it would be invisible. For this reason, the sun – made of light and itself the source of light – cannot be seen. From what source would the light needed to see the sun come?"

I nod – guessing where this is going – and he continues, encouraged:

"Now, by analogy, he asks us to consider what is necessary to 'judge' an idea. Again, three things: the idea itself, the mind to perceive it and the understanding of goodness which allows the idea to be judged. But, like the sun, goodness cannot be used to judge itself. Do you understand?"

I don't want to disappoint the man – he seems so earnest – so I say only, "I have never been entirely comfortable with analogies."

"But that's it!" he says, leaning dangerously forward from the chariot with his arms outstretched like a gull's and droplets of blood leaking from his punctured palms. "You and I are the same. We are sources – you of light, and I of goodness. It may be philosophically impossible for the people to look at us!"

We travel through black vacuum lit by impassably distant stars. Apep has won. I feel the Demon King's cold chaos everywhere in this nowhere. All I can do is shine on and hope that my shining is enough to keep the old nemesis at bay for the women and men and children ceding to sleep on that tiny spinning marble. To the wounded man, I say:

"You are an idea. I am a thing. Ideas and things are not the same."

He seems to deflate. Half turned away from me, the man removes his crown of thorns and examines it thoughtfully. On distant Earth, belief flickers, weakens. They do not look at us.

Ideas and things are not the same.

"Perhaps not," he says, and then he vanishes.

I am alone, thereafter. There is no driver, no chariot, and day and night are only the turning of the Earth. I will not see my lioness mother again – if, indeed, she existed at all. Distance is measured by time. Three light-minutes to the planet Mercury, five light-hours to the planet Pluto. Eight light-minutes to the imperiled planet of the city-builders, still orbited by my ex-wife like a white dove circling a foamy sea.

All the light-hours in between are vacuum and dust and void.

Meanwhile, the city-builders discover electricity. They revolutionize agriculture and medicine and communication and war. They take to the air themselves. When they build a spaceship and visit my ex-wife, touching so delicately down on her cratered face, I am moved by an obscure emotion, loneliness and shame and longing and jealousy accreted together as a pearl accretes around the seed of an old hurt.

They send a probe arcing my way, scintillant, a dust-mote turning through curtains of radiation in the gyre of gravity. At first, I think it is a mislaunch, more space junk, but it doesn't burn up. As the probe approaches, whipping around Venus, I see through its carbon-composite heat shield and its strange flux-measuring molybdenum dish, and I am filled with sudden astonishment and a boundless, welling gratitude.

It is an eye. Far-flung, engineered, a thing like a prayer whispered to the starry night, but better than a prayer.

The city-builders have built an eye and sent it to look at me.

Afterword

This story was inspired by NASA's launch of the Parker Solar Probe. Advances in heat shielding allow it to get much closer to the sun than any measuring device before. In 2024, the probe will make its nearest approach to date, close enough to "touch" the sun's corona.

The Sun and the Moon

From the Krachi people, west Africa

THE SUN AND THE MOON fell in love and decided to marry. For a time they were very happy together and produced many children whom they christened "stars". But it was not long before the moon grew weary of her husband and decided to take a lover, refusing to conceal the fact that she greatly enjoyed the variety.

Of course, the sun soon came to hear of his wife's brazen infidelity and the news made him extremely unhappy. He attempted to reason with the moon, but when he saw that his efforts were entirely fruitless, he decided to drive his wife out of his house. Some of the children sided with their mother, while others supported their father. But the sun was never too hard on his wife, in spite of their differences, and saw to it that their possessions were equally divided up.

The moon was always too proud to accept her husband's kindness, however, and even to this day, she continues to make a habit of trespassing on his lands, often taking her children with her and encouraging them to fight the siblings who remain behind with their father.

The constant battles between the star-children of the sun and the star-children of the moon produce great storms of thunder and lightning and it is only when she becomes bored of these confrontations that the moon sends her messenger, the rainbow, into the field, instructing him to wave a cloth of many colours as a signal for her children to retreat.

Sometimes the moon herself is caught by the sun attempting to steal crops from his fields. Whenever this happens, he chases after his estranged wife and if he catches her he begins to flog her or even tries to eat her.

So whenever a man sees an eclipse, he knows that things have come to blows once again between husband and wife up above. At this time, he must be certain to beat his drum and threaten the sun very loudly, for if he does not, the sun might finish the job, and we should certainly lose the moon forever.

Sun Chaser

E.C. Robinson

THE SKY DISTRACTS ME from rehearsal. There's a square blinking in blue and I study the glitch while I sing, squinting against the glare of the noon-bright setting. The rest of the school choir sings with earnest focus. They either don't see the error, or don't care, or care more about singing beautifully tomorrow. But I can't stop staring.

Barely in time, I notice the cue for my solo. *Gloria gloria gloria.* When the others join me, our crescendo echoes across the field.

The parents waiting nearby clap when our voices fade. Mrs. Harris's feedback starts immediately: the rhythm drags here, stagger the breath, warm up the timbre on this phrase. I try, and fail, to pay attention. Nothing is as it should be. The sky is broken; I sing songs for a faith I don't believe in; the Solstice decorations clutter our already-cramped field. I feel taut, a stretched string. Pluck me and I'll thrum.

"Evie—" Mrs. Harris interrupts my thoughts. "Acceptable, but breathy. Watch your pitch. And don't be late on your entrance."

I nod, and our rehearsal ends.

"She hates us," Tess whispers as we walk towards our parents. Papa waits away from the others, flipping through papers on a clipboard. "She never says anything nice. It's always fix this, change that. Nothing is good enough."

"She doesn't want to be embarrassed," I say. "Everyone comes to the Solstice."

"She could be nicer about it."

I shrug, listening absentmindedly to her familiar complaints, then hug her goodbye. "Gorgeous," Papa says.

"I was flat."

"I couldn't tell."

Mrs. Harris could, but I shrug, then point. "Something is wrong with the sky."

He turns, adjusting the glasses that perpetually slip down his nose, and groans when he locates the error. A small square of pixels flipping between blue and not-blue in the ceiling twenty feet above.

"They'll want it fixed for tomorrow. Do you mind waiting?"

His voice is tired, and he flips through the papers on his clipboard to make a note on a form labeled *Sky Maintenance*. I shake my head, and we cross the field to stand beneath the flicker. I look up. Sometimes, if the field is empty and I stare at the right spot in the digital sky, the metal walls of the field drop away and I can pretend I am outside. Today, though, the field is crowded, loud. I notice the walls, the corners, the squares of fake grass beneath my feet.

"Can't you do anything about the temperature," Celia's voice cuts through the chatter. She's been at the field all day, supervising the preparations for tomorrow. As she strides towards Papa and me, her white robes billow like clouds. A disk of hammered gold gleams beneath her throat. I know her from school, as we overlapped during her final year, when

I was eight and she was eighteen. After she graduated she joined the Solacers, the religious group who have ruled the Complex for the past twenty years.

"The heat is killing me," Celia fans her face. "I know it's supposed to be summer but it's too hot to breathe. I can't take another second of it, and with what's happening tomorrow—" her voice cracks, but she barrels on. I can't tell how she feels about her role in the ceremony. "It'll be even hotter during the ceremony, with everyone here. It has to be cooler."

"I'll see what I can do," Papa says. "I can add a scent, too, if you want. I have sunscreen haze, BBQ, strawberry popsicle—"

Celia shakes her head sharply. "Keep those godawful things out of here. I've made multiple complaints about them because of my allergies but it usually makes no difference. The Lord Solacer says people *need* those scents. But, for once I get to decide – I am the Sun Chaser after all – and I don't want any. Just fix the temperature levels."

"No scents, yes ma'am, I'll make a special note of that."

"Great. Thanks so much."

Celia heads towards Mrs. Harris, who has conscripted the boys in the choir into re-positioning the risers. When she is out of earshot, Papa laughs, a rough bark nothing like his normal chuckle.

"We'll have to go above," he says, tapping a pencil against his clipboard.

We walk across the field, passing the elevators that connect the Complex's levels, and head towards a side door. Papa unlocks it with a key card. Inside, the room is small, musty. A metal ladder is screwed to the wall, leading to the maintenance level above the sky. Excitement drums beneath my skin. A new room to explore.

I go first. Papa breathes heavily behind me. The climb is long and tiring, but my eagerness only grows. I haven't been here yet; the novelty is intoxicating. Walls I have not seen, floors I have not walked, air I have not tasted. And, because the field is the Complex's highest level, with each step up the ladder I get closer and closer to the outside.

When I reach the top, I flop to the side and Papa heaves himself over. The room is dimly lit and as large as the field below, but it is a mess of circuit boards, whirring machinery, the occasional cardboard box. Rather plain, almost disappointing – but still extraordinary in its newness.

Papa consults his clipboard, then crosses the room until he reaches the sky's broken section. He kneels, popping a panel off the floor with a grunt, and reaches into the hole. The movement causes the tools on his belt to jangle together, sending a metallic twang into the air.

I begin to wander; I have to see everything I can. I head towards the room's farthest side, where the choir's risers are in the field below. All of the Complex lies below me; the sky is the closest it has ever been. I walk the level's perimeter, running fingertips along the walls. The walls are rough stone instead of the other levels' buffed metal. Soon, my hands are wonderfully grimy.

Eventually I discover the staircase. It is a small thing, twisting in a tight spiral through the ceiling. Padlocked chains and a crisscross of yellow tape block the entrance. And it goes up.

Towards the sun.

I itch with curiosity. I've never seen it. No one my age has. We never got the chance to. The observatories, which are located on the highest level in the Complex and contain rooms to safely view the sky, were shut years ago, before we were born. Now, a sight of the real sky is a gift reserved only for the Sun Chaser.

But here – here is a staircase, which likely leads to one of those rooms. A staircase that is accessible if you have a key card. Like Papa does. Like Mama did.

My few memories of Mama are sun-kissed. The last is sun-ruined, but I avoid thinking about that. Tomorrow, it will be inescapable. For Mama the sun was divine; she named his colors like a prayer. The gold, the honey, the amber. She tsked at our fake sky, called our digital sunrises heresy.

"All our technology and we can't mimic the sun," she'd tell me. "If only you could feel it – the *real* one, not this blown-out circle of pixels. Maybe one day, someday, we'll stand beneath it together."

That sun-struck hope killed her. I resent her for it. Papa does too. How could she leave us? How could she love the sun more? But now, as I stand here, tempted by the mere promise of a sky sounding above, drawn by siren-call of what it would feel like to look up and not see walls, I understand her a little more.

I have to see.

I duck beneath the locked chains, bound up the steps. I peer up. The stairs rise into blackness, a soaring mystery. I step higher—

"*EVE*," Papa's voice booms. I whirl around to find him at the base of the stairs. My foot slips, and I catch myself against the railing. He holds his arms out. "Come down right now."

"But—" I protest. There's such a thumping in my body, such a need to climb higher.

"It's not safe, Evie."

"I only want to look."

"That's the danger," he says. "Once you've looked, you can't go back. That's what makes it hard."

"I'm not Mama," I tell him.

"I know sweetie, I know. Please, come here."

He looks so worried I step down and as soon as I reach the bottom he folds me into a hug. The edges of the key card, clipped to his belt, press into my stomach.

"Promise me you'll never go up there." His hands are on my shoulders and he stares into my eyes with alarming intensity. "Promise me."

"I promise."

I sit beside him while he repairs the sky, and later, when we ride the elevator down to our level, he gently squeezes my hand, as if to convince himself I am still here.

* * *

In the morning, I put on a mass-issued choir dress for the Solstice. The dress is black, floor-length with puffy sleeves, and so tight through the shoulders I can't raise my arms. I've washed it countless times but it still smells like someone else's sweat.

We arrive to the soft light of a pre-dawn sky. The field throngs with people, but despite the bright decorations, the giggles of children as they play, and the scent of sage sausage and cinnamon buns, there is a weight to the air, some half-tick to the smiles, a jaggedness to the laughter. It is an ugly hope that marks the crowd.

I take my place beside Tess on the risers. Mrs. Harris stands before us, face tight. The others, like Tess, probably assume she is nervous, but I remember last year's Solstice, when her husband was the Sun Chaser. Her eyes, I think, blaze with furious grief, not nerves.

Celia sits on the Sun Chaser's throne beside the risers. She wears saffron robes and a short hood covers her hair. The other Solacers, clad in their usual white, incline their heads as they take their place around her.

I see no hesitation on her face – in fact, she looks proud, maybe even excited, the way all the other Sun Chasers seemed to be – but I don't know what I'd do if I *did* notice regret or fear. The Solstice would continue, no matter what I do. The Lord Solacer would make sure of it. Today, I can't escape the ugly weight of my powerlessness.

The Lord Solacer waits at the podium, a shock of thick white hair framing a narrow face. His robes have saffron thread stitched at the collar, hem and cuffs and his disk shines like a golden, unblinking eye.

He quiets the crowd, which has gathered before us. Everyone in the Complex usually attends and I recognize many faces, even if I can't remember their names. I notice many look eager, gazing at the Lord Solacer and Celia in adoration, but others seem angry, or sad.

"Welcome, welcome," the Lord Solacer speaks in a reverent voice that rings across the field. Papa says the man can't resist the chance to perform, especially before an audience of five hundred. "It has been a hard year, and I know how hard you have all worked, how tired you must feel. Today, let us give thanks and celebrate."

He beckons to our sky, arms sweeping wide in a theatrical gesture.

Dawn blooms – and an almost universal gasp sounds across the crowd. It must be sublime, and maybe I would think so too if I hadn't seen it before. Since Papa maintains the sky, I know all about its various programs, even the ones that haven't officially been played yet.

This is Sunrise #43: clouds kissed in pink, stars winking out like birthday candles, a hint of apricot before the sun arrives. I crank my head back, tracking the spread of light as the sun rises like a golden disk from the farthest edge, starting at the crease between wall and ceiling. I wait for the best part – for the shadowed V of geese to fly across. A recording of their honks fills the field, and my eyes close.

I try to imagine what wind feels like, what it tastes like – horizon, dirt, eternity. I pretend I can feel sun-soaked air on my skin and inhale it until it colors my voice golden. I wonder what it would feel like to live freely, to sing freely, without a Solacer's permission.

The crowd's applause brings me back and I open my eyes. My throat tightens. The Lord Solacer gestures to Mrs. Harris.

We start on the downbeat sweep of her hands. Our voices ring like bells, a high unbroken melody falling and rising through the air in simple tones. The field brightens with our music and the rising sun. When we finish, the crowd claps and Mrs. Harris bows.

I prepare for what happens next. I think of Mama and her Solstice, of Celia's likely fate. I can't stand it. I fist my hand, fighting to keep my face calm, still, as it continues. Tess glances at me. I must look awful because she mouths, *You okay?* then covers my fist with a gentle hand.

I look across the crowd and see frowns, crossed arms, shaking heads. This year there are more than ever before. I wish they said something. Maybe that would stop it. From singing I know many voices sounding together are stronger than one. Maybe if we joined ours, others would listen.

The crowd splits in two lines to create a passage from the throne to the elevator. The Lord Solacer bows to Celia, who walks down the crowd-made aisle at a slow, measured pace. We sing a chant for the Sun Chaser, a harmonious, wordless round that arcs in an evocation of the rise and fall of day.

Celia reaches the open elevator, lowering her hood as she turns to face us.

"Be well," she tells us with a smile. "I take your tidings to the Sun."

She is still smiling as the doors shut.

Our chant is the only sound. All eyes are fixed on the elevator doors. It takes at least three minutes for the elevator to rise to the surface, one minute of exposure, then an additional five for it to sink below. Above us, the sky settles into a soft morning glow.

I stop singing. Tess squeezes my hand when she notices. I take comfort in Mrs. Harris's blazing eyes as she conducts, in Tess's friendship beside me, in Papa's steadiness. Why do we do this?

The elevator's ding is violent. The doors open, revealing what remains. All that ever remains.

A body of blistered red skin.

* * *

During dinner, I ask Papa the question I ask every year.

"Why did Mama do it?"

Papa doesn't answer at first, taking another bite of pasta before patting his mouth clean with a napkin. "Your mother had a hard time adjusting. A lot of people did. That's why we built the observatories. But for some people, looking at the sky only made it worse. It reminded them of what we lost, what we couldn't have because the surface wasn't safe anymore. It drove them crazy."

"The first Sun Chasers."

Papa nodded. "It happened about a year after the Complex sealed and we couldn't visit the outside. Some people couldn't take it anymore and went up. They died, and we decided to close all the observatories. It was too risky to keep them open. Thing is, the claustrophobia didn't go away. The man who became the Lord Solacer knew that, so now we have – this." He gestures with his fork.

"So Mama was like Celia?"

Papa sighs. I can tell the question bothers him, too. "I don't know. Maybe. She used to say there isn't enough color to build a life down here."

I already knew Papa's answers but hearing them again cut like a fresh wound. Who was I to compete with the sun?

* * *

That night I can't sleep. The elevator's ding sounds over and over, an obnoxious bell that wakes me each time I begin to drift away. Memories of today and years ago swirl and merge until it is Mama I send off with my voice, Mama who is wrapped in a shroud, Mama who is canonized.

Eventually, it's almost dawn and I've had hours of blistered dreams. My thoughts are muddled with grief; they return to the staircase. The curiosity ruins me.

I steal Papa's key. Pluck it from where it's clipped to his belt, place it in my pocket, and slip away with a flashlight and backpack.

Sneaking in is easy with the key. I hurry up the ladder and find the staircase. I pause before the yellow tape.

My stomach churns. I did promise Papa – and I know it will break his heart when he learns what I've done. But I can't go back. I'll never understand Mama until I see for myself.

So I break my promise. I was – am – a liar. Maybe that is the way of promises. Maybe all promises are lies until you make them truths.

I duck under the padlocked chains, sprint up the stairs into blackness. I settle into a rhythm, nearly dizzy from the stairs' unrelenting twist, climbing higher and higher, backpack thumping against my waist, flashlight illuminating the grate beneath my feet. It's lonely in the darkness so I begin to hum as I climb. The music brightens my path and I realize that is its true power: music lets us craft suns of our own, even in the deep belly of the earth, below meters and meters of dirt.

Soon I am belting, loud as I can, voice flung far and free, and it doesn't matter when I squeak at the high notes or land flat on the quick drops. I trill, I soar, I rise. The melody speeds my feet, turning me upwards, upwards, upwards—

My voice stops when I reach a large rectangular room. I shine the flashlight around. Benches line the uneven stone walls and overlapping metal panels cover the ceiling. An observatory. Forgotten, but now mine.

A long chain, connected to the panels, hangs in a corner. I walk to it, hold the flashlight between my teeth, and tug.

It is rusted, heavy, stiff. I brace my feet and yank, dropping my weight to the ground. Eventually, after much straining, the chain screeches into motion. The panels squeal as they slide apart. Sweat trickles down my forehead, my arms burn. I think of Mama and her colors, music and its promise, the sun and its pulsing song. I'll never unsee, never unhear it.

Darkness gradually lightens from onyx to charcoal to gray and then: light falls around me. Honey, amber. *Gloria gloria gloria*. Warm but so bright it needles. I can't see. I shut my eyes and drop the chain.

The sun beckons. Come closer. Come see. I feel for a bench and stand on top of it, then climb higher still by placing my hands and feet on the rocks jutting out from the walls. Eventually I reach up, brush fingers across smooth glass.

I look. The sky hums gold.

The Sun Ensnared

From Native American folklore

AT THE VERY BEGINNING of time, when chaos and darkness reigned and hordes of bloodthirsty animals roamed the earth devouring mankind, there remained only two survivors of the human race. A young brother and sister, who managed to flee from the jaws of the ferocious beasts, took refuge in a secluded part of the forest where they built for themselves a little wooden lodge. Here, they carved out a meagre existence, relying on nature's kindness for their survival. The young girl, who was strong and hardworking, bravely accepted the responsibility of keeping the household together, for her younger brother had never grown beyond the size of an infant and demanded her constant care. Every morning she would go out in search of firewood, taking her brother with her and seating him on a comfortable bed of leaves while she chopped and stacked the logs they needed to keep a warm fire burning. Then, before heading homeward, she would gather the ripest berries from the surrounding hedgerows and both would sit down together to enjoy their first meal of the day.

They had passed many pleasant years in this way before the young girl began to grow anxious for her brother's future, fearing that she might not always be able to care for him. She had never considered it wise in the past to leave him alone while she went about her chores, but now she felt she must take that risk for his own good.

"Little brother," she said to him, "I will leave you behind today while I go out to gather wood, but you need not be afraid and I promise to return shortly."

And saying this, she handed him a bow and several small arrows.

"Hide yourself behind that bush," she added, "and soon you will see a snowbird coming to pick worms from the newly cut logs. When the bird appears, try your skill and see if you can shoot it."

Delighted at the opportunity to prove himself, the young boy sat down excitedly, ready to draw his bow as soon as the bird alighted on the logs. But the first arrow he shot went astray and before he was able to launch a second, the creature had risen again into the air. The little brother felt defeated and discouraged and bowed his head in shame, fully expecting that his sister would mock his failure. As soon as she returned, however, she began to reassure him, offering him encouragement and insisting that he try again on the following day.

Next morning, the little brother crouched down once more behind the bush and waited for the snowbird to appear. He was now more determined than ever to prove his skill and, on this occasion, his arrow shot swiftly through the air, piercing the bird's breast. Seeing his sister approach in the distance, he ran forward to meet her, his face beaming with pride and joy.

"I have killed a fine, large bird," he announced triumphantly. "Please will you skin it for me and stretch the skin out to dry in the sunshine. When I have killed more birds, there will be enough skins to make me a fine, long coat."

"I would be very happy to do this for you," his sister smiled. "But what shall I do with the body when I have skinned it?"

The young boy searched for an answer, and as he stood thinking his stomach groaned with hunger. It seemed wasteful to burn such a plump bird and he now began to wonder what it would be like to taste something other than wild berries and greens, "We have never before eaten flesh," he said, "but let us cut the body in two and cook one half of it in a pot over the fire. Then, if the food is good, we can savour the remaining half later."

His sister agreed that this was a wise decision and prepared for them their very first dish of game which they both ate with great relish that same evening.

The little brother had passed his very first test of manhood and with each passing day he grew more confident of his ability to survive in the wilderness. Soon he had killed ten birds whose skins were sewn into the coat he had been promised. Fiercely proud of his hunting skills, he wore this new garment both day and night and felt himself ready to meet any challenge life might throw at him.

"Are we really all alone in the world, sister?" he asked one day as he paraded up and down the lodge in his bird-skin coat, "since I cannot believe that this great broad earth with its fine blue sky was created simply for the pair of us."

"There may be other people living," answered his sister, "but they can only be terrible beings, very unlike us. It would be most unwise to go in search of these people, little brother, and you must never be tempted to stray too far from home."

But his sister's words only added to the young boy's curiosity, and he grew more impatient than ever to slip away quietly and explore the surrounding forests and countryside for himself.

Before the sun had risen on the following morning, he grabbed his bow and arrows and set off enthusiastically in the direction of the open hills. By midday, he had walked a very great distance, but still he hadn't discovered any other human beings. At length, he decided to rest for a while and lay down on the grass in the warmth of the sun's golden rays. He had happened upon a very beautiful spot, and was soon lulled gently to sleep by the tinkling sound of the waters dancing over the pebbles of a nearby stream. He slept for many hours in the heat of the brilliant sunshine and would have remained in this position a good while longer had he not been disturbed by the sensation that something close to him had begun to shrink and shrivel. At first, he thought he had been dreaming, but as he opened his eyes wider and gazed upon his bird-skin coat, he soon realized that it had tightened itself upon his body, so much so that he was scarcely able to breathe.

The young boy stood up in horror and began to examine his seared and singed coat more closely. The garment he had been so proud of was now totally ruined and he flew into a great passion, vowing to take vengeance on the sun for what it had done.

"Do not imagine that you can escape me because you are so high up in the sky," he shouted angrily. "What you have done will not go unpunished. I will pay you back before long." And after he had sworn this oath, he trudged back home wearily to tell his sister of the dreadful misfortune that had befallen his new coat.

The young girl was now more worried than ever for her little brother. Ever since his return, he had fallen into a deep depression, refusing all food and laying down on his side, as still as a corpse, for a full ten days, at the end of which he turned over and lay on his other side for a further ten days. When he eventually arose, he was pale and drawn, but his voice was firm and resolute as he informed his sister that she must make a snare for him with which he intended to catch the sun.

"Find me some material suitable for making a noose," he told her, but when his sister returned with a piece of dried deer sinew, he shook his head and said it would not do. Racking her brains, she searched again through their belongings, and came forward with a bird skin, left over from the coat she had made.

"This won't do either," her brother declared agitatedly, "the sun has had enough of my bird skins already. Go and find me something else."

Finally, his sister thought of her own beautiful long hair, and pulling several glossy strands from her head, she began to weave a thick black cord which she handed to her brother.

"This is exactly what I need," he said delightedly and began to draw it back and forth through his fingers until it grew rigid and strong. Then, having coiled it round his shoulders, he kissed his sister goodbye and set off to catch the sun, just as the last light began to fade in the sky.

Under cover of darkness, the little brother set his trap, fixing the snare on a spot where he knew the sun would first strike the land as it rose above the earth. He waited patiently, offering up many prayers. These were answered as soon as the sun attempted to rise from its sleepy bed, for it became fastened to the ground by the cord and could not ascend any higher. No light twinkled on the horizon and the land remained in deep shadow, deprived of the sun's warm rays.

Fear and panic erupted among the animals who ruled the earth as they awoke to discover a world totally submerged in darkness. They ran about blindly, calling to each other, desperate to find some explanation for what had happened. The most powerful among them immediately formed a council and it was agreed that someone would have to go forward to the edge of the horizon to investigate why the sun had not risen. This was a very dangerous undertaking, since whoever ventured so close to the sun risked severe burning and possible death. Only the dormouse, at that time the largest animal in the world, taller than any mountain, stood up bravely, offering to risk her life so that the others might be saved.

Hurriedly, she made her way to the place where the sun lay captive and quickly spotted the cord pinning it to the ground. Even now, though the dormouse was not yet close enough to begin gnawing the cord, her back began to smoke and the intense heat was almost overwhelming. Still she persevered, chewing the cord with her two front teeth while at the same time her huge bulk was turned into an enormous heap of ashes. When, at last, the sun was freed, it shot up into the sky as dazzling as it had ever been. But the dormouse, now shrunken to become one of the tiniest creatures in the world, fled in terror from its light and from that day forward she became known as Kug-e-been-gwa-kwa, or Blind Woman.

As soon as he discovered that the sun had escaped his snare, the little brother returned home once more to his sister. But he was now no longer anxious to take revenge, since his adventure had brought him greater wisdom and the knowledge that he had not been born to interfere with the ways of nature. For the rest of his life, he devoted himself to hunting, and within a very short time had shot enough snowbirds to make himself a new coat, even finer than the one which had led him to challenge the sun.

A Sun Fable

Caroline Winge

FOUR RINGS COMPRISED my emperor's palace: one for the guards, one for the servants, one for his court, and the innermost chambers that only we could enter. His ancestors had built it thus to keep him safe, or so said his advisors. He could never leave it, and neither would I – ever again – once we were married. For now, I was merely his betrothed, but I hadn't seen sunlight in a week.

The palace was a single building with no doors to the outside, except at the first gate. There were few windows. Endless passages curled around themselves like a serpent; you followed them in and out of rooms without ever going *out*, only *in*, until you were drowning in *innerness*.

Even the patter of rain barely reached us in the inner courtyard to which my emperor had taken me, but a sliver of white dawn showed through a narrow opening high on the wall, between two stone bars.

If I were a bird…. Useless daydreams.

When I squinted, I could make out the faintest dampness on the window ledge. I don't think rain ever came in there. Neither did people, for dust powdered the floor and the bench where we sat. We might've been the only ones to step in this room in a decade.

Still it rained, a muted but pervasive sound, and it was a relief to know of rain, to hear it, to see a sky. I let its song wash over me, while my emperor's face puckered in anxiety.

His quiet voice broke the silence. "It isn't here today."

We'd been waiting there because something troubled him. In this courtyard, one morning, magic had visited him.

Out of the greyness of dawn, in streaks of lilac and red – a powerful spell, as he described it – a golden coin had appeared, guided by some magician's hand to his window. An *enchanted* coin. Everything it faced was turned into gold: the floor, the bench, the walls. His soft skin was gilded. His clothes, already rich, were made into a marvel. For a short while, he watched in wonder as all glittered and gleamed around him, even the dust motes in the air.

Yet it ended too soon.

Suddenly the spell was broken. The invisible magician snatched away the coin, and everything felt drab in its absence.

They had taunted him, then left. The light was once again common and pale. The window lay empty.

I looked at my emperor's face. *He must be mocking me.* Yet his sorrow seemed genuine, and I'd had enough time by then to realize his naivety.

After all, he was a baby when his parents were assassinated, and his guardians forbid him to ever set foot outside, so he was raised, safe and secluded – an unknowing captive – under their power. No one intervened. His inner circle held a special kind of courtier, who didn't mind living in a labyrinth lit by scented candles, never tasting fresh air, never feeling the touch of grass or rain or sunlight, only to have their emperor's ear.

To me they were more wolves than people. If all lights went out, I could picture their eyes glowing red in the dark.

I had been seeing too much of them since my parents arranged my betrothal. Sometimes I cursed at my mother and father for subjecting me to this powerless prestige.

They called this a palace, but it was the stuffiest and loneliest cage, which I would soon be sharing with my husband. For how long? Who knew. Our whole lives, but our regents would decide how long – or short – these might be.

My emperor's problems, now mine too, were far more serious than magic. He had no idea, as he prattled on to me of what he thought to be a *coin*.

"I came back a thousand times to see it. Every time, I ask it to stay, but I can't tempt the magician." He hung his head. "I don't understand what they want me to offer. I just know I can't command them or their golden spell."

In the faint light of overcast dawn, I nearly missed his tears, only noticing them by the wetness on my fingers when I touched his face.

I brushed them away; I kissed his cheek and lay his head on my shoulder. His body felt so small and frail in my arms.

I hadn't arrived at court expecting to love him, but he was young and lonely and in danger. I was also young and grieving my old life. When I held him like this, my heart broke for both of us. And then how could I stop love from sneaking into the wound? My emperor burrowed into my chest, seeking my warmth, and I wanted to close around him like a shield.

I loved him as much as I hated his palace. Because we were fellow prisoners, that didn't cause any contradiction yet.

At that moment, though, he raised his face to mine with such hope! To his eyes, I was a hero. I could do anything.

He breathed out the words that freed me and doomed us: "Would you bring me that golden coin?"

For a moment, all I could hear was my own heart singing. A door opened. There would be open air and rain falling outside, and I longed to rush into its embrace.

I should've known better, but I tricked myself into believing we were living in the kind of story where lovers take on impossible missions as a wedding gift, vanquish them, and come back unharmed. We would go into poems and be remembered for the ages.

I also told myself I needed only a moment outside. One last look at the world I was leaving behind. After that, I would return to him with his miracle.

"I will," I gave him my word.

Then reason caught up with my tongue, and I crashed back to reality. Had I gone mad? How could I bring my love the sun?

* * *

Our resident magicians told me there was a palace of the Sun. They showed me charts and incantations and gave me a box carved with spells to trap it at dawn, while it was still drowsy.

Their words were honeyed; they smiled and praised the lovely wedding gift I would surely bring our emperor, but their mocking gazes told me otherwise, so I paid them a gold piece each and forgot the box somewhere. I didn't trust the way they licked their lips as I left, anticipating the chance of picking my bones clean. I was better off on my own luck.

There was one single task left before I went, but when I sought my emperor to say goodbye, I found him sobbing in the courtyard.

A fist squeezed my heart.

"Why are you crying?" I put on a smile and wiped away his tears. "Aren't you pleased? I will bring your magic coin."

He clung to me. "But you're leaving."

"I'll come back."

Somehow, as I puffed my chest in a show of bravery for him, I managed to pretend even to myself that I *could* find a palace of legend and bring him the Sun trapped between my fingers. The urge to run out of his palace doors was too strong, although a mild discomfort prickled through my defenses like a badly placed hairpin.

A little voice within me whispered I could only die searching. If I left, I would never return to his side, and it would be *glad* to have its tomb out in the open, far away from this den of carrion eaters. I closed my ears to its chilling prophecies.

I kissed my emperor's brow, combing his hair with my fingers. I kissed his cheeks. Cupping his face in my hands, I kissed him full on the lips.

He tasted of salt, like sorrow.

When I drew back, he kept leaning towards me. One last kiss – softer now – and I left him.

* * *

I passed many villages and walked countless miles, but it was all for nothing. There's no use dwelling on it.

Wherever I went, the wealthiest and highest officials of our empire greeted me. They invited me to their houses, to dine and drink with them; they bade me stay as long as I wished, and their smiles congealed like old fat on their faces, when I asked them the way to the palace of the Sun. From them, I never had any answer.

I went on and told my story to travelers, tinkerers and roaming priests. Sometimes I received a wary nod the way they'd come. Best not to anger a mad noble.

When I found a cottage, I stopped farmers' wives in their work to question them. They giggled at me behind their hands and pointed east. Surely that's the Sun's home, where it rises each morning?

So I kept walking and asked the children playing by fields or village wells. They conferred solemnly among themselves before taking me to the most magical place they knew. This way, they told me, *must* lead to the palace of the Sun.

Still I couldn't find it.

* * *

I was as far away from my own nightmare palace as anyone could go when my legs finally folded beneath me on a dusty stretch of road with nothing to see but marshes from horizon to horizon. I dropped crying to the dirt, too tired to go on. Not even the giddiness of freedom could carry me any farther.

Then, I had to face everything I'd been hiding from myself. There was no palace of the Sun. My quest was doomed, and my heart was about to fail.

Back by my emperor's side, dying hadn't seemed possible – not while I was stepping on clouds, so eager to leave I would entrust myself to any fool's hope. Yet my lips weren't parched back then.

I hadn't been able to find the simplest homestead for days. I couldn't remember when I'd last eaten. Every night I shivered out in the weather.

Now I could feel death coming, so I feared it. I didn't want to die alone, half a world away from him.

I was gripped, at once, by both the need to go back and a fear of returning. If I were *lucky*, return would mean being walled alive until I crumbled over myself from old age.

It would be torture…though torture was also the thought of my love crying for me, alone in his palace of wolves, without a shield, without even a hand to hold. Soon he might be dead too: my emperor couldn't fend for himself if his advisors tired of him.

Do you understand my impasse?

It tore my heart in two. I watered the dust of that road with my tears; I beat it with my fists, and then I started laughing, sobbing, until my stomach and my chest both hurt. I couldn't breathe, but I couldn't stop either. What a ridiculous way to die!

Imagine one who has everything: an emperor. Above him, only a god.

Yet here were we: my beloved, who never knew anything but darkness. Myself, trapped in the same prison while trying to bring him some light.

I wanted some for myself too, instead of wasting away in that crypt of a palace. Who was I, though, to think I could escape reality and write down a better story?

"He never felt sunlight on his face. There are no windows…. There is no air in his palace." Hoarse ironic laughter mingled with my tears. "Everyone has a piece of the sun, even the poorest peasant.

"Can't I have just a piece to take him? He'd be happy with a coin. Is that too much? Doesn't the Sun have enough treasures?" Dropping my forehead to the road, I fell into mumbling and quiet tears that tasted like dirt.

I missed him. I didn't want to die like this. I also prayed: if only I could go back, I would brave even that palace, for as long as it took.

As the thought crossed my mind, though, it also struck me with its uselessness. I was dying. There would be no going back.

My eyes were about to flutter closed when it happened.

Would you take it for love? a little voice whispered in my ear.

I opened my eyes and then lifted myself off the dust, for a miracle stood before me.

A path of glittering cobblestones led off the road, over the marshes, towards a palace of bright yellow and red brick floating high above the ground. A halo of light surrounded it, blindingly strong.

It looked like a mirage. I thought it must be a dream.

Yet when I rose slowly and unsteadily to my feet and stepped onto the path, it held my weight. On and up, away from the ground and the mortal world, I followed it like a sleepwalker. If I glanced back over my shoulder, the road through the marshes faded in the bright haze as if the earth were the dream.

The bridge of light ended at the golden doors of the Sun, which lay open for me to enter. So I did, wandering into a grand hall of gold marble that was completely empty.

There I stood in a daze until my eyes found the stairs at the back. My gaze climbed its steps. At the very top, about six feet off the floor, there floated a golden orb of light.

I drifted towards it.

That little voice whispered to me: *The light of the Sun. It has been stolen many times. For greed…. For power. Yes, even for love, but beware. There is always a price.*

As I ascended the steps, I saw it. I watched a creature of monstrous beauty and scorching light holding the Sun in its hand. It flew over the land, and behind it, the fields were cast into gloom. Starved of sunlight, the earth turned winter-barren. Crops failed and babies died from the cold.

I watched a queen of old in her treasury. She also held the undistilled power of the Sun. Everything it touched – coins and cups, wood and tile, even her skin – turned to gold. She danced and hopped in joy, but outside her palace walls, an angry crowd gathered. There's only so much the strongest gates can take before they fall and the hallways overflow with peasants coming for your head.

They caught and killed her. I tried not to see my emperor's face on hers, her head at the tip of a spear, a metal tongue jutting, bloody, out of her mouth.

It could have been us.

All of it could *become* us.

The voice challenged me: *Take it if your love is true to the bitterest end. You chose it. You swore it.*

If I were to go back, I needed the Sun, and I didn't wish to die out here in the wilderness. I *wanted* to go back.

Even then I hesitated with my hand half-outstretched. This wasn't what I intended. To doom him.

Did it have to end in tragedy either way?

Steeling myself, I reached up; I took the orb, and it burned me. Sunlight poured into my veins, down my arms, over my chest, through my bones. My body couldn't hold it all, so it splashed onto the marble tiles, scalding my feet. I would have screamed if my throat weren't gilded and burning.

Molten gold blurred my vision instead of tears. My back itched, then arched, and I fell to the floor. Something grew between my shoulder blades.

I held onto the Sun, pressing it tight to my chest despite the pain, and slowly its touch became bearable. Either I was growing warmer, or it was growing colder. Maybe both. The orb gleamed fainter every second, winking, about to expire in my hands.

In a moment, it would all be mine, that cruelty and those horrors ours to inherit, because I said I would bring him the Sun. It was this or exile.

I don't know if I love my emperor more than my own freedom or my life. At that moment, though, I realized it wasn't mere pity that bound me to him. It wasn't duty: a promise. I thought again of bringing him his death, and I shivered.

I *did* love him.

I couldn't deliver him such an ill fate.

So I let go of the light and all my hopes of returning.

The orb floated back to its place. Slowly, despite my abuses, it built up light and heat. The halls of the palace of the Sun were again drenched in sunlight, which flooded out of doors and windows, into the world.

I waited for the magic in me to also fade, but nothing seemed to happen. Golden sunlight coursed my veins and shone faintly through my skin. The tears I wiped away were still molten gold hardening on my fingertips. Wings of light fluttered on my back.

The realization slowly dawned on me.

"Are we free?" I whispered.

No voice answered me this time.

* * *

With my golden sun wings, I flew through what was left of the day and well into the night, looking like a falling star, probably, to any who saw me go by. The whole world stretched beneath me, from horizon to horizon.

So many miles I had walked in my journey. It had taken me weeks. Now I covered the same distance in a day and a night, and as the cock crowed in the dark before dawn, I alighted at the window of my emperor's inner courtyard: back to the beginning.

My skin let only a faint gleam onto the floor many feet below, but even that seemed bright in my love's palace. As long as I stayed, nearby dust motes might be gold.

And I wasn't alone.

Someone else was also up before daybreak, sitting on that bench. My heart nearly leapt out of my mouth when he lifted his gaze to me.

On my way to him, I must admit, I'd feared his reaction. I looked changed.

Yet he rushed to the window, and under my pale beam of sunlight, his face glowed with amazement. His eyes were puffy and rimmed with red, but they twinkled up at me.

"You are back! Have you found it?"

I nodded and, leaning down, I offered him my hand. "I can show you, and all the rest too. The whole world for seeing."

On my lips, unsaid, were the words, *If you want to come*, and a plea, *Escape with me*.

Love is something, isn't it? I would go to the ends of the earth and beyond – to the palace of the Sun – for him. And he would follow me anywhere on trust alone.

He reached up and took my hand. With my new Sun strength, I hoisted him up to the window. The stone bars were spaced barely wide enough for a slip of a young emperor to pass between them and flee.

Had his guardians thought he might try, they would have made those even narrower, but now it was too late. Away we could go, anywhere. We could roam this beautiful world until we tired, and then rest in an otherworldly palace.

"You're warm. I missed you," he mumbled, his face buried in my shoulder.

I kissed his head and wrapped my arms around him. As I fell away from the ledge, my Sun wings carried us both into the sky.

This is how I spirited away an emperor.

This is our story.

The Sun in His Sky

Stewart Moore

"CORPSES AREN'T GRATEFUL," said Neforet. She stood between the brightly painted pillars, looking down into the stairwell, into the tombs.

"Future corpses are," said her brother Petobastet. He nodded toward their father leading two honey-skinned customers in Greek capes on a tour. The copper skin of Neforet's family marked them as lower class in all ways except for caring for the dead. In that respect, Egyptians reigned supreme.

The sound of the Great Sea on the other side of the dunes kept time, as remorseless as her brother holding out the broom to her. At least the air smelled clean up here, scoured by the salt. Neforet half turned away, as much as she dared. Her brother was quick and accurate with that broom handle.

"I would give anything to spend a day in the sun. I'm sure Re hardly knows me."

"The Sun knows everyone." He thrust the broom into Neforet's hands. "Now go sweep the cat poop out of that tomb."

Neforet groaned. "I swear cats are more important than people in this city."

"What benefits the cats, benefits us. Bastet smiles on us, and besides, they keep out the bats. Bat shit is much worse. Now go."

She furtively made a rude gesture with two fingers. Petobastet either missed it or ignored it. Neforet picked up the clay lamp by the archway and held it before her as she descended into the dark.

Immediately one of the little furry minions of the cat-Goddess rubbed against her legs. She wasn't fooled. The cat was only saying that Neforet, like everything else down here in the dark tunnels, belonged to it. The sour smell of cat urine competed with the spice-and-leather smell of the hundreds of guests spending their afterlives in her family's care.

Coming to the bottom of the stairs, Neforet heard a chorus of meows. The sound of so many cats agreeing with each other stirred her curiosity. She followed the chorus down one hall, another, and then another. She came upon them at last, sitting in a ring like an audience, looking up at a jackal-headed statue of Anubis. Occasionally a cat would stretch up on its hind legs, swipe at the air, and sit back down. She followed their gaze, and jumped.

A falcon sat on Anubis's arm, hiding its head in its wing.

Neforet had never seen such a thing. She tiptoed through the cats, who all began purring, a sound like washing waves. Gently she stroked the falcon's wing. Its feathers trembled but it did not raise its head.

"Little Horus, what are you doing here? Let me take you back outside. Don't be scared...."

The bird lowered its wing and looked at Neforet. Looked at her with brown human eyes out of a tiny, pale human face. The hair on the head was light brown and done up in a Greek woman's bun and ringlets. Nevertheless, a small, pointed beard sprouted from her chin.

Neforet barely avoided collapsing into the theater of cats. She knew what she saw, though she'd never expected to see one in this world. But weren't there pictures of them on every tomb? This was the part of the soul called the *ba*, which carried a family's offerings from the mummified body, the *ka*, to the glorified spirit in the Netherworld.

"Whose are you?" she whispered. The *ba* opened her mouth, and a chirruping, chittering sound fell out. Neforet had always assumed the language of the dead would be Egyptian, but this was no language at all.

A cat jumped up and dug its claws into Neforet's shoulder. Containing a shriek behind gritted teeth, she gently pressed a hand in its face until it jumped back to the ground. Other cats, meowing, approached with the same intention. But she wielded her broom, swatting them back despite the real risk of offending Bastet. This little miracle would not end up as cat poop. She scattered the crowd, which ran meowing down half a dozen tunnels into the dark. Baleful eyes gleamed just at the edge of her light.

"Hello?" someone called down the tunnel in Egyptian. A stranger, and therefore a customer – and therefore still alive.

"Stay here," Neforet said to the *ba*. "I'll come right back." She hurried up the twists and turns towards the atrium at the bottom of the stairs, where a young man stood. He was not much older than Neforet, hardly more than a boy, with deep brown skin, wearing the white linen kilt of a junior priest. He cradled a wine jar of exceptional quality, glazed and covered with geometric patterns. White light filtered down the tightly winding staircase to cast a dim, shadowless glow on his freshly shaven face and scalp. He looked around at the divine statues along the wall. A mix of human and animal heads gazed back at him.

Neforet bowed her head. "Honored servant of the Gods, for whom do you seek?"

He swallowed hard. She worked in a tomb; she knew the sound of grief. His thick voice rang from the walls. "Her name was Berenike. She was buried here last week."

I remember her, Neforet thought. *And her huge Greek family. Even then I wondered, "What are they doing here?" They barely knew how to pronounce the Gods' names properly, and the dead have to know the name of every door and doorpost of the Netherworld to be let in.*

Unable to contain a positively feline curiosity, Neforet asked, "May I know your relationship to the Glorified One, sir?"

"I don't...." His voice broke. "I don't see what relevance that has."

Neforet bowed her head again. "Of course. Follow me."

She led him through the halls to Berenike's tomb, retracing the steps of the funerary procession. Neforet's father had sold them a fine and deeply cut niche just a couple of months ago: barely in time, as it turned out. The Gods could be cruel.

Berenike resided now in a new chamber, with many empty niches around her opening up onto a darkness almost nothing could penetrate. She lay behind a large square stone, carved with her image, so vividly painted it had clearly been taken from life. *So young, to sit for a death portrait – and yet, so wise.* Below the portrait was her name, both in Greek letters and hieroglyphs.

Neforet gave him space. "She will hear you here, and rejoice."

The man stood in front of the tomb for a long time before he unstopped the jar and began pouring it out, little by little, into the dust and cat hair. He let the wine splash on his fingers, and with them gently stroked Berenike's stone face. Her cheeks would be permanently rosier. Neforet could see his lips moving, but he didn't make a sound.

She wished she could hurry back to the *ba*. She did not trust cats any more than she trusted Bastet. The Goddess had a wicked sense of humor. But the security of the deceased was paramount, and the bereaved could be unpredictable.

"There wasn't time," the man whispered.

Neforet kept silent, trained by a life lived among the dead, who listened well.

"We never should have met, but we did. We were in the marketplace, both of us running errands. Her family was well-off, but not rich enough to afford to lock a youngest daughter away from the world. Our eyes met. Neither of us could look away. We moved toward each other, dancing around the people milling everywhere. We talked in the sunlight, alone in the crowd all around us. Only Re truly saw us and knew us. We met day after day. We talked in Greek, but from the beginning I taught her Egyptian, a word here and there.

"She told me about what eternity means to the Greeks: dryness and dust and darkness, for ever and ever. I told her about the wonders of our Netherworld, where the sun shines at night and the colors never fade. I began to teach her the names of the doors. Somehow, she convinced her family to buy this place for her. Because we couldn't be together in this life." The man laid his hand on the lip of the niche beside Berenike's. He left wine-purple prints. "I was saving to buy this niche here. But there wasn't time. And now she's lost in the Netherworld."

As if it were too heavy for him, as if everything were too heavy for him, he bent to set down the jar. A drop of wine ran down the painted face of Berenike, hanging from her chin like a tiny beard. Neforet looked closer, and almost dropped her lamp. Berenike's face was the face of the *ba*. The beard had thrown her, but of course, every *ba* has Osiris's beard.

"I know where she is," she said.

"What?" Confusion and anger and hope wrestled on his face.

"What's your name, sir?"

"What?"

"Your name!"

"Ahmose," he said, stepping back.

The next words died on Neforet's lips. The cats had fallen silent. She seized his hand. "Come with me, Ahmose, quickly." Before they could take a step, she heard a seething hiss, like a wave approaching. All the cats in the tombs came running past them, silent and intent. Neforet heard them running up the stairs Ahmose had descended, and they were gone.

"I've never seen so many cats do the same thing," Ahmose whispered, his face fading into gloom. Neforet realized her light was failing. The flame burned as high as ever, but it simply put forth less light. The darkness crept closer, its depths already obscuring her feet. She could barely see Ahmose's face. Now he noticed the dark too. He looked at the lamp between them, the obvious question on his face, not daring to give it voice.

Then the light went out completely. The darkness both compacted on her skin and extended outward forever. Neforet felt that if she reached out to the walls, she'd touch nothing...or worse than nothing. She couldn't speak, or she might attract the attention of something terrible. She couldn't hear Ahmose breathing. If she tried to touch him, she was sure he wouldn't be there.

Stone screamed under unseen claws. The raking, splintering sound went on and on. It was a world away; it was right next to her. She didn't dare move, didn't even dare to tremble. Something enormous, something far too large for these tunnels, huffed and clicked its teeth and shuffled past her. It left an awful odor both musky and reptilian.

Slowly, so slowly, light returned to the world. The faint flame of the lamp seemed as bright as the sun. Ahmose's face emerged from the shadows that swirled like living things. He stared at the light the way a drowning person holds onto a rope.

The lamp grew brighter still, and now they could see Berenike's tomb. Something had smashed her capstone portrait, and gouged out her names. The darkness inside her tomb lay exposed.

"What...." breathed Ahmose.

"It was a God," said Neforet. "Berenike is in terrible danger. We need help." She pressed the lamp into Ahmose's hands and reached into the niche. She whispered to anyone who might be listening, "Forgive me."

She first found the shreds of a scroll. She could see it was a *Book of Going Forth by Day*, which the Greeks crudely called the "Book of the Dead." Berenike's name should have been written in hieroglyphs in every other verse, but those symbols were gone, burned away.

Further back she could feel linen wrappings. She pulled on them, and they came out in a loose tangle redolent of preservative frankincense. The mummy too was gone, ground to nothingness between teeth too awful to contemplate.

"Where is she?" Ahmose croaked. "Where is she!"

"We can still save her. She's lost her anchor in this world, but I promise we can save her. We can make another *ka*, but you have to come with me now."

Neforet hurried down the passageway, Ahmose stumbling in the gloom behind her. The corners seemed to bend in unnatural angles, and she twice took the wrong path, a thing she hadn't done in years. Finally she found herself before Anubis once more.

She gasped with relief. Berenike's *ba* still clung to the God's arm. It burbled at her in an incoherent but friendly way. She recognized one word: "Ahmose," *child of the moon*.

"And she is the sun in your sky," Neforet said.

Ahmose stumbled forward like a man both bewitched and besotted. "How is this possible?"

"Your wife has been attacked by an evil God, probably Seth. So we need the help of another God to fight him. And who better than the messenger of the dead?" She raised her arms. "Anubis! We pray to you. Save this soul of Berenike from evil and destruction. Come fight for...."

Frankly, Neforet expected to have to pray for a long time. The Gods liked hearing their own praises, and rarely interrupted. And when they answered, they gave omens and dreams. They did not make their statues move, as this one did now, with a grinding, stony sound. Their statues did not bend down to fix their worshippers with black and shining eyes. Their carven mouths did not open like this one did, to snarl, "No."

Anubis tried to grasp the *ba*, but she flapped away, panicked. Instinctively, Neforet put her arm up for Berenike to land. The falcon's talons punctured Neforet's skin. Blood dripped on the floor. Neforet fought the urge to shake her arm free. The *ba* burbled and chirped wildly. Ahmose jumped in between them, but the God slapped him to the ground.

"Why are you doing this?" Neforet cried. "You're the protector of the dead!"

Anubis took one foot off his pedestal and stepped heavily onto the ground. "Of the *Egyptian* dead. These Greeks, they have the Book, but they can't read it. They don't know the answers to the questions. They don't know the names. I am tired of it. Ammit, the Eater of Souls, will take care of their remains in this world and the next, with claws and teeth." His other foot crunched down on the lamp. Burning oil squirted across the floor and guttered out.

Neforet backed up, holding the *ba* away from his unseen hands. "No! We promised her! When she bought this place, we made a promise!"

"And what to me is your promise, child of Egypt?" said Anubis, his voice like a great door closing. "For what do you sell your birthright in the Netherworld to such as these?"

Ahmose groaned. "Your name is Anubis." His voice rose in the air as he stood. "Your mother's name is Nephthys. Your father's name is Seth. You weigh my heart against the feather of Ma'at. You stand before Osiris, and behind him stand Meskhenet and Renenet." His words slurred, as if he'd drunk Berenike's libation instead of pouring it out. "I know the names. I know the Book. I know the answers to the questions. I was born in Egypt! My beloved was born in Egypt! I would have taught her the names. But there was no time!"

The sound of rocks grinding came inexorably forward. The *ba* on Neforet's arm shivered. That, at last, made her furious.

"We promised her," she hissed fiercely. "My family promised her this home forever! If you won't give one to her, then let us! We'll provide her libations and offerings. We'll teach her the names. She has a place in the afterlife, here. She won't die a second time!"

Silence reigned. Neforet's ears rang, searching for some sound.

Light erupted in the blackness. Neforet shielded her eyes with her free hand. Still the light grew brighter, as if the Sun had come down into the tombs. From somewhere, from everywhere, the jangle of sistrums played, like in a procession of the Gods.

"Children," said the Sun in the tombs.

Ahmose's knees thumped into the dust. "Lord Re?"

"Guardian of the dead," the Sun God said.

Stone sighed as Anubis responded. "Yes, my Lord?"

"No." Re's voice hummed through Neforet's body. Her skin stretched tight in the heat. "I speak to my younger servant."

Neforet's throat locked. "Yes?" she choked.

Re laughed gently. "Will you teach this *ba* the names and the answers?"

She took a deep breath. "I will."

"Good. But how many *bas* can you teach?"

Neforet thought of all the niches in all these tunnels. And in all the other tombs in this cemetery, and in all the other cemeteries by the long, long Nile. Her heart fluttered, but she stepped forward into the glare. "As many as will come! I will not turn back anyone who will truly be a child of Egypt!"

Re laughed. "A generous heart. Truly, lighter than a feather." The light blinked out. Neforet opened her eyes, but saw only red. The sound of stone grinding on stone had fallen silent, though Neforet listened a long time. The *ba* clenched her claws and burbled, "Ahmose. Ahmose."

Neforet often bragged to her family that she could find her way in the tombs without a light. Now, she clasped Ahmose's hand in the dark and did it. Though she was blind, the corners and angles did not betray her. By the time they came to the place where Berenike's tomb once was, Neforet's eyes recovered from the Sun's rays. She could see the wine jar by the light coming down the stairs. She picked it up, and liquid splashed in the bottom. She poured it out.

"I pour this libation for the spirit of Berenike. May it nourish her in this world…and the next."

Violet light rose up from the puddle. The *ba* inhaled deeply, more deeply than such a little thing should have been able to, and the light went inside her until all was gone.

As they climbed the stairs, Neforet wondered what she'd say to her family, to anyone, about the *ba*. She rehearsed various introductions, but couldn't think of anything equal to the moment.

They came up into the sunlight. A breeze brought the sound of the sea, the fresh salty smell. Neforet squeezed her eyes almost shut, but underneath the splashing waves she heard a great cooing like a flock of doves.

Ahmose whispered, "By the God."

"Which one?"

"Any one," he said.

She shaded her eyes until she could finally see.

On the roof of every mausoleum, stretching down the gentle slope to the road into the city, sat hundreds and hundreds of *bas*. They watched her, each quietly chittering to itself. In the sand sat one cat for every *ba*, cool curious eyes watching feathers ruffle. What thoughts passed behind those eyes, only Bastet knew.

Neforet tamped down the panic that rose in her chest. She would teach the *bas*. She would start, as she had with her youngest siblings, with "Please" and "Thank you" in Egyptian. She could and she would.

Her mother and father and sisters and brothers stared at them all. She straightened her back and started toward them.

"I guess we'll need more wine," she said.

The Sun-Goddess

From Japanese mythology

AMA-TERASU, THE SUN-GODDESS, was seated in the Blue Plain of Heaven. Her light came as a message of joy to the celestial deities. The orchid and the iris, the cherry and the plum blossom, the rice and the hemp fields answered to her smile. The Inland Sea was veiled in soft rich colour.

Susa-no-o, the brother of Ama-terasu, who had resigned his ocean sceptre and now reigned as the Moon-God, was jealous of his sister's glory and world-wide sway. The Heaven-Illuminating Spirit had but to whisper and she was heard throughout her kingdom, even in the depths of the clear pool and in the heart of the crystal. Her rice-fields, whether situated on hillside, in sheltered valley, or by running stream, yielded abundant harvests, and her groves were laden with fruit. But the voice of Susa-no-o was not so clear, his smile was not so radiant. The undulating fields which lay around his palace were now flooded, now parched, and his rice crops were often destroyed. The wrath and jealousy of the Moon-God knew no bounds, yet Ama-terasu was infinitely patient and forgave him many things.

Once, as was her wont, the Sun-Goddess sat in the central court of her glorious home. She plied her shuttle. Celestial weaving maidens surrounded a fountain whose waters were fragrant with the heavenly lotus-bloom: they sang softly of the clouds and the wind and the lift of the sky. Suddenly, the body of a piebald horse fell through the vast dome at their feet: the "Beloved of the Gods" had been "flayed with a backward flaying" by the envious Susa-no-o. Ama-terasu, trembling at the horrible sight, pricked her finger with the weaving shuttle, and, profoundly indignant at the cruelty of her brother, withdrew into a cave and closed behind her the door of the Heavenly Rock Dwelling.

The universe was plunged into darkness. Joy and goodwill, serenity and peace, hope and love, waned with the waning light. Evil spirits, who heretofore had crouched in dim corners, came forth and roamed abroad. Their grim laughter and discordant tones struck terror into all hearts.

Then it was that the gods, fearful for their safety and for the life of every beautiful thing, assembled in the bed of the tranquil River of Heaven, whose waters had been dried up. One and all knew that Ama-terasu alone could help them. But how to allure the Heaven-Illuminating Spirit to set foot in this world of darkness and strife? Each god was eager to aid, and a plan was finally devised to entice her from her hiding-place.

Ame-no-ko uprooted the holy *sakaki* trees which grow on the Mountain of Heaven, and planted them around the entrance of the cave. High on the upper branches were hung the precious string of curved jewels which Izanagi had bestowed upon the Sun-Goddess. From the middle branches drooped a mirror wrought of the rare metals of the celestial mine. Its polished surface was as the dazzling brilliancy of the sun. Other gods wove, from threads of hemp and paper mulberry, an imperial robe of white and blue, which was placed, as an offering for the goddess, on the lower branches of the *sakaki*. A palace was also built, surrounded by a garden in which the Blossom-God called forth many delicate plants and flowers.

Now all was ready. Ame-no-ko stepped forward, and, in a loud voice, entreated Ama-terasu to show herself. His appeal was in vain. The great festival began. Uzume, the goddess of mirth, led the dance and song. Leaves of the spindle tree crowned her head; club-moss, from the heavenly mount Kagu, formed her sash; her flowing sleeves were bound with the creeper-vine; and in her hand she carried leaves of the wild bamboo and waved a wand of sun-grass hung with tiny melodious bells. Uzume blew on a bamboo flute, while the eight hundred myriad deities accompanied her on wooden clappers and instruments formed of bowstrings, across which were rapidly drawn stalks of reed and grass. Great fires were lighted around the cave, and, as these were reflected in the face of the mirror, "the long-singing birds of eternal night" began to crow as if the day dawned. The merriment increased. The dance grew wilder and wilder, and the gods laughed until the heavens shook as if with thunder.

Ama-terasu, in her quiet retreat, heard, unmoved, the crowing of the cocks and the sounds of music and dancing, but when the heavens shook with the laughter of the gods, she peeped from her cave and said, "What means this? I thought heaven and earth were dark, but now there is light. Uzume dances and all the gods laugh." Uzume answered, "It is true that I dance and that the gods laugh, because in our midst is a goddess whose splendour equals your own. Behold!" Ama-terasu gazed into the mirror, and wondered greatly when she saw therein a goddess of exceeding beauty. She stepped from her cave and forthwith a cord of rice-straw was drawn across the entrance. Darkness fled from the Central Land of Reed-Plains, and there was light. Then the eight hundred myriad deities cried, "O, may the Sun-Goddess never leave us again."

The Sun-Horse

From Hungarian-Slovenish fairy tale

THERE WAS ONCE upon a time a country, sad and gloomy as the grave, on which God's sun never shone. But there was a king there, and this king possessed a horse with a sun on his forehead; and this sun-horse of his the king caused to be led up and down the dark country, from one end to the other, that the people might be able to exist there; and light came from him on all sides wherever he was led, just as in the most beautiful day.

All at once the sun-horse disappeared. A darkness worse than that of night prevailed over the whole country, and nothing could disperse it. Unheard-of terror spread among the subjects; frightful misery began to afflict them, for they could neither manufacture anything nor earn anything, and such confusion arose among them that everything was turned topsy-turvy. The king, therefore, in order to liberate his realm and prevent universal destruction, made ready to seek the sun-horse with his whole army.

Through thick darkness he made his way as best he could to the frontier of his realm. Over dense mountains thousands of ages old God's light began now to break from another country, as if the sun were rising in the morning out of thick fogs. On such a mountain the king came with his army to a poor lonely cottage. He went in to inquire where he was, what it was, and how to get further. At a table sat a peasant, diligently reading in an open book. When the king bowed to him he raised his eyes, thanked him, and stood up. His whole person announced that he was not a man like another man, but a seer.

"I was just reading about you," said he to the king, "how that you are going to seek the sun-horse. Journey no further, for you will not obtain him; but rely on me: I will find him for you." "I promise you, good man, I will recompense you royally," replied the king, "if you bring him here to me." "I require no recompense; return home with your army – you're wanted there; only leave me one servant."

The next day the seer set out with the servant. The way was far and long, for they passed through six countries, and had still further to go, till in the seventh country they stopped at the royal palace. In this seventh country ruled three own brothers, who had to wife three own sisters, whose mother was a witch. When they stopped in front of the palace, the seer said to his servant, "Do you hear? You stay here, and I will go in to ascertain whether the kings are at home; for the horse with the sun is in their possession – the youngest rides upon him." Therewith he transformed himself into a green bird, and, flying on the gable of the eldest queen's roof, flew up and down and pecked at it until she opened the window and let him into her chamber. And when she let him in he perched on her white hand, and the queen was as delighted with him as a little child. "Ah, what a dear creature you are!" said she, as she played with him; "if my husband were at home he would indeed be delighted with you; but he won't come till evening; he has gone to visit the third part of his country."

All at once the old witch came into the room, and, seeing the bird, screamed to her daughter, "Wring the accursed bird's neck, for it's making you bleed!" "Well, what if it should make me bleed? it's such a dear; it's such an innocent dear!' answered the daughter. But the witch said, "Dear innocent mischief! here with him! let me wring his neck!" and dashed at it. But the bird cunningly transformed itself into a man, and, pop! out through the door, and they didn't know whither he had betaken himself.

Afterwards he again transformed himself into a green bird, flew on the gable of the middle sister, and pecked at it till she opened the window for him. And when she let him in he flew onto her white hand, and fluttered from one hand to the other. "Oh, what a dear creature you are!" cried the queen, smiling; "my husband would indeed be delighted with you if he were at home; but he won't come till tomorrow evening; he has gone to visit two thirds of his kingdom."

Thereupon the witch burst into the room. "Wring the accursed bird's neck! wring its neck, for it's making you bleed!" cried she as soon as she espied it. "Well, what if it should make me bleed? it's such a dear, such an innocent dear!" replied the daughter. But the witch said, "Dear innocent mischief! here with it! let me wring its neck!" and was already trying to seize it. But at that moment the green bird changed itself into a man, ran out through the door, and disappeared, as it were, in the clap of a hand, so that they didn't know whither he had gone.

A little while afterwards he changed himself again into a green bird and flew on the gable of the youngest queen's roof, and flew up and down, and pecked at it until she opened the window to him. And when she had let him in he flew straight onto her white hand, and made himself so agreeable to her that she played with him with the delight of a child. "Ah, what a dear creature you are!" said the queen; "if my husband were at home he would certainly be delighted with you, but he won't come till the day after tomorrow at even; he has gone to visit all three parts of his kingdom."

At that moment the old witch came into the room. "Wring, wring the accursed bird's neck!" screamed she in the doorway, "for it is making you bleed." "Well, what if it should make me bleed, mother? it is so beautiful, so innocent," answered the daughter. The witch said, "Beautiful innocent mischief! here with him! let me wring his neck!" But at that moment the bird changed itself into a man, and pop! out through the door, so that none of them saw him more.

Now the seer knew where the kings were, and when they would arrive. He went to his servant and ordered him to follow him out of the town. On they went with rapid step till they came to a bridge, over which the kings were obliged to pass.

Under this bridge they stayed waiting till the evening. When at even the sun was sinking behind the mountains, the clatter of a horse was heard near the bridge. It was the eldest king returning home. Close to the bridge his horse stumbled over a log of wood, which the seer had thrown across the bridge. "Ha! what scoundrel was that who threw this log across the road?" exclaimed the king in anger. Thereat the seer sprang out from under the bridge and rushed upon the king for "daring to call him a scoundrel," and, drawing his sword, attacked him. The king, too, drew his sword to defend himself, but after a short combat fell dead from his horse. The seer bound the dead king on the horse, and gave the horse a lash with the whip to make him carry his dead master home. He then withdrew under the bridge, and they waited there till the next evening.

When day a second time declined towards evening, the middle king came to the bridge, and, seeing the ground sprinkled with blood, cried out, "Somebody's been killed here! Who has dared to perpetrate such a crime in my kingdom?" At these words the seer sprang out from under the bridge and rushed upon the king with drawn sword, exclaiming, "How dare you insult me? Defend yourself as best you can!" The king did defend himself, but after a brief struggle yielded up his life under the sword of the seer. The seer again fastened his corpse upon the horse, and gave the horse a lash with the whip to make him carry his dead master home. They then withdrew under the bridge and waited till the third evening came.

The third evening, at the very setting of the sun, up darted the youngest king on the sun-horse, darted up with speed, for he was somewhat late; but when he saw the red blood in front of the bridge, he stopped, and gazing at it exclaimed, "It is an unheard-of villain who has dared to murder a man in my kingdom!" Scarcely had these words issued from his mouth when the seer placed himself before him with drawn sword, sternly bidding him defend himself, "for he had wounded his honour." "I don't know how," answered the king, "unless it is you that are the villain." But as his adversary attacked him with a sword, he, too, drew his, and defended himself manfully.

It had been mere play to the seer to overcome the first two kings, but it was not so with this one. Long time they fought, and broke their swords, yet victory didn't show itself either on the one side or on the other. "We shall effect nothing with swords," said the seer, "but do you know what? Let us turn ourselves into wheels and start down from the hill; the wheel which breaks shall be the conquered." "Good!" said the king; "I'll be a cartwheel, and you shall be a lighter wheel." "Not so," cunningly said the seer; "you shall be the lighter wheel, and I will be the cartwheel;" and the king agreed to it. Then they went up the hill, turned themselves into wheels, and started downwards. The cartwheel flew to pieces, and bang! right into the lighter wheel, so that it all smashed up. Immediately the seer arose out of the cartwheel and joyfully exclaimed, "There you are, the victory is mine!" "Not a bit of it, sir brother!" cried the king, placing himself in front of the seer; "you have only broken my fingers. But do you know what? Let us make ourselves into flames, and the flame which burns up the other shall be the victor. I will make myself into a red flame, and do you make yourself into a bluish one." "Not so!" interrupted the seer; "you make yourself into a bluish flame, and I will make myself into a red one." The king agreed to this also. They went into the road to the bridge, and, changing themselves into flames, began to burn each other unmercifully. Long did they burn each other, but nothing came of it. Thereupon, by coincidence, up came an old beggar with a long grey beard, a bald head, a large scrip at his side, leaning upon a thick staff. "Old father!" said the bluish flame, "bring some water and quench this red flame; I'll give you a penny for it." The red flame cunningly exclaimed, "Old father! I'll give you a shilling if you'll pour the water on this bluish flame." The old beggar liked the shilling better than the penny, brought water and quenched the bluish flame. Then it was all over with the king. The red flame turned itself into a man, took the sun-horse by the bridle, mounted on his back, called the servant, thanked the beggar for the service he had rendered, and went off.

In the royal palaces there was deep grief at the murder of the two kings; the entire palaces were draped with black cloth, and the people crowded into them from all quarters to gaze at the cut and slashed bodies of the two elder brothers, whose horses had brought them home. The old witch, exasperated at the death of her sons-in-law, devised a plan of vengeance on their murderer, the seer. She seated herself with speed on an iron rake, took her three daughters under her arms, and pop! off with them into the air.

The seer and his servant had already got through a good part of their journey, and were then crossing desert mountains, a treeless waste. Here a terrible hunger seized the servant, and there wasn't even a wild plum to assuage it. All of a sudden they came to an apple-tree. Apples were hanging on it; the branches were all but breaking under their weight; their scent was beautiful; they were delightfully ruddy, so that they almost offered themselves to be eaten. "Praise be to God!" cried the delighted servant; "I shall eat one of those apples with an excellent appetite." "Don't attempt to gather one of them!" cried the seer to him; "wait, I'll gather some for you myself." But instead of plucking an apple, he drew his sword and thrust it mightily into the apple-tree; red blood spouted out of it. "There," said he, "you would have come to harm if you had eaten any of those apples, for the apple-tree was the eldest queen, whose mother placed her there to put us out of this world."

After a time they came to a spring; water clear as crystal bubbled up in it, all but running over the brim and thus attracting wayfarers. "Ah!" said the servant, "if we can't get anything better, let us at any rate have a drink of this good water." "Don't venture to drink of it!" shouted the seer; "but stay, I'll get you some of it." Yet he didn't get him any water, but thrust his drawn sword into the midst of it; it was immediately discoloured with blood, which began to flow from it in mighty waves. "That is the middle queen, whose mother placed her here to put us out of this world," said the seer, and the servant thanked him for his warning, and went on, would he, in hunger and thirst, whithersoever the seer led him.

After a time they came to a rose-bush, which was red with delightful roses, and filled the air round about with their scent. "Oh, what beautiful roses!" said the servant; "I never saw such beauties in all my life. I'll go and gather a few of them; I will at any rate comfort myself with them if I can't assuage my hunger and thirst." "Don't venture to gather one of them!" cried the seer; "I will gather them for you." With that he cut into the bush with his sword; red blood spurted out, as if he had cut the vein of a human being. "That is the youngest queen," said the seer to his servant, "whom her mother, the witch, placed here with the intention of taking vengeance upon us for the death of her sons-in-law." They then went on.

When they crossed the frontier of the dark realm, flashes flew in all directions from the horse's forehead, and everything came to life again, beautiful regions rejoiced and blossomed with the flowers of spring. The king didn't know how to thank the seer sufficiently, and offered him the half of his kingdom as a reward, but he declined it. "You are king," said he; "rule over the whole realm, and I will return to my cottage in peace." He took leave and departed.

The Sunchild

From Greek mythology

ONCE THERE WAS a woman who had no children, and this made her very unhappy. So she spoke one day to the Sunball, saying, "Dear Sunball, send me only a little girl now, and when she is twelve years old you may take her back again."

So soon after this the Sunball sent her a little girl, whom the woman called Letiko, and watched over with great care till she was twelve years old. Soon after that, while Letiko was away one day gathering herbs, the Sunball came to her, and said, "Letiko, when you go home, tell your mother that she must bethink herself of what she promised me."

Then Letiko went straight home, and said to her mother, "While I was gathering herbs a fine tall gentleman came to me and charged me to tell you that you should remember what you promised him."

When the woman heard that she was sore afraid, and immediately shut all the doors and windows of the house, stopped up all the chinks and holes, and kept Letiko hidden away, that the Sunball should not come and take her away. But she forgot to close up the keyhole, and through it the Sunball sent a ray into the house, which took hold of the little girl and carried her away to him.

One day, the Sunball having sent her to the straw shed to fetch straw, the girl sat down on the piles of straw and bemoaned herself, saying, "As sighs this straw under my feet so sighs my heart after my mother."

And this caused her to be so long away that the Sunball asked her, when she came back, "Eh, Letiko, where have you been so long?"

She answered, "My slippers are too big, and I could not go faster."

Then the Sunball made the slippers shorter.

Another time he sent her to fetch water, and when she came to the spring, she sat down and lamented, saying, "As flows the water even so flows my heart with longing for my mother."

Thus she again remained so long away that the Sunball asked her, "Eh, Letiko, why have you remained so long away?"

And she answered, "My petticoat is too long and hinders me in walking."

Then the Sunball cut her petticoat to make it shorter.

Another time the Sunball sent her to bring him a pair of sandals, and as the girl carried these in her hand she began to lament, saying, "As creaks the leather so creaks my heart after my little mother."

When she came home the Sunball asked her again, "Eh, Letiko, why do you come home so late?"

"My red hood is too wide, and falls over my eyes, therefore I could not go fast."

Then he made the hood narrower.

At last, however, the Sunball became aware how sad Letiko was. He sent her a second time to bring straw, and, slipping in after her, he heard how she lamented for her mother. Then he went home, called two foxes to him, and said, "Will you take Letiko home?"

"Yes, why not?"

"But what will you eat and drink if you should become hungry and thirsty by the way?"

"We will eat her flesh and drink her blood."

When the Sunball heard that, he said, "You are not suited for this affair."

Then he sent them away, and called two hares to him, and said, "Will you take Letiko home to her mother?"

"Yes, why not?"

"What will you eat and drink if you should become hungry and thirsty by the way?"

"We will eat grass and drink from streamlets."

"Then take her, and bring her home."

Then the hares set out, taking Letiko with them, and because it was a long way to her home they became hungry by the way. Then they said to the little girl, "Climb this tree, dear Letiko, and remain there till we have finished eating." So Letiko climbed the tree, and the hares went grazing. It was not very long, however, before a lamia came under the tree and called out, "Letiko, Letiko, come down and see what beautiful shoes I have on."

"Oh! my shoes are much finer than yours."

"Come down. I am in a hurry, for my house is not yet swept."

"Go home and sweep it then, and come back when you are ready."

Then the lamia went away and swept her house, and when she was ready she came back and called out, "Letiko, Letiko, come down and see what a beautiful apron I have."

"Oh! my apron is much finer than yours."

"If you will not come down I will cut down the tree and eat you."

"Do so, and then eat me."

Then the lamia hewed with all her strength at the tree, but could not cut it down. And when she saw that, she called out, "Letiko, Letiko, come down, for I must feed my children."

"Go home then and feed them, and come back when you are ready."

When the lamia was gone away, Letiko called out, "Little hares! little hares!"

Then said one hare to the other, "Listen, Letiko is calling;" and they both ran back to her as fast as they could go. Then Letiko came down from the tree, and they went on their way.

The lamia ran as fast as she could after them, to catch them up, and when she came to a field where people were working she asked them, "Have you seen anyone pass this way?"

They answered, "We are planting beans."

"Oh! I did not ask about that; but if anyone had passed this way."

But the people only answered the louder, "Are you deaf? It is beans, beans, beans we are planting."

When Letiko had nearly reached her home the dog knew her, and called out, "Bow wow! see here comes Letiko!"

And the mother said, "Hush! thou beast of ill-omen! wilt thou make me burst with misery?"

Next the cat on the roof saw her, and called out "Miaouw! miaouw! see here comes Letiko!"

And the mother said, "Keep silence! thou beast of ill-omen! wilt thou make me burst with misery?"

Then the cock spied, and called out, "Cock-a-doodle-do! see here comes Letiko!"

And the mother said again, "Be quiet! thou bird of ill-omen! wilt thou make me burst with misery?"

The nearer Letiko and the two hares came to the house the nearer also came the lamia, and when the hare was about to slip in by the house door she caught it by its little tail and tore it out. When the hare came in the mother stood up and said to it, "Welcome, dear little hare; because you have brought me back Letiko I will silver your little tail."

And she did so; and lived ever after with her daughter in happiness and content.

The Ten Suns of Dijun and Xihe

From Chinese mythology

THE GOD OF THE EAST, Dijun, had married the Goddess of the Sun, Xihe, and they lived together on the far eastern side of the world just at the edge of the great Eastern Ocean. Shortly after their marriage, the Goddess gave birth to ten suns, each of them a fiery, energetic, golden globe, and she placed the children lovingly in the giant Fusang tree close to the sea where they could frolic and bathe whenever they became overheated.

Each morning before breakfast, the suns took it in turns to spring from the enormous tree into the ocean below in preparation for their mother's visit when one of them would be lifted into her chariot and driven across the sky to bring light and warmth to the world. Usually the two remained together all day until they had travelled as far as the western abyss known as the Yuyuan. Then, when her sun had grown weary and the light had begun to fade from his body, Xihe returned him to the Fusang tree where he slept the night peacefully with his nine brothers. On the following morning, the Goddess would collect another of her suns, sit him beside her in her chariot, and follow exactly the same route across the sky. In this way, the earth was evenly and regularly heated, crops grew tall and healthy, and the people rarely suffered from the cold.

But one night, the ten suns began to complain among themselves that they had not yet been allowed to spend an entire day playing together without at least one of them being absent. And realizing how unhappy this situation made them feel, they decided to rebel against their mother and to break free of the tedious routine she insisted they follow. So the next morning, before the Goddess had arrived, all ten of them leapt into the skies at once, dancing joyfully above the earth, intent on making the most of their forbidden freedom. They were more than pleased to see the great dazzling light they were able to generate as they shone together, and made a solemn vow that they would never again allow themselves to become separated during the daytime.

The ten suns had not once paused to consider the disastrous consequences of their rebellion on the world below. For with ten powerful beams directed at the earth, crops began to wilt, rivers began to dry up, food became scarce and people began to suffer burns and wretched hunger pangs. They prayed for rains to drive away the suns, but none appeared. They called upon the great sorceress Nu Chou to perform her acts of magic, but her spells had no effect. They hid beneath the great trees of the forests for shade, but these were stripped of leaves and offered little or no protection. And now great hungry beasts of prey and dreaded monsters emerged from the wilderness and began to devour the human beings they encountered, unable to satisfy their huge appetites any longer. The destruction spread to every corner of the earth and the people were utterly miserable and filled with despair. They turned to their Emperor for help, knowing he was at a loss to know what to do, but he was their only hope, and they prayed that he would soon be visited by the God of Wisdom.

Yi, the Archer, Is Summoned

Dijun and Xihe were horrified to see the effect their unruly children were having upon the earth and pleaded with them to return to their home in the Fusang tree. But in spite of their entreaties, the ten suns continued on as before, adamant that they would not return to their former lifestyle. Emperor Yao now grew very impatient, and summoning Dijun to appear before him, he demanded that the God teach his suns to behave. Dijun heard the Emperor's plea but still he could not bring himself to raise a hand against the suns he loved so dearly. It was eventually settled between them, however, that one of Yao's officials in the heavens, known as Yi, should quickly descend to earth and do whatever he must to prevent any further catastrophe.

Yi was not a God of very impressive stature, but his fame as one of the most gifted archers in the heavens was widespread, for it was well known that he could shoot a sparrow down in full flight from a distance of fifty miles. Now Dijun went to meet with Yi to explain the problem his suns had created, and he handed the archer a new red bow and a quiver of white arrows and advised him what he must do.

"Try not to hurt my suns any more than you need to," he told Yi, "but take this bow and ensure that you bring them under control. See to it that the wicked beasts devouring mankind are also slain and that order and calm are restored once more to the earth."

Yi readily accepted this challenge and, taking with him his wife Chang E, he departed the Heavenly Palace and made his descent to the world below. Emperor Yao was overjoyed to see the couple approach and immediately organized a tour of the land for them, where Yi witnessed for himself the devastation brought about by Dijun's children, as he came face to face with half-burnt, starving people roaming aimlessly over the scorched, cracked earth.

And witnessing all of this terrible suffering, Yi grew more and more furious with the suns of Dijun and it slipped his mind entirely that he had promised to treat them leniently. "The time is now past for reasoning or persuasion," Yi thought to himself, and he strode to the highest mountain, tightened the string of his powerful bow and took aim with the first of his arrows. The weapon shot up into the sky and travelled straight through the centre of one of the suns, causing it to erupt into a thousand sparks as it split open and spun out of control to the ground, transforming itself on impact into a strange three-legged raven.

Now there were only nine suns left in the sky and Yi fitted the next arrow to his bow. One after another the arrows flew through the air, expertly hitting their targets, until the earth slowly began to cool down. But when the Emperor saw that there were only two suns left in the sky and that Yi had already taken aim, he wisely remembered that at least one sun should survive to brighten the earth and so he crept up behind the archer and stole the last of the white arrows from his quiver.

Having fulfilled his undertaking to rid Emperor Yao of the nine suns, Yi turned his attention to the task of hunting down the various hideous monsters threatening the earth. Gathering a fresh supply of arrows, he made his way southwards to fight the man-eating monster of the marsh with six feet and a human head, known as Zao Chi. And with the help of his divine bow, he quickly overcame the creature, piercing his huge heart with an arrow of steel. Travelling northwards, he tackled a great many other ferocious beasts, including the nine-headed monster, Jiu Ying, wading into a deep, black pool and throttling the fiend with his own bare hands. After that, he moved onwards to the Quingqiu marshes of the east where he came upon the terrible vulture Dafeng, a gigantic bird of unnatural strength with a wingspan so enormous that whenever the bird took to the air, a great typhoon blew up around it. And on this occasion, Yi knew that his single remaining arrow would only wound the bird, so he tied a long black cord to the shaft of the arrow before taking aim. Then as the creature flew past, Yi shot him in the chest and even though the vulture pulled strongly on the cord as it attempted to make towards a place of safety, Yi dragged it to the ground, plunging his knife repeatedly into its breast until all life had gone from it.

All over the earth, people looked upon Yi as a great hero, the God who had single-handedly rescued them from destruction. Numerous banquets and ceremonial feasts were held in his honour, all of them attended by the Emperor himself, who could not do enough to thank Yi for his assistance. Emperor Yao invited Yi to make his home on earth, promising to build him the a very fine palace overlooking Jade Mountain, but Yi was anxious to return to the heavens in triumph where he felt he rightly belonged and where, in any event, Dijun eagerly awaited an account of his exploits.

The Third Book of the Popol Vuh

From Maya mythology

THE BEGINNING OF the third book finds the gods once more in council. In the darkness they commune concerning the creation of man. The Creator and Former made four perfect men. These beings were wholly created from yellow and white maize. Their names were Balam-Quitzé (Tiger with the Sweet Smile), Balam-Agab (Tiger of the Night), Mahucutah (The Distinguished Name), and Iqi-Balam (Tiger of the Moon). They had neither father nor mother, neither were they made by the ordinary agents in the work of creation. Their creation was a miracle of the Former.

But Hurakan was not altogether satisfied with his handiwork. These men were too perfect. They knew overmuch. Therefore the gods took counsel as to how to proceed with man. They must not become as gods (note here the Christian influence). Let us now contract their sight so that they may only be able to see a portion of the earth and be content, said the gods. Then Hurakan breathed a cloud over their eyes, which became partially veiled. Then the four men slept, and four women were made, Caha-Paluma (Falling Water), Choimha (Beautiful Water), Tzununiha (House of the Water), and Cakixa (Water of Aras or Parrots), who became the wives of the men in their respective order as mentioned above.

These were the ancestors of the Kichés only. Then were created the ancestors of other peoples. They were ignorant of the methods of worship, and lifting their eyes to heaven prayed to the Creator, the Former, for peaceable lives and the return of the sun. But no sun came, and they grew uneasy. So they set out for Tulan-Zuiva, or the Seven Caves, and there gods were given unto them, each man, as head of a group of the race, a god. Balam-Quitzé received the god Tohil. Balam-Agab received the god Avilix, and Mahucutah the god Hacavitz. Iqi-Balam received a god, but as he had no family his god is not taken into account in the native mythology.

The Kichés now began to feel the want of fire, and the god Tohil, the creator of fire, supplied them with this element. But soon afterwards a mighty rain extinguished all the fires in the land. Tohil, however, always renewed the supply. And fire in those days was the chief necessity, for as yet there was no sun.

Tulan was a place of misfortune to man, for not only did he suffer from cold and famine, but here his speech was so confounded that the first four men were no longer able to comprehend each other. They determined to leave Tulan, and under the leadership of the god Tohil set out to search for a new abode. On they wandered through innumerable hardships. Many mountains had they to climb, and a long passage to make through the sea which was miraculously divided for their journey from shore to shore. At length they came to a mountain which they called Hacavitz, after one of their gods, and here they rested, for here they had been instructed that they should see the sun. And the sun appeared. Animals and men were transported with delight. All the celestial bodies were now established. But the sun was not as it is today. He was not strong, but as reflected in a mirror.

As he arose the three tribal gods were turned into stone, as were the gods – probably totems – connected with the wild animals. Then arose the first Kiché city.

As time progressed the first men grew old, and, impelled by visions, they began to offer human sacrifices. For this purpose they raided the villages of the neighbouring peoples, who retaliated. But by the miraculous aid of a horde of wasps and hornets the Kichés utterly routed their enemies. And the aliens became tributary to them.

Now it came nigh the death-time of the first men, and they called their descendants together to hearken unto their last counsels. In the anguish of their hearts they sang the Kamucu, the song "We see," that they had sung when it first became light. Then they took leave of their wives and sons, one by one. And suddenly they were not. But in their place was a huge bundle, which was never unfolded. And it was called the "Majesty Enveloped." And so died the first men of the Kichés.

To Banish the Light

Owen Morgan

Egypt, 2400 BCE

THE LAST TWO CENTURIES were ones of plenty; the age of man dawned; the gods forgotten. Soon madness reigned in the cities, a blight of the mind; prophets spoke of the end of days, for none could predict how long the sun or moon dominated the sky, whether the moon would be in command, under the cloak of night when the monsters stirred from the cave and grave or by the sun, bright, terrible and endless. The learned ones prayed and argued for a month and finally decided to seek the counsel of the gods. The Priests of the Dawn dispatched a disciple into the Sea of Sand, isolated and dangerous, for they valued their lives. The acolytes assembled in the temple and the one who plucked the green date from a clay jar would head into the wilderness and make peace with the gods.

Menes, slight of stature and too young to shave, picked the green date and set out to find the forgotten Temple of Mun, Goddess of the Sun. If he failed in his task, no one would notice, and another would be sent in his place. As a Lantern Bearer, he was blessed and cursed by the gods, for he radiated light from his face, guiding his way at night but drawing the attention of dark and sinister things.

Street vendors and merchants plied him with sweet and juicy fruits, filled his wine skins, and charged him full for his meals. After three nights, he stepped onto the sands, a land devoid of people and plants, where he braved strange and ferocious beasts. Many thought them mythical; however, their teeth and claws proved real. Flying snakes with venomous talons and fangs zipped over the trackless land, feeding on vultures and eagles. The Dervish, a cloud of dust, scoured and flayed flesh if one approached too close. Ageless guardsmen who did not know their duty was finished patrolled the dunes, attacking anyone who ventured too close to long dead kings and queens.

A slab of granite, like a decayed tooth, jutted out of the desert. Sand wisped from the jagged roof, swirling like disturbed specters from their eternal slumber. Menes stooped under the cracked stone mantle of the temple; grayish cobwebs clung to his nose and chin with his passing. The cool night air failed to match the subterranean chill inside the narrow passage. He balled his hands until a soft glow emanated from his fists, driving away the darkness.

At the end of a corridor, a cracked stone door was rent asunder; a fissure split the surface, slumping inside the frame under the weight of ages. He traced the crack with a light finger, loosening stone, and disturbed a colony of baby spiders, who retreated on eyelash-thin legs to safety. Pulling a hammer and chisel from his belt, he thumped and drove the thin tool into the break. Powder floated in the glow of his hands until the top of the door fell into the room beyond.

Moaning, stagnant air erupted from the blackness, while little whirlwinds of dust swirled around his sandaled feet as he stepped into a pentagon-shaped chamber, the walls covered in hieroglyphs of jackal-headed men flanking elegant women decanting red wine from clay jugs. In the center of the room, a circular dais held a slender spire of stone topped by a thin disk with a small aperture in the middle. A candlesnuffer, which resembled a pair of scissors for cutting a wick, rested on the plate.

Behind the dais rested a stone oil lamp, its edges adorned with orange paint. Menes decanted the oil into the opening, a flame no more than a finger length guttered; the yellow light provided no warmth and only brightened the disk.

An eye outlined in charcoal blinked inside the flame, the thick eyebrow pressed low in concentration. "The time of choosing is at hand." A feminine voice, both enticing yet, firm filled the room.

Menes's face blazed with a fierce light, greater than the light in his hands. "I am a lowly servant of the gods; what is your will?"

"Abase yourself when speaking with a goddess. One would think your education would have imparted the minimum understanding of etiquette between a god and mortal."

Falling to his knees, he clipped his nose on the disk before pressing his forehead against the cool flagstones. "Please forgive me. A thousand apologies in this life and in the next one to come."

"You require faith and function, for they are like your sandals and feet. You always go further than if you use only one. However, you have come a vast distance from the capital and should be commended. And you shall bear witness to a universal victory."

Warm blood bubbled inside his nose and dripped onto his interlaced hands. He sniffed, trying to staunch the runny wound. "Victory, Goddess, what victory do you speak of?"

"Your actions will be scratched into papyrus, for by your hand, you will determine who shall prevail and rule the sky. The people will note and rejoice, and you will be the first among mortals and no doubt the favored of the Kings of the Upper and Lower River Kingdoms."

"How can I bring victory? I am not a warrior."

"Not all victories come by spear and sword. In this sanctum, you will decide between the sun and the moon. Truly, you have received a heroic calling, and the Priests of the Dawn have misjudged you; and were they not encumbered by hubris, one might be in your place."

Menes brushed his tender nose with the back of his illuminated hand. "I do not desire such an honor. Should I send for a priest?"

"The sandstorm gathers this night, and it is too late for the grains of sand to deny their destiny. Steal your heart and make the choice."

"Choice? You're the Sun Goddess, and I wouldn't choose against you."

Musical laughter flitted around him, wafting up into the dark ceiling. "You're the son of a priest; your family has been priests for twenty generations. You must know what is expected. Your whole life has come down to this moment: all the expensive tutoring provided by the temple, the fasting, examinations, and prayer. Don't flag or falter now."

Menes raised his head from his blood-spotted hands and rose, relieving the tension in his back. He poured the oil into the disk, watching the liquid run into the opening. The flame burned higher and brighter, as did the eyes of the hieroglyphic characters on the walls.

"Good," the goddess purred. "The faithful are always rewarded. Now complete the ceremony, and you will return to the city as a herald of the sun."

Menes grabbed the candlesnuffer and held it high. The voice of his tutor filled his mind to smash the relic and cement the primacy of the brilliant light of the sun over the pale, cool reflected luminance of the moon.

"Order," he murmured.

"Why do you hesitate? You must assure the primacy of the sun."

"My whole life has been devoted to order, a natural cycle. I can't allow the sun to dominate, for crops would wilt in intense heat and the wells would run dry. No, there must be balance."

The flame-wreathed eye narrowed. "You dare to stand before the Goddess of the Sun? What malady has possessed you?"

"I am not sickened by the sun, despite its brilliance, nor do I fear the dark. I cannot allow one to hold dominion for eternity. The people must have both."

"Then the people shall pay for your obstinacy. For if you represent their mind; they must have a blot on their souls."

"Behold." The eye shut, and the flame vanished; darkness engulfed the room. Something massive smashed the far wall, allowing starlight to fill the crumbling chamber. Striding into the vast desert was a cow, white as washed marble, a massive red disk floating between curving horns. "I'm Sekhmet, vengeance given form."

Menes wheezed from thousands of years of dust filling his lungs as he tried to keep pace with the behemoth's strides. He dropped to his knees from exhaustion. The giant cow crested a dune, outlined by the cool lunar white light, marching in the direction of Kephus, a fishing village of over a thousand souls, and gateway to the kingdom's southern border.

After an hour of coughing, he ran, staggering over the shifting sands, until he stood on a rocky hill. In the distance, the herald of the Sun Goddesses's fury strode across the wide river like a child splashing through a puddle. The flaming sphere between its horns flashed and turned midnight to midday, sending a spear of fire into the village, setting scores of mud-brick homes to the torch. People caught in the conflagration were reduced to twisting, blackened wicks.

Menes followed for three nights as the vengeful avatar laid waste to all. The choking, roiling smoke visible for miles served as a warning and allowed the able-bodied to flee, while the elderly and infants fell to hoof and flame.

The King of the Upper and Lower Kingdoms arrayed his army and stood at its head, resplendent in his war crown, mounted on his chariot, a recursive bow in his hand, and a driver at his side. Thousands of archers and spearmen covered the land; each battalion carried a totem of their district; none spoke as the ground trembled. Enormous clouds of dust swirled, marking the advance of the destructive creature. At the king's command, chariots and cavalry crept forward, building speed, and at the maximum range of their bows, they let loose. A dark rain of barbed arrows pricked the beast's back, but still it came on, unfazed. Horses bore their riders beneath the cow, striking with long spears at the udders and groin.

A bellow issued from its massive maw, and the red disk burned bright, sending a tongue of flame racing toward a square of infantry. The heat seared men, blackening skin and sending them to the underworld. The remaining footmen swarmed, slashing with hooked swords and plunging daggers into the vulnerable hamstrings.

Menes huddled in the merciful shade of a date palm inside a walled garden, abandoned by the owners. He watched the battle unfold, as the masses of soldiers hurled spears, which appeared no more than twigs, and stabbed with kitchen knives against the titan. To his left, the main gate opened, and a bedraggled youth stepped into the courtyard, his tunic torn and sweat-stained, clutching a shivered spear shaft.

"Who are you?" Menes said.

"I am Prince Khufu, the leader of," he paused. "I was the leader of a squad of soldiers, but they are no more; I have failed my father and king."

"Do not be so harsh on yourself. There is still time to make amends."

"How? We have no means at our disposal to dispatch a god's emissary."

"The cow is consumed with bloodlust, and we must give a substitute so its madness may pass."

"What will appease it?"

"We need thousands of jugs painted red, each filled with red wine, giving the appearance of blood. It will see them and drink. With luck, it shall be as a man and slumber after slaking its thirst."

"A wise stratagem; we should make haste to the capital."

The young prince and priest stalked through the land. From miles away, the cow's thunderous bellowing carried over the dunes, and smoke roiled overhead, blotting out the stars. On the third night, they approached the city and found the streets engulfed in panic. Menes returned to the Temple of the Dawn and proposed his plan; at first the priests rebuffed him, but the prince lent his support, and they yielded, though with distain etched into their wrinkled faces. Workers and slaves gathered over four thousand clay jars and filled each with a potent wine.

Khufu gave a curt nod at the remarkable collection of pottery. "Impressive, but how do we guarantee the cow will consume the wine?"

"I shall be the sun in the night," Menes said.

"By Mun's light, do you mean to make use of your gift as a Lantern Bearer?"

"I do, for while I cannot bring back the dead, I can allow those who remain to rebuild and mourn those who have died. I will bring the cow down on me."

"I forbid this; we have lost too much already. I shall not lose such a noble person."

"My prince is kind and brave, alas you possess no other means of stopping the death and destruction. Why have the gods if there is no one to venerate them?"

The rampaging nightmare appeared the following night, its red disk and eyes blazing in the inky night. It stomped over the city walls and smashed the southgate.

In the city center, a light winked in the dark. Menes waved his arms, the symbol of the Sun Goddess clenched in a tight fist. The animal snorted and stomped forward, crushing and scattering dozens of dwellings. It glared at the acolyte and shook its head, letting loose a gout of flame, and burning him to ash. When the light vanished, it drank from thousands of jars and toppled, smashing into the Temple of the Dawn. A glow enveloped the slumbering cow until it reshaped into a female form. Her name emblazoned overhead: Hathor, the Benevolent. She waved, and the blood leached into the sand, the smoke dissipated, and the sun and moon enjoyed equal time.

The prince leaned against a shattered column that once held up the temple and frowned at a Priest of the Dawn. "The gods have seen fit to stop her rampage and restore balance to the heavens, but we have lost the light."

To Be Seen by the Sun

Maddox Emory Arnold

Log entry: Stella No. 35
Orin

They always told us it was just a matter of entropy. The slow, excruciating burn of a dying star that never truly got to live. Order devolving into chaos. Simple. Inevitable.

I never believed them.

* * *

A thin beam of Sunlight reached down through the eternal gloom to dance across Orin's skin, soft and warm as it painted a shadow behind him. It curled around his body with a playful glimmer, a spotlight waiting for its star performer to open his mouth to sing.

But, of course, there was no song. There was only fear, icy cold despite the Sun's gentle heat. Orin would have preferred the oppressive darkness of Pluto's lower caverns if it meant salvation from the light that illuminated him now.

If the Sunlight was a feather's touch, then the eyes of Orin's fellow Plutonians were claws raking down his back, their hatred bundled into a rusted knife pressed against his throat. He could do nothing but stare up at the thin crack in the cave ceiling, blocked only by a sliver of quartz glass: the source of the light, and his undoing.

"No." His mother spoke softly.

His father did not. "*No!* This cannot be."

The bludgeon of his father's voice was enough to finally pull Orin's attention down from the unseen sky and its ragged Sunlight no one had felt for five years. He looked to his parents, and from their alarmed stares he knew they saw nothing but a stranger where he had been standing mere moments ago. It was as if the Sunlight had rendered him unknowable. Another knife, this one in his chest.

He heard the whispers begin around him. They started small, barely audible above the constant hiss of the heaters and oxygen filters, but they soon rose up to lash at him.

"He's a traitor!"

"It's him! The Sun's claimed him!"

"The Torch's son, a Stella!"

The Torch's son, a Stella. The last knife. Rammed through his skull.

* * *

Log entry: Stella No. 1
Marigold

I have been given a new name to suit my purpose.

We left Pluto behind in order to protect the few humans who survived the solar storm. They think I'm dangerous, you see – not a marvel of evolution, but a threat to be terminated.

The researchers on board with me are afraid. They suggested I write these logs, "to record my own observations," but I suspect they merely want to keep me busy. Although, after everything that's happened, I must admit I'm afraid too.

I did not choose the name, yet it seems I have no choice but to accept it, lest the others act upon their fear. So, in the interest of diplomacy:

Signing off,
Stella

* * *

Orin's mother, ever the politician, recovered first. His father just continued to stare at him, a mounting fury outlined in the tight set of his jaw, the few extra lines at the corners of his eyes. Orin resisted the urge to shrink beneath that gaze.

"Please, if we could all remain calm, I'm sure we can find some explanation for this," Orin's mother called. The Torch and her family stood in their customary place on a platform at the front of the main cavern. It was elevated just enough for the Plutonians to see their leader as one of them, while still demonstrating her self-appointed superiority.

Orin had always hated standing up there. And with the entire colony's wrath reverberating off the stone walls, it was worse than ever. They all loved his mother, the shuttle engineer turned politician, and his father had won them over with manufactured charm and a healthy vitriol for the Stellae. Orin, on the other hand, had been a constant disappointment. Not pretty enough to be the face of the colony. Not clever enough to follow in his mother's footsteps. Not pious enough to become a Prism, or spiteful enough to lead the Stella ceremony. Just a simple communications technician, monitoring the constant static from space. Alone in the dark with an outgoing signal that would never be heard, for anyone who could have listened was long dead.

And now, the Sun had ripped him out of that darkness to cast him in Her light, condemning him through simple illumination.

The Torch continued her attempts at calming her people. "I'm sure there's been a mistake. Perhaps if we wait for the Sun to rise in full—"

"What do you mean, *mistake*?" a man shouted from somewhere nearby. "He's a Stella, same as the others. The light does not lie!"

More voices took up the call, and Orin's mother fell silent. She turned to him, eyes full of anger and pain, though Orin was unsure whether she grieved the imminent loss of her son, or the imminent demise of her political career. She bowed her head, and the enraged clamor only grew.

The Sun had made Her choice. The light still shone upon Orin's skin, a bare thread of brilliance against the dark. In the sea of bitter hostility that surged to claim him, that thread became the only lifeline in sight.

* * *

Log entry: Stella No. 2
Rowan

> *They sent me out here to die.*

> *Bastards.*

* * *

The Stellae had always fascinated Orin. Mysterious outcasts, too dangerous to keep on the dwarf planet, yet not so much of a threat that they would ever refuse to leave. Orin supposed most of the Stellae had truly believed they were destined to destroy what little life humans had salvaged on Pluto, and so they went quietly.

But under the diluted shimmer of Sunlight and jagged contempt of his people, Orin felt himself waver. He didn't feel like an undercover agent of chaos. He didn't feel like the Sun's chosen vicar. No. As the noise in the cavern crashed over him and threatened to pull him beneath a riptide, Orin simply felt helpless.

There was nothing he could do.

Orin's father was the one who ended it. He grabbed Orin's wrist and lifted both their hands into the air. Silence descended upon the humans of Pluto; the sudden quiet was thick and full of static. In contrast to the emptiness of the space-static that Orin watched on the comms, this was the pressurized moment before a lightning strike.

"The Sun has identified a Stella among our ranks. He…." His father's voice folded up on itself. But only for a moment. "He has been marked by Her light."

The silence that blanketed the cavern shifted until it was thick and deadly, the static replaced with a feverish cloud of disdain. It clung to Orin's skin and threatened to choke him.

And yet, somehow, he remained unscathed, for Sunlight still sheathed his body in a dim glow. Even as his own father called for his exile, the distant Sun provided a barrier from any malice thrown his way. As Orin realized this, something within him seemed to *respond* to the light that fluttered around him. A pulling sensation at the base of his neck, like a string pulled taut around his spinal cord.

How curious.

Orin's father continued the ceremony. "As we have done since the Sun destroyed the Earth, this Stella will be sent through the Shadow to join his kind. We must sacrifice a living star in order to maintain what light remains to us."

As his father spoke the words that sealed his fate, the string at the base of Orin's neck began to vibrate gently, a thrumming harmony to join the Sun's unheard song.

* * *

Log entry: Stella No. 13
Crimson

> *It really is beautiful out here. I suppose, if there is one good thing in all of this, it's that the Stellae are the only humans who still get to travel the stars. If only for a little while.*

I was worried the shuttle wouldn't make it past the Shadow, but the Sun led me through the gap. It's strange, but it felt like Her light protected me from danger, keeping the debris at bay. As though She still has some control over what's left of Her solar system. I like to think I passed some wreckage from Earth on my way through.

My body has already begun to change. I am alone, for which I am grateful, as I wouldn't like for anyone else to witness this. Or to suffer the consequences. My mind, too, seems to have been altered; I dream of those who came before. Beacons of light, relegated to different corners of the galaxy. In my own corner, there is a flare behind my sternum, liquid gold spreading through my veins. I had expected pain, but oddly there is none.

There is only light.

* * *

Orin said nothing during the short journey up to the icy surface, where a shuttle was already waiting for him. His parents accompanied him, as was tradition. The sound of their footsteps echoing off the stone tunnel was their only accompaniment.

As they emerged from the caves, the weak Sunlight filtering through the Shadow above sent a mere breath of warmth down through the stasis dome that surrounded them. The first humans on Pluto had described it as similar to twilight on Earth – a dim, melancholic half-light. It shone through a small gap in the ever-present debris field orbiting Pluto, remnants of moons and planets long dead, a Shadow forever cast to hide them from the Sun.

The light was dim, yes, and yet it was just enough to set Orin's skin alight once more. The cord at his neck sent shivers across his body, through his mind, as the light brushed against him. Flashes of white burst across his vision without warning, blinding stars orbited by specks of blue and green.

He kept his gaze forward, resisting the urge to look up toward the Sun, but also to avoid having to look at his parents, afraid of what they might see in his eyes. This made it impossible to ignore the looming shuttle ahead. The lanterns around it cast shadows across its metal frame, and in the semi-darkness it looked like a creature waiting to strike.

A Prism stood beside it. He stiffened as he caught sight of Orin and his parents, seemingly struck by the sight of the Torch's son reduced to a measly Stella. By the time they stood before the Prism, however, the man's uncertainty was masked behind a smokescreen of self-righteousness and tradition.

The Prism nodded graciously to the Torch and smoothed his gray robes. His eyes flitted to meet Orin's for only a moment before he shifted his gaze up to the sky to begin the Rites of the Stellae. He did not look at Orin again as he spoke.

"Since humans arrived on Pluto," the Prism entoned, "we have lived according to the whims of a Sun that views us with disgrace. She hides her face behind the destruction caused by our ancestors, who tampered with a power that was not theirs to claim and damned us to a life beneath the Shadow's orbit. As a reminder that She is one among the cosmos, the only natural light we may seek beyond our machinery and machinations, She burdens us, too, with the Stellae.

"On this, the thirty-fifth Stella naming day, She has appeared to us to reach through the Shadow and touch the skin of one of Her chosen descendants, as has been her way on each quinquennial since Earth's death. Her chosen Stella must join Her in Her celestial domain."

The Prism turned to Orin, his eyes somber. "Did you feel Her light upon your skin?"

Orin said nothing, for as soon as the question was spoken, the cord at the base of his skull thrummed again and seemed to wrap more tightly around his neck. It forced his chin up until he stared at the Sun, still visible through the gap in the Shadow. His parents shifted uncomfortably.

The Prism cleared his throat and tried again. "Orin, did—"

"Yes," Orin cut in. "I did. I do."

The rest of the Prism's words were lost to Orin beneath the music of the Sun. The rhythm vibrated through his entire being. He saw the same bursts of light flash before his eyes, winking at him across galaxies.

* * *

Log entry: Stella No. 20
Jax

Five years ago, they sent my sister. Now, it's my turn. Our father was beside himself, begged to go in my place. Who knows, maybe he'll get chosen in another five years when the Sun's orbit lines up with the Shadow's. Maybe we can have a family reunion out here.

Not likely.

I can see a couple of stars, tiny dots that are billions of miles away. I wonder if she's out there, waiting for me.

I still talk to her from time to time, as though she were still here. It's strange, but ever since the shuttle launched, whenever I say her name the stars out there seem to shine a little brighter, a little closer....

* * *

When the Rites were finished, the Prism moved a respectful distance away from Orin and his parents to give them a chance to say goodbye. But still, nobody spoke. They all simply stared at one another. Shock melted into pain, which hardened into cold resolve that lasted only seconds before coming back around to grief.

Orin met his parents' eyes, and understood that there was nothing to be said. Neither of them seemed inclined, or able, to speak to their son, who had become what they most hated. There was worry in their eyes, yes, but it warred with anger and confusion. Their silence was stiff and halting compared to the Sun's gentle melody.

Orin was used to this kind of quiet, the absence of what should be. Every day at the comms, waiting for a message that would never come, had taught him how to survive such emptiness. He had been the subject of ridicule for years since taking the job no one wanted, made a victim by those who did not understand the importance of hope. His mother may have been the politician, his father the strategist, but Orin…. He had always been the dreamer.

He had long dreamed that the radio silence from lightyears of empty space would one day be filled. For others, that static was devastating, a sign of complete isolation in a hostile galaxy. But for Orin, it was a slow intake of breath, a vacuum pulling in air, and he listened for the voice that would finally let out a scream of confirmation that the Plutonians were not, in fact, alone. That was Orin's chosen silence. But it was not for him to break.

And so, Orin did not break this silence either. Instead, with pale Sunbeams draped across his shoulders, he turned and walked resolutely into the shuttle that would carry him away, into the aether.

* * *

Log entry: Stella No. 28
Lark

Everybody told me space would be cold. It's not, though. I think the light under my skin is too hot to let the cold in. That's a good thing, I guess.

I'm still just a little mad, you know? My mom said it's okay to be mad, that she was mad too. She didn't want me to go, but the Prism said I had to. So I'm mostly mad at him.

I don't like the way the light feels. It hurts my eyes and makes my skin feel too tight. But I turned 15 yesterday, so that's cool, I guess. I couldn't have a party, obviously.

But I had a dream about stars. And that made me feel a little better.

* * *

The shuttle's interior was cold and austere. Dull gray panels, a seat at the front window, a small bunk, a refuse pod. Not even a control panel – the autopilot would take Orin far away into an empty pocket of space, using up all of its fuel in one prolonged light-jump to put as much distance between him and Pluto as possible. Nearly all the fuel humans could produce in five years' time, wasted on a single, one-way trip.

Soon after the door slid closed behind him, the engine began to hum, and Orin strapped himself into the seat. Despite still being on solid ground, anchored above everyone and everything he had ever known, Orin felt utterly alone. Adrift, even before liftoff.

The metal casket around him shuddered and groaned as it slid out of the stasis dome, then left solid ground behind. Orin didn't dare look down to the rocky surface and the people who lived below it. Instead, he kept his eyes forward, gathering speed as his shuttle approached the gap in the Shadow, moving ever toward the distant Sun.

The further he went, the warmer his skin became, until the Sunlight that reached in through the window was met with a similar glow, emanating from his own cells, from his very core. It was as weak as the meager Sunlight Pluto received, but against the gunmetal gray of the shuttle, it was glorious.

The flashing lights in Orin's mind began to spin a little faster.

* * *

Log entry: Stella No. 32
Janelle

> *So, here it is. No one will see these words aside from you, dear Stella. Testimonies from previous sacrifices to keep you company on your way to absolution. We must store the records somewhere back home, but it's a little too late for me to go looking. I'm not exactly tech-savvy, and these death shuttles don't have a how-to guide for interstellar communications. Maybe you will know better than I do.*

> *I think I finally understand. I can see us, now, discarded across the galaxy. This is what happens when you remove a Stella from the Sun's reach.*

> *We become what was lost. What was taken from us.*

* * *

Up close, the gap in the Shadow was much larger than Orin had expected. In his head, he had imagined a wild obstacle course of dodging and weaving to make it through unscathed, but it was as simple as threading a tiny wisp of yarn through a moon-sized needle.

And the Sun shone through it still.

The shuttle sailed through the gap, and Orin's entire universe opened up around him. He reached out to place a hand against the window as the Shadow disappeared and a new kind of freedom lodged itself in his mind. An endless expanse of blackness, glittering jewels in the distance winking at him and welcoming him into the sheer vastness they had always known.

And presiding over it all was the Sun. She was small at this distance, but brighter than any other star in sight. Orin's breath left his lungs as he saw her in all her glory, with nothing between them to block Her light. The glow emanating from his skin melded with the Sunlight, and sparks danced through the air as photons collided.

He had always wondered what would happen if the Stellae were allowed to stay on Pluto. Wasn't it strange that, as soon as humans were provided with a new organic light source, they sent it away? Once she started to glow, the first Stella had been banished under the excuse of an experiment in isolation; she even had a team of researchers with her. When none of them returned, that was the end of it.

But still…. What if? Was it the Sun's touch that determined the Stellae's fate? Or was it the pain of exile from the only home they knew? As if in answer to his question, Orin's vision faded and the bursts of light took hold once more. They were clearer. More lustrous. Pulsating with a power known only to the celestial. And there were thirty-four of them.

Orin returned to the present, suspended between the Sun and a frozen ex-planet as the shuttle prepared to leave this solar system behind. An exile, alone and alight and rejected by every remaining member of his species. Yet all of a sudden, he had the feeling that home was ahead of him, rather than behind.

* * *

Log entry: Stella No. 35
Orin

I think I'm close to the end, now. The shuttle is breaking down from all the heat pouring out of me. I don't feel any pain. Don't feel much of anything, really. I have moments of lucidity, but mostly…I just drift. Finally letting entropy take over. But even now, as my skin cracks and lets out streams of burning light and molten hydrogen, I still don't think entropy is the driving force here. I can't help but remember the Sun, and how Her rays brushed my skin. It wasn't an accusation, but an invitation.

I've read the logs. I didn't realize we saved them all. I took a peek into the comms system before it was too bright for me to see, and I found where they're copied and sent back to Pluto, to rot in a storage server until they get beamed out with the next unlucky Stella. I don't even think anyone else ever reads them.

I've decided to change that. Never say a comms tech isn't good for anything. It was as simple as switching the target location from a dusty, hidden server to every piece of personal tech left to the colony. Everyone will see what became of us.

I found all of their names, too, and made sure they were included with each entry. Filling the silence as best I can. I just want people to read our words, our stories. To see if our lives might start to mean something to them.

I keep seeing the same thing in my mind: every Stella who's ever been banished, now a star, with a collection of planets in orbit that sustain a wealth of life. Maybe entropy is what got them there, but the chaos has become something beautiful. I hope it's beautiful for me too. I hope life finds me soon, so I can see what it's supposed to be like. Until then, I'll just have to wait for the right atoms to collide at the right time. For the beautiful coalescence of a dying star, ready to live once more.

The Two Suns

From Kenya, east Africa

MANY HUNDREDS OF YEARS AGO, in the land now known as Kenya, the animals could speak just as well as human beings. At that time, the two species lived in harmony and agreed on most things. They even shared the same grievances, and were equally fond of complaining about the darkness, although they readily admitted that they were more than satisfied with the daylight.

"We cannot see at night," complained the men. "It is impossible to look after our cattle in the dark and we are often afraid of the great shadows that appear out of nowhere."

The animals agreed with the men and soon they arranged a meeting to decide what to do. The great elders of the people were the first to speak and they outlined various plans to defeat the darkness, some suggesting that huge fires should be lit at night throughout the land, others insisting that every man should carry his own torch. At length, however, the man considered wisest among the elders stood up and addressed the crowd:

"We must pray to God to give us two suns," he announced. "One that rises in the east and one that rises in the west. If he provides us with these, we will never have to tolerate night again."

The people immediately shouted their approval and all were in agreement with this plan, except for one small hare at the back of the crowd who ventured to challenge the speaker a little further:

"How will we get any shade?" he asked in a tiny voice.

But his question met with an impatient roar from the wisest elder who demanded to know the identity of the creature who had dared to oppose him.

"It was the Hare who spoke," said one of the warriors in the crowd, noticing that the Hare was trying to hide himself away under the bushes. Soon he was hauled out to the middle of the gathering, visibly shaking under the gaze of the people.

"How dare you disagree with me," said the elder. "What do you know of such matters anyway?"

The Hare bowed his head silently and began to whimper.

"Speak up, great prophet," said another of the elders. "Let us hear your wise words of counsel."

The people and the animals laughed loudly at the spectacle before them, all except for the warrior who had first spotted the Hare.

"Don't be afraid of them," he said gently. "Go on! Speak! Be proud of what you have to say."

The Hare stared into the eyes of the tall warrior and his courage began to return. Then, clearing his throat and raising himself up on his hind legs, he spoke the following words:

"I only wanted to say that if we had two suns there would never be any shade again. All the waters of the rivers and lakes will dry up. We shall never be able to sleep and our cattle will die of heat and thirst. There will be fires and hunger in the land and we shall all eventually perish."

The people listened and a great silence descended upon them as they considered the words of the little Hare.

At last, the wisest of the elders arose and patted the Hare warmly on the shoulder.

"Indeed you have shown greater wisdom than any of us," he said. "We are fortunate to have you among us."

Everyone agreed, and to this day the people of Kenya say that the hare is the cleverest of all animals. And they still have day and night; they still have only one sun and nobody has ever complained about it since that day.

White Cloud's Visit to the Sun-Prince

From Native American folklore

ONCE UPON A TIME, when there were no large cities in the western world, all the land being forest or prairie, five young men set out to hunt. They took with them a boy named White Cloud. He was only ten years old, but he was a swift runner and his sight was keen, so there were many ways in which he was useful to them.

They started before daylight, and had travelled a long way when, on reaching the top of a high hill, the sun suddenly burst forth. The air was free from mist, and there being but few trees or tall bushes near, the brightness dazzled then as it had never done before, and they exclaimed, "How near it is!"

Then one of them said, "Let us go to it," and they all agreed. They did not wish to take White Cloud with them, but he insisted upon going. When they continued to refuse he threatened to tell their parents and the Chief, who would surely prevent them from undertaking such a journey. Finally they consented, and each went home to make preparations. They shot some birds and a red deer on the way so as not to arouse the suspicions of their friends.

Before they parted they agreed to get all the moccasins they could and a new suit of leather apiece, in case they should be gone a long time and might not be able to procure clothes.

White Cloud had most difficulty in getting these things, but after coaxing to no purpose, he burst out crying and said, "Don't you see I am not dressed like my s companions, they all have new leggings?" This plea was successful, and he was provided with a new outfit.

As the party went forth the next day they whispered mysteriously to one another, taking care that such phrases should be overheard as "a grand hunt," and "we'll see who brings home most game." They did this to deceive their friends.

Upon reaching the spot from which they had seen the sun so near on the previous day, they were surprised to find that it looked as far away as it did from their own village. They travelled day after day, but seemed to come no nearer. At last they encamped for a season and consulted with one another as to the direction in which they should go. White Cloud settled it by saying, "There is the place of light (pointing towards the east), if we keep on we must reach it some time."

So they journeyed toward the east. They crossed the prairie and entered a deep forest, where it was dark in the middle of the day. There the Prince of the rattlesnakes had his warriors gathered round him, but the eldest of the party wore a "medicine" of snakeskin, so he and his companions were allowed to go through the woods unharmed.

They went on day after day and night after night through forests that seemed to have no end. When the Morning Star painted her face, and when the beautiful red glowed in the west, when the Storm-fool gathered his harvest, when the south wind blew silver from the dandelion, they kept on, but cane no nearer to their object.

Once they rested a long time to make snowshoes and more arrows. They built a lodge and hunted daily until they had a good store of dried meat, as much as they could carry, and again they went on their way.

After many moons they reached a river that was running swiftly towards the east. They kept close to it until it flowed between high hills. One of these they climbed and caught sight of something white between the trees. They hurried on and rested but little that night, for they thought surely the white line must be the path that leads to the splendid lodge of the sun.

Next morning they came suddenly in view of a large lake. No land was on any side of it except where they stood. Some of them being thirsty, stooped to drink. As soon as they had tasted, they spat out the liquid, exclaiming, "*Salt* water!"

When the sun arose he seemed to lead forth out of the farthest waves. They looked with wonder, then they grew sad, for they were as far away as ever.

After smoking together in council, they resolved not to go back, but to walk around the great lake. They started towards the north, but had only gone a short distance when they came to a broad river flowing between mountains. Here they stayed the night. While seated round their fire, someone thought to ask whether any of them had dreamed of water.

After a long silence the eldest said, "I dreamt last night that we had come wrong, that we should have gone towards the south. But a little way beyond the place where we encamped yesterday is a river. There we shall see an island not far out in the lake. It will come to us and we are to go upon it, for it will carry us to the lodge of the sun."

The travellers were well pleased with the dream and went back towards the south. A few hours' journey from their old camp brought them to a river. At first they saw no island, but as they walked they came to a rise of ground and the island appeared to them in the distance. As they looked, it seemed to approach.

Some were frightened and wanted to go away, but the courage of White Cloud shamed them, and they waited to see what would happen. They saw three bare trees on the island, such as pine trees that have been robbed of their leaves by fire. As they looked, lo! a canoe with wings that flapped like those of a loon when it flies low down to the lake, left the island. It came swiftly over the water, and when it touched the land, a man with a white face and a hat on, stepped upon the shore and spoke to them, but they could not understand what he said. He motioned to them to mount the bird canoe, which they did, and were carried to the island.

There was a horrible noise and rattle like that made by the magician when he conjures the evil spirit from a sick man, then white wings sprang from the bare tree trunks, and they felt themselves moving over the water, as the deer bounds across the trail in the forest.

The night came and they saw the familiar stars above them, so they lay down to sleep, fearing nothing.

When the day dawned, they could see no shore anywhere, only the water of the lake. The Pale-faces were kind, and gave them food and drink, and taught them words, such as they said to one another.

One moon had passed and another had come and nearly gone, when the Pale-face Chief said they would soon find the shore, and he would take them to his Prince, who would direct them to their journey's end.

The Prince lived in a beautiful lodge of white stone. The walls were of silver, hung with silver shields and arrows. His throne was of white horn carved with many figures. His robe was ermine, and he had many sparkling stones in his headdress.

He talked to White Cloud and listened to the story of their wanderings, their dreams and their disappointments, and spoke gently, trying to persuade them to' give up their purpose. "See," said he, "here are hunting-grounds, and fat deer, and game and fish enough for you, and none shall make war or trouble you, why go farther?"

But they would not stay. Whereupon, the Prince proved himself a magician, for he told them in what direction they should go, and what would befall them. At the last they would come to the wigwam of the great wizard, Tangled Hair. They would hear his dreadful rattle three days before they reached his lodge, and the wizard would do his best to destroy them.

The Prince tried again to keep them, but as they would not stay, he gave them presents of food and clothing, and his warriors led them to the end of his country.

They went through many forests, but the trees were strange to them. They saw flowers springing in their path and vines upon the rocks and about the trees, but none were those they knew. Even the birds were strange, and talked in voices which they could not understand. But all this made them believe they wire getting nearer to the Sun-Prince.

After many moons the clothing which the Prince of the Pale-faces had given was worn out, so they put on their leather dresses again. Hardly had they done this, when they heard a fierce rattle and knew that they were near the wigwam of the wizard. The noise was dreadful and seemed to come from the centre of the earth.

They had travelled far that day. The ground had been rough and stony and in many places covered with water through which they had been obliged to wade. They lighted a fire and sat down to dry their clothes and to rest. The noise of the rattle continued and increased so much that they broke up their camp and went toward the place which they knew must be Tangled Hair's lodge.

It was not a wigwam, but a lodge with many fireplaces, and it had eyes which glared like their campfire. Two of the travellers wished to go back or to try to get around the lodge, but White Cloud said, "Let the wizard see we are no cowards." So they went up to the door.

There they were met by Tangled Hair himself, who said, "Welcome, my grandsons!"

When they were seated in his lodge, he gave each some smoking mixture, and as they sat and smoked he said that he knew their history, and had seen them when they left their village. He took the trouble to do this so that they might believe what he was about to say.

"I do not know that all of you will reach your journey's end, though you have gone three-fourth's of the way and are very near the edge of the earth. When you reach that place you will see a chasm below you and will be deafened by the noise of the sky descending upon the world. It keeps moving up and down. You must watch, and when it lifts you will see a little space. You must leap through this, fearing nothing, and you will find yourselves on a beautiful plain."

The wizard then told them who he was and that they had no need to fear him if they were brave men. He was not permitted to help weak men and cowards.

When the first arrow of daylight came into the lodge, the young men started up and refused to rest longer, so Tangled Hair showed them the direction they were to take in going to the edge of the world. Before they left he pointed out a lodge in the shape of an egg standing upon its larger end and said, "Ask for what you want and he who lives in that lodge will give it to you."

The first two asked that they might live forever and never be in want. The third and fourth asked to live longer than many others and always to be successful in war. White Cloud spoke for his favourite companion and for himself. Their wish was to live as long as other braves and to have success in hunting that they might provide for their parents and relatives.

The wizard smiled upon them and a voice from the pointed lodge said, "Your wishes shall be granted."

They were anxious to be gone, more especially when they found that they had been in Tangled Hair's lodge not a day, as they had supposed, but a year.

"Stop," cried Tangled Hair, as they prepared to depart, "you who wished to live forever shall have that wish granted now." Thereupon he turned one of them into a cedar tree and the other into a grey rock.

"Now," said he to the others, "you may go."

They went on their way trembling, and said to one another, "We were fortunate to get away at all, for the Prince told us he was an evil spirit."

They had not gone far when they heard the beating of the sky. As they went nearer and nearer to the edge it grew deafening, and strong gusts of wind blew them off their feet. When they reached the very edge everything was dark, for the sky had settled down, but it soon lifted and the sun passed but a short distance above their heads.

It was some time before they could get courage enough to jump through the space. White Cloud and his friend at last gave a great leap and landed on the plain of which they had been told.

"Leap, leap quickly," called White Cloud to the others, "the sky is on its way down."

They reached out timidly with their hands, but just then the sky came down with terrific force and hurled them into the chasm. There they found themselves changed into monstrous serpents which no man could kill, so their wish was granted.

Meanwhile, White Cloud and his companion found themselves in a beautiful country lighted by the moon. As they walked on all weariness left them and they felt as if they had wings. They saw a hill not far off and started to climb it, that they might look abroad over the country.

When they reached it, a little old woman met them. She had a white face and white hair, but her eyes were soft and dark and bright in spite of her great age.

She spoke kindly and told them that she was the Princess of the Moon, that they were now halfway to the lodge of her brother, the Sun-prince. She led them up a steep hill which sloped on the other side directly to the lodge of the Sun.

The Moon-princess introduced them to her brother, who wore a robe of a rich, golden colour, and shining as if it had points of silver all over it. He took down from the wall a splendid pipe and a pouch of smoking mixture, which he handed to them.

He put many questions to them about their country and their people, and asked them why they had undertaken this journey. They told him all he wished to know, and in return asked him to favour their nation, to shine upon their corn and make it grow and to light their way in the forest.

The Prince promised to do all these things, and was much pleased because they had asked for favours for their friends rather than for themselves.

"Come with me," he said, "and I will show you much that you could not see elsewhere."

Before starting he took down from his walls arrows tipped with silver and with gold, and placed them in a golden quiver. Then they set out on their journey through the sky.

Their path lay across a broad plain covered with many brilliant flowers. These were half hidden many times by the long grass, the scent of which was as fragrant as the flowers it hid. They passed tall trees with wide spreading branches and thick foliage. The most luxuriant were on the banks of a river as clear as crystal stone, or on the edge of little lakes which in their stony trails looked like bowls of water set there for the use of a mighty giant.

Tribes of waterfowl flew about, and birds of bright plumage darted through the forest like a shower of arrows. They saw some long, low lodges with cages filled with singing birds hanging on the walls, but the people were away.

When they had travelled half across the sky, they came to a place where there were fine, soft mats, which the young men discovered were white clouds. There they sat down, and the Sun-prince began making preparations for dinner.

At this place there was a hole in the sky, and they could look down upon the earth. They could see all its hills, plains, rivers, lakes and trees, and the big salt lake they had crossed.

While they were looking at a tribe of Indians dancing, something bright flew past them, downwards through the hole in the sky and struck the merriest dancer of them all, a young boy, son of a great chief.

The warriors of his tribe ran to him and raised him with great cries and sounds of sorrow. A wizard spoke and told them to offer a white dog to the Sun-prince.

The animal was brought, and the master of the feast held the choicest portion above his head, saying, "We send this to thee, Great Spirit," and immediately the roasted animal was drawn upwards and passed through the sky. Then the boy recovered and went on dancing.

After White Cloud and his companion had feasted with the Sun-prince, they walked on till they saw before them a long slope that was like a river of gold, flowing across silver sands.

"Keep close to me," said the Sun-prince, "and have no fear. You will reach your home in safety."

So they took hold of his belt, one on either side of him, and felt themselves lowered as if by ropes. Then they fell asleep.

When they awoke they found themselves in their own country, and their friends and relatives were standing near them, rejoicing over their return. They related all their adventures, and lived many years in honour and in plenty, the Sun-prince smiling upon them in all their undertakings.

Why the Sun and the Moon Live in the Sky

From southern Nigeria, west Africa

MANY YEARS AGO the sun and water were great friends, and both lived on the earth together. The sun very often used to visit the water, but the water never returned his visits. At last the sun asked the water why it was that he never came to see him in his house, the water replied that the sun's house was not big enough, and that if he came with his people he would drive the sun out.

He then said, "If you wish me to visit you, you must build a very large compound; but I warn you that it will have to be a tremendous place, as my people are very numerous, and take up a lot of room."

The sun promised to build a very big compound, and soon afterwards he returned home to his wife, the moon, who greeted him with a broad smile when he opened the door. The sun told the moon what he had promised the water, and the next day commenced building a huge compound in which to entertain his friend.

When it was completed, he asked the water to come and visit him the next day.

When the water arrived, he called out to the sun, and asked him whether it would be safe for him to enter, and the sun answered, "Yes, come in, my friend."

The water then began to flow in, accompanied by the fish and all the water animals.

Very soon the water was knee-deep, so he asked the sun if it was still safe, and the sun again said, "Yes," so more water came in.

When the water was level with the top of a man's head, the water said to the sun, "Do you want more of my people to come?" and the sun and moon both answered, "Yes," not knowing any better, so the water flowed on, until the sun and moon had to perch themselves on the top of the roof.

Again the water addressed the sun, but receiving the same answer, and more of his people rushing in, the water very soon overflowed the top of the roof, and the sun and moon were forced to go up into the sky, where they have remained ever since.

Why the Sun Sets

From the Aboriginal people of Australia

OUT ON THE MURRUMBIDGEE there is a tale about the setting sun. The country there is very different from what it is where the aborigines had a story of the Escapees.

It is flat.

It seems to be below, far below, the level of the sea.

And the sun can be seen setting.

The land which contains the great, dreary salt lakes-Frome, Eyre, Gardiner, Amadeus, Torrens, and a lot of others named and unnamed, is really below the sea's level, and if ever a canal is cut from the head of Spencer Gulf to the bed of those lakes a vast extent of territory will become an ultra-salt inland sea.

But though the country through which the greater part of the Murrumbidgee and the Lachlan and the Darling flow seems very low, it is still above the level of the great oceans.

It seems to be a disc, like a huge plate.

Turn which way one will, the horizon is sharp and level and lies all around. In the summer (and summer sets in in October and lasts until the end of March) the sun rises a huge fiery red ball. Before he appears he sends his torrid shafts, and the earth is dried and heated. With his horrible advance agents of wilting beams the flies are a wracking buzz and a stinging poison as they wing their nauseous way about, and all the other insect life starts into pestering being.

The smell of baked earth rises, and the dried grasses stand stiffly and starkly.

The level east lightens; and slowly, surely, and relentlessly the great red disc ascends and throws long shadows across the ground.

The dwarfed and gnarled gums seem to beg for some respite. The sombre Murray Pines cluster in masses as if seeking the solace and protection of one another's company.

By the advent of the first month of summer the few orchids that bloomed in the short spring have gone, and the glowing grasses have seeded and died.

It is now a bare and browned and sere world.

The sun changes from red to grey, and as he wends his solemn way up to the zenith he pours out molten light.

Lazy clouds of dust rise up from the new-formed roads, stirred by wagoned teams, and flatten and float out over the trees.

Shadows grow less and less until they are only patches directly below the bushes.

Life is a dreary and painful process.

Horses stand mutely, head to tail, close to any tree stumps that may be there; sheep huddle, panting, out in the glaring sun; birds sit on the boughs with wings opened and mouths agape; nothing lives in the wilting day – everything crouches in whatever of shade can be found.

Over and above passes the molten ball, and as he slowly descends towards the horizon of the west, and the east begins to blacken, life stirs again, and all beings long for the cool of night.

Many nights are but little cooler than the day.

The gay, glowing flowers of the sandstone elevations are not here. No epacrids, no boronias, no waratahs!

The deep restful greens of the laurels, and the glowing browns of the turpentines and woollybutts and ironbarks and lilly-pillies do not show. The banksias are stunted. Only the hardiest trees grow, and the most transient of the grasses, and they are poor and bare all except the annual grasses. They are the saving of the land.

It was not always so.

The aborigines have a legend born of their stricken condition, and of that wonderful and unexplainable knowledge of their past history as is revealed to us by our geologists and scientists which tells of a time when the earth was not parched by such a sun; when it was ever day, but the daylight was the radiance of a human ancestor, and when the trees and shrubs and flowers were as bright and plentiful as they are now in the regions that are not wilted by our sun.

The sun, they say, is an ancestor – a human that was not understood, and he retired in sorrow and became a god and thus came light – so came the setting sun.

A family which claimed the sleeping lizard as its totem was camped in a scrub of Murray Pine (a callitris); and, with wurleys built against a number of seared logs, lived, not far away, a family of which the brown-banded snake was the totem.

During the winter months good rains had fallen, and the ground was clothed with many beautiful grasses and much wild parsley, and rearing its pretty pink three-leaved and fringed flowers amongst the grasses was the Thysanotus tuberosus, or Fringed Violet.

The Kennedya and the Hardenbergia clambered over the old time-worn stumps, and the acacias poisoned the air with their pollen.

Down on the ground were the purple and white wild violets. The sleeping lizards fraternized good-naturedly with the snake-people, and all "was merry as a marriage bell".

There was a plethora of foods, birds, animals, roots and berries.

Amongst the snake people two young men strove for the one maiden, and there had been many quarrels because no one seemed to know to which she had been promised.

Meeting after meeting had been called, and the clamour at every one was great.

At last it was decided that he who made the finest stone spearhead for presentation to the father of the girl should have her.

She often spent many hours running from one to the other and she was not innocent of jeering and jibing at both the anxious workmen.

When the proofs of their handicraft were brought to the wurley of the father he pretended to fly into a great rage. He denounced the young men and scoffed at the spearheads – all of them. He rushed to the King and implored him to condemn the lot. He spat on them and flung them amongst the women, who picked them up and flew into as big a pretence of anger as the man.

The contest was renewed and it continued until the pleasant weather had gone, and the light that came from whatever member of the priesthood held the power to so propitiate the light-giver as to vouchsafe day to the world, began to wane, and it was nearly time for another magician to be appointed to carry on.

To the surprise of everyone, one of the contestants proclaimed himself to be the proper magician.

Now the duties pertaining to such an office were many and arduous.

The priest had to spend long periods in prayer and meditation out on the plain by himself. He had to submit to much indignity even flagellation, and he had to ostracize himself in other ways.

There were not many natives who cared to be considered the special emissary to the ancestor of the light.

And in this young man's case it meant giving up the girl.

But the dispute was not to be settled.

Withdrawing from the contest did not give the other man the right to his claim.

If winning in the set competition could not happen, then some other way must be chosen by the priest.

And he was not in any hurry to give a pronouncement.

In the meantime, the girl did not cease her teasing.

She still jeered at both the newly announced magician and the other contestant.

This became distasteful to the old women, whose charge she was, and they set her to perform many tasks that otherwise would not have fallen to her lot.

Perhaps never before did so young a girl have to grind the grass seeds. She had to find out for herself how to hold the stone between the calves of her legs and how to use the grinder.

She became a wife without being married, for it was a wife's duty to make most of the cakes.

One day she found her suitor to be busy making a shield.

He was drawing the circles and the radiating lines that represented the light of day.

But in it he drew the sleeping lizard.

It was meant as sarcasm, and it was hoped that this piece of portrayed scorn would bring some evil to his rival. He would much have preferred to go on with the competition until one or the other had won. He was becoming anxious to secure the wife, and this delay was beginning to annoy him.

The newly recognized magician was out somewhere in communion with the saints or the spirits or whatever it is that such people have found when they come back with tales of supernatural visitations while they are either figuratively or really eating locusts and wild honey.

Now the artistry of the young man was good.

The girl was really interested.

She sat beside him watching intently every mark.

And as they sat thus the old lightmaker died, and the new one emerged from his solitude and commenced the ceremony of light making so that it would continue.

As he was so young the light nearly went out. The semi-darkness that ensued was bewildering and it struck terror into everyone.

The tribe implored the young magician to put forth every endeavour, and his answer was that without the girl he could not make more light than there was then.

The people looked all around, but they could not see the wanted girl. No one knew where she had gone.

Then they saw that the young lover was missing also.

The light maker grew very angry.

All the gesticulations, all the genuflexions, all the grotesque dancing that were resorted to in anger, he indulged in.

His anger grew very real and it communicated itself to his people. Even the King himself became as the rest.

That feeling gave way to despair. Women sat in groups and beat themselves and one another and inflicted severe wounds. Priests hurriedly drew sacred totemic marks on the ground and drew similar designs on the bodies of those whose right it was to bear them. Mitres were fashioned and put on the heads of the higher clergy. Fires were lit to augment the lessened light of the day.

After a while a hunting party was organized to hunt up the missing people, and upon being blessed they seized their spears and shields and bounded off.

The lightmaker forgot his mission. He yearned for the girl, and without saying a word he betook himself off to search.

After a very long time he found her.

She was living in a slight depression – a crabhole – that is pointed out today by all who know this story.

The man with whom she was living was away at the time, and the lightmaker appealed to her to come to him.

So together they ran, and all the light of day went with them. The further they went the less the light grew until they were right on the edge of the world.

There a son was born to them, and because of the wrong, the father and mother died.

Never since the beginning of the trouble had the daylight been so clear or so strong as before it, and now it was leaving the earth forever. No one else could ever receive the instructions that would make him a lightmaker. The great ancestor needed a mediator between himself and the world, and it had to be a lizard man, and now no lizard man knew what to do.

The daylight faded right away.

In its going it was much more beautiful than ever before. Long streaks of gold spread over the sky, and as that faded everything became awestricken, and the world was hushed.

Even now there is that period "while the air 'twixt dark and daylight's standing still."

But the baby that was born away over there grew and became at once a light man. He held direct communion with the great ancestor and he gathered great quantities of light in his hands.

So he set out to find his way back to where he knew his people dwelt. There was one thing he did not do.

He was born with his back to his people, and he did not turn round. He just walked on and on.

He had great waters to travel over, and great beds of sand to travel through, and great forests to find his way in, and great mires to wade across, but he kept going.

He was determined to find his people and to bring them light. So a time came when the tribe saw light breaking away over in the east. It had disappeared on the one hand and it reappeared on the other.

They were overjoyed.

But the priests counselled great caution.

No one knew what to say or do.

The priests and the King said that if they made the wrong ceremony they would lose the light.

So they waited mutely and watched it. There was no welcoming shout. The birds sang to it. The trees nodded to it. Flowers bowed to it. Dewdrops left the earth and flew to it. But men and women were mute because they were afraid that they may do the wrong thing and it would leave them forever and all their days would be dark and they could not live.

Therefore the lightmaker sailed over their heads. He went on to the edge of the world where he was born.

The priests said that when they had found out how to worship him he would come down out of the sky and remain with them forever, but while in ignorance in that respect he would continue to go over their heads and disappear.

They are still in ignorance. That is why there is no sun worship.

The new sun man became more beloved than any had been before, and so the ancestor made him a god like himself, even if the father and mother did do wrong.

And the ancestor sometimes gives him huge quantities of light, and as it is thrown down to the earth it burns and sears and scorches.

So we have summer. If we could only find out how to carry out the proper ceremony of sun worship then there would be no more great heat waves.

This is the tale of the aborigines who live in those parts where the summer is scorching. It accounts for more things than will be seen at first reading.

When the light is not being thrown in large quantities the days are not scorching and the grass is green and the trees are not so dry and the great cracks in the ground are closed up and the little flowers are blooming and all is gay.

Why the Sunset Is Sometimes Red and Stormy

From the Ekoi people, Nigeria and Cameroon

IN THE BEGINNING OF THINGS, Obassi Osaw and Obassi Nsi lived in towns some distance apart. The former had no sons, but the latter had three. The first of them was a great thief, the second was the same, and when they stole anything their Father had to pay for it.

Now Obassi had great farms and plantations outside the town. Sometimes cows ate his yams; so one day he came home and put powder in his gun but no shot, meaning to frighten the beasts away next time they came. During his absence the two bad sons went and put shot in the gun. So when he fired at the cows one of them died.

Obassi Nsi cried out, and went back to the town. When he reached it he told the owner, "I shot your cow by accident; "but the man replied:

"Then I must kill you, just the same as my cow."

A meeting was held, and the townsfolk begged the man to accept another cow in exchange for the one he had lost, but he refused to do so, and still said that Obassi must die.

Next morning, therefore, Obassi said to his third son, "I have to die today; "but the latter cried:

"How can you die. First son and second son are fully grown, but I am still small. Do not leave me till I am grown up."

Obassi said, "Here is a key. The room to which it belongs shall be your own, so that you have somewhere to run to, and be safe from your brothers."

In the evening he called the boy again, and said:

"Do no evil thing in the town, and when I am dead kill a cow and give it to the people." That night he died.

The third son killed the cow as he had been bidden, but the first and second sons were very angry, and beat him, and said, "The cow belonged to us." They took away the key of his room, so that small boy had nowhere to go, and they seized all the goods for themselves, so he was left penniless. After that they went away from their father's land.

The boy went out sadly and walked through the town. He met an old woman, who asked "Whither are you going?" He said, "I am the small son of Obassi Nsi, and I have nowhere to go."

The old woman answered, "Do not trouble. Stay here with me," and to this the boy agreed. One day he found an old knife in the ground; this he cleaned and sharpened till it became all right again. Next morning he went to the bush and set native traps. In one of these he caught an Iku (water chevrotain), which he brought home and gave to the old woman. She said, "I cannot eat this meat; perhaps you have stolen it; "but he answered, "No, I will take you to the place where the traps are set." She went with him, and saw that it was as he had said; so agreed to eat the meat.

Next morning the boy said, "I wish to go and clear my farm." When he got to the plantation he saw some slaves of Obassi Osaw coming towards him. When they arrived they said:

"We have come to take charge of the goods of Obassi Nsi." On this the boy answered, "They are not in my hands. First and second sons have taken everything." So the men returned empty-handed.

Next day six more came and asked the same thing, but the lad said, "Wait a minute and I will see what can be done.' Then he went to the old woman and told her what had happened. She said, "Go to Porcupine, and get him to practise the charm."

When this was done the Diviner said, "Go to the middle compound of your father's town, and under the floor of the inner room you will find what will content the messengers."

The boy did as he was told, dug up the goods and gave them to the men to carry to Obassi Osaw.

When Obassi saw that his slaves brought back the goods, but not the boy, he was angry and said, "I told you to bring me the young son also. Why have you not done this?"

Next day, therefore, two more men were sent to bring the boy. No sooner did he arrive than the sky people brought him fruits, and all kinds of rich gifts, together with some very beautiful slaves. In spite of all that Osaw could do, however, the boy was not happy, but said, "I wish I could go back to earth once more."

Then Obassi Osaw was vexed, and his eyes began to glow, and from their gleam the sky grew red and stormy. That is the reason why we see Tornado sunsets. Obassi grows angry and his eyes become red. The storm always follows, for Tornados are the sound of the wrath of Obassi Osaw.

Biographies & Sources

Aesop
The North Wind and the Sun
Aesop (*c.* 620–564 BCE) was a Greek storyteller credited with many collections of fables, however his existence is disputed. It is very difficult to track his history, and older spellings of his name include Esop and Isope. Unfortunately, no writings by Aesop have survived, but have instead been gathered from different countries across the world, in many different languages, often through oral storytelling. It is likely that Aesop was a legendary figure created as a pen name for the many authors of fables.

Hartley Burr Alexander
The Creation Story of the Four Suns
(Originally Published in *The Mythology of All Races: Latin American, Vol. XI*, 1920)
Hartley Burr Alexander (1973–1939) was a philosopher, author, scholar, educator, iconographer, and poet. Born in Nebraska to a Methodist family, Alexander came to distrust Christianity and developed an interest in First Peoples of the Americas, their religions and spirituality. Alexander wrote prolifically on the subjects of Native American philosophy, lore, mythology and art. One of his best-known works is the poem 'To a Child's Moccasin (Found at Wounded Knee)', which stood in stark contrast to the prevailing negative views and treatment of Native Americans by the US government and American society at the time.

Rasmus Bjørn Anderson
The Creation, from the 'Younger Edda'
(This translation originally Published in *The Younger Edda*, 1901)
Rasmus Bjørn Anderson (1846–1936) was an American author, editor, translator, professor, diplomat and businessman. Born in Albion, Wisconsin, to Norwegian parents, Anderson grew up steeped in the culture of his ancestral Scandinavia. Later, as a professor at the University of Wisconsin–Madison, he became the founding head of the Department of Scandinavian Studies. Anderson also founded a publishing company called the Norroena Society, which republished Scandinavian texts. He authored several Scandinavian-themed books, including *The Scandinavian Languages* (1873) and *Norse Mythology* (1875).

Maddox Emory Arnold
To Be Seen by the Sun
(First Publication)
Maddox Emory Arnold (he/they) is a writer and educator based in Southeast Michigan. His work explores queerness, gender, mental health and otherness with a speculative twist. He particularly enjoys seeking the horrific, surreal and/or fantastical in mundane spaces and experiences. His prose and poetry have previously appeared in *If There's*

Anyone Left, HAD, NonBinary Review and elsewhere. In what little free time he has, Maddox enjoys baking, reading and hiking the Midwest wilderness. You can find him online at maddoxemoryarnold.com/home or on Twitter @maddox_emory.

Emilie Kip Baker
Apollo and King Admetus; Apollo the Musician; Iris and Aurora; The Love of Apollo
(Originally Published in *Stories of Old Greece and Rome*, 1913)
Emilie Kip Baker (1873–1951) was an American author and a significant figure in the realm of education and literature of her time. Taking a scholarly approach to her retellings of ancient myths and stories, her work gained popularity among both academics and ordinary readers alike. She is the author of the popular collection *Stories of Old Greece and Rome* (1913), as well as *Stories from Northern Myths* (1914).

Beston Barnett
The Sun and the City-Builders
(First Publication)
During the day, author Beston Barnett designs and builds furniture in San Diego. At night, he plays Romani jazz. The rest of the time, he writes quirky little stories in which he struggles – rarely successfully – to leave his characters living happily ever after. He has placed stories with *Asimov's, Strange Horizon* and *Clarkesworld*, and is a graduate of the 2018 Clarion Workshop.

Algernon Blackwood
A Desert Episode
(Originally Published in *Day and Night Stories*, 1917)
Algernon Henry Blackwood (1869–1951) was a writer who crafted his tales with extraordinary vision. Born in Kent but working at numerous careers in America and Canada in his youth, he eventually settled back in England in his thirties. He wrote many novels and short stories including 'The Willows', which was rated by Lovecraft as one of his favourite stories. Blackwood is credited by many scholars as a real master of imagery who wrote at a consistently high standard.

Vladimir Bogoraz
The Boy Who Married the Sun
(Originally Published in *Chukchee Mythology*, 1910)
Vladimir Bogoraz (1865–1936) was a Russian author, anthropologist and revolutionary. He was born in Ovruch, Russia, the son of a Jewish school teacher. Converting to Christianity as an adult, he changed his birthname, Natan, to Vladimir. Later arrested for revolutionary activity, his exile to north-eastern Siberia introduced him to the culture of the region's indigenous Chukchi people, who he came to study, and about whom he published several literary works under the pseudonym N.A. Tan. He is best known for his collection *Chukchee Tales* (1899) and *Chukchee Mythology* (1910).

E.A. Wallis Budge
Hymn III: A Hymn to Ra, the Sun God; The Legend of Râ and Isis
(Originally Published in *The Literature of the Ancient Egyptians*, 1914)
E.A. Wallis Budge (1857–1934) was an English Egyptologist, Orientalist, philologist

and author, born in Bodmin, Cornwall. With a fascination for languages from childhood, he studied Biblical Hebrew and Syriac in his spare time while working for WHSmith from the age of twelve. Making connections with the British Museum through his tutor, Budge came to work in its Department of Egyptian and Assyrian Antiquities in 1883. He published several works on the ancient Near East and Egyptology.

Margaret Compton

White Cloud's Visit to the Sun-Prince
(Originally Published in *Snow Bird and the Water Tiger and Other American Indian Tales*, 1895)
Margaret Compton (1852–1903) was an American author. With a strong interest in Native American cultures and folklore traditions, she published several works on the subject. Her book *American Indian Fairy Tales* (1907) collects a number of Native American stories. Her short fiction includes the stories 'How Mad Buffalo Fought the Thunder-Bird' (1895), 'Snowbird and the Water Tiger' (1895), and 'The Adventures of Living Statue' (1895).

F. Hadland Davis

Ama-terasu and Susa-no-o
(Originally Published in *Myths & Legends of Japan*, 1912)
Frederick Hadland Davis was a writer and historian – author of *The Land of the Yellow Spring and Other Japanese Stories* (1910) and *The Persian Mystics* (1908 and 1920). His books describe these cultures to the western world and tell stories of ghosts, creation, mystical creatures and more. He is best known for his book *Myths & Legends of Japan* (1912).

Elphinstone Dayrell

Why the Sun and the Moon Live in the Sky
(Originally Published in *Folk Stories from Southern Nigeria and West Africa*, 1910)
Elphinstone Dayrell (1869–1917) collected his tales after hearing many first-hand from the Efik and Ibibio peoples of South-eastern Nigeria when he was District Commissioner of South Nigeria. His collections of folklore include *Folk Stories from Southern Nigeria* (1910) and *Ikom Folk Stories from Southern Nigeria*, the latter published by the Royal Anthropological Institute of Great Britain and Ireland in 1913.

Parker Fillmore

The Flaming Horse: The Story of a Country where the Sun Never Shines
(Originally Published in *Czechoslovak Fair Tales*, 1919)
Parker Fillmore (1878–1944) was an American author born in Cincinnati, Ohio. Upon taking a job as a teacher in the Philippines, Fillmore was given no textbooks to teach his students English, and so he crafted his own stories for this purpose, launching his career in writing. Returning to the US and moving to a primarily Czech neighbourhood in New York City, he gained a great passion for the Czech folklore that his neighbours shared with him. This led to his publication of several collections of these stories, including *Czechoslovak Fairy Tales* (1919) and *The Shoemaker's Apron* (1920).

Mary Frere

How the Sun, the Moon and the Wind Went Out to Dinner

(Originally Published in *Old Deccan Days, or Hindoo Fairy Legends Current in Southern India*, 1868)

Author Mary Frere (1845–1911) was born in Bitton, in Gloucestershire, England. The daughter of a Baronet who worked in the colonial government of Bombay, India, and later became its governor, Frere grew up with a fascination for Indian culture. She later took trips to India with her father, during which she began collecting Indian folklore. In addition to her best-known work *Old Deccan Days*, Frere also published a play and a number of poems.

Cara Giles

Baba Yaga's Red Rider

(First Publication)

Cara Giles is a fantasy writer with a deep love of folklore and fairy tales. Baba Yaga has always loomed large in her imagination. Raised in Los Angeles, Cara now makes her home in sunny southern Utah. When she's not writing, you can find her treasure-hunting in thrift stores with her husband and exploring libraries with their two daughters. Her work has appeared in *Enchanted Living Magazine*. This is her first fiction publication.

Ralph T.H. Griffith

Hymns to the Sun God Surya

(This translation originally Published in *The Rig Veda*, 1896)

Ralph T.H. Griffith (1826–1906) was an English Indologist and translator. Born in Corsley, Wiltshire, Griffith later earned a BA from Queen's College, where he was elected Boden Professor of Sanskrit in 1849. He was one of the first Europeans to translate the Vedas into English. In addition, he translated numerous other works of Sanskrit literature, including a verse version of the Ramayana and the Kumara Sambhava of Kalidasa. He spent much of his life in India.

H. Rider Haggard

Extracts from King Solomon's Mines

(Originally Published in *King Solomon's Mines*, 1885)

Sir Henry Rider Haggard (1856–1925) was born in Norfolk, England. Best known for his adventure novels set in exotic locations, Haggard is considered a pioneer in the Lost World literary genre. He spent some years in South Africa, after which he wrote his most famous novel *King Solomon's Mines*, which was the first English adventure novel set in Africa. Later on in his life Haggard was appointed as a Knight Bachelor and Knight Commander for his services to the British Empire.

Professor Ravit Helled

Foreword

Ravit Helled is a full Professor for Theoretical Astrophysics at the Department of Astrophysics, University of Zurich, whose lectures include such topics as 'The Sun and Planets'. Professor Helled is an international expert in planetary science and has made breakthrough contributions to the understanding of the formation, evolution and internal structure of planets. She stands out by contributing to both Solar System and exoplanet science and their connection. Professor Helled is involved in various ESA and NASA space missions. She is a frequent invited speaker in scientific conferences, and serves in various international committees and science panels.

Francis Hickes
An Extract from Lucian's 'True History'
(This edition Published in *Lucian's True History*, 1902)
Francis Hickes (1566–1631) was an English translator, born in Barcheston, Warwickshire. After studying at Oxford University, where he earned a BA in 1583, he began work as a translator of Greek. His translated works include *Certaine Select Dialogues of Lucian: Together with His True Historie, Translated from the Greeke into English* (1634).

William Hope Hodgson
Extracts from 'The House on the Borderland'
(Originally Published in *The House on the Borderland*, 1908)
William Hope Hodgson (1877–1918) was born in Essex, England, but moved several times with his family, including living for some time in County Galway, Ireland – a setting that would later inspire *The House on the Borderland*. Hodgson made several unsuccessful attempts to run away to sea, until his uncle secured him some work in the Merchant Marine. This association with the ocean would unfold later in his many sea stories. After some initial rejections of his writing, Hodgson managed to become a full-time writer of both novels and short stories, which form a fantastic legacy of adventure, mystery and horror fiction.

James A. Honey
Horse Cursed by Sun
(Originally Published in *South-African Folk-Tales*, 1910)
James A. Honey (1888–1951) was an American author and journalist. He was born in Texas and later studied journalism and literature at the University of Missouri. Working for the Associated Press and the New York Times as a journalist, Honey also produced fictional works and collected folk and fairy tales. He is best known for his popular 1903 novel *The Riddle of the Sands*.

Amanda Ilozumba
Of Myths and Gods – Anyanwu, the Sun God
(Originally Published in *Black Phoenix Ink*, and won first place in the Black Phoenix Ink Writing Competition, 2020)
Amanda Ilozumba is a speculative fiction writer from Nigeria. She won the 2023 Sevhage Prize for fiction and is a Miles Morland Foundation Scholarship Finalist, a Republic New Voices Essay Competition Shortlistee and a 2023 Utopia Award for fiction nominee. She received honourable mentions in the Writers of the Future contest and was longlisted for the Awele Creative Trust award. Her works have appeared or are forthcoming in Reckoning Press, *Lolwe, Solarpunk Magazine, Utopia SF, Black Phoenix Ink*, Sevhage Publishers, Flametree, *Lunaris, Year's Best African Spec Fiction (Vol. 3)* and others. Amanda likes to think of herself as three owls disguised as a human. She is currently dabbling in scriptwriting for animations. Find her on Twitter @amandailozumba and Instagram @amandailozumba.

J.A. Johnson
Sol Invictus
(First Publication)
J.A. Johnson is the author of the creature feature series, *The Beasts of Oceanus*, published by Raven Tale Publishing, and *The Reckoner*, published by Dusty Saddle Publishing. Other works include the *Nereus Project*, a deep-sea thriller series (with K.G. McAbee), *Legends of the Coast*, a fantasy novel in the classic tradition, and *Treasure of the Jaguar King*. His story, 'Where the Nereids Play', appeared in *Merciless Mermaids: Tails from the Deep*, published by Wordfire Press. J.A. lives in South Carolina with his wife and son. He is currently busy on multiple projects.

Andrew Knighton
Breaking Bread Against the Dark
(First Publication)
Andrew Knighton is an author of short stories, comics, novellas and the forthcoming fantasy novels *The Executioner's Blade* and *Forged for Destiny*. As a freelance writer, he's ghost-written over forty novels in other people's names, as well as articles, history books and video scripts. He lives in Yorkshire with an academic and a cat, growing vegetables and dreaming about a brighter future. You can find more of his work at andrewknighton.com.

Andrew Lang
The Death of the Sun-Hero
(Originally Published in *The Yellow Fairy Book*, 1894)
The Sister of the Sun
(Originally Published in *The Brown Fairy Book*, 1904)
The Sunchild
(Originally Published in *The Grey Fairy Book*, 1900)
Poet, novelist and anthropologist, Andrew Lang (1844–1912) was born in Selkirk, Scotland. He is now best known for his collections of fairy stories and publications on folklore, mythology and religion. Inspired by the traditional folklore tales of his home on the English-Scottish border, Lang compiled twelve coloured fairy books which collected 798 stories from French, Danish, Russian and Romanian sources, among others. This series was hugely popular and had a wide influence on increasing the popularity of fairy tales in children's literature. His fairy tale collections include *The Red Fairy Book* (1890), *The Lilac Fairy Book* (1910), and *The Book of Dreams and Ghosts* (1897).

Jean Lang
Apollo and Daphne; Clytie; Hyacinthus; Icarus; Idas and Marpessa; King Midas of the Golden Touch; Niobe; Phaeton
(Originally Published in *A Book of Myths*, 1914)
Scotland's 'Jeanie' Lang has all but disappeared from view biographically, but her works survive her, and remain much read. (Not just retellings of the great Greek myths, but also stories from Edmund Spenser's *Faerie Queene* (1590) and a life of Scottish King Robert the Bruce.) This would have been how she wanted it: she would have succeeded, she said, if any of her readers felt that – even for a little while – they had "left behind the toilful utilitarianism of the present day".

Joshua Lim
The Frog Who Swallows the Sun
(First Publication)
Born and raised in Klang, Malaysia, Joshua Lim is a writer of speculative fiction with a passion for local myths and folklore. His work is published or forthcoming in *Fantasy Magazine, PodCastle, The Dark, Reader Beware* and also in various anthologies across the US, UK and Malaysia. He is currently a third-year medical student who spends too much time writing stories instead of studying. You can find him at joshualimwriter.wordpress.com or follow him on Instagram @joshualimwriter.

Amy Lowell
Many Swans: Sun Myth of the North American Indians
(Originally Published in 1920)
Amy Lowell (1874–1925) was an American poet and prose author. She was born in Boston, Massachusetts. Lowell read avidly as a child and travelled widely throughout her life, becoming a poet in her 30s. Joining the Imagist movement, Lowell embraced the movement's return to classical values, its precision of imagery and its clarity of language. She was also an early adopter of free verse. In 1926 she posthumously won the Pulitzer Prize for Poetry.

Lucian of Samosata
An Extract from Lucian's 'True History'
(This translation originally Published in *Lucian's True History*, 1902)
Lucian of Samosata (*c.* 120 CE–*c.* 200 CE) was a satirist and pamphleteer, known for his sarcasm and humour. His works were written in Ancient Greek, however his native language was likely Syriac, as he originated from the city of Samosata, in the Roman province of Syria. Little can be confirmed about his life – what we do know derives from his writings – however he was likely apprenticed to become a sculptor but, unsuccessful, ran away to pursue his education, later becoming a teacher and writer.

Clements Markham
The Shepherd and the Daughter of the Sun
(Originally Published in *The Incas of Peru*, 1910)
Sir Clements Markham K.C.B. (1830–1916) was an English geographer, writer and explorer. Serving as secretary of the Royal Geography Society from 1863 to 1888, and later as the society's president for a further twelve years, Markham organized the British National Antarctic Expedition of 1901–04. He is known for spurring the nineteenth-century revival of Britain's interest in exploring the Antarctic, as well as his prolific writings on geography, travel and history. He also produced English translations of numerous Spanish works including Pedro Sarmient de Gamboa's *History of the Incas*.

Frederick H. Martens
Sky O'Dawn
(Originally Published in *The Chinese Fairy Book*, 1921)
Frederick H. Martens (1874–1932) was an American translator and music journalist. His translation work mainly consisted of books for children, and he worked several times

with the author Clara Stroebe to translate her collections of stories and fairy tales into English. Martens was the translator of Stroebe's *Norwegian Fairy Book* (1922) and *The Swedish Fairy Book* (1921). He also translated Elsie Spicer Eells' *Brazilian Fairy Book* (1926) and R. Wilhelm's *Chinese Fairy Book* (1921). His original works include *Violin Mastery* (1919) and a number of newspaper and magazine articles.

Minnie Martin
Morena-Y-A-Letsatsi, or the Sun Chief
(Originally Published in *Basutoland: Its Legends and Customs*, 1903)
Minnie Martin was the wife of a government official, who arrived in South Africa in 1891 and settled in Lesotho (at that time Basutoland). In her preface to *Basutoland: Its Legends and Customs* (1903) she explains that "We both liked the country from the first, and I soon became interested in the people. To enable myself to understand them better, I began to study the language, which I can now speak fairly well." And thus she wrote this work, at the suggestion of a friend. Despite the inaccuracies pointed out by E. Sidney Hartland in his review of her book, he deemed the work "an unpretentious, popular account of a most interesting branch of the Southern Bantus and the country they live in".

Ondine Mayor
The Daughter of the Universe
(First Publication)
Ondine Mayor is an emerging author born and raised on a small island off the coast of Vancouver, Canada, and is currently residing in the Czech Republic. Much of her time is spent reading, taking her inspiration from the works of Terry Pratchett and Jane Austen. She's someone whose every thought will end up on paper. Sometimes it turns into something special, and sometimes it remains the scribbling on the back of a receipt. Ondine has a special interest in long-form fiction and is currently editing her first novel, while writing short stories in her free time.

Damien Mckeating
Ribbon Red Ribbon White
(First Publication)
Damien Mckeating was born and a short time after that he developed a love of fantasy and the supernatural. He has written for radio, comics, film and prose, and worked as a lyricist and bass player for the peculiar folk band Hornswaggle. He has short stories included in different anthologies, ranging from modern takes on Irish mythology to SF adventures for young readers. Right now, he's busy preparing for the publication of his debut novel, *Tallulah Belle*. He is fond of corvids and is currently the oldest he has ever been. Sometimes he remembers to blog: skeletonbutler.wordpress.com.

James Mooney
The Daughter of the Sun; The Journey to the Sunrise; Origin of Strawberries
(Originally Published in *Myths of the Cherokee*, 1902)
James Mooney (1861–1921) was an American ethnographer, born in Richmond, Indiana, and the son of Irish Catholic immigrants. He was a pioneer in the emerging field of ethnography, becoming a self-taught scholar in Native American cultures. Much of his

knowledge he gained first-hand during his long stays with various tribes, including the Cherokee. Mooney worked with the Bureau of American Ethnology in compiling the names of tribes across the country. He studied Native American groups in the southeast and the Great Plains, and he conducted studies on the Ghost Dance. His published works include *The Sacred Formulas of the Cherokees* (1891), and *Myths of the Cherokee* (1900).

Stewart Moore
The Sun in His Sky
(First Publication)
Stewart Moore has had short fiction published in anthologies edited by Ellen Datlow (*The Beastly Bride*, 2010) and Paula Guran (*Halloween*, 2011), and published by Air and Nothingness Press (*O+EU*, 2022); in the magazines *Mysterion* (2018), *Diabolical Plots* (2019) and *Lady Churchill's Rosebud Wristlet* (2020); and in the podcast *Pseudopod* (2020). He earned his Ph.D. in Hebrew Bible from Yale in 2014, focusing on Jewish ethnic identity and interethnic relationships in Hellenistic Egypt. This story is based in part on that research, and he is indebted to his dissertation advisor, John J. Collins.

Owen Morgan
To Banish the Light
(First Publication)
Owen Morgan lives in Steveston, British Columbia. He is an avid reader of fantasy and science fiction and has a particular fondness for the works of Tracy Hickman, Margret Weis and Terry Brooks. He has authored several short stories, including 'George Washington: The Loyalist', 'Splicers', 'Steamships of the Northwest Frontier', 'The Angel's Lamp', 'Attack of the Federation', 'On Wings of Thunder', 'Perchance to Sleep Perchance to Dream', 'Roman Hibernia', 'Eternal Love', 'Apocalypse by Internet', 'A Ripple in Space' and 'Space Battle'. You can find him online at owenmorgan.net, and on Twitter (X) at @owen_morgan1066.

Christopher R. Muscato
The Flight of Nikaros
(First Publication)
Christopher R. Muscato is a Pushcart-nominated writer from Colorado, USA. He is the former writer-in-residence of the High Plains Library District and a graduate of the Terra.do climate activism fellowship. He specializes in nomadic solarpunk, or nomadpunk, and is working with climate activists around the world to promote nomadism as a viable form of climate resilience. His recent fiction can be found in *Hexagon Magazine*, *Shoreline of Infinity* and *Solarpunk Magazine*, among other places.

Simon Newcomb
The End of the World
(Originally Published in *McClure's Magazine*, Vol. 21, Issue 1, 1903–05)
Simon Newcomb (1835–1909) was a Canadian-American scientist, author and self-taught polymath. Born in Wallace, Nova Scotia, he left for Massachusetts at the age of 19, where his father was teaching. He earned a Bachelor of Science at Harvard University in 1858, and he went on to work as Professor of Mathematics in the United States Navy

and at Johns Hopkins University. Outside of this career and his own experiments and studies, his passion for science also took the form of creative writing, emblematic in his short story 'The End of the World'.

Rob Nisbet
The Last Human
(First Publication)
Rob Nisbet has had over 100 stories printed in anthologies and magazines ranging from romance (using his wife's name) to horror. His wife has recently turned to crime. His first love, though, is science fiction, where he can have his characters explore wild concepts, the challenge being to make the stories relatable to the reader. He also writes audio drama. He has adapted work by Philip K. Dick for radio and has had, to date, seven audio scripts produced by Big Finish / BBC for their Doctor Who range.

Mary F. Nixon-Roulet
The Mirror of the Sun Goddess
(Originally Published in *Japanese Folk Stories and Fairy Tales*, 1908)
Mary F. Nixon-Roulet (1866–1930) was an American author, writing mainly for children and for Christian readers. She was born in Indianapolis, Indiana, and grew up in a religious and academic family. Nixon-Roulet's works largely comprise biographies of Catholic saints, as well as contributions to the "Our Little Cousin..." children's book series. Her short stories were also published in various magazines and newspapers including the New-York Tribune.

C.W. Peck
Why the Sun Sets
(Originally Published in *Australian Legends*, 1925)
C.W. Peck was an Australian author and teacher from Thirroul, New South Wales. He held a great affinity for the Aboriginal peoples of Australia, and he recorded and published many of their folk tales and mythologies. Travelling frequently throughout Australia, he befriended numerous Aboriginal people and came to learn of their various cultures. One such friend, Ellen Anderson, was a contributor of many of the stories which Peck published in his collection *Australian Legends*. Peck Anglicised the stories, often causing a loss of context, however his work has led to a modern rediscovery of some stories.

Katherine Quevedo
Ree in the Domain of Scavengers
(First Publication)
Katherine Quevedo was born and raised just outside of Portland, Oregon, where she works as an analyst and lives with her husband and two sons. Her fiction has been nominated for the Pushcart Prize and appears in Flame Tree Publishing's *Christmas Gothic Short Stories, Nightmare Magazine, Fireside Magazine, On Spec* and elsewhere. When she isn't writing, she enjoys watching movies, playing old-school video games, singing, belly dancing and making spreadsheets. Find her at katherinequevedo.com.

Peter le Page Renouf

Hymns to the Sun God Ra

(This translation originally Published in *The Egyptian Book of the Dead*, 1892)

Peter le Page Renouf (1822–1897) was a British professor, Egyptologist, translator and museum director. He was born in Guernsey on the Channel Islands, and attended Elizabeth College, Guernsey. Going on to study at Oxford University in 1840, Renouf later became Keeper of Oriental Antiquities at the British Museum. Among his best-known contributions to the field of Egyptology are his 1879 lectures, *The Religion of the Egyptians*, and his English translation of *The Egyptian Book of the Dead*.

Frank Rinder

The Sun-Goddess

(Originally Published in *Old-World Japan*, 1895)

Joseph Francis Rinder (1863–1937), who wrote under the pseudonym Frank Rinder, was a Scottish author and art critic. He was born in Camsbay, Caithness, but later lived and worked in London. He wrote art criticism for the Glasgow Herald, and he wrote about and collected early 20th-century prints. His published works include his collection of retold Japanese myths and folklore, entitled *Old-World Japan* (1895).

E.C. Robinson

Sun Chaser

(First Publication)

E.C. Robinson grew up in west Texas, where she developed a lifelong love for open spaces and big skies. She received a B.A. with high honours from The University of Texas at Austin and a M.A. and Ph.D. from Arizona State University. She now lives with her family in Boston. 'Sun Chaser' is her first fiction publication. She can be reached at ecrobinsonfiction@gmail.com.

Faye Snowden

The Long Night

(First Publication)

Faye Snowden is the author of southern gothic mysteries with strong (and flawed) women characters. *A Killing Rain* (Flame Tree, 2022), the second book in her noir mystery *Killing* series, was named by Crimereads as one of the best southern gothic mysteries of 2022, and was longlisted for the CWA Gold Dagger. Rain won gold in the 2022 Foreword Indies Book of the Year Award in the Thriller and Suspense category. Two of her short stories have been anthologized in *The Best American Mystery Suspense* (2021 and 2023). Learn more at fayesnowden.com.

Lewis Spence

The Third Book of the Popol Vuh

(Originally Published in *The Popol Vuh*, 1908)

James Lewis Thomas Chalmers Spence (1874–1955) was a scholar of Scottish, Mexican and Central American folklore, as well as that of Brittany, Spain and the Rhine. He was also a poet, journalist, author, editor and nationalist who founded the party that would become the Scottish National Party. He was a Fellow of the Royal Anthropological

Institute of Great Britain and Ireland, and Vice-President of the Scottish Anthropological and Folklore Society.

Henry M. Stanley

The Search for the Home of the Sun

(Originally Published in *My Dark Companions*, 1893)

"Dr Livingstone, I presume?" Welshman Sir Henry Morton Stanley (1841–1904) is probably most famous for a line he may or may not have uttered, on encountering the missionary and explorer he had been sent to locate in Africa. He was also an ex-soldier who fought for the Confederate Army, the Union Army, and the Union Navy before becoming a journalist and explorer of central Africa. He joined Livingstone in the search for the source of the Nile and worked for King Leopold II of Belgium in the latter's mission to conquer the Congo basin. His works include *How I Found Livingstone* (1872), *Through the Dark Continent* (1878), *The Congo and the Founding of Its Free State* (1885), *In Darkest Africa* (1890) and *My Dark Companions* (1893).

Flora Annie Steel

The Mother and Daughter Who Worshipped the Sun

(Originally Published in *Tales of the Punjab: Folklore of India*, 1894)

Flora Annie Steel (1847–1929) was born in Sudbury, England. Marrying a member of the Indian Civil Service in 1867, she moved to India and lived primarily in Punjab. Staying there for 22 years, Steel became deeply interested in Indian life and culture. She advocated for educational reforms and supported Indian arts and handicrafts. She also compiled folk stories, which she published in her collection *Tales of the Punjab: Folklore of India* (1894). She published many other works including *From the Five Rivers* (1893) and *On the Face of the Waters* (1896).

Rose Strickman

After the Storm

(First Publication)

Rose Strickman is a speculative fiction writer living in Seattle, Washington. She has been published over 50 times, in anthologies such as *Sword and Sorceress 32*, *Rattus Futura* and *Beneath the Yellow Lights*. She has also appeared in several e-zines and has self-published a number of novellas. Please see her Amazon author's page at amazon.com/author/rosestrickman.

Snorri Sturluson

The Creation, from the 'Younger Edda'

(This translation originally Published in *The Younger Edda*, 1901)

The Prose Edda, also known as *The Younger Edda*, is a collection of old Norse stories generally attributed to the Icelandic scholar Snorri Sturlson from around 1220, after the close of the Viking age. The collection recounts stories of giants, dwarfs, elves and gods all battling for survival in pagan Iceland and is generally considered one of the most influential works of mythology, inspiring fantasy writers such as J.R.R. Tolkien. It is of wide interest as it presents one of the first attempts to provide a rational explanation for mythological events, such as creation and the end of humanity.

Alyza Taguilaso
Birthday
(First Publication)
Alyza Taguilaso is a resident doctor training in General Surgery from the Philippines.
She usually writes poetry but occasionally dabbles in fiction. Her work has been
shortlisted for a Rhysling Award and other contests like the Manchester Poetry Prize
and Bridport Poetry Prize. Her poems have been published in several publications,
including *Electric Literature, Crazy Horse, The Deadlands, Canthius, Fantasy
Magazine, Strange Horizons, Orbis Journal, Voice* and *Verse and Luna Journal PH*,
among others. You may find her online via Wordpress (@alyzataguilastorm), Instagram
(@ventral), and Twitter/X (@lalalalalyza).

Percy Amaury Talbot
How the Sun Came into the Sky; Why the Sunset Is Sometimes Red and Stormy
Originally Published in *In the Shadow of the Bush*, 1912)
Anthropologist and academic, Percy Amaury Talbot (1877–1945) was a British colonial
district officer who served in southern Nigeria in the early twentieth century. He
authored several works chronicling the legends of the Nigerian, Ekoi and Chad people,
including *In the Shadow of the Bush* (1912), which includes creation stories and
animal fables. An enthusiastic anthropologist, Talbot donated to the British Museum
and the Pitt-Rivers Museum. His story 'The Treasure House in the Bush' is thought
to be a Nigerian version of 'Ali Baba and the Forty Thieves' from *One Thousand and
One Nights*.

Lauren C. Teffeau
The Siege of Zonstrale
(First Publication)
Lauren C. Teffeau is a speculative fiction writer based in New Mexico. Her
environmental fantasy *A Hunger with No Name* will be published by the University of
Tampa Press in the Fall of 2024. Her novel *Implanted* (Angry Robot) was shortlisted
for the 2019 Compton Crook award for best first SF/F/H novel and named a definitive
work of climate fiction by Grist. She has published over twenty short stories in
speculative fiction magazines and anthologies, including the Bram Stoker-nominated
Chromophobia: A Strangehouse Anthology by Women in Horror. To learn more,
please visit laurencteffeau.com.

Mark Twain
Extracts from A Connecticut Yankee in King Arthur's Court
(Originally Published in *A Connecticut Yankee in King Arthur's Court*, 1889)
Mark Twain (1835–1910) was born in Missouri in the United States. Dubbed by William
Faulkner as the "father of American literature", Twain is considered one of the greatest
American authors of all time, having contributed numerous works to the Western
literary canon. His best-known novels include *The Adventures of Tom Sawyer* (1876)
and *Adventures of Huckleberry Finn* (1884). He used his writing as a means of making
social commentary and criticism of the era, and his masterful style helped establish a
distinctly American voice in the realm of literature. He was also a humourist, lecturer,
publisher, and entrepreneur.

Jules Verne

Extracts from The Mysterious Island
(This translation originally Published in *The Mysterious Island*, 1874)
Jules Verne (1828–1905) was born in Nantes, France. As a novelist, poet and playwright, he wrote adventure novels and had a big impact on the science fiction genre. Along with H.G. Wells, Verne is considered one of the founding fathers of science fiction. His most famous adventure novels formed the series *Voyages Extraordinaires*, and include *Journey to the Centre of the Earth* and *Twenty Thousand Leagues Under the Sea*. His works remain popular today, and Verne ranks as the most translated science fiction author to date, with his works often reprinted and adapted for film.

H.G. Wells

The Further Vision, from 'The Time Machine'
(Originally Published in *The Time Machine*, 1895)
Herbert George Wells (1866–1946) was born in Kent, England. Novelist, journalist, social reformer, and historian, Wells is one of the greatest ever science fiction writers, and along with Jules Verne is sometimes referred to as a 'founding father' of the genre. With Aldous Huxley and, later, George Orwell, he defined the adventurous, social concern of early speculative fiction, where the human condition was played out on a greater stage. Wells wrote over 50 novels, including his famous works *The Time Machine, The War of the Worlds, The Invisible Man*, and *The Island of Doctor Moreau*, as well as a fantastic array of short stories.

Alice Werner

The Daughter of the Sun and Moon; The Man Who Would Shoot Iruwa; Sudika-Mbambi the Invincible
(Originally Published in *Myths and Legends of the Bantu*, 1933)
Alice Werner (1859–1935) was a writer, poet and professor of Swahili and Bantu languages. She travelled widely in her early life, but by 1894 had focused her writing on African cultures and languages. She later joined the School of Oriental Studies, working her way up from lecturer to professor. *Myths and Legends of the Bantu* (1933) was her last main work, but others on African topics include *The Language Families of Africa* (1915), *Introductory Sketch of the Bantu Languages* (1919), *The Swahili Saga of Liongo Fumo* (1926), *A First Swahili Book* (1927), *Swahili Tales* (1929), *Structure and Relationship of African Languages* (1930) and *The Story of Miqdad and Mayasa* (1932).

W.D. Westervelt

Maui Snaring the Sun
(Originally Published in *Legends of Ma-ui: A Demi God of Polynesia and of His Mother Hina*, 1910)
W.D. Westervelt (1849–1939) was an American author and pastor. He settled in Hawaii in 1899 and served as the Corresponding Secretary for the Hawaiian Historical Society beginning in 1908. His enormous interest in Hawaiian mythology and culture led him to publish numerous articles and books on the subject. His best-known works include *Legends of Gods and Ghosts (Hawaiian Mythology)* (1915), *Legends of Old*

Honolulu (1915), and *Hawaiian Legends of Volcanoes* (1916). He is considered one of the foremost authorities on Hawaiian folklore in English.

R. Wilhelm
Sky O'Dawn
(Originally Published in *The Chinese Fairy Book*, 1921)
R. Wilhelm (1873–1930) was a German sinologist, theologian and missionary. He was born in Stuttgart and attended the University of Frankfurt. Wilhelm lived in China for 25 years and was fluent in both spoken and written Chinese. He is best known for his translation of the *I Ching*, which is considered one of the finest translations, and for his translation of Chinese philosophical works into German.

Ethel Mary Wilmot-Buxton
How All Things Began; The Story of Balder the Beautiful
(Originally Published in *Told by the Northmen: Stories from the Eddas and Sagas*, 1908)
Ethel Mary Wilmot-Buxton (1870–1923) was an English author. Mainly writing accessible scholarly works for younger audiences, Wilmot-Buxton focused on creating educational narratives based on historical literature and events. An example is her book *The Story of the Crusades* (1911). She sought to combine the scholarly with the entertaining, making her works both accurate and readable. They were also shaped by the Victorian values of the time.

Caroline Winge
A Sun Fable
(First Publication)
Caroline Winge is a South Brazilian writer who loves world mythology, folklore and fairy tales. She has a Bachelor's Degree in Translation from Universidade Federal do Rio Grande do Sul, earned by adapting medieval poetry to Portuguese. When she isn't working grading essays or writing, her favourite pastimes are gardening on windowsills, reading, knitting and being a pillow for the cuddliest black cat in the world, Kikinha. Her friends attest that she can't be found online, only via summoning spells.

Albery Henry Wratislaw
The Sun-Horse
(Originally Published in *Sixty Folk-Tales*, 1889)
Albert Henry Wratislaw (1822–1892) was an English clergyman and Slavonic scholar. He was born in Rugby, Warwickshire, and later studied at Trinity College, Cambridge, then Christ's College. He studied the Czech language while living in Prague in 1849, and went on to translate numerous works from Czech to English. His published works include *Adventures of Baron Wenceslas Wratislaw of Mitrowitz* (1862), and *The Native Literature of Bohemia in the Fourteenth Century* (1878).

FLAME TREE PUBLISHING
Epic, Dark, Thrilling & Gothic

New & Classic Writing

Flame Tree's Gothic Fantasy books offer a carefully curated series of new titles, each with combinations of original and classic writing:

A Dying Planet • African Ghost • Agents & Spies • Alien Invasion • Alternate History
American Gothic • Asian Ghost • Black Sci-Fi • Bodies in the Library • Chilling Crime
Chilling Ghost • Chilling Horror • Christmas Gothic • Compelling Science Fiction • Cosy Crime
Crime & Mystery • Detective Mysteries • Detective Thrillers • Dystopia Utopia • Endless Apocalypse
Epic Fantasy • First Peoples Shared Stories • Footsteps in the Dark • Haunted House
Heroic Fantasy • Hidden Realms • Immigrant Sci-Fi • Learning to be Human
Lost Atlantis • Lost Souls • Lost Worlds • Lovecraft Mythos • Moon Falling • Murder Mayhem
Pirates & Ghosts • Robots & AI • Science Fiction • Shadows on the Water • Spirits & Ghouls
Strange Lands • Sun Rising • Supernatural Horror • Swords & Steam
Terrifying Ghosts Time Travel • Urban Crime • Weird Horror

Also, new companion titles offer rich collections of classic fiction, myths and tales in the gothic fantasy tradition:

Charles Dickens Supernatural • George Orwell Visions of Dystopia • H.G. Wells
Sherlock Holmes • Edgar Allan Poe • Bram Stoker Horror • Mary Shelley Horror
Lovecraft • M.R. James Ghost Stories • Algernon Blackwood Horror Stories
Robert Louis Stevenson Collection • The Divine Comedy • The Age of Queen Victoria
Brothers Grimm Fairy Tales • Hans Christian Andersen Fairy Tales • Moby Dick
Alice's Adventures in Wonderland • King Arthur & The Knights of the Round Table
The Wonderful Wizard of Oz • Ramayana • The Odyssey and the Iliad • The Aeneid
Paradise Lost • The Decameron • One Thousand and One Arabian Nights
Persian Myths & Tales • African Myths & Tales • Celtic Myths & Tales
Greek Myths & Tales • Norse Myths & Tales • Chinese Myths & Tales • Japanese Myths & Tales
Native American Myths & Tales • Aztec Myths & Tales • Egyptian Myths & Tales
Irish Fairy Tales • Scottish Folk & Fairy Tales • Viking Folk & Fairy Tales
Heroes & Heroines Myths & Tales • Gods & Monsters Myths & Tales
Beasts & Creatures Myths & Tales • Witches, Wizards, Seers & Healers Myths & Tales

Available from all good bookstores, worldwide, and online at
flametreepublishing.com

See our new fiction imprint
FLAME TREE PRESS | FICTION WITHOUT FRONTIERS
New and original writing in Horror, Crime, SF and Fantasy

And join our monthly newsletter with offers and more stories:
FLAME TREE FICTION NEWSLETTER
flametreepress.com

GOTHIC FANTASY

For our books, calendars, blog
and latest special offers please see:
flametreepublishing.com